A show that flopped in prime time became the greatest syndication success in television history. For twenty years, it wouldn't die. It was so successful in syndication that it finally spawned a series of high-budget theatrical motion pictures. Successful films have from time to time spawned TV series, but only *Star Trek* has reversed the process.

Indeed, incredibly enough, *Star Trek* now exists in three simultaneous incarnations. You can go to a movie theater and see a *Star Trek* film, go home, turn on the tube and catch *Star Trek: The Next Generation*, and, with a little button pushing on your remote, probably tune in reruns of the original show too!

How could this possibly happen? After all, hundreds of TV series have run three seasons or more and gone into syndication, but none has taken on a life after prime time death like *Star Trek*'s. Perhaps the Hollywood powers that be should be pardoned for failing to anticipate the incredible.

How could they have known?

The conditions that created this phenomenon didn't exist when it began. Before *Star Trek*, there *was* no mass audience for science fiction.

Star Trek created it.

—From the introduction
by Norman Spinrad

STAR TREK®

THE CLASSIC EPISODES 3

adapted by James Blish

with J. A. Lawrence

Introduction by NORMAN SPINRAD

BANTAM BOOKS
NEW YORK · TORONTO · LONDON · SYDNEY · AUCKLAND

STAR TREK : THE CLASSIC EPISODES 3
A BANTAM BOOK 0 553 29140 8

First publication in Great Britain

PRINTING HISTORY
Bantam Books edition published 1991
Bantam Books edition reprinted 1992

Bantam Books are published by Transworld Publishers Ltd,
61–63 Uxbridge Road, Ealing, London W5 5SA, in Australia by
Transworld Publishers (Australia) Pty Ltd, 15–23 Helles Avenue,
Moorebank, NSW 2170, and in New Zealand by Transworld
Publishers (NZ) Ltd, 3 William Pickering Drive, Albany,
Auckland.

Printed and bound in Great Britain by
Cox & Wyman Ltd, Reading, Berks.

CONTENTS

STAR TREK IN THE REAL WORLD

BY NORMAN SPINRAD

> Far too little attention has been paid to *Star Trek* as the pivotal work in the growth of SF cinema into a dominant force, and the concurrent growth of SF publishing into what it is today. . . .
>
> The creation of the *Star Trek* concept . . . was a cunning and audacious stroke of genius that changed the relation of SF to popular culture forever. . . .
>
> *Star Trek* imprinted the imagery of science fiction on mass public consciousness, where it had never been before, opening, thereby, the languages and concerns of science fiction to a mass audience for the very first time . . . so that years and a generation of Trekkies later, George Lucas could confidently begin *Star Wars* with a full-bore space chase and take the largest film audiences in history with him from the opening shot.
>
> —*Science Fiction in the Real World,*
> Norman Spinrad

You must pardon me for beginning this essay by quoting myself, but the above words were written long before I was asked to write this introduction; they appeared not in a piece on *Star Trek* itself but as part of a chapter on cinematic science fiction in a critical book exploring the relationship of science fiction to the wider world around us, and for purposes of this discussion, *that* is as important as the words themselves, or who happened to be the author thereof.

In science fiction, and in the real world, there has never

1

been a phenomenon quite like *Star Trek*. One scarcely knows where to begin. Consider perhaps the most improbable event of all.

Star Trek's third and final season as a network prime-time show was nearly a decade in the past when the first test-bed model of a Space Shuttle was rolled out of the hangar.

Presiding at the roll-out ceremony of the Space Shuttle *Enterprise* was the President of the United States. Gerald Ford and his people had not planned to name the prototype Shuttle *Enterprise*; in fact there was no little derision when the notion was first broached.

That was before the letters came pouring in.

And even when the inevitable decision was finally made, the powers that be insisted that in the time-honored military tradition, this first true spaceship had been named in honor of a previous vessel, the aircraft carrier *Enterprise* of World War II fame.

Sure it was.

Nevertheless, when the Space Shuttle *Enterprise* was rolled out, there beside the President of the United States was the captain of what the whole nation knew as the real *Enterprise*, along with representatives of his bridge crew, and the music they played was the theme from *Star Trek*.

Trekkies made him do it.

Just as they had kept the show on the air in prime time for two and a half seasons after NBC had tried to cancel it after the first thirteen weeks.

By the network numbers, *Star Trek* was a flop. It never rose much above twentieth place in the weekly Nielsens. NBC decided to pull the plug and told Paramount and Gene Roddenberry that no new episodes would be ordered. After the thirteenth week, *Star Trek*, like hundreds of failed series before it, would be dead.

But Roddenberry did something utterly unprecedented. He refused to take no for an answer. He decided to fight the network, to save his show using tactics that Hollywood had never seen.

He contacted a number of well-known science fiction writers, myself among them, and asked us to join a committee to save *Star Trek*. All Gene really wanted was our permission to use our names on a letterhead, and so most of us readily agreed.

Armed with this letterhead, he hired Bjo and John Trimble, well-connected science fiction fans, to use the "writers' committee" to put together a campaign to convince science fiction fans to write letters to NBC and Paramount demanding that the show be allowed to continue.

He succeeded beyond what must have been even his own wildest expectations.

When a network received a couple of thousand letters in praise of a TV show, they sat up and took notice. If they got 5000, they were mightily impressed.

Science fiction fans dumped upward of 75,000 letters on Paramount and NBC in a few short weeks. Fans picketed the studio and the network. It became a TV news item. Dumbfounded by this totally unprecedented outpouring of public opinion, NBC capitulated.

They literally didn't know what had hit them.

Particularly since the ratings never really improved.

What did Gene Roddenberry know that the network and studio mavens didn't?

It had taken Roddenberry years to get *Star Trek* on the air. He himself had written a ninety-minute pilot that didn't sell. He didn't give up. He hired Samuel Peeples to write another script, changed Spock's makeup a bit, recast the role of Captain Kirk with William Shatner, and shot another pilot that finally sold.

During this whole process, Roddenberry did what no other producer had ever done. He made the rounds of the science fiction conventions, made speeches, sat on panels, socialized with the writers and fans, treated the science fiction community to early screenings of both pilot films. He took the fans and the writers inside. He campaigned for support within the science fiction community, and he got it.

What Roddenberry knew that NBC and Paramount didn't was that while there were perhaps no more than ten or fifteen thousand committed science fiction fans in the United States, they were highly organized, literate, and voluble in print. Scores of science fiction conventions were held every year. Fans published hundreds of amateur "fanzines" filled with articles and letters from readers.

By tapping into this existing network, he was able to generate far more letters than there were fans. What NBC and Paramount didn't know was that those 75,000 letters were written for the most part by a comparatively small universe of committed people.

But, contrary to popular belief, network and studio heads are not *complete* idiots. When the first-season ratings didn't improve, they tried to cancel the show again, and when they were bombarded by another blizzard of letters, even they began to realize that something, in the immortal words of Mr. Spock, did not compute, especially when the second-season ratings were no better.

Roddenberry, however, had boxed them into a corner. The numbers said "cancel this show." But the continued letter-writing campaigns and the attendant well-managed publicity would have made them seem like high-handed antidemocratic monsters if they did.

They were royally pissed off. It almost seemed as if they had set out to assassinate *Star Trek* at the beginning of the third season, to make sure that the ratings would be so bad that no reasonable person could blame them for finally canceling it.

Their demographic studies told them that *Star Trek*'s main audiences were young children, teenagers, and young adults in their twenties. So they slotted the show at 10:00 P.M. on Friday night, when most of the kiddies had been put to bed, and most of the teenagers and young adults were out on weekend dates.

This time, the powers that be finally had their way. The third season's ratings were so bad that no amount of letter writing could save the show again, *Star Trek* was canceled, and no doubt they thought that was the end of it.

How wrong they were.

Network and studio heads may not be idiots, but they're not exactly Einsteins either. In the case of *Star Trek*, they failed to understand the true implications of their own numbers.

True, *Star Trek* had always been a ratings failure by network prime-time standards. But this "failure" still was watched by *twenty million people* a week for three years.

Ironically enough, the fact that Roddenberry was able

to beat the system for three full seasons ended up enriching Paramount enormously. Three seasons worth of programs is what you need to sell a viable syndication package, and from the time of its cancellation as a prime-time show until the present day, for over twenty years, *Star Trek* reruns have been a staple of local syndication markets.

A show that flopped in prime time became the greatest syndication success in television history. For twenty years, it wouldn't die. It was so successful in syndication that it finally spawned a series of high-budget theatrical motion pictures. Successful films have from time to time spawned TV series, but only *Star Trek* has reversed the process.

Indeed, incredibly enough, *Star Trek* now exists in three simultaneous incarnations. You can go to a movie theater and see a *Star Trek* film, go home, turn on the tube, and catch *Star Trek: The Next Generation*, and, with a little button-pushing on your remote, probably tune in reruns of the original TV show too!

How could this possibly happen? After all, hundreds of TV series have run three seasons or more and gone into syndication, but none have taken on a life after prime-time death like *Star Trek*'s. Perhaps the Hollywood powers that be should be pardoned for failing to anticipate the incredible.

How could they have known?

The conditions that created this phenomenon didn't exist when it began. Before *Star Trek*, there *was* no mass audience for science fiction.

Star Trek created it.

At the time that Gene Roddenberry began putting together the *Star Trek* project, science fiction had long languished in cultural obscurity.

The genre had been born as an offshoot of the pulp adventure magazines in the 1920's, and in the middle of the 1960's, there were a handful of science fiction magazines, none of them with a circulation much above 100,000, and less than 200 science fiction books published annually. Five thousand copies was quite a nice sale for an SF hardcover, and 100,000 sales made a paperback a big winner.

There had been a few successful major SF films like *Metropolis*, *The War of the Worlds*, and *The Day the Earth*

Stood Still, and some artistically successful B-movies like *Forbidden Planet*, *This Island Earth*, and *The Power*, but generally speaking, SF films, or "sci-fi flics," as they were more generally known, were B-movies featuring tacky monsters from outer space or other venues, typified by *The Creature from the Black Lagoon* and *The Thing*, in which John W. Campbell's subtle masterpiece *Who Goes There?* was turned into a monster movie featuring James Arness as a savage carnivorous carrot.

When it came to TV, *The Twilight Zone* had been a big long-running success, though most of the episodes were only borderline SF, and *The Outer Limits*, while it had done some serious SF, had relied heavily on monsters.

True, the hard core of regular readers knew that inside the sleazy covers of those magazines and paperbacks there existed a universe of literally infinite literary possibility, that some of the finest American writers had done their best work therein for decades, that what passed for "sci-fi movies" was only a pale shadow of the real stuff.

But the general public, when it thought of science fiction at all, thought of mad scientists, crazed robots, and bug-eyed monsters, and the Hollywood powers that be viewed SF as low-budget monster movies aimed at a modest-sized cult audience.

How this situation evolved could be and has been the subject of whole books, *Science Fiction in the Real World* being one of them, and is far too complex a story to go into here, but for present purposes, the point is that by the 1960s science fiction had evolved into something largely impenetrable to anyone who was not a regular science fiction reader.

The real stuff dealt with alien civilizations, faster-than-light space travel, mutated consciousness, time travel, alternate universes, relativity theory, synthetic religions, outré biology, the frontiers of psychology, speculative science, political theory, cybernetics. And because it had been written for a limited, educated, in-group audience for so long, it had long since come to be written without compromise, without any real attempt to make it transparent to anyone unfamiliar with the conventions, imagery, and secret language.

This, in a way, was a literary strength. Most science fiction writers felt they had no chance of reaching a general audience, so they felt free to write for a theoretical ideal audience—the fans and regular readers, who understood the conventions and the special language, for whom the recondite imagery held meaning, who were generally speaking scientifically literate, who did not have to be persuaded that space travel lay in the realm of the realistic possible, who were already convinced that there must be other intelligent beings out there somewhere. This enabled science fiction writers at their best to produce work without intellectual compromise.

But this literary strength was a commercial weakness. It made much of even the best SF largely incomprehensible to a general audience. And when writers *did* try to reach a wider audience, they usually did it by watering the stuff down, by simplifying it, bringing it closer to the here and now; in a way, by patronizing the general public.

These were the conditions that Gene Roddenberry faced when he set out to do a science fiction TV series. And two further problems as well, which were interrelated.

The first problem was that the anthology series was a dead form as far as prime-time TV was concerned; that is, the series in which each episode was a self-contained story with its own cast of characters. Since science fiction is inherently a literature built around surprise, novelty, and the attendant sense of wonder, the anthology series was the ideal form for televised SF, and indeed, the only two successful SF TV series, *Twilight Zone* and *The Outer Limits*, had been anthologies.

But what the networks wanted was series that used *familiarity* to retain and build audience share, episodic series in which the same main characters appeared each week in a familiar format and setting, characters who could not really be changed by the events of each week's episode, and this would seem to be the esthetic antithesis of the central appeal of science fiction.

Then too, science fiction was *expensive* to film. Spaceships. Other worlds. Alien civilizations. No problem when you're writing short stories and novels, but when you have to build the sets, create the costumes and the makeup, do the special-effects processing, the budget becomes prohibitive when you're talking about a time when $200,000 was about the top for an hour-long show. Not to mention the problem of doing it all on a timetable that must enable you to do twenty-six episodes a season on a six-day shooting schedule for each.

The genius of Gene Roddenberry was that he was able to look at these problems, these creative restrictions, and, by making one big leap of faith, let them determine a series format that turned them into strengths.

It would be futile to attempt a science fiction anthology series. The networks weren't buying anthologies, and besides, you simply couldn't create sets, makeup, and special effects for a new science fiction setting every week at $200,000 an episode without descending to tacky sleaze. No, it had to be an episodic series, and it had to use mostly re-usable standing sets. But then how could you create the sense of novelty and sense of wonder each week that was the core esthetic effect of science fiction?

The answer to that one was the solution to all the problems via the required leap of faith.

Set the whole thing aboard a single spaceship. You could then do most of your shooting on standing sets. Irwin Allen had done much the same thing with a futuristic submarine in the series *Voyage to the Bottom of the Sea*. Network executives love one-line descriptions of a new concept told in terms of old shows when it's time to pitch—*"Voyage to the Bottom of the Sea* in outer space!"

Or better yet, "Captain Cooke in outer space." A starship on a long voyage of exploration, completely out of touch with the Earth so you don't have to show the complex civilization of the far future, so that each week the same cast of characters can confront almost anything that the writers can dream up. You can set many of the stories entirely within the standing spaceship sets. You can use the same spaceship models over and over again, even a library of standard space shots and effects.

In retrospect, it all seems quite obvious, but to conceive it at all required one big leap of faith—namely that you *could* persuade a mass general audience to accept an interstellar spaceship as the setting for a TV series.

Roddenberry approached this problem from two directions, one dramatic, the other purely cinematic.

Give a general audience familiar character types and

well-worn traditional character relationships they can readily understand, and they'll swallow your setting, no matter how outré, for it is character relationships that draw an audience into a story, not the physical backdrop.

So . . . The Heroic Captain—call him . . . Kirk. His sidekick, the Crusty Old Sea Doctor Bones—call him . . . McCoy. The Pragmatic Grumbling Engineer—call him . . . what else, Scotty.

Any audience will accept such characters, familiar as they are from tales of the sea, and from there it's not such a great leap to transfer them from a sailing ship to a ship of space.

As for the spaceship itself, well, seeing is believing, one picture is worth a thousand words, work off the familiar conventions, give them a spaceship they can understand, a transmogrified ship of the sea.

A bridge, of course, the main and most elaborate set, where most of the action will naturally take place. An engine room to serve as Scotty's domain. A sick bay for Dr. Bones. A captain's cabin. A wardroom that can easily be redressed into anything. A corridor set to provide a sense of the ship's complex interior.

Voilà, the starship *Enterprise*, its five-year mission to seek out new worlds and new civilizations, to boldly go where no man and no TV series has gone before!

But not quite yet *Star Trek*.

Roddenberry could have stopped there and, having cracked the basic problems, probably gotten his science fiction series on the air. But it wouldn't have been *Star Trek*, and it wouldn't have become the phenomenon that created the present mass audience for science fiction both literary and cinematic. It would have indeed been merely *Voyage to the Bottom of the Sea in Outer Space*, a good format for a successful TV series maybe, but not something that would pass into the collective popular unconscious.

But Gene Roddenberry, unlike Irwin Allen, took science fiction seriously. He wanted *Star Trek* to appeal to a naive audience, but he wanted it to have credibility with the SF cognoscenti too. He wanted it to be a genuine work of science fiction.

The original series guide, the so-called bible, makes

that almost maniacally clear. Roddenberry consulted experts and the *Enterprise* was designed and even blueprinted down to the smallest niggling detail, to the point where NASA even took a look at his plans to pick up some tips on spaceship ergonomics. The ship was utterly real for Roddenberry, as I learned during the story conferences for "The Doomsday Machine."

Similarly with the details of the rest of the *Star Trek* universe. The phasers, the communicators, the shuttlecraft, the chain of command, and of course the implications of the famous Prime Directive, which by now has attained the real-world credibility of Asimov's Three Laws of Robotics. When the writers sat down to do their episodes, all of this was as predetermined as a street map of contemporary New York, and if you got something wrong, you had to change it, even if it meant altering the story to make it fit *"Star Trek* reality."

The result was that the layout, hardware, capabilities, and limitations of the *Enterprise*, the parameters of the *Star Trek* universe, remained consistent from episode to episode. Gene Roddenberry knew his ship and its universe, and if you watched enough episodes, so did you. It allowed this imaginery spaceship to become psychologically real, seemingly complex, and seemingly familiar in every detail, even though all you really ever saw was less than a dozen sets. No fictional spaceship has ever surpassed the *Enterprise* for this kind of detailed solidity, and not much on the NASA drawing boards either.

As a result, over three seasons, the *Enterprise* became as familiar as Dodge City or Gilligan's Island or Lucy Ricardo's living room to twenty million regular viewers. And over time, the reruns made it familiar to scores of millions more, to the point that by the time the Space Shuttle *Enterprise* was rolled out, an overwhelming majority of the American people were as at home on the bridge of what they psychologically regarded as the *real Enterprise*, the one commanded by James T. Kirk that half of them had known all their adult lives, as they were in their own living room.

Indeed, the *Enterprise* was an extension of the collective national living room, just as the battlefields of Viet Nam had been for eleven long years, via the magic window of the tube.

Endless TV coverage had quite literally brought Viet Nam home, given it a psychological reality that no war had ever had before, altering, over time, the national psyche, by demystifying war, leaching it of glory, revealing the reality as the grubby horror that it truly was.

So too did endless exposure to the science fiction universe of *Star Trek* via the familiar confines of the *Enterprise* demystify science fiction, imprint its imagery on the public consciousness, make an entire generation feel at home in outer space, precisely because it brought outer space into the home.

Thus did *Star Trek* create a mass general audience for science fiction. The technology of the *Enterprise* and all that it implied—faster-than-light travel, matter transmission, alien beings, human colonization of other planets—had passed into folklore, had become familiar, had become as American as apple pie, or Gerald Ford's desire not to offend the Trekkie voting bloc.

Thus was the beaming presence of Captain Kirk and the *Star Trek* theme music required to give *NASA's* new spaceship media credibility.

Thus could George Lucas open *Star Wars* with a simple type frame reading ''Once upon a time, in a galaxy far, far away,'' cut to a space battle shot, and take the largest film audience in history with him.

Thus did major science fiction films become a Hollywood staple, indeed for a time quite dominating the industry. Thus did literary science fiction come to crash the best-seller lists, and eventually come to represent about 20 percent of all fiction published in the United States.

Star Trek opened the way.

Or rather, the *Star Trek* phenomenon opened the way. If the show had died after three first-run seasons and the usual few years of syndication, none of this would have happened, and the world would probably be very different. It took time, a decade of reruns, for *Star Trek* to alter the attitude of the American mass audience toward science fiction.

Josef Goebbels had declared that even the biggest lie will come to be believed if it is repeated often enough, and gone on to prove it.

If lies, why not images of the future, which, by their very nature, are neither false nor true? It was the endless repetitive exposure to *Star Trek* that did the deed.

But why didn't *Star Trek* die after the show was canceled? Easy enough to see how *Star Trek* created the mass audience for science fiction via decades of reruns, but *that audience didn't yet exist* when *Star Trek* went into syndication. How could a show that had flopped in prime time survive long enough in syndication to become the staple of popular culture that it is today? How did it create the mass public audience for *itself* in the first place?

By the time the show was finally canceled, the letter-writing campaign had already spawned *Star Trek* fan clubs and huge *Star Trek* conventions, fanzines, the whole Trekkie subculture. While there were never enough Trekkies to make the show successful in prime time, there were enough to keep the tie-ins going even after the show had died, something quite unprecedented.

Star Trek fans continued to buy books like the one you are now reading, *Star Trek* toys, games, comics. They continued to hold conventions, which actually got *bigger* after the show was canceled. They continued to publish fanzines, they started writing their own *Star Trek* stories, even whole novels. Even *Star Trek* religions sprang up.

In short, *Star Trek* transcended television. It was no longer defined as those seventy-eight episodes of a canceled TV show running over and over again. It had become a popular myth imprinted upon mass culture, as surely as Robin Hood, or Billy the Kid, or Cinderella, a modern legend, a set of mythic archetypes, the dramatic material for books, a cartoon series, a film series, a spin-off TV series, paintings, even a strange sort of underground pornographic literature.

To the point where any character in any contemporary story who finds himself in trouble can look skyward, cry "Beam me up, Scotty," and everyone will know just what he means.

Clearly then, one cannot entirely explain the *Star Trek* phenomenon by detailing the process that gave it birth and the consequences. That can tell you *how* it happened, but not *why*. Clearly one must deal with *Star Trek* as dramatic literature in order to understand the power of its appeal in the first place.

We have come a long way into this discussion without really considering Mr. Spock. Kirk, the Heroic Captain, Scotty and Bones, the loyal sidekicks, Uhura, Chekov, and Sulu, the gallant crewpeople—these are a traditional cast of shipboard characters as old as the tale of the sea, individuated and made memorable really only by the scripts and the actors' interpretations.

But Spock is . . . something else.

Whereas the rest of the *Star Trek* format may be seen as Gene Roddenberry's clever reinterpretations and combinations of preexisting elements into a coherent and successful whole, Mr. Spock is Roddenberry's act of literary genius, a character unlike any other, a new mythic archetype, and an exceedingly complex one.

Physically, with his pointed ears and green skin, Spock evokes the image of Satan and—with his ability to mind-meld, his physical powers, and his superior intellect—certainly possesses power beyond that of mortal men.

But far from being an egoistic Faustian power-tripper, a tempter, a figment of evil, Spock, at least on the surface, *has* no ego. As a creature of pure logic, he may represent science, but with his total loyalty to the ship, his captain, his duty, he represents social virtue, not overweening intellectual pride, a kind of scientific angel in devil's clothing, a being of pure intellect serving the cause of good because it is the logical thing to do.

And that's only the surface. Beneath the surface, Spock's cold logicality is the product of his people's long and finally successful battle with their own savage nature. Vulcan dedication to pure logic is, paradoxically enough, ultimately a religious belief, not a genetic inevitable. Vulcans have *chosen* to suppress their emotional life, although not entirely, as witness their behavior when they come into sexual heat. Logical Vulcan society still seems rather ritualized and even mystical whenever we see it, and perhaps it is no accident that Vulcan features tend to evoke the orient in western eyes, with implications of Zen, Taoism, transcendent states of being achieved through spiritual discipline.

Nor is that the end of it. For Spock is half-human, though he dislikes being reminded of it, and the two halves of his being are shown to be in continual conflict. Over and over again, Spock surrenders to human emotions against his will, but almost always when these emotions represent human virtues like loyalty, empathy, compassion, rather than vices.

Surely Mr. Spock is the most complex character ever to appear in a prime-time TV series. And more than that, he is that science fictional rarity, a fully realized intelligent alien, with an inner life at least as complex as that of any human, but one that is truly *different*. A character that is, on many levels, and in Spock's own oft-repeated words, "quite fascinating."

William Shatner was hired as the star, but Kirk was never the central character in *Star Trek*, and never could be. Whether Roddenberry intended it or not, Mr. Spock is the central figure of *Star Trek*, and in the end, it is the character of Spock that has enabled *Star Trek* to transcend television, to survive, in one incarnation and another, for a quarter of a century, to pass into the collective consciousness of popular culture as surely as Superman, and take science fiction with it.

Did Roddenberry really know what he was doing when he created the character of Spock? Somehow I doubt it, for Spock, in the end, is a collaborative creation, the parameters of his character outlined by Roddenberry, interpreted by Leonard Nimoy, elaborated by the writers of the individual episodes, given additional reality by the imagination of the audience.

Spock is many things to many people. To those of a certain scientific beat, he represents not merely the intellectual but the moral and even spiritual superiority of the logical scientific viewpoint. To those of a more mystical inclination, he represents higher consciousness, mental and spiritual clarity achieved by a continuous conscious act of will. To the humanist, he epitomizes the struggle toward a balance between logic and intuition, emotion and intellect.

Finally, Mr. Spock is a sexual fantasy figure of great power and considerable complexity. Physically, he resembles Satan, Dracula, the Mysterious Dark Stranger, the Dark Side of the sexual force, the deliciously dangerous Dream Lover.

Yet, unlike such Satanic sex symbols, Spock is controlled, logical, loyal, trustworthy, admirable, virtuous. As a sexual fantasy figure, Spock is like no other, allowing the frisson of dark danger, *within* the safe limits of spiritual and moral virtue; Albert Einstein in Jim Morrison's tight black leather clothing, a Mick Jagger that a girl can bring home to meet Mother.

It is the presence of this great character that in the end has elevated a canceled television series to the status of a modern myth, a contemporary legend, a new literary archetype that has entered the collective unconscious, opening thereby the way for science fiction itself.

And in the end, perhaps, this opening up of the mass public consciousness to the things of science fiction by *Star Trek* goes deeper than mere familiarization with the imagery and the formerly secret language.

For Mr. Spock, alien though he is, is admirable, not menacing, humanity's ally, not its nemesis. His friendship with Kirk represents the possibility of empathy between the Self and the Other, between our own evolving species, and the very different beings we are likely to meet when we venture out into the Final Frontier. Even McCoy, who seemingly represents humanity's conservative reticence to love the Stranger, warms up to Spock in his heart of hearts, though neither of them are about to admit it.

This positive emotional openness to the new and the strange, this empathy for the alien, defines the heart and soul of science fiction. And up until a certain stage in human evolution, this acceptance of the alien, the foreigner, the Other, ran counter to the emotional attitude of our mass culture, and perhaps it was this divergence, as much as the unfamiliar settings, bizarre imagery, and secret language, that prevented the acceptance of science fiction as part of the literary and cinematic mainstream.

Ultimately, then, *Star Trek*, despite the literary flaws of so many of its episodes, films, books, and assorted spin-offs, succeeds on a moral level. In some small (or perhaps not so small) way, it has served the cause of our spiritual evolution as a species.

Clever format, fanatically loyal fans, marketing strategies, letter-writing campaigns, all explain how *Star Trek* has survived through a quarter of a century in all its many incarnations.

But when it comes to *why Star Trek* has survived to attain a kind of permanent place in our cultural life, and why it will probably still be with us in the twenty-first century, in the end, perhaps, it can be simply said that it deserved to.

THE LAST GUNFIGHT

(aired as Spectre of the Gun)

Writer: Lee Cronin
Director: Vince McEveety
Guest stars: Ron Soble, Rex Holman

As the *Enterprise* approached the Melkotian system, her sensors picked up an orbiting buoy which Captain Kirk thought it best to investigate. He had orders to contact the Melkotians "at all costs"—no explanation, just "at all costs"—but he was a peaceable man, and it was his experience that peoples who posted buoys around their planetary domains had a tendency to shoot if such markers were passed without protocol.

The buoy's comments were not encouraging. It said: "Aliens. You have encroached on the space of the Melkot. You will turn back immediately. This is the only warning you will receive."

Kirk's unease at the content of this message was almost eclipsed by his surprise in receiving it in English. The uneasiness returned full force when he promptly discovered that Spock had heard it in Vulcan, Chekov in Russian, and Uhura in Swahili.

"True telepaths," Spock summed up succinctly, "can be most formidable."

This was inarguable, as was the fact that absolutely nothing was known about the Melkotians but the fact of their existence. The orders were also inarguable. Kirk broadcast a message of peaceful intent, and getting no answer—not that he had expected any—proceeded, wondering what in the Universe a race of true telepaths could be afraid of.

When the ship was in range, Kirk beamed down to the planet, accompanied by Spock, McCoy, Scott and Chekov. The spot on which they materialized was a sort of limbo—a place of twisting fog, unidentifiable shapes, feelings, colors. Spock's tricorder refused to yield any further information; it was as though they were in some sort of dead spot where no energy could flow, or at least none could enter. To Kirk it felt rather more like the eye of a hurricane.

Then the Melkotian materialized—or partially materialized, almost like an image projected against the fog. He was essentially humanoid: a tall, thin, robed figure, with cold pale features, a high forehead, and piercing eyes that seemed to be utterly without feeling.

"Our warning was plain," he said in his illusion of many languages. His lips did not move. "You have disregarded it. You, Captain Kirk, ordered this disobedience. Therefore from you we shall draw the pattern of your death."

"Death!" Kirk said. "For trespassing? Do you call yourselves civilized?"

"You are Outside," the figure said. "You are Disease. We do not argue with malignant organisms; we destroy them. It is done."

The figure winked out. "Talk about your drumhead court martials," Scott said.

No one heard him, for the limbo had winked out at the same time. Instead, the five men appeared to be standing in a desert, in bright, hot sunlight. As they stared, a wooden building popped into existence; then another, and another. None of them were more than two storeys high, generally with porches at the second storey. One of them bore a sign reading, "Saloon," another, "Tombstone Hotel." Within seconds they were surrounded by a town.

"Spock," Kirk said quietly. "Evaluation."

"American frontier, circa 1880," Spock said.

"And what's this?" Chekov said, holding out a gun. It was not a phaser. A quick check showed that none of them any longer had a phaser, or a communicator; only these pieces of ironware, slung low around their hips from belts loaded with what appeared to be ammunition. Their uniforms, however, had not changed.

"That," Kirk said, "is a Colt .45—perfect for the period. My ancestors came from a background like this."

"Perfect, but dangerous, Captain," Spock said. "I suggest we dispose of them."

"Certainly not, Mr. Spock. Whatever the Melkotians plan for us, it's not likely to be pleasant. And at close range, these things are as deadly as phasers. We may have to use them as such."

"Jim, that shack over there calls itself Tombstone Epitaph," McCoy said. "Sounds like a newspaper. And there's a bulletin board on it. Let's see if we can pick up a little more information."

The bulletin board carried a copy of the day's paper. It was dated Tombstone, Arizona, October 26, 1881.

"Back in time, Mr. Spock?" Kirk said.

"And an instantaneous space crossing as well, Captain?" Spock said. "I don't care to entertain the notion of so many physical laws being violated at the same time. The energy expenditure alone would be colossal—far beyond anything we've ever detected on Melkot. I suspect we are exactly where we were before."

"Then what's the purpose of this—this setup?"

"As I understand it, Captain," Spock said gently, "the purpose is an execution."

"We can always depend on you for a note of cheer," McCoy said.

There was something about the date that nagged at Kirk's mind. As he was trying to place it, however, an unshaven man came around a corner, saw the five men, and stared. Then he said:

"Well, I'll be jiggered! Ike! Frank, Billy, Tom!" He came closer. "I was afraid you weren't going to make it."

"I beg your pardon?" Kirk said.

"But I knew you wouldn't let 'em scare you away. They're a lot of hot air, if you ask me. But now they'll have to fight, after the way they've shot off their mouths."

"Look here," Kirk said. "Obviously you think you know us. But we don't know you. We've never seen you before."

The unshaven man winked solemnly. "I getcha. I ain't seen you today, neither. That's what I like about you, Ike, you always see the funny side. And nobody can say Johnny Behan doesn't have a sense of humor."

"I'm a barrel of laughs," Kirk said. "But look, Mr. Behan . . ."

"Just one thing," Behan said. "I wouldn't take them too lightly if I was you. They may shoot wild, but they're gonna have to shoot."

As if alarmed by what he himself had said, Behan shot a glance over his shoulder and scuttled off. At the same instant, Kirk grasped the memory he had been struggling for.

"The Earps!" he said. Spock looked baffled; so did the others.

"He called me Ike," Kirk said. "And he called you Frank, and Bones, Tom, and Chekov, Billy. That's Ike Clanton, Frank and Tom McClowery, Billy Claiborne and Billy Clanton."

"Captain," Spock said, "I know something about this segment of Earth history, but those names mean nothing to me."

"Me either," McCoy said.

"All right. Try Wyatt Earp. Morgan Earp. Virgil Earp. Doc Holliday." There was no reaction. "It goes like this. In the late nineteenth century, in Arizona, two factions fought it out for control of the town of Tombstone. The Earps were the town marshals. The Clantons were lined up with Billy Behan, the County Sheriff. And on October 26, they had it out."

"And?" Chekov said.

"The Clantons lost, Mr. Chekov."

There was silence. At last Spock said, "This is certainly a most fanciful method of execution. But what did they mean by . . ."

A woman's scream cut through the still, hot air. From the direction of the saloon came a roar of men's voices and the unmistakable sounds of a brawl. Then a man stumbled backwards out of the swinging doors and fell down the steps into the street. Another man came after him like a flash.

As the first man picked himself up out of the dust, he reached quickly for his holster. He was way too late. His pursuer's gun went off with an astonishingly loud noise, like a thunderclap, and his twisted body was hurled back almost to Kirk's feet. The second man turned and went back through the swinging doors without another glance.

McCoy knelt beside the body and took its pulse. "Cold-blooded murder," he said angrily.

"I believe the phrase," Spock said, "is 'frontier justice.'"

"I can't believe it's real," Chekov said. "It's all just some sort of Melkotian illusion."

"Is the man dead, Bones?"

"Very dead, Jim."

"Well," Kirk said grimly, "that seems to be at least one thing that's real here."

From the saloon came a burst of music—a piano, recognizable in any era—and a shout of laughter. The five from the *Enterprise* looked down at the lonely dead man, and then, in almost a nightmare of compulsion, at the saloon.

"I think," Kirk said, "we'd better find out what's happening."

"Go in *there*?" Chekov said.

"Has anybody a better idea?"

There was a bartender, a pretty and very young waitress, and about a dozen customers; most of the latter were clustered around the killer of a moment before, who sat at a table. He rose slowly as the five came through the doors.

"Ike, Tom," the bartender said. He seemed both pleased and scared to see them. Here, at least, the Clantons had some sort of friend. "Hiya, boys. Didn't think we'd see you again."

The waitress turned. "Billy!" she cried with delight, and flinging herself on the astonished and delighted Chekov, kissed him thoroughly. "Billy, baby, I knew they couldn't keep you out of town."

"I didn't have much choice," Chekov said.

The girl led them toward a table a good distance away from that of the killer. "But maybe you shouldn't have," she said.

"And passed up the chance to see you? Don't be silly."

"But it's takin' crazy chances, with Morgan right in the same room."

Kirk, who had sat down, rose slowly again to get a closer look at the first of the men at whose hands they had been condemned to die. "Of course," he said. "The gentleman who kills on sight. Morgan Earp."

Earp did not move, but he watched Kirk with stony intentness.

"Captain," Spock said, *sotto voce*, "since we have seen that death is the one reality in this situation, I seriously advise that you reseat yourself without moving a muscle of either hand. Otherwise you will find yourself involved in something called 'the fast draw,' if I remember correctly. The results would be unfortunate."

Kirk sat down. As he did so, the bartender called, "You boys want your usual?"

"Absolutely," Scotty said enthusiastically. "Half a liter of Scotch."

"You know we ain't got nothin' but bourbon. 'Less you want gin."

"I don't think we've got the time for a party," Kirk said. He looked at Chekov, in whose lap the girl was now sitting. "Of any kind."

"What can I do, Captain? You know we're always supposed to maintain good relations with the natives."

"That's all right," the girl said, getting up. "I know you boys have got some palaverin' to do. Billy Claiborne, you be careful." She hurried away.

"Mr. Spock," Kirk said, "except for these handguns we're wearing, we haven't changed. Not even our clothing. Yet these people see us as the Clantons."

"I don't find that such a bad thing, Captain," Chekov said, his eyes still following the waitress.

"The day is still young, Ensign," Spock said.

"Now then, what have we got? We're in Tombstone on the day of the fight at the OK Corral, and we're the Clanton gang. Morgan Earp there will tell his brothers we're here."

"And history will follow its course," Spock said.

"It will not," Kirk said angrily. "I have no intention of letting a bunch of half-savage primitives kill us."

"May I ask, Captain, how you plan to prevent it?"

Without replying directly, Kirk got up and went over to the bar. "You, Mr. Bartender. You claim to know us."

"Ain't makin' no big claims about it to nobody," the bartender said. "Jest so happens."

"Well, you're wrong. You think I'm Ike Clanton. I'm not. I'm James T. Kirk, Captain of the Starship *Enterprise*.

And these men are some of my officers. We're not really here
at all; in fact, we haven't been born yet.''

There was a roar of laughter from the onlookers, and
somebody said, "Don't you jest bet he wishes he hadn't
been.''

Kirk whirled to the nearest man. "Here, you. Feel the
material of my shirt." The man snickered, but complied.
"Doesn't it feel any different from yours?''

"Reckon it does,'' the cowboy said. "A mite cleaner,
I'd jedge.''

"Have you ever seen men wearing clothes like these
before?''

The cowboy thought a moment. Then he said earnestly,
"Sure. On the Clantons.''

There was another outburst of laughter and thigh-
slapping.

"Looka here, now,'' the cowboy said. "You was always a great one for jokin', Ike. But I know you. Ed here,''
indicating the barkeeper, "knows you. That Sylvia, she sure
knows Billy Claiborne. Now, if'n you want to pertend you're
somebody else, that's your business. Only, if you've turned
yellow, what'd you come back to town for at all?''

Kirk frowned and tried to think, twirling his gun absently. The cowboy turned pale and backed away à step. Realizing belatedly what he had done, Kirk returned the gun to
its holster and swung back to the barkeeper.

"Ed . . .''

"It's okay with me, Ike,'' Ed said placatingly. "Anything you say. It don't make no difference who I think you
are. Your problem is—who does Wyatt Earp think you are?''

Hopelessly, Kirk returned to the table. His men looked
at him strangely. What was the matter with *them*, now?

"Well, scratch that,'' he said, sitting down. "I can't
get through to them.''

"Captain.''

"Yes, Mr. Spock.''

"We know that the Melkotians are true telepaths. And
the Melkot said that it was from you that he would 'draw the
pattern' of our deaths.''

"Are you suggesting that because I'm familiar with this
part of American history . . . ?''

"He looked into your mind, and selected what he considered to be the best time and place for our punishment. Yes, Captain. While you were pacing back and forth up there at the bar, I was recalling certain tapes in the computers. All unconsciously, you are adopting the true gunfighter's slouch. And a moment ago, you were handling the weapon like an expert."

"Some inherited characteristic?" McCoy said. "Ridiculous. Acquired characteristics can't be inherited."

"I know that, Dr. McCoy," Spock said stiffly. "The suggestion was yours, not mine. On the other hand, the possibility of ancestral memories—archetypes drawn from the collective unconscious, if such a thing exists—has never been disproved. And you observed the Captain's behavior yourself. As a further test, would you care to draw your own gun and twirl it, then return it smoothly to its holster, as the Captain did?"

"I wouldn't dare," McCoy admitted. "I'd be better off with a club."

"Let me make sure I understand this," Kirk said. "Do you further suggest that the Melkot is counting on me to act completely like one of these frontiersmen? To respond instinctively to the challenge of the Earps, and so bring about our—end?"

"Not instinctively, Captain, but certainly unconsciously. It's a possibility you must be on guard against."

"I'll bear it in mind. Now, has anybody any other suggestions for breaking this pattern?"

"Why don't we just get out of town, Captain?" Chekov said.

"There is no such place as 'out of town,'" Spock said. "Bear in mind, Ensign Chekov, that we are actually on the planet of the Melkots. Were we to leave this area, they would have no more difficulty in returning us to it than they did in putting us in it in the first place."

"Logic again," McCoy said. "Why don't you forget logic for a while and try to think of something that *would* work? If we only had a phaser—or better yet, a communicator! It'd be a pleasure to see the faces of those Earps as we were beamed back to the ship exactly thirty seconds before the big blow-down, or whatever it's called."

"Bones, you have a point," Kirk said. "Mr. Spock, when we were thrown back in time from the City on the edge of Forever, you managed to construct a functioning computer out of your tricorder. And you've got a tricorder here."

"But we were thrown back then to the Chicago of the 1930's," the First Officer said. "In those days, the technology was just barely up to supplying me with the necessary parts and power. Here we have no gem stones to convert to tuning crystals, no metals to work, not even a source of electricity."

"He's quite right there, Captain," Scott said. "I couldn't turn the trick myself, under these conditions."

"Then," Kirk said, "it would appear that we're limited to contemporary solutions."

"Maybe not," McCoy said thoughtfully. "We have gunpowder in these shells. And surely there are drugs of some kind in town. One of the Earp crowd is called 'Doc' . . ."

"He was a dentist," Kirk said.

"Nevertheless, he must have drugs, herbs of some kind. Cotton wadding. A mortar and pestle. Alcohol—we can use whisky for that if we have to."

"What do you have in mind?" Kirk said.

"What would happen if we turned up at the OK Corral with no guns at all—just slingshots—*and tranquilizing darts*?"

Slowly, Kirk began to grin. "A fine notion. What's the first step, Bones?"

"I'll go and see Doc Holliday."

"But he's one of the opposition. We'd better all go."

"Absolutely not," McCoy said. "That would start shooting for sure. I'll go by myself, and see what I can talk him out of, as one medical man to another. And the rest of you, if I may so suggest, had better drop out of sight until I get back."

"All right, Bones," Kirk said slowly. "But watch yourself."

"I'll do that," McCoy said. "It's myself I'm fondest of in all the world."

Doc Holliday's office, as it turned out, was in a barbershop. As McCoy entered, he had a patient in the chair. Doc Holliday was pulling; the patient was kicking and hollering. McCoy stared with fascination over Holliday's shoulder.

Holliday had evidently never heard of white coats. He was wearing a black frock coat, tight pants, a flat hat, and a string tie—a more elaborate version of the outfit McCoy had seen on Morgan Earp.

After a moment of watching the dentist sweat, McCoy said, "Impacted, I gather."

Holliday grunted abstractedly. Then apparently recognizing the voice, he leapt back, clearing his coat tail from his gun. He glared at McCoy.

"You want it now, McClowery?"

"Actually, the family name is McCoy."

"Look Doc," the patient said, looking up impatiently. "Are you going to pull it now, or—" Then he, too, recognized McCoy and turned white as milk. "Boys, please, no shootin'! Doc, put away your gun."

He tried to get out of the chair; Holliday slammed him back into it. "Sit!" the dentist said. "I ain't been through all that for nothin'. As fer you, McClowery, if you're goin' t'backshoot a medical man in the performance of his duties . . ."

"Not at all. I'm interested in medical matters myself. Mind if I take a look?" McCoy pried open the patient's mouth and peered in. "Hmm, that tooth is in sad shape, all right. What do you use for anesthetic, Preliform D? No, of course you don't have that yet. Chloroform? Is it possible you actually use chloroform? If so, why isn't the patient asleep?"

"What do you know about it, McClowery?"

"I've pulled a few teeth myself."

"I use whisky," Holliday said. "I never heard of chloroform."

"Tricky stuff, alcohol. You think the patient's too drunk to know his own name, and then there's a little pain, and bang! He's cold sober. Especially with a badly impacted tooth like that. Probably needs some root canal work, too."

"Whisky's all I got," Holliday said, a little sullenly.

"Well, actually, you don't need an anesthetic at all. Simple matter of pressure. A Vulcan friend of mine showed it to me. If you don't mind—" he took the crude pliers from Holliday, examined them, and shrugged. "Well, they'll have to do."

"Now look, McClowery . . ."

"No, you look, Doctor." McCoy thrust a finger into the patient's mouth. "There's a pressure point above the superior mandible—right here. Press it—hard, mind you—then you . . ."

He reached in with the pliers, closed, tugged. In a moment he was holding the tooth before Holliday's astonished face.

"Hey!" said the patient. "What happened? Did you—it's gone! It's gone—and I didn't feel a thing!"

"Nothing?" Holliday said incredulously.

"Not a thing."

"Where'd you learn that trick, McClowery?"

"You'd never believe me if I told you. Doctor, you're from the South, aren't you?"

"Georgia."

"Is that a fact! I'm from Atlanta myself."

"Is that so? I never knew that," Holliday said. "Now that's a cryin' shame, me havin' to kill another Georgia man, with this place crawlin' with Yankees and all."

"Actually, I could do you a favor, if I had time. You're not well, Doctor. Those eyes—that pallor—by George, I've never seen a case before, but I do believe you have tuberculosis. If I could run a quick physical . . ."

With a roar of rage, Holliday slammed his six-shooter on the table top. The patient sprang from the barber's chair and ran.

"One more peep out of you," Holliday said, "and you won't even hold water!"

"Why? What are you so mad about?"

"I may have bad lungs, but I've got a good aim!"

"Doctor," McCoy said, "if I had my kit here, I could clear those lungs up with one simple injection. One shot, twelve hours of rest, and the disease would be gone. Without the kit, it'll have to take more time."

"Time is just what you're short on," Holliday said. "You seem like a halfway decent sort, though. Why don't you play it smart and come in with us?"

"What—double-cross Kirk?"

"No, just the Clantons."

"Can't do it," McCoy said. "But if you don't mind

our parting friends for the moment, I'd like to borrow a few drugs.''

Holliday gestured expansively. ''A favor for a favor. Just don't expect me to shoot wild at five o'clock tonight.''

It was just that casually that McCoy learned the hour of their death.

As he emerged into the street, the sunlight blinded him for a moment. Then he became aware that Sylvia was crossing the street near him, her eyes averted. He was puzzled at the apparent cut—after all, she had seemed friendly enough to the Clantons in the saloon—and then realized that there were three other men on his side of the street, lounging outside the Marshal's office. All three were wearing the same kind of outfit as Holliday, and since one of them was Morgan, it did not take much guessing to figure out that the other two must be Virgil and Wyatt Earp.

McCoy stepped back into the doorway of the barbershop. At the same time, Morgan grinned, nudged one of his brothers, and stepped out to cut Sylvia off.

''What's the matter, honey?'' he said, taking her elbow.

Sylvia tugged at her arm. ''Let me go!''

''I'm just letting you get a jump on things. After tonight, there ain't goin' to be any Billy Claiborne.''

Both the watching brothers tensed suddenly, their grins fading. McCoy followed the direction of their stares. To his horror, he saw Chekov coming down the middle of the street, jaw set, face flushed.

Morgan saw him too. He gently thrust the girl to one side, still holding her with his left hand. ''Well,'' he said. ''Here he is—the baby who walks like a man.''

''Take your hands off her, you . . .''

Morgan abruptly thrust Sylvia away. Chekov went for his gun, but there was only one shot; Chekov's gun didn't even clear his holster. With a look of infinite surprise, he clawed at the growing red stain on the front of his tunic, and then pitched forward on his face.

McCoy was already running, and as he hit the dirt, he saw Kirk and Spock rounding a corner at top speed. Morgan Earp stepped back a few paces, contemptuously. McCoy fell to his knees beside Chekov, just in time to feel the last feeble thrill of life flutter out.

He looked up at Kirk. Scotty was there too; God knew where he had arrived from.

"Bones?" Kirk whispered, his face gray.

"I can't do a thing, Jim."

Kirk looked slowly toward the smiling Earps. Fury began to take possession of his face. McCoy heard the grating noise of the barbershop door opening; evidently Doc Holliday was coming out to join his confreres.

"Well, Ike?" Wyatt Earp said softly. "Want to finish it now?"

Kirk took a step forward, his hand dropping toward his gunbutt. Spock and Scott grabbed him, almost simultaneously. "Let me go," Kirk said, in a low, grinding voice.

"Yeah, let him go," Morgan said. "Let's see how much stomach he's got."

"Control yourself, Captain," Spock said.

McCoy rose slowly, keeping his own hand near his gun, though it felt heavily strange and useless on his hip; it occurred to him that the thing was at least three times as heavy as a phaser. "Easy, Jim," he said. "You wouldn't have a chance. None of us would."

"They murdered that boy! You think I'm going to . . ."

"You've got to," Scott said intensely. "You lose *your* head and where would the rest of us be? Not just the laddie, but . . ."

"More data," Spock said. "Jim, listen to me. We need more data."

"Smart, Clanton," Wyatt said. "Get as much living in as you can."

Slowly, slowly, Kirk allowed himself to be turned away. His face was terrible with grief.

In a back room of the saloon, Spock fitted nail points to darts; McCoy dipped the points into a mortar which contained a tacky brown elixir—his improvised tranquilizing drug. Five even more improvised slingshots lay to hand, as did an almost denuded feather duster—supplied by Sylvia—from which Spock had fletched the darts.

"I can only hope these will fly true," Spock said. "A

small hand-driven wind tunnel would help, but we have no time to build one."

"Somehow I can't seem to care," Kirk said. "Sometimes the past won't let go. It cuts too deep. Hasn't that ever happened to you?"

"I understand the feeling, Captain."

" 'I understand the feeling,' " McCoy mimicked angrily. "Chekov is dead and you talk about what another man feels. What do *you* feel?"

"My feelings are not a subject for discussion."

"There aren't any to discuss," McCoy said disgustedly.

"Can that be true?" Kirk said. "Chekov is dead. I say it now, yet I can hardly believe it. You knew him as long as I did, you worked with him as closely. That deserves its memorial."

"Spock will have no truck with grief," McCoy said. "It's human."

"I did not mean any disrespect to your grief," Spock said from behind his mask. "I, too, miss Ensign Chekov."

There was silence for a moment. Dully, Kirk realized that they had been unfair to the First Officer. No matter how often we run into the problem, he thought, we'll never get used to Spock's hidden emotional life.

Upstairs, a grandfather clock struck four. Time was running out.

"Captain, I've been thinking," Spock said. "I know nothing about the history of the famous gun battle we seem about to be engaged in. Was the entire Clanton gang involved?"

"Yes."

"Were there any survivors?"

"Let me think—yes. Billy Claiborne—*Billy Claiborne*!"

"Thus we are involved in a double paradox. The real Billy Claiborne was in the battle. 'Our' Billy Claiborne will not be. The real Billy Claiborne survived the fight. 'Ours' is already dead. History has already been changed."

"And maybe we can change it again," Kirk said with dawning hope. "Bones, how long will that tranquilizer goo of yours need to take effect?"

"No more than three or four seconds, I think. But of course it hasn't been tested. No experimental animals."

"Try it on me," Scotty suggested. "I have an animal nature."

"Well—a dilute solution, maybe. Okay. Roll up your sleeve."

"Captain," Spock said, "may I propose that this is also an opportunity to see how the darts fly? We can put Dr. McCoy's dilute solution on one."

"Too dangerous. Slingshots can kill at short range. Remember David and Goliath."

"Vaguely. But I do not propose to use a sling—only to throw the dart by hand."

Scott ambled across the room to a bureau, on which he leaned like a man leaning on a bar, imaginary glass in hand, his hip thrust out. "How's this?"

"A prime target." Spock threw the dart, gently, underhand. It lodged fair and square in Scott's left buttock. He said, "Oof," but held the pose. They watched him intently.

Nothing happened. After five long minutes, McCoy went over to him and withdrew the dart. "It penetrated the muscle," he said. "It should have worked by now. Feel anything, Scotty?"

"Nothing at all."

"No sweating? No dizziness? No palpitations?"

"I never felt better in my life."

McCoy's face fell. "I don't understand it," he said. "Full strength, that stuff should knock out a charging elephant."

"Fascinating," Spock said.

"Fascinating!" Kirk exploded. "Mr. Spock, don't you realize that this is our death warrant? There isn't time to devise anything else!"

"It is nevertheless fascinating," Spock said slowly. "First a violation of physics, then a violation of history—now a violation of human physiology. These three violations cannot be coincidence. They must contain some common element—some degree of logical consistency."

"Well, let's see if we can think it through," Kirk said. "But there's one last chance. We may be able to violate history again. Ten minutes from now, it's all supposed to end at the OK Corral. Very well—we are not going to be there. We are going to sit right here. We are not going to move from this spot.''

Spock nodded slowly, but he was frowning. The others braced themselves, as if daring anyone to move them.

Flip!

Sunlight blazed upon them from a low angle. They were in the OK Corral.

"Let's get out of here!" Kirk said. He vaulted over the fence, hearing the others thump to the ground after him, and dashed into an alley. At the other end, he paused to reconnoiter.

Ahead was the corral, with a wagon box and several horses tied in front of it. Kirk started, momentarily stunned.

"Must have gotten turned around," he said. "This way."

He led the way back up the alley. Its far end debouched onto the main street. They crossed quickly into another alley, jogging, watching the blank wooden buildings that hemmed them in.

At the end of the alley was the OK Corral.

"They're breeding like pups," Scotty said.

"Down that way . . .''

But 'down that way' also ended at the OK Corral.

"They've got us," Kirk said stonily. "The Melkotians don't mean for us to miss this appointment. All right. Remember that these guns are heavier than phasers. Pull them straight up—and drag them *down* into line the minute you've fired off the first shot.''

"Captain," Spock said, "that is suicide. We are none of us skilled in the use of these weapons. Nor can we avoid the OK Corral, that is quite clear. But—very quickly—let me ask you, what killed Ensign Chekov?''

"Mr. Spock, he was killed by a bullet.''

"No, Captain. He was killed by his own mind. Listen to me, please; this is urgent. The failure of Dr. McCoy's drug was the clue. *This place is unreal.* It is a telepathic forgery by the Melkotians. Nothing that happens here is real. Nothing at all.''

"Chekov is dead," McCoy said grimly.

"In this environment, yes. Elsewhere—we cannot know. We can judge reality only by the responses of our senses. Once we are convinced of the reality of a given situation, our minds abide by its rules: the guns are solid, the bullets are real, they can kill. But only because we believe it!"

"I see the Earps coming toward us," Kirk said. "And they look mighty convincing—and deadly. So do their guns. Do you think you can protect us just by disbelieving in them?"

"I can't protect anybody but myself, Captain; you must entertain your own disbelief—totally. One single doubt, and you will die."

The three Earps, side by side, black-clad and grim, walked slowly down the street, their faces expressionless. Pedestrians scurried away from them like startled quail.

"Mr. Spock," Kirk said, "we can't turn disbelief on and off like clockwork. I know you can; but we're just human beings."

"The Vulcanian mind meld," Dr. McCoy said suddenly.

"Yes, Dr. McCoy. I could not have suggested it myself; I have cultural blocks against invading another man's mind. But if you will risk it . . . ."

"I will."

McCoy hesitated. Then he stepped back until his back was against the wagon box. Spock came to him, closer and closer, his fingers spreading. Face to face, closer and closer.

"Your mind to my mind," Spock said softly. "Your thoughts to my thoughts. Listen to me, Bones. Be with me. Be one with me."

McCoy closed his eyes, and then slowly, opened them again.

The three Earps had been joined by Doc Holliday. He was holding a double-barreled, sawed-off shotgun under his frock coat. He fell in step with the brothers. Funereal in look and aspect, grim and unsmiling, rhythmic as a burial procession, they came down the street, real, the quintessence of death.

Spock's fingers moved to Kirk's face. "They are un-real—without body," he whispered. "Listen to me, Jim. Be with me. They are only illusion, shadows without substance. They cannot affect you. My heart to your heart, I promise you.''

The Earps and Holliday marched on across the lengthening shadows. The shotgun barrel swung periodically under Holliday's coattails. Their cheeks were hollow, their eyes dark as pitch. The street behind them was frozen, and the sky was darkening.

''Scotty,'' Spock said, his voice suddenly taking on a dark, Caledonian color, as deep as that of a prophet's. ''Listen to me. Clouds these are without water, carried about by winds. They are trees whose fruit withereth, twice dead, plucked up by the roots; wandering stars, to whom is reserved the blackness of eternity, forever.''

The spectral stalkers halted, perhaps ten paces away. Wyatt Earp said, ''Draw.''

Kirk looked at his people. Their expressions were glassy, faraway, strange, like lambs awaiting the slaughter. With a slight nod, he dropped his hand toward his gunbutt.

The Earps drew. It seemed as though twenty pistol shots rang out in as many seconds—two shotgun blasts—another pistol shot. The street fogged with the smoke and stench of black powder. Every single shot had come from the Earps' side.

''Thank you, Mr. Spock,'' Kirk said tranquilly, staring into the eyes of the astonished gunmen. ''And now, gentlemen, if you please, let's finish this up—fast, hard and good.''

The four from the *Enterprise* moved in on the Earps. The gunmen were accustomed to shoot-outs and to pistol-whipping and to barroom brawls; but against advanced space-age karate techniques and Spock's delicately precise knowledge of the human nervous system's multiple vulnerabilities, they had no defense whatsoever. Within moments, 'history' was a welter of unconscious black-clad bodies in the dust . . .

. . . And Tombstone, Arizona, wavered, pulsed, faded, and vanished into a foggy limbo.

In the fog, Kirk became aware that Chekov was standing beside him. He had to swallow twice before he could manage to say, ''Welcome back, Ensign.''

He had no time to say more, for the transparent figure

of the Melkot was forming against the eerie backdrop of the mists.

"Explain," the Melkot said.

"Glad to," Kirk said, in a voice far from friendly. "What would you like explained?"

"To you the bullets were unreal. To the players we put against you, the bullets were real, and would kill. But you did not kill them."

"We kill only in self-defense," Kirk said. "Once we saw that it was unnecessary to kill your players, we protected ourselves less wastefully, on all sides."

"Is this," the Melkot said, "the way of your kind?"

"By and large. We are not all alike. But in general, we prefer peace—and I speak not only for my species, but for a vast alliance of fellow creatures who subscribe to the same tenets. We were sent here to ask you to join it."

There was a long silence. And as they waited, the familiar fading effect began again—and then they were on the bridge of the *Enterprise*.

Uhura was at her post. She did not seem at all surprised to see them. In fact, her manner was so matter-of-fact as to suggest that they had never left at all.

Chekov began to react, but Kirk held up his hand in warning. Puzzled, Chekov said in a low voice, "Captain— what happened? Where have I been?"

"Where do you think?"

"Why—right here, it seems. But I remember a girl . . ."

"Nothing else?"

"No," Chekov said. "But she seemed so real . . ."

"Perhaps that explains why you're here. Nothing else was real to you."

Chekov looked more baffled than ever, but evidently decided to leave well enough alone.

"Captain," Lt. Uhura said, "I'm getting a transmission from the Melkot buoy."

"Cycle it for sixty seconds. Mr. Spock, has any time elapsed since the—uh—last time we all sat here?"

"The clock says not, Captain."

"I suspected not. Did it happen?"

"I cannot give a yes or no answer, Captain. It is a matter of interpretation."

"All right, Lt. Uhura. Let's hear what the Melkotian buoy has to say."

The buoy said: "Aliens! You have entered the space of the Melkot. We welcome you and promise peaceful contact."

"Very good. Lt. Uhura, ask them to specify a meeting place. Mr. Spock, a word with you in private, please."

Spock obediently drew to one side of the bridge with his Captain.

"Mr. Spock, once again we owe you our thanks for quick, thorough and logical thinking. But I will tell you something else. Privately, and for no other ears than yours, I think you are a sentimental bag of mush."

"Sir!"

"I heard what you said to me, and to the other men, when you were convincing us not to believe in the Melkotian illusions. Every word was based upon the most intimate understanding of each man involved—understanding—and honest love."

"Captain," Spock said, from behind his mask, "I did what was necessary."

"Of course you did. Very well, Mr. Spock—carry on."

But as Spock went stiffly back to his library-computer, the commandatorial eyes which followed him were not without a certain glitter of amusement.

ELAAN OF TROYIUS

Writer: John Meredyth Lucas
Director: John Meredyth Lucas
Guest stars: France Nuyen, Jay Robinson

Kirk's orders were simple. He was to "cooperate" in all matters pertaining to the mission of his passenger, the Ambassador of the planet Troyius.

It was the implications of his orders that were complicated. First, the Ambassador's mission was top secret. Second, his negotiations involved the notoriously hostile people of Elas, a neighbor planet. As if such "cooperation" weren't enough of a headache, both planets were located in a star system over which the Klingon Empire claimed jurisdiction. By entering the system, the *Enterprise* was inviting Klingon retaliation for trespass.

Kirk was frankly irritated as he swung his command chair to Uhura. "Inform Transporter Room we'll be beaming-up the Elas party at once. Ask Ambassador Petri to meet us there."

"Yes, Captain."

At his nod, Spock, McCoy and Scott followed him into the elevator. Kirk said, "Some deskbound Starfleet bureaucrat has cut these cloak-and-dagger orders."

The intercom spoke. "Bridge to Captain." It was Uhura's voice.

"Kirk here."

"Captain, signal from the Elas party. They're ready to beam aboard but demand an explanation of the delay."

"Here we go," Kirk said. "What delay are they talking about? All right. Forget it, Lieutenant Uhura. Beam them aboard."

Spock said, "The attitude is typical of the Elasians, sir. Scientists who made the original survey of the planet described their men as vicious and arrogant."

"That's the negative aspect," McCoy said. "I've gone over those records. Their women are supposed to be something very special. They're said to possess a kind of subtle— maybe mystical—power that drives men wild."

Spock gave McCoy a disgusted look. It was still on his face when the elevator door opened to reveal the waiting Troyian envoy. Kirk addressed him immediately. "Ambassador Petri, suppose you drop this diplomatic secrecy—and tell me what this mission of yours is really about."

"That must wait until the Dohlman of Elas is aboard, Captain."

"Dohlman?" Kirk said as they all entered the Transporter Room. "What the devil is a Dohlman?"

"The thing most feared and hated by my people. Our most deadly enemy," Petri said.

The Transporter Room's hum deepened—and three figures sparkled into substance on the platform. They were soldiers. Breast plates covered their chests. Weapons of no recognizable variety hung from the barbaric chains around their necks. The biggest Elasian soldier, thick-jawed, heavy-browed, covered the *Enterprise* group with his strange weapon.

"Welcome. I am the Ambassador of Troyius," Petri said.

The ape-jawed giant ignored him. "Who runs this ship?"

Kirk said, "The *Enterprise* is under my command. I am Captain Kirk."

"And I am Kryton of Elas. That Troyian there is a menace. I must know that all is secure here before the Dohlman is brought aboard."

Spock lowered his voice. "Captain, the weapons resemble twenty-first century nuclear disintegrators."

Kirk spoke to the bellicose Kryton. "My ship *is* secure. What's more, we are equipped to repel any hostile act." He turned his back on the Elasian to say to the Transporter Room technician. "Energize!"

The center transporter platform went luminous. The

three Elasians dropped to one knee. Glaring at Kirk, Kryton growled, ''Quickly! To your knee! Do honor to the Dohlman of Elas!''

Kirk's jaw tightened. Beside him, acquiescent, Petri sank to one knee. ''It is their custom,'' he muttered. ''To stand is a breach of protocol.''

Spock looked at Kirk. Annoyance on his face, Kirk nodded. The Vulcan hesitated; then, he, too, bent his knee. The sight increased Kirk's annoyance. It was abruptly dissipated. On the center platform the ''deadly enemy'' of Troyius had appeared. The Dohlman was a silver blonde. Her skin had the pearly tone of dreams. So was her body the stuff of dreams. Nor was it hidden. The scanty metallic scarves she wore served no purpose but suggestion of beauty too overwhelming for complete revelation.

Kryton said, ''Glory to Elaan, Dohlman of Elas!''

''Glory is right,'' Kirk thought, controlling an impulse to kneel himself. Instead, he bowed. Then, raising his head, he looked again at the Dohlman of Elas. Under the silver blonde hair, her eyes were dark. Aflame with contempt, they swept over the kneeling men. At a snap of her fingers, her soldier bodyguards got to their feet. Kryton, addressing Spock and Petri, said, ''Now you may stand.''

She came forward, Kryton towering behind her, tense, his weapon at the ready. Her own hand rested on the elaborately jeweled hilt of a dagger suspended from a golden chain she wore around her slim waist.

''Odd,'' Kirk said to Spock. ''Body armor and nuclear weapons.''

''Not without precedent, sir. Consider the Samurai customs of old Earth's Japanese. Even we Vulcans preserve some symbolic remnants of our past.''

Kryton growled again. ''Permission to speak was not given!''

Before Kirk could retort, Elaan said to Spock, ''You rule this ship?'' The voice was husky, infinitely feminine.

''I am the ship's First Officer. This is Captain Kirk.''

She made no sign of acknowledgment. Petri interposed hastily. ''Your glory, I am Petri of Troyius. In the name of my people, I bid you welcome to—''

''Your mission is known to me,'' she said with negligent scorn. Then, turning to Kirk, she added, "You are permitted to show the accommodations."

He pulled himself together. "I think we'd better have an understanding right—"

"*Please*, Captain," Petri begged.

Kirk said, "My First Officer, Mr. Spock will show you to your quarters." He turned to leave. "Ambassador Petri, I want to speak to you."

Elaan's words came like a whip. "You have not been dismissed."

Incredulous, on the edge of explosion, Kirk gave his response second thought. He decided to shrug. "May I have your glory's permission to leave?" he asked silkily.

"You are all dismissed," she said.

Outside in the corridor Kirk wheeled on Petri. "All right, Ambassador! What exactly are we supposed to be doing?"

Petri drew him aside. "She—that woman is to be the wife of our ruler. The marriage has been arranged to bring peace. Our two warring planets now possess the capability of mutual destruction. Some method of coexistence had to be found."

"Then we return to Troyius?"

"Yes. But slowly, Captain. I will need time. My mission is to teach her civilized manners before we reach Troyius. It must be clear to you now why I'll need time. In her present savage condition my people would never accept her as queen."

"You've got yourself quite a mission," Kirk said.

"Those are my orders. I must ask you and your crew to tolerate this Elasian impudence for the sake of future peace. It is vital that friction now be kept to a minimum."

"That I can understand," Kirk said.

"There's another thing you should understand, Captain. You have as much at stake as I have. Your superiors know that failure of this mission would be as catastrophic for Federation planning as it would be for our two planets. The peace we'd gain by accepting such an untutored wife for our ruler would not be peace." He drew a deep sighing breath. "I will take her the official gifts I bear. Perhaps they will change her mood."

Kirk said, "I hope so." But what he thought was: "Shrew, termagant—a knockout fishwife is what I've got on my ship!"

Troubled, he stopped at Sulu's station as he re-entered the bridge. "Mr. Sulu, lay in a course for Troyius. Impulse drive-speed factor point zero three seven. Take us out of orbit."

Sulu looked startled. "Impulse drive, Captain?"

"That is correct, Mr. Sulu. Sub-light factor point zero three seven."

Scott looked up from his station. "Captain, you'll not be using the warp drive? All the way on impulse?"

"Correct, Mr. Scott."

"That'll take a great deal of time."

"Are you in a hurry, Mr. Scott?"

"No, sir."

"That's it, then." But he'd scarcely reached his command chair when Spock hurried to his side. "Captain, the Dohlman is dissatisfied with her quarters!"

Overhearing, Uhura turned indignantly. "What's the matter with them?"

"Nothing that I was able to see," Spock said. "But all the Elasians seem to be most irrational."

"I gave up my quarters," Uhura said, "because—"

"*I* appreciate your sacrifice, Lieutenant," Kirk told her. He got up. "I'll talk to the lady myself."

He heard the screams of rage before he reached Uhura's cabin. Its door was wide open. But it took a moment to take in the scene. A crystal box was flying through the air—and struck Petri in the chest. "Swine! Take back your gifts! Your ruler cannot buy the favor of the Dohlman of Elas!"

Petri retrieved the box, stuffing delicate lace back into it. "Your glory," he said, "this is your wedding veil." He backed up to what he clearly hoped was a safe distance to raise the lid of a begemmed gold casket. "In this," he said, "are the most prized royal jewels of Troyius. This necklace is a gift from the bridegroom's mother to adorn your lovely throat . . ."

The necklace seemed to be composed of diamonds and emeralds. Elaan seized it. Then she hurled it at Petri with a wild aim that barely escaped hitting Kirk in the face. "I would strangle if I wore the bauble of Troyian dogs around my neck!"

Kirk stepped over the glitter at his feet and into the cabin. She saw him and shrieked, "Kryton!" The huge guard rushed in. "By whose permission has *he* come here?"

"He came in answer to your summons, your glory."

Kirk said, "I understand you are not happy with your quarters."

She waved a hand, dismissing Kryton. "Quarters?" She leveled a perfect leg at a cushioned chair. "Am I a soft, pewling Troyian that I must have cushions to sit on?" She kicked the chair over. Her own action inflamed her rage. She ran to the cabin window, ripping down its draperies. "These female trappings in here are an offense to me!"

Kirk said, "My Communications Officer vacated these rooms in the generous hope you would find them satisfactory."

"I do not find them so." She pointed at Petri. "And I find this—this Ambassador even less satisfactory! Must my bitterness be compounded by his presence aboard your ship?"

Petri, red with suppressed fury, said, "I've explained to her glory that her Council of Nobles and the Troyian Tribunal jointly agreed that I should instruct—make her acquainted with the customs and manners of our people."

"Kryton!" Elaan called. She indicated Petri. "Remove him!" The guard fingered his weapon. Petri bowed; and was moving to the door when she cried, "And take that garbage with you!" He bowed again, stooped lower to collect the gifts she'd flung to the floor and gratefully made his exit.

"That he should dare to suggest I adopt the servile manners of his people!" Elaan stormed.

"Your glory doesn't seem to be responding favorably to Troyian instruction," Kirk said.

"I will never forgive the Council of Nobles for inflicting such a nightmare on me! By the way, *you* were responding to my demand for better quarters!"

"There are none better aboard," Kirk said. "I suggest you make the best of it."

Aghast at this effrontery, she glanced at Uhura's dressing table for some object she could smash. "You presume to suggest to *me*—"

Kirk said, "Lieutenant Uhura's personal belongings have all been removed from the cabin. But if smashing things gratifies you, I will arrange to equip it with breakable articles."

"I will not be humiliated!"

"Then behave yourself," Kirk said. He went to the door; and she screamed, "I did not give you permission to leave!"

"I didn't ask for it," he said, slamming the door behind him.

An agitated Petri was waiting for him in the corridor. "Captain, I wish to contact my government. I cannot fulfill my mission. I would be an insult to my ruler to bring him this incorrigible monster as a bride."

"Simmer down, Ambassador. Your mission is a peace mission."

"There cannot be peace between the Elasians and us. We have deluded ourselves. The truth is, when I am with these people, I do not want peace. I want to kill them."

"Then you're as bad as she is," Kirk said. "You're not obliged to like the Elasians. You're obliged to do a job."

"The job's impossible. She simply won't listen to me."

"*Make* her listen," Kirk said. "Don't be so diplomatic. She respects strength. Come on strong with her, Ambassador."

"I, too, have pride, Captain. I will not be humiliated."

"You're on assignment, Ambassador. So am I. We're under orders to deliver the Dohlman in acceptable condition for this marriage. If it means swallowing a bit of our pride—well, that's part of the job."

Petri sighed. "Very well. I'll make another try."

"Strong, Ambassador. Remember, come on strong with her. Good luck."

A knockout fishwife. What she needed was a swift one to her lovely jaw. Kirk, re-entering the bridge was greeted by Uhura's hopeful question: "Does she like my quarters any better now, Captain?"

"She's made certain . . . arrangements, Lieutenant. But I think things will work out."

The intercom spoke excitedly. "Security alert! Deck five! Security alert!"

Kirk ran for the elevator. On deck five, Security Officer Evans met him as he stepped out. "It's Ambassador Petri, sir. They refuse to explain what happened but—"

At the door to Elaan's quarters, two *Enterprise* security men were confronting the three Elasian guards. "Stand aside, please," Kirk said to Kryton.

The ape-jawed giant said, "Her glory has not summoned you."

Behind him Elaan opened the closed door. "Have this Troyian pig removed," she said.

Petri lay on the cabin floor, face down in a pool of his own blood. The jeweled dagger had been buried in his back.

In Sickbay McCoy looked up at Kirk. "The knife went deep, Jim. He's lost a lot of blood."

Kirk bent over the patient. What he received was a glare. "If I recover," Petri said weakly, "it will be no thanks to you."

"I said talk to her. Not fight her."

"I should have known better than to enter that cabin, unarmed. But you forced me to. I hold you responsible for this."

"Captain!" It was Uhura. "A message from Starfleet Command just in. Class A security, scrambled. I've just put it through the decoder."

"What is it, Lieutenant?"

"The Federation's High Commissioner is on his way to Troyius for the royal wedding."

McCoy whistled. "Whew! Now the fat's really in the fire. When the Commissioner learns the bride has just tried to murder the groom's Ambassador . . ."

"What a comfort you are, Bones!" But McCoy had returned to the patient whom Nurse Christine was preparing for an air hypo. As she applied it, she said, "If the Elasian women are this vicious, sir, why are men so attracted to them? What is their magic?"

"It's not magic," Petri said scornfully. "It's biochemical—a chemical substance in their tears. A man whose flesh is once touched by an Elasian woman's tears is made her slave forever."

"What rot!" Kirk thought. "The man's a fool." The

failure of his mission was about to be exposed to the Federation's High Commissioner—and here he was going on about Elasian females' tears. He walked over to the bed. "Ambassador, I have news for you. The Federation's High Commissioner is on his way to this wedding."

"There will be no wedding. I would not have our ruler marry that creature if the entire galaxy depended on it. And I want nothing more to do with you."

"I didn't ask you to have anything to do with me. I asked you to do your job with her." He turned to McCoy. "Bones, how long will it take to get him back on his feet?"

"A few days. Maybe a week."

Petri raised his head from his pillow. "Captain, in this bed you put me. And in this bed I intend to stay. Indefinitely. I have nothing further to say to you."

Kirk looked at McCoy. Then he shrugged. Uhura and McCoy followed him out to the corridor. "I don't know what to do with him, Jim. He's as bad as she is. They're all pigheaded. And they just plain hate each other."

Uhura said, "You've got to admit he's got the better reason for hate. Captain, can't you explain to the High Commissioner that it's just impossible to—"

"High Commissioners don't like explanations. They like results. How do you handle a woman like that, anyway?"

"You stay away from her, Captain. As far away as—"

She broke off. From the recreation room they were passing came the sound of poignantly haunting music. Uhura's face lighted. "Captain, it used to be said that music hath charms to soothe the savage breast. The Dohlman has a very savage breast. Suppose you—"

"Soothing that woman is asking a lot of any music," McCoy said.

But Kirk was looking reflectively at the recreation room door. He opened it. Spock, sitting apart from the other crew members, was strumming his Vulcan lyre. Its unearthly tones suited the room decorations—its carpet of pink grass, wall vines that broke into drooping, long-stamened blossoms, the fountain spraying purple water into the air.

"Spock, what's that music you're playing?"

"A simple scale. I was just tuning the lyre."

"You can play tunes on that contraption?" McCoy said.

"I took second prize in the all-Vulcan music competition."

"Who took the first one?"

"My father."

"Can you play a love song?" Kirk said.

"A mating song. In ancient times the Vulcan lyre was used to stimulate the mating passion."

"We need some form of such stimulation on this ship," Kirk said. "A mating on Troyius is supposed to take place if we could just persuade the bride to participate in it."

"Inasmuch as she's just knifed her teacher in the bridegroom's etiquette, teaching it to her seems something of a baffler," McCoy said.

"Appoint another teacher," Spock said.

"You, Spock?"

"Certainly not. Logic dictates that the Dohlman will accept only the person of highest rank aboard this vessel."

Everybody looked at Kirk. He looked back at them, considering all the elements involved in Elaan's capitulation to reason.

"All right. Spock, give me five minutes and then start piping that music of yours into the Dohlman's quarters." He left; and as Spock's fingers moved over the strings of his instrument, Uhura sighed. "Mr. Spock, that music really gets to me."

"Yes, I also find it relaxing."

"Relaxing is the very last word I'd use to describe it," Uhura said. "I'd certainly like to learn how to play that lyre."

"I'd be glad to give you the theory, Lieutenant. However, to my knowledge no non-Vulcan has ever mastered the skill."

In Elaan's cabin Kirk was wishing he could give her the theory of acceptable table manners.

He watched her lift a wine bottle from her sumptuously spread dinner table, take a swig from it and wipe her mouth with a lovely arm. She swallowed, and replacing the bottle on the table, said, "So the Ambassador will recover. That's too bad." Then she grabbed a roasted squab from a plate. She bit a mouthful of breast meat from it; and tossing the rest of the delicacy over her shoulder, added, "You've delivered your message. You have my leave to go."

He was fascinated by the efficiency with which she managed to articulate and chew squab at the same time. "I'd like nothing better," he said. "But your glory's impetuous nature has—"

"That Troyian pig was in my quarters without permission. Naturally I stabbed him."

Kirk said, "You Elasians pride yourselves on being a warrior race. Then you must understand discipline—the ability to follow orders as well as to give them. You are under orders to marry the Troyian ruler and familiarize yourself with the habits of his people."

"Troyians disgust me," she said. "Any contact with them makes me feel soiled."

Her cheek was soiled by a large spot of grease from the squab. "It's my experience," Kirk said, "that the prejudices people feel disappear once they get to know each other."

Spock's music had begun to filter into the cabin. "That has not been my experience," she said, reaching for a rich cream pastry.

"In any case, we're still faced with a problem."

"Problem?"

"Your indoctrination in the customs of Troyius."

"I have eliminated that problem."

"No. You eliminated your teacher. The problem remains."

The luscious mouth smiled grimly. How, he couldn't figure out. "And its solution?" she said.

"A new teacher."

"Oh." She placed her dagger on the table. "What's that sickening sound?" The pastry in her hand, she rose, went to the intercom and switched off the Vulcan music. Licking cream from the pastry, she said, "And you—what can you teach me?"

"Table manners for one thing," he said.

He picked up a napkin, went to her, removed the pastry; and wiped her mouth, her cheek and fingers. "This," he said, "is a table napkin. Its function is to remove traces of the wine and food one has swallowed instead of leaving them on the mouth, the cheek, the fingers—and oh yes, the arm."

He wiped her arm. Then, grasping it firmly, he led her over to the table.

"And this," he said, "is a plate. It holds food. It is specifically made to hold food, as floors are not. They are constructed to walk on." He poured wine into a glass; and held it up. "This is a glass," he said, "the vessel from which one drinks wine. A bottle, your glory, is merely intended to hold the wine."

She seized the bottle and took another swig from it. "Leave me," she said.

"You are going to learn what you've been ordered to learn," he said.

"You will return me to Elas at once!"

"That is impossible."

She stamped her foot. "What I command is always possible! I will not go to Troyius! I will not be given to a fat pig of a Troyian as a bride to stop a war!" She lifted the wine bottle again to her mouth. Kirk grabbed it.

"You enjoy the title of Dohlman," he said. "If you don't want the obligations that go with it, give it up!"

Her shock was genuine. "Nobody has ever dared to speak to me in such a manner!"

"That's your trouble," he said. "Nobody has ever told you the truth. You are an uncivilized little savage, a vicious, bad-tempered child in a woman's body . . ."

Her fist leaped out and connected with Kirk's jaw. She had pulled her arm back to strike him again when he grabbed it and slapped her as hard as he could across the face. The blow sent her sprawling back on the bed. Shaking with rage, Kirk shouted, "You've heard the truth from me for the first time in your spoiled life!"

He made for the door—and her dagger hissed past his ear to stick, quivering, in a wall plaque beside his head. He pulled it free; and tossing it back to her, said, "Tomorrow's lesson, your glory, will be on courtesy."

As he jerked the door closed behind him, she yanked wildly at the table cover. He didn't turn at the sound of crashing crockery.

He got out of the bridge elevator to see Spock absorbed in his sensor viewer. "Captain, look at this. At first I defined it as a sensor ghost. But I've run checks on all the instrumentation. The equipment is working perfectly.''

Kirk examined the shadow. ''Hydrogen cloud reflection?''

''None in the area. The ghost appears intermittently.''

''Speculation, Mr. Spock?''

''None, sir. Insufficient data.''

''It's not an instrument malfunction, not a reflection of natural phenomena. A space ship, then?''

The intercom beeped. Scott's voice was thick with anger.

''Captain, must I let these—these passengers fool around with my equipment? I know what you said about showing them respect but . . .''

''Hang on, Scotty. And be pleasant no matter how it hurts. I'm on my way.''

He was startled himself when he opened the door to Engineering. Elaan and her three guards had their heads bent over the warp-drive mechanism. Scott had somehow got his fury under control. He was saying, ''I suppose, ma'am, that even our impulse drive must seem fast—''

''We are interested in how ships are used in combat, not in what drives them. Engines are for mechanics and other menials.''

Scott choked. ''Menials? How long do you think—''

''Mr. Scott!'' Kirk said sharply.

He strode to Elaan. ''Why didn't you tell me you wanted a tour of the engine room?''

''Do I not own the freedom of this ship? I have granted your men permission not to kneel in my presence. What more do you want?''

''Courtesy.''

''Courtesy is not for inferiors.''

Kirk said, ''Mr. Scott, our chief engineer has received you into his department. That was a courtesy. You will respond to it by saying, 'Thank you, Mr. Scott.' ''

He thought she was going to spit at him. Then she said tightly, ''Thank you, Mr. Scott.'' Her guards stared, dumbfounded. She pushed one. ''Come,'' she said to them and swept out.

Scott said, "Your schooling, sir, seems to be taking effect."

A buzz came from the intercom beside them. Spock's voice said, "Bridge to Captain."

"Kirk here."

"That sensor ghost is moving closer, sir."

"On my way."

His guess had been right. The sensor ghost was a space ship. Kirk studied the instrument for a long moment. Then he raised his head. "The question is, Mr. Spock, whose space ship is it?"

"No data yet, sir."

"Captain!" Sulu called. "A distant bearing, sir. Mark 73.5."

"Maximum magnification," Kirk said.

The main viewing screen had been merely showing a telescopic blur of a normally stationary star field. Now there suddenly swam into it the sharp image of an unfamiliar but strangely evil-looking space ship.

"Our ghost has materialized, Captain," Spock said.

Kirk nodded soberly. "A Klingon warship."

He returned to his command chair, the gravity in his face deepened. He turned to look at the screen again. "Any change, Mr. Spock?"

"Negative, sir. The Klingon ship has simply moved into contact range. She's pacing up, precisely matching our sub-light speed."

Though the bridge screen was equipped to show what was moving outside the *Enterprise*, it was not equipped to show what was moving inside it. Thus, Kirk could not see Kryton move stealthily into the engineering room—and take cover behind the huge mount where Second Engineer Watson was working. In perfect secrecy, the Elasian silently removed the main relay box cover, took a small dial-studded disk from his uniform pouch, adjusted the dials and placed the disk in the relay box. It was as he fitted it that Watson sensed something amiss. Tool in hand, he confronted Kryton, shouting, "What are you doing in here?"

Kryton's fist came up under his chin like a uncoiled spring. Watson crumpled. In a flash, Kryton had the body hidden and huddled behind the mount. Then he went back to work in the relay box.

In the bridge, Kirk, still concentrated on the Klingon ship's doings, turned to Uhura. "Lieutenant, open a hailing frequency. Identify us and ask his intentions."

She plugged into her board, shook her head. "No response, sir. Not on any channel."

"Then continue to monitor all frequencies, Lieutenant." He paused a moment. Then he said to Sulu, "Phaser crews stand by, Mr. Sulu." He waited another moment before he added "Maintain yellow alert." He rose from his chair. "Mr. Spock, it's time."

Down in Engineering, still unknown, unheard, Kryton's disk made contact. The lights in the matter-anti-matter grille flickered before they returned to full strength. Kirk, on deck five, was walking down the corridor to Elaan's cabin. As he'd expected, two guards stood at her door. But neither was Kryton. A little uneasy he said, "Where is Kryton?"

"On business," said a guard. Both lifted their weapons. "No one may enter the Dohlman's presence," one said.

"Inform her glory that Captain Kirk requests the honor of a visit."

"The Dohlman has said I shall be whipped to death if I let Captain Kirk pass through this door." Kirk pushed past them. The weapons leveled. A beam flashed twice. The guards fell; and Spock, phaser in hand, came out of the opposite door. "Have them taken to the Security Holding area, Mr. Spock."

Spock said, "Captain, how did you anticipate that she would deny you admittance? The logic by which you arrived at your conclusion escapes me."

"On your planet, Mr. Spock, females are logical. No other planet in the galaxy can make that claim."

He opened Elaan's door to see her sitting before a mirror. She was absorbed in combing the shining hair. As she saw his reflection in the glass, she flew to the bed where she'd discarded her belted dagger. Holding it high, she rushed at Kirk, its point at his heart. He seized her wrist and she shrieked, "You dare to touch a member of the royal family of Elas?"

"In self-defense, I certainly do." He removed the dag-

ger and she tried to rake his face with her nails. He closed
with her, holding her arms immobilized.

"For what you are doing the penalty is death on Elas!"

"You're not on Elas now. You are on my ship. I command here."

She bit his arm. The pain took him off guard. His hold
on her loosened—and she was gone, fled into the adjoining
bathroom, its door clicking locked behind her.

"That's your warning, Captain!" she called through it.
"Don't ever touch me again!"

"All right," Kirk shouted in answer. "Then I'll send
in Mr. Spock or Dr. McCoy! But I'll tell you one thing!
You're going to do what you've been ordered to do by Coun-
cils, Tribunals and bureaucrats . . ."

He'd had it. A Klingon warship in the offing—and here
he was, stuck behind a bathroom door trying to make sense
to an overindulged brat who had no sense. "I'm leaving!"
he yelled. "I'm through with you!"

She opened the door. "Captain . . ." She hesitated.
"There . . . is one thing you . . . can teach me . . ."

"No, there isn't!" he roared at her. "You were right
the first time! There's nothing I want to teach you! Not any
more! You know everything!"

She began to cry. "I don't know everything. I don't
know how to make people like me. Everybody hates me . . ."

He was startled into contrition. Genuine tears flooded
the dark eyes. It was a sight he'd never thought to see. "Now
look . . ." he said. "It's not that anybody hates you . . ."

"Yes, they do," she sobbed. "Everybody does . . ."

He went to her and wiped the tear-wet cheeks with his
hand. "Stop crying," he said. "It's just that nobody likes to
be treated as though they didn't exist . . ."

He was suddenly conscious of heat. "Something's
wrong with the ventilation of this room . . . I—I need some
air . . . we'll have a short recess, your glory."

"Captain . . ." He turned from the door. The luscious
mouth was smiling at him, the pearl-toned arms outstretched
to him. He stared at her for a long moment. Then he went
straight into the arms. He kissed her—and the world, the
Klingon ship, the High Commissioner, all he'd ever known
in his life before was as though it had never existed.

She whispered, "You . . . slapped me."

Unsteadily, Kirk said, "We'll . . . talk about it later . . ." His mouth found hers again.

Uhura, checking her dials, pushed the intercom button. "Bridge to Captain," she said. She glanced over at Spock. "Mr. Spock, I'm getting—"

"I have it on my sensor," Spock said.

"Bridge to Captain," she repeated, frowning. "Come in, Captain. Captain Kirk, please answer."

Kirk's voice came, unfamiliar, dazed. "Kirk here."

"Captain, I'm picking up a transmission from inside the *Enterprise*. It's on a tight beam aimed at the Klingon vessel."

Elaan was nibbling at the lobe of Kirk's ear. "Transmission?" he echoed vaguely. Her lashes were black. They should have been silver blonde but they weren't. He said, "Stop that." She kissed the ear; and he was able to focus his attention on the intercom long enough to ask, "Can you pinpoint the source of the transmission, Lieutenant?"

"Spock here, Captain. I am triangulating now. It's coming from the engine room, sir."

The news broke through his entrancement. "Security to engineering! An intruder! Security alert all decks!"

He ran for the door and the elevator. In the engine room, Scott met him, his face stricken. He pointed to the body of Watson. "Watson must have discovered the devil after he'd sneaked in here. He got killed for it. He had this in his hand when I found him. It looks like some kind of transmitter."

Kirk took it. "It's Klingon," he said.

McCoy rose from Watson's body. "Neck snapped clean, Jim."

Kirk walked over to where two Security guards, their phasers trained on Kryton, held the ape-jawed Elasian in custody.

"What signal did you send that Klingon ship? What was your assignment?"

Impassive, his small eyes bright with scorn, Kryton said, "Captain, you must know I will say nothing. Our interrogation methods are far more excruciating than anything you people are capable of.''

"I'm aware you're trained to resist any form of *physical* torture." Kirk moved to the intercom. "Kirk to Spock."

"Spock here, Captain."

"Mr. Spock, it is Kryton who's been transmitting. He refuses to talk. I'll need you to do the Vulcan mind-meld."

"Captain!" It was Evans, one of the Security guards. "The prisoner—he's sick . . ." Kirk whirled to see Kryton clutch at his stomach. The Elasian sagged at the knees—and his hand whipped out to seize Evans' phaser. He reversed it, fired it at himself and disappeared.

Stunned, Evans said, "Captain, I'm sorry. But he really seemed—"

"What was he hiding that was so important he had to die to keep it secret?" Hard-faced, Kirk turned to Scott. "He didn't come in here just to use a transmitter. Scotty, I want you to check every relay you've got."

"Captain, do you realize how many relays there are in Engineering?"

"Don't waste time telling me. Do it!"

He wasted no time himself in getting back to Elaan's cabin. She took the news of Kryton's suicide quietly. "He's been half out of his mind ever since the announcement of my wedding. He was of noble family—and he loved me."

"Then he sold out to the Klingons out of jealousy?"

"Probably." She laid her hand on his heart. "It is mine, is it not? Let us not speak of unimportant matters."

"There's a Klingon warship out there," he told her. "What is it there for? It isn't keeping pace with us just to prevent your marriage."

She put her silver blonde head on his shoulder. "We should welcome their help against the marriage," she said.

He grasped her upper arms. "Elaan, two planets, the stability of an entire star system depends on your marriage. We both have a duty to forget what happened."

"Could you do that? Give me to another man?"

"My orders—and yours—say you *belong* to that other man. What happened between us was an accident."

"It was no accident. I chose you and you chose me." Before he could speak, she added, "I have a plan. With this

ship you could utterly obliterate Troyius. Then there would
be no need for the marriage. Our grateful people would give
you command of the star system.''

He stared at her in horror. "How can you think of such
a monstrous thing?''

"He is Troyian," she said. And was in his arms again.
"You cannot fight against this love . . . against my love.''

"Captain!" It was Spock on the intercom. There was
a pause before he said, "May we see you a moment?''

Kirk didn't answer. The witch in his arms was right.
He could not fight against this love, this passion, this fatal-
ity—whatever it was, whatever name one chose to give it.
Nameless or named, it held him in thrall. His lips were on
hers again—and the door opened. Spock and McCoy stood
there, staring in unbelief.

"Jim!"

Kirk raised unseeing eyes.

"*Jim!* May I have a word with you, please?''

Kirk pulled free of the clinging arms; and moved toward the door with the slow, ponderous walk of a man walking under water. He looked back at Elaan. Then he stumbled
out into the corridor.

"Captain, are you all right?" Spock said.

He nodded.

"Jim, did she cry?''

"What?''

"*Did she cry?* Did her tears touch your skin?''

Kirk frowned. "Yes.''

McCoy sighed. "Then we're in trouble. Jim, listen to
me. Petri told Christine that Elasian women's tears contain a
biochemical substance that acts like a super, grade A love
potion.''

Kirk was staring at the hand that had wiped the tears
from Elaan's cheek. "And according to Petri, the effects don't
wear off," McCoy said.

"Bones, you've got to find me an antidote.''

"I can try but I'll need to make tests of—''

The corridor intercom spoke. "Bridge to Captain!''

"Kirk here.''

Sulu's anxious voice said, "Captain, the Klingon ship
has changed course! It's heading toward us at warp speed!''

All look of bemusement left Kirk's face. "Battle stations!" he ordered crisply. "I'm on my way."

Klaxon alarm shrieks filled the bridge as he stepped from the elevator. A fast glance at the screen showed the swiftly enlarging image of the Klingon ship. "Stand by, phasers!" he ordered, running to his command chair.

"Phasers, ready, sir," Sulu reported.

Spock called, "His speed is better than Warp Six, Captain!"

Eyes on the screen, Kirk said, "Mr. Chekov, lay in a course to take us clear of this system. If he wants to fight, we'll need room to maneuver."

"Course computed, sir," Chekov said.

"And laid in, Captain."

"Very well, Mr. Sulu. Ahead, Warp Two and—"

The intercom beeped to the sound of Scott's agitated voice. "Captain! The matter-anti-matter reactor is—"

Before Scott had uttered the next word, Kirk had barked, "Belay that order, Mr. Sulu!"

Sulu jerked his hand from the button he was about to push as though it were red-hot. Spock left his station to come and stand beside Kirk.

"What is it, Scotty?"

Everyone on the bridge could hear Scott say, "The anti-matter pod is rigged to blow up the moment we go into warp drive."

Moments went by before Kirk spoke. Then he said, "That bomb he planted, Scotty. Can you dismantle it?"

"Not without blowing us halfway across the galaxy."

Like a blow Kirk could feel the pressure of the eyes focussed on him. He drew a deep breath. "Then give us every ounce of power you've got from the impulse drive. And find a solution to that bomb."

It was into this atmosphere of repressed excitement that Elaan stepped from the bridge elevator. On the screen the Klingon ship was growing in size and detail. "Mr. Sulu, stand by to make your maneuvers smartly. She'll be sluggish in response."

Kirk turned back to the screen and saw Elaan. Absorbed though he was in crisis, he had to fight the impulse to go to her by grasping the arms of his chair. Spock moved closer to him; and Sulu said tonelessly, "One hundred thousand kilometers."

Time ambled by. Then Sulu said, "Ninety kilometers."

"Hold your fire," Kirk said.

Sulu moistened his lips. "Sixty. Fifty."

On the screen the Klingon ship blurred in a burst of speed. "She's passed us without firing a shot," Sulu said very quietly.

"Captain, I don't think they meant to attack us," Spock said. Now that the crisis had passed, Kirk was conscious again only of the presence of Elaan. He rose from his chair as though pulled to her by an invisible chain. Watchful, Spock said warningly, "*This* time we have been fortunate."

The invisible chain snapped. Kirk sank back in his chair. "Yes, their tactics are clear now. They were trying to tempt us to cut in warp drive. That way we'd have blown ourselves up. Their problem would have been solved for them without risking war with the Federation. Very neat."

"Very," Spock said. "But why do they consider the possession of this system so vital?"

"A very good question, Mr. Spock."

"I have another question, sir. Isn't the bridge the wrong place for the Dohlman to be at a time like this?"

"I'll be the judge of—" Kirk began. He met Spock's eyes. "You're right, Mr. Spock. Thank you."

He strode over to Elaan. "I want you to leave the bridge and go to Sickbay. It's the best-protected part of the ship."

"I want to be with you," she said.

"Your presence here is interfering with my efficiency—my ability to protect you."

"I won't go."

Gripping her shoulders, he propelled her toward the elevator. Over her head, he looked at Spock. "You have the con, Mr. Spock."

As the elevator door slid closed, she flung her arms about his neck. "I love you. I have chosen you. But I do not understand why you did not fight the Klingon."

"If I can do better by my mission by running away, then I run away."

"That mission," she said, "is to deliver me to Troyius."

"Yes, it is," he said.

"You would have me wear my wedding dress for another man and never see me again?"

"Yes, Elaan."

"Are you happy at that prospect?"

"No."

The intercom buzzed. "Scott to Captain."

"Kirk here."

"Bad news, Skipper. The entire dilythium crystal converter assembly is fused. No chance of repair. It's completely unusable."

"No way to restore warp drive?"

"Not without the dilythium crystal, sir. We can't even generate enough power to fire our weapons."

"Elaan, I've got to get back to the bridge. *Please* go to Sickbay. There's its door. Down this corridor."

She stood on tiptoe to kiss his forehead. "Yes, my brave love."

He watched her move down to the Sickbay door. Whatever chemical substance it was in the tears he had wiped from her cheek, it was powerful stuff.

Mysteriously baffling was how McCoy was finding it. Twenty-four tests—and analysis of it was as elusive as ever.

Petri watched him examine a read-out handed him by Nurse Christine. "You're wasting your time," he said. "There is no antidote to the poison of Elasian tears. The men of Elas have tried desperately to locate one. They've always failed." He had leaned back against his pillow when Elaan opened the Sickbay door. She addressed McCoy. "The Captain asked me to come here for safety."

Petri raised his head again. "And our safety? What about that with this woman around? How do you estimate our chances for survival, Dr. McCoy?"

"That's the Captain's responsibility," McCoy said.

Petri looked soberly thoughtful. After a long moment, he reached down into the gold casket he'd placed under his bed and withdrew the necklace Elaan had rejected. He pulled on his robe and walked slowly over to her.

"I have failed in my responsibility to my people," he

said heavily. "With more wisdom I might have been able to prepare you to marry our ruler. Now that we may all die, I again ask you to accept this necklace as a token of respect for the true wish of my—of our people—for peace between us."

"Responsibility, duty—that's all you men ever think about!" she said angrily.

But she took the necklace.

When Kirk got back to the bridge, it was for more bad news. It was Uhura who had to give it to him. "A message from the Klingon ship, sir. We are ordered to stand by for boarding or be destroyed. They demand an immediate reply."

"So he's going to force a fight," Kirk said.

Back in his command chair, he struck his intercom button. "Kirk to Engineering. Energy status, Scotty?"

"Ninety-three percent of impulse power, Captain."

"We can still maneuver, sir," Spock said.

"Aye, we can wallow like a garbage scow," Scott said. "Our shields will hold out for a few passes. But without the matter-anti-matter reactors, we've no chance against a starship. Captain, can't you call Starfleet in *this* emergency?"

"And tell the Klingons they've succeeded in knocking out the warp engines?" Kirk retorted. "No, we'll stall for time."

He swung around to confront the taut faces in the bridge. "We will proceed," he said, "on course; in hope that the Klingons can be bluffed—or think better of starting a general war. Lieutenant Uhura, open a hailing frequency."

He seized his speaker. "This is Captain James Kirk of the *USS Enterprise* on Federation business. Our mission is peaceful but we are not prepared to accept interference."

The hoarse Klingon voice filled the bridge. "Prepare to be boarded or destroyed."

"Very effective, our strategy," Kirk muttered.

"Captain, the Klingon is closing in on an intercept course!" Sulu exclaimed. "Five hundred thousand kilometers." He added, "Deflector shields up!"

It was the moment Elaan chose to step out of the bridge elevator, radiant in the shimmering white of her wedding dress, the Troyian necklace of pellucid jewels around her neck. Kirk tore his eyes from the vision she made—and hit the intercom with his fist. "Mr. Scott, can you deliver even partial power to the main phaser banks?"

"No, sir. Not a chance."

Elaan was beside Kirk. Averting his eyes from her, he said, "I told you to stay in Sickbay."

"If I'm going to die, I want to die with you."

"We don't intend to die. Leave the bridge."

She drifted away toward the elevator and stopped to lean her head back against the wall.

Sulu shouted, "One thousand kilometers!"—and the ship shuddered under impact by a Klingon missile. As it burst against a deflector shield, its flash bathed the *Enterprise* in a multi-colored auroral light.

"He's passed us," Spock said. "All shields held."

"Mr. Sulu, come to 143 mark 2. Keep our forward shields to him."

"Here he comes again, sir," Sulu said.

"Stay with the controls. Keep those forward shields to him." On the screen the Klingon ship was an approaching streak of speed.

"He's going for our flank, Mr. Sulu. Hard over! Bring her around!"

The force of the second missile shook every chair in the bridge. "Sulu!" Kirk shouted.

"Sorry, Captain. She won't respond fast enough on impulse drive."

"He's passed us again," Spock said. "There's damage to number four shield, sir."

"How bad?"

"It won't take another full strike. Captain, I'm getting some very peculiar readings on the sensor board."

"What sort of readings, Mr. Spock?"

The Vulcan had seized his tricorder and was scanning the bridge area with it. Suddenly, he leaped from his chair to point to Elaan. "*She* is the source!" he cried.

"She?" Kirk said. "You mean Elaan?"

"The necklace, Captain!"

Both men ran to her. "What kind of jewels are in that thing?" Kirk demanded.

Bewildered, she fingered the necklace. "We call the white beads radans. They are quite common stones."

Spock scanned the diamonds with a circular device on his tricorder. Under it, they glowed and sparkled with an unearthly fire.

"It's only because of its antiquity that the necklace is prized," Elaan said.

"Common stones!" Kirk said. "No wonder the Klingons are interested in this star system! May I have that necklace, your glory?"

"If it can be of any help—of course," she said.

"You may just have saved our lives," Kirk said. "Mr. Spock, do you think Scotty could use some dilythium crystals?"

"There's a highly positive element in your supposition, Captain." The necklace in hand, Spock entered the elevator.

"He's coming in again, sir," Sulu cried.

"Mr. Sulu, stand by my order to turn *quickly* to port. Try to protect number four shield. *Now*, Mr. Sulu! Hard to port!"

Again the shields reflected the brilliant interplay of multi-colored light as the ship vibrated under shock by the Klingon attack. "Shields holding but weakened," Sulu called.

"Captain, message coming in," Uhura reported. At Kirk's nod, she hit the speaker.

The guttural Klingon voice had triumph in it. "*Enterprise*, our readings confirm your power extremely low, your shields buckling. This is your last chance to surrender."

Sulu said. "Number four shield just collapsed, sir. Impulse power down to 31 percent."

Kirk walked over to Uhura's station. "Lieutenant, open a channel." He seized the microphone. "This is Captain Kirk. I request your terms of surrender." ·

"No terms. Surrender must be unconditional and immediate."

Kirk struck the intercom button. "Scotty, what's the estimate?"

"We're fitting it now, sir. We'll need to run a few tests to make sure—"

"We'll test it in combat."

Spock said, "Those are crude crystals, sir. There's no way to judge what the unusual shapes will do to energy flow."

Scott used the intercom to add his caution. "Captain, a hitch in the energy flow could blow us up just as effectively as—"

Kirk cut him off. "Let me know when it's in place." He returned to Uhura. "Hailing frequency again, Lieutenant." Back of his command chair, he said into his speaker, "This is the USS Enterprise. Will you guarantee the safety of our passenger, the Dohlman of Elas?"

The harsh voice repeated, "No conditions. Surrender immediate."

"Captain, he's starting his run!"

"I see, Mr. Sulu." Standing before the screen, Kirk felt a quiet hand laid on his arm. Elaan watched with him as death in the form of the Klingon ship neared them, itself a black missile made vague by speed. Then Scott spoke from the intercom. "It's in place, sir—but I can't answer for . . ."

"Get up here fast!" Kirk said. He wheeled from the screen. "Mr. Sulu, stand by for warp maneuver. Mr. Chekov, arm photon torpedoes."

"Photon torpedoes ready, sir."

"Warp power to the shields, Captain?"

"Negative, Mr. Sulu. His sensors would pick up our power increase. The more helpless he thinks we are, the closer he'll come. It's as he passes I want warp drive cut in. You'll pivot at Warp Two, Mr. Sulu, to bring all tubes to bear."

"Aye, sir."

"Mr. Chekov, give him the full spread of photon torpedoes."

Scott rushed into the bridge to take his place at his station and Sulu said, "One hundred thousand kilometers, sir."

"Mr. Scott, stand by to cut in warp power."

The engineer looked up from his control. "Fluctuation, Captain. It's the shape of the crystals. I was afraid of that."

"Seventy-five kilometers," Sulu said.

"He'll fire at minimum range, Mr. Sulu."

"Forty," Sulu said.

Scott's worried eyes were on the flickering lights of his board. "It won't steady down, Captain."

The mass of the Klingon ship nearly filled the screen. Kirk said, "Warp in, Scotty. Full power to the shields. Mr. Sulu, warp two. Come to course 147 mark 3."

The Klingon ship fired. The *Enterprise* swerved, began to rotate dizzily in the dazzle of the now familiar auroral blaze reflected from its wounded shields.

"We're still here!" Scott cried, unbelieving.

"Fire photon torpedoes! Full spread!"

They waited. Elaan's hand found Kirk's. Then it came. From far out in space there came the shattering roar of explosion, of tearing metal. Another one detonated.

"Direct hit amidship by photon torpedo!" Sulu yelled.

Spock lifted his head. "Damage to Klingon number three shield, Captain. Number four obliterated. They've lost maneuver power, sir."

Chekov turned. "He's badly damaged. Retreating at reduced speed, sir."

"Secure from general quarters," Kirk said.

Elaan, her eyes shining with proud excitement, looked at him, startled. "You will not pursue and finish him off?"

"No." His eyes met hers. It was a long moment before he was able to say, "Mr. Sulu, resume course to Troyius."

Having said it, he looked away from the dead hope in her face.

In the Transporter Room, Petri had taken his place on the platform. As Elaan entered in her wedding dress, she touched the Troyian necklace she wore and smiled at him. "The two missing stones in this," she said, "saved all our lives, Ambassador Petri." He bowed deeply.

She went to Kirk. "You will beam-down for—the ceremony?"

"No."

She detached the jeweled dagger from her belt. "I wish you to have this as a personal memento. You have taught me that such things are no longer for me." She stooped and kissed his hand. "Remember me," she whispered.

"I have no choice," he said.

"Nor have I. All we've got now is duty and responsibility."

She took her place on the platform, her two guards beside her. "Good-bye, Captain James Kirk." Her voice broke.

"Good-bye," Kirk said. He walked swiftly to Scott at the transporter desk. "Energize," he said. Scott turned the dial and the figure of Elaan began to shimmer. He turned for his last look at her. Her eyes were on his, bright with tears.

McCoy met him excitedly as he walked out of the bridge elevator. "Jim, I've finally isolated the poisonous substance in that woman's tears. I think I've found the antidote."

"There's no need for it, Doctor," Spock said. "The Captain has found his own antidote. The *Enterprise* infected the Captain long before the Dohlman's tears touched him."

Kirk said, "Mr. Sulu, take us out of orbit. Ahead Warp Two."

Was the *Enterprise* the antidote to Elaan? McCoy and Spock seemed very sure it was. He was not so sure. Not now, anyway.

THE PARADISE SYNDROME

Writer: Margaret Armen
Director: Jud Taylor
Guest stars: Sabrina Scharf, Rudy Solari

Doom was in the monster asteroid hurtling toward the planet on a collision course.

It was a fate which Kirk refused to accept. Stately pine trees edged the meadow where he, Spock and McCoy had materialized. There was the nostalgic fragrance of honeysuckle in his nostrils mingled with the freshness of wild roses. From somewhere nearby he could hear the murmur of a brook bubbling over pebbles. Violets, he thought. Their flat, sweet green leaves would carpet its damp banks, the flowers hidden among them.

"It's unbelievable," he said, suddenly homesick, Earth-sick. He stooped to pick a buttercup. "How long, Bones, since you saw one of these?"

"At least three years, Jim."

"It seems like three hundred." But the planet's similarity to Earth was less of a mystery than the astounding fact of its survival. It was located in a sector of its solar system where an asteroid belt had succeeded in smashing all other planets into dusty, drifting desolation.

"Two months from now when that giant asteroid hits this place—" McCoy began.

"We're here to see that it doesn't hit it," Kirk said. "Spock, how much time do we have to investigate?"

"If we're to divert the asteroid, Captain, we must warp out of orbit within thirty hours. Every second we delay in reaching the deflection point will compound the problem, perhaps past solution."

McCoy halted. "What in blazes is *that*?" he exclaimed.

Ahead of them, topping a shallow hill stood a tall tower, obelisk-shaped, composed of some gleaming metal. Wild flowers were heaped around its base. Nearing it, they could see that its surface was inscribed with curious, unreadable symbols.

"Analysis, Mr. Spock."

Spock was readjusting a dial on his tricorder. He frowned. "Incomplete, sir. It's an alien metal of some kind—an alloy resistant to probe. Readings can't even measure its age accurately."

"Any theories about what it could be?"

"Negative, Captain. But alloys of this complexity are found only in cultures that parallel our own—or surpass it."

"Buttercups in a meteor area but no meteor craters," McCoy said. "The whole place is an enigma, biologically and culturally."

"Thirty hours," Kirk said. "Let's not waste them. This Paradise may support some life-forms."

It did. Below the obelisk's hill lay a clearing. Copper-skinned people were moving about in it with an ease which declared it to be their home. In its center a large, circular lodge lifted to a roof that seemed thatched with reeds. Animal hides had been sewn together and stretched to compose its walls. A woman, children around her, was mixing meal with water she dipped from a crude pottery bowl with a gourd. Near her an old man, a heap of what looked like flint arrow heads beside him, was bent over his work. To his right, younger men, magnificently muscled, bows slung over their shoulders, were gathered around a painted skin target, engaged in some amiable argument. Perhaps it was the way the russet tone of their bodies blended with the hue of their beaded leather clothing that explained the sense of peace that lay like a blessing over the whole settlement. Here was man at one with his environment.

"Why, they look—I'd swear they are American Indians!" cried McCoy.

"They are," Spock said. "A mixture of advanced tribes—Navajo, Mohican, Delaware."

"It's like coming on Shangri-La," Kirk said. "Could

there be a more evolved civilization on this planet, Spock? One capable of building that obelisk—or developing an asteroid-deflector system?''

"The sensors indicate only one form of life type here, Captain.''

"Shouldn't we tell them, Jim?''

"What, Bones? That an asteroid is going to smash their world to atoms?''

Spock said, "Our appearance would only serve to frighten and confuse them, Doctor.''

"All right," Kirk said abruptly. "We've got a job to do. Let's get back to the *Enterprise*.'' But as he turned away, he looked back at the Indian village, his face wistful, a little envious.

"Something wrong, Jim?''

"What?'' Kirk said absently. "Oh, nothing. It just looks so peaceful and uncomplicated. No problems, no command decisions. Just *living*.''

McCoy smiled. "Back in the twentieth century it was called the 'Tahiti syndrome,' Jim— a typical reaction to idyllic, unspoiled nature. It's especially common to overpressured leader types like Star Fleet captains.''

"All right, Bones. So I need a vacation. First let's take care of that asteroid.''

Kirk moved on toward the obelisk. Stepping on to its pediment, he flipped open his communicator. "Kirk to *Enterprise*!''

"Aye, Captain.'' It was Scott's voice.

The order for beam-up was on Kirk's lips when the metal under his feet gave way. What appeared to be a panel in the pediment slid open and tumbled him down a steep flight of stairs. In the narrow shaft of daylight that shone through the gap, he had barely time to note that the panel's underside was dotted with vari-colored control buttons. Then the panel closed silently. Groggy, he raised his head—and his shoulder hit one of the buttons. A shrill buzz sounded. A blue-green beam flashed out. It widened and spread until he was completely bathed in blue-green luminescence. It held him, struggling. Then he fell down the rest of the steep stairs—and lay still.

* * *

Spock was the first to notice his disappearance. Appalled, McCoy joined him. They circled the obelisk, their anxiety mounting in them. When Spock had raked the empty meadow with his eyes to no effect, he opened his communicator, reported the news to Scott and ordered beam-down of a Security Guard search party. But neither the Guards nor their sensor probes succeeded where the Vulcan's sharp eyes had failed. The panel gave no hint of its existence. Stern-faced, Spock gave the meadow another rake with his eyes before he made his decision. He jerked open his communicator to say curtly, "Prepare to beam us all back up, Mr. Scott. We're warping out of orbit immediately."

"Leaving? You can't be serious, Spock!" McCoy said.

"That asteroid is almost as large as your Earth's moon, Doctor—"

"The devil with the asteroid!" McCoy shouted. "It won't get here for two months!"

"If we reach that deflection point in time, it may not get here at all," Spock's face was impassive.

"In the meantime, what about Jim?"

"As soon as the asteroid is diverted, we will return and resume the search."

"That'll be hours from now! He may be hurt! Dying!"

Spock faced him. "If we fail to reach that deflection point at the exact moment, we will not be able to divert it. In such case, Doctor, everyone on this planet, including the Captain, will die."

"Can a few minutes more matter?"

"In the time it has taken for this explanation, the asteroid has sped thousands of miles closer to this planet—and to the Captain." Imperturbable, he spoke into his communicator. "Beam us up, Mr. Scott."

Scott's voice was heavy with disapproval. "Beaming up, Mr. Spock."

The object of their concern wasn't dying; but he was breathing painfully, slowly. He seemed to be in a large, vault-like chamber; but the dizziness in his head made it as hard for his eyes to focus as it made it to remember where he'd come from or how he'd got here. He was sure of nothing but the vertigo that swayed him in sickly waves when he tried to stand up. In his fall, he'd dropped his phaser and communicator. Now he stumbled over them. He picked them up, staring at them without recognizing them. After a moment, he stopped puzzling over them to start groping his way up the metal stairs. As he stepped on the first one, a sharp musical note sounded. He accepted it with the same dazedness that had accepted the unfamiliarity of his phaser and communicator. Then his reaching hand brushed against some button in the panel above him. It slid open as silently as it had closed; and he hauled himself up through it into the daylight.

The three girls, flower baskets in their arms, startled him. So did their bronze skins. They were staring at him, more astonished than he was. One was beautiful, he thought. Under the long, black hair that glittered in the sunshine, she bore herself with the dignity of a young queen, despite the amazement on her face.

In their mutually dumbfounded silence, he decided he liked her high cheekbones. They emphasized the lovely, smooth planes of her brow, cheeks and chin. The other two girls seemed frightened of him. So was she, he suspected; but she didn't turn to run away. Instead, she made a commanding gesture to her companions—and dropped to her knees at Kirk's feet. Then the others knelt, too. All three placed their palms on their foreheads.

Kirk found his voice. It was hoarse. "Who—are you?" he said.

"I am Miramanee," the queenlike girl said. "We are your people. We have been waiting for you to come."

But her ready welcome of him wasn't repeated so quickly from the elderly chief of the Indian village. Kirk's greeting into the communal lodge was courteous but reserved. It was primitively but comfortably furnished with mats and divans of deerhide. Tomahawks, spears, skin shields and flint knives decorated its walls. There was a fire pit in its center, embers in it still glowing red. The chief sat beside it. Flanking him, three young braves kept their black eyes fixed on Kirk's face. One wore a gleaming silver headband, embossed with an emblem into which a likeness of the obelisk had been etched. Miramanee made her obeisance to the chief; and turning to Kirk, said, "This is Goro."

The old man gestured to a pile of skins across from him.

"Our priestess has said you appeared to her and her handmaidens from the walls of the temple. So it is that our legend foretells. Though we do not doubt the words of Miramanee, these are troubled times. We must be sure."

"I'll answer any questions I can," Kirk said, "but as I told your priestess, many things are strange to me."

The warrior who wore the emblemed headband cried out, "He doesn't even know our danger! How can he save us?"

"Silence, Salish! It is against custom to interrupt the tribal Elder in council! Even for the Medicine chief!"

But Salish persisted. "Words will not save us when the skies darken! I say he must *prove* he is a god!"

"I will have silence!" Goro addressed Kirk. "Three times the skies have darkened since the harvest. Our legend predicts much danger. It promises that the Wise Ones who placed us here will send a god to save us—one who can awake the temple spirit and make the skies grow quiet. Can you do this?"

Kirk hesitated, searching frantically through his emptied memory for some recollection that would make sense of the question. He saw the suspicion in Salish's eyes hardening into open scorn. "I came from the temple," he said finally. "Just as Miramanee has told . . . but I came from the sky, too. I can't remember this clearly, but—"

His stumbling words were interrupted by a stir at the lodge entrance. A man entered, the limp body of a boy in his arms. Both were dripping wet. Miramanee, her hand on the boy's soaked hair, cried, "A bad thing has happened! Salish, the child does not breathe! The fish nets pulled him to the bottom of the river. Lino has brought him quickly but he does not move!"

Rising, the Medicine chief went to the boy, and bending his ear to the chest, listened intently. Then he pried open an eyelid to peer into the pupil. After a moment, he straightened. "There is no sound in the body," he announced, "and no light in the eyes. The child will move no more."

Lino had laid the small body on a heap of skins. Kirk glanced around at the shocked, stricken faces. He got up,

moved quickly to the child and raised the head. "He is still
breathing," he said. Then he stooped to place his mouth on
the cold lips. Breathing regularly and deeply, he exhaled air
into them. After a moment, he seized the ankles; and began
to flex them back and forward against the chest. Salish made
a threatening move toward him. He held up a restraining hand
and Goro called, "Wait!"

The keen old ears had heard the slight moan. The child
stirred feebly—and began to retch. Kirk massaged him
briskly. There was a gasping breath. The eyes opened. Kirk
stood up, relief flooding through him. "He will be all right
now," he said.

Goro placed his palm on his forehead. "The people are
grateful."

"It's a simple technique. It goes away back . . . away
back to—"

His voice trailed off. Away back to where? He couldn't
remember. This "simple technique"—where had he learned
it? Now that the emergency's tension had passed, it was replaced by an anguish of frustration. How had he been marooned in a present that denied him any past? Who was he?
He felt as though he were dissolving, his very being slipping
through his fingers like so much water.

In a dream he heard Goro say, "Only a god can breathe
life into the dead." In a dream he saw him turn to the three
young braves. "Do you still question that the legend is fulfilled?"

Two shook their heads. Salish alone refused to touch
palm to forehead. Goro turned to Miramanee. "Give the
Medicine lodge to the god."

Still in his nightmare of non-being, Kirk felt the silver
band of the Medicine chief placed on his head.

It was Scott's angry opinion that too much was being
asked of his engines.

"I can't give you Warp Nine much longer, Spock."
Calculated disrespect went into the engineer's intercom. "My
engines are showing signs of stress."

"Stress or not, we cannot reduce speed, Mr. Scott."

"If these circuits of mine get much hotter—"

The nervous systems of the *Enterprise* bridge personnel

were also showing signs of stress. Their circuits were getting hot under pressure of the race against time being made by the asteroid. Spock alone preserved his equanimity. But even his quiet eyes were riveted to the main viewing screen where a small luminous blip was becoming increasingly visible. The irregular mass of the thing grew larger and larger, its dull though multiple colors revealing themselves more distinctly with every moment.

"Deflection point minus seven," Chekov said.

"Full power, Mr. Scott," Spock said into his intercom.

"The relays will reject the overload!"

"Then bypass the relays. Go to manual control."

"If I do that, we'll burn out the engines!"

"I want full power," Spock said tonelessly.

"Aye, sir."

The First Officer swung the command chair around to Sulu. "Magnification, factor 12, Mr. Sulu."

Sulu moved a control switch—and the image on the screen jumped into enormous contour. For the first time the asteroid's ominous details could be seen, malignantly jagged—a sharp-fanged mass of rock speeding toward them through the trackless vacuum of space.

"Deflection point minus four," Chekov said.

Spock looked away from the frightful immensity on the screen and Chekov said, "Minus three now, sir."

The Vulcan hit his intercom button. "All engines stop. Hold position here, Mr. Scott."

"All engines stopped, sir."

"Prepare to activate deflectors."

"Aye, sir."

There was an irregular cracking sound, acutely heard in the sudden silence usually filled by the engines' smooth humming. The ship vibrated.

"Power dropping, sir!" cried Sulu.

"Engineering section! Maintain full power. *Full power!*"

Scott's voice was hard. "Dilythium circuits failing, sir. We'll have to replace them."

"Not now," Spock said.

"Zero! Deflection point—we've reached it, sir!"

"Activate!" Spock said sharply.

On the screen the monstrous mass glowed redly. Then the glow flickered and faded.

"Degree of deflection, Mr. Sulu?"

"Insufficient, sir."

It was defeat. Horrified silence held the bridge in thrall.

The composure of Spock's voice came like a benediction. "Recircuit power to engines, Mr. Scott. Maximum speed. The heading is 37 mark 010."

"That heading will put us right in the asteroid's path, sir."

"I am aware of that, Mr. Chekov. My intention is to retreat before it until we can employ all our power on our phaser beams."

"What for?" McCoy demanded.

"To destroy it." Spock turned his chair around as though he were addressing the entire personnel in the bridge. "A narrow phaser beam," he said, "that is concentrated on a single spot of that rock will split it."

"It's also likely to cripple the ship," McCoy said. "Then we'll be crushed by the thing."

"Incorrect, Doctor. We could still evade its path by using our impulse power."

"Jim won't be able to get out of its path!"

"That is another calculated risk we must take," Spock said.

Miramanee, her arms full of new buckskin garments, was approaching Kirk's Medicine lodge when Salish stepped out from behind a pine tree.

"Where are you going?" he said.

"It is my duty to see to the needs of the god," she said quietly.

Salish tore the clothing from her. "You should be working on our ritual cloak!"

She retrieved the clothing. "There will be no ritual between us now, Salish." She spoke gently.

"You cannot go against tradition!"

"It is because of tradition that we cannot now be joined," she said.

"You are promised to *me*!"

"That was before he came."

"Tribal priestess and Medicine chief are always joined!"

"*He* is the Medicine chief." She paused. "Choose another, Salish. Any maiden will be honored to join with you."

"I do not wish another."

Genuine compassion came into her face. "You have no choice," she said.

"And if you had a choice, Miramanee, would you choose me?"

She didn't answer. His face darkened. He wheeled and strode off into a grove of sycamore trees. She shook her head sadly as she watched him disappear. Then her black eyes lit. She walked quickly toward the Medicine lodge; and Kirk, roused from his brooding by her entrance, looked up at her and smiled.

"Perhaps you would like to bathe before you clothe yourself in these." She placed the Indian garments at his feet.

"Miramanee, tell me about the Wise Ones."

"Tell? But a god knows everything."

"Not this god," Kirk said wryly. "Tell me."

She knelt beside him, fingering his uniform wonderingly. "The Wise Ones? They brought us here from far away. They chose a Medicine chief to keep the secret of the temple and to use it when the sky darkens." She reached to touch the back of his uniform. "There are no lacings here," she said, puzzled. "How is it removed?"

He knew he was flushing and felt like a fool. Gently he removed her hand. "And the secret was passed from father to son? Then why doesn't Salish use the secret? Why are the people in danger?"

Still puzzled, she was seeking a way to loosen his belt. "The father of Salish died before he could tell him the secret."

Kirk had taken her hands in his when two girls, accompanied by Goro, came into the lodge. They placed their baskets of fruit at his feet; and Goro, touching his forehead respectfully, said, "The people honor your name. But they do not know what you wish to be called."

Kirk felt the anguish of frustration again. "What do I want to be called?" equaled "Who am I?"—that "I" of his

without a Past, without identity. He was sweating as he fought
to dredge up one small clue to the Past that was hidden from
him—and suddenly one word advanced from its blackness.
He said, "Kir . . . Kirk. I wish to be called Kirk."

"Kirok?" Goro said.

Kirk nodded. He was exhausted. Something in his face
frightened the fruit bearers. They had hoped for the god's
approval, not this look of lostness. They withdrew; and Goro,
anxious, asked, "Have the gifts displeased you?"

"No. They are good."

"Then it must be ourselves—the way we live. Perhaps
we have failed to improve as quickly as the Wise Ones
wished."

Kirk could take no more. He found what he hoped were
comforting words. "Your land is rich and your people are
happy. The Wise Ones could not be displeased with you."

"But there is something," Goro insisted. "Tell us and
we will change it."

"I—I can't tell you anything. Except that I have been
peaceful and glad here."

Mercifully, Goro seemed satisfied. When he'd left, Kirk
turned almost angrily to Miramanee. "Why are they so sure
I can save them?"

"You came from the temple. And did you not return
life to the dead child?"

He placed his tortured head in his hands. "I—need
time," he said, "time to try and remember . . ."

She placed the buckskin garments on his knees. "Here
is much time, my god. Much quietness and much time."

The simplicity with which she spoke was oil on his
flayed soul. The strain in it relaxed. "Yes," he said. "Thank
you, Miramanee."

The *Enterprise* and the asteroid were speeding on a
parallel course. A terrible companion, it traveled with them,
a voracious menace that devoured the whole area of the
bridge's main viewing screen.

"Coordinates, Mr. Chekov?"

"Tau—eight point seven, sir. Beta—point zero four
one."

"That's our target, Mr. Chekov—the asteroid's weakest point."

Chekov gave Spock a look of awed respect. "Yes, almost dead center, sir."

"Lock all phasers on that mark, Mr. Sulu. Maximum intensity, narrow beam. I want that fissure split wide open."

"You sound like a diamond-cutter, Spock," McCoy said.

"An astute analogy, Doctor."

"Phasers locked, sir," Sulu said.

"We will fire in sequence. And will continue firing as long as Mr. Scott can maintain power."

"Standing by, sir."

"Fire phasers!"

The ship trembled. "Phaser one firing!"

Sulu hit another button. "Phaser two fired!"

On the screen the rocky mass loomed larger than the ship. Fragments erupted from it as the phasers' blue beams struck it.

"Phaser three fired, sir! Phaser four!"

Another cloud of rock segments, sharp, huge were torn from the asteroid.

"All phasers fired, sir."

The stillness of Spock's face gave impressive poignancy to the tone of bitter disappointment in his voice. "Rig for simultaneous firing, Mr. Sulu."

In the engineering section, Scott muttered to an assistant, "That Vulcan won't be satisfied till all these panels are a lead puddle!" As he spoke there was a sharp metallic click—and one of his main relays began to smoke.

"Main relay's out again, Mr. Scott!" cried the assistant.

"Machines are smarter than people," his chief said. "At least they know enough to quit before they blow themselves up!"

"Commence simultaneous bombardment." As Spock's order was heard on the intercom, a white-hot flash leaped from the engine compartment. There was the roar of an explosion that hurled Scott back against the opposite bulkhead. Spread-eagled, clinging to it, he was close to tears as he watched the death of his friends—his engines. "My bairns," he said brokenly. "My poor bairns . . ."

"Kirok."

It was a soft whisper but it roused Kirk from his uneasy doze. Kneeling beside him, Miramanee said, "The ritual cloak is finished."

She was very close to him. Under his eyes the long black hair drooped. "If it pleases you, I will name the Joining Day."

"The Joining Day?"

"I am the daughter of chiefs," she said. "Tribal law gives me to our god."

Kirk looked at her, uncomprehending. She bowed her head. "If there is another in your heart, Kirok . . ."

"There is no one else, Miramanee. In my mind or in my heart."

She was still disturbed by what she feared was his lack of response. "A god's wish is above tribal law. If you do not wish—"

Kirk reached for her. "Miramanee, name the Joining Day."

The shining lashes lifted. "The sooner our happiness together begins, the longer it will last. I name—tomorrow."

The Past was a darkness, cold, impenetrable. If he was a prisoner of the Present, at least it offered this warmth, this glow in the black-lashed eyes. Kirk drew her fiercely to him. He bent his head to her mouth.

Spock had retreated to his quarters. McCoy, entering them without knocking, found him staring at his viewer. "I told you to *rest*, Spock! For the love of heaven, quit looking at that screen!"

The intercom spoke. Scott said furiously, "Our star drive is completely burned out! So don't ask for any more Warp Nine speed! The only thing you've left us, Spock, is impulse power!"

"Estimated repair time?" the Vulcan asked the intercom.

"Hanging here in space? Forever. The only way to fix my engines is to get to the nearest repair base!"

McCoy snapped off the intercom. He laid his hand on Spock's shoulder. "You took that calculated risk for us, for that planet—and for Jim. That you took it is important. That you lost it—well, losing it was in your calculation."

"I accept the full responsibility for the failure, Doctor."

"And my responsibility is the health of this crew. You are to stop driving yourself so hard."

Spock switched the intercom back on. "Resume heading 883 mark 41, Mr. Chekov."

"Why, that's back to the planet!" McCoy cried. "Without warp speed, getting to it will take months!"

"Exactly 59.223 days, Doctor. And the asteroid will be four hours behind us all the way."

"Then what's the use? Even if the Captain is still alive, we may not be able to save him! We may not be able to save anything—not even the ship!" McCoy hit the wall. "You haven't heard a word I have said! All you've been doing is staring at that damn—" He strode over to the screen and struck the image of the obelisk that had appeared on it.

"Another calculated Vulcan risk, Doctor."

Miramanee was radiant in her bridal finery. She was surrounded by women who had crowded into the tribal lodge. As one placed a chaplet of flowers on the shining black hair, she said, "This Joining Day is the end of darkened skies."

Salish dropped the hide back over the lodge's entrance. On his moccasined feet, he walked swiftly toward the obelisk where the god-groom in festive dress was submitting his face to the paint Goro was applying to it from a gourd.

Goro handed the gourd to a young brave. "It is I who must tell the priestess you will follow," he said. "Wait here until I have walked the holy path to the tribal lodge."

When Goro had disappeared down the sun-dappled path, Kirk, smiling, stepped from the obelisk to make his way to the lodge and Miramanee. Salish, dropping from a pine bough above him, stood facing him, blocking the trail. His face was raw with hate.

"Get out of my way," Kirk said.

"Kirok, even though you are a god, I will not permit

this joining." Salish pulled a flint knife. "Before I permit it, you must strike me dead."

"I don't wish to strike anybody dead," Kirk said. But Salish jumped him. Kirk sidestepped the lunge; and Salish, rushing him again, scraped the knife across his cheek.

"You bleed, Kirok! Gods do not bleed!" He drove at Kirk with the knife, murder in his eyes. They grappled; and Kirk wrenched the knife from his grasp. Salish flung himself to the ground. "Kill me, Kirok! Kill me now! And I will return from the dead to prove to the people you are no god!"

Kirk looked at the maddened face at his feet. Placing the knife in his belt, he stepped over the prone body and moved on down the path. This imposed god-role of his had its liabilities. On the other hand it had brought him Miramanee. At the thought of her he hastened his stride toward the lodge.

Two braves greeted him at its entrance. A magnificent feathered cloak was placed around his shoulders. Miramanee moved to him; and on instruction, he enfolded her in the cloak to signify the oneness of marriage. Goro struck a stone chime with a mallet. There were shouts of delight from the people. Beads rattled in gourds, tom-toms beat louder and louder—and Miramanee, slipping from under the cloak, ran from the lodge. At the entrance, she paused to look back at him, her flower-crowned face bright with inviting laughter. This time Kirk didn't need instruction. He sped after her, the feathered cloak flying behind him.

She'd reached the pine woods when he caught her. She fell to the soft bed of scented needles and he flung himself down beside her.

He grew to love the pine woods. It was pure happiness to help Miramanee gather their fragrant boughs for the fire pit in their Medicine lodge. He loved Miramanee, too; but sometimes her black eyes saw too deeply.

They were lying, embraced, beside the fire pit when she lifted her head from his shoulder. "Each time you hold me is more joyous than it was on our Joining Day. But you—"

He kissed her eyelids. "It's the dreams," he said.

"I thought they had gone. I thought you no longer looked for the strange lodge in the sky."

He released her. "The dreams have returned. I see faces, too. Even in daylight, I see faces. They're dim—but I feel that I know them. I—I feel my place is where they are. Not here—not here. I have no right to all this happiness . . ."

She smiled down into his troubled face. "I have a gift for you." She reached her hand under the blanket they lay on and withdrew the papoose board she'd hidden under it. She knelt to lay it at his feet.

"I carry your child, my Kirok."

Kirk was swept by a sense of almost intolerable tenderness. The lines of anxiety in his face softened. He drew her head back to his shoulder.

Again without knocking, McCoy entered Spock's quarters.

"I thought I told you to report to Sickbay," he said belligerently.

Spock didn't so much as glance up from his small cabin computer. "There isn't time," he said. "I've got to decipher those obelisk symbols. I judge them to be a highly advanced form of coding."

"You've been trying to do that ever since we started back to the planet! That's fifty-eight days ago!"

Spock passed a hand over his tired eyes as though to wipe a mist away from them. He had grown gaunt from fatigue. "I'm aware of that, Doctor. I'm also aware that we'll have barely four hours to effect rescue when we reach the planet. I feel those symbols are the key."

"You won't decipher them by killing yourself!" McCoy adopted the equable tone of reason. "Spock, you've hardly eaten or slept for weeks now. If you don't let up on yourself, it is rational to expect collapse."

"I am not hungry, Doctor. And under stress we Vulcans can do without sleep for weeks."

McCoy aimed his medical tricorder at him. Peering at it, he said, "Well, I can tell you your Vulcan metabolism is so low it can hardly be measured. And as for the pressure of that green ice water in your veins you call blood—"

To straighten Spock had to support himself by clutching his console. "My physical condition is not important. That obelisk is."

"My diagnosis is exhaustion caused by overwork and guilt. Yes, *guilt*. You're blaming yourself for crippling the ship." McCoy shook Spock's shoulder. "Listen to me! You made a command decision. Jim would have made the same one. My prescription is rest. Do I have to call the Security Guards to enforce it?"

Spock shook his head. He moved unsteadily to his bunk and lay down. No sooner had McCoy, satisfied, closed the door behind him than he got up again—and returned to his viewer.

Kirk was trying to improve the lighting of his lodge by constructing a crude lamp. But Miramanee could not grasp the function of the wick.

"It will make night into day?" she said wonderingly. "And I can cook more and pre—pre . . ."

"Preserve food," Kirk said.

"For times of famine." They smiled at each other. "Ah," she said, "that is why you are making the lamp, Kirok. So I shall be forever cooking."

His laugh ended abruptly. Miramanee's face had gone tight with terror. A gust of wind pulled at the lodge's hide door. "There is nothing to fear," he said. "It is just wind."

"Miramanee is a stupid child," she said. "No, there is nothing to fear. You are here." But she had moved to the lodge door to look nervously up at the sky. She turned. "It is time to go to the temple, Kirok. The people will be there waiting for you."

"Why?"

"To save them," she said simply.

"Wind can't harm them." But the gravity in her face didn't lighten. "The wind is just the beginning," she said. "Soon the lake will go wild, the river will grow big. Then the sky will darken and the earth will shake. Only you can save us."

"I can't do anything about the wind and the sky."

She removed the lamp from his hand, seized his arm pleadingly to pull him toward the door. "Come, Kirok. You must come."

A sense of threat suddenly oppressed him. "Miramanee, wait—"

She pulled harder at him, her panic mounting. "We must go before it is too late! You must go inside the temple and make the blue flame shine!"

Kirk stared at her, helpless to reach her understanding. "I don't know how to get inside the temple!"

"You are a god!"

He grabbed her shoulders roughly. "*I am not a god.* I am a man—just a man."

She shrank from him. "No! No! You are a god, Kirok!"

"Look at me," he said. "And *listen*. I am not a god. If you can only love a god, you cannot love me. I say it again—I am a *man*!"

She flung her arms around his neck, covering his face with frantic kisses. "It must be kept secret, then! If you are not a god, the people will kill you!"

A fiercer gust of wind shook the poles of the lodge. Miramanee screamed. "You must speak to the people—or they will say you are not a god. Come, Kirok, come!"

The tribe had gathered in the central lodge. Under the onslaught of the rising wind, shields, spears, knives had been torn from their places on the hide walls. Women were screaming, pulling at children, shoving them under heaps of skins. Salish fought his way through the maddened crowd to comfort Kirk.

"Why are you not at the temple, Kirok? Soon the ground will begin to tremble!"

"We shall all go to the caves," Kirk said.

"The caves!" Salish shouted. "Is that the best a god can do for his people?"

Goro spoke. "When the ground trembles, even the caves are unsafe, Kirok. You must rouse the spirit of the temple—or we will all die!"

"What are you waiting for, god?" Salish said.

Kirk unclasped Miramanee's arms from his neck and placed her hand in Goro's. "Take care of her," he said. "I will go to the temple."

Outside, the gale tore his breath from his lungs. Somewhere to his left a pine tree crashed. Thunder rumbled along the horizon in a constant cannonade. And the sky was darkening. Boughs whipped across his face as he groped his half-blind way down the worn trail to the obelisk. The enigmatic tower told him nothing. Its inscrutable symbols held their secret as remorselessly as ever. Kirk beat at the hard metal with his fists, shouting, screaming at it, "I am Kirok! I have come! Open to me!"

The words were drowned by the screams of the un-hearing wind.

McCoy stopped dead at the door of Spock's quarters.

Strains of unearthly music were coming from the cabin. "Maybe *I've* broken," McCoy thought. "Maybe I've died, gone to heaven and am hearing the music of the spheres." It wasn't music of the spheres. It was music got from an oddly shaped Vulcan harp. Spock, huddled over his computer, was strumming it, his face tight with concentration.

"I prescribed sleep," McCoy said.

"Inaccurate, Doctor. You prescribed rest." The mu-sician looked up from his instrument. "The obelisk symbols are not letters. They are musical notes."

"You mean a song?"

"In a way. Certain cultures, offshoots of our Vulcan one, use musical notes as words. The tones correspond roughly to an alphabet." He laid the harp aside. "The obe-lisk is a marker left by a super race on that planet. Appar-ently, they passed through the galaxy, rescuing primitive cultures threatened by extinction—and 'seeded' them, so to speak, where they could live and grow."

"Well," said McCoy. "I must admit I've wondered why so many humanoids were scattered through this galaxy."

"So have I. I judge the Preservers account for a num-ber of them."

"Then these 'Preservers' must have left that obelisk on the planet as an asteroid-deflector."

Spock nodded. "It's become defective."

"So we have to put it back in working order. Other-wise . . ."

"Precisely, Doctor."

The earth around the obelisk was shaking. Villagers, panicked to the point of madness, had fled to their temple in

a last hope of salvation. Kirk, backed against it, wiped blood
from his cheek where one of their stones had gashed it.

"False god, die!"

It was Salish. As though his cry of hate were the words
they had been waiting to hear spoken, the crowd broke out
into roars of accusation. Women screamed the enormity of
their sense of betrayal. "Die, liar, die! Die as we all will
die!" Men stooped for rocks. Goro shrieked, "Impostor!
Liar!"

Miramanee flung herself before Kirk, her arms spread
wide. "No! No! You are wrong! He can save us!"

Kirk pushed her away. "You cannot help me. Go back
to them, Miramanee! Go back to them!" Salish burst from
the crowd and seized her.

"Kirok! Kirok! I belong to you!" She wrenched free
from Salish and flew back to Kirk.

"Then you die, too! With your false god!"

His rock struck her. She fell. There was a hail of stones;
she elbowed up and crawled to Kirk. Before he could lift her
to shield her with his body, Salish hurled another rock. It
caught her in the abdomen.

"Miramanee . . ." Kirk was on his knees beside her.
The crowd closed in for the kill when there came a shimmer
of luminescence on the obelisk pediment. The Indians fell
back, their stones still in their hands—and Spock and McCoy,
in their *Enterprise* uniforms, materialized on each side of the
kneeling Kirk.

"Kirok . . . Kirok . . ."

McCoy stooped over Miramanee. "I need Nurse
Chapel," he told Spock shortly. The Vulcan had his communicator ready. "Beam down Nurse Chapel with a supple-
mentary surgical kit, Mr. Scott."

Kirk tried to rise and was pushed gently back by
McCoy. "Easy, Jim. Take it easy."

"My wife . . . my wife—is she all right?"

"Wife?" Spock looked at McCoy. "Hallucinations,
Doctor?"

"Jim . . ."

"Miramanee," Kirk whispered. He looked at her face
and closed his eyes.

The *Enterprise* nurse rose from the Indian girl's crum-

pled body. She joined McCoy who was making a last diag-
nostic pass over Kirk's unmoving form. "He hasn't
recognized us," she said.

Spock was with Miramanee. "The nurse has given you
medicine to ease the pain. Why were the people stoning
you?"

"Kirok did not know how to get back into the temple."

"Naturally," Spock said. "He didn't come from
there."

She lifted her head. "He did. I saw him come out of
the temple."

Spock looked at her thoughtfully. Then he spoke to
McCoy.

"The Captain, Doctor?"

"His brain in undamaged. Everything's functioning but
his memory."

"Can you help him?"

"It will take time."

"Time, Doctor, is the one thing we do not have." He
spoke into his communicator. "Spock here. Mr. Sulu?"

"Tracking report, sir. Sixty-five minutes to end of
safety margin."

"Report noted." He returned to Kirk. "Do you think
he's strong enough for a Vulcan mind fusion, Doctor?"

"We have no choice," McCoy said.

Spock stooped to place a hand on each side of Kirk's
head. He spoke very slowly, with repressed intensity, his eyes
boring into Kirk's closed ones. "I am Spock," he said with
great distinctness. "You are James Kirk. Our minds are moving toward each other, closer . . ." His face was strained
with such concentration, he seemed to be in pain. "Closer,
James Kirk . . . closer . . . closer . . ."

Kirk moaned. "No . . . no . . . Miramanee . . ."

Spock increased the pressure against Kirk's temples as he
fought to reach the lost memory. He shut his eyes, all his powers
centered on the struggle. "Closer, James Kirk, closer . . ."

He gave a sudden hoarse cry of agony and Kirk's body
galvanized. Spock was breathing heavily, his voice assuming
the entranced tone of one possessed. "I am Kirok . . . I am
the god of the metal tower." Spock's agonized voice deep-

ened. "I am Kirok . . . I am Kiro—I am Kir—I am Spock! *Spock!*"

He jerked his hands away from Kirk's temples, his face tortured. Kirk lay still, his eyes closed.

"What's wrong?"

"He—he is an extremely dynamic personality, Doctor."

"So it didn't work," McCoy said hopelessly. He shook his head—and Kirk's eyes opened, full awareness in them.

He sat up. "It did work. Thank you, Mr. Spock."

"Captain, were you inside the obelisk?"

"Yes. It seemed to be loaded with scientific equipment."

"It's a huge deflecting mechanism, Captain. It is imperative that we get inside it at once."

"The key may be in those symbols," Kirk said. "If we could only decipher them."

"They are musical notes, Captain."

"You mean entry can be gained by playing notes on some musical instrument?"

"That's one method. Another would be placement of tonal qualities stated in a proper sequence."

Kirk said, "Give me your communicator, Mr. Spock." He paused a moment. "Tonal control! Consonants and vowels. I must have hit the control accidentally when I contacted the ship to ask Scotty for beam-up!"

"If you could remember your exact words, Captain . . ."

"Let's see if I can. They were 'Kirk to *Enterprise*'. Then Scotty said, 'Aye, Captain'."

The carefully smoothed panel in the obelisk slid open. As Spock stepped into it with him, Kirk looked back at Miramanee. "Stay with her, Bones."

The silence within the obelisk was absolute. As they examined the buttoned panel, Spock said, "From its position this button should activate the deflection mechanism."

"Careful!" Kirk warned. "I hit one and the beam it emitted was what paralyzed my memory."

"Probably an information beam activated out of sequence."

"Look, Spock. Over there—the other side of the vault.

More symbols; and like those on the outside of the tower. Can you read them?''

Spock nodded. "I have an excellent eye for musical notes, Captain."

"Then activate, Mr. Spock!"

The Vulcan pressed three lower buttons in swift succession. Above them the wind-swept darkness was sliced by a wide streak of rainbow-colored flame that sprang from the tower's peak like a giant's sword blade. There was a screaming explosion that deafened them even in their underground insulation.

"That was the sound of deflection impact, Captain. The asteroid has been diverted."

Spock was right. They emerged from the obelisk into calm air, fresh but windless. The sky had lightened to pure blue.

Kirk dropped to his knees beside Miramanee. "How is she, Bones?"

"She was pregnant and there were bad internal injuries, Jim."

"Will she live?"

McCoy's face was his answer. Kirk swayed, fighting for control. Miramanee, her face bloodless under the high cheekbones he loved, opened her eyes and recognized him.

"Kirok. It is—true. You *are* safe."

"And so are your people," Kirk said.

"I knew you would save them, my chief. We . . . we will live long and happily. I will . . . bear you many strong sons. And love you always."

"And I will love you," he said. He kissed her; and she said weakly, "Each kiss is like the . . . the first . . .''

Her voice failed on the last word. The hand on his fell away.

He bent again to kiss the dead face.

McCoy laid a hand on his shoulder.

"It's over, Jim. But in our way we kept their peacefulness for them."

THE ENTERPRISE *INCIDENT*

Writer: D. C. Fontana
Director: John Meredyth Lucas
Guest star: Joanne Linville

Operating under sealed orders, Kirk had found from long experience, almost always meant something messy. It became worse when the orders, once opened, demanded that they be kept secret from his own officers during the initial phases. And it was worst of all when those initial phases looked outright irrational.

Take the present situation. Here was the *Enterprise*, on the wrong side of the neutral zone, in Romulan space, surrounded by three Romulan cruisers which had simply popped out of nothingness, undetected by any sensor until far too late. Her presence there was a clear violation of a treaty; and since the Romulans were now using warships modeled on those of the Klingons, she was also heavily outgunned.

Kirk had worked out no way of making so suicidal a move on his part explicable except that of becoming irritable and snappish, as though his judgment had been worn down by fatigue. It was a bad solution. His officers were the best in Starfleet; sooner or later they would penetrate the deception, and conclude that whenever Kirk appeared to be worn down to the point of irrationality, he was operating under sealed orders.

And when the day came when he actually *was* too tired to know what he was doing, they would obey him blindly anyhow—and scratch one starship.

"Captain," Uhura said, her voice distant. "We are receiving a Class Two signal from one of the Romulan vessels."

"Put it on the main viewing screen, Lieutenant. Also, code a message to Starfleet Command, advising them of our situation and including all log entries to this point. Spock, your sensors read clear; what happened?"

"Sir, I have no more than a hypothesis . . ."

"Signal in," Uhura said. The main screen flickered briefly, then clarified to show a Romulan officer, with his own bridge behind him, carefully out of focus. He looked rather like Spock, and spoke like him, too.

"You have been identified as the Starship *Enterprise*. Captain James T. Kirk last known to be in command."

Kirk picked up a hand mike and thumbed its button. "Your information is correct. This is Captain Kirk."

"I am Subcommander Tal of the Romulan Imperial Fleet. Your ship is surrounded, Captain. You will surrender immediately—or we will destroy you."

Kirk flicked the switch and turned his face away toward Spock. He rather doubted that the Romulan could lip-read a foreign language, but there was no point in giving him the chance.

"Spock, come here. What do you make of this? They want something, or they would have destroyed us by now."

"No doubt, Captain. That would be standard procedure for them."

"It's my ship they want, I assume. And very badly."

"Of course. It would be a great prize. An elementary deduction, Captain."

"Skip the logic lessons." Kirk opened the mike again. "Save your threats, Subcommander," he said harshly. "If you attempt to board my ship, I'll blow her up. You gain nothing."

Tal had apparently expected nothing else, but a slight frown cut across his forehead nonetheless. "May I ask, Captain, who is that beside you?"

"My First Officer, Commander Spock. I'm surprised by your ignorance."

"You mean to insult me, but there is nothing discreditable in not knowing everything. Finding a Vulcan so highly placed in the Federation fleet does surprise me, I readily grant. However . . ."

He was interrupted by a beeping noise and hit an invisible control plate. "Yes, Commander? Excuse me, Captain . . ."

The screen dissolved into traveling moiré patterns. Then Tal was back.

"No one should decide quickly to die, Captain," he said. "We give you one of your hours. If you do not surrender your ship at the end of that time, your destruction is certain. We will open to communication, should you wish it."

"You understand Starfleet Command has been advised of our situation."

"Of course," Tal said, somewhat condescendingly. "But a subspace message will take three weeks to reach Starfleet—and I think they would hesitate to send a squadron in after you, in any event. The decision is yours, Captain. One hour."

His image winked out, and was replaced by stars.

"Lt. Uhura," Kirk said, "order all senior officers to report to the Briefing Room on the double."

"All right," Kirk said, surveying the group. Spock, McCoy and Scott were present; Chekov and Sulu on the bridge with Uhura. "Spock, you had a theory on why your sensors didn't pick up the Romulan ships, until they were right on top of us."

"I believe the Romulans have devised an improved cloaking system which renders our tracking sensors useless. You will observe, Captain, that the three ships outside are modeled after Klingon cruisers. Changing ship designs that drastically is expensive, and the Klingon cruiser has no important inherent advantages over the Romulan model of which we are aware—unless it is adaptable to some sort of novel screening device."

"If so, the Romulans could attack into Federation territory before we'd know they were there; before a planet or a vessel could begin to get its defenses up."

"They caught *us* right enough," Scott said.

"A brilliant observation, Mr. Scott," Kirk snapped. "Do you have any other helpful opinions?"

Scott was momentarily nonplussed. Then he pumped his shoulders slightly in a shrug. "We've not got many choices . . ."

"Three. We can fight—and be destroyed. Or we can destroy the *Enterprise* ourselves to keep her from the Romulans. Or—we can surrender." There was a stir among the other officers; Kirk had expected it, and overrode it. "We might be able to find out how the Romulans' new cloaking device works. The Federation *must* have that information. Opinions?"

"Odds are against our finding out anything," Scott said. "And if the *Enterprise* is taken by the Romulans, they'll know everything there is to know about a starship."

"Spock?"

"If we had not crossed the Neutral Zone on your order," Spock said coldly and evenly, "you would not now require our opinions to bolster a decision that should never have had to be made."

The others stared at him, and then at Kirk. McCoy leaned forward. "Jim, *you* ordered us—? But you had no authority—"

"Dismissed, Doctor!"

"But Jim . . ."

"Bridge to Captain," Uhura's voice broke in.

"Kirk here."

"The Romulan vessel is signaling again, sir."

"Put it on our screen here, Lieutenant."

The triangular Briefing Room viewscreen lit up to show the Vulcan-like features of Tal. He said without preamble, "My Commander wishes to speak with you, Captain Kirk."

"Very well," Kirk said, slightly surprised. "Put him on."

"The Commander wishes to see you and your First Officer aboard this vessel. It is felt that the matter requires—discussion. The Commander is a highly placed representative of the Romulan Star Empire."

"Why should we walk right into your hands?"

"Two of my officers will beam aboard your vessel as exchange hostages while you are here."

"There's no guarantee they'll transport over here once we've entered your ship."

A faint, cynical smile seemed to be threatening to break over Tal's face. "Granted we do not easily trust each other, Captain. But *you* are the ones who violated our territory.

Should it not be we who distrust *your* motives? However, we will agree to a simultaneous exchange.''

Perfect—and yet at the same time, impossible to explain to his worriedly watching officers. After appearing to consider, Kirk said, ''Give us the transporter coordinates and synchronize.''

Tal nodded and his image faded.

''I must insist on advising against this, Captain,'' protested Scott. ''The Romulans will try something tricky . . .''

''We'll learn nothing by staying aboard the *Enterprise*,'' Kirk said. ''One final order. Engineer Scott, you are in charge. If we do not return, this ship must not be taken. If the Romulans attempt it, you will fight—and if necessary, destroy the *Enterprise*. Is that clear?''

''Perfectly, Captain.'' In point of fact, Scott looked as though it was the first order he had understood in days. Well, with any luck, he'd understand all the rest later—if there was going to be any ''later.''

''Very well. Alert Transporter Officer.''

Kirk and Spock were conducted to the quarters of the Romulan Commander by two guards, after having been relieved of their weapons. Had the necessity existed, those two guards would never have known what had hit them, sidearms or no, but nothing was to be gained now by overpowering them; Kirk merely noted the overconfidence for possible future use.

Then the door snapped open—and the Romulan Commander, standing behind a desk, was revealed to be a woman. And no ordinary woman, either. Of course, no ordinary woman could become both a ranking officer and a government representative in a society of warriors; but this one was beautiful, aristocratic, compelling—an effect which was, if anything, heightened by the fact that she was of Vulcanoid, not human stock. Kirk and Spock looked quickly at each other. Kirk had the impression that if Spock could whistle, he would.

''Captain Kirk,'' she said.

''I'm honored, Commander.''

''I do not think so, Captain. But we have a matter of importance to discuss, and your superficial courtesies are the

overture to that discussion.'' Her eyes swung leveling to
Spock. ''You are First Officer . . . ?''

''Spock.''

''I speak first with the Captain.''

Spock flicked a glance at Kirk, who nodded. The First
Officer tilted a half bow toward the Commander, and Kirk
entered the office. The door snapped shut behind him.

''All right,'' he said. ''Forgetting the superficial courtesies, let's just have at it. I'm not surrendering my ship to
you.''

''An admirable attitude in a starship captain;'' she said
coolly. ''But the matter of trespass into Romulan space is one
of galactic import—a violation of treaties. Now I ask you
simply: what is your mission here?''

''Instrument failure caused a navigational error. We
were across the Zone before we realized it. Your ships surrounded us before we could turn about.''

''A starship—one of Starfleet's finest vessels. You are
saying instrument failure as radical as you suggest went unnoticed until your ship was well past the Neutral Zone?''

''Accidents happen; cutoffs and backup systems can
malfunction. We've been due in for overhaul for two months,
but haven't been assigned a space dock yet.''

''I see. But you have managed to navigate with this
malfunction?''

''The error has been corrected,'' Kirk said. He knew
well enough how transparent the lie was, but the charade had
to be played out; he needed to seem thoroughly outgunned—
in all departments.

''Most convenient. I hardly believe it will clear you of
espionage.''

''We were not spying.''

''Your language has always been difficult for me, Captain,'' the woman said drily. ''Perhaps you have another word
for it?''

''At worst, it would be nothing more than surveillance.
But I assure you that you are drawing an unjustified . . .''

''Captain, if a Romulan vessel ventured far into Federation territory without good explanation, what would a Star
Base commander do? It works both ways—and I strongly
doubt you are the injured party.'' She pressed a button and

the door opened. "Spock, come in. Both the Federation Council and the Romulan Praetor are being informed of this situation, but the time will be long before we receive their answer. I wish to interrogate you to establish a record of information for them in the meantime. The Captain has already made his statement."

"I understand," Spock said.

"I admit to some surprise on seeing you, Spock. We were not aware of Vulcans aboard the *Enterprise*."

"Starfleet is not in the habit of informing Romulans of its ships' personnel."

"Quite true. Yet certain ships—certain officers—are known to us. Your situation appears most interesting."

"What earns Spock your special interest?" Kirk broke in.

"His species, obviously. Our forebears had the same roots and origins—something you will never understand, Captain. We can appreciate the Vulcans—our distant brothers. Spock, I have heard of Vulcan integrity and personal honor. There is a well-known saying that Vulcans are incapable of lying. Or is it a myth?"

"It is no myth."

"Then tell me truthfully now: on your honor as a Vulcan, what was your mission?"

"I reserve the privilege of speaking the truth only when it will not violate my honor as a Vulcan."

"It is unworthy of a Vulcan to resort to subterfuge."

"It is equally unworthy of a Romulan," Spock said. "It is not a lie to keep the truth to one's self."

That was one sentence too many, Kirk thought. But given Spock's nature and role, it could hardly have been prevented. The woman was wily as well as intelligent.

"Then," she said, "there is a truth here that is still unspoken."

"You have been told everything that there is to know," Kirk said. "There is nothing else."

"There is Mr. Spock's unspoken truth. You knew of the cloaking device that we have developed. You deliberately violated Romulan space in a blatant spy mission on the order of Federation Command."

"We've been through that, Commander."

"We have not even begun, Captain. There is of course no force I can use on a Vulcan that will make him speak. But there are Romulan methods capable of going into a human mind like a spike into a melon. We use them when the situation requires it."

"Then you know," Spock said, "that they are ineffective against humans with Command training."

"Of course," said the Commander. "They will leave him dead—or what might be worse than dead. But I would be replaced did I not apply them as Procedure dictates. One way or another, I will know your unspoken truths."

To Kirk, Spock's iron expression never seemed to change, but now he caught a very faint flicker of indecision which must have spoken volumes to the Romulan woman. Kirk said hastily, "Let her rant. There is nothing to say."

Spock did not look at him. "I cannot allow the Captain to be any further destroyed," the First Officer said in a low monotone. "The strain of command has worn heavily on him. He has not been himself for several weeks."

"There's a lie," Kirk said, "if ever I heard one."

"As you can see," Spock continued evenly, "Captain Kirk is a highly sensitive and emotional person. I believe he has lost his capacity for rational decision."

"Shut up, Spock."

"I am betraying no secrets. The Commander's suspicion that Starfleet ordered the *Enterprise* into the Zone is unacceptable. Our rapid capture demonstrates its foolhardiness."

"Spock—damn you, what are you doing?"

"I am speaking the truth for the benefit of the Enterprise and the Federation. I say—for the record—that Captain Kirk took the *Enterprise* across the Neutral Zone on his own initiative and his craving for glory. He is not sane."

"And I say," Kirk returned between tightly drawn lips, "that you are a filthy traitor."

"Enough," the Commander said, touching a control plate on her desk. "Give me communication with the *Enterprise*."

After a long moment, Scott's voice said, *"Enterprise*; Acting Officer Scott."

"Officer Scott, Captain James T. Kirk is formally

charged with espionage. The testimony of First Officer Spock has confirmed that this intrusion into Romulan space was not an accident; and that your ship was not under orders from Starfleet Command or the Federation Council to undertake such a mission. Captain Kirk was solely responsible. Since the crew had no choice but to obey orders, the crew will not be held responsible. Therefore I am ordering Engineer Scott, presently in command of the *Enterprise*, to follow the Romulan flagship to our home base. You will there be processed and released to Federation Command. Until judgment is passed, Captain Kirk will be held in confinement.''

There were a few moments of dead air from the *Enterprise*, but Kirk had no difficulty in guessing what Scotty was doing: ordering the two Romulan hostages to be put in the brig. When he came on again, his voice was almost shaking with suppressed rage.

"This is Lt. Commander Scott. The *Enterprise* follows no orders except those of Captain Kirk. We will stay right here until he returns. And if you make any attempt to commandeer or board us, the *Enterprise* will be blown to bits along with as many of you as we can take with us. Your own knowledge of our armament will tell you that that will be quite a good many.''

"You humans make a very brave noise," the Commander said. She sounded angry herself, although her face was controlled. "There are ways to convince you of your errors.''

She cut off communication with a flick of a switch. Kirk swung on Spock.

"Did you hear, you pointy-eared turncoat? You've betrayed everything of value and integrity you ever knew. Did you hear the sound of human integrity?''

"Take him to the Security Room.''

The guards dragged Kirk out.

"It was your testimony that Captain Kirk was irrational and solely responsible that saved the lives of your crew," the Romulan Commander said. "But don't expect gratitude for it.''

"One does not expect logic from humans," Spock said. "As we both know.''

THE *ENTERPRISE* INCIDENT

"A Vulcan among humans—living, working with them. I would think the situation would be intolerable to you."

"I am half Vulcan. My mother was human."

"To whom is your allegiance, then?" she asked with cool interest. "Do you call yourself Terran or Vulcan?"

"Vulcan."

"How long have you been a Starfleet officer, Spock?"

"Eighteen years."

"You serve Captain Kirk. Do you like him? Do you like your shipmates?"

"The question is irrelevant."

"Perhaps." She drew closer, looking into his eyes challengingly. "But you are subordinate to the Captain's orders. Even to his whims."

"My duty as an officer," Spock said rigidly, "is to obey him."

"You are a superior being. Why do you not command?"

Spock hesitated. "I do not desire a ship of my own."

"Of course you believe that now, after eighteen years. But is it not also true that no one has given you—a Vulcan— that opportunity?"

"Such opportunities are extremely rare."

"For one of your accomplishments and—capabilities— opportunities should be made. And will be. I can see to that—if you will stop looking at the Federation as the whole universe. It is not, you know."

"The thought has occasionally crossed my mind," Spock said.

"You must have your own ship."

"Commander," Spock said pleasantly, "shall we speak plainly? It is you who desperately need a ship. You want the *Enterprise*."

"Of course! It would be a great triumph for me to bring the *Enterprise* home intact. It would broaden the scope of my powers greatly. It would be the achievement of a lifetime." She paused. "And naturally, it would open equal opportunities to you."

The sound of an intercom spared Spock the need to reply. It was not an open line; the Commander picked up a handset and listened. After a moment she said, "I will come

there,'' and replaced it. Spock raised his eyebrows inquir-
ingly.

"Your Captain," she said with a trace of scorn, "tried
to break through the sonic disruptor field which wards his
cell. Naturally he is injured, and since we do not know how
to treat humans, my First Officer asked your ship's surgeon
to attend him. The man's first response was, 'I don't make
house calls,' whatever that means, but we managed to convince him that it was not a trick and he is now in attendance.
Follow me, please."

She led the way out of the office and down the corridor,
followed by the omnipresent, silent guards.

"I neglected to mention it," she added, "but I will
expect you for dinner. We have much yet to discuss."

"Indeed?" Spock said, looking at her quizzically.

"Allow me to rephrase. Will you join me for dinner?"

"I am honored, Commander. Are the guards also invited?"

For answer she waved the guards off. They seemed
astonished, but were soon out of sight. A moment later she
and Spock reached a junction; to the left, the corridor continued, while to the right it brought up against a single door
not far away; it was guarded. There was a raised emblem
nearby, but from this angle Spock could not read the device
on it. He moved toward it.

"Mr. Spock!"

He stopped instantly.

"That corridor is forbidden to all but loyal Romulans."

"Of course, Commander," Spock said. "I will obey
your restrictions."

"I hope," she said, "soon there will be no need for
you to observe *any* restrictions."

"It would be illogical to assume that all conditions remain stable."

They reached the Romulan brig; a guard there saluted
and turned off the disruptor field. When they entered the cell,
he turned it on again. McCoy was there—and so was Kirk,
sitting slumped and blank-eyed on the bed, hands hanging
down loosely between his knees.

"You are the physician?" the Commander said.

"McCoy—Chief Medical Officer."

"Captain Kirk's condition?"

"Physically—weak. Mentally—depressed, disoriented, displays feelings of persecution and rebellion."

"Then by your own standards of normality, this man is not fully competent?"

"Not now," McCoy said reluctantly. "No."

"Mr. Spock has stated he believes the Captain had no authority or order to cross the Neutral Zone. In your opinion, could this mental incapacity have afflicted the Captain earlier?"

"Yes—it's possible."

"Mr. Spock, the Doctor has now confirmed your testimony as to the mental state of your Captain. He was and is unfit to continue in command of the *Enterprise*. That duty has now fallen upon you. Are you ready to exercise that function?"

"I am ready."

McCoy looked aghast. "Spock—I don't believe it!"

"The matter," Spock said, "is not open for discussion."

"What do you mean, not open for discussion? If . . ."

"That's enough, Doctor," the Commander broke in. "As a physician, your duty is to save lives. Mr. Spock's duty is to lead the *Enterprise* to a safe haven."

"There is no alternative, Doctor," Spock added. "The safety of the crew is the paramount issue. It is misguided loyalty to resist any further."

Kirk raised his head very slowly. He looked a good deal more than disoriented; he looked downright mad. Then, suddenly, he was lunging at Spock, his voice a raw scream:

"Traitor! I'll—kill—you!"

With the swift precision of a surgeon, Spock grasped Kirk's shoulder and the back of his neck in both hands. The raging Captain stiffened, cried out inarticulately once, and collapsed.

Spock looked down at him, frozen. The guard had drawn his sidearm. McCoy kneeled beside the crumpled Captain, snapped out an instrument, took a reading, prepared a hypo in desperate haste.

"What did you do to him?" McCoy demanded. He

administered the shot and then looked up. His voice became hard, snarling. *"What did you do?"*

"I was unprepared for his attack," Spock said. "He— I used the Vulcan death grip instinctively."

McCoy tried a second shot, then attempted to find a pulse or heartbeat.

"Your instincts are still good, Spock," he said with cold remoteness. "He's dead."

"By his own folly," said the Romulan Commander. "Return the corpse and the Doctor to their vessel. Mr. Spock, shall we proceed to dinner?"

"That," Spock said, "sounds rather more pleasant."

It was pleasant indeed; it had been a long time since Spock had seen so sumptuously laden a table. He poured more wine for the Commander.

"I have had special Vulcan dishes prepared for you," she said. "Do they meet with your approval?"

"I am flattered, Commander. There is no doubt that the cuisine aboard your vessel far surpasses that of the *Enterprise*. It is indeed a powerful recruiting inducement."

"We have other inducements." She arose and came over to sit down beside him. "You have nothing in Starfleet to which to return. I—*we* offer an alternative. We will find a place for you, if you wish it."

"A—place?"

"With me." She touched his sleeve, his shoulder, then his neck, brushing lightly. "Romulan women are not like Vulcan females. We are not dedicated to pure logic and the sterility of non-emotion. Our people are warriors, often savage; but we are also many other—pleasant things."

"I was not aware of that aspect of Romulan society."

"As a Vulcan, you would study it," she said softly. "But as a human, you would find ways to appreciate it."

"You must believe me, I do appreciate it."

"I'm so glad. There is one final step to make the occasion complete. You will lead a small party of Romulans aboard the *Enterprise*. You will take your rightful place as its commander and lead the ship to a Romulan port—with my flagship at its side."

"Yes, of course," Spock said impatiently. "But not

just this minute, surely. An hour from now will do—even better. Will it not, Commander?''

She actually laughed. "Yes, it will, Mr. Spock. And you do know that I have a first name."

"I was beginning to wonder."

She leaned forward and whispered. The word would have meant absolutely nothing to a human, but Spock recognized its roots without difficulty.

"How rare and how beautiful," he said. "But so incongruous when spoken by a soldier."

"If you will give me a moment, the soldier will transform herself into a woman." She rose, and he rose with her. Her hand trailed out of his, and a door closed behind her.

Spock turned his back to it, reached inside his tunic, and brought out his communicator. Snapping it open, he said quietly, "Spock to Captain Kirk."

"Kirk here. I'm already on board—green skin, pointed ears, uniform and all. Do you have the information?"

"Yes, the device is down the first corridor to the left as you approach the Commander's office, closely guarded and off limits to all but authorized personnel."

"I'll get it. Will you be able to get back to the *Enterprise* without attracting their attention?"

"Unknown. At present . . ."

"Somebody coming. Out."

Spock replaced the communicator quickly, but it was a long minute before the Commander returned. The change was quite startling; compared to her appearance in uniform, she seemed now to be wearing hardly anything, although this was in part an illusion of contrast.

"Mr. Spock?" she said, posing. "Is my attire now more—appropriate?"

"More than that. It should actually stimulate our conversation."

She raised her hand, fingers parted in the Vulcan manner, and he followed suit. They touched each other's faces.

"It's hard to believe," she said, "that I could be so stirred by the touch of an alien hand."

"I too—must confess—that I am moved emotionally. I know it is illogical—but . . ."

"Spock, we need not question what we truly feel. Accept what is happening between us, even as I do."

"I question no further."

"Come, then." Taking his hand, she turned toward the other room.

The outside door buzzed stridently. Had Spock been fully human, he would have jumped.

"Commander!" Tal's voice called. "Permission to enter!"

"Not now, Tal."

"It is urgent, Commander."

She hesitated, looking at Spock, but her mood had been broken. She said; "Very well—you may enter."

There were two guards behind Tal. It would have been hard to say whether they were more surprised by Spock's presence or by their Commander's state of undress, but discipline reasserted itself almost at once.

"Commander. We have intercepted an alien transmission from aboard our own vessel."

"Triangulate and report."

"We have already done so, Commander. The source is in this room."

She stiffened and turned to Spock. Gazing levelly at her, he reached under his tunic. Tal and the guards drew their weapons. Moving very slowly, Spock brought out his communicator and proffered it to her. Trancelike, without looking away from his face, she took the device. Then, suddenly, she seemed to awaken.

"The cloaking device! Send guards . . ."

"We thought of that also, Commander," Tal said. The slight stress on her title dripped with contempt. It was clear that he thought it would shortly pass to him. "It is gone."

"Full alert. Search all decks."

"That will be profitless, Commander," Spock said. "I do not believe you will find it."

Her response was a cry of shock. "You must be mad!"

"I assure you, I am quite sane."

"Why would you do this to me? What are you that you could do this?"

"I am," Spock said, not without some regret, "the First Officer of the *Enterprise*."

She struck him, full in the face. Nobody could have mistaken it for a caress. The blow would have dropped any human being like a felled ox.

He merely looked at her, his face calm. She glared back, and gradually her breathing became more even.

"Take him to my office. I shall join you shortly."

She was back in uniform now, and absolutely expressionless. "Execution for state criminals," she said, "is both painful and demeaning. I believe the details are unnecessary. The sentence will be carried out immediately after charges are recorded."

"I am not a Romulan subject," Spock said. "But if I am to be treated as one, I demand the Right of Statement first."

"So you know more about Romulan custom than you let appear. This increases your culpability. However, the right is granted."

"Thank you."

"Return to your station, Subcommander," she said to Tal. "The boarding action will begin on my order."

Tal saluted and left. The Commander took a weapon from her desk, and laid it before her. She seemed otherwise confident that Spock would make no ignominious attempts at escape; and indeed, even had the situation been as she thought, such an attempt would have been illogical.

"There is no time limit to the Right of Statement, but I will not appreciate many hours of listening to your defense."

"I will not require much time," Spock said. "No more than twenty minutes, I would say."

"It should take less time than that to find your ally who stole the cloaking device. You will not die alone." She tapped a button on the desk console. "Recording. The Romulan Right of Statement allows the condemned to make a statement of official record in defense or explanation of his crime. Commander Spock, Starfleet Officer and proven double agent, demands the right. Proceed, Commander Spock."

"My crimes are espionage, and aiding and abetting sabotage. To both of these I freely admit my guilt. However, Lords Praetori, I reject the charge of double agentry, with its

further implication of treason. However I may have attempted
to make the matter appear, and regardless of my degree of
success in such a deception, I never at any point renounced
my loyalty to the Federation, let alone swearing allegiance to
the Romulan Empire.

"I was in fact acting throughout under sealed orders
from Starfleet Command, whose nature was unknown to anyone aboard the *Enterprise* except, of course, Captain Kirk.
These orders were to find out whether the Romulans had in
fact developed a rumored cloaking device for their ships, and
if so, to obtain it by any possible means. The means actually
employed were worked out in secret by Captain Kirk and
myself."

"And so," the Commander said with bitter contempt,
"the story that Vulcans cannot lie is a myth after all."

"Of course, Commander. Complex interpersonal relationships among sentient beings absolutely require a certain
amount of lying, for the protection of others and the good of
the whole. Among humans such untruths are called 'white
lies.' A man's honor in this area is measured by whether he
can tell the difference between a white lie and a malicious
one. It is a much more delicate matter than simply charging
blindly ahead telling the truth at all times, no matter what
injury the truth may sometimes do. And there are occasions,
such as the present one, when one must weigh a lie which
will cause personal injury against a truth which would endanger the good of the whole. Your attempt to seduce and
subvert me, Commander, was originally just that kind of
choice. If it became something else, I am sorry, but such a
danger is always present in such attempts."

"I can do without your pity," the Commander said,
"and your little moral lecture. Pray proceed."

"As you wish. The oath I swore as a Starfleet officer
is both explicit and binding. So long as I wear the uniform it
is my duty to protect the security of the Federation. Clearly,
your new cloaking device presents a threat to that security. I
carried out my duty as my orders and my oath required."

"Everyone carries out his duty, Mr. Spock," the Commander said. "You state the obvious."

"There is no regulation concerning the content of the
statement. May I continue?"

"Very well. Your twenty minutes are almost up."

"I trust that the time consumed by your interruptions and my answers to them will not be charged against me. Interrogation in the midst of a formal Statement is most irregular."

The Commander threw up her hands. "These endless quibbles! Will you kindly get back to the point?"

"Certainly. The Commander's appeal to my Vulcan loyalties, in the name of our remote common racial origin, was bound to fail; since beyond the historic tradition of Vulcan loyalty there is the combined Vulcan/Romulan history of obedience to duty—and Vulcan is, may I remind you, a member of the United Federation of Planets. In other words . . ."

Under his voice, a familiar hum began to grow in the room. The Commander realized instantly what was happening—but instead of picking up the sidearm and firing, as she had plenty of time to do despite all Spock's droning attempt to dull her attention—she sprang forward and threw her arms around him. Then both were frozen in a torrent of sparks . . .

And both were in the Transporter Room of the *Enterprise*.

As the elevator doors opened onto the bridge, Kirk's voice boomed out.

"Throw the switch on that device, Scotty!"

"I did, sir," Scott's voice said. "It's not working."

The Commander looked in Kirk's direction and a muffled exclamation escaped her as Spock escorted her out. Kirk had not yet removed his Romulan Centurion's uniform, let alone bothered to change his skin color or have his surgically altered ears restored to normal human shape. Obviously, the other half of the plot was now all too clear to her.

Spock left her and crossed to his station. Behind him, her voice said steadily, "I would give you credit, Captain, for getting this far—but you will be dead in a moment and the credit would be gratuitous."

The Captain ignored her. "Lt. Uhura, open a channel to the Romulan command vessel; two-way visual contact."

"Right . . . I have Subcommander Tal, sir."

Tal seemed quite taken aback to see what appeared to be one of his own officers in the command chair, but must have realized in the next second that any Centurion he did not recognize had to be an imposter. He said almost instantly, "We have you under our main batteries, *Enterprise*. You cannot escape."

"This is Captain Kirk under this silly outfit. Hold your fire. We have your Commander with us."

Tal shot a look toward where his own main viewscreen evidently was located. "Commander!"

"Subcommander Tal," the woman said, "I am giving you a direct order. Obey it. *Close and destroy!*"

Uhura cut off transmission, but not fast enough. It was a risk that had had to be taken.

"Come on, Scotty, we've run out of time."

"Captain, I'm working as fast as I can."

"You see, Captain," the Commander said, "your effort is wasted."

"Mr. Spock. Distance from the Romulan vessels."

"One hundred fifty thousand kilometers and closing rapidly."

"Stand to phasers. You'll forgive me if I put up a fight, Commander."

"Of course," the woman said. "That is expected."

"One hundred thousand kilometers," Spock said. "They'll be within maximum range within six seconds . . . five . . . four . . ."

"Scott, *throw the switch!*"

"It'll likely overload, but . . ."

". . . two . . . one . . ."

"Functioning, Captain!"

"Mr. Chekov, change course to 318 mark 7, Warp Nine."

"Nine, sir? . . . Done."

Spock turned toward Kirk. "They have opened fire at where we were last, sir, but the cloaking device appears to be operating most effectively. And the Commander informed me that even their own sensors cannot track a vessel so equipped."

"Thank you, Mr. Spock," Kirk said in a heartfelt voice. He turned to the Commander. "We will leave you at a Federation outpost."

"You are most gracious, Captain. If I may be taken to

your brig, I will take my place as your prisoner. Further attendance here is painful to me.''

Kirk stood, very formal. ''Mr. Spock, the honor of escorting the Commander to her *quarters* is yours.''

The two opposing forces bowed formally to each other, and Spock led the Commander back toward the elevator. Behind them, Sulu's voice said, ''Entering Neutral Zone, Captain.''

''I'm sorry you were made an unwilling passenger,'' Spock said. ''It was not intentional. All they really wanted was the cloaking device.''

''They? And what did you want?''

''That is all I wanted when I went aboard your vessel.''

''And that is exactly all you came away with.''

''You underestimate yourself, Commander.''

She refused to hear the hidden meaning. ''You realize that we will very soon learn to penetrate the cloaking device. After all, we discovered it; you only stole it.''

''Obviously, military secrets are the most fleeting of all,'' he said. ''I hope we exchange something more permanent.''

She stepped into the elevator; but when Spock tried to follow her, she barred the way. ''You made the choice.''

''It was the only choice possible. Surely you would not have respected any other.''

She looked at him for a long moment, and then smiled, slightly, sadly. ''That will be our—secret. Get back to your duty. The guards had best take me from here.''

Spock beckoned to two guards. She could probably incapacitate both in a matter of seconds, but they were well out of Transporter range of any of the Romulan ships now—and her mood did not seem to be one which would impel her to illogical action. In a way it was a pity that she obviously did not know that Vulcans were cyclical in their mating customs, and immune to sexual attraction at all other times. Or had she been counting on his human side? And—had she been right to do so?

The elevator swallowed her down. Spock went back to his post.

''Sickbay to Captain Kirk. If all the shouting's over up there, I want you to report to me.''

"What for, Bones?"

"You're due in surgery again. As payment for the big act of irrationality you put over on me, I'm going to bob your ears."

Kirk grinned and touched the ears, which apparently he had forgotten in the heat of operations, and looked over at Spock.

"Please go, Captain," Spock said in a remote voice. "Somehow, they are not aesthetically pleasing on a human."

"Are you coming, Jim?" McCoy's voice said. "Or do you want to go through the rest of your life looking like your First Officer?"

And McCoy had the last word again.

AND THE CHILDREN SHALL LEAD

Writer: Edward J. Lakso
Director: Marvin Chomsky
Guest stars: Melvin Belli, Craig Hundley

From standard orbit, the planet Triacus appeared perfectly normal, even placid. But Starfleet Command had received a distress call. No details had been included.

"Isn't Triacus where Professor Starnes and his expedition are working?" asked Captain Kirk.

Mr. Spock nodded. "It's the only M-type planet in the system. According to the records, Dr. Starnes and his colleagues found it sufficiently pleasant to bring their families along."

"Starnes taught at the Academy. I remember him—nice old fellow. And knew his stuff."

"He is a very capable scientist, Captain."

"Prepare the Transporter Room. You and I and Dr. McCoy will beam down in ten minutes."

"Certainly, Captain."

It was a dry, dusty sort of place to have chosen to set up camp. Rock formations emerged from the flat ground, the sun casting sharp shadows. The few listless shrubs were drab, except for the spatters of bright red blood.

Picks and water bottles lay scattered among the fallen bodies of men and women. Shocked, McCoy knelt to examine a crumpled shape that still held a weapon pointed at its own ruined head.

"Dr. Starnes!" Kirk's shout burst the stunned silence. Over the rock stumbled a wild-haired middle-aged man who fell to his knees as his shaking hands held a phaser pistol aimed straight at the Captain.

"Dr. Starnes! It's me, Kirk!" Unprepared, Kirk groped for his own weapon. But with an agonized twist, the man dropped and lay still. Kirk started toward him; McCoy was there before him.

"He's dead, Captain."

"He didn't seem to know me," said Kirk wonderingly. "He tried to kill me." He picked up the pistol, and nearly tripped over a woman whose body was contorted beneath her bluish face. He stooped and pried a plastic capsule from her hand. He sniffed at it doubtfully.

"Cyalodin!"

McCoy examined the capsule, then the woman. "Self-inflicted," he said briefly. "What's been going on here?"

Mr. Spock had been searching the body of the professor. Now he brought over the tricorder that had been over the shoulder of the dead man, and flipped the switch.

". . . me . . . must destroy ourselves. The alien . . . upon us, the enemy from within . . . the enemy . . ." came in a painful, choking voice. Spock snapped it off. Kirk stared around at the scene of desolation.

"All this—self-inflicted?"

McCoy nodded. "A mass suicide."

As Spock was removing the tapes from the professor's tricorder, there was a giggle. The rising trill of children's laughter sounded from behind the shrubs.

A girl and four boys poured over the rock and stopped at the sight of the *Enterprise* crew.

"Hi. Who are you?" said the tallest boy, with complete self-possession.

"Kirk, of the Starship *Enterprise*."

"I'm Tommy Starnes. This is Mary, and Steve, Ray and Don."

"Come on, play with us!" said Mary, dancing around Kirk's legs. Kirk and the others stared around them at the grisly battlefield and found themselves seized by their hands and pulled into a wild ring-around-the-rosy, pocketful of posy, and dragged into helpless crouching at "all fall down!" among the dead.

They buried the members of the Starnes exploration party in the shadow of the rock. The inscription:

STARNES EXPLORATION PARTY
STAR DATE 5039.5
IN MEMORIAM
O'Connell
Tsiku
Linden
Jaworski
Starnes
Wilkins

still glowed warm where it had been burned into the rock with phasers. Kirk reverently placed the United Federation of Planets green-and-red flag, with its circle of UFP symbols around a center of stars, upon the grave. The *Enterprise* men were respectful and silent; the burial detail had been profoundly shocked.

The children, standing in a stiff row, tried to look solemn, and succeeded only in looking bored. Steve nudged Mary restlessly. Mary whispered something in Don's ear. They glanced at Kirk.

Finally, Mary said in a not-quite whisper, "Let's go and *play*!" and the five disappeared in a flurry of shouting.

"What's the matter with them? No sign of grief at all," said Kirk.

"No, Jim, no indication of any kind," said McCoy gravely.

"Or fear?"

"They *seem* completely secure and unafraid. But it's possibly the effect of traumatic shock."

"I can't believe it. For a child to suppress the fact that both parents are dead . . ."

The dry voice of Spock remarked, "Humans do have an amazing capacity for choosing what they wish to believe—and excluding that which is painful."

"Not children, Spock. Not to this extent. It's incredible."

"What those children saw is incredible, Jim." McCoy was quietly insistent. "The way these deaths occurred, any reaction is possible, including lacunar amnesia. That's my diagnosis, until specific tests can be made.''

Kirk shook his head. ''I'll have to be guided by that for the present, Doctor. But surely I can question them.''

''No. Certainly not until the fabric of traumatization has weakened, or you can find another explanation for their behavior. Forcing them to see this experience now could cause permanent damage. Such amnesia is a protection against the intolerable.''

Kirk had to accept this. ''But, Bones, whatever happened here is locked up inside those children.''

The cheerful sounds of children at play had been present throughout. Now Tommy was tying a blindfold around the eyes of Steve, the smallest boy, and the others dashed for cover behind the rocks as Tommy turned him round and round. As Steve began to grope, Tommy tiptoed backward softly—and tripped. Steve jumped gleefully on top, crying, ''Tommy, Tommy! I caught you!'' The others danced out of hiding, shouting all at once.

Kirk detached Steve from Tommy's back and helped the tall boy to his feet.

''Hurt yourself?''

''Nah. I'm okay.'' The others were trying to reach Tommy's head with the blindfold.

''It's Tommy's turn, it's Tommy's turn!''

It was all Kirk could do to outshout them. ''Children! It's time to leave here and go up to the ship.''

''Oh, no, not yet. We're just beginning to have some fun! Not now, please?'' came a chorus of protest.

Kirk searched their faces for some other reaction. ''I'm sorry. It's getting late. You'll have to go with Dr. McCoy.''

But all they did was grumble, disappointed. ''Only five more minutes, huh, please? It's still Tommy's turn and everything! . . . And I didn't have a turn yet . . .''

McCoy took charge of them. They didn't look back toward the camp at all.

Kirk and Spock stood for a moment by the graves. The flag fluttered peacefully.

''If it's not lacunar amnesia that's blanking out their minds, there may be something here that is doing it.''

"The attack on Professor Starnes's party must surely have been unprovoked," said Spock musingly.

"Attack? It seems to be mass suicide."

"I stand corrected, Captain. 'Induced' would be a more precise term. Induced by an outside force."

Alert, Kirk said, "Such as?"

"The release of bacteria. Or a helpless mental depression. A state of suicidal anxiety. These could be chemically induced."

"What would make the children immune?"

"I do not know. But it is a possibility, Captain. A severe form of schizophrenia leading to a helpless depressive state could be chemically created."

"With the children intentionally free."

Spock nodded. "A valid hypothesis."

"We shall have to investigate this place more thoroughly. We'll go aboard now."

Animals and children start off on the right footing in a new environment when provided immediately with a little something to stave off the pangs of starvation. Nurse Christine Chapel mounted an expedition to the Commissary. When it comes to ice cream flavors, a computer can outdo a fairy godmother.

"All right, children," said Christine, holding out a fistful of colored cards. "Each color means a different flavor. Take your pick and the computer will mix it; just call out your favorite."

The five voices clamored in urgent delight. "Orange-vanilla-cherry-apricot-licorice-CHOC'LIT!" she handed two cards to each child. Four of them dashed to the insert slot and jammed their cards in. The smallest, Steve, was clearly stuck. His face conveyed agonies of indecision.

"Would you like to be surprised, Stevie?" asked Nurse Chapel gently.

Relieved, he nodded. She inserted two cards at random. The read-out panel twinkled and the computer hummed, and eagerly Steve opened the little window and withdrew a heaping dish.

He looked up at her from somewhere around her knees

with tear-filled eyes. He said sorrowfully, "But it's coconut and vanilla. It's all *white!*"

She patted him. "There, there now, Stevie. There are unpleasant surprises as well as pleasant ones. That was your unpleasant surprise. Now what would you like for the pleasant one?"

There is nothing like knowing what you don't want, after all, for clarifying a decision. Stevie said, loud and clear, "Chocolate wobble and pistachio."

"Coming right up." The crisis was past.

"And peach."

Trying not to think about it, Christine submitted the required cards to the machine. "Oh, this is going to be a wonderful surprise."

Not vastly surprised, Steve accepted the huge mound of colors with satisfaction and trotted off to join the others at the table. The clinking of spoons and chatter overwhelmed the voices of Kirk and McCoy, who stood watching in the doorway.

"The tests show no evidence of tension due to lying," said McCoy glumly. "They behave as if nothing were wrong. Physically, they check out completely sound. And there's no sign of any biochemical substance to account for their present state. I have no answers, Jim."

"There has to be an answer." Kirk stared at the laughing group, absorbed in ice cream.

"Why can't it wait till we get to Starbase Hospital, where they can be checked by a child specialist? I'm no pediatrician."

"We're not leaving here till I know what went on—or what's going on."

McCoy shrugged. "Well, I won't *forbid* you to question them. But it could harm them."

"It could be far worse for them if I don't—and for us too."

McCoy gave him an uncertain glance. "Be careful, Jim."

Kirk nodded and eased his way over to the table, where there was much scraping of last bits from bottoms of bowls.

". . . and after this we can play games," Christine Chapel was saying cheerfully.

"Mmmm, yeah . . . that was fun . . . some *more* . . ."
surfaced from the general babble.

"Well, well," said Kirk, smiling. "You seem to be
having such a good time over here, I think I'll join you. Is
that all right?"

"Please do," said Mary formally.

"I'll have a dish too—a little one. A very little one,"
he said to Christine.

"Of course."

"*Very* little," he said meaningfully. And then to the
children, "This is better than Triacus, isn't it?"

Five faces turned to him with the look of disappointed
resignation that children give to hopeless adults.

"That dirty old planet?" said Don scornfully.

Ray's snub nose wrinkled so hard as to nearly disappear. "What's to like about that place?"

Mary explained. "You weren't there very long, Captain. You don't know."

"I don't think your parents liked it much either."

"Yes, they did," said Tommy quickly, echoed by,
"Mine sure did. Mine too."

Don summed it up. "Parents like stupid things."

Christine Chapel saw an opportunity. "I don't know
about that. Parents like children."

"Ha," said Mary. "That's what you think."

"I'm sure your parents loved you," said Kirk. "That's
why they took you with them all the way to Triacus, so you
wouldn't be so far away for so long a time. That would have
made them unhappy; they would miss you. Wouldn't you miss
them too?"

The children looked at each other, and away. They
squirmed. Tommy looked thoughtful for a split second and
then said, grinning, "Bizzy! Bizzy, bizzy!"

It exploded into laughter as they all joined in. "Bizzy-
bizzy-bizzy-bizzy . . ." They jumped up and chased around
the room, bumping each other and shouting, "Bizzy, bizzy,
bizzy!" Don called, "Guess what we are?"

"A swarm of bees!" said Christine.

They shook their heads and screamed with laughter.
Mary's voice rose above them all, crying, "Watch out! I'll
sting you!"

"A swarm of adults," said Kirk softly. The laughter missed a beat, and rose shrilly. Kirk caught Mary as she careened into him with a face of near-fury. "Now wait a minute . . ."

Tommy said hastily. "Can we have some more ice cream, please?"

"I don't think so," said Kirk, slowly releasing the little girl. "It would spoil your dinner."

"See what I told ya? They *all* say it." The children gathered behind Tommy, who stood there, a young captain ready to defend his crew, Kirk thought. The boy was a leader. But why this . . . sense of opposition?

"All right, children," he said. "You've had a full day. I think you could use some rest. Nurse Chapel will see you to your quarters."

"A very good idea, Captain," said Christine with some relief. There had been tension building up in the room. She herded them toward the door through the "Awwws" and "Do we have tos."

Kirk called to Tommy. "Just a moment. I'd like to ask you something." McCoy had quietly joined the Captain at the table. Tommy reluctantly sat down on the other side.

"Tommy, will you tell me what you saw?"

"Saw where?"

"By the rocks. On Triacus."

Tommy shrugged. "You were there," he said indifferently.

"Did you see your father today?"

"I saw 'm."

"Did he seem upset?"

"Yeah, he was very upset."

"What about?"

"I didn't ask him." How could he get through this almost sullen resistance and reach the boy?

"What was going on that would have upset him?"

Tommy looked at Kirk distantly. "How should I know? He was always upset. Just like you, Captain Kirk."

"I'm not upset with you or your friends, Tommy. We invited you aboard the *Enterprise*. Why would I do that if I didn't like you?"

"You had your reasons," said the boy in a voice too old for him.

Kirk tried another tack. "Are you unhappy about leaving Triacus?"

"That place? That's for adults."

"Aren't you sorry about . . . about leaving your parents?"

"My parents?" said Tommy, amazed. "They love it down there. Always bizzy. They're happy." He wriggled to his feet. "Can I please go now? I'm tired too, you know."

Kirk sighed. "Yes, certainly. I'll take you."

"I know the way."

They let him go. "Round one to the young contender," said McCoy.

"Almost a knockout," agreed Kirk. "It's as if the parents were strangers to them. But—" he flipped the switch on the communicator. "Kirk to Security. Post a guard on the children. They're to be kept under constant watch."

But neither officers, guards nor crew heard the soft sound of chanting from Tommy's room:

> Hail, hail, fire and snow,
> Call the angel, we will go,
> Far away, far to see,
> Friendly angel, come to me.

Perhaps they were saying their prayers.

Kirk passed a restless night. The memory of little Mary dancing on her mother's grave kept returning to haunt him. If he had not seen the tragedy, he would never have suspected any trouble at all from the children's attitude. It was all very well to talk of lacunar amnesia, but there was an undercurrent of horror that he could not shake.

And the doctor had found no signs of Spock's "chemically induced" derangement.

The viewscreen on the bridge showed the expected image of Triacus, just distant enough for the details of the landscape to be blurred.

"Mr. Sulu?"

"Maintaining standard orbit, Captain," said Sulu,

pleased to give an "all's well" report to the tired face of his commander.

"Lieutenant Uhura, is there any report from the planet security team?"

"Everything is quiet, sir." Everything quiet, everything in order. Why this sense of unease?

Mr. Spock appeared at his elbow. "Captain, I have extracted the salient portion of Professor Starnes's tapes."

"Good." Kirk moved to Spock's console.

"Among the technical facts he gathered, Professor Starnes also offers some rather . . . unscientific hypotheses." Spock's voice expressed distrust.

"Let's see them, Mr. Spock."

". . . *Log date, 5025.3. Ever since our arrival on Triacus, I've had a growing feeling of uneasiness.*" The distinguished man on the screen glanced around him. "*At first, I attributed it to the usual case of nerves commonly associated with any new project. However, I found that the rest of my associates were also bothered by these anxieties.*"

Kirk and Spock exchanged a puzzled glance. On the screen, Dr. Starnes licked his lips and hurried on.

"*The only ones not affected are the children, bless them, who are finding the whole thing an exciting adventure.*" For a moment, the trouble left his face and he smiled. "*Ah, to be young again!*"

"Are there more of these unscientific hypotheses, Mr. Spock?"

Spock nodded briefly.

". . . *5032.4 The feeling of anxiety we've all been experiencing is growing worse. It seems to be most intense close to the camp, in fact. There is a cave in the rocks in which we have been sheltering part of the time; I have ordered Professor Wilkins to begin excavating. There are signs that the area was once inhabited, and perhaps there is an explanation to be found.*"

Spock switched off the tricorder. "There is another portion, Captain, which I believe you'll find particularly interesting." He adjusted the mechanism.

". . . *5038.3 Professor Wilkins completed his excavation today. Although whatever civilization that might have been here was destroyed by a natural catastrophe, as de-*"

scribed in notebooks 7 through 12 of our records, it would appear that . . . took refuge in the cave . . . all our efforts, we are becoming more apprehensive . . . as if some unseen force . . . influ- . . .'' The recording had gradually begun fading and bleeping. Now the professor's mouth went on moving, but only a high whistling emerged from the tricorder. As Spock bent over it to try to adjust the settings, even the image blurred.

"What happened?" said Kirk.

"Unknown," replied Spock, frowning over his instrument. Kirk heard a soft step behind him.

Tommy smiled, all boyish freckles.

"I didn't see you come in, Tommy," said Kirk.

"I had something to say to you, Captain. After we leave here, can you take us to Marcos Twelve?"

"No, Tommy, we'll probably take you to a Federation Starbase."

Urgently, Tommy said, "But I have relatives on Marcos Twelve."

"I'm sorry, but Marcos Twelve isn't within our patrol area. Mr. Spock, we'll continue in my quarters." Spock was still inspecting the tricorder. He now removed the tape.

"Oh, Captain," said Tommy, looking wonderingly around the bridge at the consoles, the flashing lights, the complex equipment. "Can I stay here and watch?" For a moment, Kirk forgot the problem the boy represented, and remembered his own enchantment the first time he had been taken aboard a Starship. "I'll be very quiet," the boy added hopefully.

"All right, Tommy. Lieutenant Uhura, please ask Dr. McCoy to report to my quarters for a brief conference."

The last Kirk saw of Tommy, he was heading for Kirk's own chair—going to play Captain. Kirk smiled at Mary as he and Spock passed her at the door.

"I wonder where the rest of them are?"

"Playing, no doubt," said Spock, still looking at the malfunctioning tricorder as they walked. "It seems to be a thing they do. Most illogical."

"Of course, Mr. Spock."

* * *

Mr. Scott woke up ten minutes late and just a little irritated with himself. He stomped to the Engineering Room and picked up his clipboard, glaring at the two technicians who were on duty. Suddenly, he stopped dead in front of an indicator.

"And when did we change course?"

One of the technicians turned and looked at him curiously. "We haven't changed course."

"What d'ye mean we haven't changed course? Look at your bridge control monitor!"

Mildly puzzled, the technician replied, "We're still in orbit, sir."

"Have you gone completely blind? Tha's no' orbiting position!" Scott reached over to the controls.

The technician seized his hand and thrust it aside. "Don't touch the controls, sir," he said quietly.

"What the devil d'ye think ye're doin'?" Scott snatched his hand back.

"We must remain in this orbit until the bridge orders are changed."

"You blind fuil, can't ye see what's in front of ye? We're not *in* orbit!" Mr. Scott lunged toward the controls again.

"I will not disobey an order from the bridge," reiterated the technician firmly. He placed himself squarely before the console, barring Scott.

"You *are* disobeying an order from the bridge! Now step aside!" What ailed the man? Triacus was nowhere in sight; the readings showed the *Enterprise* moving through space at Warp Two.

"You're losing control of yourself, sir," said the second technician carefully and very gently.

"Not yet!" Scott's voice had become a growl as he drew back his fist. He ducked the blow aimed at his chin and connected satisfyingly with the solar plexus of the first technician, who doubled up and backed away. The second man was on Scott at once, and furiously Scott swung and knocked him down.

Unfortunately, the first man had recovered and dispatched Mr. Scott with a neat blow from behind. The two technicians glanced at his fallen body and turned back to their consoles.

Little Don stared down at the big man lying on the floor. HIs white teeth flashed in a proud grin.

In Kirk's quarters, the tricorder was functioning again.

"*. . . I'm being influenced to do things that don't make sense. I've even gone so far as to call Starfleet Command to request a spaceship to be used as a transport.*" Professor Starnes had entirely lost composure; his eyes had grown dull in deep caverns under his brows. "*It was only when I couldn't tell them what I wanted to transport that I began to realize that my mind was being . . . directed. I decided to send a dispatch to Starfleet, warning them. . . . God forgive us! We must destroy ourselves . . . The alien is upon us! The enemy from within, the enemy . . .*" The cracked voice faded.

"He never completed the entry. And that dispatch was never sent—only scenes of family life, games and picnics with the children. That is the complete record." Spock was sober as he rewound the tapes. "Whatever overwhelmed them must have done so with incredible speed, or the professor would have provided details of the experience. He was an excellent scientist and tireless in the pursuit of the truth."

"A high tribute coming from you, Mr. Spock. But that could be what destroyed him."

Spock stared at Kirk. "The truth destroy? I don't follow that, Captain. It seems to be a non sequitur. The pursuit of truth is the noblest activity."

"Of course, of course. But the revelation of truth had often been fought, and fought hard."

"He's only too right, Spock," said McCoy.

"Unfortunately, I am compelled to agree. Evil seeks to maintain power by the suppression of truth." Slowly, Spock added, "Or by misleading the innocent."

With a sense of nearing enlightenment, Kirk said, "I wonder . . . ?"

"Do you mean the children?" said McCoy.

"Yes, Doctor."

There was a short silence, broken by the Captain. "Spock, what do we know about the race that lived here?"

"Legends, Captain. They say that Triacus was the seat of a band of marauders who made constant war throughout the system of Epsilon Indi. After many centuries, these destroyers were themselves destroyed by those they had preyed upon.''

''Is that the end of it?''

''No. Like so many legends, this too has a frightening ending. It warns that the evil is awaiting a catalyst to set it in motion once again and send it marauding across the galaxy.''

The three officers looked at one another. ''Is it possible that this . . . evil . . . has found its catalyst?''

''I was speaking of a legend, Captain,'' said Spock severely.

''But most legends have their bases in fact, Mr. Spock.''

''I think I read you, Jim,'' said McCoy. ''But as Medical Officer, I must warn you that unless the normal grief is tapped and released from these children, you're treading dangerously.''

''I'll respect your diagnosis, Bones. But not to the exclusion of the safety of the *Enterprise*. Thank you. Mr. Spock, what other expeditions have visited Triacus?''

''According to Federation records, this is the first.''

''What was that about an 'unseen force'? Starnes said it was influencing him, he had recognized and was beginning to fight it . . .''

''And he had canceled his request for a ship,'' said Spock.

''The ship! Yes, a ship for Triacus. But why? Transport was wanted, but by whom?''

With decision, Kirk addressed the communicator. ''Security Detachment. Ready for relief duty on Triacus. Assemble in the Transporter Room immediately.'' He added, more to himself than to the others, ''I'll have some questions for the first detachment as soon as they've beamed up. It's about time we found out whether Starnes's 'enemy within' is on the planet below—or here on board.''

In the Transporter Room, two guards were already standing on the platform. Spock went to the controls. As Captain Kirk told the men that their tour of duty would be one hour, they looked at each other with astonishment—and then uneasiness. ''Be ready with your communicators at all times to report any signs of alien beings. Don't wait to investigate. Is that clear?" The men nodded. "Beam down the guards."

Mr. Spock pulled the lever; the guards shimmered, began to fade and were gone. "Beam up the Security Detachment from Triacus."

The flickering figures on the platform faded, returned, faded. Where there should have been two solid security guards, there was only scintillating light.

"What's wrong?" said Kirk sharply.

"I am unable to lock on to the proper coordinates, Captain."

"Why not?"

"It appears we are no longer orbiting Triacus."

"But that's impossible." As the information sank in, Kirk said with horror, "If we're not orbiting Triacus, those men I just beamed down are dead."

"Captain, we are no longer orbiting Triacus."

"Activate the bridge monitor screen." Mr. Sulu was sitting placidly at his console, with Tommy watching interestedly. Uhura was smiling at little Mary. "Captain to bridge. Mr. Sulu, we are not in orbit around Triacus."

"With all respects, Captain," replied Sulu, surprised, "you're wrong. I have Triacus on my screen right now."

"You're off course. I'm coming up there."

He merely glanced at the children as he hurried to Sulu's station, followed by Spock.

"Mr. Sulu, your controls are not in orbiting position."

"But we *are* in orbit. Look." The screen showed the planet serenely below them.

"So it would appear," said Spock.

Behind them, the children had begun to play some game. Mary's voice chanted, *"Hail, hail, fire and snow . . ."* as the other three gathered in the doorway. They formed a circle and joined hands, clasping and unclasping in a complicated pattern. Kirk was aware of them only as a background distraction.

"Mr. Scott! This is Kirk. Look at your course override. What is our heading?"

The answer came blandly through the intercom. "Marcos Twelve, Captain."

Marcos Twelve! Kirk glanced at the circle of children. *". . . Far away, far to see . . ."*

"Why have you changed course, Mr. Scott?"

"According to your order, Captain." The intercom clicked off.

". . . Friendly angel, come to me . . ."

"Mr. Scott! Scotty!"

The lights on the bridge dimmed slightly and took on a greenish tinge. In the circle of children, something was forming in the air, not with the familiar shimmer of a transporter beam, but eerily, gradually, the figure of a silver-haired, sweet-faced manlike being clad in a glittering cloak took shape. It spoke to the children.

"You have done well, my friends. I, Gorgan, am very proud. You have done what you must do. As you believe, so shall you do."

Softly, the children replied in chorus, *"As we believe, so shall we do."*

"Marcos Twelve has millions of people on it. Nearly a million will be our friends." The figure smiled benignly. *"The rest will become our enemies. Together with our friends, we will destroy them as we destroyed our enemies on Triacus."* It glowed with satisfaction. *"A million friends from Marcos Twelve will make us invincible. We can do anything we wish in the whole universe. It will be all ours to play in, and no one can interfere. All ours, my friends!"*

It spread out its hands. *"Now we have come to a moment of crisis. The enemy has discovered our operation. But they are too late! They no longer control the ship—we do. We shall prevail! They will take us wherever we desire.*

"As you believe, so shall you do."

The children, gazing raptly at the figure, replied, *"As we believe, so shall we do."*

"Each of you will go to your stations. Maintain your controls. If resistance comes, you know what to do. Call upon their Beasts! Their Beasts will serve us well. In each one of our enemies is the Beast which will consume him.

"Remember how it was on Triacus? If they resist, so shall it be on the Enterprise. *If you need me, call me, and I, Gorgan, will appear. We make ready for our new beginning on Marcos Twelve. We must not falter . . .*

"As you believe, so shall it be, so shall it be. . . ."
The creature smiled sweetly upon the children and slowly
faded.

Mr. Spock's eyebrow lifted in astonishment. Kirk was
unable to move for a paralyzed moment, and in that moment,
Tommy whispered orders to the others.

"Go to your stations. Mary, you remain here with me."
Don, Steve and Ray whisked out the door as Mary seated
herself near Uhura.

Kirk spoke gently to Sulu. "Helmsman, disregard what
you see—whatever you think you see—on your screen. Set a
course for Starbase 4." Sulu's hands jerked. He froze, blood
draining from his face as he stared at the screen.

"Helmsman, do you hear me?"

Sulu managed to whisper, "Yes, sir." Kirk, relieved,
ignored Tommy's mutter.

". . . See, see, what shall he see . . ." The boy's eyes
glittered with concentration.

"Lieutenant Uhura, contact Starbase 4. Tell them we
are bringing the children back. Tell Starfleet Command that
I suspect them of being alien in nature and I want a thorough
investigation made on our arrival."

"Aye, aye, sir," said Uhura briskly and turned to her
board. She stopped. She began shivering as her hands went
to touch her face, her eyes fixed on her console.

"Lieutenant!" said Kirk sharply. Then more gently,
"What are you staring at?" Uhura moaned.

"My death," whispered the beautiful Bantu. "A long,
long death. Ancient with disease and pain. Disease and
death." Her voice rose to a scream. "I see my death!"

Kirk stared at her console. For a fleeting second, he
saw Uhura's face, hideously disfigured and nearly bald, a
gray mass of wrinkles. But as he blinked, the station was its
usual neat assembly of equipment.

"There's nothing there but your communicators," he
said.

She was whimpering. "God help me. Please don't let
it, Captain. Don't let it be!"

Kirk's glance fell on Mary, hunched up in total concentration. She was singing very softly. *". . . shall she see
. . . a dying old hag where a girl should be . . ."*

Uhura moaned, touched her smooth young face and stared in paralyzed horror.

"Spock, you make the call to Starfleet." Kirk turned helplessly away from Uhura's anguish, only to see Sulu's eyes staring wildly at his screen.

"Sulu, I ordered you to change course!" Kirk strode to the station and reached for the controls.

Sulu struck his hand away. "Captain! Sir!" His eyes never strayed from his screen. "Stay away from the controls! Or we'll be destroyed!"

"But Mr. Sulu, there's nothing there!" said Kirk angrily.

"Can't you see them? The missiles? They're coming at us by thousands!"

"There are no missiles, Mr. Sulu." Kirk reached for the console. Sulu struck him away.

"Leave them alone! If we touch anything, we will be hit! You'll kill us all!"

Spock's voice came coolly from behind him. "Captain, why are we bothering Starfleet?"

What had happened to his crew? Could nobody take an order at all—even Spock? His First Officer met his look defiantly.

"This bridge is under complete control," said Spock. "There's no need to alert Starfleet."

"Take a look around you," said Kirk. Sulu, staring fixedly at his viewscreen, blind to everything but the terror-image before him; Uhura, crouching in agony at her console; and Tommy, whose freckled boy-face had taken on a look of unrelenting hardness. Spock closed his eyes. Kirk watched him anxiously as he stood shuddering very slightly, fighting to regain control of his mind.

Tommy too began to shudder. Spock opened his eyes and returned to the Communications station. He reached for the instruments. His hands stopped.

"I cannot obey your order, Captain," he said.

Kirk opened the intercom. "Send up two security guards." When they appeared in the doorway, he said, "Take Mr. Sulu to his quarters."

The guards looked at him blankly.

"You wanted us, sir?"

"Take Mr. Sulu to his quarters. Now!" The guards simply stood there, looking bewildered. Kirk began to grow angry. "I gave you an order. Take Mr. Sulu to his quarters at once and don't just stand there like a couple of . . . What the hell's the matter with you?" The guards looked at one another and shrugged.

"Must be some sort of joke," said one.

Kirk shouted furiously. "Can't you hear me? I will have my orders obeyed immediately, d'you hear?" He lunged at the guard. The man shoved him back calmly and the two coolly departed. Kirk started after them, only to find himself restrained by Mr. Spock. He stood for a moment, undecided. His eye fell on Tommy.

Kirk knew who to blame for this mess. He strode toward the boy, his hand raised. If ever any kid was asking for a good walloping . . .

And he couldn't do it. He couldn't hit a little boy. The little boy smiled with satisfaction.

Kirk turned back to Spock. His knees buckled in reaction to the waves of adrenalin that had been pouring through him. He had to hold Spock's arm for support.

"Captain, we must get off this bridge." Spock guided him, stumbling, into the elevator.

Kirk felt cold sweat on his forehead. Not even Spock obeyed orders. The ship was out of control. His crew had gone mad, or mutinous. He was losing command, even of his own legs. Fear grew in him, and he lurched, clinging to Spock. He couldn't trust Spock, though. He couldn't trust anyone. He couldn't command a single crewman. He had lost the *Enterprise.*

"I'm losing command," he muttered, sweating again, the heat of fear overcoming the coldness. His legs were strong, strong, but wouldn't hold him up. He stared at the treacherous satanic face of his First Officer. "I'm alone, I'm alone. This ship . . . it's sailing on and on . . . without me . . ." He touched the wall of the elevator, trying to get a grip on it. "I'm losing command. I'm losing command! My ship . . . my ship . . ."

"Captain."

"I've lost the *Enterprise.* No . . . no . . ." he sobbed. Spock caught him as he sagged, and held him upright.

"Jim."

The shock of that voice calling him by name was a shower of cold water. Slowly, the hysteria began to ebb.

"I've got command?" he whispered, looking to the Vulcan for reassurance. Spock nodded with vast conviction.

"I've got command." Kirk's own voice was regaining strength.

"Correct, *Captain*," said Spock firmly, allowing no further doubt. "I am awaiting orders, *Captain*. Where to?"

Kirk tested his legs. They were steady. He let go of Spock and stood up. "*. . . in each one . . . is the Beast which will consume him.*" Well, he had met his Beast. So had Spock. Between them they had conquered the enemies within—themselves. Now the enemy within the *Enterprise* remained.

"To Auxiliary Control, my Vulcan friend. This ship is off course."

They entered the Engineering Room. Scotty looked up, smiled blandly and nodded.

"Mr. Scott. I want you to override the bridge navigation system and plot a course for Starbase 4."

"I can't do that, sir!" said Scott with indignation.

"Why not?"

"These are vurra sensitive instruments. I'll no' have you upsetting their delicate balance." There was a hint of panic underlying the burring voice. "There'll be no tamperin' with the navigation system of this ship, Captain."

"I'm not asking you to tamper with it. I'm ordering you to plot a course!"

"You're ordering suicide. We'd all be lost, forever lost!" Scott grabbed a wrench from the tools stacked nearby. The two technicians loomed supportively behind him.

Spock looked at the corner of the room. Steve was quietly watching.

"I've given you men an order," said Kirk.

Scott crouched over his console, brandishing the wrench.

"You go 'way now. Go away or I'll kill you!" Kirk could not believe such words coming from his Chief Engineer, who was coming more and more to resemble a caveman with upraised club.

"Scotty, listen to me," the Captain urged. "The *Enterprise* has been invaded by alien beings. Its destination is now Marcos. If we go there, millions will die, the way they died on Triacus."

Scott snarled and lunged. The technicians jumped Spock, undeterred by his strength. Neither Spock nor Kirk was prepared to inflict serious damage on the men, but the Engineering crew had no such qualms. At last, thanks to the Vulcan nerve pinch and some quick dodging, they managed to make their way to the elevator.

Spock stared searchingly at Kirk. Still panting from the scuffle, Kirk knew what the question was.

"It's all right, Spock. My . . . Beast . . . is finished. It won't return."

Spock acknowledged this with a nod. "But, Captain, as long as those children are present, there is danger. They are the carriers."

Sometimes, Kirk thought, Spock was more human than at other times.

"But they're children, Spock. Not alien beings. Only children, being misled."

"They are followers. Without followers, evil cannot spread."

This was definitely one of the other times. "They're *children*," Kirk said helplessly.

"Captain, the four hundred and thirty men and women on board the *Enterprise*, and the ship itself, are endangered by these . . . *children*." Spock was grim.

"They don't understand the evil they're doing."

"Perhaps that is true. But the evil within them is spreading fast, and unless we can find a way to remove it—"

Reluctantly, Kirk faced it. "We'll have to kill them." He knew Spock was right. As they turned the corner, the way was blocked.

Ensign Chekov, armed with a phaser and flanked by three crewmen, stood in front of them.

"Captain Kirk," said Chekov nervously.

"What is it, Ensign?"

"I have been instructed to place you and Meester Spock under arrest."

"By whose order?"

"Starfleet Command, sir." With his free hand, he thrust a printed communication at the Captain, who glanced at it and looked back at the young officer.

"Where did you hear this order?" Chekov's face was working with some inner torment. Down the corridor, Tommy waited.

"Now listen to me," said Kirk firmly. "This order is false. I want you and your men to return to your stations."

"I am sorry, Captain, but I must inseest that you and Meester Spock come weeth me to the detention section."

"Listen to me!" said Kirk, taking a step toward him. The rifle rose and pointed at his heart.

"Do not force me to keel you, sir. I weel if I have to," said Chekov desperately. Heavy perspiration ran down his forehead. "Will you come peacefully?"

"*Listen* to me. This is a false order."

"I have never disobeyed an order, Captain," cried Chekov. "Never, never!"

"I know that, Ensign. You have never disobeyed an order. But an alien being is aboard this ship—"

"I cannot disobey, I cannot disobey an order," wailed Chekov, the rifle wavering. Spock had worked his way around the group and suddenly seized the weapon. It was a signal for the other crewmen to attack, and once again Kirk and Spock found themselves entangled in flying fists and vicious blows.

Tommy watched, concentrating and strained, as the rifle traveled from hand to hand.

Suddenly, Spock emerged from the melee holding the phaser. Tommy had vanished.

Feeling his bruises, Kirk said, "Mr. Spock, take these men to detention and then join me on the bridge." Spock gestured with the phaser and the others slowly started moving, looking dazed.

The bridge was as he had left it: Uhura rocking back and forth, keening, Sulu staring.

"Marcos Twelve in sight, sir," he said dully.

"Mr. Sulu, we are not going to Marcos Twelve. I want you to change course."

"No, Captain, no!" As Kirk approached the console, Sulu drew his pistol.

"Sulu, there is no collision possible. It's being planted in your mind, on your screen."

Sulu growled. Kirk stopped, startled. Spock and McCoy entered on this tableau.

"The prisoners are in the deten . . ." Spock's voice trailed off as he took in the impasse at Sulu's console. He stepped toward Kirk. Sulu raised his pistol to cover both of them.

"Stand back, Mr. Spock."

Kirk nodded. Then he looked at Mary, and at Tommy.

"The *Enterprise* will never reach Marcos Twelve. You will not be landed there."

"The crew will take us," said Tommy contemptuously. "The crew believe us."

"The crew! They don't understand. When they understand as I do, they will not take you to Marcos."

"They will!" cried Mary passionately. "They-will-they-will-they-will!"

Tommy's head was high. "We are going to Marcos. We are all going to Marcos. The crew will follow our friend."

Kirk spoke compassionately. "Your friend. Oh, yes, your friend. Where is that stowaway? Why does he hide?"

"He'll come if we call him," said Mary stoutly.

"But we won't," Tommy broke in. "We don't need him. We're not afraid of you."

"Good," said Kirk. "I'm glad you're not afraid of me. But your . . . er . . . leader is afraid. What's he so afraid of?"

"He's not afraid of anybody!"

"He's not afraid of anything!"

"He's afraid to be seen. When the crew see and hear him, they will know he is not their friend, and they will no longer follow."

Tommy shouted, "He *is* our friend!"

"Then let him show himself. Bring him out. Let him prove that he's MY friend and I'll—I'll follow him to Marcos Twelve and the end of the universe!"

"No!" cried Tommy. He was beginning to doubt.

An idea struck Kirk. "Mr. Spock, play back the chant.

The one the children sang before, when the alien appeared."
Unmistakably, Spock conveyed approval. Dr. McCoy shook
his head doubtfully.

The chant began:

> *Hail, hail, fire and snow,*
> *Call the angel, we will go,*
> *Far away, far to see,*
> *Friendly angel, come to me.*
>
> *Hail, hail, fire and snow . . .*

As the chant replayed, Steve, Don and Ray came in
slowly. The children drew into a group. This time, they didn't
seem to want to join hands.

"The time has come to see the world as it is," said
Kirk.

The shimmering form of the alien began to gather
strength.

"Who has summoned me?" The deep resonant voice
penetrated even the nightmare in which Uhura was lost.

"I did, Gorgan. My Beast has gone. It lost its power
in the light of reality. I command again. And I ordered you
here." It was high time, thought Kirk, that we met this an-
tagonist face to face.

The alien smiled with infinite sweetness. *"No, Captain. I command here. My followers are strong and faithful.
And obedient."* He beamed on the children, who huddled
closer together. *"That is why we can take what is ours, wherever we go."*

Spock said, "You can only take from those who do not
know you."

"And we know you," said Kirk.

"Then you know I must win, Captain."

"Not if we join together to fight you."

The alien shook its silver head calmly. *"Foolish, foolish. You will be destroyed. I would ask you to join me, but
you are too gentle. A grave weakness."*

"We are also very strong."

*"But your strength is neutralized by gentleness. You are
weak and full of goodness."* The alien face had no difficulty

in conveying contempt. *"You are like the parents. You must be eliminated."*

The children stared silently at this confrontation. Kirk wondered if they were beginning to hear the hollow crack of breaking promises. They certainly looked as if the words of their "angel" were not quite what they had expected.

"Children," said Kirk suddenly, not taking his eyes off the alien, "I have some pictures of some of you on Triacus. I'd like to show them to you."

Tommy appeared to hesitate; it must have seemed an odd time for home movies. But events were moving too fast for him. The other children were frankly bewildered.

"Mr. Spock, the pictures."

"I forbid it!" said Gorgan.

"Why should you fear it?"

"I fear nothing!"

"So we were told. Mr. Spock, the children are waiting."

The film on the big screen showed Tommy and his father playing volleyball with the others. The remains of a picnic were strewn on the ground. Tommy stumbled and fell, and before he could decide whether or not to howl, his father had run to him and picked him up tenderly.

"There's me!" cried Mary. The children murmured as they recognized themselves.

The picture changed to the charnel house scene that had met the *Enterprise* officers on Triacus. There was a collective gasp; then the graves and the inscriptions. Tommy rubbed his eyes. The little ones were very still.

"They would not help transport us. They were against us." Was the creature's voice acquiring a whine? *"They had to be eliminated."*

"Tommy's father would have destroyed you, but he recognized you too late," Spock stated flatly.

Gorgan ralli' d. *"You are also too late. The kind ones always are."*

"Not always. Not this time." Kirk looked at the children. Were those very bright eyes filling with tears at last? "You can't hide from them. They see you as you are. Even the children learn."

Gorgan summoned up an erratically brighter light

around his cloaked body. He called to the children. *"You are my future generals. Together we will raise armies of followers. Go to your posts! Our first great victories are upon us! You will see, we have millions of followers on Marcos Twelve!"*

The children looked at the flickering figure with tear-blind eyes. The alien began to shout.

"We shall exterminate all who oppose us!"

"As you believe so shall it be." As their belief waned, doubt began to creep as if it were an ugly bruise over the face of the "angels." The sweet false face was curdling.

"Don't be afraid," said Kirk. "Look at him!" McCoy was bending over the little group of sobbing children. The picture of the graves still hung on the screen. Tommy looked from the screen to the writhing alien, and back; he was holding his lower lip hard with his teeth.

"We must exterminate! Follow me!" Gorgan's head had erupted with hideous blotches.

"Without you, children, he is nothing," said Kirk. "He can no longer hide the evil Beast within himself."

"I command you, I command you . . ." the mellifluous voice cracked and roughened. *". . . to your posts . . . carry out your duties, or I will destroy you. You too will be swept aside . . ."* quavered the dreadful thing in the shimmering cloak.

"How ugly he really is. Look at him, and don't be afraid." Kirk's hand was on Tommy's shoulder, which was shaking.

"Death, death, death to you all . . ." it died away in a scream of pure, weak anger.

McCoy looked up. "They're crying, Jim. They're finally crying! It's good to see."

Tommy was clinging to Kirk. He had broken down and was weeping convulsively. "M—my father—"

"It's all right, Tommy. It's all right. It is, isn't it, Bones?"

"Yes," replied the Doctor, picking up the nearest child. "We can help them now."

Trembling, Uhura raised her head and looked uncertainly at her console. She touched it wonderingly. But her attention was claimed by a very small nose being blown on her small skirt.

Sulu, in his own voice but sounding puzzled, said, "Marcos Twelve is dead ahead, sir."

"Reverse course, Mr. Sulu."

"Aye, aye, sir!" Slowly he reached for the controls, wary eyes on his screen.

"Course reversed!" he announced with triumph.

"Set a course for Starbase 4." How many times today had he given that order, Kirk wondered. It was good to see it obeyed.

He had command.

SPOCK'S BRAIN

Writer: Lee Cronin
Director: Marc Daniels
Guest star: Marj Dusay

The curiously elegant spaceship depicted on the *Enterprise*
screen had failed to respond to any hailing frequency or to
approved interstellar symbols.

Nor was its shape familiar. Scanning it, Spock said,
"Design unidentified. Ion propulsion, neutron conversion of
a unique technology."

Kirk said, "Magnification Ten, Mr. Chekov."

But the close-up revealed the ship as mysterious as before—a long, slender, needle-thin splinter of glow against the
blackness of space.

"Well, Scotty?"

"It beats me, Captain. I've never seen anything like it.
But isn't she a beauty?" He whistled in awed admiration.
"And ion propulsion at that. Whoever they are, they could
show us a thing or two."

"Life form readings, Mr. Spock?"

"One, sir. Humanoid or similar. Low level of activity.
Life support systems functioning. Interior atmosphere conventional nitrogen oxygen." He peered more closely at his
scanner. "Just a minute, Captain . . ."

"Yes, Mr. Spock?"

"Instruments indicate a transferal beam emanating from
the humanoid life form."

"Directed to where?"

"To here sir—the bridge of the *Enterprise*."

People moved uneasily at their stations. Kirk spoke into
the intercom. "Security guard! To the bridge!"

But even as he issued the order, a figure had begun to take shape among them. It gathered substance. A superbly beautiful woman stood in the precise center of the bridge. She was clad in a short, flowing, iridescent tunic, a human woman in all aspects save in her extraordinary loveliness. On her arm she wore a bracelet, studded with varicolored cabochon jewels or buttons. She was smiling faintly.

Her appearance, no Transporter Room materialization, was as mysterious as the ship.

Kirk spoke. "I am Captain James T. Kirk. This is the Starship *Enterprise.*"

She pressed a button on the bracelet. There was a humming sound. The bridge lights dimmed, brightened, dimmed again; and with the look of amazement still on their faces, Kirk, Spock and Scott went stiff, paralyzed. Then they crumpled to the floor. The humming sound passed out into the corridor. Again, lights flickered. Three running security guards stumbled—and fell. The humming grew louder. It moved into Sickbay where McCoy and Nurse Chapel were examining a patient. Once more, lights faded. When they brightened, McCoy, the nurse and the patient had slumped into unconsciousness.

Silence flowed in on the *Enterprise.*

Still smiling, the beautiful intruder glanced down at Kirk. She stepped over him to examine Scott's face. Then she left him to approach Spock. The smile grew in radiance as she stooped over him.

Nobody was ever to estimate accurately the duration of their tranced state. Gradually, as awareness returned to Kirk, he saw that other heads around him had recovered the power to lift themselves.

"What—where—" he asked disconnectedly.

Sulu put the question. "What happened?"

Kirk pulled himself back up into his command chair. "Status, Mr. Sulu?"

Mechanically Sulu checked his board. "No change from the last reading, sir."

"Mr. Spock?"

There was no Mr. Spock at the Vulcan's station to reply. Perplexed, Kirk looked at Scott. "The girl," Scott said dazedly, "she's gone, too."

"Yes," Kirk said, "that girl . . ."

His intercom buzzed. "Jim! Jim! Get down here to Sickbay! Right now! Jim, hurry!"

McCoy's voice had an urgency that was threaded with horror. In Sickbay the *Enterprise*'s physician was trying to force himself to look at his own handiwork. Within its life function chamber, he had encased Spock's motionless body with a transparent bubble device. There was a small wrapping about the upper part of the cranium. Frenziedly working at his adjustment levers, he said, "Now?"

Nurse Chapel, at her small panel, nodded. She threw a switch that set lights to blinking. "It's functioning," she said, her voice weak with relief.

"Thank God."

McCoy was leaning back against the table as Kirk burst through the door.

"Bones, what in the name of—" Kirk broke off. He had seen through the transparency of the bubble. "Spock!" He glanced swiftly at the life indicator. It showed a very low level. "Well?" he demanded harshly.

It was Nurse Chapel who answered him. "I found him lying on the table when I recovered consciousness."

"Like this?"

"No," McCoy said. "Not like this."

"Well, what happened?"

"I don't know!" McCoy shouted.

"You've got him under complete life support at total levels. Was he dead?"

McCoy raised himself by a hand pushed down on the table. "It starts there," he said.

"Damn you, Bones, talk!"

"He was worse than dead."

"What do you mean?"

"Jim—" McCoy spoke pleadingly as though he were appealing for mercy from his own sense of helplessness. "Jim—his brain is gone."

"Go ahead."

"Technically, the greatest job I ever saw. Every nerve ending of the brain neatly sealed. Nothing torn, nothing ripped. No bleeding. A surgical miracle."

"Spock's brain—" Kirk said, fighting for control.

"Gone." McCoy had given up on professional composure. His voice broke. "Spock—his incredible Vulcan physique survived until I could get the support system to take over. The body lives—but it has no mind."

"The girl," Kirk said.

"What girl?"

"She took it. I don't know where—or why. But she took Spock's brain."

"Jim . . ."

"How long can you keep the body functioning?"

"Several days at the most. And I can't guarantee that."

"That's not good enough, Bones."

"If it had happened to any of us, I could say indefinitely. But Vulcan physiology limits what I can do. Spock's body is much more dependent than ours on that tremendous brain of his for life support."

"I ask you—how long, Dr. McCoy. I have to know."

Wearily, McCoy reached for the chart. "He suffered a loss of cerebral spinal fluid in the operation. Reserves are minimal. Spock's T-Negative blood supply—two total exchanges." He looked up from the chart. "Three days—no more."

Kirk moved over to the bubble. He could feel his heart cringe at the sight of the paper-white face inside it. Spock, the friend, the dear companion through a thousand hazards— Spock, the always reliable thinker, the reasonable one, the always reasonable and loyal one.

"All right, then—I've got three days."

At the naked anguish in his face, McCoy motioned the nurse to leave them alone.

"Jim, are you hoping to restore him his brain? How are you going to find it? Where are you going to look? Through the entire galaxy?"

"I'll find it."

"Even if you do find it, a brain can't be replaced with present surgical techniques."

"If it was taken, it can be put back. Obviously, there are techniques."

"I don't know them!" The cry was wrenched from McCoy.

"The thief who took it has the knowledge. I'll force it out of her! So help me, I'll get it out of her!"

It was Sulu who located the ion trail of the mystery ship.

"Look, Mr. Scott. I've got it again!"

Scott was jotting numbers down on the board in his hand. "Aye, an ion trail. It's from that ship of hers all right."

"Where does it lead, Mr. Chekov?" Kirk asked.

Chekov studied the panel at Spock's library computer. "It leads to system Sigma Draconis, sir."

"Lock on," Kirk said. "Maximum speed without losing the trail, Mr. Sulu."

"Aye, Captain. Warp six."

"Mr. Chekov, a complete readout on Sigma Draconis."

Sulu turned to Kirk. "Arrival, seven terrestrial hours, twenty-five minutes at warp six, sir."

"No mistake about the trail, Scotty?"

"No mistake, Captain."

Chekov called from Spock's station. "Coming into scanning range of the Sigma Draconis system, sir."

Alarm rang in Sulu's voice. "Captain, I've lost the trail!"

Kirk leaped from his chair. "You've lost the trail to Spock?"

"It's gone, sir. At warp six there was a sudden deactioned shift."

"No excuses, if you please," Kirk said. "All right, her trail is gone. But she was heading into this star system. She must be somewhere in it." He moved to Chekov. "Put a schematic of Sigma Draconis on the viewing screen."

The nine planets comprising the system took shape and position on the screen. "Readout, Mr. Chekov," Kirk said.

"Sun, spectral type, G-9. Three Class M planets showing sapient life. First planet rated number 5 on the industrial scale. Second Class M planet rated number 6."

"Earth equivalent, approximately 2030," Kirk estimated.

Scott broke in. "But that ship, Captain. Either it was

thousands of years ahead of us—or the most incredible design fluke in history.''

"Third Class M planet, Mr. Chekov?"

"Aye, sir. No signs of industrial development. Rated number 2 on the industrial scale of 20. At last report in a glacial age. Sapient life plentiful but on a most primitive level.'' Chekov turned around to face Kirk. "Of course, sir, in none of these cases has a detailed Federation survey been made. All the information is the result of long-range scanning and preliminary contact reports. We don't know how accurate it is.''

"Understood, Mr. Chekov. There are three Class M planets, not one of which owns the capability of launching an interstellar flight. Yet one of them has obviously accomplished it.''

Chekov, who had been punching up reports on the whirring computer, was too puzzled by the last one to note Kirk's irony. He compared it with what he saw on the screen before he said, "Captain, it's odd. I'm picking up high-energy generation on Planet 7.''

"That's the primitive glaciated one, isn't it?"

"Yes, sir.''

"Its source, Mr. Chekov?"

"It could be natural—volcanic activity, steam, any of a dozen sources, sir. But the pulsations are very regular.''

"Surface readings again?"

"No signs of organized civilization. Primitive humanoids in small groups. Apparently a routine hunter-predator stage of social development.''

"With very regular pulsations of generated energy?"

"I can't explain it, Captain.''

Kirk turned to address all members of the bridge crew. "This time,'' he said, "there is no time for mistakes. We've got to pick the right planet, go there—and get what we came for. Mr. Chekov, your recommendation.''

"Planet 3, sir. It's closest and the heaviest population.''

Scott said, "With a technological rating of 5, it couldn't have put that ship we saw into space.''

"None of these planets could,'' Chekov said.

"You've got to put your money where the odds are,''

Scott retorted. "Captain, my guess is Planet 4. Technologically it's ahead of 3."

"Yes," Kirk said. "But ion propulsion is beyond even our technology. Can you really credit theirs with its development?"

Uhura spoke up. "And what would they want with Mr. Spock's brain?"

"What?" Kirk said.

"I said what would they want with Mr. Spock's brain? What use could they make of it? Why should they want it?"

Kirk stared at her. "A very interesting question, Lieutenant. Why indeed should they want it? Planet 7. It's glaciated, you say, Mr. Chekov?"

"Yes, sir. For several thousand years at least. Only the tropical zone is ice-free—and that would be bitterly cold. Humanoids exist on it; but only under very trying conditions."

"But the energy, Mr. Chekov. It's there."

"Yes, sir. It doesn't make sense—but it's there."

Kirk sat back in his chair. Three days—and Spock's body would be a dead one. Choice. Choice again. Decision again—command decision. He made it.

"I'm taking a landing party down to Planet 7," he said.

Scott stirred uncomfortably.

"Well, Mr. Scott?"

"Nothing, sir."

"Very well. We'll transport down immediately."

Kirk had seen some bleak landscapes in his time; but this one, he thought, would take the cake at any galactic fair.

What vegetation there was scarcely deserved the name, sparse as it was, brown, crackling under the feet with hardened frost. No green, just rocks, black under the sprinkling of snow that clung to their harsh crags, their crannies. A constant icy wind blew. He shivered, hoping that the rest of his party—McCoy, Scott, Chekov and two security guards—were as grateful as he was for their lightweight, thermal cold-weather clothing.

"Readings, Mr. Scott." His warm breath congealed in a mist as he spoke.

"Scattered life forms, widely spaced. Humanoid all right. On the large side."

"Watch out for them. They are primitives. Readout, please, Mr. Chekov."

Chekov unslung his tricorder, and went to work on the rocky plateau where they had materialized. His explorations acquired a witness. Above him was an escarpment, broken by a gulch, sheltered by an overhang of stunted scrub. A fur-clad figure, armed with a crude knobbed club, had scrambled through the gulch; and was lying now, belly-flat, at the edge of the cliff to peer through the overhang at what went on below.

Chekov returned to his party. "No structures, Captain. No surface consumption of energy or generation of it. Atmosphere OK. Temperature—say a high maximum of forty. Livable."

"If you've got a thick skin," McCoy said.

The figure on the cliff had been joined by several other skin-clad creatures, their faces hidden by parkalike hoods. They moved, gathering, from rock to rock as though closing in. Most carried the heavy clubs. One bore a spear.

"Captain!" Chekov cried. "There's someone—something up there. There—up on that cliff . . ."

"Phasers on stun," Kirk ordered. "Fire only on my signal."

Chekov looked up again from his tricorder. "I register six of them, sir. Humanoids. Big."

"Remember, I want one of them conscious," Kirk said.

As he spoke, a huge man, savagely bearded, rose up on the cliff; and swinging his club in an arc over his head, hurled it downward. It struck a security guard a glancing blow. He yelled in surprise and alarm. The alarm in the yell brought the other five to their feet. They all clambered up to shower the *Enterprise* with rocks and clubs.

Aiming his phaser at one of them, Kirk fired. The man fell and rolled down the cliff's slope, stunned. Shouting to each other, the rest disappeared.

The prisoner belonged to a hardheaded lot. Consciousness returned to him with astonishing swiftness. He struggled to rise, but Scott seized him with a judo hold that suggested the reprisal of pain for struggle. The man (and he was a man) subsided. He looked up at Kirk, terror in his eyes. Extending his empty hands in a gesture of friendship, Kirk said, "We mean you no harm. We are not enemies. We want to be your friends."

The terror in the eyes abated slightly. Kirk spoke again. "We will not hurt you. We only want to talk to you. Let him go, Mr. Scott."

"Captain, he could twist your head off."

"Let him go," Kirk repeated.

The man said, "You are not The Others?"

"No," Kirk said. "We are not The Others. We come from a far place."

"You are small like The Others. I could break you in two."

"But you won't," Kirk said. "We are men. Like you. Why did you attack us?"

"When The Others come, we fight. We thought you were The Others."

"Who are The Others?"

"They are the givers of pain and delight."

"Do they live here with you?"

"They come."

"Where do you see them when they come?"

The man spread his arms wide. "Everywhere. On the hunt, when we eat, at the time of sleep."

"The Others—where do they come from?"

Kirk got a heavy stare. "Do they come from the sky?" he asked.

"They are here. You will see. They will come for you. They come for all like us."

"Jim, ask him about women," McCoy said. He spoke to the man himself. "Do The Others come for your women, too?"

"Women?"

"The females of our kind," Kirk said.

The man shrugged. "Your words say nothing."

Kirk tried again. "We are looking for a—lost friend."

"If he is here, The Others have him."

"Will you take us where we can find The Others?"

"No one wants to find The Others."

"We do. Take us to them and we will let you go."

"Captain!" Chekov, his tricorder switched to full power, was pointing excitedly to the ground. "Right where we're standing, there's a foundation below the surface! And masonry debris! There are registrations all over the place!"

"Buildings?"

"Unquestionably, sir. Immensely old and completely buried. I don't know how our sensors misread them."

"Then somewhere below us is where The Others live," Kirk said. "Mr. Scott, check it out."

Scott and a guard were moving away when a hoarse cry came from the fur-clad man. "Don't go!" he screamed. "Don't go!"

Chekov and McCoy tried to calm him. He refused calm. He pulled madly out of their hold, shrieking with terror. "Release him," Kirk said. They obeyed.

"Don't go!" The last warning was almost a sob. Then he was gone, frantically hauling himself back up the cliff. Chekov said, "What have these Others done to cause such fear?"

"We may know soon enough," was McCoy's sober reply.

"Bones, what was it he said The Others give? It was 'pain and delight,' wasn't it?"

"A peculiar mixture, Jim."

"Everything's peculiar," Kirk said. "A dead and buried city on a planet in the glacial age . . ."

"And a man," said Chekov, "who doesn't know the meaning of the word 'women.' "

"There's a thread somewhere that ties it all together," Kirk said thoughtfully. "Right now I wish I had Spock here to find it for me. No offense, Mr. Chekov."

Chekov said fervently, "I wish it, too, sir."

"It's beginning to look as though your hunch was right, Jim. If there was a city here, maybe millions of years ago . . ."

Kirk nodded. "Then it could have developed a science capable of building that ship we saw."

"Captain, over here, sir." Scott and a security guard were standing near a spur of rock jutting out from the cliff. Under it was an opening, large enough to make entrance accessible to even one of the huge, shaggy, fur-clad men. It led into a cave. Or a room. Or something else. "I've looked inside," Scott said. "There's food in there, Captain."

"Food?"

"And a whole pile of other stuff. Some kind of cache. You'd better look, sir."

The place was about twelve feet square. It should have been dark. It wasn't. It was quite light enough to see the food, mounds of it, laid out neatly along one wall. Furs were stacked against another along with clubs, metal knives, tools, hatchets. "A storehouse," McCoy said, "for our muscular friends."

"I don't think so, Bones."

Kirk picked up a crude metal ax. "Forged," he said, "tempered. Our savage brothers did not make this." He returned to the cave's entrance to run his fingers along its edges. They were smooth. He came slowly back to examine the place more closely. Then he saw it—a light which alternately glowed and faded. It came from a small cell set into the wall behind the piled food. He waited. The light went into glow— and shot a beam across the food to a cell in the opposite wall.

"Scotty, Bones," he called. As they approached him, he barred their forward movement with an arm. The light glowed—and he gestured toward the beam. "What do you think?"

"It could be a warning device to keep those beast boys away from the food," Scott said.

"You think that beam could kill?" McCoy asked him.

"It very well might."

"How about this?" Kirk looked thoughtful. "The food is a lure to bring those primitive men into this place."

"In that case, Captain, the beam might be serving as a signal of their arrival."

"And this cave," Kirk said, "could be a trap."

"It could trap us, too, then, Captain," Chekov said nervously.

"Yes," Kirk said. "So you and the security team will remain at the entrance. We will maintain contact with you. If you don't hear from us within five hours, you will return to the *Enterprise* and contact Starfleet Command. Understood?"

"Yes, sir."

"Then return to the entrance."

"Yes, sir."

At Kirk's nod, Scott and McCoy checked their communicators. McCoy slung his tricorder over his shoulder. Then all three stepped over the beam. Kirk turned. Behind them metal doors had dropped over the cave's entrance.

"Phasers on stun," he said.

A loud hum broke the silence. Its pitch increased to a whine—and the whole cave moved bodily under their feet, descending as a descending elevator descends. It continued its smooth downward plunge; and Scott, checking his tricorder, said, "Captain, that power we picked up before—we're getting closer to it."

"A lot of power?" Kirk asked.

"Enough to push this planet out of orbit."

The whining noise was diminishing. "Natural or artificial, Mr. Scott?"

"Artificial, I'd say, sir."

"And the source?"

"Either a nuclear pile a hundred miles wide or . . ."

"Or what, Mr. Scott?"

"Ion power."

Kirk smiled thinly. Ion power—it had stolen Spock. He had to fight against an uprush of rage. Then he decided to let it happen to him. He'd use it to sharpen every sense he had. He succeeded. The door of the cave-elevator had been fitted so deftly into it that he alone spotted it before it slid silently open. A young girl was facing them. Kirk's eyes looked for and found the button-studded bracelet on her arm. Her face had tightened in surprise and fear. But before she could stab at her bracelet, Kirk fired his phaser. She fell.

Scott stood guard while Kirk removed the bracelet. "Is she all right, Bones?" he asked as McCoy rose from her stunned body.

"I'll have her talking in a minute—if she talks."

The pretty eyelids opened. At once her right hand went to her left arm. Kirk dangled the bracelet in her face. "We've had enough of that trick," he said.

She was instantly on her feet to make a grab for the bracelet. As McCoy's firm hold convinced her of her helplessness, she said, "You do not belong here. You are not morg."

Kirk ignored that. "Take us to the one in charge," he said. "We must talk to him."

"Him? What is him?" said the girl. "I am Luma and I know no him."

"Who is in charge here?" Kirk's patience was slipping. "Where is the brain? Where was it taken? Do you understand me?"

"You do not belong here. You are not morg or eymorg. I know nothing about a brain."

"I'll say you don't!" Kirk said. "I have no time for stupid lies!"

"Jim—she's not lying. I've checked her. She really doesn't know." McCoy reslung his tricorder over his shoulder; and the girl seized her moment to make a wild dash for a door at the end of the corridor. Kirk caught her just as she reached it, but she had managed to press a photo cell built into the door jamb. Spinning her around, he barred her way through it.

"What is this place?" he demanded.

"This place is here."

"Who are you?"

"I say before I am Luma. I am eymorg. You are not eymorg. You are not morg. What you are I do not understand."

"Well," Kirk said, "they certainly seem to be in bad need of brains around here. Watch her, Scotty."

"You'll get nothing out of that one, Captain. She's got the mind of a child."

"Then she's got a sister who isn't retarded!" Kirk said. "One that she can take us to! I've had all I'm taking of these pleas of ignorance!"

He flipped the dial on his communicator. "Captain Kirk to Chekov—Kirk to Chekov. Come in, Mr. Chekov!"

There was no response. He altered the dial adjustment and tried again. "Kirk to Chekov. Come in, Mr. Chekov . . ."

"Fascinating. Activity without end. But with no volition—fascinating."

Kirk froze. A chill shook him from head to feet. It was Spock's voice, familiar, loved, speaking very slowly.

"Fascinat—" Kirk shouted into the communicator. "Spock! Spock! Is that you?"

"Captain? Captain Kirk?"

"Yes, Spock! Yes!"

"It's good to hear a voice, especially yours."

Wordless, his hands shaking, Kirk handed his communicator to McCoy. Joy in his voice, McCoy cried, "Where are you, Spock? We're coming to get you!"

"Is that you, Dr. McCoy? Are you with the Captain?"

"Where else would I be?" In his turn McCoy silently passed the communicator to Scott.

"Where are you, Mr. Spock?"

"Engineer Scott, too? Unfortunately, I do not know where I am."

Kirk grabbed the communicator. "We'll get to you, Spock. It won't be long. Hold on."

"Good. Captain. It seems most unlikely that I will be able to get to you."

McCoy spoke again. "If you don't know where you are, do you know what they're doing with you? That could help us."

"Sorry, Doctor. I have not been able to achieve any insight into that."

"They are using you for something," insisted McCoy.

"Perhaps you are right. At the moment I do not feel useful. Functional in some ways—but not useful."

"Spock," Kirk said, "keep concentrating. The use they are making of you will determine where they have you. Keep concentrating on the use they are making of you—and we'll get to you."

The door beside them slid open. Two of the shaggy men came through it. Metal bands encircled their brows. They were welded into other bands that passed over their heads and down to cup their chins. Behind them stood the beautiful passenger of the ion-propelled spaceship.

She motioned the men toward Kirk, McCoy and Scott. They didn't move. She pushed a red stud on her bracelet. The banded men writhed in torment. In a paroxysm of mixed pain and frustrated fury, they charged the *Enterprise* party. Mc-

Coy, caught off guard, felt a rib crack under the pressure of two massively muscular arms. Kirk had pulled free of his attacker's grip. He bent his back under the next maddened assault and his man slid over it into a somersault. He found his phaser, fired it—and the morg, the man, lay still. Then he felled Scott's adversary with a karate blow.

This time the beautiful lady chose to depress a yellow button on her bracelet. Kirk's phaser dropped from his hand as unconsciousness flooded over him. Like the two morgs, like Scott and McCoy, he lay still.

The five male bodies, helplessly stretched at her feet, pleased the lady. When the girl Luma joined her, the spectacle pleased her, too.

It was a woman's world under the planet's surface.

In its Council Chamber, women, all physically attractive, sat at a T-shaped table. As the still triumphantly smiling lady took her place at its head, they rose, bowed and caroled, "Honor to Kara the Leader!" Beside each woman knelt a man, sleek, well fed, docile as a eunuch. Occasionally a woman stroked a man as one pats a well-housebroken pet.

At Kara's signal a door opened. Two of the muscular kitten-men pushed Kirk, McCoy and Scott into the room and up to the head of the table. The metal bands had now been fixed to their heads. Their masculinity caused a stir among the women; but it was the response, not of adult women, but of children on their first visit to a zoo.

Scott was the first to recognize Kara. "She's the one who came to the *Enterprise*," he whispered to Kirk.

Kirk nodded. "It's the smile I remember," he said.

She spoke. "You have a thing to say?" she asked pleasantly.

"Just one thing," Kirk said. "What have you done with the brain of my First Officer?"

"We do not know your First Officer."

"His brain," Kirk said. "You have Spock's brain."

Something registered in what passed for Kara's brain. "Ah, yes! Brain! You spoke to Luma also of brain. We do not understand."

They *are* retardates, Kirk thought. Getting through to whatever gray matter existed in that beautiful head was going to be tough. Temper, temper! he said to himself. Speaking slowly, very distinctly, "You were on my Starship," he said. "You were there to take Spock's brain. What's more, you took it. So what's this talk of not understanding what I mean by brain?"

"We do not know these things you speak of. We are only here below and here above. This is our place. You are not a morg. You are stranger."

Kirk's temper refused to heed his exhortation. "You came to my ship . . ."

McCoy put a restraining hand on his arm. "Jim, she may not remember. Or even really know. Dissociation may be complete. One thing is sure. She never performed that operation."

"If it required intelligence, she certainly didn't," Kirk said.

Kara pointed to Luma. "You hurt her. It is not permitted again to hurt anyone."

"We are sorry," Kirk said. "We did not wish to hurt."

"You wish to return to your home? You may go."

Kirk rallied all the charm he'd occasionally been accused of possessing. "We wish to stay here with you. We wish to learn from you. And tell you about us. Then we will not be stranger."

The women were delighted. They smiled and nodded at each other. McCoy decided to toss his charm into the pot. "Above," he said, "it is cold, harsh. Below here with you, it is warm. Perhaps it is your beauty that freshens the air."

They liked that, too. They liked it so much that Scott was encouraged to say, "There is no sun. Yet there is light—the light of your loveliness."

Kirk had lost his last shred of patience. "I want to meet those in charge," he said.

"In charge?" echoed Kara.

She looked so puzzled that he added, "The leader of your people."

"Leader? I am Leader. There is no other."

Dumbfounded, Scott said, "Who runs your machines?"

Kirk drew a deep breath. "This is a complex place," he said. "Who controls it?"

"Control?" she said. "Controller?"

The shocked look on her face told him the word had meaning for her. He tried to subdue his rising excitement. "Controller! Yes! That is right. We would like to meet—to see your controller!"

Kara's fury was as abrupt as it was intense. "It is not permitted! Never! Controller is apart, alone! We serve Controller! No other is permitted near!"

"We intend no harm," Kirk said hastily.

But he had exploded a volcano. "You have come to destroy us!" Kara screamed. The women around her, infected by her panic, twittered like birds at the approach of a snake. They all rose, their fingers reaching for their bracelets. Appalled, Kirk cried, "No! No! We do not come to destroy you! We are not destroyers!" McCoy came to stand beside him. He put all the reassurance at his disposal into his voice. "All we want," he said, "is to talk to somebody about Spock's brain."

"Brain! And again, brain! What is brain! It is Controller, is it not?"

McCoy said, "Well, yes. In a way it is. The human brain controls the individual's functions." He was beginning to suspect the significance of the hysteria. He looked at Kirk. "And the controlling power of the Vulcan brain, Jim, is extraordinarily powerful."

Scott, too, had realized that Kara identified the word "brain" with controlling power. "Is it possible they are using Spock's brain to—" He didn't complete the sentence.

"The fact that it is a Vulcan brain makes it possible," McCoy said.

Kirk suddenly flung himself to his knees. "Great Leader! We have come from a far place to learn from your Controller . . ."

"You lie! You have come to take the Controller! You have said this!"

Still on his knees, Kirk said, "He is our friend. We beg you to take us to him."

But the fright in the women's faces had increased. One began to sob. Kara stood up. "Quiet! There is no need to fear. We know they can be prevented." The women refused consolation. As though the very sight of the *Enterprise* men filled them with horror, they pushed their benches back and fled the Council Chamber.

Kirk made a leap for Kara. "You must take us to him!" he shouted.

She touched the red stud on her bracelet. The bands cupping their heads were suddenly clawed with fiery spindles. They stabbed their temples with an excruciating agony that obliterated thought, the memory of Spock, of the *Enterprise*, the world itself. The torture widened, spread to their throats, their chests, devouring their breath. Choking, Kirk tore at the band and collapsed. Beside him, McCoy and Scott had lost consciousness.

"I must learn what to do!"Kara cried. "Keep them here!"

Her two servant morgs hesitated. She moved a finger toward her bracelet. The gesture was sufficient. They lumbered over to the slumped bodies to take up guard positions on either side of them.

The pain had ceased. Kirk opened his eyes to see McCoy stir feebly. "Are you all right, Bones?" McCoy nodded, his eyes bloodshot. "I—I wouldn't have believed the human body could have survived such pain," he whispered. Revived, Scott was pulling at his headband. "They're attached to us by a magnetic lock of some kind."

"No wonder the morgs are so obedient," Kirk said. He struggled back to his feet. "What beats me is how this place is kept functioning. What keeps the air pure and the temperature equable?"

"It's clearly not the men," McCoy said. "They live on the frozen surface like beasts. So it must be the women. They live down here with all the comforts of an advanced society."

"Not one of those women could have set up the complex that keeps the place going," Scott said. "That would call on engineering genius. There is no sign of genius in these females."

"They're smart enough to have evolved these headbands," Kirk said. "What a way to maintain control over men!"

" 'Pain and delight,' " McCoy quoted. "I'm sure you've noticed the delight aspect in these surroundings, Jim."

"Yes. Beauty, sex, warmth, food—and all of them under the command of the women."

"And how does Spock's brain fit into this woman-commanded underground?" Scott asked.

Kirk didn't answer. The guard morgs had left them to go and stand at a corner table. On it, neatly arranged, were their tricorders and communicators. Only their phasers were missing. "Bones," Kirk said, "do you see what I see over there?"

"The equipment is only there, Jim, because the women don't understand its use."

"Gentlemen," Kirk said, "wouldn't you say that science holds the answer to the problem of recovering our equipment?"

"Aye," Scott said. "Let's go, Captain!"

They went for the morgs. Kirk gripped the jaw of one in a hard press. There was a bellow of pain. Terrified that it had been heard, the other morg looked apprehensively toward the door. Then he made a jump for Scott. Both guards were paragons of muscular strength; but their long training in docility had destroyed their ability to use it effectively. Kirk downed his Goliath with a jab to the throat. Scott's rabbit punch disposed of the other rabbit. Scientific fighting indeed held the answer to their problem. Within forty seconds the two guards were out for the count.

Kirk hastily adjusted the high-power dial on his communicator. "Spock! Spock! This channel reached you. Come in, Spock! Kirk here."

"Yes, Captain." It was Spock's voice. "I am also here. But I begin to feel extended almost to infinity. Have you returned to the *Enterprise*?"

"No! We were just temporarily out of—communication."

"You have not been seriously injured, I trust?"

"No! Spock, have you discovered what use you are being put to? Is it medical or . . ."

"I am not sure, sir. I seem to have a body that stretches into endlessness."

"Body?" Scott blurted. "You have no body!"

"No body? But then what am I?"

"You are a disembodied brain," McCoy said.

"Really? Fascinating. That could explain much. My medulla oblongata is apparently directing my breathing, pumping my blood and maintaining a normal physiological temperature.''

"Spock," McCoy said, "keeping a detached brain alive is a medical miracle. But keeping it functioning, that's impossible.''

"I would agree with you, Doctor, if it were not the present fact. It seems incontrovertible that my brain *is* functioning, does it not?''

"It does, Spock, I must admit. And gladly, for once.''

"How was the operation accomplished?''

"We don't know.''

"Then why are you endangering your lives by coming here?''

"We've come to take you back," Kirk said.

"Back where? To my body?''

"Yes, Spock.''

"Thoughtful, Captain. But probably impractical. My body . . .''

McCoy took the communicator. "Don't you think I had the sense to slap it into our life support chamber?''

"Of course. But I do not believe you own the skill or knowledge to replace a brain, Doctor. That skill does not yet exist in the galaxy.''

Kirk removed the communicator from McCoy. "The skill that removed the brain exists right here. The skill to replace it may exist here, too.''

"Captain, how much time has elapsed since my brain was removed?''

"Forty-eight hours.''

"Sir, Dr. McCoy must have told you that seventy-two hours is the maximum my body can be . . .''

"I know, Spock. That leaves us fourteen hours.''

"It seems all too brief a time to develop the required skill, Captain.''

"Very brief. One question, Spock. Pain-causing bands have been fixed to our heads. Do you know how to get us free of them? They have to come off.''

"I shall consider it, sir," the voice said.

"Give it top priority. And stay with us, Spock. Kirk out.''

They moved cautiously out of the Council Chamber into the corridor. It was empty. Kirk spoke soberly. "As the lady said, gentlemen, we are not morg. We are disciplined men, intelligent, committed to a purpose. We will remain committed to it in spite of any pain inflicted upon us."

His communicator crackled. "I have the answer for you, Captain. Your pain bands are manually controlled. A blue button on a bracelet releases them. That doesn't make much sense but . . ."

"Oh yes, it does," Kirk said. "Thank you, Spock."

A blue button. He must remember. They were extremely color-prone in this place. The ornamented door at the end of the corridor blazed with color like a stained-glass window. It seemed to possess other qualities. Though they were approaching it slowly, McCoy's tricorder had begun to buzz loudly. With every careful step they took, the volume increased in intensity until McCoy said, "I'm tuning out. The power is too great for the tricorder."

"Spock," Kirk said into his communicator, "do you know whether you are close to the power source?"

"I can't tell that. But you, Captain, are very close to it."

It was a credible statement. Near now to the elaborate door, they could see that its colored bosses were radiating a dazzling luminescence. They pushed it open to be faced by a wall banked with shining instrumentation. The room might have been the laboratory of magicians versed in the mysteries of some arcane technology. Another wall was a gigantic control board, topped by a helmetlike device. Near it a large black box set on a metallic pedestal was massed with photoelectric cells, all adjusted to correspond to similar cells on the control board. They flashed together in a constant interchange of energy.

Kara, her body taut, was standing before the black box, her back to them.

She heard them, despite their care. She whirled, her hand instantly touching her bracelet. The agony seared them, ripping a scream from Scott. They stumbled on, their legs rubber, their chests on fire. Kirk reached her, tore her hand from her bracelet and wrenched it off her arm. The blue button. He pressed it—and their headbands snapped. Kara gave a wild cry.

It echoed and re-echoed endlessly. Then they saw what stretched beyond the room—a vast machinery that extended for hundreds of underground miles, utterly alien, gleaming, no element in its panels and coils familiar. Awed into silence, Scott finally found his voice. "Captain, it is the ultimate. I think that is an air recirculation unit—but I'm not sure. I'm not even sure this is a hydroponic regulator. It all seems to have been contrived for life support—but it's a work of genius that is beyond me."

Kirk had his eyes on the black box. It glittered under the light rays that streamed to it from all sections of the great control board. How he knew what he knew he didn't know. He walked up to it. "Spock," he said, "you are in a black box tied with light rays to a complex control panel."

The voice sounded very close. "Incredible!" it said.

"Spock, you said you were breathing, pumping blood, maintaining temperature. Are you also recirculating air, running heating systems, purifying water?"

"Indeed, Captain, that is exactly what I'm doing."

Kara had broken free of McCoy's grip. Frenzied, she rushed at Kirk, trying to push him away from the box. He seized her; and she sagged, screaming, "We will die! You must not take the Controller! We will die! The Controller is young, powerful—perfect!"

"Extremely flattering," said the black box.

She flung herself to the floor, groping for Kirk's knees. "Leave him with us! He will give life to us for ten thousand years!"

"You will find another Controller," Kirk said.

She was sobbing. "There exists no other in the world. The old one is finished. Our new one must stay with us!"

Spock's voice spoke. "Captain, there seem to be rather complex problems. My brain is maintaining life for a large population. Remove it—and the life support systems it supports come to a stop."

McCoy looked somber. "Jim, here his brain is alive. If you remove it from the connections that are feeding it now to turn it over to me, it may die."

"That is the risk," Spock said. "Captain, much as I long for reunion with you and the *Enterprise*, the prospect of betraying such a dependent society is disturbing to a conscience like mine."

"Rubbish!" said Kirk. "Pure rationalization. It's always provoked by a weeping woman. She took your brain out—and she can put it back!" He shook Kara roughly. "How did you remove the brain?"

"I do not know."

"She couldn't know, Jim. Her mental faculties are almost atrophied. The Controller has done all her thinking for her."

"She took it out!" Kirk shouted. He shook Kara again. *"How did you do it?"*

"It was—the old knowledge," she whimpered.

"How did you get the knowledge?"

"I put—the teacher on my head."

"What teacher?"

She pointed to the helmetlike device. "What did you do with it?" Kirk demanded. "Show us!"

She shrieked in horror. "It is forbidden! The ancients forbade it. Only on the command of the ancients can I know."

"Show us," Kirk said.

Hysterical tears swelling her face, Kara got to her feet, went to the control board and reached for the helmet. Lifting it reverently down, she slowly lowered it over her head. Over the sobs that convulsed her, Spock's voice said, "If I may explain, Captain. She referred to the taped storehouse of knowledge accumulated by the builders of this place. It is a most impressive store. I scan it. The tapes are circuited to lead into the helmet. When placed over the head of the priestess leader, their information penetrates her mind. It is used rarely—and only when predetermined by the builders."

It was another credible statement. Under the helmet, Kara's face had changed. It had been wiped clean of her infantile hysteria. Into her eyes had come a searching look, the alertness of active thinking. Even her voice had taken on the vibrancy of intelligence. She spoke with clipped clarity. "That explanation is essentially correct. However, the Controller gives no credit to me. I deserve it. I provide the means by which the knowledge is used. Without me, Captain of the *Enterprise* . . ."

This Kara was a woman to take into account. McCoy acknowledged the difference. "That is true. Without you the miracle that has kept Spock's brain alive could not have occurred."

She bowed with dignity. "Thank you, Doctor."

Kirk said, "We all appreciate your contribution."

"Good," she said. "Then you will also appreciate your own contribution—*this* . . ."

A phaser was in her hand.

"Captain!" Scott cried. "It's on the kill mark!"

"So it is," she said. "And that is the knowledge *you* have given to me—how to kill!"

Kirk was the first to rally. "You knew how to kill before we came. You are killing Spock by keeping his brain."

She laughed. "The Controller die? He will live ten thousand years!"

"But Spock will be dead. Even now his body is dying. Soon it will be too late to restore him life."

"No. Only the vessel that once contained the Controller will be dead."

"But the body and the brain comprise a being," Kirk said.

The phaser didn't waver in its aim. Above it, her eyes were very bright. "Spare me such opinions. You will stay here quietly with me until the vessel is dead. Then we shall say good-bye and you can return to your ship."

"Your ancients are using you to murder," Kirk said.

She smiled. "Their commandment is being obeyed."

"Commandments older than your ancients' forbid murder," Kirk said.

She was shaken by the cold intensity of his voice. "Why do you not understand? My people need their Controller more then you need your friend."

A sense of the righteousness of his wrath swept over Kirk like a great wave. For the first time in his life he understood the meaning of "towering" rage. It seemed to lift him up to a great height. He extended a finger at her. "No one may take the life of another. Not for any purpose. It is not allowed."

He stepped forward. The phaser lifted. Then it drooped. Behind her, Scott quietly reached an arm over her shoulder—and took the phaser. Her eyes filled with silent tears.

"The commandment," she whispered, "should be fulfilled."

"You will help us," Kirk said. "How long does the knowledge last?"

"Three kyras," she said.

"You will restore what you stole," Kirk said.

"And betray my people? No."

"Jim—if the helmet worked for her, it might work for me." McCoy moved to Kara, lifted the helmet from her head—and Spock's voice spoke. "The configurations of her brain are alien, Doctor. It could burn your brain right out."

"I am a surgeon. If I can learn these techniques, I might retain them."

"Bones, how long can we keep the brain functioning once we remove it from its current environment?"

"Five or six hours."

"When it's tied to our life support system, will it give us any more time?"

"A few more hours."

Spock's voice said, "I cannot allow such risk to the Doctor."

McCoy handed the helmet to Kirk. He went to the box. "Spock. Spock, didn't you hear me? I may retain the memory of these techniques to pass on to the world! Isn't that worth the risk to me? *You* would take such a risk! Would you deny the same right to me?"

Kirk said, "Take the helmet, Bones. Put it on."

Slowly McCoy lowered the device over his head. From the black box words came. "Mr. Scott, go to the left lower quarter of the control board . . ."

"Yes, sir."

"Have you located a small lever in that sector?"

"Yes, Mr. Spock."

"Depress it exactly two notches and force it sharply into the slit on the right."

A low humming sounded. As power moved from the control board into the helmet's circuitry, McCoy's hand went to his throat. His body and his face seemed to disconnect.

His face glowed as though he'd been struck with some final illumination, but his body convulsed in torture. Then he blacked out and keeled over. Scott hastily pulled the lever back into its original position, then he and Kirk rushed to McCoy and gently lifted the helmet from his head. Kirk sat down, holding the unconscious body—and McCoy's eyes opened.

The vagueness in them disappeared. They began to brighten, first in wonder, then in exaltation. He gave a great shout of pure joy. "Of course—of course—a child could do it. A little child could do it!"

"Good luck to you, Dr. McCoy," said the black box.

In the *Enterprise*'s Sickbay, the operating room had been prepared.

Spock lay on its sheet-shrouded table, a shield screening the upper section of his head. Behind the shield, Nurse Chapel, a look of amazement on her face, was concentrated on every move made by the surgical instruments in McCoy's rubber-gloved hands. He was working with an authority she'd never seen before in a human surgeon. She took the time to wish that Kirk and Scott could see what she was privileged to see. But they, with Kara, had been placed behind a grille.

She went to the grille to whisper to Kirk. "Captain, don't worry. It's not to be believed—the way he's fusing ganglia, nerve endings, even individual nerves almost too small to see—and as if he'd been doing it all his life."

"How much longer?" Kirk said.

"I can't tell, sir. He's going so much faster than is humanly possible."

"Time is important," he said. "There's no way of knowing how long we can count on this increased surgical knowledge to last."

Kara suddenly sobbed. Kirk placed an arm about her shoulder. "What is it?" he said.

"You will have him back. But we are destroyed."

He led her out into the corridor. "No," he said, "you are not destroyed. You'll have no Controller and that will be fine. You will have to come up from below and live on the surface."

"We will die in the cold."

"No, you won't. We will help you until you can help

yourselves. You will build houses. You'll learn to keep warm by working to keep warm. You'll learn how to be women instead of hothouse plants.''

''Captain Kirk!''

Nurse Chapel was at the Sickbay door. ''You'd better come quickly, sir!''

McCoy had stopped working. He had backed away from the operating table. He looked sick. ''I—can't. I—I can't . . .''

''He's forgetting, Captain,'' said Nurse Chapel.

''Bones!'' Kirk called through the grille.

McCoy stumbled toward him. ''All the ganglia—the nerves—a million of them—what am I supposed to do with them? The thalamus—the pallium . . .''

''Bones! You can't stop now!''

Nurse Chapel, her eyes on the life support indicator, said, ''Doctor—the cerebral spinal fluid is almost exhausted.''

McCoy groaned. ''But—I don't know what to do. It's gone—I don't remember—no one can replace a brain!''

''But you could, Bones! It was child's play just a short while ago!''

''It's all gone, Jim. He's going to die—and I can't stop it!''

''Dr. McCoy.''

Half-strangled, choked, it was nevertheless Spock's voice. They stared at the body on the sheeted table. McCoy was astounded into asking, ''Spock, did you speak? How did you speak?''

''If you will finish connecting my vocal chords, I may be able to help.''

McCoy rushed behind the shield. He chose an instrument. Then he discarded it, picked up another one and gave a brisk order to Nurse Chapel. Spock suddenly coughed. The voice came a little stronger. ''Good. One thing at a time. Now, Doctor, try the sonic separator. No discouragement . . .''

''No, Spock—it's been like trying to thread a needle with a sledgehammer.''

''No discouragement,'' Spock repeated. ''I already have feeling, sensation. Now stimulate the nerve endings and observe the reactions. I shall tell you when the probe is correct. When I tell you, seal the endings with the trilaser connector.''

Kirk spoke to McCoy. ''Well?''

His answer came in a slight hum from behind the shield. Through the grille, he could see Spock's arms move, moving normally, up and down, bending normally at the elbow.

''Very good,'' Spock said. ''Now, Doctor, please move to reconnect the major blood vessels. Begin with the carotid artery.''

HIs face drawn with strain, McCoy glanced over at Kirk. ''Even if this works,'' he said, ''I'll never live it down—this confounded Vulcan telling me how to operate!''

Relief swamped Kirk. They were back at the old bickering. McCoy had paused to allow Nurse Chapel to wipe the sweat from his forehead. He returned to work and Spock said, ''They are sealed, Doctor.''

''Are they, Bones?''

McCoy raised his head. ''How do I know? He knows. I've probably made a thousand mistakes—sealing individual nerve endings, joining ganglia. The fluid balance is right but—I don't know.''

Nurse Chapel was wiping his forehead again when Spock's eyelids flickered. The eyes opened. Spock lifted his head and his eyebrows went up into the arch McCoy thought never to see again. He shouted, ''Jim!''

Kirk strode behind the shield. Spock was sitting up. ''Gentlemen,'' he said, ''it is a pleasure to see you again.''

''Spock—Spock,'' Kirk said—and swallowed. ''How do you feel?''

''On the whole, I believe I am quite fit, sir.''

He started to get off the table. ''For the Lord's sake, take it easy!'' Kirk yelled.

Spock winced under a twinge of pain. ''Perhaps you are right, Captain. I seem to have something of a headache. Perhaps I had better close my eyes.''

''You are going to sleep and sleep and sleep,'' Kirk said.

Spock sleepily closed his eyes and immediately opened them in obvious surprise. ''The eyelids work,'' he said.

"Fascinating! It would seem, Doctor, that few of your connections were made in error."

"I performed a miracle of surgery on you to get you back into one piece," McCoy said.

"Doctor, I regret that I was unable to provide you with a blueprint."

McCoy turned to Kirk. "What I'll never know is why I reconnected his mouth to his brain."

Scott came out of the bridge elevator.

"Our technical aid teams have been beamed down to Planet 7, Captain."

"First reports, Mr. Scott?"

Scott rubbed his chin. "Well, sir, restoring friendly relations between its males and females won't be easy. Neither sex trusts the other one."

"How very human," commented Spock.

"And very cold," McCoy put in. "Especially the women. However, the aid parties have provided the ladies with a tool for procuring food, furs and fuel from the men."

"Oh?" Kirk turned from one to the other. "Money?"

"No, sir," Scott said. "Perfume."

"I'm not given to predictions, gentlemen, but I'll venture one now," Kirk told them. "The sexual conflict on Planet 7 will be a short one."

"I fail to see what facts you base your prediction on, Captain," Spock said.

"On long, cold winter nights, Mr. Spock—on the fact that cuddling is so much warmer than wood fires."

"Cuddling, sir?"

"A human predilection, Spock," McCoy said. "We don't expect you to know about it."

"Of course not, Doctor. It is a well-known fact that we Vulcans propagate our race by mail." He grinned.

"Spock!" McCoy shouted. "You smiled! No, by George, you positively grinned!"

"Another tribute to your surgery, Doctor. I was endeavoring to sneeze."

"Well, of all the ungrateful patients I—" McCoy began indignantly. It was with a real effort that Kirk maintained the gravity that seemed appropriate to the old, familiar, comfort-

able occasion. And sure enough, Spock nodded politely to
the outraged McCoy and returned to his station.

    In the end, Kirk couldn't maintain it. He laughed—a
laugh of delighted affection. To the smiling Sulu beside
him, he said, ''We're through here, Mr. Sulu. Warp factor
three.''

IS THERE IN TRUTH NO BEAUTY?

Writer: Jean Lisette Aroeste
Director: Ralph Senensky
Guest stars: Diana Muldaur, David Frankham

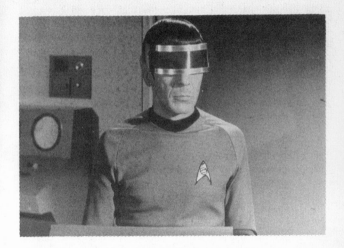

The civilian named Lawrence Marvick stepped from the Transporter platform of the *Enterprise*, aggression in every line of his square-jawed face. Kirk, moving forward to greet him, thought, *What's the man afraid of?* But his voice was smoothly cordial. "Welcome aboard, Mr. Marvick. I am James Kirk, the Cap—"

Marvick cut him off. "Kirk, what are you doing here? You'll have to leave, you know, before the Medeusan Ambassador arrives!"

"I am aware of that, Mr. Marvick. We have taken all precautions. This is Mr. Spock, our First Officer."

Marvick eyed Spock briefly. "Oh, yes, you're the Vulcan. It's all right for you to remain here but you, Kirk, and that other officer . . ."

Scott came from the Transporter console to shake the guest's hand with enthusiasm. "Montgomery Scott, Chief Engineer, Mr. Marvick. Call me Scotty!"

Recovering his hand, the new arrival addressed Spock. "Have you got your vizor? You must have it. Humans who get even a glimpse of Medeusans have gone insane."

Spock bowed. "Thank you, Mr. Marvick. I shall be wearing the vizor."

Marvick's authoritative manner was beginning to rile Kirk. "We mustn't keep the Ambassador waiting," he said. "Mr. Marvick, will you go with Mr. Scott now, please? You two should have a good deal in common."

As Scott ushered the man out, Kirk heard him say, "It's

a rare privilege to meet one of the designers of the *Enterprise*. I appreci—''

The door closed and Kirk crossed to the intercom. ''Lieutenant Uhura, inform the Ambassador and Dr. Jones that we're ready to beam them aboard.'' He turned to see Spock removing a red safety vizor from his belt. ''You're sure that thing will work?''

''It has proved entirely effective for Vulcans, sir.''

''It's your human half I'm worried about. Report to me when the Transport has been completed.''

''Yes, Captain.''

Left alone as the Captain returned to the bridge, Spock adjusted the vizor. It covered not only his eyes but the whole upper half of his face. At the Transporter console, he manipulated the beam-up buttons. On the platform sparkles gradually assumed the slim shape of a young woman. The sheen of embroidery on her long, graceful gown matched her cloud of silver-blond hair. Beside her was a box of medium size. Removing her red vizor, she revealed black-lashed eyes of a vivid blue. Then, to Spock's astonishment, a white arm was lifted in the Vulcan salute.

An eyebrow slightly raised, Spock returned it. ''Welcome aboard, Ambassador Kollos,'' he said. ''I am First Officer Spock.''

She stepped from the platform. ''And I am Dr. Jones— Dr. Miranda Jones.'' She gestured to the box still on the platform. ''The Ambassador is honored to meet you.''

Quiet and undisconcerted, Spock went to the box, affixing anti-gravs to it. When they were firmly clamped into place, he made his report to Kirk. ''Ready to proceed, Captain.''

Kirk, on the bridge, swung to Uhura. ''Lieutenant, open channels to all decks.''

''All channels open, sir.''

Kirk reached for his speaker. ''This is the Captain. All ship's personnel, clearance plans now in effect. Vacate corridors immediately. The Ambassador will be escorted at once to his quarters.'' He moved an intercom button. ''Mr. Spock, all decks are now clear. You may proceed.''

The box was clearly the habitat of the Medeusan Ambassador. As Spock lifted it carefully out of an elevator, he

said, "Dr. Jones, may I offer you my congratulations on your
assignment with Ambassador Kollos?"

She bowed. "The assignment is not yet definite. It will
depend upon my ability to achieve a true mind-link with the
Ambassador."

"You should find it a fascinating experience."

A flicker of resentment flashed in her blue eyes. "I
wasn't aware that *anyone* had ever succeeded in a mind-link
with a Medeusan!"

"Nobody has," Spock said. "I was merely referring
to mind-links I have attempted with other species."

"Surely," she said, "your duties as a Starship officer
do not permit you the luxury of many such experiments!"

He regarded her gravely. "My duties as a Starship officer permit me very few luxuries of any kind."

She reached for a conciliatory tone. "You make it quite
obvious that the *Enterprise* is your paramount interest." She
paused before she added, "You know, Mr. Spock, I have
heard you turned down this assignment with Ambassador
Kollos."

"I could not accept it," he said. "As you've pointed
out, my life is here. And the Ambassador's quarters are also
here." He indicated a cabin on their right.

There was a pedestal in the cabin. Setting the habitat
down on it, Spock removed the anti-gravs. At the room's
intercom, he said, "Spock to bridge. We have reached the
Ambassador's quarters, Captain."

"Thank you, Mr. Spock. Lieutenant Uhura, notify all
hands to return to stations." Kirk sighed with relief as he
turned to Sulu. "All right, helmsman. Let's take her out.
Warp factor two."

"Warp factor two, sir."

In the cabin, Spock, vizored like Miranda, was eyeing
the alien habitat. "Dr. Jones," he said, "I should very much
like to exchange greetings with Ambassador Kollos."

She smiled. "I am sure the Ambassador will be
charmed."

Both of them placed a hand on the box. Then they went
perfectly still, each absorbed in deep concentration. After a
long moment the lid of the box lifted very slightly—and a
light of purest blue streamed through the crack. Leaning for-

ward, Spock peered into the box. Instantly, he recoiled; but after pausing to recover from the sight, he looked into it again. His lips moved in a smile of an almost childlike wonder.

The girl saw the smile. Once more resentment flashed in her eyes. The lid of the box fell. Unsmiling now, Spock said, "I almost envy you your assignment, Dr. Jones."

"Do I read in your thoughts that you are tempted to take my place, Mr. Spock?"

"No. But I feel your mind trying to touch mine, Doctor. Were you born a telepath?"

She nodded. "Yes. That is why I had to study on Vulcan."

"Of course," he said. "May I now show you to your quarters?"

"I'd better remain here a bit. Ambassador Kollos sometimes finds the process of Transport unsettling."

"Our ship's surgeon often makes the same complaint." He pointed to the intercom. "Call when you are ready."

He bowed and left the cabin. Miranda turned back to the habitat. She removed her vizor roughly, her beautiful face disturbed, doubtful, even apprehensive. In the solitude of the cabin, she cried out fiercely, "What did he see when he looked at you, Kollos? I have to know! I have to know!"

The *Enterprise* had done itself proud. Though dinner was over, hosts and guests still lingered over their brandy at a table elegant with crystal, candlelight, arrangements of fresh-cut flowers. All the officers wore dress uniforms; and Miranda, in silver-embroidered blue velvet, glowed like a blond pearl in the candlelight. Marvick, in civilian white tie and tails, was quiet but observant.

Kirk refilled the girl's brandy goblet. "I can't understand," he said, "why they're letting you go with Kollos."

"*They*, Captain?"

"The male population of the Federation. Didn't anyone try to talk you out of it?"

The black lashes drooped. "Well . . . now that you ask, yes."

"I'm glad he didn't succeed," Kirk said. "If he had, I'd never have met you." He raised his glass to her. "Tell me, Dr. Jones, why isn't it dangerous for you to be with Kollos? Spock I can understand. Nothing makes any impression on him."

"Why, thank you, Captain," Spock said.

"Not at all, Mr. Spock." He turned back to Miranda. "No other human is able to look at Kollos without going mad, even when vizored. How do you manage?"

"I spent four years on Vulcan studying their mental disciplines."

McCoy spoke. "You poor girl!" he cried with heartfelt sympathy.

Spock looked down the table at him. "Indeed, Doctor! I would say that the lady is very fortunate!"

"Vulcan disciplines are hardly *my* idea of fun."

"On Vulcan," the girl said, "I learned to do what it is impossible to learn anywhere else."

Smiling, Kirk asked, "How to read minds?"

"How *not* to read them, Captain."

"I'm afraid I don't understand," Kirk said.

Spock interposed. "Dr. Jones was born a telepath, Captain."

Miranda laughed. "Vulcan was necessary to my sanity, Captain! I had to learn how to close out the thoughts of others."

Spock nodded. "What humans generally find it impossible to understand is the need to shut out the bedlam of others' thoughts and emotions."

"Not to mention the bedlam of even one's *own* emotions," Miranda said. "On Vulcan one learns to do that, too." She reached out to touch a medallion pinned to Spock's breast. McCoy watched her fingers move over it.

Spock pulled back, fearful of scratching her. "Forgive me," he said. "I forget that dress uniforms can injure."

She leaned toward him. "I was merely interested in your Vulcan IDIC, Mr. Spock. Is it a reminder that you could mind-meld with the Ambassador much more effectively than I could?"

There was an uncomfortable pause. She broke it hastily, explaining, "It would be most difficult for a Vulcan to see a mere human take on this exciting challenge, gentlemen."

"Interesting," McCoy said. "It's a fact, Spock, that you rarely wear your IDIC."

"Bones," Kirk said, "I doubt that our First Officer would don the most revered of all Vulcan symbols merely to annoy a guest."

Spock spoke for himself, looking straight at Miranda. "In fact, I wear it this evening to honor you, Dr. Jones."

"Indeed?" she said.

"Yes," he said, "indeed. Perhaps, despite those years on Vulcan, you missed the true symbology of the IDIC." He placed his hand on the medallion. "The triangle and the circle . . . different shapes, materials, textures . . . they represent any two diverse things which come together to create truth or beauty." He rose, brandy glass in hand. "For example—Dr. Miranda Jones, who has combined herself with the disciplines of my race to become greater than the sum of both!"

Suddenly uneasy, Kirk saw that his lively guest appreciated neither the grace nor the sincerity of Spock's gallantry. He changed the subject. "Back to your mission, Dr. Jones. Do you feel a way can be found to employ Medeusan navigators on Starships? It would solve many of our present navigational problems."

"The key is the mind-link learned on Vulcan. Once we learn to form a corporate intelligence with Medeusans, designers of Starships—and that's where Larry Marvick comes in—can work on adapting instruments."

McCoy stirred in his chair. "I don't care how 'benevolent' the Medeusans are supposed to be. Isn't it suicidal to deal with something ugly enough to cause madness? Why do you do it?"

"Dr. McCoy," Spock said, "I see that you still subscribe to the outmoded notion held by your ancient Greeks—the one which insists that what is good must also be beautiful."

Marvick spoke for the first time. "And the obverse of it—that what is beautiful is automatically expected to be good."

"I suppose," Kirk reflected, "that most of us are naturally attracted by beauty as we are repelled by ugliness. It's the last of our prejudices. But at the risk of sounding prejudiced—'' He paused to raise his glass to Miranda. "Here's to Beauty!"

All the men rose and drank. McCoy lifted his glass a second time. "To Miranda Jones—the loveliest woman ever to grace a Starship!" He looked around at his fellow males. "How can one so beautiful condemn herself to look upon ugliness for the rest of her life? Will we allow it?"

His answer was a general shout of "No!"

McCoy sat down. "We must not permit her to leave us!"

Miranda was smiling at him. "How can one so full of the love of life as you, Dr. McCoy, condemn himself to look upon suffering and disease for the rest of his life? Can we allow *that*, gentlemen?"

McCoy tipped his glass to her, sipping from it. "I drink to whatever it is you want most, Miranda."

As Kirk joined in the toast, he noticed how intently Marvick was staring at the girl. He was about to offer her more brandy when he was halted by the look of terror that had abruptly come into her face.

She rose to her feet, crying, "There's a murd—" She broke off and the flower she had been holding dropped to the table.

Kirk caught her arm. "Dr. Jones, what is it?" But McCoy was already beside her. "You're ill," he said. "Let me help you. . . ."

She pulled away, her face slightly calmer. "There's someone nearby thinking of murder," she said.

Shocked silence fell over the table. She was clearly serious and Kirk said, "Who is it—can you tell?"

"It's . . . not there now. I . . . I can't pick it up at all."

"Was it in this room?" Kirk said.

She looked around her. "I don't know, Captain. It's gone now." She seemed to have regained her composure. "These things are usually momentary. A common human impulse, seldom acted out."

Spock's quiet voice said, "True. Otherwise the human race would have ceased to exist."

"Captain, do you mind if I say good night now? I'd love to visit your herbarium—but another time, if I may."

"Of course, Dr. Jones. I'll see you back to—"

Spock interrupted. "Perhaps I could see you back to your quarters?"

McCoy was staring curiously at her. "Thank you, gentlemen," she said. "You make a choice impossible. Please stay here and enjoy yourselves. It was a delightful dinner."

"Sleep well, Miranda," Kirk said.

She waved a friendly good night to them. But McCoy, who was still watching her closely, went quickly to her at the door. "Are you sure you're well enough to find your way alone?"

"Yes, Dr. McCoy. Please don't worry about me."

McCoy bowed and, reaching for her hand, kissed it lightly. As the door closed behind her, he said, "Where I come from, that's what's called a 'lady.' "

"She *is* something special," Kirk agreed.

"*Very special!* I suggest you treat her accordingly!"

Marvick's sudden outburst startled them all. The man picked up a napkin and dropped it. "I—I have not known Dr. Jones for a long time. But long enough to be aware of her remarkable gifts!" He paused. "Well, it's been a long day for me . . ."

Scott said, "Would you like to stop off in Engineering, Larry? I have a few things to check; and a bottle of Scotch says you can't handle the controls you designed."

"Some other time," Marvick told him.

The door closed behind him. Turning away from it, Kirk looked Spock over. "Spock, you're really dressed up for the occasion. Very impressive."

"I genuinely intended to honor her, Captain." He moved to the door. "Good night, gentlemen."

His face unusually thoughtful, McCoy was still standing at the closed door. He looked at Kirk's handsome face. "That's not just another girl, Jim. Don't make that mistake."

Kirk grinned. "I can see that for myself, Bones. Anything else?"

"I can't say exactly what it is. She seems very . . . vulnerable."

Kirk was smiling again. "We're all vulnerable, Dr. McCoy . . . in one way or another."

"Yes. But there is something very disturbing about her."

"You'll get no argument from me, Bones. Meaning that she's quite a woman."

"Good night, Jim," McCoy said.

Alone, Kirk returned to the table. He retrieved the flower she had dropped and tucked it into the breast of his uniform.

Miranda's cabin was luxurious. She drifted around it, graceful but aimless, occasionally touching objects, perhaps because she admired them, perhaps to acquaint herself with the room's dimensions and contents. A buzz at her door sounded.

She leaned against it, calling, "Who is it?"

"Larry. I've got to talk to you."

"Larry, it's late. . . . "

"Please, Miranda. It's important."

She opened the door. "All right. Come in, then."

Marvick's face had the haunted look of a man in desperate need of a drug. Closing the door behind him, he stood silent for a moment, looking at the girl. "I thought that dinner," he said, "was never going to end."

He moved closer to her. She backed away, putting distance between them. "I rather enjoyed it," she said.

"I know you did. I didn't. You were too far away."

"Larry, I'll be further away than that soon." Her tone was intended to be soothing. But it failed to soothe. "Don't speak of that!" Marvick cried. "Don't . . . no, we have to speak of it. There is so little time . . ." He reached for her but she eluded him, maintaining the little distance. "Please, Miranda, don't go with Kollos!"

She sighed. "Larry, we've been over that time and time again. Please accept—"

Marvick tried for lightness but his hunger broke through it. "Don't I know? I've begged you in restaurants, in the laboratory, on one knee, on both knees! Miranda, how can you do this to me?"

"If you would only try to understand . . ."

"What I understand is that you're a woman and I'm a man—one of your own kind! You think that Kollos will ever be able to give you anything like this?'' He had her in his arms. The kiss crushed her lips against her teeth. Then his violence suddenly ended. He held her quietly, caressing her hair, her throat, blind to the quickened anger in her eyes.

She freed herself. ''You shouldn't have done that,'' she said coldly.

He ran a distracted hand over his face. ''I'm sorry. . . . Why, oh why did I ever meet you?''

''I have been honest with you,'' she said. ''I simply cannot love you the way you want me to. And I am going with Kollos. That is final.''

''Miranda, in God's name . . . !''

She went to the door. ''I think you'd better leave now. I find you exhaust—'' She suddenly broke off. Her hand went to her mouth to block a scream.

''So it's you!'' she cried.

He lowered his head like an animal at bay. She was at the far side of the room now, her face white with shock. ''I didn't know it was you before! Who is it you want to kill, Larry? Me? Larry, you must not keep such impulses to yourself! I can help you. . . . ''

''So now you want to 'help' me, do you? Well, now I know what a man has to do to get a response from you! A patient is what you want—not a man! Dr. Jones, the great psychologist! Just for a change of pace, try to be a woman for once in your life!''

He slammed the door behind him. Outside at the elevator, he turned and went back. At her cabin, he hesitated before moving on down the corridor. His square jaw hard, he stopped at the door of the Medeusan's quarters. Firmly and deliberately, he pushed it open.

In the cabin's center the habitat still stood on its pedestal. It emitted a steady, pulsing sound. For a moment Marvick stood, tense, his back to it, hand on the door handle. Then he turned to look at the box, his eyes blazing with hatred. The pulsing sound grew louder, as though the box's occupant had been aroused to danger.

There was an instant when fear and fascination combined to immobilize Marvick. It passed. His hand went fast to the phaser at his belt. The lid of the habitat flashed open, enveloping Marvick in blinding light. He staggered, dropping

the phaser. The Medeusan reared up. Marvick screamed as
his hand whipped up to shield his eyes from the forbidden
sight of Kollos.

Miranda sat bolt upright on her sleeping couch. Then
her hand went to her throat. Leaping from the couch, she
flew to her cabin door. Panic ran with her as she raced down
the corridor to Kollos's quarters.

In his light that still filled the room, she saw the phaser.
Tears flooded her eyes. Arms outstretched, she went close to
the habitat, crying, "Forgive me! Kollos, forgive me!"

The rhythm of the pulsing slowed.

Down in Engineering, Scott was adjusting a control, a
yeoman at work nearby. The yeoman turned as the door
opened, saw Marvick and signaled Scott. Scott beamed. "Ah,
there you are, Larry! So you couldn't resist that little wager!"

Trembling, still in shock, Miranda had found the
cabin's intercom. Kirk, listening to her incoherent whispers,
jumped from his command chair, shouting, "Lieutenant
Uhura, Mr. Spock and Dr. McCoy on the double! The Ambassador's quarters! Notify Security!"

He found two guards already at the door. He banged
on it, calling, "Miranda . . . Miranda!"

Spock was arranging his vizor as the door opened. The
girl, her own vizor in place, seemed to have recovered some
composure. Silently, she passed the phaser to Kirk, lifting
the mask from her eyes.

"Has the Ambassador been hurt?"

"No harm was done to him, Captain."

"Do you know who would do such a thing?"

"Larry Marvick."

Kirk stared. "Marvick? But why?"

"Madness prompted him."

Spock spoke quickly. "Did he see the Medeusan?"

"Yes, Mr. Spock."

"Then insanity is the certain result. Dangerous insanity, Captain."

Kirk ran for the cabin intercom. While he ordered a
Red Alert, Scott was turning the ship's controls over to Marvick. "They're all yours, Larry. That Scotch will be in your
cabin tonight if you can handle them!"

Kirk's filtered voice reached Engineering. "Captain

Kirk to all ship personnel. An attempt has been made to murder Ambassador Kollos. The man is dangerously insane. He is Lawrence Marvick. Be on the watch for him. Kirk out.''

Scott's jaw fell. Pulling himself together, he tried to push Marvick away from the controls, but the man's joined fists came crashing down on him with all the force of madness. Scott crumpled. The yeoman leaped for Marvick's back and was smashed to the deck.

The ship groaned under the lash of sudden acceleration. Staggering, Kirk, Spock and McCoy looked at each other. The ship's groan had become a whine when they raced out of the bridge elevator.

"Explain, Mr. Sulu!" Kirk shouted.

"I can't, sir. But we're traveling at warp factor eight point five."

"And still accelerating, Captain," Chekov said.

Spock looked at the helm console. "Our deflectors can't hold unless speed is immediately reduced."

"Lieutenant Uhura, put me through to Engineering!"

She turned to her console, bracing herself against the ship's shuddering. "Captain, they don't answer. . . . ''

Sulu said, "Warp factor nine, accelerating."

Kirk wheeled to Spock. "Mr. Spock, can you disengage the power from here?"

Spock already lay on his back, reaching inside a wall panel. "We shall try to, Captain. Mr. Chekov, come here, please. I need you."

Uhura turned. "I seem to have Engineering, Captain."

"Put it on the intercom, Lieutenant."

He heard Marvick's voice. It was singing. "We'll make it! We're under way now! We'll make it—and get out of here!"

A maniacal laugh echoed through the bridge.

Kirk hit the intercom. "Security! Get down to Engineering!"

Miranda appeared at his elbow. "I'll go with you," she said.

"No."

"I must, Captain. I can reach his mind."

After a moment, he nodded.

In the corridor outside Engineering, two Security

guards were trying to open the door. "He's jammed it, Captain," one said. "But with another good pull . . ."

It opened. Marvick, at the controls, was manipulating them easily and skillfully. But his dementia was unmistakable. Moans of genuine anguish were followed by seizures of uncontrollable giggles. When he saw Kirk standing quietly beside him, he chuckled. "Don't worry, Kirk. We'll be safe soon. Over the boundaries of the universe. We can hide there. . . ."

Kirk made a grab for the controls and Sulu's voice said, "Warp speed nine point five and accelerating, Captain."

Marvick had lashed out at Kirk with a thick metal tool. The guards closed in on him, pinning his furiously flailing arms behind his back. Scott, crawling to his feet, was moving groggily toward the controls when the ship broke out of the galaxy. In a flash of searing light, the shapes of people, instruments—everything—dissolved into nameless colors, confused and changing. A roar so deafening it lost the quality of sound hammered at the trembling *Enterprise*. The ship stopped, hanging suspended in a space of alien colors.

Kirk had been flung across the deck. As the roar diminished, he got slowly to his feet. Marvick, still held tight by the guards, was whispering, "We're safe. We made it. We're safe, Kirk. We made it over the boundaries of the galaxy."

McCoy was on his knees. Kirk nodded to him. Bones hauled himself up and, opening his medikit, stepped behind Marvick. But the hypo's needle had barely touched him when he made a lunge that almost broke the guards' hold.

Kirk said, "Marvick, it will help you sleep."

The tortured creature shrieked. "No! No! We mustn't sleep! Never! Never again. No sleep! Never! They come into your dreams. Then they can suffocate you! No sleep—no dreams. No! No!"

Kirk went to him. "All right, Larry. No sleep. No dreams. Just come with me. I have a better hiding place for you. I'll take you to it. Come. . . ."

Marvick made another break for the controls. "We must be ready to speed, Kirk! Speed! Speed on to the next galaxy. Away from here! Away!"

The wildly roving eyes caught sight of Miranda. Mar-

vick tore his arms free and stretched them out to her. Then he
collapsed. Kirk nodded to the guards, who released him.
Supporting the limp body in his own arms, Kirk saw that
Marvick's eyes had filled with tears. "Miranda . . . Miranda," he was whispering. "You . . . are here . . . with
me. . . ."

Kirk carried him to a bench. The girl came to kneel
beside Marvick. "Yes, Larry," she said. "I am here."

The madman cupped her face in his hands. "I didn't
lose you. My beautiful love. I thought I . . . had lost you."

"I am here, Larry."

For the first time, Kirk saw the depth of Marvick's love.
The tears were wet on the man's face and his body was trembling. Miranda looked up at Kirk. "I see what he sees," she
said and, turning back to Marvick, spoke softly. "Don't,
Larry. Don't think of what you saw. Don't think of it. . . ."

He uttered a scream of pain, pushing her away. "Liar!
Deceiver! You're not alone! He's here! He's here! You brought
him with you!"

The jealous hate rose in him again. He caught the girl
by the throat. The Security guards moved quickly to help Kirk
loosen his clutch. This time McCoy was fast with his hypo.

Kirk lifted Miranda in his arms. Watching them, Marvick spoke quietly. "Do not love her. She will kill you if you
love her. Do not love her."

Kirk looked down at the woman in his arms, the warning in his ears. He carried her to the door when the dying
man behind him called, "I love you, Miranda. . . ."

"Where are we, Mr. Spock?"

The bridge viewing screen showed only tangles of those
alien, nameless, ever-changing colors. Spock lifted his head
from hard work at his library computer. "Far outside our own
galaxy, Captain, judging from the lack of any traceable reference points."

"What you mean is we're nowhere," Chekov said.

Nowhere. Kirk moved restlessly in his command chair
as McCoy, a paper in his hand, came out of the elevator.

"May I interrupt, Jim?"

"Yes, Bones."

"I've got the autopsy on Marvick. Heart stopped: cause

unknown. Brain activity stopped: cause unknown. . . . Shall I go on?''

"You mean he simply died?"

"I mean he evidently couldn't live with what he saw."

Kirk looked unseeingly at the screen. "Or with what he felt." Remembering the mad eyes dripping tears, Kirk sighed. Nowhere. But back to business just the same. He turned to Scott. "How much damage to the engines, Scotty?"

"We'll need some repairs, sir, but the ship is basically intact."

"Mr. Spock, can you at least give us a position report?"

"Impossible to calculate, Captain. We lack data to analyze. Our instruments seem to function normally but what they tell us makes no sense." He paused. "Our records are reasonably clear up to the point at which we left our galaxy."

"We should be able to navigate back."

"We have no reference points to use in plotting a return course, Captain. We experienced extreme sensory distortion; and will do so again if we try to use warp speed. Nor can we recross the barrier at sublight speed."

"A madman got us into this and it's beginning to look as if only a madman can get us out."

"An entertaining suggestion, Mr. Chekov," Spock said. "Unhelpful, however."

Kirk rose and went to Spock. "The Medeusans have developed interstellar navigation to a fine art. Could Kollos function as a navigator in spite of the sensory distortion?"

"Very possibly, sir. The Medeusan's sensory system is radically different from ours. Perhaps, for the purpose of this emergency, I could become Kollos. And he become Spock."

"Explain."

"A fusion, Captain. A mind-link to create a double entity. Each of us will possess the knowledge and capabilities of both. We will function as one being."

"What are the hazards?"

"If the link is successful, there'll be a tendency to lose separate identity. It is a necessary risk." He hesitated, his eyes on Kirk's. "Of course, the lady will not want to give me permission to establish the link."

"I don't think she'd want *anyone* to intrude on the kind of rapport she has with Kollos," McCoy said.

"Dr. Jones," Spock said, "has shown reluctance whenever I have asked to converse with Kollos. In some ways she is still most human, Captain. Particularly in the vigor of her jealousy and her thirst for power."

Kirk didn't speak, and Spock went on. "Her telepathic powers are also formidable. If it is at all possible, her mind must be so engaged that no other thoughts will intrude on it."

"I think that can be arranged," Kirk said.

McCoy looked at him. "Jim, don't take this lightly. She's extremely sensitive. If you try to be devious with her, she'll know."

"Bones, I know what's at stake. I have no intention of playing games with Miranda."

He turned on his heel and left the bridge.

The Starship's herbarium was odorous with the mingled scents of flowers.

Kirk released Miranda's arm. "I may be sentimental, but this is my favorite room. It reminds me of Earth."

"I've never been to Earth. But what lovely flowers! May I touch them, Captain?"

He smiled at her. "Go ahead."

She moved down the path, stopping to stroke a velvety petal, a leaf. Watching her, Kirk thought: *She's a blossom herself*. But a spray of butterfly orchids disappointed her. "They have no scent," she complained, turning to Kirk.

"Try these."

They were roses, white, yellow, pale pink, some nearly black. She plunged her face into them, inhaling their perfume with delight. Suddenly she cried out, pulled away and with a grimace of pain put her hurt finger to her mouth.

Kirk took her hand. "Let me see. . . ."

"It was just a thorn," she said hastily, removing the hand. Kirk recovered it. Gently, he rubbed her finger. "I was hoping to make you forget about thorns today," he said.

"It doesn't hurt anymore."

"You mustn't blame yourself," he said. "because Marvick loved you."

Her abrupt ferocity startled him. "I don't! I didn't want his love! I couldn't return it—and I had no use for it!"

Kirk spoke slowly. "Surely, sooner or later you will want human love—a man to companion you."

She pushed aside a strand of silver-blond hair. "Shall I tell you what human companionship means to me? A battle! Defense against others' emotions! When I'm tired and my guard slips, their feelings burst in on me like a storm. Hatred, desire, envy, pity—pity's the worst of all! I agree with the Vulcans. Violent emotion is a kind of insanity."

"So you will spend the rest of your life with Medeusans to avoid human feelings?"

"Perhaps."

"A meeting of minds isn't enough. What are you going to do for love hunger, Miranda?"

She turned her back on him. "You will never understand me. I don't think you should try, Captain."

He pulled her around to face him. "Look. You are young, human. No matter how beautiful the Medeusans' minds are, they are alien to yours! You'll yearn for the sight and sound of a human like yourself—and weary of ugliness!"

The black-lashed eyes blazed. "Ugly! What *is* ugly? You have never seen Kollos! Who are you to say whether he is too ugly to bear or too beautiful to bear?"

"I did not mean to insult you. Please, Miranda. . . ."

As she ripped a leaf from the rosebush beside her, Spock was striding down the corridor to Kollos's cabin.

Kirk wasn't a man to be fazed by female tantrums. He picked up the leaf she'd flung down. "Well," he said, "we can agree upon one thing, anyway. We both like roses. I wish I had moonlight for you, too. I'd like to see what moonlight would do to that hair of yours." He reached for her but she evaded him with a little laugh.

"I see you're a very complicated man, Captain."

He had her, unresisting, in his arms. "Play fair," he whispered into the ear on his shoulder. "You're not supposed to know what I'm th'nking about. I'm supposed to show you."

He felt her stiffen. She released herself with a surprising strength. "He's with Kollos!" she cried. "Oh no, you mustn't let him do it!" She turned and ran down the path. He caught her. "Miranda! You can't leave just as . . . ."

She tore herself free. "Let me go! You don't realize! You don't know what a dangerous thing Spock is planning! Please, please, we must stop him!"

Kirk followed her at a run.

Spock was standing at the door of the Medeusan's quarters. He turned as they burst out of the elevator. Miranda tried to shove him aside. Grave, entirely composed, he looked at her. "The *Enterprise* is at stake, Dr. Jones. It is not possible for you to be involved."

"Why? I've already committed myself to mind-link with Kollos!" She whirled to Kirk. "Why do you allow him to place himself in jeopardy?"

"Mine is a duty you cannot assume," Spock said. "The vital factor to be considered is not telepathic competence. It is to pilot this ship. That is something you cannot do."

"Then teach me to pilot it! I can memorize instantly. Set any test you choose. After only one rehearsal, I shall be able to operate all the machinery on this vessel!"

McCoy had hurried out of the elevator. He rushed to the group, shouting, "Wait a minute!" He looked at the girl— and made his decision. "Miranda, I know you can do almost anything a sighted person can do—but you cannot pilot a Starship!"

She shrank back, stricken.

"What?" Kirk said.

"I'm sorry," McCoy said. "But the occasion calls for realism. You are blind, Miranda. And there are some things you just can't do."

Spock was eyeing the silvery embroidery on her sleeve. "Ah," he said. "A highly sophisticated sensor web. My compliments to your dressmaker, Dr. Jones."

The enigma unraveled for Kirk. She was safe with Kollos because she couldn't see him.

"I think I understand now," he said. "I know now why pity is the 'worst of all,' Miranda."

She flung her head high. "Pity which I do not deserve! Do you gather more information with your eyes than I do with my sensors? I could play tennis with you, Captain! I might even beat you. I am standing here exactly one meter and four centimeters from the door! Can you judge distance that accurately?''

"That won't be necessary," Kirk said gently. "Spock will make the mind-link. For your sake as well as ours.''

"No! I won't let you do this!''

McCoy said, "I appeal to you as a colleague, Dr. Jones—don't fight us like this.''

"No!''

"If none of us can persuade you, there is someone who can.'' Kirk used his command voice. "You will take this matter up with Ambassador Kollos.''

She glared at him. Jerking open the cabin door, she entered and slammed it behind her.

Kirk eyed McCoy. "Why didn't you tell me, Bones?''

"She'd have told you herself if she'd wanted you to know. I respect her privacy.''

"There's a great deal about this particular lady to resp—'' Kirk stopped at the sound of a broken cry from the cabin. Unshamed tears streaming down her face, Miranda opened its door. McCoy started to her, but thinking better of it, waited for her to make the first move. It was to drag an arm across her tear-wet face. In the gesture was a childlike quality that went straight to Kirk's heart.

Still sobbing, she said, "It . . . seems that I have no choice . . . but to obey you.''

The habitat had been removed to the bridge. A rigid metal screen hid it from all eyes but Spock's; and his were vizored. People barely breathed. Even the ship seemed to hold her breath. The sole sound was the quiet, majestic rhythm of Kollos's life support system. Alone with the black box behind the screen, Spock knelt and lifted the lid. The pure blue light flooded his face.

Hands pressed against the surface of the box, he leaned forward until his temples touched it. He backed away, gasping, eyes closed behind the vizor, his forehead beaded with sweat. A shudder shook him. Then, resolutely, he opened his eyes, inviting the light again.

Kirk's hands were wet. Still as cats, McCoy and Sulu waited. Chekov, at Spock's station, moved no buttons. Next to him, Uhura buried her face in her hands.

Somebody whispered, "Mr. Spock . . ."

Spock had stepped from behind the screen, pulling off the vizor. He looked relaxed, younger. And when he spoke, his voice was younger, warm and tender.

"How delightful to see you again!" he said. "I know you, all of you! James Kirk, my Captain and dear friend for years . . ."

He took a step toward Kirk, looking around him with interest. "And Leonard McCoy, another friend. And Uhura, whose name means freedom! Uhura who walks in beauty like the night . . ."

The shocked McCoy cried. "That can't be Spock!"

Cool and precise, Spock said, "Does it surprise you that I've read Byron, Doctor?"

"*That's* Spock!" McCoy said.

A mind-link to create a double entity. Those had been Spock's own words. "Am I . . . addressing the Medeusan Ambassador?" Kirk asked.

A radiant smile lit Spock's face. "In part—that is, that part of us that is known to you as Kollos. Where is Miranda? Ah, there you are! O, brave new world that boasts such beauty in it!"

She spoke harshly. "Tis new to thee, Mr. Spock."

His tone was that of a lover. "*My* world is next for you and me."

Kirk couldn't decipher the expression on her face, but she seemed to feel a need to hold herself under rigid control. But Spock's face was alive with such a naked tenderness that Kirk averted his eyes from it. The girl edged over to McCoy and Spock advanced to the command chair.

"Captain Kirk, I speak for all of us you call Medeusans. I am sorry for the trouble I have brought to your ship."

"We can't hold you to blame for what happened, Ambassador. Thank you for helping us now."

The smile vanished. Spock was back, efficient, composed. "Now to the business at hand. With your permission, Captain?"

Kirk said, "Mr. Sulu, release the helm to Mr. Spock, please."

"Aye, sir."

At Sulu's console, Spock made rapid adjustments of switches. "Coordination is completed, Captain."

"Go ahead, then, Mr. Spock."

The engines began to throb again. "Warp factor one in six seconds," Spock said. "Five seconds . . ."

The ship was picking up speed. "Two seconds. One. Zero. . . ."

The searing light inundated the bridge. The great roar hammered. Bolt upright at the helm, Spock took the *Enterprise* back into its galaxy. "Position report, Mr. Chekov," he called.

Chekov's eyes were agog with admiration. "Bull's eye, Mr. Spock! Our position is so close to the point where we entered the void that the difference isn't worth mentioning!"

"That completes the maneuver, Captain," Spock said. "Take over, Mr. Sulu."

As Spock vacated the helm, Kirk got to his feet. "Thank you, Ambassador. And now, Mr. Chekov, let's get her back on course."

Spock, flexing a hand, was intently examining it. The radiance shone in his face. "How compact your bodies are! And what a variety of senses you have! This thing you call language—it's most remarkable. You depend on it for so much. But is any of you really its master?" A look of infinite compassion came into his face. "But the aloneness. You are all so alone. How sad that you must live out your lives in this shell of flesh, contained and separate—how lonely you are, how lonely. . . ."

A warning bell sounded in Kirk's memory. The risk of the fusion was loss of separate identity. He turned in his chair. "Ambassador. It is time to dissolve the mind-link."

Who had answered him—Spock or Kollos? Kirk couldn't tell. But the words seemed to come from a great distance.

"So soon?"

Kirk got to his feet. "You must not delay."

"You are wise, Captain."

With a debonair wave of the hand, Spock crossed to the metal screen, disappearing behind it. Miranda slipped after him to stand near the screen, her face concentrated, unreadable.

Uhura spoke. "Captain, Starfleet is calling."

"Audio, Lieutenant."

A radio voice cried, "*Enterprise!* Where have you people been?"

Behind the screen a kneeling Spock was bathed again in the pure blue radiance. As Kollos vacated his mind, he bowed his head under an oppressive sense of bereavement. He could hear Kirk saying, "Give them our position, Lieutenant. Tell them we'll send a full report later."

"Captain!"

The horror in Sulu's voice spun Kirk around to the helm station. Spock's forgotten vizor lay in Sulu's hand.

"Spock!" Kirk shouted. "Don't look. Cover your eyes!"

His cry was lost in the scream that came from behind the screen.

The shriek came again. Instinctively McCoy started toward the screen but was stopped dead in his tracks by Kirk's gesture of absolute command. "No! Don't move!"

"But, Jim . . ."

"No one is to move!" Kirk gave himself a moment to rally before he called, "Spock, are you all right?"

Time moved sluggish and slow. Kirk waited for the seconds to crawl by. Then Spock, backed out from behind the screen, turned his face to them. It was both terrified and terrifying—totally insane.

Kirk went to him, his hands outstretched. "It's all right now, Spock. You are safe with me."

But Spock had been transported to an unreachable realm. Lowering his head, he lunged at Kirk, aiming a fatal blow. Kirk ducked—and Spock, his madness distractible and purposeless, ripped out a lever from a console, hurling it across the bridge. Roaring like a wounded beast, he raged through the room, smashing at people and objects. Kirk found position for a straight phaser shot and stunned him at close range.

McCoy ran to the stilled body. Looking up, he cried, "He's hardly breathing, Jim! I must get him to Sickbay at once!"

Again time crawled by. Spock, insane, perhaps dying

there before Kirk's eyes. As Marvick had died. Kirk covered his face with his hands to shut out the sight of the deathly white face on Sickbay's examination table. That brain of Spock's, whose magnificent resources had wrung victories out of countless defeats, deranged, lost to the *Enterprise*, lost to the friends who loved him. Behind his hands, Kirk could feel the skin of his face drawing into lines of haggard agony.

"Miranda," McCoy said. "Unless she reaches down into his mind and turns it outward to us, we will lose Spock, Jim."

Kirk could bear the sight of the world again. "Vulcan mind techniques!" Then his heart cringed. "She tried to help Marvick. He's dead."

"That was different. Marvick loved her."

Kirk paced restlessly. "Would she so much as try? Spock is her rival. He felt her jealousy of him."

"They were not rivals in love," McCoy said.

Kirk looked at him. "No. That's true. Bones, I'm taking action. Don't interfere with it. No matter what happens." He strode to the door of Sickbay and closed it behind him.

Miranda was in her cabin. And she knew what he'd come for. Telepathy, he thought grimly, had its advantages. It made explanation unnecessary. When she emerged from her bedroom, she was wearing a stark black tunic bare of the silver embroidery sensors. Truly blind now, she had to be guided to the door.

McCoy had had the examination table tilted almost upright. Spock's waxen, unmoving body was strapped to it. Kirk led Miranda over to it. "Your mind-link with him," he said. "It must bring him back from wherever he is."

Nearly as pale as Spock, she said, "You must leave us alone, Captain."

At his desk McCoy didn't speak. Once more Kirk waited. If the memories of Spock's loyal valor would only stop returning . . . but they wouldn't stop. And what was going on in that examination room? Spock had spoken of her "thirst for power."

Kirk walked into the examination room.

She looked up at the sound of the opening door. "Dr. McCoy?"

"It's I, the Captain."

"I have no news for you." She paused. "His life processes are failing."

The blue, blind eyes had groped for his. Kirk steeled himself against a wave of compassion for her. "And what are you doing about it?"

"Why . . . what I can, of course."

"It doesn't seem to be much!"

It sparked a flash of anger from her. "No doubt you expect me to wake up your Sleeping Beauty with a kiss!"

The compassion died in him. "It might be worth trying," he told her. "He's not a machine."

"He is a Vulcan!" she cried.

"Half of him. The other half is human—a half more human than you seem to be!"

She faced him, rage working in her face. "Face reality, Captain Kirk. His mind has gone too deep even for me to reach."

"And if you don't reach it, he will die. Isn't that what you want?"

She stared at him wordlessly, her mouth open. Then, in a small, unbelieving voice, she said, "Why . . . that is a lie!"

"You want him to die," Kirk said.

He caught her by the arm. "What did you do on the bridge? Did you make him forget to vizor his eyes?"

She wrenched her arm free. "*You* are insane."

He seized it again, his jaw hard. "You know your rival! He made a mind-link with Kollos—exactly what you have never been able to do!"

She struck at him, beating at his face with her fists. He immobilized her hands, holding her tight within the hard circle of his arms. "With my words," he said, "I will make you hear the ugliness Spock saw when his naked eyes looked at Kollos! Ugliness is deep in you, Miranda!"

"Liar! Liar! Liar!" she screamed.

"Listen to me. Your passion to see Kollos is madness. You are blind. You can never see him. Never! But Spock has seen him. And for that he must die. That's it, isn't it?"

She twisted in his arms. "Sadistic, filthy liar . . ."

"You smell of hatred. The stench of jealousy fills you. Why don't you strangle him as he lies there, helpless?"

Strength drained out of her. "No . . . no . . . don't say any more, please."

"Kollos knows what is in your heart. You can lie to yourself—but you can't lie to Kollos."

"Go away! Please . . . go away."

Kirk released her. She staggered but he reached no hand to help her. The door closed behind him.

In his office McCoy got up from his desk. Kirk sank into his chair and, leaning his arms on the desk, rested his head on them, shaken, exhausted.

"Are you all right?" McCoy asked.

Kirk didn't answer. McCoy laid a hand on the bowed shoulders. "What did you say to her, Jim?"

Kirk lifted his head. "Maybe too much."

"What is she doing in there? If she can't—"

"Maybe I shouldn't have gone in, Bones."

"Jim . . ."

"I went at her in the dark. In her darkness. In her blindness. If he dies. . . ."

"Don't, Jim."

"If he dies, how do I know I didn't kill him? How can I know she can stand to hear the truth?"

In the room behind them, she had moved to Spock, her fingers probing at his temples. In a whisper choked with fury, she was saying, "This is to the death—or life for both of us. Do you hear me, Spock?"

He was in a cavern, his eyes open. Over him hovered a Miranda, her hair a writhing nest of snakes. They hissed at him, their fangs dripping venom. He let it drip on his face. The Miranda laughed demoniacally. The venom stung. Then there were three Mirandas, chuckling with pleasure in his pain. When he put his hands over his ears to shut out the hideous chuckles, there were seven Mirandas. He groveled on his knees, clutching at his ears. The laughing stopped.

But the Fury wasn't finished with him. The cavern was a pool. A Miranda had him by the throat. She was very strong and he was tired. The water of the pool closed over his head. She pushed it down . . . down. His hands felt heavy, clumsy, strangely disobedient. But at last they did his bidding and tore her grasp from his throat. The water still dragged at him. Then his soul moved. He stumbled out of the water's hold;

and in a curious unsurprise, realized that the Miranda was helping him. He coughed frothy water from his lungs, and dreamily heard the Miranda say, "So you have decided to live after all. But there is one thing more—the madness. . . ."

A box lid was open, radiating a blue light he seemed to remember. He was about to look into the half-familiar box when its lid dropped.

He was very tired. There was a door in front of him. On a last spurt of strength, he opened it.

"Spock!"

It was the voice of his dear Captain.

Spock staggered to him. In his flood of returning sanity, he recognized McCoy. But as usual the Doctor was fussing. "You have no business to be out of bed! Sit here!"

He sat. His Captain left him to go somewhere else, calling, "Miranda!"

But if there had ever been a Miranda around, she was gone.

With meticulous care Spock placed Kollos's habitat on the Transporter platform. His hands lingered on the box—a final communion. Kirk looked at the hands, his eyes warm with affection. Pointing to Spock, he smiled at the woman beside him. "I have you to thank for his life," he said.

He spoke to a different Miranda—one transfigured by the same wondering innocence that had entered into Spock during his mind-link with Kollos. McCoy, moved by the new purity of her lovely face, said, "You now have what you wanted most, Miranda?"

"Yes. I am one with Kollos."

McCoy took her hand and kissed it. "I am truly sorry that you are leaving us."

She stepped back to Kirk. "We have come to the end of an eventful trip, Captain."

"I wasn't sure you'd even speak to me."

The blue radiance of the box was in her blue eyes. "I have you to thank for my future. What you said has enabled me to *see*. I shall not need my sensors any more."

He lifted a white rose from the Transporter console. "My good-bye gift to you," he said.

The rose against her cheek, she said, "I suppose it has thorns, Captain."

"I never met a rose that didn't, Miranda."

At the platform, Spock, in dress uniform, was wearing his IDIC. The girl touched it. "I understand the symbology, now, Mr. Spock. The marvel is in the infinite diversity of life."

He met her eyes gravely. "And in the ways our differences can combine to create new truth and beauty."

She took her position on the platform as Spock adjusted his vizor for the last time. Then he lifted his hand in the Vulcan salute.

She returned it. "Peace and long life to you, Mr. Spock," she said.

"Peace and long life, Miranda."

At the Transporter console, Kirk himself moved the dematerializing switches.

THE EMPATH

Writer: Joyce Muskat
Director: John Erman
Guest stars: Kathryn Hays, Alan Bergmann

The second star in the Minarian system was entering a critical period of its approaching nova phase. Accordingly, the *Enterprise* had been ordered to evacuate personnel of the research station which was established on the star to study the phenomena of its coming death. But all the Starship's attempts to contact the scientists had failed. Kirk, his urgent mission in mind, decided to beam down to the surface to try to locate their whereabouts.

He, Spock and McCoy materialized on a bleak landscape, grim and forbidding under a sky already red with the light of the imminent nova. A gust of harsh wind blew dirt in their faces. It also rattled the door of a metal hut a few yards to their right. "It's the research station," Kirk said. He led the way to it. Its door gave way under a push. The hut was deserted, but its interior, a combination of living quarters and laboratory, was neatly arranged. In a corner, Kirk spotted a video-tape recorder.

Spock ran his hand over a table. "Dust," he said. "Apparently, their instruments have not been recently in use."

The recorder still held a tape card. Kirk was about to insert it when his communicator beeped. Handing the tape to Spock, he flipped it open. It said, "*Enterprise* to Captain Kirk. Come in, please."

"Kirk here. Go ahead, *Enterprise*."

"Scott here, Captain. Our instruments have picked up a gigantic solar flare with very high levels of cosmic rays."

"How bad?" Kirk said.

"Sensors indicate cosmic-ray concentration measures 3.51 on the Van Allen scale. It'll play the devil with the crew as well as the ship, sir."

Spock spoke. "On that basis it will take exactly 74.1 solar hours for the storm to pass, Captain."

"Warp her out of orbit right now! Mr. Scott, stay at the minimum distance for *absolute* safety!"

"Aye, aye, sir. We'll beam you up in—"

Kirk interrupted, "Negative. We're staying here. The atmosphere of the planet will protect us. Now get my ship out of danger, Mr. Scott!"

"Very well, Captain. Scott out."

"Kirk out." Closing his communicator, he turned to Spock. "Mr. Spock . . . how about that tape?"

Spock had been examining it. As he inserted it into the recorder, he said, "Whatever we see and hear, Captain, happened approximately two weeks ago."

Activated, the device's viewing screen lit up. It showed two men checking equipment against the hut's background. "The one on the left is Dr. Linke," Kirk said. "The other is Dr. Ozaba. Does the speaker work, Spock?"

It worked. Linke was saying, ". . . another week in this godforsaken place . . ."

He lurched to the shaking of a brief earthquake. Ozaba grinned. "*In His hand are the deep places of the earth.* Psalm 95, Verse 4. I wish He'd calm them down. . . ."

Abruptly, sound and picture ended. The recorder emitted a deep organlike chord. It grew louder—and the picture returned to image the scientists searching for the source of the sound. Their lips moved but their voices were overwhelmed by the rising chord's reverberation. Suddenly Ozaba clutched his head, staggering in pain. As Linke rushed forward to help him, Ozaba winked out. Terrified, Linke stared around the hut. Then he too began to stagger. He disappeared. The sound faded and the screen went blank.

Appalled, McCoy cried, "Jim, what happened to them?"

As though in answer the strange sound came again, gathering around the *Enterprise* men. Spock swiftly unlimbered his tricorder while Kirk and McCoy frantically searched for some clue to the noise.

"Where's it coming from?" Kirk shouted. "Spock, can you pin it down?"

"Negative, Captain! This 'sound' doesn't register on my tricorder!" He bent his head to check the instrument when his eyes glazed. His hands went to his head as though the increasing sound were crushing it. He reeled drunkenly. Kirk, rushing to him, put out an arm to steady him. Then Spock winked out.

Kirk stared around him in horror. The sound intensified. "Bones!" Kirk yelled. "Spock—he's gone!"

But McCoy was gripping his head. Then, he too staggered. Even as Kirk raced to him, he vanished. Stunned, Kirk stood still. The hammer of sound beat at him. He began to struggle forward like a man fighting the pull of a monstrous magnet. He stumbled against a metal staircase and fell, cutting his head. As he hauled himself back to his feet, he winked out.

The triumphant sound rose higher in the empty hut.

Time passed. How much, they never knew. But something had transported them into the center of an arenalike place. When a blinding, overhead, circular light came on, they found themselves able to move. Kirk groped up to his knees. Beyond the circle of light, the arena's boundaries were lost in total darkness. The cut on his head throbbed.

"Bones . . . Spock. Spock, where are we?"

McCoy had seen the cut. He reached for his medikit and, struggling to his feet, dealt with the injury. Spock was checking his tricorder. "We are exactly 121.32 meters below the planet's surface, Captain."

"How did we get here?"

"Residual energy readings indicate that we were beamed here by a matter-energy scrambler not dissimilar to our own Transporter mechanism."

"Is that cut very painful, Jim?"

Kirk nodded, shrugging; and Spock, his eyes still on his tricorder, said, "Captain, I'm picking up a life form . . . bearing 42 mark seven."

"Could it be one of the missing scientists?"

"Negative, sir. Although humanoid, it is definitely not *Homo sapiens*."

"Identification?"

"Impossible. I can make no exact identification other than that it is humanoid."

"Then let's find out what it is. Phasers on stun!"

It was the tricorder that guided them through the dimness ahead. The brilliant light which had illuminated the arena's center didn't reach to its outer space. But, stumbling along it, they could finally discern what seemed to be a narrow, circular platform—a platform or a couch. On it lay a figure. It was very still.

Spock extended the tricorder. "The life form, Captain."

"What is it?" Kirk said.

The creature stirred. As it sat up, lights blazed in a sharply outlined circle over the couch. The being stood up. It had the body of a girl and it was clothed in a gossamer stuff that glittered with the sparkle of diamonds. Her skin was dead white. Dark hair clustered around her temples. But it was her eyes that riveted Kirk's. They were large, shining— the most expressive eyes he'd ever seen in his life.

McCoy started forward.

"Careful!" Kirk said sharply.

"She seems to be harmless enough, Jim."

"The sand-bats of Manark-4," Spock said, "appear to be inanimate rock crystals before they attack."

Kirk moved cautiously toward her. "I am James Kirk, Captain of the USS *Enterprise*." He gestured back to the others. "This is my Science Officer, Mr. Spock, and Doctor McCoy, Ship's Surgeon. We are not going to hurt you." He paused, still fascinated by the eyes. "Do you live here? Is this . . . your home?"

She didn't answer.

"Spock, analysis?"

"From what we know of gravity and other environmental conditions on this planet, a life form such as hers could not evolve here," McCoy said.

"Agreed, Doctor," Spock said. "She is obviously not of this planet."

"Why are you here?" Kirk asked her.

She shrugged. He persisted. "Are you responsible for bringing us here?" Despite her eyes, he was beginning to feel exasperated. "At least you must know how *you* got here!"

She shrank back. Aware that he had frightened her, Kirk relaxed. "Don't be afraid," he said gently. "You must not fear me." His reassurance didn't seem to reassure her. How should he approach this sensitive creature with the remarkable eyes? He turned to McCoy. "What about it, Bones? What's wrong with her?"

McCoy looked up from his readings. "She's mute . . . no vocal cords, not even vestigials. And it doesn't look like a pathological condition."

"Explain."

"As far as I can tell, she's perfectly healthy. As for the other, my guess is that the lack of vocal cords is physiologically normal for her species, whatever that is."

"A whole race of mutes . . . like the Gamma Vertis-4 civilization?"

"That's my opinion, for what it's worth."

"Without speech, how's she able to understand us? Unless she's a telepath. Could telepathic power have been used to bring us here?"

Spock said, "An unlikely possibility, Captain. Over ninety-eight percent of the known telepathic species send thoughts as well as receive them. She has made no attempt to contact our thoughts."

Kirk looked at her intently for a long moment. Then his hand went to his forehead, pressing tightly against its pulsing ache. As he sank down on the couch, something in the girl's white face moved McCoy to say, "We can't keep calling her 'she' as though she weren't here!"

"You have any suggestions?" Kirk said.

"I don't know about you two, but I'm going to call her 'Gem.' " Conscious of Spock's raised eyebrow, he added a defiant, "At least it's better than 'hey you'!"

Kirk got to his feet. "I want to know why we're here— what's going on. The girl may know. Spock, try the Vulcan mind meld."

Nodding, Spock went to the couch, hands extended to

make contact with her. But she had watched his approach
with panic. Spock, touching her arm, recoiled.

"Spock, what is it!"

"Her mind doesn't function like ours, Captain. I felt it
trying to draw on *my* consciousness. Like a magnet. I could
gain nothing from her."

High above their heads, like a theater's mezzanine, was
a semicircular construction. And like a theater director and
stage manager, placed for a different viewpoint of the actors
below them, two figures were observing the little drama being enacted on the platform-stage beneath them. An organ
chord sounded.

Kirk, Spock and McCoy whirled as one man.

Slowly the figures descended from their eminence. Tall,
clad in floor-length robes, their bodies were muscular and
agile but their faces were old, their heads bald. Among the
wrinkles of great age, their eyes blazed with a purpose that
was barren of all warmth or emotion. Each bore a curious
silver object in his right hand. It had the shape of a T. Ignoring the men, they advanced on the cowering Gem. Again,
as one man, the *Enterprise* trio moved forward protectively
in front of her.

Kirk spoke. "I am—"

He was interrupted. The figure on the left said, "We
are aware of your identity, Captain."

"Who are you? Why have you brought us here?"

The voice was as cold as death. "We are Vians. My
name is Lal. This is Thann." A finger pointed to Gem. "Do
not interfere!"

"What do you intend to do to her?"

"Delay us no longer!"

It was Thann who spoke. As he started forward, Kirk
moved swiftly to block his way to the girl. Lal raised his
silver T-bar and Kirk was hurled up and over her couch. The
crashdown reopened the cut on his forehead. It began to
bleed. Wiping blood from his eyes, he hauled himself back
to his feet and, pulling out his phaser, called "Phasers on
stun!" Then he circled the couch to confront the Vians.
"Since you already know who we are, you must also know
that we come in peace. Our prime directive specifically prohibits us from interfering with any. . . ."

The Vians directed their T-bars at the three *Enterprise* men. Their phasers, flying out of their hands, dissolved into air. They tried to reach Gem—and a pulsing, multicolored force field enveloped them.

Thann was stooping over the girl, touching his T-bar to her head. It emitted a chilling whine. They all saw that her white face was transfixed with terror. With a concerted effort, they gathered all their strength to strain against the force field. McCoy was the first to weaken. Then it was Kirk's turn. His head swam, blurring his vision so that everything— the place, Gem, the Vians, his friends' faces, spun wildly in a vertiginous mist.

"Bones . . . I . . . can't seem to stand up. . . ."

"Stand still!" McCoy said sharply. "You too, Spock! Don't fight it, don't move! Somehow this field upsets the body metabolism. . . ."

Lal's cold eyes focused on McCoy. "Not quite, Doctor. The field draws its energy *from* your bodies. The more you resist it, the stronger it becomes."

He nodded to Thann, who moved away from Gem. When he lifted his T-bar, the chord sounded. Both Vians disappeared—and the force field collapsed so suddenly that its prisoners fell to the floor.

Kirk gritted his teeth against the pain in his head. "Mr. Spock, there must be an exit from this place. See if you can find it."

"Yes, Captain." Tricorder out, Spock moved off to quarter the arena.

"Jim, that's a nasty cut," McCoy said. "Let me have another look at it."

"Don't fuss over me, Bones. They may have hurt the girl." He went to Gem on the couch. "Did they hurt you?" he asked her.

She shook her head. Then, timidly, she touched Kirk's hands. At once pain twisted her face. She drew back; but after a moment, she raised her arm to lay a finger on his throbbing head. To his amazement he saw a cut, identical in size to his own, appear on her forehead. Marveling, he looked at the deep gash. Extending a hand, he touched it gently. It was wet with blood. She took the hand, holding it quietly. And he knew that his wound was gone. At the same instant, hers vanished. Kirk stood up feeling fully refreshed and whole.

McCoy was staring. Kirk nodded. "Yes. The pain is gone. Soon after she touched my head it went."

"And the wound is completely healed! What's more, it fits in, Jim. She must be an *empath*! Her nervous system is so highly responsive, so sensitive that she can actually *feel* others' emotional and physical reactions. They become part of her."

Kirk smiled at Gem. "What does one say for what you've done? My thanks."

"Captain . . ." It was Spock returning. He pointed to the left. "In that direction my tricorder picked up a substantial collection of objects—electronically sophisticated devices. I fail to understand why the tricorder gave no previous indication of anything out there."

"It's there now, Mr. Spock. Let's check it out." They were turning to leave when Kirk looked back at Gem. "Wait a minute." He went to her. "If they find you alone here, it could be dangerous. Will you come with us?"

She nodded, rising from the couch.

Because of the dimness the going was slow. They had to edge past large, contorted rock formations that reared up out of sight. Then, ahead of them, Kirk saw a glimmer of light. As they approached it, the rocks ended and the light grew brilliantly dazzling. It shone down from the ceiling of what seemed to be an enormous laboratory. An odd laboratory. All its complex instrumentation hung in midair.

They spread out to examine it. McCoy, Gem beside him, puzzled over an octagonal, bulb-studded object. Spock had gone straight to the viewing screens; but Kirk, after a cursory glance at a blank panel, was peering into blackness that lay beyond the light's reach. Suddenly glare struck him in the face. It illuminated the lab's dark corner. He backed away, disbelief and horror struggling in his face. "Spock, Bones. *Look!*"

Two large test tubes were suspended from the ceiling. Stuffed into them were the bodies of Linke and Ozaba, their features twisted with agony. The test tubes were labeled. One read "SUBJECT: LINKE." The other said, "SUBJECT: OZABA."

McCoy's voice roused Kirk from his daze. Bones was calling, "Jim! Spock!"

They crossed to him at a run. Wordless, he was pointing to three empty test tubes. The labels they bore read: "McCOY—SPOCK—KIRK."

The chord sounded hollowly in the big room. The *Enterprise* men wheeled. T-bar in hand, Lal was facing them. He eyed their shocked faces disinterestedly. "We are on schedule," he said. "But some further simple tests are necessary."

"We've just seen the results of some of your . . . tests!" McCoy shouted.

"And I have found our missing men dead." Kirk's voice shook. "Another of your experiments?"

"You are wrong," Lal said. "Their own imperfections killed them. They were not fit subjects. Come, time is short."

"*Your* time has just about run out!" Kirk cried. "This planet is about to nova. When it does, it will finish itself, you and your whole insane torture chamber along with it! As for your experiments . . ."

The three exchanged a fast glance. Kirk and McCoy strode toward the Vian. He backed away. As the two circled him, Spock closed in with his Vulcan "neck pinch." Lal collapsed. Spock removed his T-bar control. As he rose from his stoop, the bar in his hand, his tricorder beeped. Lifting it, he said, "Readings indicate passage to the surface lies in that direction, Captain." He gestured to their right.

When the party had left the lab, Lal got to his feet. Thann appeared beside him. They stood silent, their cold eyes fixed on the passageway where the group had vanished.

Spock had found his exit to the surface. Twenty minutes of clambering over rocks had brought them into the open. The red sky was overcast and the stiff wind was blowing harder. Kirk took out his communicator. "Kirk to *Enterprise*. Come in, *Enterprise*!" There was no answer. The Starship was still out of range. Belting the communicator, Kirk saw that Spock was pouring over his tricorder.

"Report, Mr. Spock?"

Spock looked up. "The research station is six kilometers from here, Captain. Straight ahead."

"Let's get there as fast as we can. If the ship has a search party looking for us, it will be there." He took Gem's hand; but a blast of wind struck her and she halted, blinded by the whip of sand in her eyes. He made to pick her up in his arms. She shook her head, smiling; and hooking her arm under his, struggled forward again. Fiercely blowing sand became a hazard to them all. Its hard grit hit McCoy's eyes so that he stumbled over a rock that tumbled him head over heels. Spock was hauling him to his feet when Gem rushed from Kirk to help McCoy. He grinned at her reassuringly. "I'm all right," he told her. "Don't worry about me, Gem."

Kirk, shading his eyes, peered ahead through the driving sand. "How much farther?" he asked Spock.

"Just ahead, sir."

McCoy gave a shout. "Jim! Look . . . Scotty and a search party!"

Before the metal hut, Scott and two Security guards were waving to them. The howl of wind drowned their voices.

"Scotty! Scotty!" Kirk yelled.

He was racing forward when he suddenly realized that Gem had fallen behind. He turned to help—and saw the Vians standing on a rock observing them.

Gem was down, her white face wet with sweat and effort. He picked her up, pushing her after Spock and McCoy. "Keep going!" he cried.

He watched her stumble on. Then, to cover the others' retreat, he ran toward the Vians.

Lal spoke to Thann. "Their will to survive is great."

"They love life greatly to struggle so."

Lal nodded. "The prime ingredient." He pointed a T-bar at the onrushing Kirk; and at once the *Enterprise* Captain felt his strength begin to ebb. Gravity became the enemy—a monstrous leech sucking, sucking at his vitality. Weaving, he reached the foot of the rock where the Vians waited—and fell.

He opened his eyes to see Spock bending over him. Fighting the fatigue that still drained his power, he sat up, crying, "What are you doing here? What happened to Scotty?"

"Mr. Scott and the guards were a mirage, Captain."

The Vians' resources seemed as infinite as their will

was inexorable. He heard Thann speak his name. He looked up.

"We have decided that one specimen will be sufficient. You will come with us, Captain Kirk."

Kirk got to his feet. "And the others?"

"We have no interest in them," Lal said. "They may go."

McCoy had joined Spock. At the look of relief in Kirk's face, he burst into protest. "You can't go back there! You'll end up like the other two!"

Spock spoke. "Captain, I request permission to be allowed to remain. . . ."

"Denied," Kirk said.

"But, Jim . . ."

"You have your orders!"

Without a backward look, Kirk started to climb the hillock topped by the rock. Spock, McCoy and Gem moved after him.

The rock was flat as a table. As Kirk walked up to the Vians, Lal said, "You are prepared?"

"Let's get on with it!" Kirk looked into the frigid Vian eyes—and a suspicion chilled him. He turned to check on the others' whereabouts. Spock and McCoy had disappeared. For a moment a hot rage choked him so that he was unable to speak. Then he said, "Where are my friends?"

"They are safe."

"*Where are they?* You said they'd be released! You said you needed one specimen! *One specimen!* You have it—me! Let the others go!"

Thann nodded to Lal. "Indeed the prime ingredient."

Kirk was shaking. "Never mind the ingredients! Where are my men? Tell me!" The rage broke free. He leaped at Thann. The control bar was lifted. In mid-leap Kirk winked out.

The *Enterprise* was having its troubles. The solar flares had not diminished. A worried Sulu, turning to Scott in Kirk's command chair, said, "Cosmic ray concentration is still above acceptable levels for orbiting the planet, sir."

Scott went to him. "I don't like it, Mr. Sulu. Constant

exposure to this much radiation could raise the hob with Life Support and our other vital systems.''

"Shall I change course to compensate, sir?''

"Not yet.'' Scott punched the intercom. "Bridge to all sections. We will continue to maintain our present position outside the Minarian star system. Report any sudden increase in radiation levels to the bridge immediately. Medical sections and Life Support will remain on standby alert.'' Swinging his chair to the helm station, he said, "Mr. Sulu, estimate how much longer we have until those solar flares subside.''

Eyeing his viewer, Sulu moved buttons on his console. "Readings now indicate 2.721 on the Van Allen scale, sir. At the present rate of decrease, we'll have to wait at least seventeen more hours before we can even attempt entering orbit.''

Scott nodded glumly. "Aye. Well, as long as we're stuck out here, we might just as well relax and wait till the storm has passed.''

"It has already lasted four more hours than we anticipated, sir. Do you think our landing party could be in any danger?''

"Not likely, Mr. Sulu. The planet's atmosphere will give them ample protection. If I know Captain Kirk, he's more worried about us than we are about him. . . .''

Kirk had been stripped to the waist. His arms were stretched wide, held in their spread-eagled position by two shackles. He was drenched with sweat. Gem, clinging to a laboratory table, was trembling, her eyes closed.

"All right,'' he said wearily. "What is it you want to know?''

"We seek no 'information,' as you understand the word. Your civilization is yet too immature to possess knowledge of value to us,'' Lal said.

Kirk raised his heavy head. "Our knowledge has no value but you're willing to kill to get it! Is that what happened to Linke and Ozaba?''

Thann took a step toward him. "*We* did not kill them! Their own fears did it!''

"Just exactly what did you expect from them? What is it you want from me?''

"We have already observed the intensity of your passions, Captain. We have gauged your capacity to love others. Now we want you to reveal your courage and strength of will."

Kirk's shoulders were going numb. "Why?" he said, his head drooping. He forced it up. "Why, Lal? What do you hope to prove?" The shackles were too tight. It was their bite into the flesh of his arms that was keeping him conscious. He was glad of the shackles—but tired. Very tired. "If . . . if my death is going to have any meaning, at least tell me what I am dying for."

Lal lifted his control bar. A flicker of light played over Kirk's swaying body. At the table Gem staggered.

The Vians' transporter had conveyed Spock and McCoy back to the arena. McCoy followed Spock as the Vulcan used his tricorder. "The passage out was there before, Spock! It's got to be there now!"

"I am unable to lock in on the previous readings, Doctor. I can find no exit from here."

A circle of light flared before the couch. It widened, materializing into the forms of Kirk and Gem. His wrists were torn and bleeding; and the swollen veins on his neck were blue. When Spock and McCoy rushed to him, the force field flung them back.

"Jim! What have they done to you?"

Inside the field, Gem had taken Kirk's bleeding hands in hers. Her face and body writhed with his agony. Then red stigmata, identical to his wounds, appeared on her wrists. She backed away and the marks faded. She hesitated, looking at Spock and McCoy.

McCoy stopped straining to reach Kirk. "Help him, Gem. Don't be afraid to help him."

She kept her eyes on them as though the sight of them gave her strength. Again she took Kirk's bleeding wrists—and again her own began to bleed. But this time she ignored both her pain and her wounds. She knelt down on the floor and, cradling Kirk's head on her lap, began to massage his neck and shoulders. Once more there was the strange effect of her touch. His pain visibly eased. Their injuries vanished at the same moment. Gently she laid his head on the floor.

Then she slid away from him, too weakened to get to her feet. Kirk reached out a hand to her.

The force field dissolved. Spock and McCoy hurried to them. Still dazed, Kirk struggled to rise. "Gem?" he whispered.

"Lie still!" McCoy said. "I'll check her out right now."

He had to carry her to her couch. Her eyes were closed. McCoy was staring at his medical tricorder, incredulous. The body he'd laid on the couch had been almost transparent, as though entirely drained of life. Now, before his eyes, it was recovering its solidity. Smiling, Gem looked up at McCoy. He smoothed the soft hair back from her forehead and left her to go to Kirk.

He was sitting up. "Is she all right?"

"She seems fine again."

"Bones, can you explain what happened?"

McCoy spoke excitedly. "Complete empathy—that's what it was! She must be a totally functional Empath! Her nervous system actually connected to yours to counteract the worst of your symptoms. With her strength she virtually sustained your physiological reactions."

"It weakened her," Kirk said. "I could feel it. Does this ability endanger her life?"

"It's impossible to say yet. Supplying life support to you *did* drain her."

Spock said, "She was afraid to approach the Captain after the first sharp impact of his pain. It was only your urgent plea, Doctor, that caused her to continue."

"Fear would naturally be the first reaction, Spock." McCoy went to the couch and took Gem's hands. Smiling at her, he said, "She doesn't know our Captain well enough— not yet—to offer up her life for him."

"Could the strain really have killed her?" Kirk persisted.

"I would assume that her instinct for self-preservation would take over to prevent that, Jim." He returned to Kirk. "How do you feel?"

"Tired . . . just tired."

"Captain, can you recall what happened?"

Kirk spoke slowly. "I'm not sure. I remember the laboratory . . . there was something they wanted to know. What it was I can't remember." His voice rose. "I wish I could! I can't!"

"Easy does it, Jim. Take it easy."

"What's wrong with me, Bones?"

McCoy studied his tricorder, frowning. "You have all the symptoms of the 'bends.' Nitrogen bubbles in your blood caused the pain. But how did you get the bends down here?"

"You'll have to ask the Vians." Vigor was returning to his voice. "Will I live?"

"You could still use some time in a decompression chamber. Otherwise your recovery is just about miraculous. I wish that I could take the credit for it, but Gem did most of the work."

Spock was examining the control bar he'd taken from Thann. "Captain," he said, "I noted that a circle of light preceded you at the moment you were returned here from the Vians' laboratory."

"Spock, do you have to get so analytical? At a time like this?"

"Bones, Spock is right. Continue, Mr. Spock."

"I conclude that such a light is an energy transfer point linking this device to the power source."

"Can you tap into it?"

"If I can determine the frequency at which this device operates I could cause it to function for us."

"And get us out of here the same way they brought us here."

"I would say so, Captain."

"Then get started, Mr. Spock."

But the organ chord that invariably heralded some new Vian mischief sounded once more. The two long-robed creatures stood just outside the circle of light that still shone down before Gem's couch.

Lal addressed Kirk. "You are called 'Captain.' You are responsible for the lives of your crew. Is this correct?"

"It is correct," Kirk said.

Thann stepped forward. "We find it necessary to have the cooperation of one of your men in our efforts."

"We will not cooperate," Kirk said.

Lal continued as though he hadn't spoken. "When we

resume our interrogations, you will decide which of your men we shall use. There is an 87 percent possibility that the Doctor will die. And though Commander Spock's life is in no danger, the large probability is that he will suffer brain damage resulting in permanent insanity."

They vanished.

Still weakened by his ordeals, Kirk had centered his hopes on Thann's T-bar. He crossed to where Spock was working on it to discover its operating frequency. "How's it coming, Spock?"

"I do not know, Captain. I begin to understand the principles by which it functions—but that is all."

Responsible for the lives of his crew. Lal's definition of *his* function. How to fulfill it? For Bones—probable death in that laboratory. For Spock—derangement of that exquisitely precise organ of his: his mind.

McCoy joined them. "Spock, it won't be too long before those Vians come back. You'd better find out how that thing works—and soon!"

Kirk gave his own words back to him. "Easy does it, Bones. Take it easy."

"Men weren't intended to be this far underground! It's not natural!"

"And space travel is?" Kirk asked.

Without looking up from his task, Spock said, "I must disagree, Doctor. Witness the men who pass a majority of their lives in mines beneath the surface."

"I'm a doctor, not a coalminer!"

Now Spock looked up from the T-bar. "Doctor, I have recorded my theories and procedures on the tricorder. Should the Vians return, there is sufficient data for you and the Captain to complete the adjustments."

McCoy's anxiety exploded in irritation. "I'm no mechanic! I couldn't get that thing to work no matter how many notes you left!"

"Possibly not. But you and the Captain *together* are capable of doing so."

"In any case, you, Spock, are the *logical* choice to leave with the Captain. I am the man who should go with the Vians."

Kirk intervened. "The decision is mine! If there are

any decisions to be made, *I'll* make them!'' He paused. ''If and when it becomes necessary.''

Gem had been listening intently. Wearily Kirk sat down on the couch beside her. The combinations of mental and physical strains had exhausted his last reserves of strength. He rested his head in his hands, shutting his eyes. A hypo hissed against his shoulder. He didn't move. ''What is it, Bones? I don't need any—''

''I'm still Chief Medical Officer of the *Enterprise*. Would you rather have the bends? . . . Still dizzy?''

''A little.''

''Lie down until the hypo takes effect. Gem, sit beside him. Watch him.''

Kirk lay down, too tired to argue. As his breathing assumed the quiet regularity of sleep, McCoy nodded his satisfaction and Spock, looking up again from the control bar, said, ''How long will he be asleep?''

''Between the emotional drains and that attack of the bends, he's in pretty bad shape, Spock.''

''I am not criticizing your action. Doctor. On the contrary, I am grateful for it. The Captain will not be additionally strained by making so difficult a decision. You have simplified the situation considerably.''

McCoy looked at him warily. ''How?''

''While the Captain is asleep, it is I who am in command. When the Vians return, I shall go with them.''

The appalled McCoy looked down at his hypo. ''You mean if I hadn't given him that shot . . . ?''

''Precisely. The choice would have been the Captain's. Now it is mine.'' He bent over the control bar, his face expressionless as ever. McCoy stared at him a moment. Then, returning to Kirk, he checked him over. Satisfied, he replaced the hypo in his medikit. Cursing under his breath, he gave Spock a savage glance. It was noted by Gem, who'd been taking in the argument. She rose now to move noiselessly until she was standing between Kirk and Spock. Kirk stirred restlessly, fighting the unconsciousness of the drug. Spock looked over at him, hesitated, then resumed his work. Gem went to him, touching his shoulder. He didn't look up. She withdrew the hand, looking at it. Then the shining eyes returned to Spock. In her face was a look of wondering love.

She had seen past the coldly logical front Spock presented to the world to what the Vulcan officer kept carefully hidden—his love for his Captain and McCoy.

McCoy had seen the look on her face. His own changed abruptly as he came to a decision of his own. Apology in his eyes, he glanced at the impassive Spock, took out his hypo; and crossing to Kirk as though to check him, suddenly whirled—and injected Spock.

Spock stared at him in angry comprehension. "Your actions are highly unethical! My decision stands! I am in command and. . . ." He slumped forward.

McCoy put a hand on his shoulder. "Not this time, Spock," he said softly.

The organ notes sounded. The Vians had returned.

McCoy spoke quickly. "The choice has been made." He extended his hand back to Gem. "You stay with my friends. They will take care of you." He turned. "Do you understand, Gem?"

She looked at him. Thann, exchanging a glance with Lal, said, "Come, then."

McCoy started toward them. Then he looked back toward the sleeping Kirk and Spock. The look was a silent farewell. Tears filled Gem's eyes. They were merciful tears. They dimmed the sight of McCoy as he followed the Vians.

The shackles were stained with Kirk's blood. The Vians had not been content with McCoy's outstretched arms or the threat of his imminent death. They had placed him so as to force his eyes to the empty test tube with his name on it.

A master of the art of suspense, Lal made a speech. "Doctor, please understand that if there were any other way to accomplish our purpose, we should employ it."

McCoy could feel the veins in his neck swelling. "Get on with it!" he told them.

They advanced on him. Thann raised a control bar.

A white-faced Kirk was prowling the arena. "Spock, why . . . *why* did you let him do it?"

The composed voice said, "I was convinced in the same way you were, Captain—by the good Doctor's hypo." Spock looked up, meeting Kirk's eyes. A message flashed between them. Kirk nodded slightly to their mutual recognition of McCoy's devotion. Then a dissonant chord rang from Spock's control bar. Kirk hurried to him, asking, "Anything, Spock?"

Spock leaned back, regarding the bar with admiration. Extending it to Kirk, he said, "A most unusual device. It is a control unit but *not* a control mechanism. It is, in fact, a mechanical device."

"What exactly is it?"

"The control is attuned to only one pattern of electrical energy—the pattern produced by the mental impulses of the person who possesses it. It is activated solely through mental commands."

"Can it be adapted or . . . or reattuned to our brain patterns?"

"I am attempting to do so." Spock paused. "However, it is not possible to adjust the control for more than one pattern at a time. As I am most familiar with my own pattern, with your permission, Captain . . ."

"Do whatever you think best to get it working. What disturbs me is why the Vians have allowed it to remain in our possession."

Spock bent again over the bar. "Understandable, sir. They must know that we are capable of comprehending the control and of making use of it."

"They must know we will use it to escape."

Spock nodded. "The only logical assumption is that they wish to let us go."

"While they still have McCoy?"

"It is evidently their intention, Captain."

Kirk paced the length of the arena. Turning, he looked at Gem. Then slowly he went to her. "Somehow you are the crux . . . the focal point of all this." He wheeled to Spock. "Even before we got here, she was a prisoner. Yet they haven't hurt her. They haven't even made threats."

"Indeed, Captain, the facts indicate that she is essential to their purpose."

"Yes . . . there is purpose. *But what is it?*"

Kirk, taking Gem's hands in his, looked intently into the sensitive face, as though it held his answer. "Gem, did those who preceded us die . . . for you? Has all this . . . this pain and terror . . . happened—or been made to happen—for you?''

Spock broke into his concentration. "Completed, Captain. The adjustments are delicate. They may not survive more than one use. Even so, there should be sufficient power to return us to the *Enterprise*."

"Will it take us to McCoy?"

"If you so desire, sir."

Kirk spoke briskly. "The best defense is a strong offense. And I intend to start offending!"

The circle of light still lay before Gem's couch. Kirk stepped into it. Spock followed him. Silently, Gem joined them, McCoy's medikit in her hand. She passed it to Kirk. He looked at her, his face drawn with anxiety. "Aim for the lab," he said to Spock.

Spock stared down at the bar he held, eyes fixed in concentration. The arena vanished. They were in the lab. Kirk looked around it. Then, stunned, he saw what he had to see.

McCoy hung limply from ropes attached to the ceiling. HIs features were battered to a pulp. Blood dripped from his open wounds and through the remnants of his uniform.

Kirk broke out of his shocked horror. He ran to the tortured body, supporting its weight in his arms. When Spock had removed the shackles, they carried it to a table, easing it down gently. Kirk reached for a torn wrist. "The pulse is almost gone." Spock, at the head of the table, was busy with a medical tricorder.

"Spock, what are the readings?"

"Heart, severely damaged; signs of congestion in both lungs; evidence of massive circulatory collapse."

From the corner where she huddled, Gem was watching their every move. In the harsh lab light McCoy's face was colorless, his lips faintly blue. His eyes shuddered open, stared blankly, then focused.

Kirk found water. Raising McCoy's head, he poured some into the smashed lips. "Don't try to talk, Bones." He laid the head back on the table. "Don't try to speak. Don't think. Just take it easy until we can get back to the ship. Don't—"

"Captain . . ."

Something in Spock's tone caught Kirk's alarmed attention. "What is it? What's the matter?"

With a visible effort Spock looked up from the tricorder. "Captain, I . . . he's dying. We can make him comfortable but that is all."

"No! You can't be sure, Spock! You're not a doctor."

McCoy whispered, "But . . . I am. Go on, Spock. . . ."

Spock moved the tricorder over the entire body. "Internal injuries; bleeding in chest and abdomen; hemorrhages of the spleen and liver; 70 percent kidney failure. . . ."

"He's right, Jim." McCoy grinned weakly. "Being a doctor has its drawbacks. . . . I've always wondered—" A bout of coughing silenced him. Kirk supported his head until it passed. Then he tore a piece from McCoy's mangled shirt. Dipping it in the water, he dampened the hot forehead.

"Thanks . . . Jim . . ."

Kirk, his face suddenly appearing ten years older, looked at Spock. "How long?"

Spock hesitated; but at McCoy's faint nod, he said, "It could happen at any time, Captain."

The broken mouth moved in a smile. "The correct medical phrase, eh, Spock?" Coughing assailed him again, this time so violently that he seemed unable to breathe. It ceased abruptly, leaving him motionless.

"Doctor!" Spock felt for the neck pulse. He found it. Straightening, he rested his hand briefly on McCoy's head. McCoy opened his eyes, met Spock's—and their unspoken loyalty was wordlessly spoken. Then a spasm of pain twisted McCoy's face. He writhed on the table, coughing. The fit lasted so long that it suffocated him.

"Can't we do something?" Kirk said.

"I'm afraid not, Captain." As Spock spoke, McCoy lost consciousness.

Kirk said, "Gem!" They both turned toward her. "Gem could help him!" Kirk cried. "As she helped me!"

She was cowering in her corner. At the sight of her overwhelming fear, Kirk hesitated. "Could his nearness to death also kill her?"

"The Doctor's analysis of her life-support reactions assumed that the instinct for self-preservation would prevent that. However, he could not be positive.''

"If she could just strengthen him to keep him from sinking further into death, we could take over, Spock, with Bones directing us.''

They had started toward her when the chord suddenly reverberated at full power. The force field encircled them.

The Vians' arms were lifted in nameless threat. Lal's T-bar was extended downward. "No interference will be permitted!" he said.

Imprisoned, Kirk spoke from within the field. He was openly pleading. "She can save his life! Let us help her go to him!"

"She must neither be forced nor urged to take action.''

"All must proceed without interference,'' Thann added.

"The purpose that brought us together—'' Lal began.

"What purpose?'' Kirk shouted. "What purpose can any of this serve except the satisfaction of some sick need of yours?''

"We have but one need left in life,'' Lal said. "It is to see the completion of the final moment of our test.''

"Be patient,'' Thann urged.

"Patient!'' Kirk's scorn was fierce with fury. "Our friend is dying!''

"Perhaps,'' Thann said.

"What purpose will our friend's death serve other than your pleasure in it?'' Spock's voice had never been so toneless. "Surely beings as advanced as you know that your solar system will soon be extinct. This star of yours will nova.''

"We know,'' Thann said.

"Then you know that the many millions of inhabitants on its planets are doomed.''

The chill voice of Lal said, "That's why we are here.''

Kirk swept the laboratory with a gesture. "This place of death you have devised for your pleasure—will it prevent that catastrophe?''

"No, it will not. That is true. But it may save Gem's planet. Of all the planets of Minara, we are empowered to transport to safety only the inhabitants of one.'' Thann's eyes fixed on Kirk's. "If Gem's planet is the sole one to be saved, we must make certain beyond all doubt that its people are worthy of survival.''

"And how will that be served by the death of our friend?''

Lal answered. "His death will not serve it. Only Gem's willingness to give her life for him will. You were her teachers.''

"Her teachers? What did she learn from us?''

"Your will to survive; your love of life; your passion to know. These qualities are recorded in her being.'' He paused. "Each one of you has been ready to give his life for the others. We must now find out whether that instinct has been transmitted to Gem.''

The laboratory equipment rattled. The earth rumbled under the pressures of another quake. Thann spoke to Lal. "Time is growing short.''

Spock looked down at McCoy's ravaged face. "You were correct, Captain. Everything that has occurred here has been caused to happen by them. This place has been a great laboratory and we have been the subjects of a test.''

"No!'' Thann said. "Only the circumstances were created by us. They were necessary.''

Lal stepped toward Kirk. "Your actions have been spontaneous. What is truest and best in any species of beings has been revealed by you. Yours are the qualities that make a civilization worthy to survive. We are grateful to you.''

"Look!'' Thann cried.

Gem had left her corner. She moved to McCoy, passing through the force field as though it didn't exist. She passed her hands gently over the wounds on his face and body. Staring at her, hope returned to the *Enterprise* men.

Thann turned to Lal. "This is most significant. An instinct new to the essence of her being is generating. We are seeing it come to birth. . . .''

Lal nodded. "Compassion for another is becoming part of her functioning life system.''

The fearful injuries on McCoy's face were transferring themselves to Gem's. His eyes fluttered open, their pupils still glazed. Tensely, Kirk watched for some body movement. It didn't come. But the wounds on his face had begun to heal; and those on Gem's were disappearing. McCoy moved his head. Looking at Gem, recognition replaced the glaze in his eyes.

She was growing weak. Fear came into her great eyes. She withdrew from the table and staggered back toward her corner. McCoy's wounds began to bleed again.

"She is saving herself," Lal said. "She does not yet possess the instinct to save her people."

"We have failed," Thann said.

Spock spoke to Kirk. "Captain, the Doctor's life is not solely dependent on Gem. The Vians also must have the power to give him back his life."

Lal addressed Spock directly. "Your friend's death is not important. We must wait to see whether her instinct for self-sacrifice has become stronger than her instinct for self-preservation."

Watching, Kirk could see signs of the anguished internal struggle in the girl. Then her white face cleared with decision. She returned to McCoy, her step firm and determined. Kneeling beside the table, she took his limp hands in hers. Again, his wrists' gashes transferred to hers. McCoy's body moved—but life once again seemed to be draining from her.

McCoy lifted his head. "Don't touch me," he told her. "Stay away."

He tried to look around. "Jim . . . Spock . . . are you here?"

"Yes, Bones."

"Don't let her touch me. She will die."

He hauled himself to his knees, struggling to pull his hands from Gem's. The effort exhausted him. He fell back, looking pleadingly at Kirk. "Make her leave me . . . Jim . . . Spock. . . . I will not destroy life. Not even to save my own. You know that. Please . . . make her leave me."

Gem placed her hand on his heart. Color, faint but visible, came into McCoy's face.

"Captain!"

"Yes, Spock."

"The intensity of emotion that is exhausting us is building up the force field around us!"

"I know. It draws its energy from us."

"In spite of what we see, sir, all emotions must be eliminated. This may weaken the field."

"I'll try, Spock."

Both closed their eyes. A complete calm was in Spock's face. Even concentration was absorbed by his serenity. His hand went through the force field. He moved through it and quietly approached the Vians. Still held by the field, Kirk tried to still his tumult of anxieties. He looked at the Vians. They were so tense with their will to power that they failed to note Spock's position behind them. The Vulcan's arm rose; and lashed down in a judo chop that sent Lal's T-bar flying. The force field broke. As Kirk raced out of it, Spock retrieved the T-bar. Physically helpless now, the Vians hesitated, their essential test threatened with final disaster.

Gem was swaying with increasing weakness. McCoy dragged himself to his knees, crying, "No! No! I won't let you do it!" He shoved her away in a momentary influx of strength. Frightened by his sudden violence, she shrank from the table. As McCoy tried to move further away from her, his wounds reopened. He fell back, lying still. Gem stumbled back to her corner.

Kirk took the T-bar from Spock. He was rushing to McCoy with it when Lal spoke. "You cannot use our powers to change what is happening."

Kirk looked at the deathly white face on the table. Then he went to the Vians. "You must save the life of our friend."

"No. We will not," Lal said. "Her instinct must develop to the full. The test must be complete."

"It *is* complete." Spock joined Kirk. "Gem has already earned the right of survival for her planet. She has offered her life."

"To offer is insufficient proof," Lal said.

"If death is the only proof you can understand, then here are four lives for you." Kirk proffered the T-bar to Lal.

The Vian stared at him. "We will not leave our friend," Kirk said.

Lal took the bar. Turning, the two *Enterprise* officers strode back to McCoy.

At the table, Kirk faced around. "You are frauds," he said. "You have lost the capacity to feel the very emotions you brought Gem here to experience! You don't know the meaning of life. Compassionate love is dead in you! All you are is arid intellect!''

Lal's face went rigid with shock. Thann began to tremble. Their very bodies seemed to dwindle as Kirk's words struck home. They looked at each other, lost, the values of their lifetime dissolving. Lal was the first to move. Thann followed him to the table. They stood there a long moment, looking down at McCoy. Then Lal passed the T-bar over him. McCoy sat up, whole.

Nobody spoke. The Vians went to Gem. They lifted her in their arms. With her head on his shoulder, Lal turned, the first glint of warmth in his aged face. "The one emotion left to us is gratitude," he said. "We are thankful that we can express it to you. Farewell."

They chose to vanish slowly, changing into mist. Gem, looking back at the *Enterprise* trio, was the last to disappear.

The bridge viewing screen held the images of the immortal stars. Kirk turned away from it. Among them was a mortal star about to die.

"Strange . . ." he said.

Beside him, Spock said, "What puzzles you, Captain?"

"Puzzled isn't the word, Mr. Spock. I think I am awed."

"I'm with you, Jim," McCoy said. "She awed me."

"I wasn't thinking of Gem," Kirk said. He looked back at the viewing screen. "I was thinking of the fantastic element of chance that out in limitless space we should have come together with the savior of a planet."

Spock said, "The element of chance, Captain, can virtually be eliminated by a civilization as advanced as the Vians'."

Scott spoke from his station. "Not to dispute your computer, Mr. Spock—but from the little you have told me, I would say she was a pearl of great price."

"What, Scotty?"

"You know the story of the merchant . . . that merchant 'who when he found one pearl of great price, went and sold all he had and bought it.' ''

"She was that all right, Scotty," Kirk said. "And

whether the Vians bought her or found her, I am glad for her and the planet she will save."

"Personally," McCoy said, "I find it *fascinating* that with all their scientific knowledge and advances, it was good old-fashioned *human emotion* they valued the most."

"Perhaps the Vulcans should hear about this," said Scott.

"Mr. Spock, could you be prevailed upon to give them the news?"

Spock looked at them blandly. "Possibly, Captain. I shall certainly give the thought its due consideration."

"I am sure you will, Mr. Spock." Kirk turned to Sulu. "Helmsman, take us out of orbit. Warp factor two."

At high speed the *Enterprise* left the area of the dying star.

THE THOLIAN WEB

Writer: Judy Burns and Chet Richards
Director: Herb Wallerstein

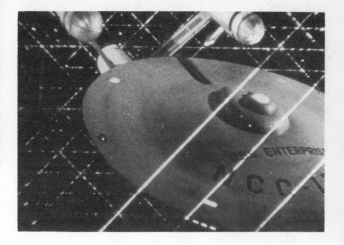

The bridge was at full muster—Kirk, Scott, Spock, Uhura, Chekov, Sulu—and extremely tense. The *Enterprise* was in unsurveyed territory, approaching the last reported position of the Starship *Defiant*, which had vanished without a trace three weeks ago.

"Captain," Spock said, "I have lost the use of all sensors. Were I to believe these readings, space itself is breaking up around us."

"A major failure?"

"Not in the sensors, sir; I have run a complete systems check. The failure is mine; I simply do not know how to interpret these reports."

"Captain," Scott added, "there may be no connection, but we're losing power in the warp engines."

"How bad is it?"

"We can hardly feel it now, but it's richt abnormal all the same. I canna find the cause."

Now it was Chekov's turn. "Captain, we have visual detection of an object dead ahead. It *looks* like a starship."

It did, at that, but not a starship in any condition to which they were accustomed. It was visibly shimmering.

"Mr. Spock, what's wrong with it?"

"Nonexistence, to put the matter in a word, Captain. There is virtually no radar return, mass analysis, radiation traces. We see it, but the sensors indicate it isn't there."

"Mr. Chekov, narrow the field and see if you can bring up the identification numbers. It's the *Defiant*, all right. Mr.

232

Sulu, impulse engines only. Close to Transporter range. Lieutenant Uhura, open a hailing channel."

"I've been trying to raise them, sir, but there's no response."

Chekov shifted the viewing angle again. The other ship showed no gaping holes or other signs of damage. It was just ghostly—and silent.

"Within Transporter range, sir."

"Thanks, Mr. Sulu. Lieutenant, order Dr. McCoy to the Transporter Room. Mr. Spock, Mr. Chekov, I'll want you as well. Environment suits all around; O'Neil to handle the Transporter. Take over, Mr. Scott."

The Transporter was locked onto the bridge of the *Defiant*. The lighting there turned out to be extremely subdued; even some monitor lights were not functioning. But the situation was all too visible, nonetheless.

A man somewhat older than Kirk, wearing a captain's stripes, lay dead in his command chair, a number one phaser clutched in one hand. The other hand was twisted in the hair of a junior officer. The junior was also dead, with both his hands locked around the Captain's neck.

Chekov was the first to speak. "Has there ever been a mutiny on a starship before?"

"Technically," Spock said, "the refusal of Captain Garth's fleet to follow his orders when he became insane was a mutiny. But there has never been any record of an occurrence like this."

McCoy stopped to examine the bodies. "The Captain's neck is broken, Jim."

"This ship is still functioning," Spock said after a quick check of the communications console. "It is logical to assume that the mutineers are somewhere aboard. Yet the sensors show no sign of life anywhere in the vessel."

"Odd," Kirk said reflectively. "Very odd. Spock, you stay here with me. Chekov, get down to Life Support and Engineering. Dr. McCoy, check out sickbay. I want some answers."

The two men moved off. As they did so, Scott's voice sounded in Kirk's helmet. "Captain, Mr. Sulu reports that he can't get an accurate fix on the *Defiant*, but it seems to be drifting away. Should he correct for range?"

Still odder. How could one ship be moving relative to the other when neither was under power? "Keep us within beaming range, but not too close."

"Chekov reporting, Captain. All dead in Life Support and in Engineering as well."

"Right. Get back up here. Bones?"

"More bodies, Jim. Proximate cause of deaths, various forms of violence. In short, I'd say they killed each other."

"Could a mental disease possibly have inflicted all of the crew at once?"

"It may still be here, sir," Chekov said, reappearing. "I feel pretty funny myself—headachy, dizzy."

"I can't answer the question," McCoy's voice said. "According to the medical log, even the ship's surgeon here didn't really know what was going on. The best I can do for you is take all the readings I can get and analyze them later. Now what the devil . . . ?"

"Bones! What's happening?"

There was a brief silence. Then: "Jim, this ship's beginning to dissolve! I just put my hand right *through* a corpse—and then through the wall next to him."

"Get back up here on the double. Kirk to *Enterprise*. Mr. Scott, stand by to beam us back."

"Captain, I can't. Not all at once, at least."

"What do you mean? What's going on over there?"

"Nothing we can understand," Scott's voice said grimly. "The *Defiant* is fading out, and it's—well, something is ripping the innards out of our own ship. It's jamming our Transporter frequencies. We've got only three working, and I can't be sure about those. One of you has got to wait."

"Request permission to remain," Spock said. "I could be completing the data."

"It's more important to get what you already have into analysis on the *Enterprise*. Don't argue. I'll probably be right after you."

But he was not. Within moments after Spock, Chekov and McCoy materialized aboard the *Enterprise*, the *Defiant* had vanished.

* * *

Scott was at the consoles with the Transporter officer. Spock joined them, removing his helmet, and scanned the board.

"See anything I don't?" Scott said.

"Apparently not. Everything is negative."

McCoy took off his own helmet. "But he's got to be out there somewhere. If the Transporter won't grab him, what about the shuttlecraft? There must be some way to pick him up."

"There is no present trace of the Captain, Doctor," Spock said evenly. "The only next possible action is to feed the computer our data and see what conclusions can be drawn."

The computer was the fastest of its kind, but the wait seemed frustratingly long all the same. At last its pleasantly feminine voice said: "Integrated."

"Compute the next period of spatial interphase," Spock told it.

"Two hours, twelve minutes."

Spock shut the machine off. Scott was staring at him, aghast. "Is that how long we have to wait before we can pick up the Captain? But, Spock, I don't think I can hold the ship in place that long. The power leak is unbalanced and I haven't been able to trace it, let alone stop it."

"You will have to keep trying," Spock said. "The fabric of space is very weak here. If we disturb it, there will be no chance of retrieving the Captain alive."

Chekov was looking baffled; worse, he was looking positively ill. "I don't understand," he said. "What's so special about this region of space?"

"I can only speculate," Spock said. "We exist in a universe which coexists with a multitude of others in the same physical space, but displaced in time. For certain brief periods, one area of such a space overlaps an area of ours. That is the time of interphase when we connect with the *Defiant*'s universe."

"And retrieve the Captain," Uhura added.

"Perhaps. But the dimensional structure of each universe is totally dissimilar to the others. Any use of power would disturb what can at best be only a tenuous and brief connection. It might also result in our being trapped ourselves . . ."

"And die like them?" Chekov said raggedly. Suddenly his voice rose to a yell. "Damn you, Spock . . ."

He sprang. Spock, surprised, was knocked backward, Chekov's hands around his neck. Sulu attempted to drag Chekov off; the enraged man struck out at him. Scott promptly grabbed him by that arm. It was all that they could do to handle him, but the distraction enabled Spock to get in a neck pinch.

"Security guards to the bridge," Spock said to the intercom. "Dr. McCoy, will you also please report?"

McCoy appeared almost at once, taking in the scene at a glance. "He jumped you? My fault, I should have checked him the minute he said he was feeling funny, but there was so much else going on. Anybody notice any spasms of pain? Ah. What about his behavior? Hysterical? Frightened?"

"He looked more angry than frightened to me," Uhura said. "But there was nothing to be angry about."

"Nevertheless," Spock said, "there were all the signs of a murderous fury. After what we have seen aboard the *Defiant*, the episode is doubly disturbing."

"I'll say it is," McCoy said. "Guards, take him to sickbay. I'll see what I can find out from seeing the thing in its first stages. Spock, on the other subject, what makes you think Captain Kirk is still alive?"

"The Captain was locked in the Transporter beam when the *Defiant* phased out, Doctor. It is possible that he was saved the shock of transition. If we do not catch him again at the precise corresponding instant in the next interphase, he will die. There is no margin for error; his environmental unit can supply breathable air for no more than another three point twenty-six hours."

"Mr. Spock," Sulu called from the helm. "A vessel is approaching on an intercept vector."

Spock walked quickly to the command chair, and Scott went back to his post. "Status, Mr. Sulu," Spock said.

"Range, two hundred thousand kilometers and closing. Relative velocity, zero point five one C."

"Red alert," Spock said. The klaxon began to sound throughout the ship. At the same instant, Uhura captured the intruder on the main viewing screen.

The stranger was crystalline in appearance, blue-green

in coloration, and shaped like a tetrahedron within which a soft light seemed to pulsate. As the scene materialized, Sulu gasped.

"Stopped dead, Mr. Spock. Now, how do they do that? Range, ninety thousand kilometers and holding."

"Mr. Spock," Uhura said. "I'm getting a visual signal from them."

"Transfer it to the main viewer."

The scene dissolved into what might have been the command bridge of the alien vessel. Most of the frame, however, was occupied by the upper half of an unknown creature. Like its vessel, the alien was almost jewel-like in appearance, multifaceted, crystalline, though it was humanoid in build. A light pulsated rapidly but irregularly inside what seemed to be its head.

"I am Commander Loskene," the creature said at once in good Federation Interlingua. "You are trespassing in a territorial annex of the Tholian Assembly. You must leave this area immediately."

Spock studied Loskene. The pulsating light did not seem to be in synch with the voice. He said formally, "Spock, in command of the Federation Starship *Enterprise*. Commander, the Federation regards this area as free space."

"We have claimed it. And we are prepared to use force, if necessary, to hold it."

"We are not interested in a show of force. The *Enterprise* has responded to a distress call from one of our ships and is currently engaged in rescue operations. Do you wish to assist us?"

"I find no evidence of a disabled ship. My instruments indicate that ours are the only two vessels in this area."

"The other ship is trapped in an interspatial sink. It should reappear in one hour and fifty minutes. We request that you stand by until then."

"Very well, *Enterprise*. In the interest of interstellar amity, we will wait. But we will not tolerate deceit."

The view wavered, and then the screen once more showed the Tholian ship. Now there was nothing to do but wait—and hope.

* * *

The moment of interphase approached at last. As before, Scott personally took over the Transporter console. In the command chair, Spock watched the clock intently.

"Transporter Room."

"Aye, Mr. Spock. I'm locked onto the Captain's coordinates."

"Interphase in twenty seconds . . . ten seconds . . . five, four, three, two, one, energize!"

There was a tense silence. Then Scott's voice said, "The platform's empty, Mr. Spock. There's naught at all at those coordinates."

"Any abnormality to report, Mr. Sulu?"

"The sensor readings don't correspond to those we received the last time we saw the *Defiant*. Insofar as I can tell, the Tholian entry into the area has disturbed the interphase."

"McCoy to bridge," said the intercom. "Has the Captain been beamed aboard, Mr. Spock?"

"No, Doctor. And the interphase period has been passed. We will have to wait for the next one."

"But he hasn't got enough air for that! And there's been another case like Chekov's. I have had to confine my orderly to sickbay."

"Have you still no clues as to the cause, Doctor?"

"I know exactly what the cause is," McCoy's voice said grimly. "And there's nothing I can do to stop it. The molecular structure of the central nervous system, including the brain, is being distorted by the space we are in. Sooner or later the whole crew will be affected—unless you get the *Enterprise* out of here."

"Mr. Spock!" Sulu broke in. "We're being fired upon!"

The announcement came only seconds before the bolt itself struck. The *Enterprise* lurched, but did not roll.

"Damage control, report," Spock said.

"Minor structural damage to sections A-4 and C-13."

"Engineering, hold power steady. Mr. Sulu, divert all but emergency maintenance power into the shields."

"Sir," Sulu said, "that will reduce phaser power by fifty percent."

Almost as if it had heard him, the Tholian ship darted forward. It seemed to be almost within touching distance before it fired again. This time, the shock threw everybody who was not seated to the floor.

"Engineering to bridge. Mr. Spock, we can't take another like that. We'll either have to fight or run."

"Mr. Sulu, lock in phaser tracking controls. Divert power to the phaser banks and fire at the next close approach. Lieutenant Uhura, open a channel to the Tholians."

McCoy came onto the bridge, his face masklike. On the main viewing screen, the pyramidal ship looped around and began another run.

"Spock, what's the use of this battle?" McCoy demanded. "You've already lost the Captain. Take the ship out of here."

Spock, intent upon the screen, did not answer. The pyramid zigzagged in. Then both vessels fired at once.

The *Enterprise* rang like a gong and the lights flickered, but the screen showed that the Tholian, too, had sustained a direct hit. There was no visible damage, but the pyramid had again stopped dead, and then began to retreat.

"A standoff," Spock said. "Mr. Scott, status?"

"Convertors burned out," Scott's voice said. "We've lost drive and hence the ability to correct drift. I estimate four hours in replacement time."

"By that time," Sulu said, "we'll have drifted right through that—that gateway out there."

"Are you satisfied?" McCoy said, picking himself up off the deck. "Spock, why did you do it?"

"To stay in the area for the next interphase," Spock said, "required for disabling the Tholian ship."

"But you're ignoring the mental effects! How can you risk your whole crew on the dim chance of rescuing one officer—one presumed dead, at that? The Captain wouldn't have done that!"

"Doctor, I hardly believe that now is the time for such comparisons. Get down to your laboratory at once and search for an antidote to the mental effects. Since we must remain here, that is your immediate task. Mine is to command the *Enterprise*."

McCoy left, though not without an angry glare.

"Mr. Spock, something has just entered sensor range," Sulu said. "Yes, it's another Tholian ship. Loskene must have contacted them at the same time they intercepted us. Loskene is moving back out of phaser range."

"Lieutenant, attempt contact again."

"No response, sir."

On the screen, the two Tholian ships joined—literally joined, base to base, making what seemed to be a single vessel like a six-sided diamond. Then they began to separate again. Between their previously common bases a multicolored strand stretched out across space.

Spock rose and went to the library computer station. The Tholians met again, separated, spinning another thread. Then another. Gradually, a latticework of energy seemed to be growing.

"Switch scanners, Mr. Sulu."

The screen angle changed. The tempo of the Tholian activity was speeding up rapidly. From this point of view, it seemed that the *Enterprise* was already almost a third surrounded by the web and it kept on growing.

Spock pulled his head out of the hooded viewer. "Fascinating," he said. "And very efficient. If they succeed in completing that structure before we are repaired, we shall not be able to run even if we wished to."

Nobody replied. There seemed to be nothing to say.

There was a service for Kirk. It was brief and military. Spock, as the next in command, spoke the eulogy. The speech was not long, but it was interrupted all the same, by another seizure of madness striking down a crewman in the congregation. Afterward, the tension seemed much greater.

As the rest filed out, McCoy stopped Spock at the doorway. "There is a duty to be performed in the Captain's cabin," he said. "It requires both of us."

"Then it will have to wait. My duties require my immediate return to the bridge."

"The Captain left a message tape," the surgeon said. "It was his order that it be reviewed by both of us should he ever be declared dead—as you have just done."

"It will have to wait for a more suitable moment," Spock said, putting his hand on the corridor rail.

"Why? Are you afraid it will change your present status?"

Spock turned sharply. "The mental and physical state of this crew are your responsibility, Doctor. As I have observed before, command is mine."

"Not while a last order remains to be obeyed."

For a moment Spock did not reply. Then he said, "Very well. To the Captain's quarters, then."

McCoy had evidently visited Kirk's quarters before the service, for laid out on a table was the black velvet case which contained Kirk's medals, and it was open. The surgeon looked down at them for a long moment.

"He was a hero in every sense of the word," he said. "Yet his life was sacrificed for nothing. The one thing that would have given his death meaning is the survival of the *Enterprise*. You have made that impossible."

Spock said glacially, "We came here for a specific purpose."

"Maybe not the same one. I came to find out, among other things, really why you stayed and fought."

Spock closed the box. "The Captain would have remained to recover a man at the risk of his own life, other things being equal. I do not consider the question closed."

"He wouldn't have risked the ship. And what do you mean, the question isn't closed? Do you think he may be still alive after all? Then why did you declare him dead—to assure your own captaincy?"

"Unnecessary. I am already in command of the *Enterprise*."

"It's a situation I wish I could remedy."

"If you believe," Spock said, "that I remained just to fire that phaser and kill James Kirk or this crew, it is your prerogative as Medical Officer of this ship to relieve me of duty. In the meantime, I suggest that we play the tape you referred to, so I can get back to the bridge and you can resume looking for an antidote for the madness."

"All right," McCoy turned to Kirk's viewer and flipped a switch. The screen lit; in it, Kirk was seated at his desk.

"Spock. Bones," Kirk's voice said. "Since you are playing this tape, we will assume that I am dead, the tactical situation is critical and you two are locked in mortal combat.

"It means also, Spock, that you have control of my ship and are probably making the most difficult decisions of

your career. I can offer only one small piece of advice, for
what it's worth. Use every scrap of knowledge and logic
you've got to save the ship, but temper your judgment with
intuitive insight. I believe you have that quality. But if you
can't find it in yourself, then seek out McCoy. Ask his advice.
And if you find it sound, take it.

"Bones, you heard what I just told Spock. Help him if
you can, but remember that *he* is the Captain. His decisions,
when he reaches them, are to be obeyed without further question. You might find that he is capable of both human insight
and human error, and they are the most difficult to defend.
But you will find that Spock is deserving of the same loyalty
and confidence that you all have given me.

"As to the disposal of my personal effects . . ."

McCoy snapped the switch, and turned. For a moment
the two men studied each other, less guardedly than before.
Then McCoy said, "Spock, I'm sorry. It hurts, doesn't it?"

Spock closed his eyes for a moment. Then he turned
and left. McCoy remained for a moment longer, thoughtful,
and then stepped out into the corridor.

He was greeted by a stifled scream. Turning, he saw Uhura
running toward him, half out of uniform, her normally unshakable calm dissolved in something very close to panic. She saw
McCoy and stopped, gasping, trying to get words out; but before they could form, a stab of pain seemed to go through her
and her knees buckled. She grabbed the rail for support.

The signs were all too clear. McCoy surreptitiously got
out his hypospray, and then went to steady her.

"Lieutenant!" he said sharply. "What is it?"

"I—Doctor, I've just seen the Captain!"

"Yes, he just left a moment ago."

"No, I don't mean Mr. Spock. The captain. He's
alive!"

"I'm afraid not. But of course you saw him. We would
all like to see him."

Her legs were still shaking, but she seemed somewhat
calmer now. "I know what you're thinking. But it isn't that.
I was looking into my mirror in my quarters, and there he
was. He was—sort of shimmering, like the *Defiant* was when
we first saw it. He looked puzzled—and like he was trying to
tell me something."

McCoy brought the hypospray up. Uhura saw it and tried to fight free, but she was too wobbly to resist. "I did see him. Tell Mr. Spock. He's alive, he's alive . . ."

The hypospray hissed. "I'll tell him," McCoy said gently. "But in the meantime, you're going to sickbay."

One of Scott's crewmen attacked him within the same hour. The effect was spreading faster through the ship. The Tholian web was now two-thirds complete, and the *Enterprise* was still without impulse drive, let alone the thrust to achieve interstellar velocity.

The crewman's attack failed; but a shaken Scott was on the bridge not ten minutes later.

"Mr. Spock—I've just seen the Captain."

"Spock to McCoy; please come to the bridge. Go on, Mr. Scott."

"He was on the upper engineering level—sparkling, rather like a Transporter effect. He seemed to be almost floating. And I think he saw us. He seemed to be breathing pretty heavily—and then, hey presto! he winked right out."

The elevator doors snapped open and McCoy came out, fast enough to pick up most of Scott's account. He said, "Scotty, are you feeling all right?"

"Och, I think so. Tired, maybe."

"So are we all, of course. Don't fail to see me if you have any other symptoms."

"Right."

"Lieutenant Uhura told a similar story before she went under," Spock said. "Perhaps we ought not to discount it entirely. Yet in critical moments, men sometimes see exactly what they want to see, even when they are not ill."

"Are you suggesting," McCoy said, "that the men are seeing the Captain because they've lost confidence in you?"

"I am making no suggestions, but merely stating a fact."

"Well, the situation is critical, all right. And there have been more assaults on the lower decks. And if Scottie here's being affected, that will finish whatever chance we have to get the *Enterprise* out of here."

"Have you any further leads on a remedy?"

"A small one," McCoy said. "I've been toying with

the idea of trying a chlortheragen derivative. But I'm not ready
to try anything so drastic, yet.''

''Why not?''

''Well, for one thing . . .''

''Gentlemen,'' Scott said quietly. ''Mr. Spock. Look
behind you.''

At the same moment, there was a chorus of gasps from
the rest of the personnel on the bridge. Spock turned.

Floating behind him was an image of Captain Kirk, full
length but soapily iridescent. He seemed to recognize Spock,
but to be unable to move. Kirk's hand rose to his throat, and
his lips moved. There was no sound.

Spock—hurry!

The figure vanished.

The Tholian web continued to go up around the *Enterprise*, section by section. The pace had slowed somewhat;
Loskene and his compatriots seemed to have concluded that
the *Enterprise* would not or could not leave the area.

Aboard the ship, too, the tension seemed to have
abated, if only slightly. It was now tacitly accepted that the
apparition of the Captain on the bridge had not been a part
of the lurking madness, and that he had been, therefore, alive
then.

Spock and Scott were having another computer session.

''So your reluctance to use the phasers now stands en-
dorsed,'' the Engineering Officer said. ''They blasted a hole
right through this crazy space fabric and sent the *Defiant*
heaven only knows where.''

''And would have sent the Captain with it, if we had
not had a Transporter lock on him during the first fade-out.
As of now, only the overlap time has changed; the next interphase will be early, in exactly twenty minutes. Can you be
ready?''

''Aye,'' Scott said, ''she'll be back together, but we'll
have only eighty percent power built up.''

''It will have to do.''

McCoy came up behind them, carrying a tray bearing
a flask and three glasses. ''Compliments of the house, gen-

tlemen," he said. "To your good health and the health of your crew. Drink it down!"

"What is it?" Spock said.

"Generally, it's an antidote-cum-preventive for the paranoid reaction. Specifically, a derivative of chlortheragen."

"If I remember aright," Scott said, "that's a nerve gas used by the Klingons. Are you trying to kill us all, McCoy?"

"I said it was a derivative, not the pure stuff. In this form it simply deadens certain nerve inputs to the brain."

"Any good brand of Scotch will do that for you."

"As a matter of fact," McCoy said, "it works best mixed with alcohol. But it does work. It even brought Chekov around, and he's been affected the longest of any of us."

Scott knocked his drink back, and made a face. "It'll nae become a regular tipple with me," he said. "I'll be getting back to my machines."

Spock nodded after him and crossed to the command chair. A moment later Chekov himself entered, beaming, and took his regular position. Uhura was already at her post, as was Sulu.

"Your absence was keenly felt, Ensign," Spock said. "To begin with, give me an estimated time for completion of the Tholian tractor field."

"At the enemy's present pace, two minutes, sir."

"Mr. Sulu, I have the computers programmed to move us through the interspatial gateway. Stand ready to resume the helm as soon as we emerge on the other side—wherever that may be."

"Transporter Room."

"Scott here."

"Ready for interphase in seventy-five seconds."

"Aye, sir, standing by."

"Mr. Spock," Sulu said, "the Tholians are getting ready to close the web. It seems to be contracting to fit the ship."

"Counting down to interphase," Chekov said. He now had an open line to the Transporter Room. "One minute."

"Mr. Scott, have we full power?"

"Only seventy-six percent, Mr. Spock."

"Can the computer call on it all at once?"

"Aye, I think she'll stand it."

"Thirty seconds."

Suddenly, on the viewing screen, between the *Enterprise*, a tiny figure in an environmental suit popped into being.

"I see him!"

"He's early!"

"It's the Captain!"

The webbing began to slide across the screen in a heavy mesh. Behind it, stars slid past as well.

"Tractor field activated," Sulu said. "We're being pulled out of here."

"Try to maintain position, Mr. Sulu."

The ship throbbed to the sudden application of power at the computer's command. Heavy tremors shook the deck.

The web vanished.

"We broke it!" Chekov cheered.

"No, Ensign, we went out through the interdimensional gateway. Since we went through shortly after interphase, we should still be in some part of normal space. Compute the distance from our original position."

"Umm—two point seventy-two parsecs." Chekov looked aghast. "But that's beyond Transporter range!"

"You forget, Mr. Chekov, that we have a shortcut. Mr. Scott, are you still locked on the Captain?"

"Aye, sir, though I dinna understand how."

"You cam beam him in now—we have broken free."

"Aye, sir—got him! But he's unconscious. McCoy, this is your department."

"I will be down directly," Spock said. "Mr. Sulu, take over."

As it turned out, no elaborate treatment was needed; taking Kirk's helmet off to let him breathe ship's air removed the source of the difficulty, and once he had been moved to his quarters, an epinephrine hypospray brought him quickly to consciousness. For a moment he looked up at Spock and McCoy in silence. Then McCoy said, "Welcome home, Jim."

"Thanks, Bones. You know, I had a whole universe to

myself after the *Defiant* was thrown out. There was absolutely
no one else in it. Somehow I could sense it.''

"That must have been disorienting," McCoy observed.

"Very. I kept trying to get through to the ship. I think
I did at least three times, but it never lasted. I must say I like
a crowded universe much better. How did you two get along
without me?''

"We managed," McCoy said. "Spock gave the orders.
I found the answers.''

Spock gave McCoy a curious glance, but nodded con-
firmation.

"You mean you didn't have any problems?" Kirk said,
with slight but visible incredulity.

"None worth reporting, Captain," Spock said.

"Let me be the judge of that.''

"Only such minor disturbances, Captain, as are inevitable when humans are involved.''

"Or are involved with Vulcans," McCoy added.

"Understood, gentlemen. I hope my last orders were
helpful in solving the problems not worth reporting.''

"Orders, Captain?" Spock said.

"The orders I left for you—for both of you—on tape.''

"Oh, those orders!" said McCoy. "There wasn't time,
Captain. We never got a chance to listen to them.''

"The crisis was upon us and then passed so quickly,
Captain, that . . .''

"I see," Kirk said, smiling. "Nothing worth reporting
happened, and it all happened so quickly. Good. Well, let's
hope there will be no similar opportunity to test those orders
that you never heard. Let's get to work.''

FOR THE WORLD IS HOLLOW AND I HAVE TOUCHED THE SKY

Writer: Rik Vollaerts
Director: Tony Leader
Guest stars: Kate Woodville, John Lormer

That "Bones" McCoy was a lonely man, Kirk knew. That he'd joined the service after some serious personal tragedy in his life, Kirk suspended. What he hadn't realized was the fierce pride in McCoy that made a virtual fetish of silence about any private pain. So he was startled by his violent reaction to the discovery that Nurse Chapel had exceeded what McCoy called her "professional authority."

Entering Sickbay, Kirk found her close to tears. "You had no business to call Captain Kirk!" McCoy was storming at her. "You're excused! You may go to your quarters!"

She blew her nose. "I'm a nurse first, Doctor—and a crew member of the *Enterprise* second," she said, chin firm under her reddened eyes.

"I said you were excused, Nurse!"

Christine swallowed. The hurt in her face was openly appealing. She blew her nose again, looking at Kirk, while McCoy said gruffly, "Christine, please—for God's sake, stop crying! I'll give the Captain a full report, I promise."

She hurried out, and Kirk said, "Well, that was quite a dramatic little scene."

McCoy squared his shoulders. "I've completed the standard physical examinations of the entire crew."

"Good," Kirk said.

"The crew is fit. I found nothing unusual—with one exception."

"Serious?"

"Terminal."

Kirk, shocked, said, "You're sure?"

"Positive. A rare blood disease. Affects one spaceship crew member in fifty thousand."

"What is it?"

"Xenopolycythemia. There is no cure."

"Who?"

"He has one year to live—at the outside chance. He should be relieved of duty as soon as possible."

Kirk spoke quietly. "Who is it, Bones?"

"The ship's chief medical officer."

There was a pause. Then Kirk said, "You mean yourself?"

McCoy reached for a colored tape cartridge on his desk. He stood at stiff attention as he handed it to Kirk. "That's the full report, sir. You'll want it quickly relayed to Starfleet Command—to arrange my replacement."

Wordless, Kirk just looked at him, too stunned to speak. After a moment, he replaced the cartridge on the desk as though it had bit him. McCoy said, "I'll be most effective on the job in the time left to me if you will keep this to yourself."

Kirk shook his head. "There must be *something* that can be done!"

"There isn't." McCoy's voice was harsh. "I've kept up on all the research. I've told you!"

The anguish on Kirk's face broke him. He sank down in the chair at his desk.

"It's terminal, Jim. Terminal."

Though red alert had been called on the *Enterprise*, Kirk was in his quarters. A "replacement" for Bones. Military language was a peculiar thing. How did one "replace" the experience of a human being—the intimacy, the friendship forged out of a thousand shared dangers? "One year to live—at the outside chance." When you got down to the brass tacks of the human portion, you wished that speech had never been invented. But it had been. Like red alerts. They'd been invented, too. In order to remind you that you were Captain of a starship as well as the longtime comrade of a dying man.

As he stepped from the bridge elevator, Spock silently rose from the command chair to relinquish it to him.

"What is that stuff on the screen, Mr. Spock? Those moving pinpoints? A missile spread?"

"A very archaic type, Captain. Sublight space."

"Aye, and chemically fueled to boot, sir," Scott said.

"Anything on communications, Lieutenant Uhura?"

"Nothing, sir. All bands clear."

"Course of the missiles, Mr. Spock?"

"The *Enterprise* would appear to be their target, Captain."

Prepare phaser banks. Yes. Two of them. He gave the order. "Get a fix, Mr. Chekov, on the missiles' point of origin."

"Aye, Captain."

"Mr. Sulu, fire phasers."

The clutch of missiles exploded in a blinding flash. "Well, that's that," Kirk said. "Mr. Chekov, alter course to missile point of origin."

"Course change laid in, sir."

"Warp three, Mr. Sulu."

Spock spoke from the computer station. "They were very ancient missiles, Captain. Sensor reading indicates an age of over ten thousand years."

"Odd," said Kirk. "How could they still be functional?"

"They evidently had an inertial guidance system that made any other communications control unnecessary."

"And the warheads, Captain," Scott said. "Nuclear fusion type according to my readings."

Spock spoke again. "We're approaching the coordinates of the hostile vessel, Captain."

"Get it on the screen, Mr. Sulu."

The term "vessel" seemed to be inappropriate. What had appeared on the screen was a huge asteroid. It was roughly round, jagged, its rocky mass pitted by thousands of years of meteor hits.

"Mr. Spock, we've got maximum magnification. Is the object on the screen what it looks to be—an asteroid?"

"Yes, sir. Some two hundred miles in diameter."

"Could the hostile vessel be hiding behind it?"

"Impossible, Captain. I've had that area under scanner constantly."

"Then the missiles' point of origin is that asteroid?"

"Yes, sir."

Kirk got up and went to Spock's station. "Full sensor probe, Mr. Spock."

After a moment, Spock withdrew his head from his computer's hood. "Typical asteroid chemically but it is not orbiting, Captain. It is pursuing an independent course through this solar system."

"How can it?" Kirk said. "Unless it's powered—a spaceship!"

Spock cocked an eyebrow in what for him was amazement. Then he said slowly, "It *is* under power—and correcting for all gravitational stresses." He dived under his hood again.

"Power source?" Kirk asked.

"Atomic, very archaic. Leaving a trail of debris and hard radiation."

Kirk frowned briefly. "Plot the course of the asteroid, Mr. Chekov."

Once more Spock withdrew his head. "The asteroid's outer shell is hollow. It surrounds an independent inner core with a breathable atmosphere—sensors record no life forms."

"Then it must be on automatic controls," contributed Scott.

Spock nodded. "And its builders—or passengers—are dead."

Chekov said, "Course of asteroid—I mean spaceship— 241 mark 17."

Spock had stooped swiftly to his console. He pushed several controls. Then he looked up. "Sir, that reading Ensign Chekov just gave us puts the asteroid ship on a collision course with planet Daran V!"

"Daran V!" Kirk stared at him. "My memory banks say that's an inhabited planet, Mr. Spock!"

"Yes, sir. Population, approximately three billion, seven hundred and twenty-four million." He paused, glancing back at his console panel. "Estimated time of impact: thirteen months, six days."

"Well," Kirk said. "That's a pretty extensive population." He whirled to Sulu. "Mr. Sulu, match *Enterprise* speed with the asteroid ship's. Mr. Spock and I are transporting aboard her. Mr. Scott, you have the con.''

They entered the Transporter Room to see Christine Chapel handing his tricorder to McCoy. "A lot can happen in a year," she was saying. "Give yourself every minute of it."

"Thanks," McCoy said, and slung the tricorder over his shoulder. Ignoring Kirk and Spock, he stepped up on the Transporter platform, taking position on one of its circles.

Kirk walked over to him. "Bones," he said, "Spock and I will handle this one."

"Without me?" McCoy said. "You'll never make it back here without me."

"I feel it would be wiser if . . . ."

"I'm fine, thank you, Captain," McCoy brushed him off. "I want to go."

So that was how Bones wanted it played. He wasn't fatally ill. The word terminal might never have been spoken. "All right, Bones. You're probably right. If we make it back here, we'll need you with us." He took up his own position on the platform between Spock and McCoy.

They arrived on a land area of the asteroid ship. As though land on an asteroid weren't strange enough, strange plants, coiling back tendrils abounded, their strange roots sunk in deep, smoking fissures. High mountains shouldered up in the distance. Otherwise, the view showed only rubble and pockmarked rocks.

McCoy said, "You'd swear you were on a planet's surface."

Spock tossed away a stone he'd examined. "The question is, why make a ship look like a planet?"

"You wouldn't even know you were on a spaceship." Kirk jerked his com unit from his belt. "Kirk to *Enterprise*."

"Scott here, Captain."

"Transported without incident. Kirk out." He rehung his communicator on his belt, and was moving forward when, to his far left, his eye caught the glint of sunlight on metal. "Over there," he said. "Look . . ."

It was a row of metal cylinders. They were all about eight feet high, their width almost matching their height, and regularly spaced fifty feet apart. The men approached the nearest one, examining it carefully without touching it. "No apparent opening," Kirk observed.

"Spock, you found no intelligent life forms," McCoy said, "but surely these are evidence of . . ."

"This asteroid ship is ten thousand years old, Doctor. They may be evidence of the existence of some previous life forms." He checked his tricorder. "Certainly, there are no signs of life now."

They eyed the enigmatic cylinder again before they walked on to the next one. It was a duplicate of the first. As they reached the third, the two cylinders behind them suddenly opened, disgorging two groups of men, clad in shaggy homespun. Armed with short daggers and broadswords, they moved silently, trailing the *Enterprise* trio. A slim and beautiful woman followed them. She halted as the men charged.

The struggle was quick and violent. Outnumbered, Spock took several blows from sword hilts before he dropped to the ground, half-conscious. McCoy, head down, rushed a man off his feet, the momentum of his plunge crashing him into the woman. Her eyes widened in a surprise that contained no fear. Startled by her beauty, McCoy was brought up short, taking in the lustrous black hair piled on her head in fantastic loops, her glittering black leotardlike garment. Then he was stunned by a smash on the head. Kirk, going down under a swarming attack, saw the broadsword lifting up over McCoy and yelled, *"Bones!"*

The woman raised her right hand.

The broadsword was stayed in midstroke. McCoy was pulled to his feet. He shook his head, trying to clear it. Vaguely, he became aware of hands fumbling at his belt. Then his arms were jerked behind his back. Disarmed of phasers and communicators, he, Kirk and Spock were herded over to the woman.

"These are your weapons?" she asked, holding their belts in her right hand.

"Yes," Kirk said. "Of a kind. Weapons and communication devices. Let me help my friend!" He struggled to pull free. The woman made a commanding gesture. Released, he rushed over to the still groggy McCoy. "Bones, are you all right?"

"I—I think so, Jim."

The woman's dark eyes were on McCoy. "I am called Natira," she told him. "I am the High Priestess of the People. Welcome to the world of Yonada."

"We have received more desirable welcomes," Kirk said.

She ignored him. "Bring them!" she ordered their guards.

She led the way to an open cylinder. They were in an apparently endless, lighted corridor, lined by curious people in their homespun clothing. As Natira passed them, they bowed deeply. She was nearing an arched portal. It was flanked by two ornately decorated pillars, their carvings suggestive of a form of writing, cut deep into the stone. Natira, bowing herself, touched some hidden device that opened the massive door. But keen-eyed Spock had registered its location. He had also observed the writing.

The large room they entered was dim, its sole light a glow that shone from under its central dais. Its rich ornamentation matched that of the portal.

"You will kneel," Natira said.

There was no point, Kirk thought, in making an issue of it. He nodded at Spock and McCoy. They knelt. Natira, stepping onto the dais, turned to what was clearly an altar. Etched into its stone was a design that resembled a solar system. As Natira fell to her knees before the altar, light filled the room.

McCoy, his voice lowered, said, "She called this the world. These people don't know they're on a spaceship."

Kirk nodded. "Possible. The ship's been in flight for a long time."

"That writing," Spock said, "resembles the lexicography of the Fabrini."

But Natira, her arms upraised, was speaking. "O Oracle of the People, O most wise and most perfect, strangers have come to our world. They bear instruments we do not understand."

Light blazed from the altar. As though it had strengthened her to ask the question, she rose to her feet, turned and said, "Who are you?"

"I am Captain Kirk of the Starship *Enterprise*. This is

Dr. McCoy, our Medical Officer. Mr. Spock is my First Officer.''

"And for what reason do you visit this world?''

The word "world" again. Kirk and McCoy exchanged a look.

"We come in friendship," Kirk said.

The sound of thunder crashed from the altar. A booming echo of the thunder, the voice of the Oracle spoke.

"Learn what it means to be our enemy. Learn what that means before you learn what it means to be our friend.''

Lightning flashed. The three *Enterprise* men were felled to the floor by a near-lethal charge of electricity.

McCoy was taking too long to recover consciousness. He continued to lay, white-faced, in a sleeping alcove of their lavishly decorated guest quarters. Spock, who had been trying to work out muscle spasms in his shoulders, joined Kirk at McCoy's couch.

"He must have suffered an excessively intense electrical shock," he said.

"No. I don't think that's it," Kirk said. He reached for McCoy's pulse. Spock, aware of the deep concern in Kirk's face, was puzzled. "Nothing else could have caused this, sir." He paused. "That is—nothing that has occurred down *here*.''

Kirk glanced up at Spock. He knew that the Vulcan had sensed something of the real cause of his anxiety. "The shock was unusually serious because of McCoy's weakened condition," he said.

"May I ask precisely what is troubling the Doctor?''

"Yes, Mr. Spock. He'd never tell you himself. But now I think he'd want you to know. He has xenopolycythemia.''

Spock stiffened. After a long moment, he said quietly, "I know of the disease, Captain.''

"Then you know there's nothing that can be done.'' As he spoke, McCoy stirred. His eyes opened. Kirk stooped over him. "How is it now, Bones?''

"All right," McCoy said. He sat up, pulling himself rapidly together. "How are *you*, Spock?''

"Fine, thank you. The Captain and I must have received a less violent electrical charge.''

Falsely hearty, McCoy said, "That Oracle really got to me. I must be especially susceptible to his magic spells."

"Spock knows," Kirk said. "I told him, Bones."

There was relief in McCoy's face. He stood up. "Hadn't we better find this ship's control room and get these people off their collision course?"

"You're in no shape to be up," Kirk said.

"Ridiculous!" McCoy said. *"I'm up!"*

Kirk saw one of the alcove's curtains sway. He strode to it, jerking it aside. A shabby old man, fear in his face, was huddled against the wall. He peered into Kirk's face. What he saw in it must have reassured him. He moved away from the wall, hesitated, took some powder from a pouch hung over his shoulder. "For strength," he said. He held out the pouch to them. "Many of us have felt the power of our Oracle. This powder will be of benefit. You are not of Yonada."

"No," Kirk said gently. "We come from outside your world."

The old hand reached out to touch Kirk's arm. "You are as we are?"

"The same," Kirk said.

"You are the first to come here. I am ignorant. Tell me of the outside."

"What do you wish to know?"

"Where is outside?"

Kirk pointed skyward. "It's up there."

The filmed eyes glanced up at the ceiling. Like a child put off by an adult lie, the old man looked back at Kirk in mixed disbelief and disappointment. Kirk smiled at him. "The outside is up there and all around."

"So *they* say, also," the old man said sadly. "Years ago, I climbed the mountains, even though it is forbidden."

"Why is it forbidden?" Kirk asked.

"I am not sure. But things are not as they teach us— for the world is hollow and I have touched the sky."

The voice had sunk into a terrified whisper. As he uttered the last words, the old man screamed in sudden agony, clutching at his temples. He collapsed in a sprawled heap on the floor. Horrified, Kirk saw a spot on one temple flash into a pulsating glow. Then the flare died.

McCoy examined the spot. "Something under the

skin." He moved the shabby homespun to check the heart.
"Jim, he's dead."

Kirk looked down at the heap. " 'For the world is hollow and I have touched the sky.' What an epitaph for a human life!"

Spock said, "He said it was forbidden to climb the mountains."

"Of course it's forbidden," Kirk said. "If you climbed the mountains, you might discover you were living in an asteroid spaceship, not in the world at all. *That* I'll bet is the forbidden knowledge."

"What happened?"

It was Natira. She had entered their quarters with two women bearing platters of fruit and wine. At the sight of the crumpled body, their faces convulsed with terror. But Natira knelt down beside it.

"We don't know what happened," Kirk told her. "He suddenly screamed in pain—and died."

She bent her head in prayer. "Forgive him, O Oracle, most wise and most perfect. He was an old man—and old men are sometimes foolish." She rose to her feet. "But it is written that those of the People who sin or speak evil will be punished."

The severity in her face softened into sadness. She touched a wall button. To the guards who entered she said, "Take him away—gently. He served well and for many years." Then she spoke to the women. "Place the food on the table and go."

As the door closed behind them, she crossed to McCoy. "You do not seem well. It is distressing to me."

"No," he said. "I am all right."

"It is the wish of the Oracle that you now be treated as honored guests. I will serve you with my own hands." But the tray she arranged with fruit and wine was taken to McCoy. When she left them to prepare the other trays, Kirk said, "You seem favored, Bones."

"Indeed, Doctor," Spock said, "the lady has shown a preference for you from the beginning."

"Nobody can blame her for that," McCoy retorted.

"Personally," Kirk said, "I find her taste questionable." McCoy, sipping wine, said, "My charm has always been fatal,'' but Kirk noted that his eyes were nevertheless fixed on the graceful bend of the woman at the table. "If it's so fatal,'' he said, "why don't you arrange to spend some time alone with the lady? Then Spock and I might find a chance to locate the power controls of this place.''

Natira was back, holding two goblets of wine. "It is time that our other guests refresh themselves.''

Kirk lifted his goblet. "To our good friends of Yonada.''

"We are most interested in your world,'' Spock said.

"That pleases us.''

"Then perhaps you wouldn't mind if we looked around a bit,'' Kirk ventured.

"You will be safe,'' she said. "The People know of you now.''

McCoy coughed uncomfortably. She went to him swiftly. "I do not think you are yet strong enough to look around with your friends.''

"Perhaps not,'' he smiled.

"Then why not remain here? Rest—and we will talk.''

She *was* beautiful. "I should like that,'' McCoy said.

She turned to Kirk. "But you—you and Mr. Spock— you are free to go about and meet our People.''

"Thank you,'' he said. "We appreciate your looking after Dr. McCoy.''

"Not at all,'' she inclined her head. "We shall make him well.'' She saw them to the door. Then she hastened back to McCoy. As she sat down on the couch beside him, he said, "I am curious. How did the Oracle punish the old man?''

The dark lashes lowered. "I—cannot tell you now.''

"There's some way by which the Oracle knows what you say, isn't there?''

"What we say—what we think. The Oracle knows the minds and hearts of all the People.''

McCoy's forehead creased a worried frown. Concerned, Natira extended a white hand that tried to stroke the frown away. "I did not know you would be hurt so badly.''

"Perhaps we had to learn the power of the Oracle.''

"McCoy. There is something I must say. Since the moment I saw you—'' She took a deep breath. ''It is not the custom of the People to hide their feelings.''

McCoy said to himself, Watch your step, boy. But to her, he said, ''Honesty is usually wisdom.''

''Is there a woman for you?'' she asked.

He could smell the fragrance of the lustrous black hair near his shoulder. This woman was truthful as well as beautiful. So he gave her the truth. ''No,'' he said. ''No, there isn't.''

The lashes lifted—and he got the full impact of her open femininity. ''Does McCoy find me attractive?''

''Yes,'' he said. ''I do. I do indeed.''

She took his face between her hands, looking deep into his eyes. ''I hope you men of space—of other worlds, hold truth as dear as we do.''

Watching his step was becoming difficult. ''We do,'' he said.

''It is dear to me,'' she said. ''So I wish you to stay here on Yonada. I want you for my mate.''

McCoy took one of the hands from his face and kissed it. The Eagle Scout in him whispered, Brother, douse this campfire. But in him was also a man under sentence of death; a man with one year to live—one with a new, very intense desire to make that last year count. He turned the hand over to kiss its palm. ''But we are strangers to each other,'' he said.

''Is it not the nature of men and women—that pleasure lies in learning about each other?''

''Yes.''

''Then let the thought rest in your heart, McCoy, while I tell you about the Promise. In the fullness of time, the People will reach a new world, rich, green, so lovely to the eyes it will fill them with tears of joy. You can share that new world with me. You shall be its master because you'll be my master.''

''When will you reach this new world?''

''Soon. The Oracle will only say—soon.''

There was an innocence about her that opened his heart. Incredibly, he heard himself cry out, ''Natira, Natira, if you only knew how much I've needed a future!''

''You have been lonely,'' she said. She picked up the

wine glass and held it to his lips. "It is all over, the loneliness. There shall be no more loneliness for you."

He drank and set the glass aside. "Natira—there's something I must tell you . . ."

"Sssh," she said. "There is nothing you need to say."

"But there is."

She removed the hand she had placed over his mouth. "Then tell me, if the telling is such a need."

"I am ill," he said. "I have an illness for which there is no cure. I have one year to live, Natira."

The dark eyes did not flinch. "A year can be a lifetime, McCoy."

"It is my entire lifetime."

"Until I saw you my heart was empty. It sustained my life—and nothing more. Now it sings. I am grateful for the feeling that you have made it feel whether it lasts for a day—a month—a year—whatever time the Creators give to us."

He took her in his arms.

Kirk and Spock were meeting curious looks as they walked down a corridor of the asteroid ship. The more people they encountered, the clearer it became they had no inkling of the real nature of their world. Spock said, "Whoever built this ship must have given them a religion that would control their curiosity."

"Judging by the old man, suppressing curiosity is handled very directly," Kirk said. They had reached the portal of the Oracle Room. Pretending to a casual interest in its carved stone pillars, Spock eyed them keenly. "Yes," he said, "the writing is that of the Fabrini. I can read it."

"Fabrina?" Kirk said. "Didn't the sun of the Fabrina system go nova and destroy its planets?"

"It did, Captain. Toward the end, the Fabrini lived underground as the people do here."

"Perhaps some of them were put aboard this ship to be sent to another planet." Kirk glanced up and down the corridor. It was almost empty. "And these are their descendants."

They were alone now in the corridor. Kirk tried and failed to open the Oracle Room's door. Spock touched the secret opening device set into one of the pillars. Inside, they flattened themselves against a wall. The door closed behind them. Nothing happened. Kirk, his voice low, said, "The Oracle doesn't seem to know we are here. What alerted it the first time?"

Spock moved a few steps toward the central dais. "Captain, the Oracle's misbehavior occurred when Natira knelt on that platform." Kirk stepped onto the platform. He walked carefully around it. Again, nothing happened. "Mr. Spock, continue investigating. The clue to the control place must be here somewhere." But carvings on a wall had caught Spock's attention. "More writing," he said. "It says nothing to suggest this is anything but a planet. Nor is there any question that the builders of the ship are to be considered gods."

Kirk had found a stone monolith set in a niche. It bore a carved design of a sun and planets. Spock joined him. "Eight planets, Captain. Eight. That was the number in the solar system of Fabrina."

"Then there's no doubt that these People are the Fabrini's descendants?"

"None, sir. And no doubt they have been in flight on this asteroid ship for ten thousand years." As Spock spoke, there was the sound of the door opening. They hastily slid behind the monolith. Kirk cautiously peered around it to see Natira, alone, crossing the room to the platform. She knelt. As before, hot light flared from the altar.

"Speak," said the Oracle.

"It is I, Natira."

"Speak."

"It is written that only the High Priestess of the People may select her mate."

"It is so written."

"For the rest of the People—mating and bearing is only permitted by the will of the Creators."

"Of necessity. Our world is small."

"The three strangers among us—there is one among them called McCoy. I wish him to remain with the People—as my mate."

Kirk gave a soundless whistle. Bones certainly had lost no time. Spock cocked an eyebrow, looking at Kirk.

"Does the stranger agree to this?" queried the Oracle.

"I have asked him. He has not yet given me his answer."

"He must become one of the People. He must worship the Creators and agree to the insertion of the obedience instrument."

"He will be told what must be done."

"If he agrees to all things, it is permitted. Teach him our laws so that he commits no sacrilege, no offense against the People—or the Creators."

"It shall be as you say, O most wise."

Natira rose, bowed twice, backed away from the altar and walked toward the door. As Kirk watched her go, his sleeve brushed against the monolith's carved design. The Oracle Room reverberated with a high-pitched, ululating whine. Natira wheeled from the door. The whine turned to a blazing white light. It turned to focus on Kirk and Spock. They went rigid, unable to move.

Natira rushed to the altar.

"Who are the intruders?" demanded the booming voice.

"Two of the strangers."

"McCoy is one of them?"

"No."

"These two have committed sacrilege. You know what must be done."

"I know."

Guards rushed into the room. The light that held Kirk and Spock died, leaving them dazed. Natira pointed to them. "Take them," she told the guards.

As they were seized, she walked up to them. "You have been most foolish," she said. "You have misused our hospitality. And you have more seriously sinned—a sin for which death is the punishment!"

Natira withstood the storm of McCoy's wrath quietly. As he paused in his furious pacing of her quarters, she said—and for the third time—"They entered the Oracle Room."

"And why is death the penalty for that?" he shouted. "They acted out of ignorance!"

"They said they came in friendship. They betrayed our trust. I can make no other decision."

He wheeled to face her. "Natira, you must let them return to their ship!"

"I cannot."

"For me," he said. He pulled her from her couch and into his arms. "I have made my decision. I'm staying with you—here on Yonada."

She swayed with the relief of her love. Into the ear against his cheek, McCoy said, "What they did, they did because they thought they had to. You will not regret letting them go. I am happy for the first time in my life. How can I remain happy, knowing you commanded the death of my friends?"

She lifted her mouth for his kiss. "So be it," she said. "I will give you their lives to show you my love."

"My heart sings now," McCoy said. "Let me tell them. They will need their communications units to return to their ship."

"Very well, McCoy. All shall be as you wish."

He left her for the corridor where Kirk and Spock were waiting under guard. He nodded to the guards. When they disappeared down the corridor, he handed the communicators to Kirk. Kirk passed one to Spock. "Where's yours?" he asked. "You're coming with us, aren't you?"

"No, I'm not," McCoy said.

"But this isn't a planet, Bones! It's a spaceship on a collision course with Daran V!"

"Jim, I'm on something of a collision course myself."

"I order you to return to the ship, Dr. McCoy!"

"And I refuse! I intend to stay right here—on this ship. Natira has asked me to stay. So I shall stay."

"As her husband?"

"Yes. I love her." There were tears in his eyes. "Is it so much to ask, Jim, to let me love?"

"No." Kirk straightened his shoulders. "But does she know—how much of a future you'll have together?"

"Yes. I have told her."

"Bones, if the course of this ship isn't corrected, we'll have to blow it out of space."

"I'll find a way—or you will. You won't destroy Yonada and the people."

Kirk shook his head. "This isn't like you—suddenly

giving up—quitting—not fighting any more. You're sick—and you're hiding behind a woman's skirts!''

McCoy swung a fist and Kirk took it square on the chin. He staggered. Spock steadied him. McCoy was yelling, ''Sick? Not fighting? Come on, Captain! Try me again!''

Very grave, Spock said, ''This conduct is very unlike you, Doctor.''

Kirk fumbled for his communicator. ''Kirk calling *Enterprise*. Come in, *Enterprise*.''

''Scott here, Captain.''

''Lock in on our signals. Transport Mr. Spock and me aboard at once.''

''What about Dr. McCoy?''

Yes, indeed. What *about* Doctor McCoy? He looked at his friend. ''He is staying here, Mr. Scott. Kirk out.''

Spock moved to Kirk, flipping open his own communicator. McCoy backed away. They broke into sparkle—and were gone. Savagely, McCoy dragged a sleeve over his tear-blinded eyes.

Custom required him to stand alone before the Oracle. It spoke.

''To become one of the People of Yonada, the instrument of obedience must be made part of your flesh. Do you now give your consent?''

Natira came forward. She crossed to another side of the altar and opened a small casket.

''I give my consent,'' McCoy said. As she removed a small device from the casket, her dark eyes met his with a look of pure love. ''Say now, McCoy,'' she said. ''For once it is done, it is done.''

''Let it be done,'' he said.

She came to him. Placing the device against his temple, she activated it. He heard a hissing sound. There was a thudding in his head. Instinctively his hand went to the place of insertion. ''You are now one with my People,'' she said. ''Kneel with me.''

He reached for her hand. She said, ''I here pledge you the love you want and will make beautiful your time.''

''We are now of one mind,'' he said.

''One heart.''

"One life," he said.

"We shall build the new world of the Promise together, O most wise and most perfect." They rose. She moved into his arms and he kissed her.

The Oracle said, "Teach him what he must know as one of the people."

Natira bowed. Obediently, she led McCoy to the stone monolith. She touched a button—and the carved inset depicting a sun and eight planets slid aside to reveal a large book. "This is the Book of the People," she said. "It is to be opened and read when we reach the world of the Promise. It was given by the Creators."

"Do the People know the contents of the book?"

"Only that it tells of our world here. And why we must one day leave it for the new one."

"Has the reason for leaving been revealed to the People?"

"No! It has not."

Then they'd been right, McCoy realized. Yonada's inhabitants were unaware they lived on a spaceship. "Has it been revealed to you, Natira? As the Priestess of the People?"

She shook her head. "I know only of the new world promised to us, much greater than this little one—verdant and fruitful but empty of living beings. It waits for us."

"Don't you long to know the book's secrets?"

"It is enough for me to know that we shall understand all that now is hidden when we reach our home." She touched the button in the monolith. Its carved inset slid back.

"What is the law concerning the book?"

"To touch it—to allow it to be seen by a nonbeliever is blasphemy to be punished by death."

On the *Enterprise* Kirk had made his first act a report to Starfleet Command. It had to be told, not only of McCoy's critical illness, but of their failure to correct the collision course of the asteroid ship. Its Chief of Operations, Admiral Westervliet himself, appeared on the screen in Kirk's quarters to respond to the news.

"Medical Headquarters will supply you with a list of

space physicians and their biographies, Captain. You will find
a replacement for Dr. McCoy among them.''

Kirk addressed the stiffly mustached face on the screen.
"Yes, Admiral. However, Starfleet's orders to continue our
mission is creating difficulties.''

"Difficulties? Perhaps I've failed to make myself clear,
Captain. You have been relieved of all responsibility for al-
teration of the course of the asteroid ship Yonada. Starfleet
Command will take care of the situation.''

"That is the problem, sir,'' Kirk said.

"A problem? For whom?''

"My crew, sir. Dr. McCoy's illness has become generally known. His condition forced us to leave him on Yonada. His safety depends on the safety of Yonada. To leave
this area before Yonada's safety is certain would create a morale problem for the crew. It's a purely human one, of
course.''

Westervliet had a habit of attacking his mustache when
human problems were mentioned. Now it was taking a beating.

"Yes,'' he said. "Well, Captain Kirk, I certainly sympathize with your wish to remain in Dr. McCoy's vicinity.
But the general mission of the *Enterprise* is galactic investigation. You will continue with it.''

"Yes, Admiral,'' Kirk said. "One request, however.
Should a cure for Doctor McCoy's disease be discovered, will
you advise the *Enterprise*?''

"That is not a request, Captain. Between you and me,
it's an order, isn't it?''

"Yes, sir. Thank you, sir.''

Kirk, switching off the screen, sat still in his chair.
McCoy had made his choice. No appeal had been able to
change it. And who was to say it wasn't the right one? A year
of life with a woman's love against a year of life without it.
Bones. He was going to miss him. The intercom squeaked.
He rose to hit the button. "Kirk here.''

"Dr. McCoy for you, Captain,'' Uhura said. "He has
an urgent message.''

"Put him on!''

"Jim?''

"Yes, Bones.''

"We may be able to get these people back on course!" Kirk's pulse raced. "Have you located the controls?"

"No—but I've seen a book that contains all the knowledge of Yonada's builders. If you can get to it, Spock can dig out the information."

"Where is it?" Kirk asked.

A scream of agony burst from the intercom. "Bones! What's happening? Bones!"

Silence. Frantic, Kirk tried again. "McCoy, what *is* it? What has been done to you? Bones, come in . . ."

But he knew what had happened. Torture, death.

The Oracle had taken McCoy's life in exchange for his forbidden revelation.

Kirk's jaw muscles set hard. "Transporter Room," he told the intercom.

He and Spock materialized in Natira's quarters. She was cradling McCoy's head in her arms. But his face was contorted with pain. Kirk saw him struggle to lift his head. It sank back into Natira's lap.

She looked at them. Dully, her voice toneless, she said, "You have killed your friend. I will have you put to death."

"Let me help you," Kirk said.

"Until you are dead, he will think of you and disobey. While you live, my beloved cannot forget you. So I shall see you die."

She made a move to get up and Kirk grabbed her, clapping his hand over her mouth. "Spock," he said, "help McCoy."

"Yes, Captain." Spock unslung his tricorder. From it he removed a tiny electronic device. Bending over McCoy's motionless body, he pressed the device on the spot where the instrument of obedience had been inserted. When he withdrew it, the insert was clinging to it. He jerked it clear. Then he handed it to Natira. She stared at him, unbelieving. A little moan broke from her. Kirk released her. She sank to the floor. After a moment, she pulled herself up to her hands and knees and crawled over to McCoy. She touched his temple. "My beloved is again a stranger. We are no longer one life." She burst into passionate weeping. "Why have you done this to us? Why?"

"He is still yours," Kirk said gently.

The tears choked her. "It is—forbidden. He is not of
our people—now. You have released him—from his vow of
obedience."

"We have released him from the cruelty of your Oracle," Kirk said.

She closed her eyes, unhearing, her body racked with
sobs. Beside her, Kirk saw McCoy's eyelids flicker open. He
went to him quickly, bending over him. "You spoke of a
book," he said. "Where is it, Bones?"

Natira leaped to her feet with a shriek. "You must not
know! You must not know that!"

McCoy looked up into Kirk's eyes. "The Oracle
Room," he whispered.

"You will never see the Book!" cried Natira. "It is
blasphemy!" She ran to the door, calling, "Guards! Guards!"

Kirk caught her, closing his hand over her mouth again.
"You must listen to me, Natira!" She pulled away from him
and he jerked her back. "*Listen to me!* If you do not understand what I tell you, you may call the guards. And we will
accept whatever punishment is decreed. *But now you must
listen!*"

She slowly lifted the tear-wet lashes. "What is it you
wish to say?"

"I shall tell you the truth, Natira—the truth about your
world of Yonada. And you will trust it as true as a child trusts
what is true. Years ago, ten thousand years ago, a sun died
and the sun's worlds died with it. Its worlds were the eight
ones you see pictured on the stone pillar in the Oracle Room."

"Yonada is one of those worlds," she said.

"No. It was the world of your ancestors—your creators." He paused to give her time. After a moment, he quietly added, "It no longer exists, Natira."

"You are mad," she whispered. "You are mad."

"Hear me out, Natira! Your ancestors knew their world
was about to die. They wanted their race to live. So they built
a great ship. On it they placed their best people. Then they
sent them and the ship into space."

"You wish me to believe that Yonada is a ship?"

"Yes," Kirk said.

"But we have a sun! It did not die. And at night I see the stars!"

"No. You have never seen the sun. You have never seen the stars. You live inside a hollow ball. Your fathers created the ball to protect you—to take you on the great journey to the new safe world of the Promise."

In her face he could see half-thought thoughts reviving, completing themselves. But the growing perception was painful. Yet it had come. She spoke very slowly. "The truth—why do you bring it to Yonada?"

"We had to. Your ship has done well—but its machinery is tired. It must be mended. If we don't mend it, Yonada will strike and kill another great world it knows nothing about."

Belief flooded into her. With it came the realization of betrayal.

"Why has this truth not been told us? Why have we been kept in darkness?"

Kirk went to her. But she pushed him away, overwhelmed by the sense of an incredible treachery. "No! You have lied! I believe only the Oracle! I must believe!"

Kirk said, "Let us remove the instrument of obedience. Let us remove it for the truth's sake."

She was gone, fled out the door. Kirk turned to Spock. "Do you think she understood me?" he said. But Spock was at the open door. Kirk saw him nod pleasantly to a passing guard before he quietly closed the door. "She hasn't sent the guards to detain us, Captain. It is my supposition that she understood a great deal."

Behind them, McCoy had struggled shakily to his feet. Now he pushed past them. "Natira! I have to go to her. I must go to her in the Oracle Room."

She was on her knees before the altar, her eyes shut in rapt devotion.

The thunder voice spoke. "You have listened to the words of the nonbelievers."

"I have listened."

"You felt the pain of warning."

"I felt the pain of warning."

"Why did you listen further?"

"They said they spoke the truth."

"Their truth is not your truth."

She opened her eyes. "Is truth not truth for all?"

"There is only one for you. Repent your disobedience."

"I must know the truth of the world!" she cried.

At the sound of her scream, Kirk rushed into the Oracle Room. He lifted Natira from the dais, but McCoy, reaching for her, took her in his arms, holding her close. Her body was stiff under spasms of pain. As one passed, she reached out a hand to caress his face. "Your friends have told me— much."

"They spoke the truth," McCoy said.

"I believe you. I believe . . ."

Agony convulsed her again. She fought it bravely. "I believe with you, my husband. We have been kept in darkness."

McCoy extended a hand to Spock. The tiny electronic device performed its function once more. When McCoy lifted it from Natira's temple, it held the obedience insert. He held it up for her to see. The grief of a great loss shadowed her dark eyes as she lapsed into unconsciousness.

"Is she all right?" Kirk asked.

"She will be. I'll stay with her."

Kirk said, "Mr. Spock—the Fabrina inset."

They were crossing to the monolith when the Oracle spoke, a fierce anger in its voice. "You blaspheme the temple!"

Kirk turned. "We do this for the survival of Yonada's people."

"You are forbidden to gaze at the Book!"

"We must consult it to help the people!"

"The punishment is death."

Kirk looked back at McCoy. "Bones?"

"Depress the side section," McCoy said.

A blast of heat struck them. Around them the walls had turned a radiant red. Even as he pressed the side of the monolith, the air he breathed was scorching Kirk's lungs. But the inset had slid open. He seized the book and passed it to Spock. "It must contain the plan. Is it indexed?"

"Yes, Captain. Here's the page . . ."

Yellow, brittle with age, the page's parchment showed

the same idealized sun, the same planet placements as the altar design and the inset. Arrows pointed to three of the planets. Spock translated the Fabrini writing at the top of the page. "Apply pressure simultaneously to the planets indicated."

The walls were glowing hotter. Spock tossed the book aside and they raced for the altar plaque. As Kirk pushed at the three planets, the altar moved forward. Then it stopped. Spock slid into the space behind it. Before he followed him, Kirk turned back to McCoy and Natira. "Let's get out of this heat," he called.

Spock had found a short passageway. As he approached its end wall, it lifted. At once he heard the hum of electronic power. A light shone on a button-crowded console. Spock studied it for a moment. Then he pressed a button. The light went out. "I've neutralized that heating element!" he called back to the others.

The heat in the Oracle Room rapidly cooled. Kirk and McCoy sat Natira down against an altar wall. "You'll be all right here now," Kirk said. "The Oracle can no longer punish."

He saw her rest her glossy head against McCoy's shoulder. Looking up at him, she said, "Your friends have ended the punishments?" He nodded. "And will they send this—this ship on to the place of the Promise?"

"Yes," he said. "That is their promise. Now I must help them. Come with me."

"No," she said.

"There is nothing to fear now, Natira. So come. We must hurry to join them."

"No. I cannot go with you." She paused. "It is not fear that holds me. I now understand the great purpose of our fathers. I must honor it, McCoy."

He stared at her in unbelief. "You mean to stay here—on Yonada?"

"I must remain with my people throughout our great journey."

"Natira, trust me! The Oracle will not harm us!"

"I stay because it is what I must do," she said.

"I will not leave you," McCoy said.

"Will McCoy stay here to die?"

The question shocked him into silence. He fell to his knees beside her. "Natira, you have given me reason to wish to live. But wishing is not enough. I must search through the universe to cure myself—and all those like me. I wanted you with me—with me . . ."

"This is my universe," she said. "You came here to save my people. Shall I abandon them?"

"I love you," McCoy said.

She kissed him. "If it is permitted, perhaps one day you, too, will see the land of our Promise. . . ."

It was good-bye. And he knew it. He reached for her blindly through a mist of tears.

In the asteroid ship's control room, Spock had located a weakness in one of its consoles' eight tubes.

"Enough to turn it off course?" Kirk asked.

"Yes, Captain. The engine can take a check." Kirk, studying control panels, was reminded of those of the *Enterprise*. "A very simple problem," Spock called from the engine room. "And comparatively easy to repair."

He came back, holding one hand out stiffly. "I think we can now attempt the course correction, sir."

"What was wrong?"

"In creating a completely natural environment for the people on this ship, its builders included many life forms—including insects. A control jet in there was blocked by a hornets' nest."

"You're not serious, Mr. Spock?"

Spock held up a forefinger. It was swollen to twice its size. "I destroyed the nest," he said. "In doing so, I was stung." He sat down, resuming his watch of the console instruments. "The guidance system is taking over, sir. I think we can revert to automatic controls."

"She's steady on course now," Kirk said.

They released the manual controls and were heading back to the Oracle Room when Spock stopped at a screened console of complex design. "Knowledge files," he said. "Those banks are filled with the total knowledge of the Fabrini. I presume they were prepared for the people to consult when they reach their destination." He left Kirk to examine the console more closely. "They seem to have amassed a great deal of medical knowledge."

Unslinging his tricorder, he slipped a taped disk into it. He passed it over the console. "The knowledge of the builders of this ship could be extremely valuable—even though it is ten thousand years old."

McCoy spoke from behind them. "Gentlemen, are we ready to return to the *Enterprise*?"

Kirk stared at him. It was best to ask no questions, he thought. "Yes, Bones, we are," he said. He flipped open his com unit. "Kirk to *Enterprise*. Landing party ready to beam aboard."

The screen in Sickbay held a series of chemical formulas in the Fabrini writing. Kirk and Spock, watching Christine Chapel prepare another air-hypo injection, saw that her hands were shaking. She noticed it, too. To quiet her agitation, she glanced at the life indicators at the head of McCoy's bed. The steady blinking of their lights steadied her. She thrust the air-hypo into a green liquid.

"Not another one?" McCoy said as she approached his bed. He made a face as the hypo took effect. But already it had made a fast change in the life support panel.

"Excellent, Doctor," Christine said. "You're quite able to see for yourself. The white corpuscle count is back to normal." She reached an arm under his shoulders to help him check the panel behind him. He still looked pained.

"Tell me, Doctor," Kirk wanted to know. "Why are cures so often as painful as the disease?"

"Jim, that is a very sore subject with medical men."

"Dr. McCoy," Spock said reprovingly, "it seems that the Fabrini cure for granulation of the hemoglobin has seriously damaged your gift for witty repartee."

Nurse Chapel had filled the hypo again. "This is the last one, Doctor."

Spock, his eyes on the life support panel, achieved a Vulcan triumph. Joy radiated from his impassive face. "Your hemoglobin count is now completely normal, Doctor. So the flow of oxygen to all the cells of your body is again up to its abundantly energetic level."

McCoy sat up. "Spock, I owe this to you. Had you not brought back that Fabrini knowledge . . ."

"My translation abilities are one of my most minor accomplishments," Spock said. "If you consider my major ones, Doctor . . ."

"I wonder if there's a Fabrini cure for a swelled head," McCoy speculated.

Kirk intervened. "Bones, the Fabrini descendants are scheduled to debark on their promised planet in exactly fourteen months and seven days."

The grin left McCoy's face. He looked at Kirk.

"Yes," Kirk said. "I expect you'd like to see the Fabrini descendants again to thank them personally. So I've arranged to be in the vicinity of their new home at the time of their arrival. You will want to be there to welcome them, won't you?"

"Thank you, Jim," McCoy said. "Thank you very much."

DAY OF THE DOVE

Writer: Jerome Bixby
Director: Marvin Chomsky
Guest stars: Michael Ansara, Susan Howard

≡

Though the planet had said it was under attack by an unidentified spacecraft, the *Enterprise* landing party had found only black dust, white rocks and strange clumps of moving plants. Its tricorders—McCoy's as well as Chekov's—refused to report any evidence of a colony or of people who could have signaled the message. Yet they had existed.

Kirk stooped for a handful of the black, powdery soil. "An SOS from a human settlement—one hundred men, women and children. All gone. Who did it? Why?"

As if in reply, his communicator beeped. "Spock here, sir. Sensors have picked up a Klingon ship closing in fast."

"Deflectors on, Mr. Spock! Protect yourselves. Total response if attacked." He closed the communicator, his face grim. So that was the answer—Klingons. They had destroyed the settlement. But Spock had more news of the Klingon ship. "Trouble aboard her, Captain. Evidence of explosions . . . massive damage. We never fired at her."

"Maintain full alert, Mr. Spock."

Behind his group the air was collecting into dazzle. Six Klingons in their stiff metallic tabards were materializing, their weapons aimed and ready. Their leader was the first to assume full shape. His hand, slant-eyed face distorted by fury, he reached out and swung Kirk around. "You attacked my ship!" he shouted. "Four hundred of my crew—dead! My vessel is disabled. I claim yours! You are prisoners of the Klingon Empire for committing a wanton act of war against it!" He nodded to his men. "Disarm them!"

Kirk had recognized the harsh, Mongol-like features. The Klingons' Kang. "We took no action against your ship," he said.

He'd been hustled into line with Chekov and McCoy. Kang paced before them. "For three years your Federation and our Empire have been at peace . . . a treaty we have honored to the letter . . ."

Kirk protested again. "We did not attack your ship."

"Were the screams of my men imaginary? What were your secret orders? To start a war? You have succeeded! Or maybe to test a new weapon. We shall be interested to examine it!"

Kirk said, "There was a Federation colony on this planet. *It* was destroyed."

"And by what? I see no bodies, no ruins. A colony of the invisible!"

"Perhaps a new *Klingon* weapon that leaves no traces. Federation ships don't specialize in sneak attacks!"

Along the ground near Kang a small, mushroom-shaped crystal was floating. Its swirling red color was concealed by a white rock and a faint, ugly throbbing came from it.

Kirk's patience was ebbing. No denial of guilt seemed able to penetrate the heavy bones of Kang's hairless skull. "You lured my ship into ambush with a false Klingon distress call!"

Kirk stared at him. "*You* received a distress call? *We* were the ones who received it!"

"I don't propose to spend any more time arguing your fantasies, Kirk! The *Enterprise* is ours! Instruct your Transporter Room. We are ready to beam aboard."

"Go to the devil," Kirk said.

"We have no devil—but we understand the habits of yours . . ." Still hidden among the rocks, the crystal's red glow brightened as Kang burst out, "I will torture you to death, one by one! Who will be the first? You, Kirk?"

Chekov suddenly exploded into action. He charged Kang, sobbing with rage. *"Swine! Filthy Klingon murderers!"* Kirk made a grab for him, missed—and Kang's men beat him to the ground. But he still sought to get at Kang. *"You killed my brother! Piotr!"*—the Arcanis Four Research Outpost . . .

a hundred peaceful people massacred—*just as you did here! My brother, Piotr . . .''*

Kang looked down at him. "So you volunteer to join him. That is loyalty." He gestured to one of his men. A sputtering device was pushed against Chekov's neck. He writhed with agony, doubled up. Kirk, wrenching forward, was immobilized by the Klingons. The device was readjusted—and Chekov screamed.

"You win, Kang!" Kirk said. "Stop the torture!"

"Jim!" McCoy cried. "You can't hand over the *Enterprise*!"

"Help Chekov, Bones."

Kang was eyeing Kirk. "Don't plan any tricks. I will kill a hundred hostages at the first sign of treachery!"

"I'll beam you aboard the *Enterprise*. Once we're there—no tricks."

"Your word?"

Kirk nodded; and Chekov, still convulsed with pain, cried, "Captain!—we can't! . . . don't let these . . . *animals* . . . have the ship!"

"Animals?" Kang said. "Your captain crawls like one. A Klingon would not have surrendered." He turned to Kirk. "Order everyone in this area to be transported up." He said something to his men, and Kirk, ringed by weapons, opened his communicator.

"Kirk to *Enterprise*. Mr. Spock . . ."

"Here, Captain."

"We have guests," Kirk told him. "Adjust Transporter for wide-field and beam-up everyone in the target area." His finger pressed a tiny control on the communicator.

"Yes, Captain."

Everybody shimmered out, Kirk under the weapons, Chekov supported by McCoy, both glaring.

In the *Enterprise* Transporter Room, only the landing party materialized. No Klingons stood on the platform.

Kirk stepped off his pad. "Full Security on the double, Mr. Galloway! Good work, Spock!"

As Galloway hit the intercom, the bewildered McCoy said, "What—happened?"

"Landing party brought up intact," Spock told him.

At the console, Scott spoke. "All others suspended in transit. Who are the guests, by the way, Captain?"

"Klingons."

Scott grinned happily, slapping the console. "They're in here—until we decide to rematerialize them."

"Galloway?" Kirk said.

"Security squads on the way, sir."

Chekov's voice was thick with hate. "Captain! Leave them on the planet! Leave them where they are! In nonexistence. That's so many less Klingon monsters in the galaxy!"

"And that's what they would do," Kirk said. As the Security detail rushed through the door, he spoke to the Transporter Chief. "Bring them in."

The six Klingons sparkled into shape on the platform. They all stiffened, taking in the changed situation. Outnumbered by the Security men, they made no resistance as they were disarmed. The weaponless Kang looked at Kirk.

"Liar!" He spat the word.

"I said no tricks *after* we reached the ship." Kirk stepped forward, formal, terse. "You are prisoners of the United Federation of Planets against which you may or may not have committed an act of war."

"There are survivors still aboard my ship," Kang said.

Kirk nodded to the Transporter chief and Scott said, "Captain, we haven't been able to get through to Starfleet Command. All subspace frequencies are blocked. And there's too much radiation from the Klingon ship—it's a hazard to the vicinity."

"Prepare to destruct, Scotty."

"Completing the job you started!"

Kirk wheeled on Kang. "You wouldn't be standing there if I had."

The surviving Klingons were shimmering into form. Of the six, several were women. One, queenly, graceful, her dark eyes gleaming under the epicanthic fold of their Mongol lids, left the platform to go at once to Kang. He took her arm. "This is Mara—my wife and my Science officer," he told Kirk.

She ignored Kirk. "What has happened, Kang?"

"More Federation treachery. We are prisoners."

She was visibly terrified. The arm in Kang's hand trem-

bled. "What will they do to us? I have heard of their atrocities . . . their death camps! They will torture us for our
scientific and military information . . ."

Kirk addressed her. "You have some things to learn
about us, madam." He turned to Galloway. "Detain them in
the crew lounge. Program a food-synthesizer to accommodate
our . . . guests. You will be well treated, Commander Kang."

"So I have seen," the Klingon said.

Kirk bowed and left, followed by Spock, McCoy and
the still blazing Chekov. Unseen, unheard, the floating crystal
hummed over their heads as they passed into the corridor.

"What *did* attack their ship, Jim?"

Kirk didn't answer. "Mr. Spock, maintain Red Alert.
Scan this sector for other ships. Run a full check on the colony. We've got to nail this down fast . . ."

"We know what happened!" Chekov cried. "That distress call—"

Spock, speaking to nobody in particular, said, "From
their distant position, the Klingons could scarcely have attacked the colony at the time we received the call. Moreover,
they were apparently attracted there themselves by a distress
call."

"Lies!" Chekov cried. "They want to start a war by
pretending *we* attacked it!"

Entering an elevator, Kirk glanced at his overwrought
face. But McCoy was saying, "Chekov might be right. The
Klingons *claim* to have honored the truce—but there have
been incidents! . . . raids on our outposts . . ."

"We've never proved the Klingons committed them,
Bones."

McCoy was flushed with unusual vehemence. "What
proof do we need? We know what a Klingon is!"

He stormed out of the elevator. Kirk frowned, puzzled
by his belligerence; and Spock, noting his uneasiness, said,
"Our Log-tapes will indicate our innocence in the present
situation, Captain."

"Unfortunately, there is no guarantee they will be believed."

At the bridge deck, Chekov stalked to his post, his back
stiff and stubbornly unrelenting. Kirk eyed him again before
he asked for Uhura's report.

"Still unable to contact Starfleet Command, Captain. Outside communications blanketed."

"Keep at it, Lieutenant. We've got a diplomatic tiger by the tail."

He'd have liked authorization to take steps about the derelict Klingon ship. But at least he knew no lives were aboard it. He turned in his command chair. "Forward phasers locked and ready to fire, Mr. Sulu."

"Aye, sir."

"Fire phasers," Kirk said.

On the screen, the crippled vessel flared into light—and vanished. So that was that. A diplomatic tiger, indeed.

"Lieutenant Uhura?"

"No contact with Starfleet yet, sir."

Spock looked up from his mounded viewer. "Sensor sweeps reveal no other ships within range, Captain."

Had the Klingons annihilated that colony after all? There was no telling. Not now. He swung to Uhura. "Keep trying, Lieutenant. Mr. Sulu, set course seventeen mark four. Warp speed three."

"Warp three, sir."

In the crew lounge, Security guards and the "guests" were facing each other, each group wary, watchful, suspicious. Above them all the crystal drifted. Kang, Mara beside him, used an empty space for restless pacing. "When I take this ship," he said, "I will have Kirk's head stuffed and hung on his cabin wall."

"They will kill us before we can act," she warned him.

"No! They wish to question us—learn our strength, our plans. They never will."

"We are forty," she protested. "Forty against four hundred."

One of Kang's men stepped forward. "Four thousand throats may be cut in one night by a running man."

"Patience," Kang said. "Vigilance. They will make their mistake. Capture of the *Enterprise* will give us knowledge to end this war quickly."

The crystal's unheard throb moved out of the lounge and into the corridor. When it reached the bridge, its throbbing faded. Uhura, abruptly irritated, jabbed at her controls.

"Still no outside contact, sir! Carriers normal. Channels open. I don't understand! Could the Klingons be doing something—?"

The ship suddenly shuddered. Engine sound rose. Kirk whirled. "Mr. Sulu?"

"Change of course, sir! Accelerating . . ." He struggled with switches. "Helm dead. Auxiliary navigation dead!"

Kirk braced himself against another shudder. "Override."

Sulu turned. "*Nothing* responds, Captain!"

"New course?"

"Nine-oh-two mark five . . ."

It would head the *Enterprise* out of the galaxy. Kirk hit a button. "Scotty—stop engines!"

The engine sound grew to a whining roar. On the intercom, Scott's voice was high with alarm. ". . . would if I could, sir! My controls have gone crazy! Something's—taken over . . ."

The bridge trembled under the rising roar. Scott shouted, "The engines, Captain! They've gone to warp nine—by themselves!"

Uhura's board was a dazzle of wildly flickering lights. Earphones fixed, she cried, "Captain! Reports from the lower decks! Emergency bulkheads closed! Almost four hundred crewmen trapped down there!"

Furious, Kirk exploded from his seat, racing for the elevator. The crystal followed him into the crew lounge. Kang was pleased with his information. "The bulk of your crew trapped? Your ship racing from the galaxy at wild speeds? Delightful! But how did I perform this sabotage, Kirk? My men are *here*."

Frigid with rage, Kirk spoke to Galloway. "Double security. Some Klingons may have beamed aboard, undetected. Mr. Spock, get down to Engineering. Help Scott hammer things back to normal and release those crewmen!"

He eyed Kang. "Before I throw you in the brig, I owe you something!" He landed a clenched fist on Kang's jaw. The Klingon stumbled back into a console, his hand falling on a lever. It came loose, grew red—and changed into a sword. Kang, amazed, stared at it in unbelief. Then he hefted it. At the same moment, all the lounge's objects—ashtrays, vases, lamps, magazines, game equipment—went into glow, transforming into swords, shields, javelins, battle-axes. The Klingons rushed for the weapons.

Kirk's people reached for their phasers. But the phasers, too, went into glow. Then they turned into swords and maces.

Kang took a swordsman's stance. "You killed four hundred of my men, Captain Kirk. It is time that that debt be repaid . . ."

Kirk looked at the sword that had been a console lever. Molecular revolution. But explanation did nothing to solve the deadly mystery. His own phaser was a sword.

The Klingons attacked—and the fight was on. Outnumbered, the Security guards were forced to retreat. Kirk fenced expertly, and was deflecting a slash by Kang when he saw that Galloway was wounded. He battled his way to the lieutenant, got an arm around him and shoved him into an elevator. The doors whooshed shut in the faces of Kang and his men. They rang with the sound of beating, frustrated swords.

Kirk beeped Engineering on his intercom. "The Klingons are free, Scotty. And armed. They'll try to take the ship. How many men do we have?"

"I don't know, sir, but three hundred and ninety-two are trapped below decks."

"Deploy forces to protect your section and Auxiliary Control Center. Check the Armory—and try to free those trapped men."

"Doors and bulkheads won't budge, sir. We'll have to cut through—"

"Blow out bulkheads if you have to—we need numbers! Any luck regaining control of speed?"

"No, sir. She's a projectile—at warp nine. Don't ask me what's holding her together."

"Five-minute reports. Kirk out."

He went to Spock's station. "Full sensor scans of the ship, Mr. Spock. Report any movements on the part of the Klingons. The Klingon Empire has maintained a dueling tradition. They think they can beat us with swords!"

Spock coolly examined the sword that had once been his phaser. "Neither the Klingon technology nor ours is ca-

pable of this, Captain. Instantaneous transmutation of matter.
I doubt that they are responsible . . ."

"Other logical candidates?" Kirk demanded impatiently.

"None, Captain. But if they had such power, wouldn't
they have created more effective weapons—and only for
themselves?"

Kirk turned away. "Get below, Mr. Sulu. Take command of forces protecting Engineering and Auxiliary Control."

Sulu rose and Chekov rose with him.

"As you were, Mr. Chekov," Kirk said.

"*No*, sir! Let me go, too! I've got a personal score to
settle with Klingons!"

"Maintain your post. This is no time for vendettas."

"Captain, I . . ."

"Sit down, Mister."

Chekov made a break for the elevator. As he reached
it, Kirk grabbed his shoulder. Chekov wrenched away; and
Spock, at Kirk's side, reached out an arm. Ducking under it,
Chekov drew his sword. As he lifted it, Kirk and Spock
paused, unwilling to risk a tangle that might hurt him.

"Don't try to stop me, Captain! I saw what they left of
Piotr! I swore on his grave I would avenge his murder . . ."
He backed into the elevator and its doors closed.

Sulu was staring. "What's Chekov's grudge against the
Klingons? Who's—Piotr?"

"His brother," Kirk said. "Killed in a Klingon raid."

"His brother?" Sulu echoed blankly. "Chekov never
had a brother! He's an only child."

It was Kirk's turn to stare. After a long moment, he
said, "You are mistaken."

"I'm not, sir!" Sulu was very earnest. "I *know* he's an
only child. It's why he requests his shore leaves on Earth—a
good only son of his parents should visit them!"

"On your way to Engineering, Mr. Sulu."

Sulu left—and a newly troubled Kirk hit his intercom.
"Captain Kirk to Security. Find Mr. Chekov and return him
to the bridge."

Uhura swung around. "Captain—what could have made
Chekov believe he had a brother?"

"I don't know, Lieutenant. But he does believe it—and now he wants revenge for a nonexistent loss."

On the *Enterprise* bridge, mystery was compounding itself, but in its crew lounge, clarification was in order.

A Klingon had projected the Starship's plan and arrangements on the viewer. "Layout and specifications of the ship, Commander Kang."

"Enemy numbers are the same as ours," Mara said. "We have a fighting balance."

"Then we will take this ship!" Kang spoke with a ferocious determination.

"A vessel that is racing toward the edge of the galaxy is weakening," his man said. "If the humans can't control it . . ."

Kang jabbed at the diagrams on the viewer. "These points we must capture! First, their Engineering section . . ."

McCoy was working feverishly to complete his treatment of Galloway's wound. As he worked, he could hear the moans of other slashed men waiting their turn at the table.

"Those—filthy butchers!" he muttered. "There are *rules*—even in *war* . . . you don't keep on hacking at a man after he's down!" He felt sick with impotent rage. He looked at an orderly who was wiping blood from a shoulder gash. "Where's that Numanol capsule?"

Haggard and worn by Sickbay's harrowing activity, the orderly turned, only to be confronted by wheeled stretchers bearing two more injured men. McCoy went to them. A glance told him their wounds were serious. As he bent over one of them, he spoke to the orderly. "I'm convinced now the only good Klingon is a dead one," he said.

Scott was inclined to agree with him. All attempts to release the cut-off crewmen had failed. Phaser beams couldn't cut through the bulkheads. Their metal's structure had changed. He hit an intercom button to make his report.

"What about the Armory?" Kirk said.

"I'm there now, Captain. You never saw such a collection of antiques in your life . . ."

The Armory had turned into a medieval weapons' Wonderland. Crossbows, hatchets, knives, broadswords . . .

"Get back to Engineering," Kirk said. "Keep trying to reestablish engine control. And make some phasers—fast."

"Aye, sir."

He was about to leave when he spotted a sharply two-edged weapon in the rack. He removed it, fondling it. "A claymore!" Exchanging it for a sword at his waist, he murmured, "Ah, you're a beauty, aren't you?"

As he strutted out of the Armory, reinforced by Scotland's history of claymore triumphs, Spock was computing the opposing forces at an exact thirty-eight. He lifted his head from his computer. "The Klingons occupy Deck Six and starboard Deck Seven, Captain. We control all sections above." He bent to his viewer again, becoming suddenly intent. "Most curious," he said.

"What?" Kirk said.

"There appear to be more energy units aboard than can be accounted for by the presence of the *Enterprise* crew plus the Klingons. A considerable discrepancy."

"Could some more of Kang's crew have beamed aboard?"

"Their ship was thoroughly vacated, Captain." He flipped a switch. "I shall compensate for the human and Klingon readings."

The crystal had found Engineering. It hovered high in the air, as unseen as it was unheard.

Scotty, descending a ladder, stepped down into the lower level of his section. "Any signs of those treacherous devils, Mr. Sulu?"

"All clear, Mr. Scott."

Klingons, moving into the upper level, leaped down to the attack. The surprised humans fell back. But Scott was inspired by his claymore's tradition. He felled a Klingon with its haft; and then realizing that his species was hopelessly outnumbered, darted through a door into the corridor. Sulu joined him, downing the two Klingons who followed him.

Scott was breathless. "I don't know how many of these creatures are around. We'll split up here. Maybe . . . one of us . . . can make it back to the bridge."

Inside Engineering, the rest of the crew were being

shoved against a wall. As they were disarmed, a jubilant Kang strode in, Mara at his side.

It was hard going, trying to get back to the bridge. Klingons seemed to be everywhere. The canny Scott finally reconciled national glory with common sense. He hid in a lavatory. So he was in no position to see Spock zero in on an unusual but steady beeping.

"An alien life force, Captain. A single entity. I am unable to ascertain its location." He flicked a switch. "Readings diverted to the library computer for analysis . . ."

Kirk, beside him, said, "We have to make contact . . . find out what it wants!"

Calmer than custard, Spock said, "The computer report, Captain . . ."

There was a click—and the computer voice said, "Alien life force on board is composed of pure energy. Type unknown. Actions indicate intelligence and purpose."

"What purpose?" Spock said.

The metallic computer voice said, "Insufficient data for further analysis."

The computer's stark admission of inadequacy fired Kirk into new, creative thought. Out of his human memory banks he made connections. "A brother that never existed," he said. "A phantom colony—fancied distress calls! The illusion that phasers are swords! Do you begin to sense a pattern, Mr. Spock?"

Spock, loyal to facts, looked up. "If the alien has caused these phenomena, it is apparently able to manipulate matter and minds."

"Now its controlling the *Enterprise*—taking us out of the galaxy! *Why?*"

"I am constrained to point out, Captain, that as minds are evidently being influenced, we cannot know that our own memories at this moment are accurate."

Kirk faced his sole alternative. "We've got to talk to Kang and bury the hatchet!"

"An appropriate choice of terms, sir. However, once blood has been drawn, it is notoriously difficult to arrange a truce with Klingons . . ."

"A *truce?*"

It was McCoy—an outraged, infuriated McCoy. His

white surgical uniform was blood-spattered. "I've got seven men down in Sickbay—some of them dying—*atrocities* committed on their persons! And you can talk of making peace with those fiends? They'd jump us the minute our backs were turned! We know what Klingons do to prisoners! Slave labor, death planets—experiments!"

Kirk had never seen Bones so angry. "McCoy—" he began.

McCoy rushed on. "Even while you're talking, the Klingons are planning attacks! This is a fight to the death—and we'd better start trying to win it!"

"We are trying to end it, Doctor." Spock's voice was more than usually quiet. "There is an alien aboard which may have created this situation . . ."

McCoy glared at him. "Who *cares* what started it! We're *in* it! Those murderers! Let's wipe out every one of them!"

"Bones, the alien is the enemy we have to wipe out—"

Uhura cut in. "Sickbay calling, Doctor. There are more wounded men requiring your attention."

McCoy wheeled, starting back to the elevator. Then he turned again to Kirk and Spock. "How many men have to die before you begin acting like military men instead of damn fools?" The elevator doors closed on his bleakly hopeless face. Kirk looked at Spock. The Vulcan murmured, "Extraordinary."

Kang was on the intercom. Kirk spoke quickly. "There's something important we must discuss . . ."

Vindictive and triumphant, Kang's voice said, "I have captured your Engineering section! I now control this ship's power and life support systems." At Engineering's intercom he nodded to Mara. She moved a series of switches and Kang spoke again into the intercom.

"I have deprived all areas of life support except our own. You will die . . . of suffocation . . . in the icy cold of space . . ."

On the bridge, lights were dimming. Panels were going dark.

Kirk walked slowly over to Sulu's station. "Mr. Sulu, get down to Emergency Manual Control. Try to protect life support circuits and activate auxiliary power . . ."

"Aye, Captain." But as Sulu approached the elevator, Scott burst out of it. He barely acknowledged the helmsman's smile of relief at his safety. Kirk went to him. "Scotty! I'm glad you escaped . . ."

Scott was shaking. "Chekov was right, Captain! We *should've* left those slant-eyed goons in the Transporter! That's right where they belong—in nonexistence! Now they can study the *Enterprise*—add our technology to theirs—change the balance of power!" He lurched at Kirk, not in attack but in a blind misery that was seeking some shred of comfort. "You've jeopardized the Federation!"

The charge was a cry of anguish. "Scotty . . ."

Spock had joined them. "Mr. Scott, calm yourself," he said.

Scott pulled back. For one terrible moment, Kirk feared he was going to spit at Spock, such aversion showed in his face. "Keep your Vulcan hands off me! Just stay away! Your 'feelings' might get hurt, you green-blooded, halfbreed freak!"

Kirk didn't believe his ears. Appalled, he stared at Scott. Then Spock made his icy retort. "Let me say that I have not enjoyed serving with humans. I find their illogical and foolish emotions a constant irritant."

"So transfer out!" Scott shouted.

Spock moved toward Scott. He loomed darkly formidable over him—and Scott, frightened, took a clumsy punch at him. Kirk grabbed their arms; but Spock, twisting easily free, seemed about to use his great strength in an upsurge of rage he couldn't govern. Kirk tried again; and yanking them apart, crashed back into his command chair. "Spock! Scotty! Stow it!" He pinned them, panting. *"What's happening to us! What are we saying to each other?"*

Spock pushed Kirk away. Kirk braced himself, ready for some ultimate disaster. But nothing happened. Spock was himself again, perhaps a little more impassive than usual.

"Fascinating," he said to Kirk. "A result of stress, Captain?"

"We've been under stress before! It hasn't set us at each other's throats!" Scott had started forward again and Kirk pushed him back.

"This is a *war*!" Scott yelled.

"There isn't any war . . ." Kirk paused, the sound of his own words in his ears. "Or—*is* there?"

"Have we forgotten how to defend ourselves?" Scott cried.

"Shut up, Scotty." Kirk paced at the back of his command chair, frowning as he put his two's together. "What *is* happening to us? We're trained to think in other terms—than war! We're trained to fight its causes whenever possible! So why are *we* reacting like savages?" The two's were adding up. He swung around to his men. "There are two forces on this ship, armed equally. Has—a war been *staged* for us? A war complete with weapons, grievances, patriotic drumbeats?" He turned on Scott. "Even race hatred!"

Spock had nodded. "Recent events *would* seem directed to a magnification of basic human and Klingon hostilities. Apparently, it is by design that we fight. We seem to be pawns."

"In what game?" Kirk said. "Whose game? What are the rules?"

"It is most urgent," Spock said, "that we locate the alien entity, determine its motives—and some means of halting its activities."

Scott's startled thoughts had been tumbling around in his head. He was quieter now—and guilt-stricken. He spoke to Spock. "Without sensors, sir? All our power down? The thing can pass through walls. It could be anywhere."

Kirk hit his intercom. "Mr. Sulu, report!"

Sulu was at the Jeffries tube, peering up into it. "No good, Captain. Circuits are in but systems aren't responding." As he spoke, the tube's complex instruments flickered with light and settled down to a steady pattern. He heard Kirk say, "Are we getting something?"

"Aye, sir. Power and life support restored—remotes on standby . . ."

"Good work!" Kirk told him.

"But Captain—*I didn't do it!* Everything just came on by itself!"

Kirk thought, "Well, this is a gift horse I don't look too close in the mouth of." He said, "All right, Mr. Sulu. Get back to Manual Control. Kirk out."

The bridge lights had come back to normal. Panels had

resumed their humming. Spock turned. "Sensors operating again, Captain."

"Start scanning, Mr. Spock. Look for the alien."

In Engineering, a puzzled Mara was studying lights on a large board. "Their life support systems have resumed and are holding steady," she told Kang.

"Cause them to be unsteady," he said.

"They appear to be controlled from another location." For the first time her voice was uncertain. "I'm also unable to affect the ship's course—to return to our Empire."

"Some trick of Kirk's? Has he bypassed these circuits? What power is it that supports our battle, yet starves our victory? Interrupt power at their main life support couplings. Where are they?"

She looked at the diagrams on the viewer. "They are on this deck." At Kang's nod, she spoke to a Klingon. "Come with me."

Above them in the bridge, Spock had tensed. He whirled to Kirk. "Alien detected, Captain! In the Engineering level, near reactor number three!"

Kirk leaped from his chair. "Let's go!"

Mara, the Klingon behind her, was rushing down a corridor that led to the couplings. As they passed an alcove, Chekov, sword drawn, moved out of it, his face hate-filled. Two well-aimed slashes disposed of the Klingon. Mara was turning to run when Chekov grabbed her and whirled her around. She fought well; but Chekov blocked her karate blow. He pinned her back against the wall, sword at her throat. It was a lovely throat. Chekov's manner changed. He eyed her with an ugly speculation, grinning. "No, you don't die— yet," he said. "You're not human but you're beautiful, aren't you?" His grip on her tightened. "Just how human *are* you?"

She pushed at him, struggling against the grip. Chekov placed his hand over her mouth and was pressing her into the alcove when Kirk and Spock raced out of the elevator. Assault was the last thing on their minds. Hearing Mara's muffled scream, they stared at each other. Then they broke into a run, rounded a corner—and stopped dead in their tracks at what they saw.

"Chekov!"

Chekov wheeled to face Kirk, a wild beast deprived of

its prey. Mara's garment was ripped from her shoulders. Chekov spun her away. She hit a wall and dropped. He tried to dodge Kirk and failed. Kirk seized him, slapping his face forehand, backhand. Chekov sobbed; and raising his sword, made a swipe at Kirk. He was disarmed and felled with a punch. Beside himself with fury, Kirk struck him again.

Spock put a hand on Kirk's shoulder. "Captain . . . he is not responsible . . ."

Mara, crouched on the deck, was trying to pull her torn clothes together. Kirk went to her. "Listen to me," he said. "There's an alien entity aboard this ship. It's forcing us to fight. We don't know its motives—we're trying to find out. Will you help us? Will you take me to Kang . . . a temporary truce! That's all I ask!"

Mingled fear and hate blazed from her eyes. Kirk turned his back on her. "Bring her, Spock." He moved to the weeping Chekov and lifted him gently in his arms. Was this what was in store for all of them? Hatred, violence wherever they turned?

McCoy was re-dressing Galloway's wound when Kirk carried Chekov into Sickbay. He looked up, taking them all in, Kirk, the still sobbing Chekov clinging to him, a disheveled Mara, closely followed by Spock. Shaking his head, he left Galloway and hurried to help Kirk place Chekov on an exam table. He applied a device to the new patient's head.

"Brainwaves show almost paranoid mania. What happened, Jim?"

"He's—lost control—useless as a fighter." He turned to the door. "Come on, Spock . . ."

McCoy stopped him with a hand on his arm. He seemed somewhat calmer himself but his tired face was bewildered. "*Jim*—Galloway's heart wound has almost entirely healed! The same with the other casualties. Sword wounds . . . into vital organs—massive trauma, shock—and they're all healing at a fantastic rate!"

Spock spoke. "The entity would appear to want us alive."

". . . Why?" Kirk said. "So we can fight and fight—and always come back for more? Some kind of bloody Colosseum? What next? The roar of crowds?"

Galloway was listening. And he was buying none of it.

His jaw hardened. He wanted out from Sickbay and for only one reason—another crack at the Klingons.

Kirk felt the lieutenant's hostility like a tangible thing. "Spock, let's find that alien!" He looked at Mara. "You come along. Maybe we can prove to you that it exists!"

In the corridor, Spock unlimbered his tricorder. He led the way, searching cautiously, the tricorder first aimed one way, then another. When they reached a second intersection, Spock paused, gesturing to his left. They turned the corner—and they all heard the crystal's faint humming. Without speaking, Spock signaled them to look up to the right side of the corridor. The crystal was floating there, brighter than it had ever been.

Kirk shot a significant look at Mara. Now that she was forced to believe, she was staring at the thing's swirling red.

"What is it?" Kirk said.

"Totally unfamiliar, Captain."

Kirk approached the crystal. "What do you want? Why are you doing all this?" It hovered silently, persistent.

Kirk, close to blowing his stack, shouted, *"What do you want?"*

The thing glowed still brighter, bobbing slightly. Spock, noting the increased glow, whirled at a sound. Galloway, still bandaged, was coming down the corridor, a little weak but grimly determined. He hefted his sword—and started to push past them as though he didn't see them.

"Lieutenant Galloway!" Kirk cried. "What are you doing here? Did the Doctor release you?"

"I'm releasing myself!"

First, Chekov's insubordination. Now this one. It took all Kirk's strength to remember that the crystal was in the business of war, dissension and rule-breaking.

"Go back to Sickbay," he said.

"Not on your life! I'm fit and ready for action!" He shook Kirk's hand from his arm. "The Klingons nearly put me away for good! I'm going to get me some scalps . . ."

"I order you!" Kirk said.

"I've got my orders! I'm obeying orders! To Kill Klingons! It's them or us, isn't it?"

The crystal had bobbed over Galloway's head. Spock, looking up, saw it bob as Galloway pushed past him, heading for an elevator. He tagged the man with a neck pinch. Kirk saw Galloway slump, unconscious, to the deck. Spock's eyes were already back on the crystal. Its glow had faded.

"Most interesting," Spock said.

His eyes returned to Kirk. "During Mr. Galloway's emotional outburst—his expressions of hatred and lust for vengeance—the alien's life-energy level *increased*. When the lieutenant became unconscious, the alien *lost* energy."

"A being that subsists on the emotions of others?" Kirk said.

"Such creatures are not unknown, Captain. I refer you to the Drella of Alpha Carinae five—energy creatures who are nourished by the cooperation of love they feel for one another." He had neared the crystal and was looking up at it, composed and calm. "This creature appears to be strengthened by mental radiations of hostility, by violent intentions . . ."

"It feeds—on hate!" Complete illumination dawned on Kirk.

"Yes, to put it simply, Captain. And it has acted as a catalyst to create this situation in order to satisfy that need. It has drawn fighting forces together, supplied crude weapons to promote the most violent mode of conflict. It has spurred racial animosities—"

"And kept numbers and resources balanced to maintain a stable state of violence! Spock, it's got to have a vulnerable area. It's got to be stopped!"

"Then all hostile attitudes on board must be eliminated, sir. The fighting must end—and soon."

Kirk nodded. "I agree. Otherwise, we'll be a doom ship—traveling forever between galaxies . . . filled with bloodlust . . . eternal warfare! Kang *has* to listen—we've got to pool our knowledge to get rid of that thing!"

The crystal was showing agitation, bobbing as though angry that its secret was known. Now, as Kirk strode to an intercom, it moved toward him, throbbing loudly. For a moment Kirk wavered. Then he walked on. The crystal, its hum furious, approached Mara. Suddenly, without warning, she hurled herself at Kirk, biting, scratching, pushing him away from the intercom. Spock lifted her from Kirk, quietly pinning her arms to her sides.

Kirk hit all buttons. "Kang! This is Kirk! Kang! *Kang!*"

Mara shrieked, "Commander! It's a trick! They are located—"

Spock's steel hand went over her mouth. At the intercom, Kirk hit the buttons again. *"Kang!"* It was hopeless. The Klingon wouldn't answer.

"The alien is affecting his mind, Captain. Soon it will grow so powerful that none of us will be able to resist it."

The intercom beeped and Kirk hit it fast—fast and hopefully. "Kirk here!"

"Scotty, sir. The ship's dilithium crystals are deteriorating. We can't stop the process . . ."

Kirk struck the wall with his fist. "Time factor, Scotty?"

"In twelve minutes we'll be totally without engine power, sir."

"Do everything you can. Kirk out."

The crystal stopped bobbing. It glowed brilliantly, back in the driver's seat. As they watched it, it vanished through a wall. Kirk spoke to Mara. "So we drift forever . . . with only hatred and bloodshed aboard. Now do you believe?"

Her strained eyes stared into his. But she made no answer.

The dilithium crystals were still losing power. Spock, rallying all his scientific know-how, toured the bridge, examining panels. Finally, he broke the bad news to Kirk. There was nothing to be done to halt the crystals' decay.

"We have nine minutes and fifty-seven seconds before power zero," he said. "But there is a logical alternative, Captain." He was looking at Mara, his face speculative. "Kang's wife, after all, is our prisoner. A threat made to him . . ."

"*That's* something the Klingons would understand," Scott urged.

Mara had flinched, remembering the unspeakable atrocities said to be visited on Klingon prisoners by their human captors. Kirk saw her remembering them. Though the idea of using her to threaten Kang just might result in a productive discussion with him, it revolted him. On the other hand, peace between them was the sole hope now. After a long, painful moment, he said, "You're right, Mr. Spock."

He flicked on his intercom. This was going to be difficult. He harshened his voice. "Kang, Kang! This is Captain Kirk. I know you can hear me . . . Don't cut me off! *We have Mara—your wife!*"

At Engineering's intercom, Kang was listening. Kirk's voice went on. "We talk truce *now*—or she dies. Reply!"

Kang was silent.

"She has five seconds to live, Kang! Reply!"

The answer came. "She is a victim of war, Captain. She understands." Kang flicked off the intercom, his dark emotion visible to his men. He turned to them. "When we get Kirk, he is mine," he said.

The last card had been played. Kirk looked at Mara. She had stiffened, her head held high, proud, a queen awaiting death. He pointed to a seat. "Sit over there and keep out of our way. Lieutenant Uhura, guard her."

She didn't understand. ". . . you're . . . not going to . . . ?"

"The Federation doesn't kill or mistreat its prisoners. You've heard fables, propaganda." He looked away from her as though he'd forgotten her existence. "How much time now, Mr. Spock?"

"Eight minutes and forty-two seconds, sir."

Instead of taking a seat, Mara had gone to the panel Spock was studying. Reading it, she realized the dilithium situation. Near her, Uhura watched her as she turned in shocked belief. "So it was no trick . . ." she said, bewildered.

Scott spoke. "The alien has done all this. We are in its power. Our people—and yours."

Kirk rose from his chair. "We wanted only to end the fighting to save us all," he told her.

Her relief had bred a need to explain. "We have always fought, Captain Kirk. We must. We are hunters, tracking and taking what we need. There are poor planets in the Klingon systems. We must push outward to survive."

"Another way to survive is mutual trust, Mara. Mutual trust and mutual help."

"I will help you now," she said.

He'd hoped to no point too many times to feel anything but skepticism. "How?" he said.

"I will take you to Kang. I will add my plea to yours."

Scott's suspicion found voice. "Captain—I wouldn't trust her . . ."

"We can't get past the Klingon defenses in time now, anyway—" Kirk paused. "Unless . . ." He whirled to Spock. "*Spock! Intra*ship beaming! From one part of the ship to another! Is it possible?"

"It has rarely been done, sir, because of the great danger involved. Pinpoint accuracy is needed. If the Transportee should materialize within any solid object—a wall or deck . . ."

"Prepare the Transporter," Kirk said.

"Mr. Scott, please help me with the Main Transporter Board." Spock moved to a panel but Scott hesitated, worried.

"Even if it works, Captain, she may be leading you into a trap!"

"We're all in a trap, Scotty. And this is our only way out of it."

"We'll go with you, sir . . ."

"That would start the final battle." Kirk took a long-searching look at Mara. "I believe her."

Scott took one for himself. He believed her, too. "Aye, sir," he said.

Mara entered the elevator. Following her, Kirk said, "We'll wait for your signal." As the doors closed, Scott thoughtfully fingered his sword. "But she can't guarantee that Kang will listen. Right, Mr. Spock?"

But Spock was intent on the Main Transporter Board. "No one can guarantee another's actions, Mr. Scott."

The Transporter Room was empty. Entering it, Kirk deliberately removed his sword; and, disarmed, placed the weapon on the console. Mara smiled at him. Spock's voice spoke from the intercom. "Your automatic setting is laid in, Captain. When the Transporter is energized, you will have eight seconds to get to the pads."

The console was flickering with lights. As Kirk pressed a button, it beeped to every second that passed. Its hum rose and Kirk said, "I hope your computations are correct, Mr. Spock."

"You will know in five point two seconds, Captain."

Kirk and Mara went quickly into position on the platform. There were eight more beeps from the console before they shimmered out.

At their appearance in Engineering, the startled Kang exploded to his feet. "*Mara!* You are alive! . . . and you bring us a prize!" He turned, shouting, "*Guards!*"

Swords drawn, his men ringed Kirk.

"Kang—wait!" Mara cried. "He has come alone— unarmed! *He must talk to you!*"

"Brave Captain. What about?" Kang swung to his men. "Kill him."

Mara rushed into place before Kirk. "*No!* You must listen! There is great danger to us all!"

Kang paused—and Kirk moved her aside, unwilling to allow her shield to him. "Before you start killing," he said, "give me one minute to speak!"

Kang ignored him. He spoke to Mara. "What have they done to you? How have they affected your mind?" Then he spotted her torn garment, her bruised shoulder. His slanted eyes went icy. "Ah, I see why this human beast did not kill you . . ."

She flashed into action. She seized a sword and tossed it to Kirk. He caught it as Kang launched himself headlong into attack. Defending himself, he retreated before another fierce slash. Mara, held by a Klingon, was struggling, agonized by the turn events had taken.

"*They didn't harm me!* Kang, listen to Kirk!"

Kang backed away for another onrush. "With his death, we win!"

"*Nobody wins!*" Kirk shouted. "Have any of your men died?" He broke into sudden attack but only to bring himself closer to Kang. "*Listen! We can't be killed—any of us! There's an alien aboard this ship that needs us alive!*"

Kang shoved him away only to come back with another vicious onslaught.

"You *fool*!" Mara screamed.

From behind them all, the Transporter humming sounded. Spock, McCoy, Sulu and the *Enterprise* forces sparkled into shape and substance. Kang's men rushed forward, swords aimed. The Security guards, led by Sulu who uttered a yell that might have been "Banzai!" closed with them.

Kirk, downing a Klingon with a hard right to the jaw, reached Kang—and grabbed him. Nose to nose, he shouted, "*Listen* to me! Let me *prove* what I say!"

Kang wrenched free, his sword up for the lethal downsweep. Kirk parried the blow in mid-descent. Mara, huddled against a wall, covered her face with her hands, despairing. Kang came back with another vicious slash. As Kirk ducked it, he heard the triumphant throbbing. He looked up. The crystal—above their heads, brighter than he'd ever seen it—was casting its virulent red light on Kang's face.

The sight was all that he needed. He pushed Kang back, pinning him, and whirled him around to face their common enemy.

"LOOK! *Up there!*"

Kang looked. He shot a glance at Kirk—but the real meaning of what he'd seen didn't get through to him.

The fight went on, interminably. Sulu plunged his sword into an opponent's chest. The Klingon staggered, pawing at the wound. Then he rallied. He drove so straight for Sulu's heart that the *Enterprise* helmsman barely managed to escape the thrust.

Kang, his eyes on the crystal, was just beginning to get the lay of the land. Kirk pressed his advantage. ". . . for the rest of our lives, Kang! For a thousand lifetimes—fighting, this insane violence! That alien over our heads will control us forever!"

The crystal throbbed loudly. Kirk himself felt the heat of its bloody radiance. But Kang still twisted, snarling, avid for killing. Kirk smashed the sword that had reappeared in his hand. He struck it furiously against a bulkhead. It broke. Kang stared at him. Then he stepped forward, his own weapon upraised. Kirk stood his ground.

"Come on! In the brain, the heart—it doesn't matter, Kang! *I won't stay dead!* Next time the thing will see to it that I kill you. And you won't stay dead! The good old game of war—mindless pawn against mindless pawn! While something somewhere sits back and laughs . . . laughs fit to kill, Kang—and starts it all over again . . ."

The sword was at his throat.

"Jim—*jump him!*" McCoy shouted.

Spock spoke out of his wise Vulcan heritage. "Those who hate and fight must stop themselves, Doctor—or it is not stopped."

Mara had flung herself at Kang's feet. "I'm your wife—a Klingon! Would I lie for them? Listen to Kirk. He is telling the truth!"

"Then be a pawn!" Kirk said. "A toy—the good soldier who never asks questions!"

Kang looked up at the excitedly throbbing crystal. Very slowly, his hand relaxed on the sword. It dropped to the deck.

"Klingons," he told the crystal, "kill for their *own* purposes." He turned to his men, shouting. "Cease hostilities! At rest!"

They were puzzled by the order—but they obeyed. Kang yelled a Klingon away from a downed Security man. *"At rest! At rest!* You heard the order!"

Through the open door they could all hear the clashing sounds of continuing battle in other parts of the ship. *"All* fighting must be stopped, Captain, if the alien is to be weakened before our fuel is gone."

Kang had lifted Mara to her feet. They joined Kirk at the intercom as he activated it, Kang still suspicious.

"Lieutenant Uhura, put me on shipwide intercom . . ."

"Ready, Captain."

"Attention, all hands! A truce is ordered . . . the fighting is over! Regroup and lay down weapons." He stepped back, speaking urgently. "Kang! Your turn at the intercom . . ."

The Klingon hesitated, reluctant. He couldn't resist a push at Kirk as he moved to the intercom. "This is Kang. Cease hostilities. Disarm."

The crystal was bobbing wildly with anger; but its throbbing had lessened and its redness was dimmer. "The cessation of violence appears to have weakened the alien," Spock said. "I suggest that good spirits might prove to be an effective weapon."

Kirk nodded. A hard smile on his lips, he addressed the crystal. "Get off my ship!" The thing retreated, still bobbing. "You're powerless here. You're a dead duck. We know all about you—and we don't want to play your game any more."

The throbbing was fainter. Spock was right. What the invader needed was a cheerful scorn. Kirk looked up at it. "Maybe there are others like you still around. Maybe you've caused a lot of suffering—a lot of history. That's all over. We'll be on guard . . . we'll be ready for you. Now butt out!" He laughed at the crystal. "Haul it!"

McCoy waved a contemptuous hand. "Get out, already!" he yelled.

As the throbbing faded, Kirk was amazed to hear a hoarse chuckle from Kang. Then he laughed as though he weren't used to it. His gusto grew. "Out!" he shouted at the crystal. "We need no urging to hate humans!" He laughed harder at Spock's irritated glance. "But for the present—only fools fight in a burning house."

Guffawing, he raffled Kirk's teeth with a sadistic whack on the back. McCoy nudged Spock. After a moment, the Vulcan thumbed his nose at the crystal. "You will please leave," he said.

The red was now a dull flicker. They all watched it, laughing. Suddenly the crystal vanished through a bulkhead. Floating in space outside the Starship, it flared up and winked out.

The forced laughter had come hard. Kirk's relief from hours of nervous strain overwhelmed him so that he wasn't surprised to see that swords and shields had disappeared. Spock and McCoy discovered their phasers in place. McCoy made a point of drawing his; and Kang, noting the weapon, went right on chuckling. Caution—it was how things were between the Federation and his Klingon Empire.

Uhura's voice spoke. "Captain, jettisoning of fuel has stopped. The trapped crewmen are free. All systems returning to normal."

"Carry on, Lieutenant. Mr. Sulu, resume your post. Set course for—well, set it for any old star in the galaxy!"

As Sulu left, Kirk nearly knocked Kang from his feet with a mighty thump on the back. Kang spun around, blood in his eye—and Kirk grinned at him. *"Friends!"* he said.

The command chair was a place again where a man could relax. For a moment, anyway. Kirk leaned back in his seat.

"Ahead, Mr. Sulu. Warp one." He turned to Kang and

Mara. "We'll reach a neutral planet by tomorrow. You'll be dropped there. No war, this time."

He eyed Mara. A real woman, that one. If she hadn't been Kang's wife . . . if there had been time. Ah, well, no man could accommodate all opportunities . . .

Kang was saying, "Why do you humans revere peace? It is the weakling's way. There's a galaxy to be taken, Kirk, with all its riches!"

Spock looked up. "Two animals may fight over a bone, sir—or they can pool their abilities, hunt together more efficiently and share justly. Curiously, it works out about the same."

Kang turned. "One animal must trust the other animal."

"Agreed," Kirk said. "Cooperate . . . or fight uselessly throughout eternity. A universal rule you Klingons had better learn." He paused. "*We* did."

Had it got through? Maybe. At any rate, Kang's face seemed unusually thoughtful.

PLATO'S STEPCHILDREN

Writer: Meyer Dolinsky
Director: David Alexander
Guest stars: Michael Dunn, Liam Sullivan, Barbara
  Babcock

The planet was uncharted; but the sensors of the *Enterprise*, in orbit around it, had detected mineral and chemical riches under its rugged, mountainous surface. Spock looked up from his viewer to say briefly, "Kironide deposits, too, Captain."

"Record coordinates," Kirk told him.

Uhura turned. "Mr. Spock, what *is* kironide?"

"A particularly potent and long-lasting source of power, Lieutenant—very rare."

She was about to question him further when her board's lights flashed. Surprise still on her face, she reported to Kirk. "A distress signal's coming in, Captain."

It *was* disconcerting news. An uncharted planet, apparently uninhabited—and an SOS call. Kirk said, "Let's have it. Put it on audio, Lieutenant."

A woman's voice, amplified by the bridge's audio system, was loud enough for everyone to hear.

"My spouse is dying. We need a physician immediately. The situation is urgent. If there's a physician hearing this, we need you. Please make contact. My spouse is dying . . ."

Kirk said, "I thought there was no life down there, Mr. Spock."

"The sensors still read negative, sir."

But the voice was still with them. "Please help us. We are in desperate need of a physician. My spouse is dying. Acknowledge . . . acknowledge . . . please . . ."

"Mr. Spock, life forms or no life forms, that distress call sounds authentic." Kirk got up and strode to Uhura's station. "Lieutenant, acknowledge and report that we're beaming down at once. Notify Dr. McCoy to meet us in the Transporter Room."

Medikit in hand, McCoy materialized with Kirk and Spock in front of a colonnaded promenade. At first glance, there seemed to be no one around. Then Kirk spotted movement at the rear of a marble column. A dwarf, clearly frightened and wearing a short Greek robe that left one misshapen shoulder bare, broke from behind the column and scuttled to them.

"Are you from the spaceship *Enterprise*?"

Kirk looked down at him for a moment before he spoke. "That's right."

"No offense," the dwarf said hastily. He bowed low. "Alexander . . . at your service. I sing, I dance, I play all variety of games and I'm a good loser. A very good loser. And I try, I try very hard. Please bear that in mind."

It was an extraordinary speech. The *Enterprise* men looked at each other, nonplussed, and the dwarf said, "Now, if you'll accompany me . . ."

"Who inhabits this planet?" Kirk said.

The little creature bowed again. "Platonians. You've never heard of us. Our home star is Sahndara. Millennia ago, just before it novaed, we got off. Our leader liked Plato's ideas—Plato—Platonians, see? In fact, Parmen, our present philosopher-king, calls us Plato's children. Some of us think we're more like *step*children." He gave a nervous little laugh. "Now, please—they're waiting for you . . ."

He wheeled around and hurried ahead of them like a mechanical doll set suddenly into motion.

The *Enterprise* three hesitated. Then, curious but a little uneasy, they followed him.

Whoever McCoy's prospective patient was, he had done very well for himself. The dwarf ushered them into a stately, atrium-like court pillared by marble. In the center of the place, a nymph of marble dripped water from an urn into a reflecting pool. There was a game board on the left, flanked by benches, the pieces it held geometrically shaped into balls, pyramids, cylinders and cubes. Two tall robed men stood near a couch where another one reclined, his legs covered. Kirk saw a spasm of pain convulse his face. It seemed to deeply concern the dark, beautiful woman who was stooping over him. She touched his bald head gently before she hurried forward to greet the newcomers.

"Parmen and I welcome you to our Republic," she said. "I am Philana, his wife. Who among you is the physician?"

So the Platonians' philosopher-king was the patient. The startled McCoy said, "I am. What is the problem?"

She gestured to the couch. "You must do something . . ."

Following her, McCoy removed the covering from his patient's legs. An infection had swollen the left one almost to the knee. "What happened to that leg?" he said.

With a sick man's irritation, Parmen snapped, "What do you suppose? I scratched it!"

"I don't understand," McCoy said. "Why wasn't this attended to immediately?"

"Sheer ignorance. Is there anything you can do?"

The question put McCoy on guard. "We're certainly going to try. The infection is massive. Let me give you a shot to ease the pain."

McCoy opened his medikit; but before he so much as touched his hypo, it rose from the kit and sailing through the air, hovered for a moment. Kirk and Spock were looking up at it in amazement when Parmen said, "Where?"

McCoy came out of his shock. "Your arm," he said.

The hypo alighted on Parmen's upper arm, delivered the shot and replaced itself in the medikit. The sick man noted McCoy's expression. "Sorry, didn't mean to take matters out of your hands," he said. "But I can't risk any further contamination."

Watching, the dwarf touched Philana's white robe. "Mistress, they've come to help. They deserve better than to die."

Alexander had spoken so softly that Kirk didn't hear the plea. But what he saw was enough. The little man's mouth was forced open. His fist clenched and was shoved into the open mouth. Then his teeth were snapped back to bite into his knuckles.

"Alexander, you talk too much," Philana said.

The fist was left in the mouth. Over it the dwarf's tormented eyes met Kirk's.

* * *

"What is your prognosis, Doctor?"

Parmen barely managed to utter the words. His breath was coming in heavy pants and he was perspiring profusely. But McCoy, scanning him with his tricorder, had not forgotten the hypo episode. "It will be better," he said, "if I handle my instruments myself without any help from you."

His patient stifled a cry of agony. McCoy took another closer reading of his tricorder's dials. As Parmen moaned, turning on his side, Kirk approached the couch. "I don't understand how a simple scratch could get this serious," he said to McCoy.

The *Enterprise* surgeon stepped to one side. "Neither do I. But it has. And how do I knock out an infection with a tricorder that has no information on Platonian bacteria? All I can do—and it's going to take time—is match his bugs with a known strain and *hope*."

"Look at the game board," Kirk said.

The dwarf's fist had been removed from his mouth. It had been removed so that he could play a game with one of the robed academician-guests. Kirk and McCoy saw Alexander move a piece; but his opponent's piece made its countermove by itself.

"Your pyramid is in jeopardy, Eraclitus," Alexander said.

A cube rose into the air and descended into another position. "Aha! It isn't now!" Eraclitus laughed. "I won the game."

Kirk went to Philana. "This psychokinetic power of yours is unique. How long have you possessed it?"

"Two and a half millennia—ever since our arrival here on Platonius."

Spock joined them. "How is the power transmitted?" he asked.

"Brain waves," she told him.

"Do these waves cease when you're asleep?"

"No, not if they're embedded in the unconscious," she said.

"How do dreams affect them?" Kirk said.

Her anxious face moved in a coldly formal smile. "Our sleep is dreamless."

McCoy, gathering chemicals from his kit, was mixing them in a vial. Delirium's symptoms were beginning to show in the twisting, fevered Parmen. Frustrated and disturbed, McCoy called to Philana. *"Why don't you have doctors? Medicine?"*

"We've had no pressing need for the medical arts, Doctor. While still on Sahndara, we instituted a mass eugenics program. We're the result. Pared down to a population of thirty-eight, we're perfect for our utopia. Overemotionality and concern with family have been eliminated. We're bred for contemplation, self-reliance and longevity." She paused. "How old would you say I am, gentlemen? Don't be afraid. I'm not vain."

"Thirty-five," Spock said.

"That old? I . . . I stopped aging at thirty. Anyway, you missed by two thousand years. I am two thousand, three hundred years old. We married very young, Parmen and I. I was only one seventeen, he was one twenty-eight. You see, we scarcely have to move any more, let alone work."

Kirk nodded. "That's why you have no resistance."

"True," she said. "A break in the skin or a cut can be fatal." She looked over at the couch. "We went for a stroll in the moonlight—something we seldom do—and my spouse fell . . ."

Parmen gave a cry. She hurried away from them to watch McCoy. He was working fast, pulling his mixed chemicals into the hypo. Suddenly a marble bust of Socrates fell from its pedestal, and the game board, along with its geometric pieces, lifted up and went spinning through the room. McCoy was trying to shield the hypo and vial with his body when he was whirled about and sent careening across the floor.

Kirk ran to help him to his feet. Spock, rescuing the hypo and vial, said, "Captain, I believe we are experiencing the psychokinetic manifestations of Parmen's delirium."

Kirk's communicator beeped. He flipped it open and Scott's voice said, "Captain, we're fighting a storm! No discernible cause—I've never seen anything like it! Ten-scale turbulence right now, sir!"

As he spoke, the *Enterprise* gave a violent lurch. Scott turned to Sulu. "Emergency gyros and stabilizers at maximum!'' To Kirk he said, ''If it keeps up this way, we can't last, Captain!''

''Engines at full speed, Mr. Scott. Get her out of orbit and into space!''

''I've tried, sir. We're locked tight!''

''Then there's nothing you can do but batten down and weather it!''

''Right, sir . . .''

Kirk replaced the communicator in his belt. ''Parmen's mind is not only throwing the furniture around, it's tearing the *Enterprise* apart! Bones, knock him out—and fast!''

McCoy drew the last of his chemical mixture into the hypo. He tried to hold his patient still long enough to administer it; but Parmen, staring at him wild-eyed, slammed him back against the wall. McCoy barely succeeded in hanging on to the hypo. Still in his delirium, the philosopher-king caught sight of Alexander. The dwarf was smashed against another marble wall.

''Help! Save me!'' he screamed.

Unseen hands were pummeling the dwarf. They jerked him forward only to have him lashed again against the wall. He twisted, ran and was hurled once more against the wall. Kirk raced to him. Kirk seized him, shouting, ''Stay behind me!''

''It's no use. His mind will find me anyhow . . .'' He whispered, ''Don't save him! Please don't save him. Let him die. The others will all kill each other trying to become ruler . . .''

A blow meant for Alexander grazed Kirk's cheek. ''Bones, hurry up with that shot!''

McCoy, crouching too low for Parmen to see him, grabbed his arm and got the hypo home against his shoulder. Alexander was screaming again. ''Agh . . . I . . . I can't breathe! Choking . . . chok—''

''Bones, shake Parmen! Break his concentration!''

As McCoy obeyed, emptying the hypo, the invisible clutch released the dwarf's throat. A pedestal about to fall slowly righted itself. Kirk opened his communicator. Had quiet returned to the *Enterprise*?

''It's all right, Captain,'' Scott said. ''The turbulence has abated.''

"I think you'll find the orbit lock is broken as well. Assess damage, Mr. Scott, and repair what's necessary."

"Aye, sir."

Philana had seen that sleep had stilled the patient. Gracious now, she spoke to the visitors. "I don't know how I can ever thank you enough, not only for myself but for Platonius."

Kirk was brief. "No thanks are necessary."

"Alexander, show our guests to the South Wing."

"No, thank you," Kirk said. "We must return to the *Enterprise*."

McCoy spoke. "Jim, I think I should wait till the fever breaks."

Kirk hesitated. He'd had enough of Platonius and Platonians. On the other hand, McCoy was a doctor. To snatch him away from a patient for whom still more might need to be done was arbitrary action, whoever the patient was.

"Then we'll stay," he said.

The South Wing was a magnificent suite, hung with silk and decorated in the same classic Greek fashion as Parmen's atrium. Alexander scurried about, introducing them to dressing rooms and sleeping quarters. "You need anything, just say so," he told Kirk.

Kirk smiled at him. "Thanks, Alexander."

"Think nothing of it; you people saved my life." He swallowed nervously. "I . . . I think I ought to tell you . . ."

"Tell us what?" Kirk said.

The little man appeared to change his mind. He shook his head, a worried little smile on his mouth. "Just that I didn't know any people like you existed."

Kirk peered through the door into an empty corridor. "Where is everyone?" he said.

"In their chambers—meditating."

Kirk turned. "Alexander, are there other Platonians like you?"

The dwarf's face quivered. "What do you mean, 'like me'?"

"Who don't have psychokinetic ability?" Kirk said quietly.

"For a minute I thought you were talking about my . . . my size. They laugh at my size. But to answer your question,

I'm the only one who doesn't have it. I was brought here as the court buffoon. That's why I'm everybody's slave."

"How does one get this power?" Spock said.

"As far as I know, it just comes to you after you're born. They say I'm a throwback and I am. But so are you!" Fear came into his eyes. "I'm sorry. I didn't mean anything. I shouldn't have said that."

"Don't worry about it," Kirk said. "We're happy without the ability."

Alexander studied Kirk's face. "You know, I think you are," he said slowly. He paused. "Where you come from, are there a lot of people without the power . . . and my size?"

Kirk was beginning to like the little man. "Size, shape or color doesn't matter to us. And nobody has the power."

Alexander stared. "Nobody!"

Even as he stared, he was being pulled backward toward the door. He gave a miserable little laugh. "Somebody wants me," he told them. Then he was yanked out of the room.

Kirk looked at Spock. The Vulcan shrugged. "It will be pleasant to leave," he said.

Kirk began to pace. "That may not be easy. If Parmen should die . . ."

"Even if he shouldn't . . ." Spock said.

Kirk nodded. "This little Utopia of theirs is about the best-kept secret in the galaxy. Screening themselves from our sensors, locking us in orbit—*it all adds up to a pattern*, Spock—and one I do not like . . ."

McCoy, with his medical kit, came through the door. He closed it behind him.

"Well?" Kirk said.

"My concoction has actually worked. Fever's broken, and Lord, what recuperative powers! The infection's already begun to drain."

"Dr. McCoy, you may cure the common cold yet!" Spock said.

Kirk took out his communicator. "If we're going to make it out of here, this is the time." He flipped the dial. "Kirk to *Enterprise*. Scott, come in, please . . ."

"Scott here, sir."

"Standby to beam us up."

Scott spoke slowly. "I'm afraid I can't, Captain. All our instrumentations, even our phaser weapons, are frozen."

"The turbulence hit you that hard?"

"It's not the turbulence, sir. Damage to the ship is minimal."

"Then what's caused it?"

Scott's voice was despairing. "I wish I knew, sir. You tell me. I'm only reporting the facts."

Kirk eyed the door. It was still closed. "Scotty, we're up against a society that has psychokinetic energy more powerful than our machines. Did you get out into space?"

"No, Captain. The orbit lock is tighter than ever. And our subspace communication with Starfleet Command is completely severed."

Kirk spoke softly. The contrast between his voice and the fury in his face was so marked that McCoy and Spock stared at him. "I'm going to take care of this. I'll get back to you, Scotty." He closed the communicator, replaced it in his belt; and opening the door, strode out into the corridor.

He found Parmen sitting up on the couch. The philosopher-king's eyes were closed, not with weakness, but with the ravishment of aesthetic ecstasy. The deformed Alexander stood beside him, plucking a lyre as he chanted a song from an Aristophanes play . . .

> Great Pan
> Sounds his horn:
> Marking time
> To the rhyme
> With his hoof,
> With his hoof.
> Forward, forward in our plan
> We proceed as we began . . .

The wretched dwarf croaked, imitating a chorus of frogs.

He turned at the sound of Kirk's entrance. He seemed to shrink into a still smaller man at Kirk's approach to the couch.

"Your Excellency!" Kirk said.

Parmen opened his eyes, annoyed by interruption of

his artistic trance. Then Plato's views on Republican behavior calmed him. "Parmen will do," he said. "Philosopher-kings have no need of titles."

"I want to know why the *Enterprise*'s weapons and instrumentation are frozen—why the ship itself is locked in orbit!"

"Captain, please. You're mistaken, I assure you . . ."

The bland evasion enraged Kirk further. "I just spoke to my Engineer aboard the *Enterprise*," he said. "We showed our good faith. Now you show yours. I want that ship released immediately."

Alexander, in panic, was shaking his head at him, mouthing the words, "No—no . . ." Kirk saw why. Parmen was manifestly displeased. The cultivated benignity of his face had been displaced by a supercilious tightness. "The amenities, Captain," he said. "Allow me to remind you that I am the head of this Principality. Guests don't come barging in here, making demands and issuing orders!"

He looked at Kirk's phaser. The weapon left Kirk's belt and zoomed into Parmen's hand. Kirk studied the cold face with contempt. "Guests!" he said. "You don't know the meaning of the word! Guests are not treated like common prisoners!"

Parmen was more than displeased by the rebuke. His face worked with rage—a rage that held no vestige of Platonic calm. "Don't take that tone with me!" he shouted.

Kirk's hand was lifted to strike him sharply across his left cheek. Then his other hand was brought up to slap his right one. In a matter of seconds he'd lost all power to control his hands. Parmen, leaning back on the couch, watched him repeatedly slap himself across the face with one hand after the other.

Control of his communicator seemed to be also lost. Despite several calls to Scott, he couldn't raise him. Finally, he closed the communicator. His face was burning from the beating he'd given it. Like his anger. That burned, too.

Spock turned from one of the silken curtains that draped a window of their suite. "Obviously," he said, "Parmen does not want any contact made with the *Enterprise*."

McCoy protested. "He may still need the ship's medical stores. Why should he prevent contact?"

"To hide any knowledge of his brutal treatment of a Starfleet Captain," Spock said.

Kirk shook his head. "No, Mr. Spock. One thing is certain. Parmen is not concerned with either my dignity or safety."

"Agreed, Captain," Spock said. "And he would not have treated you so brutally if he had any intention of releasing you—or the *Enterprise*."

Suddenly, McCoy rose from a couch and started toward the door.

"Where are you going?" Kirk said.

"I don't want to go, Jim—but I can't help myself."

As he spoke, Kirk was yanked toward the door, too; and Spock, twisted around, was forced to follow him. The three were literally trotted into the corridor, staring down at their moving legs in horror. Will-lessly, they were propelled back into Parmen's chamber. And to the beat of a lyre and drum. At their entrance, Alexander, a one-man band, evoked a great drum roll that matched the rhythm of their trotting feet. Parmen, Philana beside him, applauded the show.

She rose from the couch and curtsied to them. "Gentle spacemen, we are eternally in your debt," she said. "Please accept some trifles as tokens of our gratitude. They stem from the very source of our inspiration. To the noble captain, a shield carried by Pericles as a symbol of his gallant leadership . . ."

She motioned to a shield on the wall. It flew into Kirk's hands. He was about to drop it; but it hovered at his hands, persistent. At last he was compelled to take it; and Philana, smiling, said, "And to our silent and cerebral Mr. Spock, that kathara from which to pluck music to soothe his ever-active brow . . ."

The instrument left a bench. It sailed over to Spock, who took it; and without looking at it, shoved it under his arm.

It was McCoy's turn to become the recipient of favor. "And lastly, the physician who saved Platonius and my spouse. To you, Dr. McCoy, that ancient collection of Greek cures, penned by Hippocrates himself . . ."

A scroll rose from a table and floated over to McCoy.

Kirk saw him begin to unroll it. He took a furious step forward. "Has my ship been released yet?" he demanded.

Parmen spoke. "Captain, wait. I know what you're thinking. My humble apologies. You were badly used. In my own defense, allow me to say that my illness was more profoundly disturbing than I myself realized."

He leaned back on his couch. A great leaner, Parmen. From his newly-relaxed position, he added, "I'm sure, Captain, that you, too, have been out of sorts; and have reacted with fits of temper and rage. Unlike you, however, what I think and feel is instantly translated into reality. Please find it in your heart to forgive me."

Kirk said, "*Has the* Enterprise *been released yet?*"

"It will be, shortly. You're free to leave the planet."

Kirk turned on his heel, speaking over his shoulder. "Good day, then. And thank you for the gifts."

"Not at all. There is, though, one final request . . ."

Kirk whirled. He'd known there was a catch in this somewhere. "Well?" he said.

But Parmen was looking at McCoy. "After my nearly fatal infection," he said, "it has become clear to us all that we cannot afford to be without a skilled physician." He paused. "We'd like you, Dr. McCoy, to remain with us."

Kirk stood very still. He heard McCoy say, "I'm sorry. That's impossible."

Parmen sat up. "Your duties will be extraordinarily light. You'll be able to read, meditate, conduct research—whatever you like. You will want for nothing."

"I'm afraid the answer is no."

"We'd like to keep this cordial—but we're determined to have you stay, Doctor."

Kirk fought to keep his voice steady. "You can bring yourself to do this after Dr. McCoy saved your life?"

"I'm losing patience, Captain . . ."

Despite all his efforts, Kirk's scorn broke through. "And you consider yourself Plato's disciple!"

The comment amused Parmen. "We've managed to live in peace and harmony for centuries, my dear Captain."

Spock's voice was icy. "Whose harmony? *Yours?* Plato wanted beauty, truth and, above all, justice."

The remark hit Parmen where he hurt. "Captain,

please! I admit circumstances have forced us to make a few adaptations of Plato. But ours is the most democratic society conceivable! Anyone at any moment can be and do just as he wishes, even to becoming the ruler of Platonius *if* his mind is strong enough!''

''And if it isn't strong enough, he gets torn apart like Alexander!''

Parmen reverted to another lean-back against his couch. ''Oh, come now, Captain, we're not children. In *your* culture, justice is the will of the stronger. It's forced down people's throats by weapons and fleets of spaceships. On Platonius we'll have none of these. Our justice is the will of the stronger *mind*. And I, for one, consider it a vast improvement.''

''Why?'' Kirk said. ''Never would we use our weapons for the kind of brutality you practice!''

Relaxation deserted Parmen again. He got to his feet. ''Farewell, Captain Kirk.''

Kirk spoke to McCoy. ''Come on, Doctor.''

He and Spock turned to leave. But McCoy was rooted to the spot where he stood. Kirk, looking back, saw him unmoving, rigid.

''Bones?''

''I—I can't move, Jim. They're going to keep me, no matter what. Leave, please!''

Before, Kirk had never understood the term ''towering rage.'' Now he did. His fury seemed to be making him twelve feet tall in height. *''No!''* he shouted. ''You're a doctor, Bones! They need your goodwill. They're just trying to—''

Parmen interrupted. ''Captain, go while you still can.''

''We're staying right here until Dr. McCoy is released!''

''This is not the *Enterprise*. And you're not in command here, Captain.''

Kirk saw Philana shrug. ''Why even discuss it, Parmen? Get rid of them.''

''But that might offend the good doctor, Philana.'' An idea—a delightful one—seemed to strike Parmen. He smiled at Kirk. ''You wish to stay? Then do, by all means. You can help us celebrate our anniversary.'' He spoke to the immobilized McCoy. "In the process, I hope we can persuade you to join our tiny Republic . . ."

McCoy's tongue was still his to use. "You won't persuade me," he said.

"I think we will," Parmen told him.

Two garlands detached themselves from a marble statue of Aphrodite; and, whirling through the air, landed at the feet of Kirk and Spock. They were forced to bend and pick them up. Their gifts fell from their hands; and the same force compelled them to place the garlands ceremoniously on each other's heads.

Parmen nodded to Alexander. The drum broke into a dancing beat. Kirk and Spock began a tap dance. Spock looked down at his shuffling feet in disgust. But Parmen's delightful idea of celebration was just beginning to be realized. The two *Enterprise* men found themselves childishly skipping around the pool, bowing to each other in mechanical precision. Then a line of a song was placed in Kirk's mouth. "I'm Tweedledee, he's Tweedledum . . ." Spock bowed to him, singing, "Two spacemen marching to a drum . . ."

It wasn't over. "We slithe among the mimsy troves," Kirk sang. Spock bowed to him again. "And gyre amidst the borogroves . . ."

The garlands were exchanged. Kirk pouted sadly at the loss of his; and Spock, grinning madly in triumph, put it on his head. They bowed stiffly to each other and were dropped to their knees.

"McCoy!" Kirk yelled. "You're not staying here, no matter what he does to us!"

Parmen made an imperious gesture. Kirk coughed. He could feel the defiance in his face replacing itself with a pleading abjectness. He heard himself reciting—

Being your slave, what should I do but tend
Upon the hours and times of your desire?
I have no precious time at all to spend,
No services to do till you require.
Nor dare I chide the world-without-end hour
Whilst I, my sovereign, watch the clock for you.
Nor think the bitterness of absence sour
When you have bid your servant once adieu . . .

There was no time for breath. The shaming words continued to stream from him . . .

Nor dare I question with my jealous thought
Where you may be or your affairs suppose,
But, like a sad slave, stay and think of naught
Save where you are how happy you make those!
So true a fool is love that in your will
Though you do anything, he thinks no ill . . .

The idiot thing was done. Kirk's head went down.

"Stop it! Stop it!" McCoy shouted.

Kirk looked up. "No matter what he makes me say, it's no. You hear me, McCoy—*no*! I . . ."

His head was almost twisted from his shoulders. He was jerked to his feet, an arm wrenched behind his back. Something grabbed him under the chin—and pulled his neck back, back until a cry of pain escaped him.

"Well, Doctor?" Parmen said.

McCoy was agonized, wavering with the torment of indecision. He was torn not only by laceration of his deep personal affection for Kirk. There was his professional obligation, too. As the *Enterprise*'s surgeon, its captain's well-being was his prime consideration. If he agreed to remain with these people, he could end the torture, serving both his love for Kirk and his duty to Starfleet service. Finally, he came to his anguished decision. He turned to Parmen. "I have my orders," he said.

Parmen's mouth tightened. "As you wish, Doctor."

Kirk was hurled to the ground. He got up, fists clenched, and rushed at Parmen. The Platonian stared at him. Kirk was frozen, a raised foot still in the air. "Is this your Utopia?" he shouted. "You haven't even . . ."

He was flung again to the floor. Then words, too, were denied him. His vocal cords went dead.

"We've had enough of your moralizing," Parmen said.

McCoy whirled. "And we've had too much of *yours*! You will never get me to stay here!"

He was smashed backward.

"You will be happy to stay," Parmen told him. "It

takes a little time, Doctor. But you will be happy to stay, I promise you."

He unfroze Spock from his knees. The Vulcan, sickened by Kirk's misery, moved toward Parmen only to be frozen in mid-stride.

Philana looked at Spock. "Perhaps you have been a bit too forceful, Parmen. There are other ways that might be more persuasive."

"I doubt that they will be as entertaining. But if you want to have a try, do so."

Spock gave a cry. Philana had sent him into a wild, stamping flamenco. He danced around and around the downed Kirk. McCoy, unseeing, was staring straight ahead.

"An excellent choice, Philana," Parmen said. He spoke to the rigid McCoy. "All you have to do is nod."

The air was filled with the clack of castanets. The viciously-heel-stamping Spock was moved in close to Kirk's head. An inch closer—and Kirk would be trampled to death. A stomping heel grazed his head. McCoy, about to make an appeal, clamped his mouth shut. Then he closed his eyes against the sight of Spock's helpless attack on Kirk.

The castanet sounds ceased. So did Spock's dancing. He froze in a finger-snapping gesture over Kirk's body. His arms dropped. He began to shake. Out of him came wild peals of laughter.

McCoy opened his eyes as he heard them. He looked, appalled, at Spock as his laughter grew wilder. He swung around to Parmen. "Mr. Spock is a Vulcan," he said. "You must not force emotion from him."

"You must be joking, Doctor," Philana said.

"It can destroy him," McCoy said.

"Come now," Parmen said. "There's nothing so wholesome as a good laugh."

Spock was battered now by the insane fits of laughter. McCoy saw him pressing at his chest to soothe the agony of the spasms. Kirk was fighting to lift himself to get to Spock. He sank back to the floor, too weak to do it. McCoy launched a fierce blow at Parmen. "You're killing Spock!" he cried.

"Then we can't let him die laughing, can we now?" Parmen asked.

The laughter ended. Slowly Spock fell to his knees, his head limp, arms dangling.

"The poor fellow does look rather miserable, doesn't he, dear wife?"

Philana encircled Parmen with her arm. "He does, dear husband. You know, nothing relieves misery like a good, honest cry."

McCoy stared at them. "He's a Vulcan! I beg you . . ."

Parmen's face was flushed with a growing excitement. "Later! Later!" he said impatiently. "That's probably not true of Vulcan men, anyway. Shall we test it, Philana?"

Spock's shoulders began to shake. His body rocked from side to side as though wracked by a sudden woe. He was looking into Kirk's pain-ravaged face. Kirk moved on the floor toward him, his arm out. "Hang on, Spock," he whispered. "Hang on! Don't let him break you open . . ." He was tense with the struggle to support Spock's repression. But it was no good. Spock's quiet face had turned into the tormented mask of tragedy. Tears welled in his Vulcan eyes and dripped down his cheeks. Unable to control his sobs, he crashed to the floor.

Alexander, trembling and outraged, hurried to the center of the chamber, his lyre in his hand. "Parmen! They saved your life!"

He was flipped back into the pool. He staggered up, soaking wet, his tears mixed with the water. From deeps he didn't know he owned, he delivered his final judgment on his society. "I'm ashamed to be a Platonian. Ashamed!"

It was a resourceful society. Kirk was lifted to his feet; and, from the pool, the dwarf was placed upon Kirk's back. Alexander's arm whipped him on as he was driven, skipping around Spock's body, its eyes vacant as Kirk passed him.

Parmen spoke sadly to McCoy. "How can you let this go on, Doctor?"

For the moment their ordeals were suspended. They'd been permitted to return to their suite. Alexander had followed them; and was now dressing himself in the dry tunic and pantaloons that were his buffoon's costume. But Spock, his eyes closed, sat apart. The total loss of emotional control had been such a violation of his Vulcan nature that he was still inwardly trembling. Kirk, resting on a couch, watched him anxiously. "Bones, can't you do anything for him?"

"There's no medicine that can help him, Jim. He has to get through this himself."

Despite his aching back, Kirk got up. As he crossed to Spock, McCoy joined him. They stood before him a moment, both quiet; and Spock, slowly becoming aware of their presence, opened his eyes. The awful experience of his turmoil was still evident in them. Kirk looked away from the painful sight of an overwrought Spock. He had no right to intrude on such private agony.

"I trust they did not hurt you too much, Captain."

"Just a sore set of muscles, Spock."

"The humiliation must have been hardest for you to bear, sir. I . . . I can understand."

He assumed his customary impassive expression. But it was belied by the tremor in his voice and hands. Kirk's fury flamed in him.

McCoy tried to be soothing. "The release of emotion is what keeps us healthy," he observed. "At least, emotionally healthy."

"Fascinating," Spock said. "However, I have noted, Doctor, that the release of emotion is frequently very *unhealthy* for those nearest to you. Emotionally, that is."

Kirk forced a chuckle. "Which proves again that there are no perfect solutions."

"It would seem so, Captain."

Spock's eyes closed again. He spoke with them closed. "Captain!"

"Yes, Spock."

"Captain, do you still feel anger toward Parmen?"

"Great anger."

"And you, Dr. McCoy?"

"Yes, Spock. Great hatred."

"You must release it somehow . . . as I must master mine."

Spock suddenly stood up, his eyes wide open. They blazed with rage. He shuddered with the effort to control it, his fists clenching. "They almost made me kill you, Captain. That is why they have stirred in me such hatred. Such great hatred. I must not allow it to go further. I must master it. I must control . . .''

He grabbed Kirk's arm. His hand tightened on it until it seemed his great strength would snap a bone. Kirk held absolutely still. Gradually, Spock relaxed. He dropped the arm. His body was quieted as though the fierce embrace of his captain's arm had been a desperately needed reassurance of the dear existence. He sat down.

McCoy, his face drawn with strain, drew Kirk aside. "Jim . . . Jim, listen. I've thought it over. This is senseless. I'm going to stay.''

"You can't, Bones."

"I have Parmen's word that you'll be safe.''

"Parmen's word! He'll let us beam up to the *Enterprise*—and then plunge the ship into this atmosphere!''

McCoy shook his head. "Why bother to trick me?''

"If he killed us outright in front of you, you'd retaliate. You're a doctor, you have the means.'' He put a hand on McCoy's shoulder. "I know you're trying to do the right thing. But if anyone of us got away, Parmen knows that Starfleet will never let this planet go unpunished. He dare not let us go. Sacrifice yourself by agreement to stay—and you'll only be signing our death warrant.''

Alexander pulled at McCoy's uniform. "The Captain is right. I didn't warn you. They treated you like they treat me. Only you fight them . . .''

The dwarf's eyes filled with tears. "All this time I thought it was me—my mind that couldn't move a pebble. They told me how lucky I was that they bothered to keep me around. And I believed them. The arms and legs of everybody's whim. Look down! Don't meet their eyes . . . Smile! Smile! Smile! Those great people . . . They were my gods . . .''

He seized a vase; and, smashing it against a column, picked up a long, jagged shard of hard earthenware. "You made me see them!'' he cried. "I know what they are now. It's not me, not my runty size! It's them. It's them!''

"Alexander, put that down,'' Kirk said.

"No! It's the best thing for them!''

Kirk and McCoy moved toward him. "I said drop it,'' Kirk said.

Alexander backed toward the door. "I'm going to cut

them up. Parmen first. They'll become infected. Only this time, no matter what they say, let them die!''

Kirk nodded at McCoy. They both rushed the little man; and, as McCoy pinned an arm, the dwarf reluctantly surrendered the weapon to Kirk. "Let me at least give them a taste of what they gave me!" he pleaded. "Please! They're going to kill you anyhow! You already know that . . .''

"There's no point in your dying, too," Kirk said.

Alexander stared at him. Then a sob broke from him.

"That's . . . the first time . . . somebody's thought of my life before his own . . .'' Remorse overwhelmed him. "But it's . . . all my fault. I should have told you right off that they were out to kill you. I knew . . . I knew—but I was afraid.'' The tears welled again.

"It's all right, Alexander," Kirk said. "We haven't given up. Maybe you can help us.''

"I'll do anything for you . . . anything. Just tell me what to do.''

"It might help us to know one thing. Did all the other Platonians always have the power?''

"No. Not before we came here to this terrible planet.''

Spock had joined them. "Then they acquired their psychokinetic power *after* coming here," Kirk said.

"I guess so.''

Spock spoke. "Is it possible for you to recall how long after you arrived here that their power began to develop?''

"How could I forget? It was exactly six months and fourteen days after we got here that they started pushing me around.''

"Would you know how many months'. supplies you brought with you?''

The dwarf's effort to remember was obvious. "I think it was four months . . . no, three. Yes, three . . .''

"That's close enough," Spock said. "Fascinating. The power developed two or three months after they started eating native foods.''

Alexander's eyes widened in surprise. "Yeah! That's right.''

Spock turned to Kirk. "Then it would be logical to assume that there is connection between their psychokinetic power and the native foods.''

McCoy puzzled over Spock's hypothesis. "Then why wouldn't Alexander have the same power as the others?"

"Perhaps his system can't absorb the crucial element, Doctor."

"Bones, I'd like you to take a reading of Alexander's blood," Kirk said.

The dwarf clutched Kirk. "Will it hurt much?"

McCoy smiled at him. "You won't know it happened," he said as he ran his tricorder over his arm.

"Bones, you still have the tricorder reading of Parmen's blood?"

"Of course. Parmen possesses the highest order of psychokinetic ability; Alexander the lowest—and under the same environmental conditions." He looked at Kirk. "I'll put both of their blood samples through a full comparative test in the tricorder."

"If our theory proves out, we've got a weapon . . ." Kirk said.

When the tricorder buzzed, McCoy read out its information on its data window. "The one significant difference between Parmen's blood and Alexander's is the concentration of kironide, broken down by pituitary hormones."

"Kironide's a high-energy source. It could be it!" Kirk said.

"The pituitary hormones confirm the assumption," Spock said. He looked at Alexander. "They also regulate body growth."

"You mean the same thing that kept me from having the power made me a dwarf?"

Spock nodded. "It is obvious now why Parmen has kept his Utopia such a secret. Anyone coming down here and staying long enough would acquire the power."

"Exactly, Mr. Spock." Kirk wheeled to McCoy. "Isn't there some way to build up the same concentration of kironide in us?"

"It'll take doing but it should be possible, Jim."

"Then what are we waiting for?"

McCoy went to work. Pulling vials from his kit, he inserted them in the tricorder. He checked a dial. Then he reached for an optical tube. More vials went into the tricorder. He hesitated. "Jim, even if the kironide has the desired effect, it still may not help us get out of here."

Kirk looked anxiously at Spock. "If all of us *do* come up with the power, what chance do we have against thirty-eight of them?"

"The point's well taken, Captain. However, the power isn't additive. If it were, with the Platonians' hostile propensities, two or three of them would have combined forces centuries ago—and deposed Parmen."

Alexander pulled at Kirk's sleeve. "He's right. Parmen says everyone has his own separate power frequency. He says whenever they try to put their power together and use it, it never works."

McCoy straightened, the hypo in his hand. "I'm ready."

"Then let's not waste time. Give us double the concentration found in Parmen's blood."

As Spock was injected, he said, "The time factor concerns me. It may take days or weeks before there's enough buildup from the kironide to do us any good."

"What about Alexander?" Kirk asked.

"Well," McCoy said, "since the kironide's already broken down and injected directly into the bloodstream, it should work on him as well as the rest of us. Better, in fact—he's acclimated."

But Alexander wanted no part of kironide. "You think the power is what I want? To be one of them? To just lie there and have things done for me—a blob of nothing! You're welcome to the power! And if you make it out of here, all I ask is that you take me with you. Just drop me anyplace where they never heard of kironide or Platonius!"

Kirk said, "All right, Alexander. All right . . ."

"Jim!"

At the tone of McCoy's voice, Kirk whirled. In the room air was shimmering with the familiar Transporter sparkle.

Unbelieving, he watched the dazzle form into the shapes of Uhura and Christine Chapel. They saw him—but when they tried to speak, their mouths were clamped shut. Then their legs moved, marching them like marionettes toward a dressing room.

"Nurse! Lieutenant Uhura!" Kirk shouted.

They didn't turn. As they disappeared into the dressing room, two lovely, sheer mini-robes floated after them.

Acidly bitter, Kirk finally spoke to his men. "The afternoon entertainment wasn't enough for them," he said.

And he stayed bitter, as arrangements were made for the evening's entertainment. *Enterprise* uniforms vanished. He and Spock were forcibly clad in short Greek tunics, knotted over one shoulder. Leaf wreaths were settled on their heads. And in the main room of the suite, a table appeared. Piled high with food, with fruit and wine, it glittered, heavy, with silver and crystal.

The dressing room door opened. A little shy in her highly becoming mini-robe, Christine hesitated. Then her pleasure in seeing them sent her smiling to them. "Are we glad to see you!"

Uhura addressed the question in Kirk's eyes. "We were forced into the Transporter and beamed down. It was like becoming a puppet for someone."

"I thought I was sleepwalking," Christine told him. "I couldn't stop myself."

"I don't understand it," Uhura said. "A simple invitation would have brought me running for this . . ." She lifted a soft fold of the golden robe that matched her exotic skin color.

"Definitely," Christine agreed. "Why use force on a girl to get her into clothes like these?" Then she paused, looking at Kirk. "Captain, what's wrong? Something's terribly wrong, isn't it?"

"Yes," Kirk said quietly.

He had heard the sound of laughter. The bewildered girls stared at each other; and Kirk said, "Spock, have you felt any reaction to the kironide shot?"

"I have experienced a slight flush, Captain."

"So did I. Shall we try a simple test? Let's concentrate on raising that cluster of grapes."

They fixed their eyes on the grapes, the girls watching them in uncomprehending silence. The grapes continued to nestle placidly between two apples.

"Didn't budge," Kirk said.

There was a fanfare of music and a burst of applause. Kirk looked up from the disappointing grapes. Panels set into the room's walls had slid aside, revealing boxes behind them. They were crowded with Platonians. Kirk caught sight of Alexander at a music stand, his instruments beside him. Parmen, Philana and McCoy occupied the center box. The philosopher-king stood up, lifting a hand.

"Fellow Academicians! Twenty-five hundred years ago a hearty band of vagabonds arrived on this barren planet. Those were times of desperate hardship and heartbreaking toil. Then a divine Providence graced our genius with the power of powers! Through it, our every need was materialized. We determined to form a Utopian Brotherhood. This is a festive occasion. For tonight, we welcome its first new member into our Brotherhood!"

Kirk used the top of his voice. "Don't count on it, Parmen! First you must win the doctor's consent!"

McCoy, shouting back, called, "I'll never give it, Jim!"

Whispering, Parmen said, "Doctor, please. You are destroying the festive mood . . ." He waved a hand. "Let the madcap revels begin!"

The four *Enterprise* people were sent whirling around the couches in a game of musical chairs. Then Uhura was dropped on one in a languorous pose. Christine's turn came. Her chin was placed on a bent hand, her body disposed in a seductive position. Kirk and Spock were each pulled to a couch. After a moment they were caused to exchange places.

Eraclitus called from a box, laughing, "Ah, how fickle and faithless! Make up your minds!"

Spock sat on Christine's couch, straining against Parmen's will-to-power. It was no use. His arms encircled Christine; and her hand was forced up to caress his face. The Platonians tittered.

"I am so ashamed, Mr. Spock." But even as her whisper reached Spock, her hand had reached into his hair to tousle it amorously. She whispered again. "Oh, stop it, Mr. Spock. Please make them stop it . . ."

But they were in a close embrace, Christine's arms entwined around him. His eyes were closed in desperate concentration. He was forced to open them in order to gaze passionately into Christine's. Their lips met. As the kiss ended, she said brokenly, "I have so wanted to be close to you. Now all I want to do is crawl away someplace and die . . ."

"Careful, Mr. Spock!" Eraclitus called. "Remember! The arrows of Eros kill Vulcans!"

Christine sank back on the couch. Spock's body followed hers to shouts of "Bravo! Bravo!"

Uhura was saying, "I am so frightened, Captain . . . so frightened . . ."

"That's the way they want you to feel, Lieutenant. It makes them think they're alive."

"I know it . . . I wish I could stop trembling . . ."

Kirk pulled her to him. Uhura looked into his eyes.

"Try not to think of them," Kirk said. "Try!"

She smiled faintly. "You know what I'm thinking, Captain?"

"What, Lieutenant?"

"I'm thinking of all the times on the *Enterprise* when I was scared to death. And I would see you so busy with your commands. And I would hear you from all parts of the ship. And then the fear would pass. Now they are making me tremble. But I am not afraid."

Her dark eyes were serene. "I am not afraid . . ."

They kissed.

The applause was scattered. And what there was of it was too loud.

Philana in her box stirred restlessly. "Parmen, let's get on with it."

"You are so impatient, my wife! Observe the doctor and learn. He is content to wait for the *pièce de résistance*."

Nevertheless, Parmen got on with it. He moved the table of food into a corner and rolled another one into its place. It was loaded with weapons—swords, a bullwhip, knives, a battle-ax. In its center a brazier, a poker thrust into it, glowed red hot. The two *Enterprise* men were lifted from the girls' couches. Kirk found the bullwhip in his hand. He saw Spock reach for the poker. Its tip of iron flamed with its adopted fire.

Kirk whirled to the boxes. "You're dead, all of you!" he cried. "You died centuries ago! We may disappear tomorrow—but at least we're living now! And you can't stand that!

You're half crazy because you've got nothing inside! Nothing!''

But Parmen was looking at the girls. Turning, Kirk realized that they had been transfixed, helpless, on their couches. The heavy whip rose in his hand and lashed out at Uhura. It flicked close to her cheek.

McCoy could bear no more. He rose in his box. "Stop it, Parmen! Stop it! I can't take any more! I can't! I'll do whatever you want!"

Apparently, his capitulation came too late. Parmen merely grinned at him. "I'll stay here with you!" McCoy cried. "I'll serve you. But stop this!"

Alexander broke from his place. Racing to the table of weapons he seized a knife and rushed at Parmen. He was stopped cold. Parmen stood up. "Alexander, again! He likes to play with knives. Very good. We'll indulge him . . ."

Slowly, relentlessly, the knife blade was pressed against the little man's throat. It halted there—and suddenly, unseen fists slammed Parmen against the back of his box.

The shaken Platonian stared around him. Staggering back, he shouted, "Who . . . who . . . who did that?"

Kirk tossed the whip away. *"I did!"*

Eraclitus was on his feet. "Impossible!"

"What's going on?" Philana screamed.

Kirk lifted his head to the boxes. "Platonians, hear this! The next one of you who tries anything will get hurt! Not only do we possess your psychokinetic ability, but we've got it at twice your power level!"

"Not twice mine!" Parmen's eyes veered to Alexander.

The dwarf was spun around; and, knife upraised, sent racing toward Kirk. Instead of evading the charge, Kirk stood still, drawing on all his strength of concentration. His new power slowed the onrush. With a supreme effort, he turned Alexander around and set him running toward Parmen. The battle of wills was joined. Parmen's cold eyes bulged with his struggle to recover control of the dwarf. But Alexander had picked up speed. He vaulted into the box, the knife extended to Parmen's heart . . .

The Platonian shrieked. "Captain, no! I beg of you.

I'll do anything you say! I do not wish to die! Do you hear me, Captain?''

Kirk arrested the knife. But Alexander, so close to vengeance for his years of suffering, fought to plunge the knife deep into his tormentor. "Let me do it!" he cried to Kirk. "Let me finish him!"

Kirk strode to the box. "Do you want to be like him, Alexander?" he said.

The dwarf's eyes met his. After a moment, he shook his head. Then he threw the knife at Parmen's feet.

The new power was exhilarating. Kirk used it to force Parmen to kneel before the dwarf. Alexander looked down at the bald, arrogant head. "Listen to me, Parmen! I could have had the power—but I didn't want it! I could have been in your place right here and now! But the sight of you and your Academicians sickens me. Because, with all your brains, you're dirtier than anything that ever walked or crawled in the whole universe!''

As he jumped from the box to Kirk's side, he turned to say, "Get up from your knees! Get up!"

Parmen, his world crashed around him, spoke to Kirk. "Captain, you knew it was my intention to destroy you and the *Enterprise*. Yet you have spared me."

Kirk eyed him for a long moment. "To us, killing is murder—even for revenge. But I am officially notifying you that other Starships will be visiting Platonius—and soon!''

He'd been right. There was nothing in these people. Once their control power was defeated, they shriveled into nothing. Their ruler was too hasty with his reassurance. "There's no need for concern, Captain. They'll be safe. Of late, I've begun to feel that we've become bizarre and unproductive. It's time for some fresh air. We'll welcome your interstellar visits.''

"I don't believe you," Kirk said. "The minute we leave, you'll lose your fear—and turn as sadistic as ever. So let me warn you. This incident will be reported in its entirety to Starfleet Command.''

His voice went icy. "Keep your power. We don't want it. But, if need be, we can create it in a matter of hours. Don't try anything again.''

All his essential weakness had appeared in Parmen's

flabby face. "Understood, Captain. And you're right. None of us can be trusted. Uncontrolled power turns even saints into savages. We can all be counted on to live down to our lowest impulses."

"You're good at making speeches," Kirk said. "I hope your last one sinks in. Stand back."

Obediently, Parmen shrank back into the box. Philana was haggard, almost looking her great age. McCoy left them to join Kirk.

"Alexander!" Kirk called.

As the dwarf hurried over to him, Kirk released his communicator from his belt. Flipping it open, he said, "Kirk to Scott. I'm bringing a guest aboard. Standby to beam us up."

Alexander looked at him, love in his long-suffering eyes.

WINK OF AN EYE

Writer: Arthur Heinemann (story by Lee Cronin)
Director: Jud Taylor
Guest stars: Kathie Brown, Jason Evers

In the space fronting the handsome building of unidentified metal, a fountain flung its sparkle of spray into the air. Kirk, abstracted, watched Security Guard Compton taking samples of its water. Nearby, McCoy was scanning the plaza's periphery with his tricorder. Necessary but time-consuming occupations, Kirk thought. And useless. They had done nothing to locate the source of that distress call that had forced their beam-down to this unexplored planet calling itself Scalos.

With abrupt impatience, he opened his communicator. "Kirk to *Enterprise*. Lieutenant Uhura, does the location of that distress signal exactly correspond to this area?"

"Yes, sir. And I am receiving visual contact with the Scalosians. I can't see you on the viewing screen but I can see them."

"Check coordinates, Lieutenant."

"The coordinates correspond, sir."

His impatience grew. "There are no Scalosians, Lieutenant. Apart from our landing party, there is nobody here."

"Their distress call is very strong, sir. They are begging for immediate assistance."

"Check circuits for malfunction. Captain out."

He looked up to meet McCoy's nod. "There *must* be a malfunction, Jim. This is a barren world—hardly any vegetation; no apparent animal life."

As though to contradict him, a shrill mosquito whine sounded near Kirk's head. He struck the invisible insect away. "But there's some kind of insect life," he said.

"My tricorder doesn't register it."

"My ears did," Kirk retorted. He dropped the subject for Spock, rounding a corner of the strangely-fluted metal building, was approaching them. "Anything, Mr. Spock?"

"Evidently a civilization of high order, Captain, rating number seven on the Industrial Scale. Humanoid in appearance, according to paintings. An abundance of literature which I shall have translated and processed. Certain structures hold signs of recent occupancy. Other ones apparently long abandoned."

"But no sign of present life," Kirk said.

As he spoke, he noted that Compton, rinsing his hands in the fountain's jet, had lifted one to knock away some unseen annoyance at his ear. At the same moment, he again heard the mosquito whine. He had to make an effort to concentrate on what Spock was saying. ". . . indication of life forms of a highly unusual intermittent nature. They have neither discernible shape nor location. A most puzzling phenomenon, sir."

"The Scalosians *were* here," Kirk said. "We saw them on the viewing screen, Mr. Spock. Lieutenant Uhura can still see them. She's still getting their distress call. What happened to them?"

"At this moment I cannot answer that, Captain."

"Mr. Spock, I want you to make a complete survey of this planet. You will use all the ship's instruments—"

He broke off at McCoy's shout. "Jim! Compton's gone! Look over there! Compton's gone!"

Emptiness was where the guard had been stooping at the fountain. McCoy was staring at its feathered plume of water dazedly. "Compton—gone," he said again.

"Bones!" Kirk said. "Snap out of it! What happened?"

McCoy's shocked eyes veered to his. "He . . . was stowing vials of that fountain's water in his shoulder bags . . . when he vanished. I was looking straight at him—and then he wasn't there. He wasn't there, Jim. He . . . just wasn't there . . ."

Had the Scalos distress signal been real? Maybe unreal like its inhabitants. Kirk, entering the *Enterprise* bridge, barked an inconsequential order to an unremembered crew member. As he sat down in his command chair, he said, "Lieutenant Uhura, start a replay of that distress call." Then he hit a switch. "Mr. Scott, are all Transporter controls still in functioning order?"

"Aye, sir. Is Mr. Spock still down on the planet's surface?"

"He's in Sickbay. Dr. McCoy is running a check on the landing party." His attention, used to dispersing itself to note any significant movement in the bridge, had registered Uhura's look as she struggled with her dials. "What is it, Lieutenant?"

She was frowning. "Malfunction, sir." She touched a switch—and her frown deepened. "Now it's corrected itself."

Sulu spoke. "Captain, there's some trouble on the hangar deck. Controls are frozen."

"Have repair crews been assigned?"

"Yes, sir."

Kirk shot a look of inquiry at Uhura. She nodded. "The tape of the distress call is ready, sir."

Spock had quietly returned to his station. Now he turned to look at the viewing screen. An upside-down image took shape on it. Then, righting itself, it showed a proud, strong male face. Its lips moved. "Those of us who are left have taken shelter in this area. We have no explanation for what has been happening to us. Our number is now five . . ."

The face on the screen took on human height and breadth. The figure moved; and around it appeared the four other Scalosians, two of them women. One was surpassingly lovely. The whole impression created by the group was that of a cultured, singularly handsome people, peaceful in purpose. Their spokesman went on. "I am Rael. We were once a nation of nine hundred thousand, this city alone holding—"

"Freeze it," Kirk said.

Uhura immobilized the tape and Spock, swinging around, said, "Perhaps this distress call was prerecorded— and what we received was a taped signal."

"Mr. Spock, the fact remains that when we beamed down, we could not find these people. They *were* there—now they're *not* there. Nor is crewman Compton."

"Some force or agent only partially discernible to our instruments may have been responsible, Captain."

Kirk nodded. "Mr. Sulu, I want this ship on standby alert while we continue the investigation." But Sulu had turned an anxious face to him. "I have a reading, sir, that our deflectors are inoperative. They do not respond to controls."

"Scotty, assist," Kirk said. He got up to go over to Spock's chair. "Mr. Spock, ever since we beamed back up from Scalos, we have suffered a series of malfunctions. I wish an investigation and an explanation. I want—"

McCoy's voice interrupted. "McCoy to Captain Kirk. The Captain's presence for examination is requested."

"Can't it wait, Bones?"

"Your orders, Jim. You're the last one."

"What do you read so far?"

"Can we discuss it in Sickbay?"

Moving to the elevator, Kirk said, "Mr. Spock, you have the con." But the elevator doors, instead of whooshing open at his approach, remained shut. Kirk wheeled, shouting, "Is this another malfunction?"

Spock jabbed hastily at buttons: and after a long moment, the doors opened slowly, grudgingly. Kirk was still fuming as he jerked off his shirt in Sickbay. "Bones! What did your examinations of the others turn up?"

"All normal. Whatever caused Compton's disappearance didn't affect anyone else."

"Has anyone experienced anything unusual since beaming back up?"

"No mention of it. No, Jim."

But Nurse Chapel looked up from the sheet she was draping over Kirk's midriff. "Yet something's going on, Captain. All the medical supply cabinets have been opened."

Kirk sat up. "Anything missing?"

"Just disordered. As if everything had been picked up and examined."

Once again that insect whine sounded close to Kirk's ear. He waited a moment before he said, "Bones, could something be causing me to hallucinate?" The urgency in his voice startled McCoy out of his concentration on his medical panels. He turned. "How—hallucinate? What do you mean?"

"Twice," Kirk said, "I've felt something touch me. Nothing was there. I just felt it again. Did I just fancy it?"

"There's nothing physically wrong with you, Jim."

"I asked you a question. Am I hallucinating?"

McCoy left his panels. "No."

Kirk leaped from the medical table. "Then we *did* beam something aboard! Something has invaded this ship!" He was making for the intercom when the alarm of a red alert sounded. Over the shrieking of its sirens, he cried, "Captain to bridge! Mr. Spock, come in!"

Spock didn't come in. Minutes passed before Kirk could hear the voice, faint, blurred. "Captain, I have a reading from the life support center . . ."

"Spock, I can't hear you! Check circuits. Is it a malfunction?"

More minutes passed. Then it was Uhura speaking, her voice also dimmed and distorted. ". . . intercom system breaking down rapidly . . ."

Kirk felt the sweat breaking out on his forehead. "Lieutenant, issue a shipwide order! Use communicators instead of the intercom. Arm all crewmen with phaser pistols. Spock, come in!"

The words were a jumble. "Reading . . . life support . . . center. Alien . . . substances . . . introduced . . ."

Kirk was shouldering into his shirt. "Mr. Spock, meet me in the life support center! On the double! Captain to Security! Armed squad to life support center at once!" He was at Sickbay's door when he saw McCoy sway. Christine Chapel, clutching the back of a chair, called, "The oxygen content is dropping, Doctor . . ."

As for Kirk himself, Sickbay, its door, its cabinets, its equipment, were all swimming into blur. He fought the dizziness that threatened to become darkness, struggling to open his communicator. "Bridge! Bridge! Scotty, where are you? Emergency life support!"

Scott's steady voice said, "Emergency on, sir."

Behind him, McCoy and Christine were gulping in lungfuls of healthy air. Kirk's vertigo subsided—and Scott said, "Condition corrected, Captain."

But the cold hand of imminent death had touched Kirk. It was a man of a different discipline who met Spock at the entrance to the life support center. As wordlessly as it was given, he took the phaser, flinging open the door to the center. Its security guards, sprawled on the floor, were kneeing back up to their feet. One, phaser out, charged to his left, only to be flung back and down again by something invisible. Kirk, staring around him, said, "How do you explain that, Mr. Spock?"

The sharp Vulcan eyes scanned their tricorder. "A force field, sir, with the nature of which I am unfamiliar. But I get a reading of alien presences similar to those obtained on the planet. They seem to have no exact location."

" 'Life forms of a highly unusual, intermittent nature'." Kirk recalled grimly. "Phasers on stun, everybody. Sweep the area."

Once more came the thin whine. Phaser beams were lacing the corridor outside. Inside, Kirk and Spock edged cautiously forward to the location of the force field. Instead of flinging them back, it yielded to them; but when a guard moved to follow them, he was struck down.

"It would seem they will allow only the two of us in to the life support unit," Spock said. "Take care, Captain."

Kirk took the advice. He opened the heavy door to the unit, his weapon at the ready. At first glance the unit appeared to be its usual self, its complex coils, squat dynamos, its serpentine tubings and compressors arranged in their customary pattern. Then Kirk saw the gleaming metal of the device affixed to one of the dynamos. The metal was fluted like that of the Scalosian building. Though alien in shape and material, the small device had been able to affect the functioning of the huge life support unit.

"Mr. Spock, what is it?"

"I cannot determine, Captain. Perhaps a Scalosian refrigerating system." He scanned the thing with his tricorder. "It would seem that installation of the device is incomplete, sir. Life support is still operational."

"Disconnect it," Kirk said.

But the hand Spock extended toward the fixture was flung back. Kirk, whipping out his phaser, heard yet again that now familiar whine. "Destroy it, Spock!" he shouted.

As their two phasers fired at the device, their weapons disappeared. One moment, they were hard, tangible in their hands; but the next, they were gone. Both men pushed forward and were thrust strongly back.

"And that wasn't a force field!" Kirk cried. "Something pushed me back. They are in here with us!" He swung around, shouting at the empty air. "You! What are you doing to my ship? Show yourselves!"

The mosquito whine shrilled. They tried again, not lunging this time to the device but approaching it. A hard shove sent them stumbling back.

Spock's voice was dry. "It seems that we may look at their mechanism—but that is all, Captain."

Kirk nodded. "A show of strength." He shouted again to the invisible enemies. "But we'll find a way to dismantle this aggressive engine of yours!"

It was more than a mere show of strength. Back on the bridge, they discovered that key systems over the entire ship had either been crossed or fused. Spock's computer alone was still operational. All doors, including those of the elevators, were jammed open. Scott greeted them with a gloom thick as a Tyneside fog. "Warp engines are losing potency, Captain. We shall be on emergency power soon—a situation that gives us at most one week of survival."

Kirk wheeled to Spock. "Have your readings been fed into the computer bank?"

"Affirmative, Captain."

"Readout."

Flipping a switch, Spock addressed the computer. "Analyze and reply. Have we been invaded?"

"Affirmative."

"Nature and description of enemy forces."

"Data insufficient."

"Purpose of the invasion."

"Immediate purpose, seizure and control of the Federation Starship *Enterprise*. Data insufficient for determination of end purpose."

"Is there a link between this seizure and Compton's disappearance?"

"Data insufficient."

"Are we at present capable of resisting?"

"Negative."

"Recommendations?"

"If incapable of resistance, negotiate for terms."

Listening, Kirk glared at the computer. Then he flushed at his own childishness. The computer was just doing its computer job. But men were not computers. "We will not negotiate for terms," he said. "Scotty, do you concur?"

"Aye, sir."

Spock, giving him an approving nod, said, "What are *your* recommendations, Captain?"

"Coffee," Kirk said. He turned to the pretty yeoman on duty. "Is a round of coffee available to bridge personnel—or have those circuits also been damaged?"

She smiled, adoration in her eyes. It shouldn't have cheered him up—but it did. Challenge hardened his jaw as he looked around him at an air made malevolent by invisible hostility. "Let them take the next step," he said. "The next move is theirs."

His cup of coffee was set on the arm of his chair. He let it wait to cool. Then, as he leaned back in the chair, his hair was suddenly stirred. He stared around him, baffled—and felt soft lips on his. He *was* hallucinating. McCoy was wrong. He put out a tentative hand, exploring the space before him. Shaking his head, he seized his cup and, after drinking its coffee, replaced it on the chair arm. At the same instant, he became abruptly aware of a change of tempo in the voices around him. They sounded too slow, like those from a phonograph that was running down. And the movements of the bridge people—they, too, seemed strangely slowed, lethargic.

He went to Spock. But Spock, who had bent to his computer, seemed unable to reach its hood.

"Mr. Spock, what's wrong?"

The Vulcan didn't answer. He sat perfectly still in his chair. Kirk wheeled, calling, "Scotty!" No reply. Scott appeared to be frozen in the very act of moving a dial. It was then he heard the feminine giggle—a very feminine giggle. It came from his left. He turned. The Scalosian beauty was standing there, her chestnut hair making a dream of her creamy skin. She wore a short garment of golden gauze that clung to a slim body of subliminally provocative appeal. She was laughing at him; and the gleam of her teeth between her rosy lips gave the lie to all poets' talk of "pearls."

Still laughing, she kissed him. She flung her arms around his neck and kissed him. He tried. He tried to remember who he was; the pressing problems of the *Enterprise*, his command responsibilities. But all he succeeded in doing was to remove the lovely arms from his neck.

"Who are you?" he said.

"Deela, the enemy," she said. "Isn't it delicious?"

He had thought he knew women. But nothing in his experience had prepared him for this dazzling combination of mischief and outrageously open attractiveness. "*You're* the enemy?"

She nodded her enchanting head. "Yes. You beamed me aboard yourself when you came up. A ridiculously long process . . ."

"*What have you done to my ship?*"

"Nothing."

He swung around to gesture to the motionless bridge people. "You call that nothing?"

"They're all right," she said. "They're just what they have always been. It's you who are different."

He stared around him. "Lieutenant Uhura . . . Mr. Sulu . . . every one of them . . ."

"Captain, they can't hear us. To their ears we sound like insects. That's *your* description, you know. Accurate, if unflattering. Really, nothing's wrong with them."

"Then what have you done to me?"

"Changed you. You are like me now. Your crew can't see you because of the acceleration. We both move now in the wink of an eye. There is a dreary scientific term for it—but all that really matters it that you can see me and talk to me and . . ." The creamy eyelids lowered over eyes the color of wet green leaves. ". . . and we can go on from there."

"Why?" Kirk said.

"Because I like you. Didn't you guess?" She came closer to him. She was ruffling his hair now; and he seemed unable to do a thing about it. The situation was out of hand . . . the presence of his crew . . . this public exhibition of endearments . . . her overwhelming beauty . . . his ship's predicament. He seized the caressing hands. They were warm, soft. It wasn't the answer.

"Is it because you like me that you've sabotaged my ship?"

"It hasn't been sabotaged. We just had to make some changes in it to adjust it to our tempo."

"'We'?"

"Of course. My chief scientist and his men. I'm their Queen. You're going to be their King. You'll enjoy living on Scalos."

"And what happens to my ship—*my* men?"

"Oh, in a few of their moments they'll realize you've vanished. Then they'll look for you. But they won't find you. You're accelerated far beyond their powers to see. So they'll go on without you . . ."

He became conscious that her hands were still in his. He released them. She smiled at him. "Don't be stubborn. You *can't* go back to them. You must stay with me. Is that so dreadful a prospect?"

He reached for his phaser. "I won't kill you—but the 'stun' effect isn't very pleasant."

"Go ahead," she said. "Fire it at me."

He fired the stun button. She stepped aside and the beam passed harmlessly by her. She laughed at the look on his face. "Don't look so puzzled. My reactions are much too fast for such a crude weapon. Besides, I'm quite good at self-defense." She pulled a small instrument from her golden belt. Pointing it at his phaser, she fired it—and its beam tore the phaser out of his hand. "It can be set for stun and destroy, too," she said. "Like yours. Please accept what's happened. There's nothing you can do to change it."

His ship. Suppose he capitulated—and went with her? Went with her on the condition she made the *Enterprise* operational again and removed the device attached to the life support system? Spock could carry on . . .

His face was somber. She saw it set into grim lines and cried, "Don't fret so! You'll feel better about it in a little while. It always happens this way . . . they're all upset at first. But it wears off and they begin to like it. You will, too. I promise . . ."

He turned on his heel and left her. She touched a medallion on the golden belt. "He's on his way to you, Rael. Be gentle with him," she said.

Kirk came at a run down the corridor to the life support center. He found what he expected. The *Enterprise* guards at its door were stiff, rigid. He skirted them; and was starting toward the door when a third guard in the Starship's uniform emerged from a corner. "Compton!" Kirk shouted.

Compton beamed at him. "Captain Kirk! So you made it here!"

"You've been accelerated, haven't you?" Kirk said.

"Yes, sir."

"Are they in there? They've got something hooked in to life support—and we've got to get rid of it. Come on!"

But Compton had barred his way with the Scalosian weapon. "Sorry, sir. Entry is forbidden."

"Who gave that order?"

"The commander, sir. You'll have to step back, please."

"*I* am your commander—and I order you to let me in."

"I am very sorry, sir. You are no longer my commander."

"Then who is? Deela? Are you working for her?"

Compton reached an arm back into the corner's shadows and drew out the other Scalosian girl. He spoke very earnestly. "At first I refused, sir—but I've never known anyone like Mira. She brought me aboard and I showed them the ship's operations, its bridge controls and life support. I didn't understand at first but I do now. I—I've never been in love before, sir."

Kirk stepped back. Then, lunging at Compton, he chopped the weapon away from him and raced for the door.

In the center, Rael, two other Scalosians beside him, was working on the small device. He looked up as Kirk plunged in. "Stun," he said to one of his men. The weapon came up; and from behind Kirk, pushing him aside, Compton hurled himself at it. His try at protection was too late. The blast caught Kirk. He collapsed. Raging, Rael felled Compton with a blow. "You were ordered to stop him! Why did you disobey?"

Compton's mouth was bleeding. "You wanted to hurt him," he said.

"He was violent and to be subdued. Why did you disobey?"

"He—he was my Captain . . ."

Compton crumpled. "Go to him, Ekor," Rael said. The man with the weapon knelt beside Compton. Mira, who had drifted into the center, joined him. When he looked up, he said, "There is cell damage." The girl, her pretty face curious, stooped over Compton. "Don't be troubled," Rael told her. "Another will be secured for you." Nodding, she strolled out of the door.

It was Uhura who first noticed the empty command chair. "The captain!" she cried. "He's gone! Mr. Spock, the captain's gone! He was sitting there just a minute ago! He'd just drunk his coffee! There's the cup—on the arm of his chair! But where's the Captain?"

Spock had already left his station. "Mr. Sulu, what did you see?"

Sulu turned a bewildered face. "That's what happened, sir. He was there, putting his cup down—and then he wasn't there!"

There was a moment's silence before Spock said, "Mr. Sulu, did you drink coffee when the yeoman brought it around?"

"Yes, sir."

Spock eyed the bridge personnel. "Did anyone else?" he said.

"I had some," Scott said.

One by one Spock lifted their cups, sniffing at them. Then he sniffed at Kirk's.

"Was it the coffee?" Scott cried. "Are we going to vanish, too, like the captain?"

"The residue in these cups must be analyzed before I can answer that, Mr. Scott."

"And by *that* time— " Scott fell silent.

"I suggest," Spock said," that we remember the Captain's words. Make them take the next step. In the meantime we must determine effective countermoves. The con is yours, Mr. Scott. I shall be in the medical laboratory."

Deela sat on the deck in life support center, the head of the still unconscious Kirk in her lap. Rael, at the device, watched her as she smoothed the hair from his forehead. "I told you," she said, "to be gentle with him."

"He was violent. We had to stun him to avoid cell damage."

She looked over to where Compton lay in a neglected huddle. "Who damaged that one? You? I might have known it. I suppose he was violent, too."

"He turned against us," Rael said.

"And you lost your temper."

"He had to be destroyed. He had not completely accepted change. It is a stubborn species."

Deela's eyes were still on Compton. "I know what happens to them when they're damaged. You will control your temper, Rael. I don't want that to happen to mine. If they're so stubborn a species, perhaps they'll last longer."

"It may be."

"I hope so. They all go so soon. I want to keep this one a long time. He's pretty."

"He is inferior, Deela!"

"We disagree, Rael."

"You cannot allow yourself to feel an attachment to such a thing!"

"I can allow myself to do anything I want!" The flare of anger passed as quickly as it had come. "Oh, Rael, don't be that way," she coaxed. "Am I jealous of what you do?"

"I do my duty."

"So do I. And sometimes I allow myself to enjoy it."

As she spoke, Kirk's dazed eyes opened. Under his head he felt the softness of feminine thighs. He shook it to clear it; and looking up, saw Deela smiling at him. "Hello," she said.

He sat up—and recognized Rael. Leaping to his feet, he turned on Deela. "Is this what you wanted us for? To take over our ship?"

She rose in one graceful movement. "We need your help. And you and your ship are supplying it."

"And what does that device of yours have to do with the supply?"

"Hush," she said. "I'll tell you everything you want to know. And you'll approve of it."

"Approve!" he shouted. "We're your prisoners!"

"Hardly," she said. "You're free to go wherever you want."

Kirk rushed to the life support unit. Instead of interfering, Rael stepped aside. "Go ahead, Captain. Our mechanism is not yet completely linked to your support system but it is in operating order. Study it if you wish. I advise you not to touch it."

Kirk's eyes narrowed. He eyed the small device; and spotting its connecting switch, extended a wary hand to it. He snatched it back, the Scalosians watching him expressionlessly. Then, despite the shock of contact with it, he grabbed it boldly with both hands. They froze on it. Deela ran to him; and, careful not to touch the switch herself, released his hands.

"He told you not to touch it!" She folded his numbed palms between hers, warming them. "The cold will soon pass," she said.

Rael spoke. "Our mechanism has its own self-defense arrangement. You should have heeded me."

Kirk jerked his still icy hands from Deela's. He'd had enough of these aliens; and, feeling a sudden compunction for Compton, sprawled and untended in his heap, he went to him quickly to kneel beside him. But what had been the young and vigorous Compton was now withered by age, mummified as though dried by a thousand years of death. He looked up in horror and Rael said, "In your struggle with Compton, you damaged some of his cells. Those newly accelerated to our tempo's level are sensitive to cell damage. They age very rapidly and die."

Kirk got to his feet. "Is this what you have prepared for us?"

"We all die," Rael said. "Even on Scalos."

Kirk looked around at the bland faces. Where was the way back into his own time . . . the time of Spock . . . of McCoy . . . of Scotty? A sense of unutterable loneliness overwhelmed him. He walked out of the center.

Behind him Deela cried, "Rael, why did you lie to him? He didn't damage the dead one! You did!"

Rael shrugged. "Perhaps he'll be less violent now."

"There was no reason to make him feel worse than he does!"

"What do you care about his feelings?"

She changed her tactics. "Rael," she said, "he's not one of us. You know he's temporary." But Rael still stooped to his work. She sighed; and touching the medallion on her belt, listened. "He's in the medical laboratory trying to communicate with the Vulcan. He likes that one of the pointed ears. His species seems capable of much affection."

"I have noted that," Rael said stiffly.

"Oh, stop sulking! Accept it. We've had to accept it all our lives! Don't make it worse!"

Rael seized her fiercely in his arms. Her hand was reaching to caress his face when she broke free, laughing and breathless. "Not now," she said. "Go back to work."

He didn't. Instead, he watched her as she followed Kirk out of the center. She found the door of the medical laboratory open. Ignoring the rigid figures of Spock and McCoy, she went to the communicator console where Kirk was dictating. "Kirk to Spock," he was saying. "I have fed all facts ascertainable into the computer banks—" He broke off as he saw Deela.

She studied him—a beautiful woman estimating a man for her own reasons. "Go ahead," she said. "It won't accomplish anything. But it may be historically valuable."

Eyes on her, he continued. "Hyper-acceleration is the key, Mr. Spock. We are in their control because of this acceleration. They are able to speed others up to their level as they did to Compton and me. Those so treated then exist at their accelerated tempo, become eventually docile but when—"

"Damaged," Deela said.

Kirk gave her a mock bow. "When damaged, they age incredibly fast as if the accelerated living—"

"Burns them out," Deela said.

"Destroys them. Compton is destroyed. The device affixed to life support produces an icy cold. It is my belief it will turn the *Enterprise* into a gigantic deep-freeze and for purposes the Scalosians alone know—"

"Quite correct," Deela said.

Kirk was ironic. "My opinion has been verified. Their mechanism has it own protective shield, preventing physical contact. I have no means of destroying it. But its destruction is imperative. I am dictating this in the presence of their

Queen who has denied none of it. Why she has permitted me to—''

Leaning forward, the cloud of her hair brushing his shoulder, Deela spoke for the record into the communicator.

''Because by the time you hear this, it will be too late. Our mechanism will be activated.''

He turned to look at the two stiffened figures of his friends. The ice would creep through the *Enterprise* to stiffen them forever in a shroud of frost. He swung to Deela. ''*Why?* Why are you doing this?''

''You really want to know? In a short time, it won't matter to you a bit. You'll be quite happy about it, as Compton was.''

''I want to know.''

''Oh dear. You *are* so stubborn. It should be obvious to one with your reasoning powers that we're doing it because we have to.'' She pushed the shining cloud of hair back. ''A long time ago, we used to be like you. Then our country was almost destroyed by volcanic eruptions. The water was polluted and radiation was released. That changed us. It accelerated us . . .''

He waited. It was possible. The long-term effects of radiation were still unpredictable. ''The children died,'' she said. ''Most of the women found they couldn't bear any more. All our men had become sterile. We had to mate outside our own people . . .''

A doomed race. Listening, Kirk seemed to know what he was going to hear. He felt a stab of pity. She gave him a sad little smile. ''So, whenever a space ship came by, we sent out calls for help. But accelerating their crews to our level burned them out . . .'' She came to him and put her head on his shoulder. ''Don't you see? Must I give you every detail? We're going to take you down with us. Maybe one or two others of your crew, too. /e have to. We'll be kind to you. I *do* like you, you know.''

''And the rest of my crew?'' Kirk said.

''It's as you said. They'll be kept frozen in a reduced animation we know how to suspend. It won't do them any harm. We'll save them for our future needs. You won't last forever. You know that.'' At the look on his face, a cry tore from her. ''Captain, we have the right to survive!''

"Not at the cost you impose," he said.

"You'd do exactly the same thing! You came charging down into that life support room just as soon as you knew it was threatened! You'd have killed every one of my people if you could have . . ."

"You had invaded my ship! You were endangering my crew!"

"There's no difference!" she cried.

"There's every difference. You are the aggressors!"

"We didn't ask for our situation. We're simply handling it the only way we know how to—the way our parents did and their parents before them . . ."

"Would you call it a real solution?"

She looked at him, silent. "Have you tried any other answer? Deela, tell your scientist to disconnect his construction—to destroy it! I promise you we'll use every skill we have to help you. We'll even move you to another planet if you want that. We'll call on the most brilliant minds in our Federation for help!"

She shook her head. "We *have* tried other ways. We tried to make the transition to your time level. Those who made the attempt died. We're trapped, Captain, just as you are now. I'm sorry for what it's going to do to you but I can't change it. And you can't change me."

The medallion on her belt beeped. She touched it and Rael's voice said, "Go to the Transporter Room, Deela. Signal me when you're there and beam down."

"With the captain?"

She was frowning, concentrated on the medallion—and Kirk grabbed his chance. He pulled his dictated tape partially out of the computer so that Spock would note it. He heard Rael say, "Yes. I'll activate our mechanism and follow you. I'm setting it to allow enough time for all of us to get off the ship. But don't delay, Deela."

Kirk had raced for the lab door. Behind him, Deela shouted, "The captain's gone!"

"Go after him, Deela!"

But his headstart had given him time to make the Transporter Room. He rushed to its console, ripped out some wire; and had it shut again to conceal the damage as Deela ran in.

"Why did you leave me?" she demanded.

"I panicked," Kirk said.

The green eyes swept over him. "I don't believe that," she said.

"Can we leave before he activates your device?" he said.

She looked at him, her smooth brow puckered suspiciously. Then she touched the medallion. "Rael, we're in the Transporter Room. You can—activate."

"Beam him down at once."

Still doubtful, she gestured Kirk to the platform. At the console, she pushed a switch. It swung, limp—and the smile in the green eyes deepened. "What did you do to the Transporter, Captain?"

"Nothing," he said. "It must be what your people did. Try the switch again."

She obeyed. Then she touched the medallion communicator. "The Transporter isn't working," she said quietly.

"What did he do to it?"

She delayed her answer. The impishness glinted in her eyes. She was enjoying herself. It was fun to pretend she didn't know what she knew. "Nothing," she told Rael. "He didn't have time. I think it's a—what do they call it? A malfunction. You'd better not activate yet." She turned to Kirk, the amusement still in her face. "What would you say it is, Captain?"

He assumed a thoughtful look. "Well, our technicians reported a loss of energy. That may be it."

She spoke solemnly to the medallion. "The captain says his technicians—"

"I heard him. Do you expect me to believe him?"

It was the Queen in her who spoke. "*I* expect you to check into all possible causes." She turned the medallion off to smile the impish smile at Kirk. "If I had a suspicious nature," she said, "I'd say you sabotaged the Transporter, Captain. To buy time."

"Of course," he said.

She laughed with delight. "Aren't we the innocent pair? I despise devious people, don't you?"

Kirk nodded gravely. "I believe in honest relationships, myself." He hesitated. "Deela, you've never seen my quarters. Before we leave, wouldn't you like to?"

Their eyes met. "Are they like you?" she said. "Austere, efficient—but in their own way, handsome?"

"Yes," he said.

In his cabin, the first thing she went to was his mirror. "Oh, I look a perfect fright! All this running about has left me a perfect fright, hasn't it?"

She lifted a brush from the dresser and flung her head over, the shining hair cascading to the floor. She parted the chestnut curtain with a finger, peeking at him. Then she laughed, tossed the hair back and began to brush it, a delicious woman attracting what she knows her preening has attracted. An electric spark flashed between them.

"Are you married, Captain?"

"No."

"No family, no attachments? Oh, I see. You're married to your career and never look at a woman."

"You're mistaken," he said. "I look, if she's pretty enough."

"I wondered when you'd say something nice to me. Am I more presentable now?"

"A bit," he said.

She was facing him, the brush still in her hand. "It was quite delightful kissing you when you couldn't see me. But now that you do see me, don't you think . . . ?"

He strode to her, took her in his arms and kissed her. She drew back—but he had felt her body tremble. Her arms were reaching for his neck when she whirled out of his embrace, her weapon out. "Unfair!" she cried. "To try and take it in the middle of a kiss!"

She thrust it back into her belt. "But I'll forgive you. I'd have been disappointed in you if you *hadn't* tried to take it!"

"Was I too crude?" Kirk said.

"Just don't try it again, that's all. You're so vulnerable to cell damage. All I have to do is scratch you." She held up pink nails. Then she lifted his arms and placed them around her waist. "You'll come around to our way of thinking sooner or later. And it will be better sooner or later. That's a promise."

* * *

In the medical lab, Spock, still functioning in normal time, was about to insert a tape of his own into the computer when McCoy called him. "Have a look at this, Spock. There's no question about it. The same substance is in the captain's coffee as in the Scalosian water. But not a trace of it in the other cups."

Spock spoke to Christine. "Nurse, program that information and see if we can isolate counteragents."

A mosquito whined. Spock, striking at air, turned to McCoy. "Did you just hear—"

"I've been hearing that whine ever since we beamed down to Scalos."

"We brought it with us. And I know what it is. I shall be on the bridge." They stared after him, puzzled, as he raced out of the lab. He was still running when he brought up short on the bridge. "Lieutenant Uhura, replay that Scalosian distress call on my viewer!"

"Yes, sir."

Rael's image appeared on the screen. Spock leaned forward in his chair, waiting for the voice. It came. "Those of us who are left have taken shelter in this area. We have no explanation for what has been happening to us. Our number is now five . . ."

It was enough. Spock twisted a dial on the viewer; and the voice, rising in pitch, became incoherent babble, went higher still until it turned into recognizable whine. Spock slowed the voice back into words, lifted it up again into the whine—and nodded. On the screen, the image, rushed faster and faster, had first blurred. Then it vanished.

"So," Spock said to nobody.

Back in the lab, McCoy had made a discovery, too. Banging away the whining mosquito at his ear, he spoke into the intercom. "McCoy to Spock."

"Spock, here."

"Did you leave a tape in the computer? I've tried reading it but I get nothing but that whine . . ."

"Bring it to the bridge at once, Doctor."

Kirk's voice. They listened to it on their separate edges of eternity, each of them reading his own fate in Compton's and Kirk's.

". . . Its destruction is imperative. I am dictating this

in the presence of their Queen who has denied none of it.
Why she has permitted me—''

Deela's voice came. "Because by the time you hear this,
it will be too late. The mechanism will be activated . . .''

Silence fell over the bridge people. Spock leaned swiftly
to his console. "I read no change in life support," he said.
"Lieutenant Uhura, alert the rest of the crew.''

Scott rose and went to him. "We could use phasers to
cut through the wall, bypass the force field and get to that
mechanism . . .''

"Mr. Scott, we cannot cope with them on our time
level.''

"Is there a way to cope with them on theirs?''

"A most logical suggestion, Mr. Scott. Please stand by
in the Transporter Room. Dr. McCoy, I should appreciate
your assistance.''

They left with him, their faces blank with bewilder-
ment. Uhura followed them with her eyes. "Mr. Sulu, if
nothing has happened yet, wouldn't it mean that the captain
has managed to buy time, somehow?''

"Yes," Sulu said. "But how much?''

Rael had restored sufficient energy to the Transporter
for a beam-down. But his success had a bitter taste. His fancy
persisted in tormenting him with present and future images
of Deela with Kirk. Finally, he touched his own medallion.

"Deela . . .''

She didn't answer. Languorously, she was combing her
hair to rights before Kirk's mirror. He watched her from a
chair. Then he got up, smiling at her reflection in the mirror.
As he kissed the back of her neck, she turned full into his
arms.

"Deela!''

Rael stood in the cabin doorway. The hot fury in him
exploded. He reached for her; and seizing a lamp, hurled it
at Kirk. Kirk ducked it. Cell damage! In his accelerated state,
this could be no ordinary fight. Deela screamed, "Rael, stop
it! Don't hurt him! Rael! Captain, get out . . .''

Grabbing her weapon, she fired it at the lamp. But Rael
lunged at Kirk again, barehanded. She fired again, spinning

him around with the force beam. "That's enough!" she cried. "Did he damage you, Captain?"

"No."

"How very fortunate for you, Rael! Don't try anything like that again!"

"Then don't torment me. You know what I feel."

"I don't care what you feel. Keep that aspect of it to yourself. What I do is necessary, and you have no right to question it." She paused to add more quietly, "Allow me the dignity of liking the man I select."

He stood sullen but subdued. "Is the Transporter repaired?" she said.

"I have more work to do."

"Then do it." He left. She remained silent, more depressed by the scene than she cared to show. After a long moment, she spoke. "He loves me. I adored him when I was a child. I suppose I still do." She made an effort to recover their former mood. "I must say, you behaved better than he did."

"I hope so," Kirk said.

Something in his manner startled her. "What did you say?"

"That I hope I behaved well."

She was staring at him. "And nothing troubles you now?"

"Why are we here?"

"Our leaving was delayed. Don't you remember? You damaged the Transporter."

"That was wrong," Kirk said.

"It certainly was."

"But we are going to Scalos?"

"Do you want to?"

"Yes."

"What about your crew? Aren't you worried about them?"

"They'll be all right here."

Her mouth twisted with distaste. "What's the matter?" Kirk said.

"You've completely accepted the situation, haven't you? You even like it."

"Am I behaving incorrectly?"

"No." Then she burst out petulantly. "Oh, I liked you

better before! Stubborn, independent . . . and irritating! Like Rael!"

"Those are undesirable qualities," Kirk said.

But she was brooding over her discovery. "Maybe that's why I liked you so much. Because you were like him."

The muscles of Kirk's face ached under the blandness of his smile. But he held it. She touched her medallion. "Rael, you don't have to worry about him. He's made the . . . adjustment."

McCoy was examining the vial of liquid he had processed. "It's finished," he told Spock wearily.

Spock took the vial; and, mixing some of its contents with the Scalosian water, exposed the result to an electronic device. "It counteracts the substance most effectively, Doctor."

"Under laboratory conditions. The question is, will it work in the human body? And the second question is, how do we get it to the captain?"

Spock poured some of the Scalosian water into a glass. He lifted the glass in a toast to McCoy. "By drinking their water." He drained the glass.

"Spock! You don't know what the effects—"

But Spock was savoring the taste. "It is . . . somewhat stimulating." He paused. "And yes, Doctor, you seem to be moving very slowly. Fascinating."

He winked out. McCoy sank down in a chair, his eyes on the vacancy where Spock had stood.

Rael, his face intent, twisted a knob on his refrigerating mechanism. When it flared into red life, he adjusted another one. He nodded to himself as it began to pulsate, its throb dimming the lights of the life support unit. He touched his communicator medallion. "The arrangement is activated, Deela. Go to the Transporter Room and beam-down at once. The others have already left."

Scott was at the console. Unseeing, unmoving, he didn't turn as Kirk entered the room with Deela. Time, time, Kirk thought—was there no way to gain more time? He looked at the Transporter platform that was to maroon him on Scalos, and Deela said, "Come, Captain. We are leaving your pretty ship. Your crew will be all right. You said so yourself."

He smiled at her. "Know something?" he said. "I think I'll make sure of it." Then he caught her; and wrenching her weapon from her belt, ran for the door.

She screamed into her medallion. "Rael! He broke away! He's armed—"

"I'm ready for him!"

Kirk was racing down the corridor to life support, ducking the stony figures of his crewmen. The beam of a phaser lanced the darkness—and he brought up short. Then he saw Spock. They didn't speak. They didn't need to. A vicious *ping* came from the open life support door. Together, they dodged, split, and, weapons out, plunged through the door.

Rael fired again, missed—and Kirk stunned him with Deela's weapon. At the same moment, Spock's phaser beam struck the Scalosian machine. It continued to flare and throb. Kirk aimed his weapon at it. It burst into flame, melted and was still.

"Nice to see you, Mr. Spock," Kirk said.

"Rael!"

It was Deela. She ran to the slumped body, feeling for its heart. Satisfied, she kissed Rael's lips. Then she looked up at Kirk. "You're very clever, Captain. You tricked me. I should have known you'd never adjust." She had Rael in her arms. "What shall we expect from you?"

"We could put you in suspended animation until we determine how to use you," he said. "What do you want us to do with you?"

She was close to tears. "Oh, Captain, don't make a game of this! We've lost. You've won. Dispose of us."

"If I send you back to Scalos, you'll undoubtedly play the same trick on the next space ship that passes."

She was openly weeping now. "There'll never be another one come by. You'll warn them. Your Federation will quarantine this entire area."

"I'm sure it will."

"And we'll die out. We'll solve your problem that way. And ours."

"Will you accept help?" Kirk said.

"We can't be helped. I've told you . . ."

"Madam," Spock said, "I respectfully suggest that as we are advanced beyond your rating on the Industrial Scale, we may be able to be of some help."

"Our best people in the Federation will work on it. Will you accept our offer, Deela, and go in peace?"

Clearly, there were aspects to Kirk's nature she had not suspected. She looked at him wonderingly. After a moment, the old mischief glinted in her green eyes. She shrugged. "What have we to lose?"

She looked down at Rael. He was recovering consciousness. "We have lost," she told him quietly. "It is you and I who will transport down to Scalos."

He smiled up at her. "Soon," he said.

As they took their places on the platform, Deela turned to Kirk at the console. "Now about your problem, Captain. I note that your Vulcan friend, too, has been accelerated."

Spock spoke. "If you will devote yourself exclusively to the concerns of Scalos, Madam, we shall be very happy to stay and take care of the *Enterprise*."

"Spock," Kirk said, "remind me sometime to tell you how I've missed you."

"Yes, Captain."

"You could find life on Scalos very pleasant, Captain," Deela urged.

"And brief," Kirk said.

"Do I really displease you so much?"

"I can think of nothing I'd like more than staying with you. Except staying alive."

"Will you visit us, Captain?"

"Energize!"

"Captain . . . Captain . . . goodbye . . ."

Spock had moved the controls. They dissolved—and were gone. Kirk stared at the empty platform a long moment. Then, turning briskly to Spock, he said, "And now, how do we get back?"

"Doctor McCoy and I have synthesized a possible counteragent to the Scalosian water, sir. Regrettably, we lacked the opportunity to test it."

"Then let's test it." He took the solution Spock gave him and swallowed it. Deela and Rael. It was all for the best.

You couldn't have everything you wanted. Sex—a peculiar magnetic field. Her eyes . . . like wet green leaves . . .

Preoccupied, he vaguely heard Spock say, "Your motion seems to be slowing down, sir."

Kirk started to speak. "Missssterrr . . . Spock!" He drew a deep breath. The counteragent had worked. They were back in their own time! Then, abruptly, he realized that Spock hadn't answered. He wheeled—and before his eyes, Spock vanished.

"Spock! Spock, where are you?"

Scott came through the door to halt in midstride. *"Captain Kirk!"* he yelled. "Where in blazes did you come from?"

There was no cause to panic. Bones would have more of the counteragent. But Vulcan physiology was a tricky thing. What had worked for him would not necessarily work for Spock. What then? A permanent isolation in an accelerated universe? Kirk had whipped out his communicator before he remembered it was useless, dead as the ship itself. The bridge! He had to get to the bridge! Search parties? Futile. They couldn't see him. If Spock were there beside him, he, Kirk himself, couldn't see him.

He ignored the bridge's hubbub of welcome. Passing Uhura's station, he snapped, "Lieutenant, try to set our recorder at maximum speed . . ."

"Yes, sir." But the lights on her console had gone mad. The rapidity of their flashing turned them into blur. And all around him other boards and panels were affected by the same dementia. Suddenly, relief engulfed him. Grinning, he spoke to Scott. "I think we've found Mr. Spock. Lieutenant Uhura, are your circuits clearing?"

Her face was startled. "Yes, sir."

"Mr. Sulu?"

"Clearing, sir."

"Lieutenant Uhura, open all channels." He seized his mike. "Captain to crew. Repairs to the ship are being completed by Mr. Spock. We will resume normal operations . . . just about immediately."

The air beside his chair seemed to thicken. It solidified. Kirk looked at the elegantly pointed ears. "Greetings, Mr. Spock. My compliments on your repair work."

"Thank you, Captain. I have found it all a most fascinating experience."

"I'm glad," Kirk said. "I'm glad on many counts." He got up to pace the round of the stations. "Malfunctions—any anywhere?" Faces beamed at him. He returned to his chair—and the viewing screen lit up. On it the five Scalosians came back into view, Deela's surpassing loveliness transcendent.

"Sorry, sir," Uhura said. "I touched the tape button accidentally."

He leaned back in his chair, eyes on the screen. Deela's face seemed to fill the world. The magnetic field between them—and susceptible to no analysis. The images winked off, leaving the screen blank.

"Goodbye, Deela," he said softly.

THAT
WHICH SURVIVES

Writer: John Meredyth Lucas
        (story by Michael Richards)
Director: Herb Wallerstein
Guest star: Lee Meriwether

The planet on the *Enterprise* screen was an enigma.

Though its age was comparatively young, its vegetation was such as could only evolve on a much older world. Nor could its Earthlike atmosphere be reconciled with the few million years of the existence it had declared to the Starship's sensors. Kirk, over at Spock's station, frowned as he checked the readings. "If we're to give Federation an accurate report, this phenomenon bears investigation, Mr. Spock. Dr. McCoy and I will beam down for a landing survey. We'll need Senior Geologist D'Amato." He was still frowning when he spoke to Uhura. "Feed beamdown coordinates to the Transporter Ensign, Lieutenant." Crossing swiftly to the elevator, he turned his head. "Mr. Sulu, you'll accompany me." At the door, he paused. "Mr. Spock, you have the con."

The elevator door slid closed; and Spock, crossing to the command chair, hit the intercom. "Lieutenant Radha, report to the bridge immediately."

In the Transporter Room, McCoy and D'Amato were busy checking equipment. Nodding to McCoy, Kirk addressed the geologist. "Mr. D'Amato, this expedition should be a geologist's dream. The youth of this planet is not its sole recommendation to you. If Mr. Spock is correct, you'll have a report to startle the Fifth Inter-Stellar Geophysical Conference."

"Why, Jim? What is it?" McCoy said.

"Even Spock can't explain its anomalies."

They had taken their positions on the Transporter platform; and Kirk called "Energize!" to the Ensign at the console controls. The sparkle of dematerialization began—and Kirk, amazed, saw a woman, a strange woman, suddenly appear in the space between the platform and the Ensign. She was dark, lovely, with a misty, dreamlike quality about her. He heard her cry out, "Wait! You must not go!" Then, just as he went into shimmer, she moved to the console, her arms outstretched. Before the Ensign could draw back, she touched him. He gasped, wrenched by convulsion—and slumped to the deck.

Kirk disappeared, his eyes blank with horror.

It remained with him as they materialized on the planet. Who was she? How had she gained access to the *Enterprise*? Another enigma. He had no eyes for the blood-red flowers around him, bright against canary-yellow grass. For the rest the planet seemed to be a place of a red, igneous rock, tortured into looming shapes. Far off, black eroded hills jutted up against the horizon. He flipped open his communicator.

"Kirk to *Enterprise*. Come in, *Enterprise*."

McCoy spoke, his voice shocked, "Jim, did you see what I saw?"

"Yes, I saw. That woman attacked Ensign Wyatt. *Enterprise*, come in."

The ground shuddered beneath their feet—and the entire planet seemed to go into paroxysm. Hundreds of miles above them, the *Enterprise* trembled like a toy in a giant's hand. There was a bright flash. It vanished.

The landing party sprawled on the ground as the planet's surface continued to pitch and buck. Then it was all over. Sulu, clambering to his feet, said, "What kind of earthquakes do they have in this place?"

Bruised, Kirk got up. "They can't have many like that without tearing the planet apart."

D'Amato spoke. "Captain, just before this tremor—if that's what it was—and it's certainly like no seismic disturbance I've ever seen—I got a tricolor reading of almost immeasurable power. It's gone now."

"Would seismic stress have accounted for it?"

"Theoretically, no. The kind of seismic force we felt should have raised new mountains, leveled old ones."

Kirk stooped for his dropped communicator. "Let's see what sort of reading the ship got." He opened it. "Kirk to *Enterprise*." He waited. Then he tried again. "Kirk to *Enterprise*!" There was another wait. "*Enterprise*, come in! Do you read me, *Enterprise*?" He looked at the communicator. "The shock," he said, "may have damaged it."

Sulu had been working his tricorder. Now he looked up, his face stricken. "Captain, the *Enterprise*—it's gone!"

D'Amato was frantically working his controls. Kirk strode to Sulu, moving dials on his instrument. Awed, D'Amato looked at him. "It's true, Captain. There's nothing there."

"Nothing there? Gone? What the devil do you mean?" McCoy cried. "How could the *Enterprise* be gone?" He whirled to Kirk. "What does it mean, Jim?"

"It means," Kirk said slowly, "we're stranded."

Hundreds of miles above, the heaving *Enterprise* had steadied. On the bridge, people struggled up from the deck. Spock held the back of his cracked head and Uhura looked at him anxiously. "Mr. Spock, are you all right?"

"I believe no permanent damage is done, Lieutenant."

"What happened?"

"The occipital area of my head impacted with the arm of the chair."

"Sir, I meant what happened to us?"

"That we have yet to ascertain, Lieutenant." He was rubbing the side of his head when the Lieutenant, staring at the screen, cried, "Mr. Spock, the planet's gone!"

Scott leaped from his station. "But the Captain! And the others! They were on it!" He eyed the empty screen, his face set. "There's no trace of it at all!"

"Maybe the whole system went supernova," Radha said, her voice shaking. "Those power readings . . ."

"Please refrain from wild speculation," Spock said. "Mr. Scott, engine status reports. Lieutenant Uhura, check damage control. Lieutenant Radha, hold this position. Scan for debris from a possible explosion."

On the planet speculation was also running wild. Sulu, staring at his tricorder, said, "The *Enterprise* must have blown up."

"Mr. Sulu, shall we stop guessing and try to work out a pattern? I get no reading of high energy concentrations around the planet. If the *Enterprise* had blown up, there would be high residual radiation."

"Could the *Enterprise* have hit us, Jim? I mean," McCoy said, "hit the planet?"

Sulu said, "Once in Siberia there was a meteor so great it flattened whole forests and—"

"If I'd wanted a Russian-history lesson," Kirk snapped, "I'd have brought Mr. Chekov. We face the problem of survival, Mr. Sulu. Without the *Enterprise*, we've got to find food and water—and find it fast. I want a detailed analysis of this planet. And I want it now."

His men returned to work.

Up on on the *Enterprise*, normal functioning had finally been restored. On the bridge, tension had begun to lessen when Uhura turned from her board. "Mr. Spock, Ensign Wyatt, the Transporter officer, is dead."

"Dead?" He punched the intercom button. "Spock to Sickbay."

"Sickbay, Dr. M'Benga, sir."

"Report on the death of the Transporter officer."

"We're not sure yet. Dr. Sanchez is conducting the autopsy now."

"Full report as soon as possible." Spock turned. "Mr. Scott, have the Transporter checked for possible malfunction."

"Aye, sir."

Radha broke in. "No debris of any kind, sir. I made two full scans. If the planet had broken up, we'd have some sign." She hesitated. "What bothers me is the stars, Mr. Spock."

He looked up from his console. "The stars?"

"Yes, sir. They're wrong."

"Wrong, Lieutenant?"

"Wrong, sir. Look."

The screen showed a distant pattern of normal star movement; but in the immediate foreground, there were no stars. Radha said, "Here's a replay of the star arrangement just before the explosion, sir." A full starfield appeared on the screen.

"It resembles a *positional* change," Spock said.

"It doesn't make any sense but I'd say that somehow—in a flash—we've been knocked a thousand light years away from where we were."

Spock went swiftly to his viewer. "Nine hundred and ninety point seven light years to be exact, Lieutenant."

"But that's not possible!" Scott cried. "Nothing could do that!"

"It is not logical to assume that the force of an explosion—even of a small star going supernova—could have hurled us a distance of one thousand light years."

Scott had joined him. "The point is, it shouldn't have hurled us anywhere. It should have immediately vaporized us."

"Correct, Mr. Scott. By any laws we know. There was no period of unconsciousness; and the ship's chronometers registered only a matter of seconds. We were displaced through space in some manner I am unable to fathom."

Scott beamed. "You're saying the planet didn't blow up! Then the Captain and the others—they're still alive!"

"Mr. Scott, please restrain your leaps of illogic. I have not *said* anything. I was merely speculating."

The intercom beeped. "Sickbay to Mr. Spock."

"Spock here."

"Dr. M'Benga, sir. You asked for the autopsy report. The cause of death seems to have been cellular disruption."

"Explain."

"It's as though each cell of the Ensign's body had been individually blasted from inside."

"Would any known disease organism do that?"

"Dr. Sanchez has ruled out that possibility."

"Someone," Spock said, "might have entered the Transporter Room after—or as—the Captain and his party left. Keep me advised, please. Spock out." He looked up at Scott. "Since the *Enterprise* still appears to be in good condition, I suggest we return to our starting point at top warp speed."

"Aye, sir—but even at that, it'll take a good while to get there."

"Then, Mr. Scott, we should start at once. Can you give me warp eight?"

"Aye, sir. And perhaps a bit more. I'll sit on those warp engines myself and nurse them."

"Such a position would not only be unfitting but also unavailing, Mr. Scott." He spoke to Radha. "Lieutenant, plot a course for—"

"Already plotted and laid in, sir."

"Good. Prepare to come to warp eight."

Kirk was frankly worried. "You're sure your report covers all vegetation, Mr. Sulu?"

"Yes, Captain. None of it is edible. It is poison to us."

It was the turn of McCoy's brow to furrow. "Jim, if it's true the ship has been destroyed, you know how long *we* can survive?"

"Yes." Kirk spoke to Sulu. "There must be water to grow vegetation, however poisonous. A source of water would at least stretch our survival. Lieutenant D'Amato, is there any evidence of rainfall on this planet?"

"No, sir. I can find no evidence that it has ever experienced rainfall."

"And yet there is Earth-type vegetation here." He looked around him at the poppylike red flowers. "Lieutenant D'Amato, is it possible that there is underground water?"

"Yes, sir."

McCoy broke in. "Sulu has picked up an organism that is almost a virus—some sort of plant parasite. That's the closest to a mobile life form that's turned up."

Kirk nodded. "If this is to be our home as long as we last, we'd better find out as much about it as we can. D'Amato, see if you can find any sub-surface water. Sulu, run an atmospheric analysis."

As the two men moved off in opposite directions, Kirk turned to McCoy. "Bones, discover what you can about the vegetation and your parasites. How do they get their moisture? If you can find out how they survive, maybe we can. I'll see if I can locate some natural shelter for us."

"Are you sure we *want* to survive as a bunch of Robinson Crusoes? If we had some wood to make a fire and some

animals to hunt, we could chew their bones sitting around
our caveman fire and—''

''Bones, go catch us a parasite, will you?''

McCoy grinned; adjusting his medical tricorder, he
knelt to study the yellow grass. Kirk got a fix on a landmark
and made off around the angle of a cliff. It wasn't too distant
from the large rock formation where Sulu was taking his readings. Setting the dials on his tricorder, he halted abruptly,
staring at them. Puzzled, he examined them again—and
grabbed for his communicator.

''Sulu to Captain!''

''Kirk here.''

''Sir, I was making a standard magnetic sweep. From
zero I suddenly got a reading that was off the scale . . . then
a reverse of polarity. Now again I get nothing.''

''Have you checked your tricorder for damage? The
shaking it took was pretty rough.''

''I've checked it, Captain. I'll break it down again. But
I've never seen anything like this reading. Like a door opened
and then closed again.''

Meanwhile, D'Amato had come upon a vein of the red
igneous rock in the cliff face. Its elaborate convolutions
seemed too complex to be natural. Intrigued, he aimed his
tricorder at it. At once its dials spun wildly—and the ground
under his feet quaked, pitching him to his knees. As he
scrambled up, there came a flash of blinding light. When it
subsided, he saw the woman. She was dark and lovely; but
the misty, dreamlike expression of her face was lost in the
shadow of the cliff.

''Don't be afraid,'' she said.

''I'm not. Geological disturbances do not frighten me.
They're my business. I came here to study them.''

''I know. You are Lieutenant D'Amato, Senior Geologist.''

''How do you know that?''

''And from the Starship Enterprise.''

''You've been talking to my friends?''

She had come slowly forward, her hand outstretched.
He stepped back and she said, ''I am for you, D'Amato.''

Recognition had suddenly flooded him. ''You are the
woman on the Enterprise,'' he said slowly.

"Not I. I am only for D'Amato."

In the full light her dark beauty shone with a luster of its own. It disconcerted him. "Lucky D'Amato," he said—and reached for his communicator. "First, let's all have a little conference about sharing your food and water."

She stepped closer to him. "Do not call the others . . . please . . ."

The voice was music. The grace of her movement held him as spellbound as her loveliness. The last thing he remembered was the look of ineffable sadness on her face as her delicate fingers moved up his arm . . .

"McCoy to Kirk!"

"Kirk here, Bones."

"Jim! I've just got a life form reading of tremendous intensity! It was suddenly just there!"

"What do you mean—just there?"

"That. All tricorder levels were normal when this surge of biological life suddenly registered! Wait a minute! No, it's gone . . ."

Kirk's jaw hardened. "As though a door had opened and closed again?"

"Yes."

"What direction?"

"Zero eight three."

"D'Amato's section!" Tensely, Kirk moved a dial on his communicator. "Kirk to D'Amato!" He paused, intent. "Come in, D'Amato!"

When he spoke again, his voice was toneless. "Bones, Sulu—D'Amato doesn't answer."

"On my way!" McCoy shouted. Kirk broke into a run along the cliff base. In the distance, he saw McCoy and Sulu racing toward him. As they converged upon him, he halted abruptly, staring down into a crevice between the cliff and a huge red rock. "Bones—here!"

The body was wedged in the crevice. McCoy, tricorder in hand, stooped over it. Then he looked up, his eyes appalled. "Jim, every cell in D'Amato's body has been—disrupted!"

Time limped by as they struggled to comprehend the horror's meaning. Finally, Kirk pulled his phaser. Very carefully he paced out the rectangular measurements of a grave.

Then he fired the phaser. Six inches of soil vaporized, exposing a substratum of red rock. He fired the phaser again—but the rock resisted its beam. He aimed it once more at another spot; and once more its top soil disappeared but the rock beneath it remained—untouched, unscarred. He spoke grimly. "Better than eight thousand degrees centigrade. It just looks like igneous rock, but it's infinitely denser."

McCoy said, "Jim, is the whole planet composed of this substance covered over by top soil?"

Kirk snapped off his phaser. "Lieutenant Sulu, it might help explain this place if we knew exactly what this rock is. I know it is Lieutenant D'Amato's field—but see what you can find out."

Sulu unslung his tricorder. As they watched him stoop over the first excavation, McCoy said, "I guess a tomb of rocks is the best we can provide for D'Amato." They were collecting stones for the cairn when Kirk straightened up. "I wonder if the Transporter officer on the *Enterprise* is dead, Bones."

"You mean that woman we saw may have killed him?"

Kirk looked around him. "Someone killed D'Amato." He bent again to the work of assembling stones. Then, silently, they dislodged D'Amato's body from the crevice. When it had been hidden under the heaped stones, they all stood for a moment, heads bowed. Sulu shivered slightly. "It looks so lonely there."

"It would be worse if he had company," McCoy said.

Sulu flushed. "Doctor, how can you joke about it? Poor D'Amato, what a terrible way to die."

"There aren't really any good ways, Lieutenant Sulu. Nor am I joking. Until we know what killed him, none of us is safe."

"Right, Bones," Kirk said. "We'd better stick together, figure this out, and devise a defense against it. Is it possible the rock itself has life?"

Sulu said, "You remember on Janus Six the silicon creatures that—"

McCoy cut in. "But our instruments recorded them. They registered as life forms."

"We could be dealing with intelligent beings who are able to shield their presence."

Sulu stared at Kirk's thoughtful face. "Beings intelligent enough to have destroyed the *Enterprise*?"

"That's our trouble, Lieutenant. All we've got is questions. Questions—and no answers."

In his apparent safety on the *Enterprise*, Scott, too, was wrestling with a question to which there seemed to be no sane answer. His sense of suspense grew until he finally pushed the intercom button in his Engineering section.

"Spock here, Mr. Scott."

"Mr. Spock, the ship feels wrong."

"*Feels*, Mr. Scott?"

Both troubled and embarrassed, Scott fumbled for words. "I—I know it doesn't . . . make sense, sir. Instrumentation reads correct—but the *feel* is wrong. It's something I . . . don't know how to say . . ."

"Obviously, Mr. Scott. I suggest you avoid emotionalism and simply keep your readings 'correct'. Spock out."

But he hesitated just the same. Finally, he crossed over to his sensor board.

Down in Engineering, Scott, frowning, studied his control panel before turning to an assistant. "Watkins, check the bypass valves for the matter-anti-matter reaction chamber. Be sure there's no overheating."

"But, Mr. Scott, the board shows—"

"I didn't ask you to check the board, lad!"

"Yes, sir." Watkins wiped smudge off his hands. Then, crossing the engine room, he entered the small alcove that housed the matter-anti-matter reaction-control unit. He was nearing its display panel when he saw the woman standing in the corner. Startled, he said, "Who are you? What are you doing here?"

She smiled a little sadly. "My name is not important. Yours is Watkins, John B. Engineer, grade four."

He eyed her. "You seem to know all about me. Very flattering. What department are you? I've never seen that uniform."

"Show me this unit, please. I wish to learn."

Suspicion tightened in him. He covered it quickly. "This is the matter-anti-matter integrator control. That's the cutoff switch."

"Incorrect," she said. "On the contrary, that is the emergency overload bypass valve which engages almost instantaneously. A wise precaution."

Frightened now, Watkins backed away from her until he was stopped by the mass of the machine. She was smiling the sad little smile again. "Wise," she said, "considering the fact it takes the anti-matter nacelles little longer to explode once the magnetic valves fail." She paused. "I'm for you, Mr. Watkins."

"Watkins! What's taking you so long?" Scott shouted.

The woman extended a hand as though to repress his reply. But Watkins yelled, "Sir, there's a strange woman here who knows the entire plan of the ship!"

Scott had raced across the Engine Room to the reaction chamber. "Watkins, what the de'il—?" As he rushed in, the woman backed against a wall, suddenly seemed to flip sideways, her image a thin, two-dimensional line. Then she vanished.

Scott looked down at the alcove's floor. His look of annoyance changed to one of shock. "Poor, poor laddie," he whispered. Then he was stumbling to the nearest intercom button. "Scott to bridge," he said, his voice shaking.

"Spock here, Mr. Scott."

"My engineering assistant is dead, sir."

There was a pause before Spock said, "Do you know how he died, Mr. Scott?"

The quiet voice steadied Scott. "I didn't see it happen. His last words . . . warned about some strange woman . . . ."

Spock reached for his loud speaker. "Security alert! All decks! Woman intruder! Extremely dangerous!"

Sulu had finally managed to identify the basic material of the planet. Looking up from his tricorder, he said, "It's an alloy, Captain. Diburnium and osmium. It could not have evolved naturally."

Kirk nodded. "Aside from momentary fluctuations on our instruments, this planet has no magnetic field. And the age of this rock adds up to only a few million years. In that time no known process could have evolved its kind of plant life."

"Jim, are you suggesting that this is an artificial planet?"

"If it's artificial," Sulu said, "where are the people who made it? Why don't we see them?"

"It could be hollow," Kirk told him. "Or they could be shielded against our sensor probes." He looked around him at the somber landscape. "It's getting dark; get some rest. In the morning we'll have to find water and food quickly—or we're in for a very unpleasant stay."

"While the stay lasts," McCoy said grimly.

"Sir, I'll take the first watch."

"Right, Mr. Sulu. Set D'Amato's tricorder for automatic distress on the chance that a spaceship might come by." He stretched out on the ground and McCoy crouched down beside him.

"Jim, if the creators of this planet were going to live inside it, why would they bother to make an atmosphere and evolve plant life on its surface?"

"Bones, get some rest."

McCoy nodded glumly.

Spock wasn't feeling so cheerful, either. Though Sickbay had reported the cellular disruption of Watkins's body to be the same that had killed the Transporter Ensign, its doctors could not account for its cause. "My guess is as good as yours," M'Benga had told him.

Guesses, Spock thought, when what is needed are facts. He spoke sharply to M'Benga. "The power of this intruder to disrupt every cell in a body . . . combined with the almost inconceivable power to hurl the *Enterprise* such a distance, speak of a very high culture—and a very great danger."

Scott spoke. "You mean one of the people who threw us a thousand light years away from that planet is on board this ship, killing our crew?"

"That would be the reasonable assumption, Mr. Scott."

Scott pondered. "Yes. Watkins must have been murdered." He paused. "I'd sent him to check the matter-anti-matter reactor. There are no exposed circuits there. It can't have been anything he touched."

"If there are more of those beings on that planet, Mr.
Scott, the Captain and the others are in very grave danger."

Danger. Kirk stirred restlessly in his sleep. Near him
the tricorder beeped its steady distress signal. Sulu, on guard,
shoulders hunched against the cold, felt the ground under him
begin to tremble. The strange light flared through the dark.
Kirk and McCoy sat up.

"Lieutenant Sulu?"

"It's all right, Captain. Just another one of those
quakes."

"What was that light?" McCoy said.

"Lightning, probably. Get some rest, sir."

They lay back. Sulu got up to peer into the darkness
around him, patrolling a wider circle. He approached the
beeping tricorder, looked down at it, and was moving on
when the signal stopped. Sulu whirled—and saw the woman.
He went for his phaser, pulling it in one swift movement.

"I am unarmed, Mr. Sulu," she said.

Hand on phaser, he advanced toward her cautiously.
She stood perfectly still, her face blurred by the darkness.

"Who are you?" he said.

"That is not important. You are Lieutenant Sulu; you
were born on the planet Earth—and you are helmsman of the
Enterprise."

"Where did you get that information?" he demanded.
"Do you live on this planet?"

"I am from here."

Then the planet *was* hollow. Rage suddenly shook him.
"Who killed Lieutenant D'Amato?"

She didn't speak, and Sulu snapped, "All right! My
Captain will want to talk to you!" He gestured with his
phaser. "That way. Move!"

The melodious voice said, "You do not understand. I
have come to you."

"What do you want?"

"To—touch you . . ."

He was in no mood for her touching. "One of our men
has been killed! We are marooned here—and our ship has
disappeared!" Her features were growing clearer. "You—I
recognize you! You were in the *Enterprise*!"

"Not I. Another." She started toward him.

"Keep back!"

But she continued her move to him. He lifted his phaser. "Stop! Or I'll fire!"

She maintained her approach. "Stop!" he cried. "I don't want to kill a woman!"

She was close to him now. He fired, vaporizing the ground before her. She still came on. Sulu turned his phaser to full charge—and fired again. The beam struck her, but made no more impression on her than it had made on the rock. He backed away, but stumbled over a stone behind him. The phaser skittered across the hard surface of the planet. He scrambled up—but she was on top of him, her hand on his shoulder. He leaped clear, screaming in agony. Then he fell to the ground, his face contorted, screams tearing from his throat. The woman reached for him, her arms outstretched.

"Hold it!"

Kirk, phaser aimed, had interposed himself between them. The woman hesitated, startled.

"Who are you?" Kirk snapped.

"I am for Lieutenant Sulu."

Sulu was clutching his shoulder, groaning. "Phasers won't stop her, Captain . . . don't let her touch you . . . it's how D'Amato died. It's . . . like being blown apart . . ."

The woman moved to go around Kirk. Again, he blocked her way to Sulu. "Please," she said. "I must. I am for Lieutenant Sulu."

McCoy had joined them. "She's mad!" he cried.

"Bones, take care of Sulu." Kirk eyed the woman, her dark loveliness, her misty, dreamlike state. He had to fight his mounting horror as he recognized her. "Please, please," she said again. "I must touch him."

Once more she advanced—and once more Kirk shielded Sulu with his body. They collided. Her outstretched arms were around his neck. He felt nothing but revulsion. Shoving her away, he said, "Why can you destroy others—and not me?"

She looked at him, her eyes tortured. "I don't want to destroy. I don't *want* to . . ."

"Who are you? Why are you trying to kill us?"

"Only Sulu. I wish you no harm, Kirk. We are—much alike. Under the circumstances—" She broke off.

"Are there men on this planet?" Kirk demanded.

"I must touch him."

"No."

She stepped back. Then she flipped sideways, leaving only a line that thinned—and disappeared.

Kirk stared at the empty space. "Did you see that, Bones? Is this a ghost planet?"

"All I know is that thing almost made a ghost of Sulu! His shoulder where she touched him—its cells are disrupted, exploded from within. If she'd got a good grip . . ."

"Why? It's true we must seem like intruders here, but if she reads our minds, she must know we mean no harm. Why the killing, Bones?"

Sulu looked up at him. "Captain, how can such people be? Such evil? And she's—she's so beautiful . . ."

"Yes," he said slowly. "I noticed . . ."

Spock had changed the red alert to an increase of security guards. Sweep after sweep had failed to show evidence of any intruder. Uhura, bewildered, turned to him.

"But how did she get off the ship, Mr Spock?"

"Presumably the same way she got on, Lieutenant."

"Yes, sir." She spoke again, anxiously. "Mr. Spock, what are the chances of the Captain and the others being alive?"

"We're not engaged in gambling, Lieutenant. We are proceeding in the logical way to return as fast as possible to the place they were last seen. It is the reasonable method to ascertain whether or not they are still alive."

Radha spoke from where she was monitoring her station's instruments. "Mr. Spock, speed is increased to warp eight point eight."

He crossed hastily to the command chair. "Bridge to Engineering," he said into the intercom.

"Scott here, sir. I see it. It's a power surge. I'm working on it. Suggest we reduce speed until we locate the trouble."

"Very well Mr. Scott." He turned to Radha. "Reduce speed to warp seven."

"Aye, sir. Warp seven." Then, as she looked at her

board, her eyes widened. "Mr. Spock! Our speed has increased to warp eight point nine and still climbing!"

Spock pushed the intercom button. "Bridge to Scott. Negative effect on power reduction, Mr. Scott. Speed is still increasing."

Scott, down in the matter-anti-matter reaction chamber, looked at the unit that had witnessed Watkins's death. "Aye, Mr. Spock," he said slowly. "And I've found out why. The emergency bypass control valve for the matter-antimatter integrator is fused—completely useless. The engines are running wild. There's no way to get at them. We should reach maximum overload in fifteen minutes."

Spock said, "I calculate fourteen point eight seven minutes, Mr. Scott."

The voice from Engineering had desperation in it. "Those few seconds won't make much difference, sir. Because you, I, and the rest of this crew will no longer be here to argue about it. This ship is going to blow up and nothing in the universe can stop it."

Around Spock, faces had gone blank with shock.

Sulu's pain had begun to ease. McCoy, still working on his shoulder, looked up at Kirk. "There's a layer of necrotic tissue, subcutaneous, a few cells thick. A normal wound should heal quickly. But if it isn't, if this is an infection . . ."

"You mean your viruses?" Kirk said.

"It couldn't be! Not so quickly!"

"She just touched me, sir," Sulu said. "How could it happen so fast?"

"She touched the Transporter Ensign. He collapsed immediately. Then she got to D'Amato and we saw what happened to him." Kirk looked down at Sulu. "Why are you alive, Lieutenant?"

"Captain, I'm very grateful for the way it turned out. Thank you for all you did."

"Jim, what kind of power do they wield, anyway?"

"The power, apparently, to totally disrupt biological cell structure."

"Why didn't she kill you?"

"She's not through yet, Bones."

* * *

Spock had joined Scott in the matter-anti-matter chamber. As the Engineer rose from another examination of the unit, he shook his head. "It's useless. There's no question it was deliberate."

"Sabotage," Spock said.

"Aye—and a thorough job. The system's foolproof. Whoever killed Watkins sabotaged this."

"You said it's been fused, Mr. Scott. How?"

"That's what worries me. It's fused all right—but it would take the power of the ship's main phaser banks to have done it."

"Interesting," Spock mused.

"I find nothing interesting in the fact we're about to blow up, sir!" Scott was glaring at Spock.

The Vulcan didn't appear to notice it. "No," he agreed mildly. "But the *method* is extremely interesting, Mr. Scott."

"Whoever did this must still be loose in the ship! I fail to understand why you canceled the red alert."

"A force able to fling us a thousand light years away and yet manage to sabotage our main energy source will not be waiting around to be taken into custody." He put the result of his silent musings into words. "As I recall the pattern of fuel flow, there is an access tube, is there not, that leads into the matter-anti-matter reaction chamber?"

"Aye," Scott said grudgingly. "There's a service crawlway. But it's not meant to be used while the integrator operates."

"However, it's there," Spock said. "It might be possible to shut off the flow at that point."

Scott exploded. "With what? Bare hands?"

"No, Mr. Scott. With a magnetic probe."

"Any matter that comes into contact with the anti-matter triggers the explosion. I'm not even sure a man could live in the crawlway—in the energy stream of the magnetic field that bottles up the anti-matter."

"I shall try," Spock said.

"You'd be killed, man!"

"That fate awaits all of us unless a solution can be found very quickly."

Scott stared at him with mingled admiration and annoyance. There was a pause. Then he said, "Aye, you're right. We've nothing to lose. But *I'll* do it, Mr. Spock. I know every millimeter of the system. I'll do whatever must be done.''

"Very well, Mr. Scott. You spoke, I remember, of the 'feel' of the ship being 'wrong'.''

"It was an emotional statement. I don't expect you to understand it, Mr. Spock.''

"I hear, Mr. Scott, without necessarily understanding. It is my intention to put an analysis through the ship's computers comparing the present condition of the *Enterprise* with her ideal condition.''

"We've no time for that!''

"We have twelve minutes and twenty-seven seconds. I suggest you do what you can in the service crawlway while I return to the bridge to make the computer study.''

Scott's harassed eyes followed him as he left. Shaking his head, he turned to several crewmen. "Lads, come with me.''

They followed him quickly.

Down on the planet Kirk had also indulged some musings. As he watched McCoy check Sulu again, he said, "If this planet is hollow—if there are cities and power sources under the surface, there should be entrances. We'll do our exploring together. Lieutenant Sulu, do you feel strong enough to move now?''

"I feel fine, Captain.''

"Is he, Bones?''

"He's back in one piece again.''

"Whatever destructive power that woman has is aimed at a specific person at a specific time. If I'm correct, when she appears again, the other two of us may be able to protect the one she's after. And simply by intruding our bodies between her and her victim. No weapons affect her.''

"But how does she know about us, Captain? She knew my name, my rank—even the name of the ship! She must read our minds—'' Sulu broke off at the sound of a whining noise that rose rapidly in pitch. "Captain! That's a phaser on overload!''

But Kirk had already whipped his weapon from his belt. "The control's fused,'' he said. "Drop.''

Sulu and McCoy hit the ground. Kirk, flinging his phaser away with the full force of his strength, also fell flat, his arms shielding his head. They acted just in time. There was an ear-splitting roar of explosion. Debris rained down on them. Then it was over. Kirk got to his feet, looking around him.

"That answers our question," he said. "She *does* read our minds. Let's go . . ."

The crawlway was dark and narrow. Scott, two of his men, beside him, peered up through it. "All right," he said. "Help me up into it." Wriggling through the cramped space, a corner faced him. He edged around it, the heat of the energy stream meeting him. It flowed over him, enveloping him in a dim glow. He spoke into the open communicator beside hi, his voice muffled. "Scott to bridge."

"Go ahead, Mr. Scott."

"I've sealed off the aft end of the crawlway. And I've positioned explosive separator charges so you can blow me clear of the ship if I rupture the magnetic bottle. I'm so close to it now that the flow around me feels like ants crawling all over my body."

"Mr. Scott, I suggest you do not engage in any further subjective descriptions. You have precisely ten minutes and nineteen seconds to perform your task."

Radha turned from her console. "Mr. Spock, we're at warp eleven point two and accelerating."

From the crawlway, Scott said, "I heard that. The ship's not structured to take that speed for any length of time."

"Mr. Scott, you now have ten minutes, ten seconds."

The hot glow in the crawlway was enervating. Every inch of Scott's body was tingling. "All right, Mr. Spock, I'm now opening the access panel to the magnetic flow valve itself. Keep your eye on that dial. If there's a jump in magnetic flow, you must jettison me. The safety control can't hold more than two seconds after rupture of the magnetic field."

"I am aware of these facts, Mr. Scott. Please get on with the job."

Spock had moved to his station, twisting dials. Now, pushing the computer button, he said, "Computer."

The metallic voice said, "Working."

"Analysis on comparison coordinates."

Three clicks came in succession before the computer said, "Unable to comply. Comparison coordinates too complex for immediate readout. Will advice upon completion."

Scott spoke again. "I've removed the access plate and I've got static electric charges dancing along the instruments. It looks like the aurora borealis in here."

Spock turned to Uhura. "You're monitoring the magnetic force?"

"Yes, sir."

"Don't take your eyes off it." His quiet face showed no sign of strain. "Lieutenant Radha, arm the pod jettison system."

"Aye, sir." She moved a toggle. "I'll jettison the pod at the first sign of trouble."

"Only on my order!" Spock snapped.

"Yes, sir. Warp eleven point nine now."

Spock used the intercom. "Mr. Scott, what's your situation?"

In the access tube, sparks were flying from all the metal surfaces. Scott himself seemed encompassed by a nimbus of flowing flames. "It's hard to see. There's so much disturbance I'm afraid any attempt to get at the flow valve will interrupt the magnetic shield."

"You have eight minutes forty-one seconds."

To himself, Scott muttered, "I know what time it is. I don't need a bloody cuckoo clock."

The three on the planet had reached a plateau of the red rock. They paused for rest; checking his tricorder, Sulu cried, "Captain! There's that strange magnetic sweep again! From zero to off the scale and then—"

"Like a door opening . . ." Kirk muttered.

From behind a jutting rock stepped the woman, the dreamy smile on her lovely mouth.

"And who have you come for this time?" Kirk said.

"For you, James T. Kirk, Captain of the *Enterprise*."

McCoy and Sulu stepped quickly in front of Kirk. "Keep behind us, Jim!" McCoy shouted.

She was standing quite still, her short, flowing garment clinging to the lines of her slim body.

Kirk spoke over McCoy's shoulder. "Why do you want to kill me?"

"You are an invader."

She moved forward and he spoke again. "We're here on a peaceful mission. We have not harmed you. Yet you have killed our people."

McCoy had his tricorder focused on her. Reading it, he said amazedly, "Jim, I get no life reading from her!"

"An android," Sulu said.

"That would give a mechanical reading. I get nothing."

Warily maintaining his place behind his men, Kirk said, "Who are you?"

"Commander Losira."

"Commander of what?"

"This base," she said.

Kirk studied her exquisite features. "You are very beautiful, Losira. You—appeal to me."

Stunned, McCoy and Sulu turned their heads to stare at him. The woman trembled slightly. Kirk noted it with satisfaction. "Do I appeal to you, Losira?"

She lowered her dark eyes. "At another time we might have—" She broke off.

"How do you feel about killing me?" Kirk said.

The eyelids lifted and her head came up. "Feel?" she asked. Then, very slowly, she added, "Killing is wrong." But nevertheless, she took another step forward. "You must not penetrate this station." Her arms stretched out. "Kirk, I must—touch you."

Behind his shielding two men, Kirk was frantically working at his tricorder. Where was the door? She must have emerged from somewhere! But as he worked, he talked. "You want to kill me?"

She stopped her advance, confused. "You *don't* want to," he said. "Then why do you do it if you don't want to?"

"I am sent," she said.

"By whom?"

"We defend this place."

"Where are the others?"

"No more." Abruptly, determination seemed to possess her again. She ran to them, arms out, struggling to get past McCoy and Sulu. They remained, immovable before Kirk, her touch leaving them unaffected.

"How long have you been alone?" Kirk said.

Her arms dropped. A look of depthless sorrow came over her face. Then, turning sideways, she was a line that vanished in a flash of light.

"Where did she go?" McCoy cried. "She must be somewhere!"

"She isn't registering," Sulu said. "But there's that power surge again on my tricorder! Right off the scale! The place must be near here."

"Like a door . . . closing," Kirk said. He moved forward toward a big, distant, red rock.

The bridge chronometer was marking the swiftly passing seconds. Spock left the helm position to hit his computer button. "Computer readout," he said.

"Comparison analysis complete."

"Continue."

"Transporter factor M-7. Reassembled outphase point zero, zero, zero, nine."

Spock's eyebrows arched in astonishment; and Radha called, "Fifty-seven seconds to go, sir."

"Understood," Spock said. Radha watched him unhurriedly study the readout—and had to struggle for calm. Nor did he raise his head from his view box when Scott's blurred voice came from the intercom. "Mr. Spock."

"Spock here, Mr. Scott."

In the crawlway sweat beaded Scott's forehead. Varicolored light played over his face as he cautiously eased two complex instruments toward the access hatch. "I'm going to try to cut through the magnetic valve. But if the probe doesn't exactly match the flow, there'll be an explosion—starting now." He crept forward with agonizing care.

Radha, her face drawn with strain, had poised her finger ready to activate the jettison button. Uhura cried, "Mr. Spock, magnetic force indicator's jumping!"

Spock came out of his scope. "Mr. Scott, ease off," he said.

As Scott withdrew his instruments, the tempo of light

fluctuation slowed. Uhura, eyes on her console said, "Magnetic force back to normal, sir."

Radha, with forced composure, spoke. "Warp thirteen point two, Mr. Spock."

If he heard, he gave no sign. "Computer, for out-phase condition, will reversed field achieve closure?"

"Affirmative if M-7 factor maintained."

Spock struck the intercom. "Mr. Scott, reverse polarity in your magnetic probe."

"Reverse polarity?"

"That is correct, Mr. Scott."

"But that'll take a bit of doing and what purpose—?"

"Get started, Mr. Scott. I shall explain. You were right in your 'feel'. The *Enterprise* was put through a molecular transporter. Then it was reassembled slightly out of phase. Reversed polarity should seal the incision."

"I've no time for theory, but I hope you're right."

Radha said, "Fifteen seconds, Mr. Spock."

In the crawlway Scott heard her. "I'm doing the best I can. Wait—it's stuck." He struggled frantically with the magnetic probe, the sweat dropping into his eyes.

"Ten seconds," Radha said.

"I'm stuck," Scott said. "Blast me loose."

"Keep working, Mr. Scott."

"Don't be a fool, Spock. It's your last chance. Push that jettison button. Don't be sentimental. Push it. I'm going to die, anyway."

"Stop talking," Spock said. "Work."

Scott retrieved the probe. The control came free. He shoved it quickly into the access hatch. "It's loose now. But there's no time. Press the button." Lights flared wildly around him as the probe sank deeper into its hole.

Spock was at Radha's station. The needle on her dial had climbed to warp fourteen point one. Uhura, looking across at him, said, "Magnetic force meter is steady, sir."

As she spoke, the needle on Radha's dial had sunk to warp thirteen. It continued to drop. Spock flipped the intercom. "Mr. Scott, you have accomplished your purpose."

Scott disengaged the magnetic probe. Then his head fell on the hot metal of the tube. "You might at least say thank you, Mr. Spock."

Spock was genuinely astounded. "For what purpose, Mr. Scott? What is it in you that requires an overwhelming display of emotion in a situation such as this? Two men pursue their only reasonable course—and you clearly seem to feel something more is necessary. What?"

"Never mind," Scott said wearily. "I'm sorry I brought it up."

The three stranded *Enterprise* men were nearing the big, red rock. And the readings on Sulu's tricorder still showed off the scale beyond their peak. Kirk approached the rock. "That closed door," he said, "must be right here."

They all shoved their shoulders against the rock. It didn't move. Panting, McCoy said, "If that's a closed door, it intends to stay closed."

The rock of itself slid to one side. It revealed a door that suddenly telescoped and drew upward. They stood in silence for a moment, peering inward.

"You think it's an invitation to go in?" McCoy said.

"If it is," Sulu said, "it's one that doesn't exactly relax me."

"The elevator door on the *Enterprise* bridge would be certainly preferable," Kirk agreed. "But whatever civilization exists on this planet is in there. And without the ship, gentlemen, in there is our sole source of food and water."

Following his lead, they cautiously moved through the doorway. It gave onto a large chamber. Athwart its entrance was a huge translucent cube. Pulsing in a thousand colors, lights flashed across its surfaces. "What is it?" Kirk said. "Does it house the brain that operates this place?" They were studying the cube when, between it and them, the woman appeared, wearing that same look of sadness. She moved toward them slowly.

"Tell us who you are for," Kirk said.

She didn't answer; but her arms rose and her pace increased.

"Form a circle," Kirk said. "Keep moving."

The woman halted. "You see," Kirk said, "you might as well tell us who you're for." He paused. "On the other hand, don't bother. You are still for Kirk."

"I am for James Kirk," she said.

McCoy and Sulu drew together in front of him as he said, "But James Kirk is not for you."

"Let me touch you—I beg it," she said. "It is my existence."

"It is my death," he said.

Her voice was very gentle. "I do not kill," she said.

"No? We have seen the results of your touch."

"But you are my match, James Kirk. I must touch you. Then I will live as your match even to the structure of your cells—the arrangement of chromosomes. I need you."

"That is how you kill. You will never reach me." Even as he spoke, he saw the second woman. Silently, unnoticed, she was moving toward them, arms outstretched. "Watch out!" he shouted.

"I am for McCoy," said the second woman.

Kirk jumped in front of Bones. "They are replicas!" he cried. "The computer there has programmed replicas!"

"They match our chromosome patterns after they touch us!" McCoy shouted.

A third woman, identical in beauty and clothing, slipped into view. "I am for Sulu," she said.

Aghast, the *Enterprise* men stared at each other. "Captain! We can no longer protect each other!"

McCoy said, "We could each make a rush at the other's killer!"

"It's worth a try," Kirk said.

Unhearing, dreamy, their arms extended, the trio of women were nearing them, closing in, closer and closer. Beside them, the air suddenly gathered into shimmer. Armed with phasers, Spock and an *Enterprise* security guard materialized swiftly. They swung their weapons around to cover the women.

"No, Spock!" Kirk yelled. "That cubed computer—destroy it!"

The phasers' beams struck the pulsing cube. There was a blast of iridescent light—and the women vanished. McCoy drew a great gasping sigh of incredulous relief. Kirk turned to Spock. "Mr. Spock, it is an understatement to say I am pleased to see you. I thought you and the *Enterprise* had been destroyed."

Spock holstered his phaser. "I had the same misgivings about you, Captain. We got back close enough to this planet to pick up your life form readings only a moment ago."

"Got back from where, Mr. Spock?"

But Spock was examining the broken cube with obvious admiration. "From where this brain had the power to send the ship . . . a thousand light years across the galaxy. What a magnificent culture this is."

"*Was*, Mr. Spock. It's defenses were run by computer."

Spock nodded. "I surmised that, Captain. Its moves were all immensely logical. But what people created it? Are there any representatives of them?"

"There were replicas of one of them. But now the power to reproduce them has been destroyed. Your phasers—" He stopped. On the blank wall of the chamber Losira's face was gradually forming. The lovely lips opened. "My fellow Kalandans, I greet you."

She went on. "A disease is decimating us. Beware of it. I regret giving you only this recorded warning—but we who have guarded this outpost for you may be dead by the time you hear it."

The voice faded. After a moment it resumed. "In creating this planet, we also created a deadly organism. I have awaited the regular supply ship from our home star with medical assistance, but I am now sickening with the virus myself. I shall set the outpost's controls on automatic. They will defend you against all enemies except the disease. My fellow Kalandans, I wish you well."

"She is wishing the dead well," McCoy said.

Spock had returned to the blasted computer. "It must have projected replicas of the only being available—Losira."

Kirk's eyes were on the dissolving image. "She was— beautiful," he said.

Spock shook his head. "Beauty is transitory, Captain. She was, however, loyal and highly intelligent."

The image on the wall had gone. Kirk opened his communicator. "Kirk to *Enterprise*. Five of us to beam up. By the way, Mr. Spock, I don't agree with you."

"Indeed, Captain?"

In Kirk's mind was the remembered sound of a voice like music, of a dark and lonely loveliness waiting in vain for the salvation of her people. ''Beauty survives, Mr. Spock. It survives in the memory of those who beheld it.''

Spock stared at him. As they dematerialized, there was a sad little smile on Kirk's lips.

LET THAT BE YOUR LAST BATTLEFIELD

Writer: Oliver Crawford (Story by Lee Cronin)
Director: Jud Taylor
Guest stars: Frank Gorshin, Lou Antonio

An airborne epidemic was raging on Ariannus; the *Enterprise* was three hours and four minutes out from the stricken planet on a decontamination mission when her sensors picked up, of all unexpected objects, a Starfleet shuttlecraft. Furthermore, its identification numbers showed it to be the one reported stolen from Starbase 4 two weeks earlier.

Its course was very erratic, and it was leaking air. There was a humanoid creature aboard, either injured or ill. Kirk had the machine brought aboard by tractor, and then came the second surprise. The unconscious creature aboard it was, on his left side, a very black man—while his right-hand side was completely white.

Kirk and Spock, curious, watched the entity, now on the surgery's examination table, while McCoy and Nurse Chapel did what seemed indicated. This, in due course, included an injection.

"Doctor," Spock said, "is this pigmentation a natural condition of this—individual?"

"So it would seem. The black side is plain ordinary melanin."

"I never heard of such a race," Kirk said. "Spock? No? I thought not. How do you explain it, Bones?"

"At the moment, I don't."

"He looks like the outcome of a drastic argument."

"I would think not," Spock said seriously. "True, he would be difficult to account for by standard Mendelian evolution, but unaccountable rarities do occur."

"A mutation?" McCoy said. "Tenable, anyhow."

"Your prognosis, Bones?"

"Again, I can't give one. He's a novelty to me, too."

"Yet," Spock said, "you are pumping him full of your noxious potions as if he were human."

"When in doubt, the book prevails. I've run tests. Blood is blood—even when it's green like yours. The usual organs are there, somewhat rearranged, plus a few I don't recognize. But—well, judge the treatment by its fruits; he's coming around." The alien's eyes blinked open. He looked as though he were frightened, but trying not to show it.

"Touch and go there for a bit," McCoy said. "But you're no longer in danger."

"You are aboard the Starship *Enterprise*," Kirk added.

"I have heard of it," the alien said, relieved. "It is in the fleet of the United Federation of Planets?"

"Correct," Kirk said. "And so is that shuttlecraft in which you were flying."

"It was?"

"Don't you usually know whose property you're stealing?"

"I am not a thief!"

"You're certainly no ordinary thief," Kirk said, "considering what it is you appropriated."

"You are being very loose with your accusations and drawing conclusions without any facts."

"I know you made off with a ship that didn't belong to you."

"I do not 'make off' with things," the alien said, biting off the words. "My need gave me the right to its use—and note the word well, sir—the use of the ship."

Kirk shrugged. "You can try those technical evasions with Starfleet Command. You'll face your charges there."

"I am grateful that you rescued me," the alien said with sudden dignity.

"Don't mention it. We're glad we caught you. Who are you?"

"My name is Lokai."

"Go on."

"I am from the planet Cheron."

"If I remember correctly," Spock said, "that is located in the southernmost part of the Galaxy, in a quarter that is still uncharted."

"What are you doing so far from your home?" Kirk asked. Lokai did not answer. "You know that upon completion of our mission, you will be returned to Starbase to face a very serious charge."

"The charge is trifling. I would have returned the ship as soon as I had—" Lokai stopped abruptly.

"Had what? What were you planning to do?"

"You monotoned humans are all alike," Lokai said in a sudden burst of fury. "First condemn and then attack!" Struggling to get a rein on his temper, he sank back. "I will answer no more questions."

"However we view him, Captain," Spock said, "he is certainly no ordinary specimen."

Lokai looked at the First Officer as though seeing him for the first time. "A Vulcan!"

"Don't think he'll be any easier on you," McCoy said. "He's half human."

"That's a strange combination."

Spock raised one eyebrow. "Fascinating that you should think so."

"You're not like any being we've ever encountered," Kirk added. "We'd like to know more about you and your planet."

"I—I'm very tired."

"I think that's an evasion. Surely you owe your rescuers some candor."

"I insist," Lokai said, deliberately closing his eyes. "I am extremely tired. Your vindictive cross-examination has exhausted me."

Kirk looked down at the self-righteous thief for a moment. Then Chekov's voice said from the intercom, "Contact with alien ship, Captain. They request permission to beam a passenger aboard. They say it's a police matter."

"Very well. I'll see him on the bridge. Let's go, Mr. Spock."

Still another surprise awaited them there. The newcomer was almost a double for Lokai—except that he was black on his right side and white on his left.

* * *

"I am Bele," he said. His manner was assured and ingratiating.

Kirk eyed him warily. "Of the planet Cheron, no doubt. What brings you to us?"

"You bear precious cargo. Lokai. He has taken refuge aboard this ship. I am here to claim him."

"All personnel on this vessel are subject to my command. No one 'claims' anyone without due process."

"My apologies," Bele said readily. "I overstepped my powers. 'Claim' was undoubtedly an unfortunate word."

"What authorization do you have and from what source?"

"I am Chief Officer of the Commission on Political Traitors. Lokai was tried for and convicted of treason, but escaped. May I see him, please?"

"He's in sickbay. Understand that since you are now aboard the *Enterprise*, you are bound by its regulations."

Bele smiled, a little cryptically. "With your permission, Captain."

There were two guards at the door of Sickbay when Kirk, Spock and Bele arrived; McCoy was inside. Lokai glared up at them.

"Well, Lokai, it's a pleasure to see you again," Bele said. "This time I'm sure your 'joining' will be of a permanent nature. Captain, you are to be congratulated. Lokai has never before been rendered so—quiescent."

Lokai made a sound remarkably like a panther snarling, which brought in the two guards in a hurry. "I'm not going back to Cheron," he said with savage anger. "It's a world of murdering oppressors."

"I told you where you were going," Kirk said. "We brought your compatriot here simply as a courtesy. He wanted to identify you."

"And you see how this killer responds," Bele said. "As he repays all his benefactors . . ."

"Benefactors?" Lokai said. "You hypocrite. Tell him how you raided our homes, tore us from our families, herded us like cattle and sold us as slaves!"

"They were savages, Captain," Bele said. "We took them into our hearts and homes and educated them."

"Yes! Just enough education to serve the Master Race."

"You were the product of our love and you repaid us with murder."

"Why should a slave have mercy on the enslaver?"

"Slave? That was changed millennia ago. You were freed."

"Freed? Were we free to be men—free to be husbands and fathers—free to live our lives in dignity and equality?"

"Yes, you were free, if you knew how to use your freedom. You were free enough to slaughter and burn all that had been built."

Lokai turned to Kirk. "I tried to break the chains of a hundred million people. My only crime is that I failed. Of that I plead guilty."

"There is an order in things," Bele said. "He asked for Utopia in a day. It can't be done."

"Not in a day. And not in ten times ten thousand years by your thinking. To you we are a loathsome breed who will never be ready. I know you and all those with whom you are plotting to take power permanently. Genocide for my people is the Utopia you plan."

Bele, his eyes wide with fury, sprang at Lokai. The guards grabbed him. "You insane, filthy little plotter of ruin! You vicious subverter of every decent thought! You're coming back to stand trial for your crimes."

"When I return to Cheron, you will understand power. I will have armies of followers."

"You were brought here to identify this man," Kirk told Bele. "It is now clear, *gentlemen*, that you know each other very well. Bringing you together is the only service this ship has to offer. It is not a battlefield."

"Captain," Lokai said. "I led revolutionaries, not criminals. I demand political asylum. Your ship is a sanctuary."

"I'll say it just once more. For you this ship is a prison."

"Captain, it is imperative that you return him for judgment."

"Cheron is not a member of the Federation. No treaties have ever been signed. Your demand to be given possession of this prisoner is impossible to honor. There are no extradition procedures to accomplish it. Is that clear, Commissioner Bele?"

"Captain," Bele said, "I hope you will be sensible."

"I'm not interested in taking sides."

"Since my vessel has left the area—I was only a paid passenger—I urge you to take us to Cheron immediately."

Kirk felt himself beginning to bristle. "This ship has a mission to perform. Millions of lives are at stake. When that is completed, I'll return to Starbase 4. You will both be turned over to the authorities. You can each make your case to them."

"I'm sorry, Captain, but that is not acceptable. Not at all!"

"As a dignitary of a far planet," Kirk said, seething, "I offer you every hospitality of the ship while you are aboard. Choose any other course, and . . ."

"You're the Captain," Bele said with sudden mildness.

"And as for you, Lokai, I suggest you rest as much as possible. Especially your vocal chords. It seems you will have a double opportunity to practice your oratory at Starbase . . ."

He was interrupted by the buzz of the intercom. "Chekov to Captain Kirk. Urgent. Will you come to the bridge, sir?"

It was urgent, all right. The ship was off course; it seemed to have taken a new heading all by itself; it was moving away from Ariannus on a tack that would wind it up in the Coal Sack if it kept up. A check with all departments failed to turn up the nature of the malfunction.

"Mr. Spock, give me the coordinates for Cheron."

"Roughly, sir, between 403 Mark 7 and Mark 9."

"Which is the way we're heading. Get Bele up here. I assigned him to the guest quarters on Deck 6."

Bele, once arrived, did not wait to be asked any questions. "Yes," he said, "we are on the way to Cheron. I should tell you that we are not only a very old race but a very long-lived one; and we have developed special powers which you could not hope to understand. Suffice it to say that this ship is now under my direction. For a thousand of your terrestrial years I have been pursuing Lokai through the Galaxy. I haven't come this far and this long to give him up now."

The elevator doors snapped open and Lokai ran out, followed by the two security guards.

"I will not return to Cheron!" he cried despairingly. "You guaranteed me sanctuary! Captain Kirk . . ."

"He cannot help you," Bele said. "You have lost, Lokai. You are on your way to final punishment."

"Stop him!"

"Not this time, you evil mound of filth. Not this time."

"My cause is just. You must help me—all of you . . ."

"The old cry. Pity me! Wherever he's gone, he has been helped to escape. On every planet he has found fools who bleed for him and shed tears for the oppressed one. But there is no escape from this ship. This is your last refuge."

With a cry of rage, Lokai leaped at him. Kirk pulled him off. "Security," he said, "take both of these men to the brig."

The guards stepped forward. In an instant, a visible wall of heat formed around both the aliens.

Bele laughed. "You are helpless, Captain."

"What a fool I am," Lokai said bitterly, "expecting help from such as you."

"This ship," Kirk said, "is going to Ariannus. The lives of millions of people make no other choice possible."

"You are being obtuse, Captain. I am permitting no choice. My will now controls this ship and nothing can break it." Every cord in Bele's body and every vein in his head stood out with the ferocity of his determination.

"Bele, I am Captain of this ship. It will follow whatever course I set for it—or I will order it destroyed."

Bele stared at him. "You're bluffing. You could no more destroy this ship than I could change colors."

Kirk turned sharply toward Uhura. "Lieutenant, tie bridge audio into master computer."

"Aye aye, sir."

Kirk sat down and hit a button on his chair. "Destruct Sequence. Computer, are you ready to copy?"

"Working," said the computer's voice.

"Stand by to verify Destruct Sequence Code One."

"Ready."

"This is Captain James T. Kirk of the Starship USS *Enterprise*. Destruct Sequence One—Code One One A."

There was a rapid run of lights over the face of the computer, accompanied by the usual beeping. Then on the upper left of the panel a yellow square lit up, with a black figure 1 in its center.

"Voice and Code One One A verified and correct. Sequence One complete."

"Mr. Spock, please continue."

"This is Commander Spock, Science Officer. Destruct Sequence Number Two—Code One One A Two B."

"Voice and code verified and correct. Sequence Two complete."

"Mr. Scott."

The sweat was standing out on Scott's brow. Perhaps no one aboard loved the *Enterprise* as much as he did. Looking straight into Kirk's eyes, he said mechanically, "This is Lieutenant Commander Scott, Chief Engineering Officer, Destruct Sequence Number Three—Code One B Two B Three."

"Voice and code verified and correct. Destruct Sequence engaged. Awaiting final code for thirty-second countdown."

"Mr. Spock, has this ship returned to the course set for it by my orders?"

"No, Captain. We are still headed for Cheron."

Bele said nothing. Kirk turned quietly back to the computer. "Begin thirty-second countdown. Code Zero-Zero-Destruct-Zero."

"Count beginning. Thirty. Twenty-nine."

"Now," Kirk said, "let us see you prevent the computer from fulfilling my commands."

"Twenty-five."

"You can use your will to drag this ship toward Cheron. But I control this computer. The final command is mine."

"Fifteen."

"From five to zero," Kirk said, "no command in the universe can stop the computer from completing its Destruct order."

"Seven."

"Waiting," Kirk said relentlessly.

"Five."

The lights stopped blinking and became a steady glare,

and the beeping became a continuous whine. Chekov hunched tensely over his board. Sulu's hand was white on the helm, as though he might put the ship back on course through sheer muscle power. Uhura looked at Kirk for a moment, and then her eyes closed peacefully. Spock and Scott were tensely impassive.

"Awaiting code for irrevocable five seconds," the computer's voice said.

Kirk and Bele stared at each other. Then Kirk turned back to the computer for the last time.

"Wait!" Bele said. It was a cry of despair. "I agree! I agree!"

Kirk's expression did not change. He said, "Captain James Kirk. Code One Two Three Continuity. Abort Destruct order."

"Destruct order aborted." The computer went silent.

"Mr. Spock, are we heading for Ariannus?"

"No, sir. The *Enterprise* is now describing a circular course."

"And at Warp Seven, Captain," Scott added. "We are going nowhere mighty fast."

"I warned you of his treachery," Lokai said. "You have weapons. Kill him!"

"We are waiting, Commissioner," Kirk said, "for you to honor your commitment."

"I have an alternative solution to offer, Captain. Simple, expedient, and, I am sure, agreeable. Captain—I am happy to have you complete your mission of mercy to Ariannus. It was madness to interfere with such a worthwhile endeavor."

Kirk listened stonily.

"Please, sir. You may proceed to Ariannus. Just guarantee me that, upon completion, you will take me and my traitorous captive to Cheron."

"Sir," Kirk said, "he is not your captive—and I make no deals about control of this ship."

Bele's shoulders sagged. He closed his eyes for a moment, his face curiously distorted, and then opened them again. "The ship's course is now in your control."

"Mr. Sulu?"

"She responds, sir. I'm resetting course for Arian-nus."

"And as for you two—let me reaffirm my position. I should put both of you in the brig for what you have done. As Lokai observed, we have weapons, from which no heat shield will protect you. But I won't do it, since you are new to this part of the Galaxy, which is governed by the laws of the United Federation of Planets. We live in peace with the fullest exercise of individual rights. The need to resort to force and violence has long since passed. It will not be tol-erated on this ship."

"You are both free to move about the ship. An armed guard will accompany each of you. I hope you will take the opportunity to get to know the ways of the Federation through some of its best representatives, my crew. But make no mis-take. Any interference with the *function* of this ship will be severely punished. That's all."

Bele, his face inscrutable, nodded and went out, fol-lowed by a guard.

Lokai said, "You speak very well, Captain Kirk. Your words promise justice for all."

"We try, sir."

"But I have learned to wait for actions. After Arian-nus—what is your justice? I shall wait to see it dispensed."

He too went out followed by a guard. Spock looked after him.

"Fascinating," the First Officer said. "Two totally hostile humanoids."

"Disgusting is what I call them," Scott said.

"That is not a scientifically accurate description," Spock said.

"Fascinating isn't one, either. And disgusting de-scribes exactly what I feel about those two."

"Your feelings, as usual, shed no light on the matter."

"Enough for one day," Kirk said. "Those two are be-ginning to affect you."

Lokai settled upon Uhura as his next hope, perhaps feeling that since he had made no headway with the white members of the crew, a black one might be more sympa-thetic. He was talking eagerly to her in the rec room, with

Chekov and Spock as bystanders. Racially, the four made a colorful mixture, though probably none of them was aware of it.

". . . and I know from my actions you must all think me a volcanic hothead—erupting lava from my nostrils at danger signals that are only figments of my imagination. But believe me, my friends, there can be no moment when I can have my guard down where such as Bele are present. And so what happens? I act the madman out of the anger and frustration he forces upon me and thereby prove his point that I *am* a madman."

"We all act incorrectly when we're angry," Uhura said.

"After all," Chekov added cheerfully, "we're only human."

"Ah, Mr. Chekov, you have used the phrase which puts my impatience into perspective—which focuses on my lack of ability to convey to your captain, and to you, yes you here in this room, my lack of ability to alert you to the real threat of someone like Bele. There is no persecution on your planet. How can you understand my fear, my apprehension, my degradation, my suffering?"

"There was persecution on Earth once," Chekov said.

"Yes," said Uhura. "But to us, Chekov, that's only something we were taught in history class."

"Yes, that's right. It was long ago."

"Then," said Lokai, "how can I make your flesh know how it feels to see all those who are like you—and only because they are like you—despised, slaughtered and, even worse, denied the simplest bit of decency that is a living being's right. Do you know what it would be like to be dragged out of your hovel into a war on another planet? A battle that will serve your oppressor and bring death to you and your brothers?"

There seemed to be no answer to that.

Bele, for reasons not to be guessed at, continued to work on Kirk—perhaps because he had developed a grudging respect for the man who had faced him down, or perhaps not. He visited the Captain's quarters whenever asked, though Kirk took care on each occasion to see that Spock was present as well.

"Putting the matter in the hands of your Starfleet Command is of course the proper procedure," Bele said on one such occasion. "Will it be long before we hear from them, Captain?"

"I expect the reply is already on the way, Commissioner."

"But Command may not arrive at the solution you anticipate," Spock added. "There is the matter of the shuttlecraft Lokai appropriated."

"Gentlemen," Bele said, almost airily, "we are discussing a matter of degree. Surely, stealing a shuttlecraft cannot be equated with the murder of thousands of people?"

"We don't know that Lokai has done that," Spock said.

"Well, the one thing we're agreed on is that Lokai is a criminal."

"We are agreed," Kirk said, "that he took a shuttlecraft—excuse me. Kirk here."

"Captain," Uhura's voice said, "I have your communication from Starfleet Command."

"Fine, Lieutenant. Read it out."

"Starfleet Command extends greetings to Commissioner Bele of the planet Cheron. His urgent request to be transported to his planet with the man he claims prisoner has been taken under serious consideration. It is with great regret that we report we cannot honor that request. Intragalactic treaty clearly specifies that no being can be extradited without due process. In view of the circumstances we have no doubt that after a hearing at Starbase, Commissioner Bele will be provided transportation, but whether with or without his prisoner remains to be determined. End of message."

Bele's face was a study in the attempt to retain a bland mask over anger. "As always," he said, "Lokai has managed to gain allies, even when they don't recognize themselves as such. He will evade, delay and escape again, and in the process put innocent beings at each other's throats—for a cause they have no stake in, but which he will force them to espouse violently by twisting their minds with his lies, his loathsome accusations, his foul threats."

"I assure you, Commissioner," Kirk said, "our minds will not be twisted by Lokai—or by you."

"And you're a leader of men—a judge of character?"

Bele said contemptuously. "It is obvious to the most simple-minded that Lokai is of an inferior breed . . ."

"The evidence of our eyes, Commissioner," Spock said, "is that he is of the same breed as yourself."

"Are you blind, Commander Spock?"

"Obviously not; but I see no significance in which side of either of you is white. Perhaps the experience of my own planet may help you to see why. Vulcan was almost destroyed by the same conditions and characteristics that threaten to destroy Cheron. We were a people like you—wildly emotional, often committed to irrationally opposing points of view, to the point of death and destruction. Only the discipline of logic saved our people from self-extinction."

"I am delighted Vulcan was saved, Commander, but expecting Lokai and his kind to act with self-discipline is like expecting a planet to stop orbiting its sun."

"Maybe you're not a sun, and Lokai isn't a planet," Kirk said. "Give him a chance to state his grievances—listen to him—hear him out. Maybe he can change; maybe he *wants* to change."

"He cannot."

"Change is the essential process of all existence," Spock said. "For instance: The people of Cheron must have once been monocolored."

"Eh? You mean like both of you?"

"Yes, Commissioner," Kirk said. "There was a time—long ago, no doubt—when that must have been true."

Bele stared at them incredulously for a moment, and then burst into uproarious laughter.

While he was still recovering, the intercom sounded. "Scott here, Captain. We are orbiting Ariannus. We're ready with the decontamination procedure and Ariannus reports all ground precautions complete."

"Very good, Scotty, let her rip. Kirk out."

"I once heard," Bele said, still smiling, "that on some of your planets the people believe that they are descended from apes."

"Not quite," Spock said. "The apes are humanity's cousins, not their grandfathers. They evolved from common stock, in different directions. But in point of fact, all advanced forms of life have evolved from more primitive stages.

Mutation produces changes, and the fittest of these survives. We have no reason to believe that we are at the end of the process—although no doubt the development of intelligence, which enables us to change our environment at will, has slowed down the action of selection.''

"I am aware of the process," Bele said, somewhat ironically, "and I stand corrected on the detail. But I have told you that we are a very old race and a long-lived one. We have every reason to believe that we *are* the end of the process. The change is lost in antiquity, but it seems sensible to assume that creatures like Lokai, of generally low intelligence and virtually no moral fiber, represent an earlier stage.''

"Lokai has sufficient intelligence to have evaded you for a thousand years," Kirk said. "And from what I've seen of you, that can't have been easy to do.''

"Nevertheless, regardless of occasional clever individuals, whom we all applaud, his people are as I have described them. To suggest that behind both of us is a monochrome ancestor . . .''

The buzzer sounded again. "Captain, Scott here again. We have completed the decontamination orbit. Orders?''

"Program for Starbase 4. We'll be right with you.''

Bele was showing signs of his strained and intense look of concentration which Kirk had no reason to recall with confidence. Kirk said, in the tone of an order, "Join us on the bridge, Commissioner?''

"Nothing I would like better.''

But when they arrived, the bridge personnel were in turmoil. They were clustered around the computer, at which Scott was stationed.

"What's wrong?" Spock asked.

"I don't rightly know, Mr. Spock. I was trying to program for Starbase 4—as ordered—but I can't get a response.''

Spock made a quick examination. "Captain, some of the memory banks are burned out.''

"See if you can determine which ones.''

"I will save you that trouble, Mr. Spock," Bele said. "They are in Directional Control and in the Self-Destruct circuit. You caught me by surprise with that Destruct procedure before." As he spoke, the fire sheath began to form around him. "Now can we go on to Cheron without any more discussion?"

"Stand clear of him," Kirk said. "Guard, shoot to stun."

The heat promptly increased. "I cannot block your weapon," Bele said, "but my heat shield will go out of control if I am rendered unconscious. This will destroy not only everyone here, but much of the ship's bridge itself."

The Cheronian was certainly a virtuoso at producing impasses. As he and Kirk glared at each other, the elevator doors parted and Lokai came storming out to the Captain.

"So this is the justice you promised after Ariannus! You have signed my death warrant! What do you do—carry justice on your tongues? Or will you fight and die for it?"

"After so many years of leading the fight," Kirk observed, "you seem very much alive."

"I doubt that the same can be said for many of his followers," Spock said.

Bele laughed contemptuously. At once, a fiery sheath also grew around Lokai.

"You're finished, Lokai. We've got your kind penned in their districts in Cheron. And they'll stay that way. You've combed the Galaxy and come up with nothing but monocolored primitives who snivel that they've outgrown fighting."

"I have given up on these useless pieces of bland flesh," Lokai raged. "But as for you, you—you half of a tyrant . . ."

"You image in a cheap mirror . . ."

They rushed together. Their heat shields fused into a single, almost solid mass as they struggled. Its edges drove the crew back, and wavered perilously near to the control boards.

"Bele!" Kirk shouted. "Keep this up and you'll never get to Cheron, you'll have wrecked the bridge! This will be your last battlefield—your thousand years of pursuit wasted!"

The combatants froze. Then Bele threw Lokai away from him, hard. Lokai promptly started back.

"And Lokai, you'll die here in space," Kirk continued. "You'll inspire no more disciples. Your cause will be lost."

Lokai stopped. Then his heat shield went down, and so, a moment later, did Bele's.

"Captain," Spock said, "I believe I have found something which may influence the decision. I can myself compute with moderate rapidity when deprived of the machine . . ."

"Yes, and beat the machine at chess, too. Go on."

"Because of our first involuntary venture in the direction of Cheron, our orbit around Ariannus was not the one originally planned. I believe we can leave it for Starbase 4 in a curve which will pass us within scanning range of Cheron. With extreme magnification, we might get a visual readout. I can feed Mr. Sulu the coordinates; he will have to do the rest of the piloting by inspection, as it were, but after the piloting he did for us behind the Klingon lines* I am convinced he could fly his way out of the Cretan labyrinth if the need arose."

"I believe that too," Kirk said. "But what I don't see is what good you think will come out of the maneuver."

"Observing these strangers and their irreconcilable hatreds," Spock said, "has given me material to draw certain logical conclusions. At present it is only a hypothesis, but I think there would be value in testing it."

Anything Spock said was a possibly valid hypothesis was very likely to turn out to be what another man would have called a law of nature. Kirk said, "It is so ordered."

The visual readout of Cheron was wobbly, but growing clearer; Sulu had sufficiently improved upon Spock's rather indefinite course corrections so that the moment of closest approach would be not much over 15,000 miles. It was an Earthlike planet, but somewhat larger, by perhaps a thousand miles of diameter. Both Bele and Lokai were visibly moved by the sight. Well, a thousand years is a long time, Kirk thought, even for a long-lived race.

"There is your home, gentlemen," he said. "Not many details yet, but if you represent the opposing factions there typically, we must be picking up a raging battle."

"No, sir," Spock said from his console. The words could not have been simpler, but there was something in his

*See *Spock Must Die!* (Bantam Books, 1970)

tone—could it possibly have been sadness?—that riveted
Kirk's attention, and that of the Cheronians as well. "No
conflicts at all."

"What are you picking up?" Kirk said.

"Several very large cities. All uninhabited. Extensive
traffic systems barren of traffic. Vegetation and lower animals
encroaching on the cities. No sapient life forms registering
at all, Captain."

"You mean the people are *all* dead?"

"Yes, Captain—all dead. This was what I had deduced
when I suggested this course. They have annihilated each
other—totally."

"My people," Bele said. "All dead."

"Yes, Commissioner," Spock said. "All of them."

"And—mine?" Lokai said.

"No one is left. No one."

The two survivors faced each other with ready rage.

"Your bands of murderers . . ."

"Your genocidal maniacs . . ."

"Gentlemen!" Kirk said in his command voice. Then,
more softly, "The cause you fought for no longer exists. Give
up your hate, and we welcome you to live with us."

Neither seemed to hear him; the exchange of glares
went on.

"You have lost, Bele. I have won."

"You always think you win when you destroy."

"What's the matter with you two?" Kirk demanded,
his own temper at last beginning to fray. "Didn't you hear
my First Officer? Your planet is dead. Nobody is alive on
Cheron just because of this kind of hate! Give it up, in heav-
en's name!"

"You have lost the planet," Lokai said. "I have won.
I have won because I am free."

Suddenly, he made a tremendous leap for the elevator.
The doors opened for him, and then, with a wild laugh, he was
gone. Bele made as if to rush after him; Kirk stopped him.

"Bele—listen! The chase is finished."

"No, no! He must not escape me!"

"Where can he go?" Spock said.

"I think I know the answer to that," Uhura said.
"Someone has just activated the Transporter."

"Oh," Kirk said. "Are we in Transporter range of Cheron?"

"Just coming into it," Spock said. "And a sentient life form is beginning to come through on the planet."

"It is he!" Bele cried. "Now I'll get him!"

He sprang for the elevator in turn. The guards, now belatedly alert, moved to stop him, but Kirk held up his hands.

"Let him go. Bele, there's no one there to punish him. His judges are dead."

"I," Bele said, "am his punisher." Then he too was gone.

There was a brief silence. Then Uhura said, "Captain, the Transporter has been activated again."

"Of course," Kirk said wearily. He felt utterly washed out. "Is he showing up on Cheron on the scanners now, Mr. Spock?"

"Some second sapient life form is registering. I see no other possible conclusion."

"But," Uhura said, "it doesn't make any sense."

"To expect sense from two mentalities of such extreme viewpoints is not logical," Spock said. "They are playing out the drama of which they have become the captives, just as their compatriots did."

"But their people are dead," Sulu said slowly. "How can it matter to them now which one is right?"

"It does to them," said Spock. "And at the same time, in a sense it does not. A thousand years of hating and running have become all of life."

"Spock," said McCoy's voice behind them, "may I remind you that I'm supposed to be the psychologist aboard this ship?"

"Spock's human half," Kirk said, turning, "is perhaps better equipped to perceive half measures taking over the whole man than the rest of us, Bones. And his Vulcan side quite accurately predicted the outcome. Hate wasn't all Lokai and Bele had at first, but by allowing it to run them, that's all they ended up with. This is their last battlefield—and let us hope that we never see its like again. Mr. Sulu, Warp Two for Starbase 4."

WHOM GODS DESTROY

Writer: Lee Erwin (Story by Lee Erwin and Jerry Sohl)
Director: Herb Wallerstein
Guest stars: Steve Ihnat, Yvonne Craig, Keye Luke

Dr. Donald Cory seemed almost effusively glad to see Captain Kirk and Spock, not very much to Kirk's surprise. There was ordinary reason enough: Kirk and Governor Cory were old friends, and in addition, Kirk's official reason for the visit was to ferry him a revolutionary new drug which might release him from his bondage. And what bondage! It would take the most dedicated of men to confine himself behind a force field, beneath the poisonous atmosphere of Ebla II, in order to tend the fourteen remaining incurably insane patients in the Galaxy.

"Fifteen, now," Cory said. He was a cheerful-looking man despite his duties, round-faced and white-haired. "You'll remember him, Jim: Garth of Izar."

"Of course I remember him," Kirk said, shocked. "He was one of the most brilliant cadets ever to attend the Academy. The last I heard, he was a Starship Fleet Captain—and there were no bets against his becoming an admiral, either. What happened?"

"Something utterly bizarre. He was horribly maimed in an accident off Antos IV. The people there are master surgeons, as you've probably heard. They virtually rebuilt and restored him—and in gratitude, he offered to lead them in an attempt to conquer the Galaxy. They refused, and he then tried to destroy the entire planet with all its inhabitants. One of his officers queried the order with Starfleet Command and, naturally, he wound up here."

"How is he responding?" Spock asked.

"Nobody here responds to anything we try," Cory said. "That in fact is the ultimate reason why they're here at all. Perhaps your new drug will help, but frankly, I'm pessimistic; I can't afford not to be."

"That's understandable," Kirk said. "I'd like to see Garth, Donald. Is that possible?"

"Of course. The security section is this way."

The security cells offered evidence, were any needed, that rare though insanity now was, it was no respecter of races. Most of the inmates behind the individual force fields were humanoid, but among them was a blue Andorian and a pig-faced Tellarite. Perhaps the most pathetic was a young girl, scantily dressed and quite beautiful; her greenish skin suggested that someone of Vulcan-Romulan stock had been among her ancestors, though probably a long time back, for she showed none of the other physical characteristics of those peoples.

As the group passed her, she called out urgently, "Captain! Starship Captain! You're making a mistake! Please—get me out of here and let me tell you what has happened!"

"Poor child," Cory said. "Paranoia with delusions of reference—closer to a classic pattern than anybody else we have here, but all the same we can't break through it. Captain Kirk is pressed for time at the moment, Marta."

The girl ignored him. "There's nothing wrong with me. Can't you see just by looking at me? Can't you tell just by listening to me? Why won't you let me explain?"

"A rational enough question, that last," Spock observed.

"I *am* rational!"

Kirk stopped and turned toward her. "What is it you want to say to me?"

The girl shrank away from the invisible barrier and pointed. "I can't tell you, not in front of him."

"You're afraid to talk because of Governor Cory?"

Her expression became sly, her tone confidential. "He isn't *really* Governor Cory at all, you know."

Kirk looked at Cory, who spread his hands helplessly. "I don't mean to sound callous," he said, "but I hear it every day. Everyone is plotting against her, and naturally I'm the chief villain. Garth's cell is around the corner. He's been unusually disturbed and we've had to impose additional restraints.''

He waved them forward. As Kirk turned the corner, he was stunned to discover what Cory had meant by "restraints." The man in the cell was shackled spread-eagled against the wall, his chin sunk upon his chest, a vision straight out of a medieval torture chamber. With a muffled exclamation, Kirk stepped forward. Surely no modern rehabilitation program could necessitate . . .

At the sound, the prisoner looked up. He was disheveled, haggard and wild-eyed, but there could be no doubt about his identity.

He was Governor Cory.

Kirk spun. The other Cory was not there. Standing at the bend of the corridor was a tall, hawk-nosed man with deep-set, glowing eyes, with a phaser trained on the two *Enterprise* officers. Behind him crowded most of the supposedly restrained inmates Kirk had previously seen, also armed.

"Garth!"

"No other," the tall man said pleasantly. "You said you wanted to see me, Captain. Well, here I am. But I suggest you step into the cell first. The screen's down—that's why we had the Governor shackled. Tlollu, put the Vulcan in the biggest empty cell. Captain, drop your weapons on the floor and join your old friend."

Kirk had no choice. As he entered, a faint hum behind him told him that the force field had gone up. He crossed quickly to Cory and tried to release him, but the shackles turned out to be servo-driven; the control was obviously outside somewhere. Cory said hoarsely, "Sorry he tricked you, Jim."

"Don't worry, we'll think of something."

"Our esteemed Governor," Garth's voice said, "reacts to pain quite stoically, doesn't he?"

Kirk turned. The green-skinned girl was also free, and clinging to Garth, who was fondling her absently.

"Garth, you've got me. What's the point in making Cory suffer like this . . ."

"You will address me by my proper title, Kirk!"

"Sorry. I should have said Captain Garth."

"Starship Fleet Captain is merely one of my minor

titles," Garth said with haughty impatience. "I am Lord
Garth of Izar—and future Emperor of the Galaxy."

Oho, this was going to be very tricky; Garth had described his own madness all too accurately. "My apologies,
Lord Garth."

"We forgive you. Of course, you think I'm a madman,
don't you, and are humoring me. But if so, why am I out
here while you two are in there?" Garth roared with laughter
at his own joke. Kirk, finding the girl, Marta, watching him
intently, forced a smile. She whispered in Garth's ear. "Later,
perhaps. Marta seems quite taken with you, Captain. Fortunately for you, I have no weaknesses, not even jealousy."

"I tried to warn you, Captain," Marta said. "Remember?"

"She did, you know," Garth said affably. "But of
course I had so arranged matters that you would not listen.
Our Marta is indeed a little unstable."

"What," Kirk said, "do you expect to accomplish with
a staff of fourteen mad creatures?"

"Now you try reason. That is better. The Izarians,
Captain, are inherently a master race. Much more so than
the Romulans and the Klingons, as their failures have shown.
When I return triumphantly from exile, my people will rally
to my cause."

"Then you have nothing to fear from Governor Cory.
Why don't you release him?"

"I fear no one; the point is well taken. You see, we
can also be magnanimous." He touched a device at his belt.
Behind Kirk, Cory's shackles sprang open with a clang; Kirk
only just managed to catch the tortured Governor before he
fell to the floor.

"Thank you, Lord Garth," Kirk said. "What have you
done with the medicine I brought?"

"That poison? I destroyed it, of course. Enough of this
chatter; it is time I took command of the ship you brought
me. You will help me, of course."

"Why should I?"

"Because I need the ship," Garth said, with surprised
patience. "My crew mutinied. So did my Fleet Captains. The
first use I will make of the *Enterprise* is to hunt them down
and punish them for that."

"My crew won't obey any such lunatic orders," Kirk said, abandoning with disgust any attempt to be reasonable with the poor, dangerous creature. "You're stuck, Garth. Give it up."

"Your crew will obey you, Captain. And you forget how easily I convinced *you* that I was your old friend Governor Donald Cory. It's a helpful technique, as you will observe. Watch."

Garth's features, even his very skin, seemed to crawl. When the horrifying metamorphosis was over—and it took only a few seconds—the man inside the false Cory's clothes was no longer Garth, but a mirror-Kirk.

The duplicate grinned, gave a mock salute, and strode off. Marta remained for a moment, giving Kirk a look of peculiar intensity. Then she too left, murmuring something under her breath.

"I—was praying you wouldn't get here at all," Cory said. "A starship is all he needs—and now he's got one."

"Not quite. And even if he does gain command of the *Enterprise*, one of my officers is bound to appeal his first crazy order to Starfleet Command, just as his own officers did."

"Jim, are you sure of that?"

Kirk realized that he was not at all sure of it. In the past, acting under sealed orders had forced him to give what seemed to be irrational orders often enough so that, tit for tat, his crew assumed any irrationality on his part was bound to be explained eventually. He had, in fact, long been afraid that that would be the outcome.

"No—I'm far from sure. But one starship is not a fleet; even if my officers obey him implicitly, there's a limit to the harm he can do."

"Those limits are pretty wide," Cory said. "He says he has devised a simple, compact method for making even stable suns go nova. I think it quite likely that he has. Can you imagine what a blackmail weapon that would be? And if the Izarians do rally to him—which wouldn't surprise me either, they've always been rather edgy and recalcitrant members of the Federation—then he has his fleet, too. It won't do to underestimate him, Jim."

"I don't. He was a genius, that I remember very well.
What a waste!"

Cory did not answer.

"How does he manage that shape-changing trick?"

"The people of Antos taught him the technique of cellular metamorphosis and rearrangement, so he could help
them restore the destroyed parts of his body. It's not uncom-
mon in nature; on Earth, even lowly animals like crabs and
starfish have it. But Garth is a long way from being a lower
animal. He can mimic any form he wishes to now. He used
it to kill off my entire medical staff—and to trap me. And
laughed. I can still hear that laugh. And to think I hoped to
rehabilitate him!"

"There's still a chance. Even masquerading as me,
Garth can't get aboard the *Enterprise* without a password—
we made that standard procedure after some nasty encounters
with hypnosis and other forms of deception."

"Where does that leave us, Jim? He's got us."

"Why," Kirk said slowly, "he will have to ask us for
help. And when that time comes, he'll get it—and it will be,
with any luck at all, not the help he thinks he wants, but the
help he needs."

"If you can do that," Cory said, "you're a better doctor than I am."

"I'm not a doctor at all," Kirk said. "But if I can get
him into McCoy's hands . . ."

"McCoy? If you mean Leonard McCoy, he's probably
Chief Medical Director of Starfleet Command by now. Hopeless."

"No, Donald. Garth is not an admiral, and McCoy is
not warming any bench on Earth, either. He's in orbit right
above our heads. He's the Medical Officer of the *Enterprise*."

Cory was properly staggered, but he recovered quickly.
"Then," he said, "all we have to do is get Garth onto the
Enterprise—which is exactly what he wants. I can't say that
you fill me with optimism, Jim."

Garth appeared outside the cell the next day, all smiles
and solicitude. "I hope you haven't been too uncomfortable,
Captain?"

"I've been in worse places."

"Still, I'm afraid I've been somewhat remiss in my duties as your host. In my *persona* as Cory, I invited you down to my planet for dinner—you and Mr. Spock. The invitation still stands."

"Where is Mr. Spock?"

In answer, Garth beckoned, and Spock was brought around the corner, surrounded by an armed guard of madmen. Among them was Marta, smiling, a phaser leveled at Spock's head.

"Nice to see you, Mr. Spock."

"Thank you, Captain."

Kirk turned back to Garth. "Isn't Governor Cory dining with us?"

"Governor Cory is undergoing an involuntary fast, necessitated by his resisting me. You will find, however, that for those who cooperate we set a handsome table."

Kirk was about to refuse when Cory said, "You can't help me by going hungry, Jim. Go along with them."

"Good advice, Governor," Garth said, beaming. "Well, Captain?"

"You're very persuasive."

Garth laughed and led the way.

The staff refectory of the Elba II station had evidently been once as drably utilitarian as such places always tend to be, but now it looked like the scene of a Roman banquet. Garth waved Kirk and Spock to places between himself and Marta. They sat down wordlessly, aware of the vigilant presence at their backs of the Tellarite and the Andorian. Kirk became aware, as well, that Marta was virtually fawning on him.

Garth glared at her. "Hands off, slut."

This only seemed to please the girl. "You're jealous, after all!" she said.

"Nonsense. I'm above that sort of thing. The Captain is annoyed by your attentions. That's all."

The girl looked sweetly at Kirk. "Am I annoying you, darling?"

This looked like a good opportunity to provoke a little dissension in the ranks of the mad. "Not really," Kirk said.

"You see? He's fascinated by me and it bothers you. Admit it."

"He said nothing of the sort," Garth retorted. "Your antics will lead to nothing but your being beaten to death."

"No, they won't. You wouldn't. I'm the most beautiful woman on this planet."

"Necessarily, since you're the only one," Garth said.

The girl preened herself. "I'm the most beautiful woman in the Galaxy. And I'm intelligent, too, and I write poetry and I paint marvelous pictures and I'm a wonderful dancer."

"Lies, all lies! Let me hear one poem you've written."

"If you like," Marta said calmly. She got up and moved to the front of the table, striking an absurdly theatrical pose. At the same time, Spock leaned slightly closer to Kirk.

"Captain," he said almost inaudibly, through motionless lips, "if you could create a diversion, I might find my way to the control room to release the force field."

Kirk nodded. The notion was a good one; all they would need would be a few seconds if Scotty had a security detail alerted—as he probably did have if Garth had already tried to pass himself off as Kirk without the password.

Garth was glaring at Marta, who, however, was looking only at Kirk. She began:

Shall I compare thee to a summer's day?
Thou art more lovely and more temperate.
Rough winds do shake the darling buds of May,
And summer's lease hath all too . . .

"*You* wrote that?" Garth broke in, shouting.

"Yesterday, as a matter of fact."

"More lies. It was written by an Earthman named Shakespeare a long time ago."

"Which doesn't change the fact that I wrote it again yesterday. I think it's one of my best poems, don't you?"

Garth controlled his temper with an obvious effort. "Sit down, Marta, you waste everyone's time. Captain, if you really want her, you can have her."

"Most magnanimous," Kirk said drily.

"You will find that I *am* magnanimous to my friends— and merciless to my enemies. I want you, both of you, to be my friends."

"Upon what, precisely," Spock said, "will our friendship be based?"

"Upon the firmest of foundations—enlightened self-interest. You, Captain, are second only to me as the finest military commander in the Galaxy."

"That's flattering, but at present I'm primarily an explorer."

"As I have been too. I have charted more new worlds than any man in history."

"Neither of these records can help a man who has lost his judgment," Spock said coldly. "How could you, a Starship Fleet Captain, have believed that a Federation squadron would blindly obey an order to destroy the entire Antos race? That people is as famous for its benevolence as for its skill—as your own survival proves."

"That was my only miscalculation," Garth said. "I had risen above this decadent weakness, but my officers had not. My new officers, the men in this room, will obey me without question. As for you, you both have eyes but cannot see. The Galaxy surrounds us—limitless vistas—and yet the Federation would have us grub away like ants in a somewhat larger than usual anthill. But I am not an insect. I am a master, and will claim my realm."

"I agree," Kirk said, "that war is not always avoidable and that you were a great warrior. I studied your victory at Axanar when I was a cadet. It's required reading at the Academy to this day."

"Which is as it should be."

"Quite so. But my first visit to Axanar was as a new-fledged lieutenant with the peace mission."

"Politicians and weaklings," Garth said. "They threw away my victory."

"No, they capped it with another. They were statesmen and humanitarians, and they had a dream—a dream that has become a reality and has spread throughout the stars. A dream that has made Mr. Spock and me brothers."

Garth smiled tightly and turned to Spock. "Do you feel that Captain Kirk is your brother?"

"Captain Kirk," Spock said, "speaks figuratively. But with due allowance for this, what he says is logical and I do, in fact, agree with it."

"Blind—truly blind. Captain Kirk is your commanding officer and you are his subordinate; the rest is sugar-coating. But you are a worthy commander in your own right, and in my fleet you will assuredly have a starship to command."

"Forgive me," Spock said, "but exactly where *is* your fleet?"

Garth made a sweeping gesture. "Out there—waiting for me; they will flock to my cause with good reason. Limitless wealth, limitless power, solar systems ruled by the elite. We, gentlemen, are that elite. We must take what is rightfully ours from the stultifying clutches of decadence."

Spock was studying Garth with the expression of a bacteriologist confronted by a germ he had thought long extinct. "You must be aware," he said, "that you are attempting to repeat the disaster that resulted in your becoming an inmate of this place."

"I was betrayed—and then treated barbarically."

"On the contrary, you were treated justly and with a compassion you displayed toward none of your intended victims. Logically, therefore, it would . . ."

Garth bounded to his feet with a strangled cry, pointing a trembling forefinger at Spock. All other sound in the hall stopped at once.

"Remove this—this walking computer!"

Spock was removed, none too gently. Kirk's abortive move to intervene was blocked by the smiling Marta, who had produced her phaser seemingly from nowhere.

Garth took the weapon from her, and instantly switched back to his parody of the affable host. "Won't you try some of this wine, Captain?"

"Thank you, but I prefer to join Mr. Spock."

"And I prefer that you remain here. We have many divertisements more diverting than Marta's poetry, I assure you. By the way, I assume you play chess?"

"Quite a lot. We have a running tournament aboard the *Enterprise*."

"Not unusual. How would you respond to Queen to Queen's Level Three?"

So—Garth had tried to fool Scotty and had been stopped by the code challenge; now he was fishing for the countersign. "There are, as you know, thousands of possible responses, especially if the move is not an opening one."

"I'm interested in only one."

"I can't for the life of me imagine which."

" 'For the life of me' is a well-chosen phrase," Garth said, smiling silkily. "It could literally come to that, Captain."

"I doubt it. Dead I'm of no use to you at all."

"I could make you beg for death."

Kirk laughed. "Torture? You were Academy-trained, Garth. Suppose *I* attempted to break *your* conditioning by such means; would it work?"

"No," Garth admitted. "But observe, Captain, that Governor Cory is not Academy-trained, and furthermore has been weakened by his recent, ah, reverses. And among his medical equipment is a curious chair which was used in the rehabilitation process. As such it was quite painless, and, I might add, also useless. It made men docile, and hence of no use to me. I have added certain refinements to it which make it no longer painless—yet the pain can be prolonged indefinitely because there is no actual destruction of tissue."

"In the midnights of November," Marta said suddenly, "when the dead man's fair is nigh, and danger in the valley, and anger in the sky—I wrote that this morning."

"Very appropriate," Kirk said grimly.

"Tell him what he wants. Then we'll go away together."

Kirk's lips thinned. It was the old double device of the carrot and the stick, and in a very crude form, at that. But it wouldn't do to reject the carrot out of hand; the girl was obviously too unstable for that.

"Torturing Governor Cory," he said, "would be quite useless. I would simply force you to kill me; if you didn't, I would intervene."

"Phasers can be set to stun."

"If I am unconscious, I can't be blackmailed by Governor Cory's pain, can I?"

Garth glared at him for a long moment with unwinking eyes. Then a spasm of pure rage twisted his face. Raising the phaser, he leveled it at Kirk and fired point-blank.

* * *

Kirk awoke to a sound of liquid gurgling quietly. Then it stopped, and Kirk felt a cup of some sort being pressed to his lips. He swallowed automatically. Wine. Pretty good, too.

"Slowly," said a woman's voice. "Slowly, my darling."

That was Marta. He opened his eyes. He was lying on a divan with the girl sitting beside him, a goblet in her hands; there was a carafe on a small table nearby.

"Rest," she said. "You're in my room." She took his hand and kissed it gently, then stroked his face.

Kirk studied her. "So he's decided to give the carrot another try?"

"I don't understand you," she said. "I was terrified that he would put you in the Chair. I told him I would discover your secret. I lied. I would have told him anything to save you from the torment."

After a moment Kirk said, "I think you mean that."

"I do." She leaned forward and embraced him, sighing and clinging. "This is where I've longed to be. I think I knew I loved you the first moment I saw you."

Kirk disengaged himself gently. "I want to help you, Marta. If I can get back to the *Enterprise*, I'll be able to."

"It's not possible."

"There's a way," Kirk said. "If I can get to the control room and cut off the force field, Garth is finished."

"Garth is my leader."

"And he'll lead you to your destruction. He has already destroyed the medicine that might have helped you. But I think my Ship's Surgeon has a sample he might be able to duplicate."

"I will help you in a little while," Marta said thoughtfully. "Your friend Spock will soon be here, and then we will see. I've arranged that much, at any rate."

Was there no predicting this girl? "How did you do it?"

"A convincing lie," she said, shrugging, "told to a guard who finds me desirable."

"Marta, let me help you, too. If I can get away from Garth, back aboard . . ."

She silenced him with a kiss, which he did not fight.

When they separated, she was breathing hard and her eyes were glittering.

"There is a way," she said. "A way in which we can be together always. Where Garth cannot harm us. Trust me and believe in me, darling."

She kissed him again, clutching at him with almost animal intensity. At the same time, he became aware that her left hand was burrowing between the cushions of the divan. He pulled away, to discover a long, thin, wicked-looking knife which she had been about to drive into his back.

He shoved her away, hard. Almost at the same instant, Spock stepped into sight and seized her upper arms from behind.

She looked back over her shoulder. "You mustn't stop me," she said reasonably, reproachfully. "He is my love and so I must kill him. It is the only way to save him from Lord Garth."

Spock pinched her neck. The knife clattered to the floor as she slumped.

"Apparently," Spock said expressionlessly, "she has worked out an infallible method for ensuring male fidelity. An interesting aberration."

"I'm glad to see you, Mr. Spock."

"Thank you, Captain. I am now armed, and I assume we will try to reach the control room. Would you like the weapon?"

"No, I'm still a little shaky; you handle it. The room will be guarded."

"Then we will blast our way in."

That was surprisingly ferocious of Spock; perhaps the attempted murder of his Captain had shaken him momentarily? "Only if it's absolutely necessary, Mr. Spock. Meanwhile, set your phaser on 'stun.' "

"I have already done so, Captain."

They stepped cautiously out of the room, then were forced to duck back in again as footsteps approached. Once the inmates had passed, they stole out into the corridor.

The guard before the control room was the Tellarite. He seemed to be in some sort of trance; Spock stunned him as easily as shooting a sitting duck. Kirk scooped up the fallen man's phaser, and they stuffed the limp body into a nearby closet.

Kirk cautiously tried the door. "Unlocked," he whispered. "I'll kick it open; you go in ready to shoot."

"Yes, Captain."

They burst in; but the place was deserted. Spock strode to the master switch and threw it. "Force field now off, Captain."

Kirk stationed himself at the console and activated the communicator. "Kirk to *Enterprise*. Kirk to *Enterprise*."

"Here, Captain," Uhura's voice said. "Mr. Scott, it's Captain Kirk!"

The view screen lit to show Scotty's face. "Scott here, Captain. You had us worried."

"Have Dr. McCoy synthesize a new supply of drug as fast as possible."

"Aye aye, sir."

"And I want a fully armed security detail here, Scotty, on the double."

"They're already in the Transporter Room."

"It would be better," Spock said, "if you were to return to the *Enterprise* at once."

"Why?" Kirk asked in astonishment.

"Your safety is vital to the ship. I can take charge of the security detail."

"I see," Kirk said. "Very well, Mr. Spock. Mr. Scott, beam me aboard on receipt of countersign."

"Aye, sir," the engineer said. "Queen to Queen's Level Three."

"Mr. Spock will give the countersign." Kirk leveled his phaser. "Go ahead, Spock—if that's who you are. Give him the countersign. You're supposed to know it."

"Security guard ready," Scott's voice said. "Mr. Sulu, lock into beamdown coordinates. Ensign Wyatt, ready to energize."

Spock reached for the master switch, his lineaments already changing into the less familiar ones of Garth. Kirk pulled his trigger. Nothing happened. The switch clicked home; the force field was reactivated.

"Blast away, Captain," Garth said. "I would not be fool enough to let you capture a charged phaser."

"Where is Spock? What have you done to him?"

"He is in his cell. And I have done nothing to him yet. But anything that does happen henceforth will be on your conscience—unless you give me the countersign."

"Captain Garth . . ."

"Lord Garth."

"No, sir. Captain—Starship Fleet Captain—is an honored title, and it was once yours."

"Quite true," Garth said, but his own phaser did not waver. "And I was the greatest of them all, wasn't I?"

"You were. But now you're a sick man."

Garth bristled. "I've never been more healthy."

"Think," Kirk said. "Think back. Try to remember what you were like before the accident that sent you to Antos IV."

"I—I can't remember," Garth said. "It's—almost as if I died and was reborn."

"But I remember you. You were always the finest of the Fleet Captains. You were the prototype, and a model for the rest of us."

"Yesss—I do remember that. It was a great responsibility—but one I was proud to bear."

"And you bore it well. Captain Garth, the disease that changed you is not your fault. Nor are you truly responsible for the things you've done since then—no matter how terrible they may seem to you, or to us."

"I don't want to hear any more of this," Garth said, but his voice was less decisive than his words. "You—you're weak, and you're trying to drain me of my strength."

"No! I want you to regain what you once had. I want you to go back to the greatness you lost."

For a moment Kirk thought he had been winning, but this was all too evidently the wrong tack. Garth stiffened, and the wavering phaser came back into line.

"I have never lost greatness! It was taken from me! But I shall be greater still. I am Lord Garth, Master of the Galaxy."

"Listen to me, dammit . . ."

"The other failed, but I will not. Alexander, Lee Kuan, Napoleon, Hitler, Krotus—all of them are dust, but I will triumph."

"Triumph or fail," Kirk said levelly, "you too will be dust."

"Not yet. Back to your cell, ex-Captain Kirk. Soon your doubts will be laid to rest. Out!"

The Tellarite and the Andorian came back for him the next day and hauled him out into the corridor, leaving Governor Cory behind. They brought him back to the refectory, where all the rest of Garth's followers—except Marta, who was not to be seen—were working to transform the hall from a banquet scene into some sort of ceremonial chamber. Garth was there, seemingly childishly happy, dividing his attention between Kirk and his minions.

"The throne must be higher—higher than anything else. Use that table as a pedestal. Welcome back, Captain. You will be needed for our coronation."

"Coronation?" Kirk said, a little dazed.

"I know that even a real throne is merely a chair, but the symbolism is important, don't you agree? And the crown will be only a token in itself; but it will serve as a standard around which our followers will rally."

"You have only a handful of men."

Garth smiled. "Others have begun with less, but none will have reached so far as we. Good, very good. Now we will want a royal carpet for our feet. That cloth will do nicely. The tread of our feet will sanctify it."

"And it will still be a tablecloth, stained by food and wine," Kirk said. "That's all."

"My dear Captain, you do refuse to enter into the spirit of the thing, don't you? Would you prefer a larger role in the ceremony? You could serve as a human sacrifice, for example."

"I'm sure I wouldn't enjoy the rest of it. And you seem to need me alive."

"That's true. All right. How about Crown Prince?"

"I'm not part of the family. Who were they again? Krotus, Alexander, Hitler, Genghis Khan and so forth?"

"Genghis Khan," Garth said reflectively. "I'd forgotten about him. Heir apparent, I believe, that's the proper role for you. Now we think we are ready. Excuse us for the moment, Captain."

Garth bowed grandly and went out. The guards remained alert; the Tellarite, who had been stunned in Garth's
earlier attempt to trick the countersign out of Kirk, was regarding the Captain with especial vigilance—and no little an-
imosity. Evidently he had forgotten, if he had ever known,
that the whole charade had been arranged by Garth himself.

Suddenly the air shook with a blast of recorded music.
Kirk did not have to be an expert to recognize it: it was,
ironically, *Ich bete an die Macht der Liebe*, by somebody
named Bortniansky, to which all Academy classes marched
to their graduation.

The refectory doors were drawn aside, and Garth, not
very resplendent in a cast-off uniform, entered solemnly, chin
up, eyes hooded. Beneath his right arm was tucked a crown
which looked as if it had been hastily cut from a piece of
sheet metal. On his right arm was Marta, swathed in trailing
bedsheets and looking decidedly subdued.

The other madmen dropped to their knees, and the cold
nose of a phaser against the back of his neck reminded Kirk
not to remain standing alone. It came just in time—he had
been almost about to laugh.

Stepping slowly in time to the processional, the "royal"
couple proceeded along the "carpet" to the "throne," which
they mounted. Garth turned and signaled his followers to
rise. The music stopped.

"Since there is no one here, or elsewhere in the known
universe, mighty enough to perform such a ceremony," he
said grandly, "we will perform it ourselves. Therefore, we
hereby proclaim that we are Lord Garth, formerly of Izar,
now Master-that-is-to-come of the Galaxy."

He settled the metal crown upon his own head.

"And now, we designate our beloved Marta to be our
consort."

Garth kissed her chastely on the forehead. She shrank
away from him, but stood her ground. Carefully, he fastened
around her throat what appeared to be a necklace with a diamond pendant; conceivably it held the diamond from Garth's
own Fleet Captain clasp, but somehow Kirk doubted that.

Garth seated himself upon the throne. "And now,
guards, remove our beloved consort and our heir apparent,
so that they may conclude their vital roles in this ritual."

They took Marta out first. As she was surrounded, she
she began to keen—an eerie, wailing dirge that chilled Kirk's
blood. They had her hands pinned behind her back.

Then the Tellarite and the Andorian were prodding him
out of the refectory, through a different door. He saw at once
where he was being driven: back to the control room. Behind
him, the music crashed out again, and the guards marched
him along in step.

"Listen to me," he said urgently, under cover of the
noise. "This may be your only chance."

They poked him with their phasers. The door to the
control room loomed ahead.

"Garth will destroy all of us if you don't help me stop
him," Kirk continued to the air before him. "He's using you.
All he wants is power for himself. I brought you something
that might have cured you, but he destroyed it."

There was no answer. Why did he continue to try reasoning with these madmen, anyhow? But at the moment there
seemed to be nothing else to try.

The control room was empty. The closing of the door
cut the music off. The blades of the force-field switch gleamed
invitingly only a few yards away.

"If I can get a patrol in here, they'll bring more of the
medicine. Garth will be finished and all of us will be safe
again. Safe, and well."

Stolidly, one of the guards waved him to a chair. Kirk
shrugged and sat down. There was what seemed to be an
immensely long wait.

Then Garth came in, still in uniform but no longer
wearing the crown. In one hand he was carrying a small flask
packed with glittering crystals.

"Well done," he said to the guards. "Kirk, your resistance has now reached the point of outright stupidity, and
is a considerable inconvenience to us. We propose to take
sterner measures."

"If it's any further inconvenience to you, I'll be happy
to cooperate."

"We shall see. Let us first introduce you to our latest
invention." He tossed the flask into the air and caught it with
the other hand. "This is an explosive, Captain, the most powerful one in history. Or, let us be accurate, the most powerful

of all chemical explosives. This flask can vaporize the entire station; in fact, the crater it would leave would crack the crust of the planet. We trust you do not doubt our word.''

"You were quite capable of such a discovery in the past," Kirk said. "I have every reason to believe you still are."

"Good. Here!" Suddenly, Garth tossed the flask to one of the guards. Since the man had only one hand free to catch it, he very nearly dropped it. He was in great haste to throw it back to Garth, who resumed juggling it, laughing.

"How are your nerves, Captain?"

"Excellent, thank you. If it happens to me, it happens to you. That's all I need to know."

"Then we are halfway toward a solution already," Garth said. "Actually, dropping the flask would not so much as break it; the explosive must be set off electrically, from the board. But in fact, I am quite prepared to do so. Do you see why?"

"I can see that you're bluffing."

"Then your logic is deficient. Perhaps we need your friend Spock to help you reason. He is a logical man. Yes, a very logical man." Garth looked briefly at the guards. "Go and bring the Vulcan here to us."

The guards went out. Kirk felt the first surge of real hope in days. To the best of his knowledge, Spock—the real Spock—had not been taken out of his cell since his first imprisonment, when he had been confronted with impossible odds; and, being logical, had allowed himself to be taken. But in hand-to-hand combat, he was also a machine of outright inhuman efficiency. Sending only two guards to fetch him—and on top of that, aliens who probably had no experience with either the human or the Vulcan styles of infighting—was folly; or so he had to hope.

"In the meantime, Captain, let us expose the logic of the situation to you. It is your responsibility to preserve Federation lives and property—not only your life, Mr. Spock's, Governor Cory's, but that of everyone here, even including our own. You need not confirm this; as a sometime officer of the Federation—as our uniform should remind you—this was once our responsibility as well."

"It still is," Kirk said stonily.

"We have higher responsibilities now. Above all, a responsibility to our destiny. To this, you hold the key. We cannot advance further until we are in command of the *Enterprise*. Nor can we expect another such opportunity to arise in the practicable future. It might be said, in short, that if you remain stubborn, we no longer have a future, and are under no further responsibility toward it. Do you follow us so far?"

Kirk was a good distance ahead of him by now, and not at all liking what he found there. Even Spock, he suspected, would have to concede that the trap was indeed logical, however insane.

There was a buzz from the console. Moving sidewise, Garth activated a screen. Kirk could not see what it showed, but Garth obligingly told him.

"Your Vulcan friend is a most ingenious fellow. He has somehow disposed of my associates—who will suffer for their inefficiency—and is coming this way, armed. This could be most amusing."

"The joke is entirely on you," Kirk said. "You'll have no chance to play logic games now. Whichever one of us you shoot first, the other one will have you."

"Our training was as good as yours; the outcome is by no means so inevitable. Indeed, it suggests an even better scheme."

Garth moved behind Kirk, out of sight. This moved him away from the console, which he evidently reconsidered, for a moment later he went back to it—changed.

There were now two Captain Kirks. Even the uniforms were in a nearly identical state of wear and tear now. Smiling, Garth threw in all his previous cards; he even put his phaser out of reach.

Kirk tensed to spring. At the same instant, the door shot open and Spock crouched in it, phaser ready. He seemed prepared for anything except, possibly, what he found; he actually blinked in surprise.

"That's Garth," Garth said urgently, pointing. "Blast him!"

"Hold it, Spock! The madman *wants* you to shoot me!"

"Look at us carefully, Spock. Can't you tell I'm your Captain?"

"Queen to Queen Three," Spock said.

"I won't answer that. It's the one thing he wants to know."

"Very clever, Garth. I was about to say the same thing."

Spock, keeping both Kirks under the gun, crossed to the master switch.

"What are you doing?"

"Arranging to beam down a patrol," Spock said. "I should be interested to hear any objections."

"They'll walk into a trap."

"That's true, Spock. Garth can destroy the whole station instantly if he wants."

The double agreement halted the Science Officer. After a moment he said, "What maneuver did we use to defeat the Romulan torchship off Tau Centi?"

"Conchrane deceleration."

"A standard maneuver with an enemy faster than one's self. Every Starship Captain knows that."

"Agreed, Captain," Spock said to both. "Or Captains. Gentlemen, whichever one of you is Captain Garth must at this moment be expending a great deal of energy to maintain the image of Captain Kirk. That energy level cannot be maintained indefinitely. Since I am half Vulcan, I can outwait you; I have time."

"I propose a simpler solution. Shoot us both."

"Wait, Spock! I agree, he's quite right. But you must *shoot to kill*. It's the only way to ensure the safety of the *Enterprise*."

Instantly, Spock whirled on Garth and fired. Kirk sprang to the console.

"Kirk to *Enterprise* . . ."

"Scott here. Queen to Queen's Level Three."

"Queen to King's Level One."

"Aye aye, sir. Orders?"

"Beam down Dr. McCoy with the new drug supply—and the security guards with him."

"Aye, sir. Scott out."

Kirk turned. "Well done, Mr. Spock. Did you damage either of the guards seriously?"

"I fear I broke the Tellarite's arm."

"A trifle. Help me haul this hulk to the treatment room."

Garth, still unconscious, was in the same chair he had once proposed to use as an instrument of torture; Cory had stripped it of his modifications.

"Dr. McCoy, how long does this drug need to take effect?"

"Reversal of arterial and brain damage begins at once, but the rate depends on the individual. I'd say you could start as soon as—great looping comets!"

Garth had still been mimicking Kirk, even while stunned, a further evidence of his enormous personal drive. But now the change back was beginning; Kirk had forgotten that McCoy hadn't seen the process before.

"All right," McCoy said, swallowing. "Start now."

The chair whined, almost inaudibly. Then Cory cut it off. "That's all I dare give him for a starter."

Garth's eyes opened. They were peaceful but vacant, as though he had no mind left at all. They passed from one captor to another, without recognition. He began to whimper.

Kirk leaned toward him. "Captain."

Garth's moans stopped. He looked pleadingly up at Kirk.

"Captain Garth—I'm James Kirk. Perhaps you remember me."

Garth's expression, or lack of it, did not change. He looked toward Spock, and frowned slightly.

"I am a Federation Science Officer, Captain," Spock said.

"We are from the Starship *Enterprise*," Kirk said. "I am her Captain."

Garth looked back at Kirk, long and hard. Something was awakening in him, after all. He struggled to speak. Finally the mumbled words became clear.

"Federation—Starship . . ."

"Yes, sir. The *Enterprise*."

Cory was watching closely. Garth slowly reached out his hand. Kirk took it.

"A—privilege, sir. My ship is—no, cancel that. I have no ship. I am a Fleet Captain."

"My honor, Captain."

"That's enough," Cory said. He put his arms under Garth's and helped him from the chair. "Thank you, gentlemen. I can manage him now, and the rest of them, I'm sure."

As they moved off, Garth turned for a last look at Kirk. It was now alarmingly penetrating, but still puzzled. "Should I know you, sir?" he asked.

Time for a new beginning. "No, Captain—no."

He was led out. Looking after him, Kirk said, "Tell me something, Mr. Spock."

"Yes, Captain."

"Why was it so impossible to tell the difference between us?"

"It was not impossible, Captain. Our presence here is proof of that."

"Yes, and congratulations. But what took you so *long*?"

"The interval of uncertainty was actually fairly brief, Captain. It only seemed long—to you. As I threatened then, I could have waited you both out, but you made that unnecessary by proposing that I kill both of you. It was not a decision Garth could have made."

Kirk felt a faint chill. "Excuse me, Mr. Spock, but I think that's wrong. He had only just finished readying himself to destroy not only both of us, but the whole station."

"Yes, Captain, I believe he was capable of that. It would have been a grand immolation of his whole scheme. But to die by himself, ignominiously, leaving followers behind to see his defeat—no, I do not believe megalomaniacs think like that."

"I see. Well, there's no doubt about how you think."

"Indeed, sir?"

"Yes, indeed—fast. *Very* fast." Kirk raised his communicator. "Kirk to *Enterprise*. Three to beam up, Scotty."

"King," Spock added without a trace of a smile, "to King's Level One."

THE MARK OF GIDEON

Writer: George F. Slavin and Stanley Adams
Director: Jud Taylor
Guest stars: Sharon Acker, David Hurst

"It appears to be Paradise, Mr. Spock," said Kirk, handing back the folder of Federation reports and stepping onto the Transporter platform. "It's taken Gideon long enough to agree to negotiating membership in the Federation."

"I'll be interested in hearing your description, Captain," said Spock, taking his place at the console. "Since they have not permitted any surveillance, or any visitors, you appear to be uniquely privileged to visit Heaven early."

"You won't have long to wait," said Kirk. Uhura's voice replied at once to Spock's request for coordinates. Spock set the levers at 875; 020; 079.

"Let's go, Mr. Spock."

"Energizing, Captain." Spock did not, of course, smile at Kirk's eagerness to be off.

The Transporter Room shimmered, then steadied. Nothing seemed to have happened.

"Mr. Spock," said Kirk, stepping from the platform. "Mr. Spock?" There was no one in the Transporter Room but himself.

He clicked the intercom button. "Mr. Spock, I have not been transported down, and why have you left your post before confirming? Mr. Spock, answer me . . ."

This was not at all according to regulations. Annoyed, Kirk stamped out of the Transporter Room and headed purposefully toward the bridge. There was nobody there either.

He hit the intercom with increasing irritation. "This is the Captain speaking. All bridge personnel report immediately." He folded his arms and waited; there had better be one hell of an explanation. Nothing happened. He switched on the intercom again, alternately calling Engineering, security, Dr. McCoy, and listening. There was only silence.

"Lieutenant Uhura, report to the bridge immediately."

The viewing screen showed only the planet Gideon exactly as he had just seen it before stepping onto the Transporter, a perfectly ordinary M-type planet peacefully poised in the screen. The readouts and lights on the bridge consoles continued to operate in their usual conformations.

"Captain Kirk." The smooth voice of Prime Minister Hodin emerged from the communication screen. "The Council is still awaiting your arrival."

A plump figure rose to its feet from among the Councillors of Gideon.

"This discourtesy is unforgivable!" he snapped. "Doesn't your Federation recognize that first impressions are most important?"

Spock blinked. "Captain Kirk was transported down minutes ago, sir."

"That's impossible."

"I transported him myself," said Spock firmly.

"He never arrived here," said Hodin, evenly. Spock stared at Scott, and turned back to the screen.

"He was beamed directly to your Council Chamber. Please check your coordinates, Prime Minister."

Hodin read out from a slip of paper, "875; 020; 079."

Scott nodded.

"Something's gone wrong with the Transporter," said Chekov. "Captain Kirk's lost somewhere between the *Enterprise* and Gideon." His voice rose; Spock's expression remained impassive. The planet hung in the viewscreen, enigmatic.

The Prime Minister was speaking insistently. "We provided you with the exact coordinates for this room, Mr. Spock. And that is all we were obligated to do. If he is not here it is your own responsibility and that of your staff."

"I do not deny that, Your Excellency. I was not attempting to blame your personnel."

"We are glad to hear that, sir." Hodin's voice sounded

almost smug. "We are, in fact, inserting it into the records of this . . . most unfortunate event."

"Your Excellency, with intricate machinery so delicately balanced as ours, there is always a margin for error," Spock said sharply. "Captain Kirk may have materialized in some other part of Gideon."

Hodin said, "Let's hope it was dry land, Mr. Spock."

"Your Excellency, to cut directly to the point, I request permission to beam down and search for the Captain."

Hodin sat back, hands on the table before him. "Permission denied, Mr. Spock. Your Federation is well aware of our tradition of isolation from all contaminating contact with the violence of other planets . . ."

"Your Excellency, the wars between star systems no longer prevail in our galaxy. If you will grant permission . . ."

"We shall institute a search immediately. In the meantime I suggest you look to your machinery."

"We have already done so, sir." Spock's voice was now extremely controlled. "With regard to permission to land . . ."

But the Council Chamber had vanished from the screen.

"We must once and for all acknowledge that the purpose of diplomacy is to prolong a crisis," said Spock, deliberately closing the switch.

"What are we waiting for, Mr. Spock? *We're* not diplomats," McCoy flung himself on a chair.

"We are representatives of the Federation, Doctor."

"That doesn't mean we have to sit here like schoolchildren and listen to a damfool lecture by some . . . dip-lo-mat."

"Unfortunately, diplomacy is the only channel open to us at the moment. This planet is shielded from our sensors; we cannot observe it. Therefore we are unable to select coordinates. They have to be given to us. We are bound by Federation's agreements with Gideon." Spock turned to Lt. Uhura. "Contact Starfleet immediately. Advise them of this problem and request permission to use every means at our disposal to locate the Captain."

"D'ye think he's there, Spock?" said Scott. "Or are there any other possibilities?"

"They are endless, Mr. Scott."

"Where do we start?" said McCoy helplessly.

Spock leaned over Sulu's console. "Institute three-hundred-and-sixty degree scan, Mr. Sulu—one degree at a time."

"You're going to scan space for him? But sir, that could take years!"

"Then the sooner you begin, Mr. Sulu, the better," said Spock grimly.

Sweating slightly, Kirk ran from the elevator and pressed a door; it did not budge. He tried to force it with no success. He tried the next door; it opened easily. Standing guardedly in the opening, he pushed it all the way open with his elbow, one hand on the butt of his phaser. It whished slightly in the silence. the tables in the lounge stood as though the crew had just been summoned; a half-finished chess game, a sandwich with a bite out of it, a book dropped carelessly on the floor. But the only sound was Kirk's own breathing. He went out into the corridor again, warily.

Two more doors, locked. The third, labeled "Captain's Quarters," opened to the lightest pressure. His familiar room suddenly seemed alien—no crackle from the intercom, the bunk neatly made up, his books orderly on their shelf; his lounging robe swung eerily in the slight breeze made by the opening door. Momentarily disoriented, he wondered for a wild moment whether he had strayed from his own body and was visiting the *Enterprise* long after he and his crew had perished from the universe.

Footsteps! Dancing footsteps, echoing in the corridor; he pivoted on his now very real heels and stared. At the end of the hall a graceful figure whirled and curtsied, feet pattering gaily on the utilitarian flooring.

She caught sight of Kirk in mid-pirouette, and stopped with a little cry. He reached, and caught her; the sight of a human form brought his sense of reality back with a bump.

"Who are . . . who are you?"

She frowned, her delicate forehead lovely even when wrinkling; suddenly she smiled.

"Odona . . . yes. My name is Odona. Why did you

bring me here?'' She indicated the ship's corridor with a wide gesture.

Kirk was startled. ''What are you doing on my ship?''

''This entire ship is yours?''

''It's not my personal property. I'm the Captain.''

''And you have all this to yourself?'' Her voice was full of wonder.

''At the moment, we seem to have it all to ourselves,'' Kirk corrected.

Odona smiled, sapphire eyes looking up from under sable lashes. ''So it seems. You're hurting me, Captain.''

Kirk hastily released her.

''Captain James Kirk. And I did not bring you here, incidentally.''

''If you didn't . . .''

''Exactly. Who did?''

She shrugged helplessly. The decorations bordering her brief tunic twinkled in the lights.

''What happened before you got here?'' said Kirk. ''Try to remember. It's important.''

She puzzled over it for a moment. ''I remember . . . it seems I was standing in a very large auditorium, crowded with people, thousands of people pressed against me so hard I could hardly breathe . . . and I was fighting for breath, screaming to get out and they kept pushing and pushing . . .'' She shuddered.

''Don't be afraid.'' Kirk placed a comforting hand on her shoulder.

''I'm not.'' She looked up at him. ''But you are troubled?''

Kirk turned away. ''I am the only one of my crew left on the *Enterprise*. Out of four hundred and thirty. I may be the only one left alive.''

''I am sorry. If only I could help.''

''You can,'' said Kirk earnestly. ''Tell me the rest. You were fighting for breath, screaming to get out, and . . .''

''And suddenly I was here on this . . . your ship. And there is so much room, so much freedom. I just wanted to float.'' She smiled impishly. ''And then, there you were.''

''How long have you been on the *Enterprise*?'' Kirk's

questions were almost random; any clue, any train of suggestion, might lead him to a solution.

"I don't know. Not long. Does it matter?"

"It might. Come on." He started back toward the
bridge.

Odona followed reluctantly.

"Do we have to leave this wonderful open place?"

Kirk glowered at the chronometer in the bridge, gripping Odona's hand. She tried to pull away from him; he held
her firmly.

"Half an hour of my life is lost."

Odona stared at him.

"Between the time I tried to leave this ship for Gideon,
and the time I found myself here alone, a full half hour disappeared—poof! What happened during that half hour?"

"What is Gideon?"

"Your home, the planet you came from . . . don't you
remember?"

"I don't know any Gideon." She looked at him, apparently utterly lost.

"That's impossible. We were in synchronous orbit over
the capital city. I was supposed to beam down. Something
went wrong. You must have been sent aboard from Gideon."

She shook her head, trying to remember.

"I do not think so."

Kirk flipped on the viewing screen. Gideon had vanished. The changing patterns of the stars indicated the forward motion of the ship. Odona moved closer, and put her
hand in his.

"We are no longer over Gideon," said Kirk in a flat
voice.

"Where are we?"

"I don't know. I don't recognize that quadrant," said
Kirk dully.

Odona bit her lip. Thinking aloud, Kirk said, "Odona,
you must realize that we are not here together by accident.
Someone must have arranged it, for a purpose, an unknown
purpose."

A small voice replied, "Captain Kirk, before I said I
wasn't afraid. Now, I think I am."

He looked at her with compassion, and they turned back to the incomprehensible pattern of stars.

"Go back two degrees, there was a pulse variation," said Spock. Sulu maneuvered the sensor screen.

"There," said Spock. "There is something. Give me a reading."

Sulu flicked switches. "I can't make it out, sir."

"Get chemical analysis and molecular structure."

Sulu pointed silently at the indicators. Scott, McCoy and Chekov watched anxiously. Spock shook his head.

"Space debris."

Sulu sighed, and resumed tracking.

"Lieutenant Uhura, has Starfleet honored our request with an answer?"

"Not yet, sir."

"Did you impress upon them that the Captain's life is at stake?"

"Of course, Mr. Spock," she said indignantly. "But they insisted that the matter had to be referred to the Federation."

"What department?"

"Bureau of Planetary Treaties, sir."

"Contact them directly."

"I already have, Mr. Spock. They insist we go through Starfleet channels."

Sulu exploded, spinning in his chair. "With the Captain missing that's the best they could come up with?"

"A bureaucrat," said Spock bitterly, "is the opposite of a diplomat. But they manage to achieve the same results."

He stared at the chronometer. The second indicator clicked on. The captain was waiting . . . somewhere. And time was passing inalterably.

Suddenly Uhura's voice broke the tense silence.

"Mr. Spock, Gideon is making contact."

McCoy said sourly, "Now we're in for another dose of doubletalk."

"Since we must learn the language of diplomacy in order to deal with our present problem, shall we just listen to what they have to tell us?" said Spock. "Then, Doctor, we can decide on the relative merits of their statements."

THE MARK OF GIDEON

Four poker-faced ministers flanked the Prime Minister as he appeared on the viewer. Courteously, Spock began, "Your Excellency, we are pleased to hear that you have news of the Captain."

"Good news!" said the smiling image. "Very good news indeed, Mr. Spock. Your Captain is definitely *not* on Gideon. We have made a thorough search, just as you requested. I am sure you will be relieved to know you may now proceed to investigate all the other possibilities, and forget about Gideon."

"But that is not what we requested!"

"It is in the records, Mr. Spock," broke in the voice of the Prime Minister. "You asked for a thorough search of Gideon. We have used every means at our disposal to accommodate you, Mr. Spock." Outraged astonishment overlaid the diplomat's usual smile.

"Your record on this subject cannot be precise, Excellency."

Hodin waved to an assistant, and took from him a thick book. With ambitious eagerness the assistant had already opened it to a specific passage.

"You do not intend, I hope, that a conference be made the subject of a dispute between Gideon and the Federation, Mr. Spock."

"Your Excellency, a dispute is farthest from our minds. It's quite unnecessary to check your documents. I am merely suggesting to you that the language of our request may not have been understood exactly as intended."

Hodin stood up, huffily indignant. He waved his puffy hand.

"Mr. Spock, you are an officer of a spaceship. In your profession you make use of many instruments, tools, and . . . weapons . . . to achieve your objectives, do you not?"

"Yes, sir."

Hodin's eyes were squinting with an apparent effort to remain diplomatically cool. His posture betrayed him.

"However," he continued, "the only tool diplomacy has is language. It is of the utmost importance that the meaning be crystal clear."

Spock's own posture was of stiff attention.

"I am basically a scientist, Excellency. Clarity of formulation is essential in my profession also."

"I am glad to hear that. Perhaps then you will make a greater effort to choose your words precisely."

The word "precisely" vibrated through the bridge like a red petticoat in a bullring. The crew was coming to a full boil; all hands were fists by now.

McCoy muttered, "Are you going to let him get away with that, Spock?"

"No matter what you say, he'll find a way to twist the meaning," said Scott.

Uhura growled, "How can you stand this, Mr. Spock?"

McCoy leaned past Spock to the viewer and spoke directly to Hodin. "Our Captain is lost out there somewhere. We don't care how much you have searched, we are going over every inch of space ourselves. He's got to be down there somewhere. We're going after him!"

Too loudly, Chekov said, "This is no time to stick to rules and regulations, this is an emergency!" McCoy gently pulled him back, and leaned toward the screen again.

"We can't leave without being absolutely positive ourselves that everything has been done," he said. "Surely you can understand our feelings."

Hodin turned back to the screen, smiling.

"Mr. Spock. Mr. Spock."

"Yes, Your Excellency?"

"Are you still there?" That smile was imperturbable. "There was considerable interference with your transmission. A great deal of noise drowned out your transmission; could you please repeat more clearly?"

McCoy retreated, baffled. "Let me apologize for the *noise*, Your Excellency," said Spock. "To summarize, I request permission to transport down to Gideon."

The Prime Minister looked at his deputies and back at Spock. They all burst out in offensive laughter.

"Forgive me, Mr. Spock," Hodin's oily voice resumed. "No criticism of your equipment is intended. But evidently it has sent your Captain on some strange journey— we all still hope a safe one, of course." He bowed formally. "But it could create for us a grave incident with your Federation. And now you propose to repeat the disaster with yet another officer? Are you mad?''

Scott shouted, "I'll not take that, Mr. Spock. The Transporter was in perfect condition . . . I pairsonally guarantee that mysel'. Transport me down there this minute and I'll be proving it to those . . . those . . . gentlemen!''

The chill in Spock's quick glance froze Scott in his tracks.

"I could not quite make that out, Mr. Spock. Would you be so good as to repeat what you said?'' Hodin gave every appearance of amusement at the antics of the crew.

"The ship's engineer was saying that the malfunction that existed has now been repaired,'' said Spock, a quelling eye on Scott. "We would like to test it immediately. I would like to transport down to your Council Chamber.''

"But, Mr. Spock, you . . .''

Spock interrupted Hodin. "Your Excellency, grant this one request.''

"You are a very persistent fellow, Mr. Spock.''

A moment of tension passed while Hodin again consulted with his staff.

"All right, Mr. Spock.'' A whistling sound passed through the bridge as the entire crew released held breath. "You shall test the skill of your . . . er . . . very excitable repairman.''

Scott's teeth ground in Chekov's ear. "He doesna ken what excitable is . . .'' Chekov grinned at him, and whispered, "But he's letting him go . . . Wait.''

"There is one further proviso. We cannot risk additional incident. You will therefore transport a member of my staff to your ship. Let us first see if that works.''

"Thank you, Your Excellency. Your proposal is accepted.'' Spock turned to Scott. "Transporter Room, Mr. Scott, on the double.''

"At once, Mr. Spock,'' said Scott, rather stiffly. He stalked to the elevator and punched the door.

On the screen, yet another assistant with a large book was talking to Hodin, who looked up.

"My assistant will provide you with the proper, what is the word?''

"Co-or-di-nates,'' said Spock, very clearly.

"Thank you. You may proceed."

The Gideonite assistant, placed himself at a corner of the Council Chamber.

"875," he said.

"875, Mr. Scott," said Spock.

"875, aye."

"020."

"020."

"709."

"709?" The last number was repeated. Spock hesitated for a moment.

"709, Mr. Scott. Energize."

"Mr. Spock, the young gentleman fron Gideon is here," Scott reported triumphantly.

"Very good, Mr. Scott." Spock turned to the screen. "Your assistant is safely arrived, Your Excellency. And now we would like to send down myself and if possible, a few technicians to follow through on . . ."

"Now, now, now, Mr. Spock. Not so fast. That is quite a different matter. We agreed to allow one representative on our soil, your Captain alone. Now you suggest a 'few technicians.' And will the Federation then demand an army of 'technicians' to hunt for these?"

Patiently, Spock said, "I will demand only one thing, Prime Minister; that I be permitted to beam down to your planet to search for the Captain."

"Your request," said Hodin, smoothly triumphant, "will be brought to the floor at the next session of Gideon's Council. Er . . . do not look forward to a favorable reply."

"Your Excellency!" Spock pressed the switch several times rapidly; the screen remained blank. He hit the intercom.

"Mr. Scott. Send the gentleman from Gideon home."

"I was just beginning to think you might find a new career as a diplomat, Spock," said McCoy.

"Do not lose hope, Doctor. Lt. Uhura, contact Starfleet Command. Demand an instant reply to our request for permission to land on Gideon."

The room was tense as Uhura operated her console.

"*Enterprise* to Starfleet Command.

"*Enterprise* to Starfleet Command."

* * *

"*Enterprise* to Starfleet Command." Kirk and Odona bent over the console, Kirk's fingers expertly flicking the controls.

"Captain Kirk here. Red Priority Alert. Do you read me? Red Priority Alert." The console impassively continued its normal light patterns.

"Isn't it working?" said Odona.

"It seems to be all right." Kirk flipped the manual control and held it open.

"Kirk here. Answer please. Red Priority Alert."

"If it is working someone must hear you," Odona said hopefully.

"There's nothing. If they do hear they aren't replying."

"Why would they do that?"

"They wouldn't." Kirk glanced quizzically at her, then crossed the bridge to Sulu's board. With a few swift motions he altered the setting so that the lights showed a different pattern.

"I'm taking the ship out of warp speed."

"Out of what?" Odona looked utterly baffled.

Kirk laughed. "Space terminology. We're no longer moving faster than light. I trimmed her down to sublight speed till we can find out where we are."

"It doesn't feel any different."

"Well, no." Kirk was amused. Abruptly, his smile faded. "Maybe it isn't." He stared at the other consoles, one by one. No change was apparent. He turned on the forward viewing screen. No motion was visible in the star-filled sky, still and remote.

"Has the ship slowed down?"

"If we can believe the screen, it has."

"Oh, don't tell me the *sky* is out of order now!"

They stood side by side watching the glittering heavens; behind them the console lights moved in rhythmic silence. Odona said softly, "It's so quiet, and peaceful."

"It isn't really, you know. Out there, it's . . ." As he turned his head to look at her he felt fingers against his lips.

"And it's beautiful," she said.

Kirk looked back at the panoply on the screen, and at the delicate oval face in its black wings of hair.

"And it's beautiful. Very beautiful."

"We're all alone here. Can it last a long, long time?"
Her eyes were raised to his, sparkling. His arm slipped around
her.

"How long would you like it to last?"

"Forever." Odona's voice was barely audible.

"Let's see now. Power; that's no problem, it regener-
ates. Food; we had a five years' supply for four hundred and
thirty. For two of us that should last . . ."

"Forever?"

Their eyes met, and her hands touched his shoulders.
He pulled her closer. She said in a trembling voice, "All my
life I've dreamed of being alone . . ."

The startling intensity of her "alone" woke Kirk; the
moment was broken. Gently he released her. She stood, her
arms still raised, eyelids lowered, her expression rapt.

"Most people are afraid of being alone," Kirk said.

She opened her eyes and looked him in the face.

"Where I live people dream of it."

"But why? What makes the people of Gideon dream
of being alone?" His voice had recovered its tone of imper-
sonal interest.

"I . . ." she caught herself. Her expression of puzzlement returned. "Gideon? I told you I don't know where my
home is." She shook her head.

"It might well be Gideon." Kirk appraised her coolly.

"Does it matter so much?" She started toward him,
her hands out.

"It might help me locate our position." She stopped.
Her hands dropped to her sides. She shrugged, almost im-
perceptibly.

"And then you might find your crew. Being here with
you, I forgot there were others. I envy your sense of loyalty."
She drew close to him. "I wish I could ease your fear for
your friends."

Kirk shook his head. "I *must* make contact with whoever is manipulating us. I've got to find a way . . ." He paced
the room, stopping in front of each of the consoles, willing
them to reveal something, the smallest clue. Suddenly he
whirled and faced the girl.

"Odona, can't you remember why your people want so much to be alone?"

A wave of utter panic swept over her face. She shivered, although there was no change in the temperature.

"Because they cannot ever be."

"Why not?"

"There are so many." He could hardly hear her reply. She lifted her head. A shuddering force seemed to rise from her slender body.

"So many . . . so many. There is no place, no street, no house, no garden, no beach, no mountain that is not filled with people. If he could, each one would kill to find a place to be alone. If he could, he would die for it."

She stared at him, tears creeping down her cheeks, supporting herself on Uhura's chair. She looked exhausted.

"Why were you sent here, Odona?" Kirk put the question compassionately.

Her head lifted proudly. "No one commands Odona. I was not sent here."

Kirk strode to her side, and took her face in his hands.

"Have you come here to kill?"

Her tearstained face was shocked; unable to answer, her lips formed a soundless "no."

"Have you come here to die?"

"I don't know. I don't care . . . I only know I am here. I only know I am happy here." She threw her arms around his neck and clung to him, desperately. The trouble in her eyes moved Kirk as her coquetry had failed to do. He kissed her, gently, then more urgently. Yet in the back of his mind the images evoked by her tormented outcry haunted him; faces of people yearning for solitude, young, old, men, women and children unable to draw a breath that was not their neighbor's.

The stars on the viewscreen ignored them.

Suddenly Kirk drew back his arm with an exclamation. She flinched.

"I have done something wrong?"

"No." Kirk smiled ruefully. But he let her go, and pulled up his sleeve. There was a bruise on his forearm. Blood made a tiny dome in its center.

"Why does it take so long?" Odona asked, peering at it.

"Long? What?"

"The bruise. It stays the same."

"And the irritation gets worse. If Dr. McCoy were here he'd take care of it with a simple wave of his medical tricorder."

It was obviously the same as if he had said "his wand" to Odona, but she said, "I would willingly give up some of this glorious space to Dr. McCoy, if he could take away your . . . irritation."

"They took Dr. McCoy, but they had to leave Sickbay," said Kirk. He took her arm and steered her to the elevator.

On the bridge of the other *Enterprise*, Uhura, Chekov, Scott and McCoy were intently scanning the viewscreen. Spock stood at attention in the Captain's position. Over the air the voice of the Starfleet Admiral, slightly distorted by its long journey, sounded extremely stern.

"I sympathize deeply, but Starfleet cannot override Federation directives in this matter."

"The crew will not understand it, Admiral."

"Damn straight," muttered McCoy.

"Has your crew suddenly become interested in provoking a war, Mr. Spock? That is hardly Starfleet's mission."

"We only want to save the life of the Captain," repeated Spock.

"You have not proved your case to the Federation, or even to Starfleet, for that matter," said the Admiral.

"What's the matter wi' them all?" said Scott in a surly voice. "Ye'd think naebody but us care at all . . ."

Spock shushed him with a wave of his hand behind his back.

"I'm positive I will be able to do so to your satisfaction, Admiral. It has been clear to me since my first exchange of, er . . . courtesies with the Prime Minister that they have taken the Captain prisoner."

"Granted, Mr. Spock."

"I know now precisely where the Captain is being held." A stunned silence gripped the crew.

"Leave it to Spock, every time," whispered Uhura. Scott nodded.

". . . If he is at the same place to which we transported him," Spock went on.

"They would not dare to harm him in the Council Chamber!" The Admiral was outraged.

"That is not where the Captain is, Admiral. He is being held nearby."

"Well! You have now answered What and Where. I now await your explanation of Why."

"Since this planet is shielded from our sensors, by Federation agreement, Admiral, we cannot possibly establish that without on-the-spot investigation."

"Mhm. What evidence have you that the Captain's life is threatened?"

"Why else would they keep him?"

"I'm afraid that's not good enough, Mr. Spock. Permission denied."

Spock took a deep breath, fists clenched. "I wish personally to go on record that this decision is completely arbitrary."

"So noted." The screen blipped off.

"Diplomats!" exploded Scott. "What did you mean, Mr. Spock? Didn't we beam the Captain into the Council Chamber?"

"Quiet, please!" Mr. Spock broke through the agitated babble. "No, Mr. Scott, Gideon supplied us with two different sets of coordinates; one for the Captain, and one for our . . . er . . . recent guest." As Scott looked doubtful, he said, "The Captain's Log is evidence enough—I hope." He turned to the ship's memory. The crew stared at the numbers on the readout.

"You're right, Mr. Spock!"

"Look at that!"

"What kind of finagle is this?" Scott turned to Spock, hands on hips and a glare in his eye.

"What now, Mr. Spock?" said McCoy. "Are we to sit here and wait with our hands folded for the Captain to reappear?"

"This is typical of top echelon isolation." Spock's dry voice conveyed disgust. "They are too far away from the elements that influence crew morale."

"At times like this I don't think they remember that there is such a thing," said McCoy furiously.

"It is unfortunate. But for the first time in my career, I am forced to violate a direct order from Starfleet."

"Hear, hear!" shouted Scott. "That's absolutely the right decision, Spock. I'm with you!"

"One hundred percent!" That was Chekov; it was very clear that if Starfleet Command could but hear them the entire crew would be tried for insubordination—at the least.

"I shall beam down there at once." Spock's resolute calm stirred everybody into action; positions were taken.

"Mr. Scott, the con is yours."

"Aye, but ye'll be needing me along," said Scott, protesting.

"The Captain will be needing all of you at your posts." This reminder had the desired effect; subdued, Scott headed for the elevator behind Spock.

"It might be taken as an invasion," McCoy whispered to Scott. "I'll pick up my medical tricorder and meet you in the Transporter Room, Mr. Spock."

"No, Dr. McCoy; I cannot assume responsibility for ordering a fellow officer to violate a Starfleet directive. I go alone."

"Well, that's just about the worst decision you'll ever make, Spock," grumbled McCoy. "I hope you won't regret it."

As he entered the elevator, Spock said, "I'm sure this won't take long." McCoy held out his hand in a good-luck gesture. Spock shook it solemnly, and the doors closed.

"Isn't that just what Captain Kirk said?"

Chekov's words echoed in the suddenly quiet room.

Odona wandered around Sickbay, fingering pieces of equipment, peering curiously at instruments, spelling out the names of chemicals.

"If I can find a medical tricorder I'll be cured in no time," said Kirk, rummaging in a cabinet.

"Cured?"

"My arm," said Kirk patiently. "The pain would be gone."

"Oh. What will happen if you do not find it? Will you become sick? Will you, uh, die?"

Kirk looked at her, astonished. "Of this little scratch? Of course not. It would heal itself, eventually. It's just a simple . . ." He looked closely at the little wound.

"Or is it?" Recollections of biological sampling, blood tests, other scientifically motivated wounds went through his mind. Had someone wanted something of his tissues? Well, there was no telling. He turned back to the cabinet.

"All this is needed to cure those who are . . . sick?" Odona was examining the autoclave. Kirk nodded.

"It is cruel. Why are they not allowed to die?"

"What did you say?"

"Why don't you let them die?"

Her hand lay on the cauterizer; Kirk jumped.

"Don't touch that!"

He was a fraction of a second too late; Odona had bumped the switch; a jet of flame streaked out. Kirk jerked her away from the machine and switched off the flame in one motion.

"Are you hurt?"

"Just my hand." Odona had not even blinked, had not cried out. Was this a spartan self-control—or something else?

"Let me see it." She covered her damaged hand.

"It's nothing."

He pulled the hand gently but firmly into the light. Her forefinger was burnt completely away.

"My God!" Kirk's grip tightened with sympathetic horror. She withdrew her hand.

"The pain is already gone. Don't worry." Her voice was quite calm.

"Sutures . . . it's already cauterized . . . shock . . ." Kirk plunged at the cabinet.

"Wait." She was utterly unperturbed. "It's already healing."

Kirk glanced at the hand she held out to him and lurched into the cabinet door. A tiny forefinger had already appeared where a moment ago had been a raw wound. As he goggled, the finger grew before his eyes. In a matter of minutes Odona's hand was as whole as ever.

"See?" she said. "Why did you worry so much? This is strange to you?"

"Regeneration . . ." he muttered. "Injuries heal themselves?"

"Just as your arm will," she said, reassuringly.

"No. I have never seen anything like this before. Do all your people have this capacity?"

"Of course."

"They do not fall sick. Or die."

Once again the fleeting expression of panic swept over her face.

"That is why they long for death," Kirk said slowly, gazing at her. "So many, no one ever dying . . ."

He became aware of a sound—a sound not due to his own or Odona's movements. It grew in his consciousness to a steady throb.

"Do you hear that?" he asked. Odona nodded. Kirk prowled the room, listening at the walls for the direction of the sound. He checked his watch; it timed at seventy-two beats per minute. Odona put her hand to her forehead.

"It sounds like an engine," she offered.

"The ship's engine makes no sound."

"But there is something wrong with the equipment. Could that be it?"

"I know every sound on this ship; this is coming from outside," said Kirk, trying to recollect what the timing had reminded him about.

"Is it a storm?"

"We wouldn't hear a storm in here. Come along, it's not coming from here, at any rate."

They moved cautiously along the corridor, Kirk leading the girl by the hand. Her hand was cold, and a little damp. She must be terrified. The pulse of sound went on, no louder and no less. Kirk stopped at a viewing port in the observation corridor.

"We can see outside from here—if it works." He depressed a button. Nothing happened. He reached for the manual control level. The panel slid open.

To his horrified amazement, the port was filled with the faces he had imagined when Odona had burst out with her passionate yearning for solitude. Silently screaming, the faces filled his vision with distress and longing. He fell back a step, glanced at Odona. When he looked at the screen again it showed only the still and starlit skies.

Sharply he asked, "What did you see?"

"People . . . the faces of people; and stars."

She turned to him, pale. "What is it? What's happening?"

The sound stopped as suddenly as it had begun. He remembered; the beat had been identical with the human heartbeat. Thousands of people outside the ship, pressing against it with their bodies.

"You said we were moving through space."

"Yes."

"Then there couldn't really be people out there."

"There could," Kirk said grimly. "Someone could be creating an illusion in our minds. Why would they want to do that, Odona?"

She shrank from him. He saw that her forehead was beaded with perspiration.

"I don't know. I don't know anything. Why do you ask me?"

"I wonder . . . if we were convinced of a location, we would stop searching. We might be content to stay here, mightn't we?"

"Be . . . content." Odona's pallor belied her calm. Suddenly he was irritated and tired of trickery.

"Where is my crew, girl? Are they dead? Have you killed them to have the ship to yourself?"

She shivered in his grasp, scarlet patches flaming her cheeks. Her sapphire eyes had lost their sparkle, looked dull and sunken.

"No, no, I don't know anything. Please, Captain, something strange is happening to me. I never felt like this . . ."

"Neither have I," said Kirk, as cold as ice.

"Am I sick? Is this . . . dying?" she whispered, clinging to a doorframe. Her weight fell on Kirk's arms as he gripped her firmly.

"You do not know of sickness," he said. "You have none on your planet. What kind of . . ."

"Now there will be . . . sickness, now there will be death!" Her voice died in a whisper as she fainted, smiling.

"What the blue . . ." Kirk caught her. Bearing her in his arms he started straight back to Sickbay. As he approached the door he was arrested by the sound of pounding feet coming down the corridor.

"Hodin!"

Guards surrounded him as Hodin ponderously walked toward Kirk and his burden.

"Yes, Captain. Our experiment has passed the first stage."

The explanation would have to wait.

"Let me by," he said urgently. "I must help her."

"No," said Hodin, quietly. "We do not want any of your medicines."

"But she's very ill. Look at her—she needs help, and at once."

"We are grateful for her illness. Thank you, Captain. You have done more than you know for us."

Kirk thought they must be mad. He looked at Odona. Her eyelids fluttered. Hodin spoke gravely.

"My dear daughter, you have done well." He took the limp form from Kirk and turned away. The deputation closed in around the baffled Captain.

"Guard him well, we shall need him for a long time," called Hodin over his shoulder.

In total perplexity Kirk marched along with his guard. What had happened to his crew? This corridor along which they were now walking was unfamiliar; not aboard the *Enterprise*, then. Well, where *was* the *Enterprise*? Why did this diplomat want his daughter to die? Perhaps he could take comfort from the fact that he alone had been tricked; perhaps crew and ship were safe elsewhere. They drew near to the "Captain's Quarters" and he heard voices. He halted, despite the guards' effort to press him along.

"I must see him," came the faint tone of Odona.

"Yes, yes. But now you must lie still." Hodin's voice had lost some of its smoothness. "Do you feel great pain?"

"My arms . . . and . . . thighs . . ."

Avid, yet tender, Hodin said, "What is it like?"

"It is like . . . like when we have seen that the people

have no hope, Father. You felt . . . great despair. Your heart
was heavy because you could do nothing. It is like that.''

"You have great courage, my daughter. I am very proud
of you." Hodin closed the door softly behind him. Kirk
stepped toward him anxiously.

"Let me see her."

"Not yet."

"You don't know what illness she has. Maybe I can
tell."

Hodin looked at him gravely. "We know. She has
Vegan choriomeningitis."

"Oh, my God." Kirk stepped back; "If she is not
treated at once, within twenty-four hours, she will die. I
know; it nearly killed me."

Hodin nodded. "Yes, Captain. We learned of your
medical history, as we did the plan of a starship, during the
negotiations. We brought you here to obtain the microorgan-
isms."

"So that's how my arm was hurt."

"My apologies. As you have learned, we have no
medical practitioners. We were unforgivably awkward to
have inflicted pain on you . . ."

"You mean you deliberately infected your own daughter . . ." Overcome with fury, Kirk turned on his guards. His
right fist shot out and caught one in the midriff; as he doubled
up with a grunt, Kirk lashed out at the other and leaped for
the door of Odona's sickroom. But the first man had recovered and dived at Kirk's feet, bringing him down; the second
guard pulled him roughly up and dragged him back to Hodin.

"We do not wish to hurt you. You will see her as soon
as we are certain she is susceptible."

"You *are* mad!" cried Kirk in frustrated rage.

"No, Captain. We are desperate. Bring him along to
the Council Chamber."

The chamber was a scene of excited chatter, the deputies of Gideon's government descending upon Hodin, demanding, "How is she? What has happened?"

Hodin waved them to their places around the table. Kirk
was brought forward between his guards.

"Your report to the Federation was a tissue of lies,"
he said angrily. "You described Gideon as a Paradise."

"And so it was . . . once. A long time ago it was as we described it. In the germ-free atmosphere of Gideon people flourished in physical and spiritual perfection, Captain. The life-span was extended and extended, until finally death comes only to the very ancient, when regeneration is no longer possible. These gifts, Captain, have been our reward for respecting life."

"Most people would envy you."

"We no longer find this condition enviable. Births have increased our population until Gideon is encased in a living mass of beings without rest, without peace, without joy."

"Then why have you not introduced measures to make your people sterile?"

"They do not work," said Hodin simply. "All known techniques are defeated by our organs' capacity to regenerate, like my daughter's hand."

"There are other ways to prevent conception, however."

"This is our dilemma, Captain. Life is sacred to our people. This is the one unshakable tradition. Yet we pay for the gifts that the worship of life has brought us, and the price is very heavy. Because of our overwhelming love of life we have the gifts of regeneration and longevity."

"And misery."

"That is the contradiction."

"The reality, Hodin."

Hodin flinched. He turned his back for a moment, then walked back and forth, the tortured confusion of his mind all too apparent.

"What are we to do? We cannot deny the truth of what has shaped us as we are. We are not capable of interfering with the Creation we love so deeply. It is against our natures."

"Yet you can kill your own daughter. How can you justify that?"

"We are not killing her. It is the disease that will or will not kill her; this is not under our control. The opportunity came to us, perhaps as a gift; we have seized upon it to readjust the life cycle of this planet. My daughter had hoped you might be brought to feel the agony of Gideon, Captain.

It is impossible; no stranger could realize the horror of existence.

"I will not ask you to understand my personal grief; nor will I parade it to gain your cooperation." Hodin had stopped pacing, and faced Kirk proudly.

"My daughter has won my pride, as she has always had my love. She has freely chosen to take this chance with her life, as all the people of Gideon are free to choose. And she cannot be sure she is right."

"This virus is rare. Where do you intend to get it?" said Kirk, grappling with the first of these problems that he felt able to handle.

The smooth diplomatic mask slipped over Hodin's face. Kirk was suddenly wary.

"Your blood will provide it, Captain. You will be staying here."

Kirk slammed the table with the flat of his hand.

"Not me, Hodin. You have other ways to solve your problem. I do not offer my life for this purpose at all; I have other commitments. And I have other hopes for Odona than death."

"My daughter hoped you would love her—enough to stay."

Kirk looked hard at him. "What passed between your daughter and me was between us alone."

"She pleaded with you to stay."

"You watched us, didn't you?"

Hodin bowed his head in admission. "We are desperate. And privacy is perhaps of less concern to us than to you."

"I'm desperate too, you . . ."

Kirk was interrupted by a buzzer. A message was delivered to Hodin, who raised his head in proud sorrow.

"You may go to her now. She is calling for you. You cannot leave quite yet, Captain, can you?"

"Spock to *Enterprise*. Spock to *Enterprise*."

"Scott here, Mr. Spock."

"Mr. Scott, I am speaking to you from the bridge of the *Enterprise*."

"Ye're what, man?"

"Speaking from the bridge of the *Enterprise*, Mr. Scott."

"Those were the coordinates you gave me!"

"They were correct. I am apparently on an exact duplicate of the *Enterprise*."

"What's that? Is it in orbit?"

"You could say so; Gideon is in orbit, this ship is on Gideon."

"Weel, that's a beginning, Spock. What about the Captain?"

"I'm sure he's somewhere here, Mr. Scott. I'm picking up life readings locally. Spock over and out."

Kirk knelt by the side of the bunk where Odona lay, flushed with fever, her cloud of silvery black hair tarnished and lifeless. He looked up at Hodin.

"If you do not let me get Dr. McCoy it will soon be too late for her."

"We have told you, Captain Kirk. It is her wish and mine that there be no interference with the natural development of this precious virus."

"What is the matter with you? If she lives, her blood would contain the virus just as mine does. She doesn't have to die."

"She must die. Our people must believe in this escape."

"She is so young . . ."

"Because she is young she will be an inspiration to our people. Don't you see, Captain, she will become a symbol for others to follow? In time, Gideon will once again be the Paradise it was . . ."

Odona's sigh pierced the shell of exaltation Hodin had erected around his consciousness. Kirk smoothed her blazing forehead; Hodin stood by her bedside in a state of misery. But Odona's weary eyes only gazed at Kirk.

"I . . . am glad you are here. Is my time short?"

"Very short," Kirk whispered.

"I asked you to make the journey last forever." She smiled wanly. "It began here, didn't it?"

Kirk spoke very clearly, hoping to penetrate the fever-ish haze that surrounded her senses.

"The journey can continue. If you will let me, I can make you well."

"Like your arm?"

He nodded hopefully. She lay still, expressionless. Then, with a slight cry, she raised her arms to embrace him. The delicacy that had given her such grace in health now gave her too much fragility in his arms. He willed her with all his might to agree to be cured.

"I am not afraid of . . . what will happen. I am not at all afraid," she murmured feebly against his shoulder. "It's only that now . . . I wish it could be . . . with you . . . forever . . ." Her voice sank. Gently Kirk laid her uncon-scious head on the pillow.

The door closed with a decisive snap.

"I am glad to see you looking so well, Captain. Ap-parently Starfleet's analysis was correct after all." Spock's cool words cut into the air.

Kirk whirled; it *was* Spock. "I'm fine," he managed to say. "But we do have a patient." He lifted Odona from the bed. Hodin stood, paralyzed.

"Spockto*Enterprise* Spockto*Enterprise* Threetobeam-up Mr.Scott," Spock slipped the words out with machine-gun speed.

"Three—? Er—same coordinates, Mr. Spock?"

Scott had obviously grasped the need for haste.

Hodin plunged at Spock with an inarticulate sound of fury.

"Your Excellency, please do not interfere." As the sparkles replaced the three figures, Mr. Spock's last, "I al-ready have enough to explain to upper echelons, Prime Min-ister," hung in the air over Hodin's impotent rage.

"I am . . . cured?" Odona's tone wavered between disappointment and wonder.

"Completely." Kirk lifted her to her feet and stood smiling down at her brightened eyes.

"Then I can now take your place on Gideon," she said gravely.

"Is that what you want to do?" Kirk was very serious,

yet a small smile crossed his face as he watched her. She touched his cheek tenderly, lightly.

"That is what I must do. I am needed there."

Kirk kissed her hand, a gesture of salute to her gallantry—and a farewell. "People like you are needed everywhere, Odona."

They walked side by side into the corridor.

"Will you sign this, please, sir?" A young crewman held out a clipboard to Kirk. He scrawled his initials, and in the bustle of traffic in the corridor he saw her watching a couple stroll hand in hand toward the lounge. As she caught his eye, the wistfulness in her face vanished. She smiled.

"It's different from our *Enterprise*."

"It's almost exactly the same," said Kirk. "Only this one works." He added wryly, "And it's crowded."

She laughed. "Does it seem so to you?"

"It does now."

"Excuse me, Captain, but before this young lady goes home we are obliged to devise some way to complete our mission. The Prime Minister, you may recall, was somewhat agitated when we last saw him." Spock was apologetic, but quite firm.

Kirk clapped a hand to his head. "Foof, I was forgetting him. Call McCoy and Scott; we'll confer on the bridge."

"Captain," said Spock very formally. "I beg leave to report that I have broken regulations. Starfleet Command gave specific orders which I, upon my own responsibility, disobeyed. In view of Prime Minister Hodin's intransigence to date . . ."

"If you mean father," said Odona, "he did not really want me to volunteer for this sickness at all. He will be grateful to have me back, and if I am carrying the virus, all will be well."

"He wanted you to be a symbol for your people," said Kirk thoughtfully. "He was quite impassioned about that, Odona."

"He had to have some way to live with himself, letting me die, Captain," said Odona gently. "I haven't died. Perhaps there may be some way to inspire our people, nevertheless."

Spock was frowning into his console. "I wonder," he said. "There are many ways to gather public approval—besides the sacrifice of . . . er . . . young women."

There was a silence; each of them cast about in his mind for alternatives. Hodin required something that would serve to call forth volunteers from his people for infection with a deadly disease; and this was a unique public relations problem for the crew of the *Enterprise* to consider.

"In the old days of medicine . . ." began McCoy. "I seem to recall that there was some sort of signal . . . illness aboard, doctor required; I don't quite remember . . ."

Spock laughed. "Bravo, Doctor!" He punched rapidly at his console. "Here it is; a distress flag, flown by seagoing vessels . . . the design sounds simple enough."

Uhura rose from her seat. "I'll see to it at once." She left the room quickly.

"What is it? What are you doing?" Odona was unable to follow their rapid trains of thought. Kirk smiled to himself. This time her puzzlement was genuine.

"What we propose, madame, is to send you home with a badge of honor," said Spock. "When you show it to your father, he can offer such badges to all your people who volunteer for the . . . service he so urgently wishes to render them. This will make it a matter of pride to have such a badge in the family, and thus serve the same purpose as your death was designed to do."

Uhura returned with a small flag, as described by Spock. Kirk took it from her, and going up to Odona, while the crew stood at full attention, he pinned it ceremoniously to her shoulder.

"For service to Gideon above and beyond the call of duty," he intoned. He hesitated, then kissed her on both cheeks. "An old custom of some of our people," he said, smiling at her blush.

"Will you stay on the ship?" she whispered.

He looked at her quickly. In that moment he recognized the ambiguity of her question, and replied unmistakably.

"On *this* ship, I will stay, Odona."

She said wistfully, "Forever?"

"Sometimes I think so," he said, very quietly. "But this is my ship, my dear." He struck at the intercom.

"Kirk to Transporter Room. One to beam down to Gideon."

Later, McCoy asked, "Captain, is the Federation really all that anxious to gain the membership of what is now more or less a plague planet?"

"That," said Kirk, with a glance at Spock, "will be for the diplomats to decide."

THE LIGHTS OF ZETAR

Writer: Jeremy Tarcher and Shari Lewis
Director: Herb Kenwith
Guest star: Jan Shutan

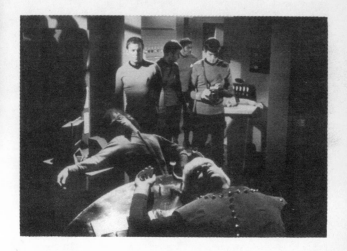

The *Enterprise* was enroute to Memory Alpha when the storm first appeared. Memory Alpha was a planetoid set up by the Federation solely as a central library containing the total cultural history and scientific knowledge of all planetary Federation members. The ship had a passenger, Lt. Mira Romaine, an attractive woman of about thirty. She was on board to supervise the transfer of newly designed equipment which the *Enterprise* was also carrying. At the moment, she was on the bridge talking to Scott at his position.

"Mr. Scott, I hope I haven't been too much trouble to you with all the questions I've asked."

"Well, I'm sorry the trip is coming to an end," Scott said. "I'm going to miss your questions."

Kirk watched them amusedly. "Present position, Mr. Chekov?"

"On course—one seventy-two mark four."

"Mr. Scott, as soon as we are within viewing range of Memory Alpha, you and Lt. Romaine will go to your stations in the emergency manual monitor. Prepare for direct transfer of equipment."

"Yes, Captain."

"We're ready, sir," Mira added.

"Lieutenant," Spock said, "may I offer my congratulations on what will be a first in the Federation."

"And good luck," Kirk added.

"Thank you, Mr. Spock, Captain."

"I didn't think Mr. Scott would go for the brainy type," Chekov said, almost too softly for Kirk to overhear.

"I don't think he's even noticed she has a brain. Has she?" Sulu said. A red light came up on his panel. "Captain, I am picking up a high intensity reading. Shall I display it?"

"Yes." Kirk looked at the main viewing screen. In the blackness of space there was a faint light source. "Is that Memory Alpha?"

"No, sir."

"Magnification eight."

The light now showed as a cloud of vaguely organic shape, almost like a brain. It sparked and flashed intermittently in varied hues, like a series of inspired thoughts.

"Is that some kind of storm?" Kirk said.

"Quite possible, Captain," Spock said. "I've never seen one of such great intensity and strange conformation."

"Captain," Sulu added, "it is approaching at warp two point six and accelerating."

"Recheck your readings, Mr. Sulu. It is impossible for a natural phenomenon to move faster than the speed of light."

"It is definitely doing so," Spock confirmed—and indeed the thing was visibly growing on the screen. "It therefore cannot be a phenomenon of nature."

"Deflector on. Condition yellow."

The light source filled the screen. The glare was almost unbearable. Then the screen went blank.

Kirk tried to snap out an order and found that he could not. The whole bridge was suddenly deathly silent. No one moved.

Then, just as abruptly, it was over. "Mr. Sulu, full scan on that turbulence or whatever it was!" Kirk noticed Scott staring uncertainly over Kirk's own shoulder. Turning to see what he was looking at, he was just in time to see Mira crumple out of sight behind the command chair.

"Mira!" Scott leapt from his post, knelt beside her and lifted her head off the floor. "Mira!"

She murmured unintelligibly. It was not that the sounds were indistinct, but as though they were in an unknown language.

"What's that you're saying?" Scott said. Kirk and

Spock were now also bending close. The strange murmuring went on.

McCoy came onto the bridge and crossed at once to the group, his tricorder already out and in use. He said, "Was she hurt by the fall or by the action of that . . . disturbance?"

"I don't know," Kirk said. "You were closest, Scotty. Did you notice?"

"She collapsed when it was over."

McCoy gave her a shot. The murmuring died away. Her expression changed from a curiously rapt look to one of relaxation. Then her eyes opened and she looked around in confusion.

"Easy now," Scott said. "You took quite a fall."

"I'm fine now," she said.

"Let me be the judge," McCoy said. "Can you walk to Sickbay?"

"Doctor, I'm fine, really I am." Again she looked around the bridge, obviously still puzzled. "Is everyone else—all right?"

"Aye, they are," Scott said. "You do just as Dr. McCoy says."

"Why? I never felt better in my—"

"Lieutenant, report to Sickbay," Kirk said. "That's an order."

"Yes, sir." She followed McCoy resignedly toward the elevator.

Scott said, "Would it be all right for me to go to Sickbay?"

"You will stay at your post, Mr. Scott. Lt. Uhura, damage report, all stations."

"All stations are operative."

"Mr. Spock?"

"Some equipment was temporarily out of order. My sensors were inoperative."

"Any damage to the warp engines?"

"None, Captain."

"Good. From the action of that—that storm, we may need all the speed we can get."

"It was not a storm, Captain," Spock said.

"Mr. Chekov, get a fix on whatever it was and try to

project its path . . . That was a novel experience for the *Enterprise*. Would you agree, Mr. Spock?''

"Unforgettable, Captain.''

"Yes? I was hoping you had an explanation.''

"None at the moment, Captain. Only a sharply etched memory of what I felt during the onslaught.''

"Memory Alpha was hailing us a moment before,'' Uhura said. "I wanted to respond, but I couldn't make my hand move.''

"It was not hands that were paralyzed, it was eyes,'' Chekov said. "I couldn't force my eyes to look down to set a new course.''

"No,'' Sulu said, "speech was affected. I couldn't utter a sound.''

"Nor could I,'' Kirk said. "You seemed to be having the same trouble, Mr. Spock.''

"Yes, Captain, I was.''

"Any explanation yet?''

"Only of the result,'' Spock said, "none of the cause. In each case, different areas of the brain were affected. Our voluntary nerve functions were under some form of pressure.''

"Or of attack?''

"Attack might be a more precise formulation, Captain.''

"Lt. Romaine seems most susceptible. Mr. Scott, perhaps you'd better go down to Sickbay after all. If she was the only one of four hundred and thirty people who passed out, we'd better find out why.''

"Aye, sir,'' Scott said, heading for the elevators with alacrity.

"I have plotted the storm's path, Captain,'' Chekov said. "On its present course it will hit the Memory Alpha planetoid as it did us.''

"Uhura, warn them of the proximity of the phenomenon. Can you give us an ETA for it, Chekov?''

"It's impossible, Captain. It has the ability to change speed.''

"Sorry, Captain,'' Uhura said, "But I'm unable to establish contact with the planetoid. Am hailing on all frequencies. No response.''

"It does not matter, Captain," Spock said. "Memory Alpha has no protective shields. When the library complex was assembled, shielding was regarded as inappropriate to its totally academic purpose. Since the information on the memory planet is freely available to everyone, special protection was deemed unnecessary."

"Wonderful," Kirk said sarcastically. "I hope the 'storm' is aware of that rationale."

"We're completing approach to the planetoid," Sulu said. "But the storm's gotten there first."

"Uhura, get through to—"

"I cannot," Uhura said. "I cannot get past the interference, sir."

"Mr. Spock, how many people are there on Memory Alpha?"

"It varies with the number of scholars, researchers, scientists, from various Federation planets who are using the computer complex."

"Mr. Chekov, maintain standard orbit."

"The storm is now leaving Memory Alpha," Sulu reported.

"And," Spock added, "the sensors give no readings of energy being generated on the planetoid."

"Any life readings?"

"None, sir."

"Check for malfunction."

Spock did so. "Sensors inoperative again."

"We'd better find out what's going on down there." Kirk turned to the intercom. "Kirk to Sickbay. Is Mr. Scott there?"

"Scott here. I was checking on the lass. She's going to be fine, though. Nothing wrong with her."

"I'm relieved to hear your prognosis. Is the doctor there with you?"

"McCoy here, Jim."

"How's the girl?"

"I think she's in good shape."

"Apparently Scotty thinks so, too. Both of you, meet me in the Transporter Room, on the double. Mr. Spock, come with me. The con is yours, Mr. Sulu."

* * *

The four materialized in a computer room on Memory Alpha. The room was utterly silent, and there was no light at all.

"Somehow," McCoy grumbled, "I find transporting into the darkness unnerving."

"Scotty," Kirk said, "can you give us some light in here?"

Scott checked the boards nearby; they could hear him fumbling. Then a small glow appeared, a safe-light of some sort. "This will have to do. The generator is inoperative. The alternative is to go back to the ship for hand torches."

Spock moved to the face of the largest computer cabinet with his tricorder, but for several moments simply stood there, doing nothing. Kirk guessed he was waiting for his eyes to become dark-adapted, a gift far better developed in Vulcans than in humans. Then he lifted the tricorder.

"Damage report, Mr. Spock?"

"It's a disaster for the galaxy, Captain. The central brain damaged—all memory cores burned out. The loss might be irretrievable."

Kirk took a step and stumbled over something large and soft. He put a hand down to it, but he too could see better now.

"Mr. Spock. I've just encountered a body. Look around the floor."

There was a long silence. Then Spock said: "There are dead men and creatures from other planets sprawled all around us. Move very carefully until you can see better. I'm scanning for a life reading . . . Yes, I have one, very faint."

"Location, Mr. Spock?"

"It is too weak to get an exact bearing, but . . ." He moved away.

"We'd better find him while he's still alive. We have to get more knowledge of this . . . enemy."

"Over here, Captain," Spock's voice called.

The other three carefully moved toward the sound of his voice. At his feet a girl, evidently a technician, was on her knees, struggling to get up. An already dead man nearby had evidently tried to help her. She was murmuring.

Spock listened intently. "The same garbled sounds,"

he said, "that Lt. Romaine was making when she fainted after the disturbance."

"Are you sure, Spock?"

"Absolutely sure."

Kirk flipped open his communicator. "Kirk to *Enterprise* . . . Mr. Sulu. Beam down Lt. Romaine immediately—and have her bring five hand torches."

"Yes, sir."

The technician's voice murmured on, but it was becoming steadily weaker. Then she pitched forward on her face.

McCoy took a reading, and then silently shook his head. Kirk said: "Can you tell what she died of?"

"Severe brain hemorrhaging due to distortion of all neural centers. Dissolution of all basic personality patterns. Even the autonomic nervous system."

"The attack, Captain, was thorough," Spock said.

"What did the others die of?"

"Each had a different brain center destroyed," McCoy said. "Just how, I can't tell you. Maybe when I get back to the ship's computer—"

The shimmer of the Transporter effect briefly illuminated the charnel chamber and Mira materialized. The beam of a flashlight leapt from her hand, but Scott moved swiftly to step into it, blocking her view of the bodies.

"Mira—the Captain has some questions. Give me the rest of the torches."

"Here you are . . . Yes, Captain?"

Kirk said gently: "Mira, while you were unconscious you were, uh, speaking."

"What did I say?" She seemed genuinely surprised.

"We don't know. You talked in a strange language we didn't understand. We found one person barely alive in here, and she was speaking in the same way—"

"Was speaking?" Before anyone could move to prevent her, she darted around the central computer and swept the beam of her flash over the floor. When she spoke again, it was in a frightened whisper. "All dead . . . just like I saw them. Captain, we must get back to the ship."

"Why?"

Her hands went to her brow. She seemed unable to answer.

"Tell me why!"

"Captain—that . . . that . . . it's returning!"

"How do you know?"

"I know. You'll be killed if we stay."

"I assure you, lieutenant," Spock said, "that unexplained phenomenon was headed away from the planetoid before we came here. It is probably seeking other victims."

"I tell you, it will kill us!" Her panic was genuine, that was clear.

Kirk's communicator beeped. "Bridge to Captain Kirk. The storm has reappeared on the long-range scanner."

"I told him it is not a storm," Spock said.

"Course, Mr. Sulu?"

"Coming back in this direction, and closing fast."

"Beam us up."

The minute he saw the Transporter Room coming into being around him, Kirk headed for the intercom, but Scott's voice stopped him.

"Captain, wait! We've lost Mira."

Kirk turned and saw that Lt. Romaine was indeed not there. Lt. Kyle was at the Transporter controls. Scott leaped to his side.

"Where is she? Stabilize her!"

"Something's interfering with the transporter signal," Kyle said. "I have her coordinates, but she's suspended in transit."

"Let me." Together the two men struggled with the controls. Suddenly, Kyle said, "Aha, it's cleared," and at the same moment Mira materialized on the Transporter platform. She stepped off, dazed but smiling.

"Mr. Scott, Lt. Romaine, you'd best go to the emergency manual monitor and see if enough new equipment is in inventory to repair at least some of Memory Alpha." Kirk hit the intercom. "Mr. Sulu, get us out of here. Mr. Spock, to the bridge, please."

In the emergency manual monitor, Mira and Scott were working side by side. The inventory had proceeded for some time in silence. Then Scott said:

"When I—thought we lost you, back there in the Transporter Room—well, you're not to do that again."

"It was so frightening," she said. "I felt pulled apart."

"You almost were. There was interference with the Transporter mechanism."

"And that's more than you can say about me," she said. What she meant by this, Scott had no idea.

"I'll tell you something. You are the sanest—the smartest—the nicest—and the most beautiful woman that has ever been aboard this ship."

"And what else?"

"Anything else, I'm keeping to myself for the moment."

"But I'm so much trouble to you."

"Trouble? What trouble? Of course, you could drive a man daft, but that's not what I call trouble."

She smiled. "Do I drive you daft, Scotty?"

"Well now—if it was me, you might have to work at it."

"I'd be willing—" Then, as if embarrassed, she turned away and resumed being busy.

"The *Enterprise* has been my life," Scott said. "I love this ship, and I love every day I've spent on it. But, until you came aboard, I didn't know how lonely it is to be free in the galaxy . . . So, don't you talk of trouble." He took her in his arms. "Now I want to forget about Memory Alpha."

It was the wrong thing to say. She pushed against his chest, her hands trembling. "Scotty . . . before that . . . I saw it—exactly as it happened."

"What of it? That happens to lots of people. There's a French term for it. They think they're seeing something before it actually occurs. But actually one eye picked it up without realizing—"

"My eyes weren't playing tricks!"

He smoothed her brow. "Then I'm sure there is some other perfectly reasonable explanation that will erase that worried frown."

"But Scotty, I saw the men dead in their exact positions—before I ever left the ship."

He put his hands on her shoulders. "Listen to me. I told you in Sickbay what strange tricks a first trip in space can play on your mind. That's all it is."

"No, Scotty."

"Have you ever had visions of future events before this?"

"Never."

"And, if you ask me, *nobody* ever has," Scott said firmly. "That seeing the future is pure bunk. You know that, don't you?"

"I always believed it."

"And you're absolutely right."

"But what is it, Scotty? What is frightening me? Ever since we've been near that—that storm, I've had such strange thoughts . . . feelings of such terror."

"Space, space, space, that's all it is."

"Then I don't have to report it?"

"If you want to spend the trip in Sickbay," Scott said. "But what good would it do? McCoy can no more cure it than he can cure a cold. It'll pass."

"When I get my permanent assignment . . . I hope it will be to the *Enterprise*."

"You just better make sure of it."

"Captain," Sulu said. "It's changing course."

"Plot it, Mr. Chekov."

"Present course will bring it across our starboard bow."

"Mr. Spock, you made a statement that that phenomenon was not a storm."

"Yes, Captain. No known conditions in space would support it as a natural phenomenon. But the sensors seem to be in working order at the moment. Perhaps this time the elusive creature will reveal something about itself." He bent into his hooded viewer. "It seems to be maintaining its distance, but matching course with us. I am receiving increasing magnitudes of energy. Yes—undoubtedly a life form. Fascinating!"

"Control your fascination, Mr. Spock. Pragmatically, what are the implications?"

"We saw the results of full contact in the deaths on Memory Alpha. The humanoid neurological system is destroyed when fully exposed to these peculiar wave patterns."

"But what *is* it, Spock?"

"Not what is it, sir. What are they. There are ten distinct life units within it, Captain. They are powerfully alive and vital."

"Who are they? Where are they from?"

"Impossible to determine without programming for computer analysis."

"Not now." Kirk shot a glance at the main viewer. "It's clear we can't outrun them. Can we shield against them?"

"I do not think so, sir."

"There must be some defensive action we can take."

"Captain, it is a community of life units. Their attack is in the form of brain waves directed against the brain that is most compatible."

"A living brain!" Kirk said. "Perhaps we can avoid a next time. Lt. Uhura, open all channels and tie in the universal translator. Maybe I can talk to them."

Uhura got to work. Indicators began to light up. "All channels open," she said finally. "Translator tied in."

Kirk looked up at the form of lights on the viewer. Incongruously, he felt wryly amused at the notion of trying to talk to an electrical cloud. "This is Captain James Kirk of the USS *Enterprise*. We wish you no harm. Physical contact between us is fatal to our life form. Please do not come any closer to this ship."

There was no response; only a faint wash of static. Spock said, "Perhaps it did not understand."

"Captain, change in velocity recorded," Sulu said. "It has accelerated its approach."

"Perhaps it will understand another language," Kirk said, beginning to feel angry. "Condition Red Alert. Prepare for phaser firing."

The Red Alert began flashing, and the distant alarm echoed throughout the ship.

"Mr. Sulu, lock in phasers for firing across their course. Do not hit them."

"Locked in, sir."

"Fire."

The phaser shot lanced to one side of the lights and on off into deep space.

"Reaction, Mr. Sulu?"

"None, sir. They are still approaching."

Apparently a shot across the bow was insufficiently convincing. "Lock to target."

"Locked on, sir."

"Fire."

The shot seemed to score a direct hit. The community of

life units dispersed in apparent confusion, and then began to reform. So they *could* be hurt—

"Captain, Captain," Scott's voice shouted from the intercom, without even waiting for an acknowledgment. "Scott here. The phaser shots—they're killing Mira."

"Killing Lt. Romaine? How—"

"When you fired, she was stunned, she crumpled. Another shot and you'll kill her."

"Get her to Sickbay at once . . . Mr. Spock, we appear to be at an impasse. Any suggestions?"

"Only one, Captain," the Science Officer said. "There seems to be only one possible defense. If we can find an environment that is deadly to the life form—and at the same time, isolate the girl from the deadly effects of it—"

"It sounds like asking the impossible." Kirk turned to the intercom. "Kirk to Dr. McCoy . . . Bones, is Lt. Romaine well enough to be talked to?"

"I think so," McCoy's voice said. "I can have her ready in a few minutes."

"Bring her and Mr. Scott to the Briefing Room as soon as possible. Bring all available biographical data on the lieutenant. . . . Mr. Spock, come with me."

In the Briefing Room, Spock went immediately to his slave console; Kirk sat at the center of the table, McCoy next to him.

"Go easy on her, Jim. She's in a bad state."

"I'll try. But this can't be postponed."

"I know. I was pretty hard on her myself the first time this happened. I needn't have been. We might know more."

"I'll be careful."

The door opened to admit Scott and Mira. He was holding her by the arm. She seemed pale and distraught. After she was seated, Scott went to his chair at the opposite end of the table.

Kirk leaned toward her and said gently: "This is not a trial, Lt. Romaine. You are not being accused of anything."

"I know," Mira said, almost in a whisper. She glanced toward McCoy. "I didn't mean to be uncooperative, Doctor."

"Of course you didn't," McCoy said. "I told the Captain that."

"I'll tell you everything I know. I trust all of you implicitly. I want to help."

"Good," Kirk said. "This investigation is prompted by two events that may be connected. The first time was when you passed out on the bridge. The second is when we fired the ship's phasers into the force that is attacking us, and we seriously injured you."

"It wasn't serious, Captain. You mustn't worry about hurting me."

"We're glad we didn't. Nevertheless, we won't take that particular defense measure again. Now, this is how we will proceed. Spock will provide everything we know about our attackers. Dr. McCoy has access to Starfleet's exhaustive file on you. A comparison of the two may turn up some unsuspected connection that will protect you—and ourselves. All right, gentlemen? Dr. McCoy, you begin. Does Lt. Romaine have any history of psychosomatic illness?"

"Occasional and routine teen-age incidence."

"Any evidence of any involuntary or unconscious telepathic abilities?"

"None."

"Any pathological or unusual empathic responses?"

"No, Captain. Not empathic. However, an exceptionally flexible and pliant response to new learning situations."

At this Spock leaned forward, but made no comment.

"There's one other thing, Captain," McCoy said. "Right after our phasers hit that thing, I gave Lt. Romaine the Steinman Standard Analysis. I don't have the results here but Nurse Chapel is having it sent down. In the meantime, I see nothing else very illuminating in the psychological file. Lt. Romaine has developed strong defenses to guard against her extreme competitiveness. Marked scientific and mathematical abilities set up an early competition with her distinguished father. It appears that the problem is still not completely resolved."

"That's not true," Mira said, tears coming to her eyes. "It was over long ago. I'm not like that—not any more."

"Everybody's record has much worse comments from the psychology majors," Kirk said. "Luckily for us, nobody ever reads ours. Pretend you didn't hear. Mr. Spock, any functional and motivating data on the life force?"

"I have asked the computer why these beings pursue the

Enterprise. The first answer was 'Completion.' When I requested an alternate formulation, it gave me 'Fulfillment' instead. I find both responses unclear, but the machine has insufficient data to give us anything better, thus far.''

The door opened and a yeoman entered with a cartridge which he handed to McCoy. The surgeon inserted it into his viewer. Almost at once, he cast a disturbed look at Mira.

''What is it, Doctor?''

''A comparison of our Steinman with Starfleet records shows that Lt. Romaine's fingerprints, voice analysis, retinal patterns, all external factors are the same as before. But according to the two encephalograms, her brain wave pattern has been altered.''

''Isn't that impossible?'' Kirk asked.

''That's what I was taught. The BCP is as consistent as fingerprints.''

''Let's see it.''

McCoy put the tape deck into the slot on the desk, and the tri-screen lit up. They all looked at it for a moment. Then Spock said, ''Doctor, I believe that's the wrong slide.''

''No it isn't, Spock. It's from tape deck D—brain circuitry pattern of Lt. Mira Romaine.''

''No, Doctor. It happens to be tape deck H—the impulse tracking we obtained on the alien life units.''

''Nurse Chapel followed this every step of the way. There can't be an error.''

Mira was staring in tense horror at the screen.

''According to your records, Dr. McCoy,'' Spock said, ''Lt. Romaine did not show abnormal telepathatic ability.''

''That's right, Spock. Exceptional pliancy *was* indicated. It might be a factor.''

''It must be. There is an identity of pattern between these alien life forms and the mind of Lt. Romaine. Their thoughts are becoming her thoughts.''

Scott said: ''Mira's tried to tell me all along that she was seeing things happen in advance—''

''Why didn't you report it?'' Kirk said.

''You don't report space sickness. That's all I ever thought it was.''

''What else did she see?''

Scott thought a moment. ''The first attack on the

ship . . . the attack on Memory Alpha . . . and—the time we almost lost her.''

"Those were all acts carried out by our attacker. Anything else?''

Scott got up and went over to Mira, who was still staring at the screen. "I thought there was another time. I guess I was wrong.''

"Was he wrong, Lieutenant?'' Kirk said.

Mira finally looked up at Scotty, who sank to one knee beside her. In a trancelike voice, she said, "Yes. There was one other time.''

"What did you see?''

"I saw Scotty,'' she said, still looking at him intently.

"Where?''

"I don't know.''

"What was he doing?''

"He was dying.'' Her hand went to Scott's face. "Now I understand what's been happening. I've been seeing through another mind. I have been flooded by thoughts that are not my own . . . by desires and drives that control me—'' Suddenly she broke completely and was in Scott's arms. "Scotty—I would rather die than hurt you. I would rather die!''

"What's all this talk of dying?'' Scott demanded. "They've called the turn on us three out of four times. That's a better average than anybody deserves. It's our turn now. We'll fight them. So let's not hear anything more about dying.''

It was a bold speech, but Kirk could think of no way that the *Enterprise* could back it up. He punched the intercom. "Ensign Chekov, what success have you had with the evasive tactics?''

"Useless, sir. They'll probably be through the shields again in a minute or so.''

Kirk turned to Mira. "They may destroy you and us as they did Memory Alpha. You are especially susceptible to their will. There is one way we might survive. Do not resist. Let them begin to function through you. If we can control that moment, we have a chance. Will you try?''

"Tell me what to do,'' she said, her voice shaky.

"Everybody down to the antigrav test unit. Follow me.''

"Attention all personnel!'' Sulu's voice barked from the intercom. "Clear all decks! Alien being has penetrated ship!''

* * *

The door to the gravity chamber opened off the interior of the medical lab. As the group from the Briefing Room entered at a run, Kirk said, "As soon as she enters the chamber, secure all ports."

But as Mira started for the chamber, the swirling colors of the life force pervaded the lab. She stopped and spun around, her hand going to her brow, her eyes blazing, her face contorted with struggle. Scott started toward her.

"Don't touch me!" It was a piercing scream. "Scotty—stay away—"

The multicolored flashes slowly and finally were gone, leaving Mira standing as if frozen. Then her lips parted, and from them came once more the sound of the unknown language.

"We've lost her to them," Scott said desperately, starting toward her once more.

"Stay where you are!" Kirk said.

McCoy added, "She could kill us all in this state."

"She will," Spock said, "unless we are able to complete what the Captain is planning."

Scott was looking at Mira in agony. "Stay with us, Mira. Stay with us, Mira Romaine!"

"I am trying," she said. It was her own voice, but coming out in smothered gasps. "I want to be . . . with you . . . They are too strong."

"Fight them now, Mira," Kirk said. "Don't lose yourself to them. Hold on."

The girl sank against the door to the gravity chamber. Her eyes closed, her body became taut with the effort at control.

"I am Mira Romaine," she said, and this time her voice was angry. "I will be who I choose to be. Let me go!"

But the struggle was too much for her. Her body went limp, and her eyes opened, inexpressibly sad. In a voice like a lost soul, utterly unlike anything, she had ever sounded before, she said:

"She cannot prevent us. You cannot stop us."

Scott lunged forward, but Kirk grabbed him. "Mira! Mira!"

"That's not Mira talking," McCoy said.

"Captain, we must deal with them directly," Spock said.

"Now, while she retains partial identity, we can speak to them. Her voice will answer for them."

"I am the commander of this vessel," Kirk said to the entranced girl. "Do you understand me?"

"We understand you. We have searched for a millennium to find the One through whom we can see and hear and speak and live out our lives."

"Who are you?"

"We are of Zetar."

"All humanoid life on Zetar," Spock said, "was destroyed long ago."

"Yes. All corporeal life was destroyed."

"Then what are you?" Kirk demanded.

"The desires, the hopes, the thoughts and the will of the last hundred from Zetar. The force of life in us could not be wiped out."

"All things die."

"At the proper time. Our planet was dying. We were determined to live on. At the peak of our plans to go elsewhere, a sudden final disaster struck us down. But the force of our lives survived. And now at last we have found the One through whom we can live it out."

"The body you inhabit has its own life to lead."

"She will accept ours."

"She does not wish it. She is fighting to retain her own identity."

"Her mind will accept our thoughts. Our lives will be fulfilled."

"Will she learn like the people on Memory Alpha learned?"

"We did not wish to kill."

"You did kill!"

"No! Resisting us killed those on Memory Alpha. We did not kill. We wanted only the technician, but she fought back."

"The price of your survival is too high."

"We wish only the girl."

"You cannot have her," Kirk said fiercely. "You are entitled to your own lives. But you cannot have another's!"

Mira herself seemed to hear this, and her eyes to respond. When she spoke again, the voice was her own. "Life was given to *me*. It is mine. I will live it out—I will . . ."

Her voice weakened, and she sank back. McCoy took a tricorder reading. "The girl's life reading is becoming a match to the—Zetarians," he said. "She is losing."

"Do not fight us."

"They will not accept their own deaths," Spock said.

"They will be forced to accept it," Kirk said.

"You will all die," said the Mira/Zetar voice.

"Captain," Spock said, "unless we can complete the plan at once, they will carry out their threat."

McCoy said, "Jim, you realize that the pressure you need to kill the Zetarians might kill her, too?"

"At least, our way she has a chance. We must get her into the antigrav chamber."

They all moved in about her, in a close circle. Scott forced himself to the front and said, "Mira will not kill me."

He stooped and quickly picked her up in his arms. He faced the opening to the gravity chamber, and his head snapped back, his face contorted in agony. Nevertheless he got her into the chamber, and the doors closed behind her. Then he crumpled to the floor. His face now, however, was relaxed. As McCoy bent over him, his eyes opened.

"I knew she wouldn't kill me," he said, with a faint smile.

Kirk and Spock went to the chamber's console, joined after a moment by McCoy. After a sweeping glance, Kirk then crossed to the bull's-eye port which gave visual access to the chamber.

"Neutralize gravity, Mr. Spock."

Mira's body lay on the floor of the chamber where Scott had put it for what seemed to be a long time. Then she moved feebly, and the motion set her to drifting weightlessly.

"The Zetarians are growing stronger," McCoy said. "The weightless state is their natural condition, after all."

"Begin pressurizing," Kirk said. "Bring it up to two atmospheres."

Spock turned a rheostat slowly. There seemed to be no change in Mira. Theoretically, there should begin to be some sort of feedback system going into operation between Mira's nervous system, as it responded to pressures on her body not natural to her, and the occupying wave patterns of the Zetarian brain; but no such effect was evident yet.

"Two atmospheres, Captain."

"Increase at the rate of one atmosphere a minute."

"Wait a minute, Jim," McCoy said. "Not even a deep-sea diver experiences pressure increases at that rate. They take it slowly, a few atmospheres at a time."

"That's just what I'm counting on, Bones. If it's something Mira can adapt to, there'll be no adverse effect on her, and hence none on them. Run it up as ordered, Mr. Spock."

His hands darting, Spock tied the pressure rheostat into circuit with a timer. "Rising now as ordered, Captain."

A quick glance at the big bourdon gauge showed this. Kirk glued his face back to the glass.

Still nothing seemed to be happening, except that Mira's head was now lolling from side to side.

"Jim, you're going to kill her at this rate!"

Kirk did not respond. The chamber was beginning to look hazy, as though water were beginning to condense out of the atmosphere inside it—but that couldn't be, because water vapor didn't condense except to a *decrease* in pressure—

The fogginess increased, and became luminescent. In a moment more, the chamber was pulsating with the multiple lights of the Zetar life force. It grew brighter and brighter for several seconds.

"Jim, you can't—"

Kirk silenced the surgeon with a savage gesture. Almost at the same moment, the lights vanished, and with them the fog.

"Cut, Spock!"

There was the snap of a toggle. Mira's eyes were now open. She looked entirely normal, though a little bewildered at finding herself floating in midair. Scott snatched up the microphone which fed the intercom in the tank.

"Don't move, Mira! It's going to be all right! They're gone—they're gone!"

Kirk turned away and gestured to McCoy to take over.

"Reduce pressure very *very* gradually, Mr. Spock," the surgeon said.

"It will tax Mr. Scott's patience, Doctor."

"We have all the time in the world, now," Scott said, his eyes glowing.

"Precisely," McCoy said. "And after all this, we don't

want to lose the subject to a simple case of the bends. Lieutenant, lie perfectly still; you're in free fall and the slightest movement may bounce you off the chamber walls—and I don't want even the slightest bruise. Don't move at all, just take deep regular breaths . . . that's it . . . Mr. Spock, restore gravity very gradually. I want her to ground without even a jar . . . Mira, don't hold your breath. Breathe deeply and continuously . . . That's it—in, out, in, out, keep it steady . . . Fine. You won't be out of there for another two hours, so you might as well relax. The battle's over, anyhow.''

There was a deep sigh all around. Perhaps Mira had given up holding her breath, but it was evident that she had not been alone.

"Spock," Kirk said, "is it possible for you to judge the long-range mental effects on the Lieutenant?"

"I am not an expert, Captain, and bear in mind that Lt. Romaine's mind was invaded by something quite inhuman. However, despite Starfleet's judgment of her pliancy, she put up a valiant struggle to retain her identity. I would propose that that augurs well.''

"Spock is right, Jim," McCoy said, to Kirk's surprise. "While the truth was hard for her to take, when it was brought out, the girl reacted well. The struggle she put up in this experience, I would say, will strengthen her whole ego structure."

"Would either of you credit Scotty's steadfast belief in her as a factor?"

Spock's eyebrow arched suspiciously. "You mean 'love' as a motivation? Humans claim a great deal for that particular emotion. It is possible, but—"

"No 'buts' at all," McCoy said. "It was a deciding factor—and will be, in the girl's recovery."

"Then, do I understand you both agree that Lt. Romaine need not return to Starbase for further treatment?"

"I would say," Spock said, "that work is the better therapy."

"Absolutely, Jim."

"Scotty, unsmash your nose from that port and give us a sober opinion. How is Lt. Romaine now?"

"Beautiful, Captain."

"Ready to return to work?"

"Positively, Captain."

There was an exchange of grins all around. Then Kirk turned to the intercom. "Kirk to bridge."

"Sulu here, Captain."

"Set course for Memory Alpha. Lt. Romaine has lots of work to do there."

THE CLOUD MINDERS

Writer: Margaret Armen (story by David Gerrold and
          Oliver Crawford)
Director: Jud Taylor
Guest stars: Jeff Corey, Diana Ewing

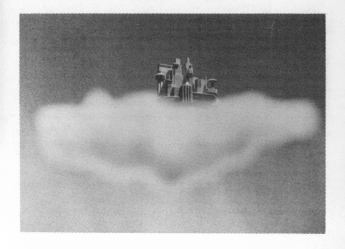

"Then there's been a mistake," Kirk said.

And he couldn't afford one, not on this mission. During a routine check of the *Enterprise*'s operational quadrant of the galaxy, they had been ordered by the Federation to make top warp speed to the planet Ardana, sole source of a trace metal able to arrest a botanical plague ravaging vegetation which made a neighboring planet habitable. It was a mission whose emergency nature was known to the High Advisor of Ardana. Yet his greeting to the *Enterprise* had contained no reference to the zenite mines. Instead, his welcome specified Stratos as the reception site.

"Stratos is their Cloud City, isn't it, Mr. Spock?"

"It is, Captain."

Kirk hit the intercom to the Transporter Room. "Mr. Scott, are you locked in on the mines of Ardana or its Cloud City?"

"The mines, Captain. That's what you ordered."

Then this mistake isn't ours, Kirk thought. The Ardanans understood the Transporter; they had it themselves. Turning to Uhura, he said tersely, "Tell the High Advisor we request that the official welcoming courtesies be dispensed with. We are beaming down directly to the mines to ensure the fastest possible transport of the zenite to Marak II. The need is desperate. Say we appreciate the honor and look forward to a visit to Cloud City in the future . . . Come with me, Mr. Spock."

But no miners were awaiting them at the mine-shaft entrance. The hill by which they'd arrived was deserted.

"I don't understand it," Kirk said. "The Troglyte miners were to make delivery when we beamed down."

"Perhaps there is another entrance," Spock suggested.

There was none. The other side of the hill was as abandoned, as bleak and forbidding as the rest of their arrival area. It was Spock who put the thought in both of their minds into words. "It would seem that the Troglytes have changed their minds about the delivery, sir."

Even as Kirk nodded there came a hiss in the air above their heads. Two heavy, noosed thongs were hurled from behind them with an accuracy that pinned their arms helplessly to their bodies. Jerks tightened the thongs, and the two *Enterprise* officers were pulled roughly around to confront four creatures, obvious Troglytes, their loose miners' overalls begrimed, their eyes begoggled, their features hidden by slitted masks. One of the Troglytes was slightly smaller than the others; but they all had long, sharp-edged mortae, the honed blades aimed in open threat.

"What is the reason for this attack?" Kirk demanded.

"Interference breeds attack," the smallest Troglyte said coldly, in a female voice. "My name is Vanna, Captain. I have need of your . . . services. Move on." The overalled arm motioned to the mine-shaft entrance.

"We are here by permission of your government Council," Kirk said. "On emergency mission."

"Move on, Captain." Ominous ice entered the voice.

Kirk felt the prod of her sharp blade in his back. Exchanging a swift glance with Spock, they burst into simultaneous action, lashing out with their feet at the two nearest Troglytes. Spock's kick caught his man in the chest. It felled him just as Kirk's foot, slamming into his captor's stomach, dropped him to the ground, knocking the wind out of him.

Vanna lunged at Kirk, but he had broken clear of his bonds and knocked her weapon out of her hand. Spock and the remaining Troglyte circled each other warily. Vanna, agile and swift, lunged at Kirk with her bare hands and they fell to the ground. In the struggle, the strap securing her goggles snapped. They slipped from her face to reveal feminine features of such surprising beauty that Kirk, lost in amazement, had no eyes for what was materializing on the Transporter coordinates.

It was her wince at the sudden glare of sunlight that brought him out of his trance. A man of patrician bearing stood behind them. He wore a togalike garment and the charismatic air of the born ruler. Two husky males, armed and uniformed in gleaming white, shimmered into sight beside him—guards.

The patrician spoke. "Troglytes! Halt!"

He was not obeyed. Vanna, unyielding, continued to writhe in Kirk's grasp. Spock was now trying to cope with two of the miners, as the third elbowed groggily from the ground where the Vulcan's first kick had landed him.

"Surrender—or we'll fire!"

Wrenching an arm free, Vanna tried to rake Kirk's face with her nails. He pulled back slightly, and seizing her chance to break his hold, she leaped to her feet and ran to the mine entrance, shouting to her companions. They joined her, racing after her amid a shower of shining pellets. One of the missiles from the guards' guns struck. Zigzagging, hunkered low, the three unwounded Troglytes disappeared into the mine entrance.

Kirk, climbing slowly to his feet, was frowning in preoccupation, his eyes following Vanna and her vanished companions. Spock stooped to retrieve the communicator which had dropped from his belt, and straightened to meet the approach of their rescuers.

"Are you harmed, gentlemen?" asked the toga-clad man.

"Just a little shaken up," Kirk said.

"I am Plasus, High Advisor for the planet Council."

Kirk acknowledged the introduction briefly. "Captain Kirk, *Enterprise*. My First Officer, Mr. Spock."

"My regrets for the unpleasantness of your welcome to Ardana, gentlemen."

"It was rather warm," Kirk said dryly.

"Unfortunately, violence is habitual with the Troglytes. I can assure you, Captain, this insult will not go unpunished."

It was Spock's turn to frown in thought as Kirk said,

"I am more concerned with that zenite consignment. Why isn't it in its specified location?"

Urbane, unruffled, the High Advisor's face with its high-bridged nose assumed a look of sadness. "Apparently the Disruptors have confiscated it, as I feared they would. They're a small group of Troglyte malcontents who hold the others under complete domination. It is the Disruptors who are responsible for the others' refusal to continue mining zenite."

"But they agreed to this delivery," Kirk protested. "It was your Council which assured us of that."

Plasus nodded benignly. "Obviously," he said, "they agreed as a ruse to get valuable hostages."

"Hostages? For what purpose?"

"To force the Council to meet their demands." Plasus turned to his guards. "Pick up the injured Troglyte for later questioning . . . Then organize a search party for the zenite consignment." Once more the urbane host, he said to Kirk, "Meanwhile, Captain, I suggest that you and First Officer Spock be our guests in Stratos City."

"I hope the search will be brief," Kirk said.

A shadow of grimness darkened the urbanity for a fleeting second. "I assure you we will do everything in our power to make it so. Now if you will just step this way, over here, our own Transporter will pick us all up."

They were led into a large, oddly designed chamber. Its floor and three of its walls glittered with a subdued iridescence. The fourth wall had been left open to the expanse of sky beyond, its border a waist-high balustrade of the same iridescent material. There was a careful carelessness about the manner in which luxuriously cushioned benches were scattered about the room, a calculated casualness that matched the surrealistic sculptural ɔrms which decorated it. Central to it was a small dais, flanked by two straggly carved poles of almost ceiling height. They struck Kirk as purposeless even as decoration.

From the balustrade, Spock called, "Captain, here, sir, please!"

The whole planet was spread out beneath them. Its surface could be only half seen through drifting mists. What was visible was dwarfed by distance to the dimensions of a relief map, its hills anonymous mounds, its valleys vague shadows. There was both beauty and terror in such eminence. It evoked a feeling of uneasiness in Kirk.

"Remarkable," Spock said. "The finest example of sustained antigravity elevation I have ever seen."

The sound of a door opening behind them made them turn. A young woman had entered the room of antigravity triumph. She was tall, willow-slim, willow-graceful, her golden hair a mist of mystery around her perfect face. She didn't walk—she glided, her approaching movement so supple it lacked all suggestion of bone or skeletal muscle. Like the clouds which obscured the planet's contours, she drifted toward the two *Enterprise* officers.

"My father," she said to Plasus, "your sentinels informed me of our honored guests' arrival. I came to extend my greetings."

"Gentlemen, my daughter—one of our planet's incomparable works of art. Droxine, Captain James Kirk and his First Officer, Mr. Spock."

Her eyes lingered for a moment on the satyr ears of the First Officer. "I have never met a Vulcan before, sir," she said demurely.

Spock bowed. "Nor I a work of art, madame."

Kirk looked at Spock with quizzical amusement and surprise. Plasus beckoned his guests back into the room from the balcony. "Come, gentlemen, there is much to see in our city. This is our Council gallery. We have some of our finest art forms assembled here for the viewing of all our city dwellers. That piece there can boast of a special—"

He stopped abruptly. The piece he had turned to was a transparent solid of flowing serpentine lines curled like coiling flames. A miner's mortae had been driven into it, webbing it with cracks.

"Disruptors again!" Furiously, Plasus jerked the tool from the sculpture and dashed it to the floor.

"They are despoiling the whole city," Droxine said.

"For what purpose?" Spock asked.

"Again, to force the Council to accede to their demands." Plasus spoke with the impatience of an adult irritated by a half-witted child.

"Just what are these demands?" Kirk said.

"Nothing you need concern yourself about, Captain."

Kirk's voice was very quiet. "I must concern myself with anything that interferes with the delivery of the zenite, Mr. Advisor."

"Mr. Advisor, plant life is the source of oxygen," Spock added. "If all plant life is destroyed on Marak II, all humanoid and animal life will end there with it."

Plasus had recovered his suavity. "I assure you, gentlemen, you will get what you came for."

"I hope so," Kirk said. He paused. "Ardana is a member of the Federation. It is your Council's responsibility that nothing interferes with its obligation to another Federation member."

"And we accept the responsibility."

Spock touched the webbed cracks in the sculpture. "But why destroy art forms? They are a loss to everybody."

"Art means nothing to the Disruptors." Plasus stooped to pick up the mortae. "*This* is the only form they understand." Rage overpowered him again. Nobody spoke as he fought to regain control of himself. "But no doubt you would like to rest. A chamber has been prepared for you. Sentinels will conduct you to it, gentlemen."

It was dismissal. Droxine's eyes followed Spock as the two from the *Enterprise* left the room.

"The Disruptors must be mad," she said, "to have attacked two such charming strangers."

"They grow more daring every day," Plasus said.

"Do you think the Captain and his very attractive officer will feel we are responsible?"

Plasus smiled indulgently down on his daughter. "Responsible for injuries done to the charming strangers—or to our diplomatic ties?"

Droxine flushed. "Oh, I was concerned about both, father."

Plasus laughed outright. "I am sure they will not blame you."

She exhaled a breath of relief. "I'm glad. I like them. They are not at all like our men of Ardana . . . Father, promise me not to find the zenite too soon?"

Before he could reply, two guards burst into the room.

Between them was a powerful man, his muscular shoulders tensed against their grip, but not struggling to free himself. That he had been doing so before was evident in the guards' panting.

"Apologies, Mr. Advisor," said one of them. "This Troglyte was apprehended leaving the city. As he lacks a transport card, we thought you would want to question him."

The man's aspect bore little resemblance to the stunted figures of other Troglytes. Despite the grime of his miner's overalls, the unkempt tangle of his shoulder-length hair, he was handsome. Proudly he drew himself to his full height, his eyes bright with scorn as they fixed on Plasus.

"What is your business in Stratos City, Troglyte?" demanded the High Advisor.

Though the flashing eyes burned with hate, the lips were silent.

"Speak! I command you!"

"My business is to repair," said the prisoner.

"Indeed. Then you must have a repair order. Where is it?"

"It was forgotten."

"Did you also forget your transport card?" The question was harsh with irony.

"It was lost when your sentinels attacked me."

"And where was your cavern mortae lost?" Plasus pointed to the empty sheath at the waist of the overalls. Then, striding to the mutilated sculpture, he plunged the mortae he still held in his hand into the hole it had made. "Here, perhaps."

"I came to make repairs," the prisoner said stubbornly.

"You shall make them—by telling me the names of the Disruptors."

"I know nothing."

"I would advise you to increase your knowledge."

An open sneer distorted the handsome face. "That is not possible for a Troglyte. The Stratos City dwellers have said so."

"Secure him to the dais," Plasus told the guards.

They tried to. But as they pushed the miner toward the dais, he knocked one guard aside and raced for the iridescent balustrade. The guards moved for their guns, but Plasus shouted, *"No!* I want him alive!"

It was too late. The prisoner had flung himself over the balustrade.

After a moment, Plasus shrugged. "How unfortunate," he said philosophically. "How unfortunate." He went out.

Droxine, as composed as her father, had been busying herself with an arrangement of goblets on a cubical table. The gold metal of one rang as she set it down, and a moment later, Spock came through the still open doors of the Council chamber.

"Mr. Spock!" the girl cried. "I thought you had accompanied Captain Kirk to the rest chamber down the corridor."

"There was some disturbance," the First Officer said. "It awakened me."

"I was but setting the table. I did not realize I would disturb you."

"Only Vulcan ears would find such a noise discernible from such a distance," Spock said.

The perfect eyelids lifted. "It seems Vulcans are fascinatingly different," said their owner. "In many ways."

Their eyes met. "The same may be said of inhabitants of Stratos," Spock observed.

"Vulcan eyes seem to be very discerning, too." She drew him down on the bench beside her.

His attention was sufficiently on this Ardanan work of art for him to fail his reputation for discerning sight for once. Behind him, a small figure draped in the clothing of Stratos crept from behind a pillar and moved stealthily down the corridor.

In the rest chamber, Kirk, breathing evenly, lay apparently asleep on a wide, billowy-pillowed dais. Vanna, crossing to him silently, drew a mortae from under her gown and laid its blade against his throat.

Kirk opened his eyes and he seized Vanna's wrist. Twisting the mortae from her grasp, he fell back with her on the bed. She kicked and writhed, but shortly he got her arms pinned back above her head.

"Well, that's better," he said, breathing evenly. "You again!" The face beneath his chest was lovelier than he remembered; but its eyes were cold as death.

"You sleep lightly, Captain," Vanna said.

"And I see you've changed your dressmaker."

"Release me," she said tonelessly.

"So you can attack me again?"

"Then call the guards," she told him contemptuously. "They will protect you."

"But I don't want protection. I find this very enjoyable."

"I do not."

Kirk grinned down at her. "All right, I'll make a bargain with you. Answer some questions, and I'll let you up."

"What questions?"

Kirk shook his head. "First, your word."

Hesitation came and went in her face. "I will answer."

Kirk released her. Panther-swift, she leaped to her feet and stooped for the mortae beside the bed. As he gripped her wrist again, he became aware that Spock's bed was empty. Where *was* Spock in this place of sudden treacheries? With that gliding girl?

The gliding girl was leaning back against a down cushion, its cream less creamy than the skin of her face. Spock, sitting very erect, was saying, "Yes, we Vulcans pride ourselves on our logic."

"Also on complete control of your emotions?"

"Emotions interfere with logic," he said firmly.

"Is that why you take mates only once in seven years?"

"The seven-year cycle is biological. At that time the mating drive outweighs all other motivation."

Droxine moved her head from the pillow and rested it against his shoulder. He looked down at the spindrift of golden hair, its fragrance in his nostrils, and their eyes locked. "Can nothing disturb the cycle, Mr. Spock?"

The Vulcan logician cleared his throat. "Exceptional feminine beauty is always disturbing, madame."

She had lifted her mouth toward his when a clang resounded from down the corridor. Spock sprang from the bench and ran for the door. Rushing into the rest chamber, he stopped dead at the sight of Vanna. Kirk had wrenched the mortae from her once more and dashed it to the floor.

"Captain, are you all right?"

From behind him Droxine cried, *"Vanna!* Why have you come here?"

Disheveled but still proud in her disarray, the Troglyte girl bent in a low bow to Kirk and Spock. "To welcome our honored guests," she said in a voice that cut with sarcasm. "Just as I was taught to do when I served in your father's household."

"It seems the Troglytes have the impression that our ship is here to intimidate them," Kirk told Spock.

"It is not an impression, Captain," Vanna said hotly. "It is truth!"

Kirk picked up her mortae and shoved it into his belt. "We are here to get that consignment of zenite. Nothing more."

"Starships do not transport cargo!" Vanna cried.

"In times of emergency they do anything," Kirk said. "And believe me, this plant plague on Marak II is an extreme emergency."

"Lies will not keep the Troglytes in their caverns, and neither will your ship, Captain."

Droxine said, "You speak like a Disruptor, Vanna."

"I speak for my people! They have as much right to the skies as you Stratos dwellers!"

"What would Troglytes do here?" asked Droxine disdainfully.

"Live! With warmth and light as everyone should!"

"Your caverns are warm," said Droxine coldly. "And your eyes are unaccustomed to light. Just as your minds are unaccustomed to reason." She moved to a wall and pressed a button. A sentinel appeared at the door; and waving a casual hand toward Vanna, Droxine said, "Take her away."

Kirk looked at Spock. "Surely," he said to Droxine, "you don't deny light and warmth to the Troglytes?"

"The Troglytes are workers," said the child of the High Advisor. "They mine zenite and till the soil. Those things can't be done here."

"In other words," Spock said, "they perform all the physical toil necessary to maintain Stratos?"

Droxine smiled at him. "That is their function in our society."

"Yet they are not allowed to share its advantages?"

"How can they share what they don't understand?"

"They could be taught to understand," Kirk said.

Droxine's answer had the sound of a lesson learned by rote. "The complete separation of toil and leisure has given Ardana a perfectly balanced social system."

Kirk was finding this conversation increasingly disturbing. He began to pace. Spock said, " 'Troglyte' is a corruption of an ancient Earth term, Captain. Its technical translation is 'cave dweller.' "

Kirk threw him a tight nod. "We should have realized—"

He was interrupted by a shriek of agony echoing from the Council gallery. He and Spock exchanged a glance of alarm and raced down the corridor to the room of luxuriously cushioned benches.

Tied tightly to its central dais, Vanna was screaming. Incandescing rays from its flanking poles flooded her face with green fire. She shrieked again.

Droxine went back to the cubical table and straightened a gold goblet, while Plasus watched. Kirk and Spock sprang to the dais to tear at the cords that bound Vanna's writhings.

"Stop it!" Kirk shouted at Plasus. There was a long moment. Then Plasus' hands came together in a faint clap. The rays faded. Still bound, Vanna slumped into unconsciousness.

"She is stubborn," Plasus said. "Physical discomfort is the only persuasion they understand, Captain."

"You have tortured her." Kirk's voice shook with anger.

"Is it preferable to spare Vanna—and allow an entire planet to be destroyed? You yourself pointed out that the search for your zenite must be short." Plasus' voice was eminently reasonable.

Spock approached Droxine. "Violence in reality is quite different from theory. Do you not agree, madame?"

"But nothing else moves the Troglytes. What else can they understand?"

"All those little things you and I understand," the Vulcan said gravely. "Such as kindness, justice, equality."

She shivered slightly. The she drew a fold of her gown around her, rose gracefully and left the gallery.

"The abstract concepts of an intellectual society are beyond the comprehension of the Troglytes, Mr. Spock." The High Advisor was angry now.

"The abstract concept of loyalty seems clear to Vanna," Kirk said.

"A few Troglytes are brought here as retainers. Vanna was one of them. They receive more training than the others."

"But obviously no more consideration," Kirk said.

Open rage thickened Plasus' voice. "I fail to see the use of this continued criticism." He beckoned to his guards and pointed to the slumped body on the dais. "Revive her!"

Kirk leaped to the dais. "The only way you'll use that device again is on both of us!"

"An imposing display of primitive gallantry, Captain. You realize, of course, that I can have my guards remove you."

"Of course," Kirk said. "But Starfleet Command seldom takes kindly to having either rays or physical force used on one of its personnel. Think twice."

Plasus did so. "Why are you so concerned about this Disruptor's well-being, Captain Kirk?"

"I want that zenite."

"Then stop interfering—and I'll get it for you. We will get it for you in our own way. Guards, take the prisoner to confinement quarters. As for you, Captain, you will return to your starship at once—or I shall contact your Starfleet Command myself to report your interference in this planet's society, in contravention of your prime directive. Should you reappear on Stratos City again, it would be only as an enemy."

The guards were removing Vanna's unconscious body from the dais. Kirk clicked open his communicator.

"Kirk to *Enterprise*."

"Scott here, Captain."

"Returning to ship. Beam us up, Mr. Scott."

The Council gallery disappeared in dazzle.

* * *

Twelve hours.

Kirk moved restlessly in his command chair. The decision that confronted him was no joke. Twelve hours—and all plant life on Marak II would be irreversibly on its way to becoming extinct. Seven hundred and twenty minutes to allow the plague to complete its lethal work—or to persuade Ardana to make good on its pledge of the zenite consignment.

He swung his chair around to Uhura. "Advise Starfleet Command that the methods being employed by the government of Ardana will not make the zenite available. It is my view that I have only one alternative. I hereby notify that I must try to reason directly with the Troglyte miners. I am assuming full responsibility for these direct negotiations."

McCoy walked over to him and laid a hand on Kirk's shoulder. "That won't be easy, Jim. Ardana has supplied us with data showing mental inferiority in the Troglytes."

"That's impossible, Bones! They have accepted personal sacrifice for a common cause. Mentally inferior beings aren't capable of that much abstract loyalty."

"I've checked the findings thoroughly," McCoy said gently. "Their intellect ratings are almost twenty percent below the planetary average."

Spock turned from his hooded computer. "But they all belong to the same species," he reminded McCoy. "Those who live on Stratos and those who live below all originated on the surface, not long ago. It is basic biological law that their physical and mental evolution must have been similar."

"True enough, Spock. But obviously the ancestors of those who live on Stratos had left the environment of the mines. That's how they avoided further effects of their influence."

"What influence?" Kirk asked.

McCoy held out a small sealed container, carefully. "This is a low zenite ore sample I had brought from the surface. If I unsealed the container, it would have detrimental effects on everybody here."

"Zenite is shipped all over the galaxy wherever there's danger of plant plague," Spock protested. "No side effects have been reported."

"After it's refined there are none. But in its natural state it emits an odorless, invisible gas which retards the cortical functioning of the brain. At the same time it heightens emotional imbalance, causing violent reactions."

"Then the mines must be full of this gas," Kirk said.

McCoy nodded. "And the Troglytes breath it constantly."

"But the Disruptors—Vanna, for instance. They've outwitted a highly organized culture, apparently for years."

"Captain," Spock said, "you will recall Vanna's experience as a servant in Plasus' household. She was removed from exposure to the gas for an apparently significant period. Perhaps without long exposure, its effects slowly wear off."

"They do," McCoy said. "The other Disruptors probably have similar histories."

"Any way of neutralizing the gas, Bones?"

"No. But filter masks would eliminate the exposure."

"Get one, Bones—or make a mock-up of one, fast—and report back here on the double. Lieutenant Uhura, call Advisor Plasus."

After a considerable interval, the Council gallery materialized on the main viewing screen. Plasus was sitting at the cubical table, drinking slowly.

"Your further communication is not welcome, Captain," he said.

"I may be able to change your mind," Kirk said. "At least, I hope so. My ship's surgeon has made a crucial discovery. He has found that zenite ore discharges a gas that impairs brain function. He thinks he can counteract it."

McCoy appeared at Kirk's elbow, a face mask in his hand. "That is the case, Mr. Advisor. This filter arrangement in my hand is a gas mask. It eliminates all gases injurious to humanoid life. If others like it are distributed to the miners, we can confidently expect them to achieve intellectual equality with Stratos inhabitants, perhaps quite soon."

Plasus dropped the goblet. "Who are you? Who are you to talk of 'intellectual equality' for—for *Troglytes*?"

"Let me present Dr. McCoy, Medical Officer of the *Enterprise*, Mr. Advisor," Kirk said. "We have checked his findings with our computers. They are absolutely valid."

"Are you saying that this comical mask can accomplish what centuries of evolution have failed to do?"

"Yes. That's what I said, Mr. Advisor."

"Centuries isn't a long time in terms of evolution," McCoy added.

"And do your computers also explain how my ancestors managed to create a magnificence like Stratos City while the Troglytes remained savages?"

"Your ancestors removed themselves from contamination by the gas," Spock said.

"Preposterous!"

"We have no time to argue," Kirk said. "I propose to inform Vanna that the filters are available."

"I doubt that even Vanna will credit such nonsense!"

"Are you afraid that the filters might work, Mr. Advisor?"

Kirk's question obviously hit home. Plasus stamped his foot on the iridescent floor. "You are here to complete an emergency mission, Captain! Not to conduct unauthorized tests!"

"I am here to collect a zenite consignment," Kirk said. "If these masks will help me do it, I will use them."

"I forbid it, Captain! Your Federation orders do not entitle you to defy local governments." Plasus reached for a switch. "This communication is ended."

As he faded from the screen, Kirk said, "My diplomacy seems to be somewhat inadequate."

"Pretty hard to overcome prejudice, Jim."

Kirk nodded. "Doesn't leave us much choice, does it?"

"Not much time, Captain," Spock said. "There are now ten hours and forty minutes left us to deliver the consignment to Marak II."

Kirk took the mask from McCoy. "Alert the Transporter Room to beam me down to Vanna's confinement quarters, Mr. Spock."

"Jim! You're returning to Stratos against government orders?"

"Unless Vanna has something definite to gain for her people, she'll die, Bones, before she turns over the zenite to us."

Spock intervened, an undertone of anxiety in his voice.

"If you are apprehended violating the High Advisor's orders, he will consider it within his rights to execute you."

Kirk grinned. "If you're about to suggest that *you* contact Vanna, the answer is negative, Mr. Spock. And that goes for you, too, Bones."

Spock said stiffly, "Allow me to point out that a First Officer is more expendable than either a doctor or a Captain, sir."

"This mission is strictly unofficial," Kirk said. "Nobody is to have any part of it—or take any responsibility for it but myself. That's an order, Mr. Spock."

Silently the Vulcan detached his phaser from his belt and handed it to Kirk. Kirk took it, saying, "You have the con, Mr. Spock. Stand by until I contact you."

Vanna's confinement quarters were narrow, barely wide enough to accommodate a slim sleep dais and a small cube table. Her face still drawn from her ordeal, she was pacing the short length of the cell when she halted in amazement at the sight of him.

"I've brought you a gift," he said, and held out the mask to her. "Listen to me carefully, Vanna. In the mines there's a dangerous gas that affects the development of the Troglytes who are exposed to it too long. This mask will prevent any further damage and allow recovery to take place."

He laid the mask on the table and waited for her surprise to subside. She made no move toward the table.

"Gas from zenite?" she said suspiciously. "It's hard to believe that something we can neither see nor feel can do much harm."

"An idea isn't seen or felt, Vanna. But a mistaken idea is what's kept the Troglytes in the mines all these centuries."

"Will all the Troglytes receive these masks?"

"I will arrange to have Federation engineers help construct them."

She faced him, her eyes pondering. "Suppose Plasus will not agree?"

"Plasus is not the whole government," Kirk said.

"But the City Council will not listen to Troglytes."

"When the zenite is delivered, we'll come back. Then

I'll request permission to mediate for the Troglytes. I give you my word.''

"Stratos," she said, "was built by leaders who gave their word that all inhabitants would live there. The Troglytes are still waiting.''

"This time you won't have to wait," he said gently. "We'll deliver the zenite in a few hours.''

Her face was tormented. "Hours can become centuries just as words can be lies.''

Kirk grasped her shoulders. "You must trust me, Vanna! If you don't, millions of people will die! A whole planet will die! The zenite is all that can save them—and the masks are all that can save the Troglytes!''

She closed her eyes for a moment, swaying. Then she said, "Very well, Captain. But the consignment is deep in the mines. I cannot tell you how to find it. I must take you to it.''

Kirk hesitated. "Valuable hostages" was the phrase Plasus had used. There was no getting away from the fact that Captain James Kirk of the *Enterprise* would qualify as a very valuable hostage. But he had asked for her trust; he would have to give her his. He took out his communicator.

"Kirk to Scott. Beam us both up, and then back down to the mines.''

Blinking in the planet's relentlessly glaring sunlight, Kirk drew the mask down over his head. Through its goggles, he could see Vanna's delicate figure, a dark shadow against the darker shadows of the mine's entrance, vanish into blackness. He followed her.

They were moving down a steeply descending tunnel. Ahead of him Kirk could discern faint glimmers of unidentifiable light. Then they were in a large cavern. Its walls glowed greenly with the phosphorescence of zenite ore lodes that etched themselves in cabalistic scribbles on the rock face like messages left by witches. Other jagged rocks jutted from the floor. The cavern might have been an underground grave-yard of magicians' tombstones.

A miner's mortae lay against one of the floor's peaked rocks. Picking it up, Vanna struck the rock three times; the rock rang like a gong. As the sound died, Kirk heard a stealthy movement from a narrow ledge high on the left wall of the cave. Two big, begrimed Troglytes were climbing down a series of crude steps, hewed into the rock, to the cavern floor.

Vanna touched their shoulders in greeting. Their faces lightened. "Anka, Midro," she said.

"Vanna. It is you." Anka, the bigger Troglyte, touched her shoulder in similar greeting. "You have returned."

"And I have brought you a hostage," she said. "Seize him!"

The Troglytes grabbed Kirk's arms so swiftly that he could not make a move in defense. They were twisted behind him as Vanna, jerking his phaser from his belt, thrust it into hers. Then she snatched his communicator and hurled it against a sharp-toothed outcropping of rock a few feet away.

Kirk found his voice, but it was unfamiliar, hoarse, distorted by the mask. "We had a bargain. Why are you breaking it?"

"Did you really think I would trust you, Captain?"

"I trusted you," he said.

"You thought you'd tricked me with your talk of unseen gas and filters. I don't believe in it any more than Plasus does."

"Then you are a fool," Kirk said. "The filters can free you just as I said they could."

"Only weapons will free us," she retorted. "And you have just furnished us with two valuable ones. Yourself—and this." She touched the phaser in her belt.

"Holding me will not help you. My men will still come for the zenite consignment."

She laughed. "Without that," she said, pointing to the communicator, "you will be hard to locate."

"They will find me," Kirk said.

"Perhaps." She removed his mask and draped it over a mortae thrust into a crevice on the wall. "I don't think you will be needing this." Then she had a second thought, and taking the mask down again, handed it to Anka. "Send this to Plasus. It will inform him that we have more to bargain with than our mortaes and thongs."

Anka's eyes brightened. "You are clever, Vanna. Very clever."

He hurried out of the cavern and she turned to Midro.

"Go to the other mines and tell the Troglytes to post watchers. Search parties may be coming soon."

Midro pointed to Kirk. "What of him?"

Vanna drew the phaser from her belt. "I will see that he does not escape."

"If we kill him," Midro said, "there'll be no need to see to that."

"A dead hostage is useless," she told him.

His face set stubbornly. "Only the Troglytes need know."

"I brought him—and I will say what is to be done."

"You're not the only Disruptor," Midro said sullenly. "I too can say."

"Can you do nothing but argue?" she cried impatiently. "Hurry—or the searchers will be here!"

"When Anka returns, we will *all* say." Nevertheless, he left.

Vanna kept the phaser leveled on Kirk. "Now, Captain, dig," she said. "Dig for zenite as the Troglytes do. I will give you a lesson in what our lives are like."

Silently, Kirk turned to the wall. It proved to be hard work. There was a bag on the floor in which he was told to put the chunks of ore; it took him a long time to get it half full. Vanna watched, smiling, as immaculate Captain James Kirk of the Starship *Enterprise* tore a nail on a bleeding finger.

"Is that what the Disruptors are working for?" he said. "The right to kill everyone?"

"Midro is a child."

"The filter masks could change that."

"Keep digging. You do it well, Captain. The unseen gas doesn't seem to be harming you."

"It takes a while for the effects to become noticeable." He straightened his aching back. "How long do you plan to keep me here? Providing Midro doesn't kill me, of course."

"Until we have help in the mines and our homes in the clouds."

"That might be quite a while." Kirk loosened another chunk of ore. "Longer than I can wait!"

He hurled the rough lump full in her face. She staggered back with a cry, and a moment later Kirk had wrested

the phaser from her. He leveled it at the cavern entrance and
fired. The boulders supporting it disintegrated, and the whole
upper portion of its walls crumbled with a crash, sealing the
entrance with a massive pile of rubble.

"You have trapped us!"

"Obviously."

"But soon the atmosphere will go! We will die!"

"Die? From something we cannot see or feel? You
astound me, Vanna." He picked his way over the rubble to
his communicator. As he had rather expected, it was unharmed; these instruments had been designed for rough use.
"Kirk to *Enterprise*."

"Spock here, Captain. Is anything wrong?"

"Nothing. Are you locked in on me?"

"Locked in, sir. Ready to beam up consignment."

"Circumstances dictate a slight variation, Mr. Spock."
Kirk eyed Vanna warily. "Hold on these coordinates. Locate
the High Advisor and beam him down to me immediately.
Without advance communication. Repeat—*without advance
communication*."

"Instructions clear, sir. We'll carry through at once.
Spock out."

"You will seal Plasus in here also?" Vanna had gone
rigid with alarm.

"I am preparing a slight demonstration of the effects
of unbelieved gas," Kirk said. He waited. After a moment,
the cavern shimmered and Plasus materialized. Such fury
shook him when he saw Kirk that at first he failed to register
the greenish darkness of his surroundings.

"Abduction of a planetary official is a serious crime,
Captain! You will pay for it, I promise!"

Awe struggled with the alarm on Vanna's face. Kirk
leveled the phaser at them both. "Not till you're convinced
of the effects of zenite gas, Mr. Advisor."

"What effects? I see no change in either of you!"

"You need closer exposure." He waved to the half-
filled bag at the cavern wall. "Fill that container."

"You suggest that *I* dig zenite?"

Kirk waved the phaser. "I insist, Mr. Advisor."

Plasus' fists clenched. "You will indeed pay for this,
Captain." After eyeing the steady phaser for a moment, he

turned to the wall, and began to scrabble at the open zenite lode. It was quickly obvious that he had never done any physical labor before in his life.

Kirk's jaw hardened, and he smiled a cold, thin smile. He felt strangely vindictive, and was enjoying it. "You too, Vanna."

She stared at him for a moment, and then obediently turned also to the wall.

Time passed. After a while the communicator beeped. "*Enterprise* to Captain."

"What is it, Spock?"

"Contact check, sir. May I remind you that there are only five hours left to—"

"Your orders were to stand by. Carry them out."

"Standing by."

Kirk clicked out. Both his laborers were beginning to show signs of exhaustion. Vanna leaned against the wall for a moment. "I grow faint," she whispered. "The oxygen is going."

"She is right," said Plasus, panting. "You must have us transported out of here."

"Dig."

"You imbecile! We'll die!" Plasus cried.

Kirk backhanded him. "I said, *dig*!"

Knocked back against the wall, arms spread, Plasus snarled, an animal at bay; all trace of the urbane ruler of Ardana had vanished. "I will take no more orders!" He lurched forward.

Kirk jerked the phaser. "Another step and I'll kill you."

Vanna stared at Kirk's distorted face. "Captain—the gas!" she choked out. "You were right! It *is* affecting you!"

Plasus took the cue. "Are you as brave with a mortae as you are with a phaser?" he taunted.

Infuriated, Kirk tossed the phaser to the floor. Plasus scooped two mortae from the rock ledge, and one in each hand, charged Kirk like a clumsy bull, slashing. Kirk dodged, grabbed Plasus' right wrist and tumbled him with a karate twist. The head struck rock. The two mortae clanged on the floor and Kirk leapt for Plasus' throat. As he fell on the High Advisor, the communicator dropped from his belt.

Vanna grabbed it and began shouting. *"Enterprise! Enterprise!"* It remained dead. Vanna shook it, and then found the switch. *"Enterprise!* Help! They will kill each other! Help us."

For a moment, nothing happened. Kirk's fingers tightened on Plasus' throat. Then the cavern shimmered out of existence, and he found himself wrestling on the Transporter platform of the *Enterprise*.

"Captain!" Spock's voice shouted. "Stop! The gas—"

Kirk let go and got groggily to his feet. "The gas? What gas?" He looked around, almost without recognition. The Transporter Room was full of armed security guards. Vanna was cowering; Plasus was crawling off the platform, all defiance fled. It had been a near thing.

The Council gallery of Stratos City resembled a first rehearsal reading of a play, Kirk thought. The whole cast was assembled. He hoped they had all learned their lines.

"I understand you are going to get what you came for," Plasus said.

"Yes, Mr. Advisor."

"The zenite will be delivered exactly as I agreed," Vanna said.

But Plasus hadn't yet learned all his lines. He turned on her. "The word 'agreed' is not in the Troglyte vocabulary."

"The Captain will have his zenite."

"No thanks to any agreement by you. It had to be obtained by force."

"Force has served your purpose at times," she said.

"And bribery," Plasus said, stubborn to the last. "Those masks."

Kirk had had enough. "The masks will be very effective, Mr. Advisor. The Troglytes will no longer suffer mental retardation and emotional imbalance."

"No," said Plasus. "They will all be like this one—ungrateful and vindictive."

As he spoke, two sentinels entered the gallery staggering under the weight of an immense box. "There," Vanna said, "is the zenite. My word is kept."

"As mine will be," Kirk said. "Thank you, Vanna."

He took out his communicator. "Kirk to *Enterprise* . . . Mr. Scott, the zenite is here in the Council gallery. Have it beamed up immediately . . . Mr. Spock—"

He broke off. Spock and Droxine had drifted to the balustrade. The hand of Ardana's incomparable work of art was on Spock's arm.

"I don't like 'filters' or even 'masks,' " she was saying. "I think the word 'protectors' is much better, don't you, Mr. Spock?"

"It is less technical," he told her. "And therefore, less accurate." He looked down at the hand on his arm. "But perhaps it is more generally descriptive of their function."

" 'Protectors' is more personal," she said. "I shall be the first to test them. I shall go down into the mines. I no longer wish to be limited to the clouds."

"There is great beauty in what lies below. And there is only one way to experience it, madame."

"Is your planet like this?" She looked up at him.

"Vulcan is quite different," Spock said. His back was stiff.

"Someday, I should like to see it."

"You cannot remain on Stratos," Spock replied, "if you wish to make a real test of . . . a protector."

Kirk judged it time to intervene. "Mr. Spock, I think it is time. We've got just three hours to get the zenite to Marak II."

Spock turned from the balustrade. Removing the white hand from his arm, he bowed over it. Then he straightened.

"To be exact, Captain," he said, "two hours and fifty-nine minutes."

THE WAY TO EDEN

Writer: Arthur Heinemann (story by Michael Richards
        and Arthur Heinemann)
Director: David Alexander
Guest stars: Skip Homeier, Charles Napier

Under Federation orders to observe extreme delicacy, the *Enterprise* had beamed aboard the six people who had stolen the cruiser *Aurora*. The son of the Catullan Ambassador was one of them, and treaty negotiations between the Federation and the Ambassador were at a crucial phase. Clearly, none of the six had known much about operating a cruiser; in the attempt to escape, they had managed to destroy the cruiser, and had only been rescued by Scott's pinpoint skill with the Transporter.

"Scotty, are they aboard?" Kirk asked his control chair intercom.

"Aye, Captain, they are. And a nice lot, too."

"Escort them to the briefing room for interview."

There were other voices in the background, rising in an increasing hubbub. Suddenly a woman's voice became clearly audible above the others. "Why should we?"

At that, Chekov's head jerked up sharply, his expression one of recognition struggling with incredulity. Then a man's voice said, "Tell Herbert it's no go."

All the voices chimed in with a ragged chant: "No go no go no go no go . . ."

"What's going on?" Kirk asked.

"They refuse, sir," Scott called over the chant.

"Why?"

"I don't know. They're just sitting on the floor, the lot of them. You can hear them yourself. Shall I send for Security?"

"No, I'll come down. Sulu, take the con."

He and Spock could hear the chanting continuing long
before he reached the Transporter Room. The six were, indeed, "a nice lot." One wore a simple robe, the others were
nearly naked or in primitive costumes, with flowers worn as
ornaments and painted on their bodies. There were three girls
and three men, all but the one in the robe in their early twenties. They were squatting on the floor with a clutter of musical instruments around them.

"We are not in the mood, Herbert," one of the girls
said; it was the same voice he had heard before. The others
resumed the "No go" chant.

"Which one of you is Tongo Rad?" Kirk shouted.

The chant died down raggedly, and the newcomers
looked curiously from Kirk to one of their number, a handsome humanoid who despite his costume had that intangible
air which often goes with wealth and privilege. He got up
and lunged forward, not answering, not quite insolent.

"You can thank your father's influence for the fact that
you're not under arrest," Kirk snapped. "In addition to pi-
racy, you're open to charges of violating flight regulations,
entering hostile space and endangering the lives of others as
well as your own."

"Hostile space?" Rad said.

"You were in Romulan territory when we yanked you
out."

"Oh," said Rad. "I'm bleeding."

"On top of which you've caused an interstellar incident
that could destroy everything that has been negotiated between your planet and the Federation."

"You got a hard lip, Herbert."

"If you have an explanation, I'm prepared to hear it."

Rad looked down at the older man in the robe, but
there was no response. Rad sat down with the others and
folded his arms.

Kirk turned to Spock. "Take them to sickbay for medical check. There may be radiation injury from the *Aurora*
explosion."

The "No go" chant started up again immediately. Kirk
started to shout, but Spock intervened.

"With your permission, Captain." He put his hands

together, index finger to index finger, thumb to thumb, forming an egg shape. "One."

The group seemed to be surprised. The man in the robe rose. "We are one."

"One is the beginning," Spock said.

One of the boys, a rather puckish youth, said, "You One, Herbert?"

"I am not Herbert."

"He's not Herbert. We reach."

Kirk was wholly bewildered. Evidently all this meant something, however, and had almost miraculously achieved calm and accord.

"Sir," Spock said to the older man, "if you will state your purpose and objectives, perhaps we can arrive at mutual understanding."

"If you understand One, you know our purpose."

"I should prefer that you state it."

The older man smiled faintly. "We turn our backs on confusion and seek the beginning."

"Your destination?"

"The planet Eden."

"Ridiculous," Kirk said. "That planet's a myth."

Still smiling, the older man said, "And we protest against being harassed, pursued, attacked, seized, and Transported here against our wishes and against human law."

"Right, brother," said the puckish youth.

"We do not recognize Federation regulations nor the existence of hostilities. We recognize no authority but that within ourselves."

"Whether you recognize authority or not, I am it on this ship," Kirk said, restraining himself with difficulty. "I am under orders to take you back to Starbase peaceably. From there you will be ferried back to your various planets. Because of my orders you are not prisoners, but my guests. I expect you to behave as such."

"Oh, Herbert," said the puckish youth, "you are *stiff*."

"Mr. Spock, since you seem to understand these people, you will deal with them."

"We respectfully request that you take us to Eden,"

the robed man said. Despite the politeness of the words, and the softness of his voice, his insolence was obvious.

Kirk ignored him. "When they're finished in sickbay, see that they are escorted to the proper quarters and given whatever care they need."

"Yes, Captain."

"We respectfully request that you take us to Eden."

"I have orders to the contrary. And this is not a passenger ship."

"Herbert," said the girl who had first spoken. The others picked it up and another ragged chant followed Kirk as he went out: "Herbert Herbert Herbert Herbert . . ."

He was in a simmering rage by the time he returned to the bridge. Taking his seat, he said, "Lieutenant Uhura. Alert Starbase we have aboard the six who took the space cruiser *Aurora*. And that the cruiser itself was regrettably destroyed."

"Aye, sir."

"Personal note to the Catullan Ambassador. His son is safe."

"Captain, sir," Chekov said hesitantly. "I believe I know one of them. At least I think I recognized her voice. Her name is Irina Galliulin. We were in Starfleet Academy together."

"One of those went to the *Academy*?" Kirk said incredulously.

"Yes, sir. She dropped out. She—" Chekov stopped. Under his accent and his stiffness, it was apparent that he still felt a painful emotion about this girl.

Kirk looked away as Spock entered, and then back to Chekov. "Do you wish to see her? Permission granted to leave your post."

"Thank you, sir." He got up fast and left; another crewman took his post.

Kirk turned to Spock. "Are they in sickbay?"

"Yes, Captain."

"Do they seriously believe that Eden exists?"

"Many myths are founded on some truth, Captain. And they are not unintelligent. Dr. Sevrin . . ."

"Their leader? The man in the robe?"

Spock nodded. "Dr. Sevrin was a brilliant research

engineer in acoustics, communications and electronics on Tiburon. When he started the movement, he was dismissed from his post. Young Rad inherits his father's extraordinary abilities in the field of space studies."

"But they reject that—everything this technology provides—and look for the primitive."

"There are many who are uncomfortable with what we have created," Spock said. "It is almost a biological rebellion. A profound revulsion against the planned communities, the programming, the sterilized, artfully balanced atmospheres. They hunger for an Eden, where Spring comes."

"We all do, sometimes," Kirk said thoughtfully. "The cave is deep in our ancestral memories."

"Yes, sir."

"But we don't steal cruisers and act like irresponsible children. What makes you so sympathetic toward them?"

"It is not so much sympathy as curiosity, Captain. A wish to understand. And they regard themselves as aliens in their worlds. It is a feeling I am familiar with."

"Hmm. What does Herbert mean?"

"It is somewhat uncomplimentary, sir. Herbert was a minor official notorious for his rigid and limited pattern of thought."

"I get the point," Kirk said drily. "I shall endeavor to be less limited in my thinking. But they make it difficult."

There were only five of the six in the examining room when Chekov came in. Four were sprawled about listening to the puckish youth, who was tuning something that looked like a zither. Apparently satisfied, he hit a progression of chords and began to sing softly.*

> Looking for the new land—
> Losing my way—
> Looking for the good land—
> Going astray—
> Don't cry.

*I much regret that I cannot reproduce the music which went with this script; it was of very high quality. The script I have does not name the composer.—J.B.

Don't cry.
Oh I can't have honey and I can't have cream
But the dream that's in me, it isn't a dream.
It'll live, not die.
It'll live, not die.
I'll stand in the middle of it all one day,
I'll look at it shining all around me and say
I'm here!
I'm here!
In the new land,
In the good land,
I'm here!

"Great, Adam," one of the others said. There was a murmur of applause.

Chekov cleared his throat. "Excuse me. Is Irina Galliulin with you?"

"Getting her physical," Adam said. He hit a chord and sang:

I'll crack my knuckles and jump for joy—
Got a clean bill of health from Dr. McCoy.

"You know Irina?" someone else said. Chekov nodded.

"Say, tell me," said Tongo Rad. "Why do you people wear all those clothes? How do you breathe?"

Nurse Chapel came out of the sickbay with two medics. She looked over the group and pointed to Sevrin. "You're next."

Sevrin sprawled, oblivious. Chapel nodded to the two medics, who stepped forward and, picking up the limp form, dragged it into sickbay. A moment later, Irina came out.

"Irina," Chekov said.

She did not seem to be surprised. She smiled, her strange, habitual smile, which rarely left her—but there was watchfulness behind it.   · ·

"Pavel Andreievich," she said calmly. "I had thought we might encounter each other."

"You knew I was on the *Enterprise*?"

"I had heard."

"Irina—why—" He stopped, all eyes upon him. "Come."

He led her out into the corridor, which was empty. He stared at her for a moment, taking in the bizarre, brief costume, the long hair, the not-quite-untidiness. When he spoke, it was almost with rage.

"How could you do this to yourself? You were a scientist. You were a—a decent human being. And now look at you!"

"Look at yourself, Pavel," she said calmly.

"Why did you do it?"

"Why did you?"

"I am proud of what I am. I believe in what I do. Can you say that?"

"Yes." Momentarily her voice was sharp; then the smile returned. Chekov took her arm and they walked toward the lounge. "We should not tear at each other so. We should meet again in joy. Today, when I first knew it was your ship that followed us, I thought of you, I wondered what I would find in you. And I remembered so much. In spite of that uniform, I still see the Pavel I used to know. Are you happy in what you do?"

"Yes."

"Then I accept what you do."

"You even talk like them."

Yeomen passed them, turning to look at the odd couple. Chekov led Irina into the lounge. "Why did you go away?" he asked.

"It was you who went."

"I came back to look for you. I looked. I looked. Where did you go?"

"I stayed in the city. With friends."

"You never felt as I did. Never."

"I did."

"You don't have it in you to feel so much. Even when we were close you weren't with me. You were off thinking of something else." She shook her head, the smile still there. "Then why did you stay away?"

"Because you disapproved of me. Just as you do now. Oh, Pavel, you have always been like this. So correct. And inside, the struggle not to be. Give in to yourself. You will be happier. You'll see."

"Go to your friends," Chekov said grayly.

After a moment she left, still with that maddening smile. There seemed to be another hubbub starting in the corridor. Chekov went after her, quickly.

The noise was coming from outside sickbay, where there was something very like a melee going on. The group from the *Aurora* was trying to get in, over the opposition of Nurse Chapel and two security guards. The group was shouting noisily, angrily, demanding entrance, demanding to see Sevrin.

Kirk came out of the elevator and forced his way through the crowd, not without a what-the-hell glance toward Chekov.

"Herbert Herbert Herbert Herbert Herbert . . ."

The sickbay doors shut automatically behind Kirk and Nurse Chapel, mercifully deadening the sound. "I thought all those animals were in their cages," she said.

Sevrin was sitting on a bed, defiant, the two medics standing ready to grab him. McCoy was finishing what had evidently been a strenuous examination.

"What's going on, Bones?"

"Trouble. Your friend here didn't want a checkup. Turns out there was a reason."

"I refuse to accept your findings," Sevrin said.

"You don't have the choice."

"They are the product of prejudice, not science."

"I don't know what this man was planning to do on a primitive planet," McCoy continued. "Assuming it existed. But I can tell you what would happen if he'd settled there. Within a month there wouldn't be enough of those primitives left to bury their dead."

"Fantasy," Sevrin said. "Fantasy."

"I wish it were. There's a nasty little bug evolved in the last few years, Jim. Our aseptic, sterilized civilizations produced it. *Synthococcus novae*. It's deadly. We can immunize against it but we haven't licked all its problems yet."

"Does he have it?" Kirk asked. "What about the others?"

"The others are clear. And he doesn't have it. He's a

carrier. Remember your ancient history? Typhoid Mary? He's immune to it, as she was. But he carries the disease, spreads it to others.''

''Is the crew in danger?''

''Probably not. They all had full spectrum immunizations before boarding. My guess is that his friends had their shots too. But a regular program of booster shots is necessary. I'll have to check on everyone aboard. There may have been some skips. Until that's done, this fellow should be kept in total isolation.''

''This is outrageous,'' Sevrin said. ''There is nothing wrong with me. You're not isolating me, you're imprisoning me. You invent the crime, find me guilty, sentence me . . .''

''Would you like to run the tests yourself, Doctor?'' There was no answer. ''You knew you were a carrier before you started out, didn't you?''

''No!''

''Then why did you fight the examination?''

''It was an infringement on my rights as a human being . . .''

''Oh, stop ranting.''

''Put him in isolation,'' Kirk said.

''Be ready for his friends' objections. They're a vocal lot.''

''I'm ready.''

There was still a crowd in the corridor; four of the *Aurora* group (one girl was missing) were sitting or sprawling on the deck; among them stood Sulu, Chekov and several crewmen. The protesters were chanting, but this time each of them had a different slogan.

''Eden now!''

''Free Ton Sevrin!''

''James T. Kirk is a brachycephalic jerk!''

''McCoy is a doctor of veterinary medicine!''

Sulu was talking to one of the girls, between slogans. He seemed confused but fascinated. Thus far no one had noticed Kirk's arrival.

''You don't belong with them,'' the girl was telling Sulu. ''You know what we want. You want it yourself. Come, join us.''

''How do you know what I want, Mavig?''

"You're young. Think young, brother." Lifting a hand to him, she gave him an egg.

"Mr. Sulu," kirk said sharply. Sulu started, stiffened with embarrassment, and hastily gave the egg back to Mavig. "Explain, Mr. Sulu."

"No explanation, sir."

Kirk turned to the group, which had gotten even noisier upon seeing him. "Dr. Sevrin will be released as soon as we determine it is medically safe."

"Herbert Herbert Herbert Herbert . . ."

Ignoring them, Kirk strode toward the elevator with Sulu, stepping over the bodies. Chekov followed. As he approached Irina, she lay back provocatively.

"Don't stay with Herbert. Join us. You'll be happier. Come, Pavel."

"Link up, Pavel," Adam said.

"Join us."

"Link up, Pavel. Link up, Pavel."

Adam struck a chord on his instrument and began to sing:

> Stiff man putting my mind in jail—
> Judge bangs the gavel, and says
> No bail—
> So I'll lick his hand and wag my tail . . .

Blessedly the elevator doors opened at this point, and Kirk, Sulu and Chekov made their escape.

The bridge was a haven of routine activity, with Spock in charge. Chekov and Sulu went to their posts. But before Kirk could settle, the intercom cut in with its signal.

"Engineering to bridge," Scott's voice said.

"Kirk here."

"Captain, I just had to give one of those barefooted what-do-you-call-ems the boot out of here. She came in bold as brass, tried to incite my crew to disaffect."

"All right, Scotty." He shut the intercom off and turned to Spock, his irritation finally breaking out. "Mr. Spock, I don't seem to communicate with these people. Do you think you can persuade them to behave?"

"I shall endeavor, sir."

"If it weren't for that Ambassador's son, they'd be in the brig."

"Yes, sir." Spock went out.

He found Sevrin sitting cross-legged in the isolation ward, in a yoga-like position, a cold, hostile figure. There was one security guard in the corridor outside. Spock stood on the other side of the isolation shield.

"Doctor, can you not keep your people from interfering with the running of the ship?"

"I have no influence over what they do."

"They respect you. They will listen to your reasoning. For their sake, Doctor, you must stop them."

The baleful eyes lifted to Spock's face, answer enough in themselves.

"Dr. Sevrin, I can assist you and your group. I can use the resources of the *Enterprise* to establish whether or not Eden exists, and to plot its exact location. I can present a case to Federation that would allow your group to colonize that planet." There was no answer. "Neither you nor they are at present charged with any crime worse than theft, plus a few lesser matters. The charges may be waived. But incitement to mutiny would tip the balance. And Federation would never allow the colonization of a planet by criminals. If they persist, they will be so charged, and forever barred from Eden."

"As I have been barred," Sevrin said softly. The voice was low, but the gleaming eyes were those of a fanatic.

Spock hesitated a moment. "Then you knew you were a carrier?"

"Of course I knew. You have researched my life. You have read the orders restricting me to travel only in areas of advanced technology, because of what my body carries."

"I fail to understand why you should disobey them."

"Because this is poison to me!" Sevrin looked around, as if seeing all the technology of the ship, representing all the technology of space. "This stuff you breathe, this stuff you live on. The shields of artificial atmosphere we have layered about every planet. The programs in those computers that run your ship and your lives for you. Those bred what my body carries! This is what your sciences have done for me! You have infected me!"

He shook his fist at the ceiling; his "you" was obviously not Spock but the whole Galaxy. He began to pace.

"Only the primitives can cleanse me. I cannot purge myself until I am among them. Only their way of living is right. I must go to them."

"Your very presence will destroy the people you seek out! Surely you know that."

"I shall go to them and be one of them. Together we will make a world such as this Galaxy has never seen. A world, a life. A life!" His passion spent, Sevrin sat down, and after a moment lifted his head to look at Spock, a faint smile on his lips. "And now you are about to assure me that your technologies will find a cure for me. And I will be free to go."

"Yes, Doctor."

"And for that reason I must persuade my friends to behave, so they too will be allowed."

"Yes."

"Send them in," Sevrin said, smiling still. "I'll talk to them."

It was an uneasy victory, whose outcome was uncertain. Spock went back to the bridge.

"They've been a lot quieter," Kirk reported. "How did you accomplish it?"

"It had nothing to do with me. Could I speak to you a moment, sir?"

Kirk rose and both went to Spock's console. "What is it?"

"Dr. Sevrin is insane. I did not consult Dr. McCoy. But I have no doubt of it."

"I'll have Bones check him again," Kirk said, stunned. "You had great respect for him. I'm sorry, Mr. Spock. But it explains some of what they've done."

"His collapse does not affect my sympathy with the movement, sir. There is no insanity in what they seek—I made a promise which I should like to keep. With your permission, I must locate Eden. I shall work in my quarters. May I have the assistance of Mr. Chekov in the auxiliary control room?"

"Mr. Chekov, assist Mr. Spock."

* * *

The auxiliary control room was deserted except for Chekov, who was at the plotting console, bent over the computer, studying.

Spock's voice came over the intercom. "Ready for your plottings, Mr. Chekov."

Chekov fed a tape into the computer. The door opened, and Irina entered, hesitantly. "Am I allowed in?" she asked.

He concentrated stiffly on his work. "Yes."

"I have been looking for you, Pavel. What room is this?"

"Auxiliary control."

"What's it for?"

"Should the main control room break down or suffer damage, we can navigate the ship from here."

"Oh."

"What do you want?"

"To apologize. I should not have teased you. It was cruel."

"It doesn't matter," Chekov said.

"But it does. It is against everything I believe in."

"Let us not discuss your beliefs."

"And I do not like having you angry with me," she said softly. "Or disapproving."

"Then why do you do such things?"

She began to wander about the room, examining the panels in seeming childlike curiosity. Chekov continued working, but his eyes followed her when she was not looking in his direction. Then she came back to him. "What are you working on?"

"I am assisting Mr. Spock in locating your Eden."

"Now you are teasing me," she said in sudden sharpness.

"I am not. These tapes contain star charts, and we project the orbits of the various known planetary systems here, determining by a mathematical process whether or not they are affected by other bodies not yet charted."

"Do you know all these things?"

"What I do not know I find out from the computer banks. If I knew nothing at all, I could navigate this ship simply by studying what is stored in there. They contain the sum of all human knowledge. They solve our problems of navigation, of control, of life support . . ."

She bent over the computer, close to him. "They tell you what to do. And you do what they tell you."

"No. We use our own judgment also."

She came still closer. "I could never obey a computer."

"You could never listen to anyone. You always had to be different."

"Not different. What I wanted to be. There is nothing wrong in doing what you want."

She faced him, smiling still. Abruptly Chekov arose, took her in his arms, and kissed her hungrily.

"I am not receiving, Mr. Chekov," said the intercom. "Spock to Mr. Chekov. Repeat. I am not receiving."

Chekov broke free and opened his intercom. "I am sorry, Mr. Spock. I was momentarily delayed."

With permission, the *Aurora* group had stored its gear and bedded down in the Recreation Room. Adam and Mavig were relaxing when Rad entered.

"His name is Sulu," Rad said. "Specialist in weapons and navigation. His hobby is botany."

"Can?" said Adam.

"Can. I reach botany. It's my favorite of studies. What's yours?"

"Vulcan. Spock is practically One now."

Irina came in; the others were instantly alert.

"Everything can be handled from auxiliary control. The computers contain all the information we need. We can do it."

"It starts to chime," Adam said.

"When will it?" Rad wanted to know.

"Soonest. Like Sevrin said, now, we should go out, swing as many over as we can."

"You suggest any special ways to swing them?"

"Just be friendly. You know how to be friendly, then they'll be friendly and we'll all be one. All right? Scatter. Remember, it's a party we're inviting them to and we're providing the entertainment."

"I like parties," Rad said.

"I like the entertainment we've planned. All hit numbers."

Adam and Rad grinned at each other. Then everyone went off, in different directions. Adam headed directly for Spock's quarters.

Spock said "Come in" absently. He was at his computer, studying the images, making notes. Adam approached him diffidently.

"Am I crossing you?" he asked. Spock shook his head. "I was wondering if—" He stopped, noting the lute hanging on the wall behind Spock. "Hey, brother. You play?"

Spock nodded.

"Is it Vulcan? Can I try it?"

Spock took the lute down and gave it to Adam, who tried several chords. "Oh, that's now. That's real now. I reach that, brother, I really do. Give."

He passed the lute back to Spock, who amusedly played a few runs.

"Hey. How about a session, you and us. It would *sound*. That's what I came for. I wanted to ask, you know, great white captain up there he don't reach us, but would he shake on a session? I mean, we want to cooperate like you asked, so I'm asking."

"If I understand you correctly," Spock said, "I believe the answer might be yes."

"I'll spread the word."

The Recreation Hall was jammed. Lights had been dimmed, with the effect of spotlighting the group. They were singing; for those crew members who could not be present, intercoms carried the music throughout the ship. The words went like this:

I'm talking about you.
I'm talking about me.
Long time back when the Galaxy was new,
Man found out what he had to do.
Found he had to eat and found he had to drink,
And a long time later he found he had to think.

(spoken)
I'm standing here wondering.

(sung)
If a man tells another man, 'Out of my way'
He piles up trouble for himself all day.
But all kinds of trouble come to an end
When a man tells another man, 'Be my friend.'

(spoken)
What's going to be?

(sung)
There's a mile wide emptiness between you and me,
Can't reach across it, hardly even see—
Someone ought to take a step one way or other.
Let's say goodbye—or let's say brother.
Hey out there
Hey out there
I see you
I see you
Let's get together and have some fun.
Don't know how to do it but it's got to be done.

There was enthusiastic applause. The three girls took up the song. The boys faded back, clapping rhythmically. The clapping soon spread throughout the audience.

On the bridge, Uhura, Sulu and Scott were at their posts, listening. When Kirk came in, Uhura turned the intercom off.

"Thank you."

"At least we know where they are and what they're doing," Scott said. "I don't know why a young head has to be an undisciplined one. Troublemakers."

"I made a bit of trouble at that age, Scotty. I think you may have."

The intercom buzzed. "Spock to bridge."

"Go ahead."

"Captain, something strange is taking place. Two of the boys slipped out of the group somewhere during the last five minutes, and now the girls are beginning to go. And it is not Haydn's Farewell Symphony they are staging, either.''

"Come to the bridge."

"Something strange here too," Sulu said. "I have no response on controls. We're going off course."

Scott crossed to Sulu's console and checked it. "It's shorted—no, it's channeled over somewhere—yes, to auxiliary control."

As Spock entered, Kirk began calling. "Bridge to auxiliary control. Bridge to auxiliary control."

"Captain," Spock said, "in my opinion someone else is running the ship."

"That's right, Captain," said Sevrin's voice from the intercom. "Someone else is running the ship. I am. All functions, Captain. Life support as well. I suggest that you do not attempt to regain control. I do not intend to return the helm to you until and unless we reach Eden. If I am in any way prevented from reaching that destination, I shall destroy the ship and all aboard."

Scott and Sulu had been frantically checking circuits. Now Scott said, "He can do it, Captain. He has got everything channeled over."

"Start a traceback on all circuits. See if you can bypass."

"Do that," Sevrin's voice said, "and I shall retaliate. I shall not warn you again."

"We are leaving the neutral zone now, Captain," Sulu said. "Bearing into Romulan space."

"Do you read any patrols, Mr. Spock?"

"No, sir."

"They'll be on us soon enough. Dr. Sevrin! You are violating Romulan space and endangering the peace of the Galaxy. They will see this as a military intrusion and attack. Bring her about. Now. If you bring her about and return to Starbase, nothing will be said about this."

"Like you said, brother Sevrin," said Adam's voice.

"If you do not, you will never reach Eden. You and this ship will be destroyed. We would be no match for a Romulan flotilla."

"He's got jelly in the belly," said Adam. "Real scared."

"Adam, Rad—you are being led by a man who is insane. You are being used by him. Spock, tell them."

"Adam," Spock said. "There is a file in the computer banks on Dr. Sevrin. You will find in it a report attesting to the fact that he is a carrier of a bacillus strain known as *Synthococcus novae*."

"Ain't that just awful?"

"You will also find a report from the same hospital giving a full psychiatric profile of him, projecting these actions of his."

"Yeah, brother."

"You know I reach you," Spock said. "I believe in what you seek. But there is a tragic difference between what you want and what he wants."

"You're making me cry," Adam said. Then he began to sing:

> Heading out to Eden—
> Yeah, brother!
> Heading out to Eden—
> Yeah, brother!
> No more trouble in my body or my mind—
> I'll live like a king on whatever I find—
> Eat all the fruit and throw away the rind—
> Yeah, brother!"

Kirk shut off the intercom; it was impossible even to try to determine a course of action through that noise. He got up and looked at Spock, who nodded.

"We are within sensor range of Eden and continuing to approach," he said.

"Whatever they're going to do, they'll do it now," Kirk said. "We have no choice left. Mr. Spock, Mr. Scott, come with me. And let's make it fast."

He led them down the corridors to auxiliary control.

"Phasers out and on full. We'll cut through the door. If Sevrin stops Life Function, we should be able to get through and start it again before any serious consequences follow—I hope. We'll take shortcuts in turn, so as not to risk killing somebody and damaging equipment when we hole through. I'll go first, then Spock, then Scott."

His phaser spat, followed by Spock's. Then another sound started, like the whine of an oscillator, going higher and higher. Spock, with his sensitive hearing, reacted first. He dropped his phaser and clapped his hands to his ears.

"Mr. Spock!" As Kirk went to him the sound stopped. "It has stopped. It's all right, Mr. Spock."

"It—hasn't stopped—Captain. It is beyond—no! Captain—they are using . . ."

Kirk's head suddenly swam. If there was an end to Spock's sentence, he never heard it.

An unknown time later, Kirk came to, finding the corridor just as before, Spock and Scott stirring to consciousness. No, not just as before; the door to auxiliary control was open, and there was no one in there.

The three of them got to their feet and staggered in. Spock pointed. "There it is. An ultrasonic generator, feeding into the ventilation system . . ."

The First Officer suddenly leaped forward and smashed the device with an iron fist.

"Why did you do that?" Kirk said. "The parts could have . . ."

"It was set to go off again in a few seconds, Captain—and this time on a killing frequency. It must have been Sevrin's work; I doubt that the youngsters would have let him do it had they known the device could be made lethal. Clearly he didn't intend us to get back to make any reports."

Kirk grabbed the intercom and began calling. "Kirk to bridge. Come in, do you read me? Engineering. Hangar deck. Transporter Room. Do you read me? Kirk to bridge."

"Captain?" Scott's voice said.

"Sulu here, Captain. What happened to us? I heard a whistle and then . . ."

"Never mind, Sulu," Kirk said. "Do we have control of the ship?"

"It's still all in auxiliary, sir," said Chekov's voice. "Some of the gear is jammed."

"Can we break orbit if we have to?"

"I think so, sir."

"Hangar deck to Captain."

"Kirk here."

"Sir, one of the shuttlecrafts has been taken. We were all knocked out . . ."

"Stand by. Mr. Spock, do you read any Romulans?"

"Negative, Captain. I am picking up the shuttlecraft, however."

"Where?"

"It has landed. Sir, except for those aboard the shuttlecraft, I read no sign of life at all. Neither animal nor humanoid. And there are only five life forms aboard the craft."

"Auxiliary control to McCoy. Bones, are you all right?"

"Yes, Jim."

"Stand by the Transporter Room. Full medical gear."

"Bridge to Captain Kirk," said Uhura's voice. "Do you wish hailing frequency, sir?"

"No. They tried to destroy us. Let them think they succeeded. I want coordinates zeroed in so that when we beam down we are not visible to them. Mr. Scott, the con is yours. If a Romulan patrol appears, hold in orbit; Lieutenant Uhura is to try to make them understand. I don't want to provoke combat. Mr. Chekov, join us in the Transporter Room. Mr. Spock, you too."

The garden was brilliant with sunshine, dazzling with flower color, opulent with heavy-laden fruit trees, one of them a giant. But it was utterly silent. The landing party looked about in awe.

"The legends were true, sir," Spock said in a low voice. "A fantastically beautiful planet."

"Eden," said Chekov.

Kirk said, "It almost—was this what they believed they'd find?" Spock nodded. "I can understand now. But why have they remained in their ship? Well, spread out and approach with caution."

The other three moved away. Kirk remained where he was, flipping open his communicator. "Dr. Sevrin, this is Captain Kirk. You are under arrest. You will debark from your ship."

The shuttlecraft remained silent, its doors shut. Then there came a whimpering little sound, in Irina's voice. "No . . ."

"You will come out at once."

"No! No!" This time it was a scream of pure terror. Kirk went after McCoy.

"Bones, you heard that? What do you make of it?"

"She sounds terrified."

"Of what?"

McCoy took out his tricorder. "I don't know, Jim. I don't read anything abnormal. Wait a minute . . ."

There was a yell of pain from Chekov. He was standing by a flowering plant, his right fist clenched to his chest, his face contorted. They got to him fast.

"What is it, Chekov?"

"The flower, sir. I touched it. It's like fire."

McCoy forced him to unclench the fist. Fingers and palm were stained and seared. The surgeon aimed the tricorder at it, then at the flower, the plant proper, the grasses.

"The sap in it is pure acid," McCoy said. "All the plant life. The grass, too." He took out his medical kit and smeared ointment over Chekov's hand.

"Their feet!" Kirk said. "They were barefoot! Don't touch a thing. Bones, will our clothing protect us?"

"For a short time."

"Captain," Spock called. "Come over here, please."

He was standing under the largest fruit tree. Kirk joined him and looked down. Adam lay dead on the ground, twisted, a half-eaten piece of fruit from the tree still clutched in his hand.

"Bones," said Kirk.

McCoy took readings. "Poison. The fruit is deadly."

Spock bent and picked up the body, his enormous strength holding it easily. He looked at Kirk. "His name was Adam."

Understanding now, Kirk walked to the shuttlecraft openly, Spock beside him. Kirk pushed a button, and the doors opened. He called in gently, "You will be cared for."

The girls and Rad came limping out, murmuring in pain.

"It hurts," Irina said.

"I know," Spock said. "It hurts us all."

Chekov went at once to Irina and held her comfortingly as McCoy began to treat her. Kirk went on inside the craft.

Dr. Sevrin sat on the deck in the yoga position, immobile, heedless of his blistered, naked feet. His injuries were shockingly worse than those of the others.

"Bones, in here, please! Dr. Sevrin—Dr. Sevrin. Look at him, Bones. How can he stand it?"

"He should be beamed aboard. He needs more attention than I can give him here."

"No!" Sevrin said suddenly. "No. We are not leaving."

"We'll take care of you aboard the ship," Kirk said.

"We are not leaving Eden. None of us."

"Be sensible, Sevrin."

"We're not leaving!" As Kirk bent to help him, Sevrin thrust him savagely aside, lunged for the door and ran, despite the agony it must have cost him. He plunged straight toward the huge fruit tree. There was no chance of stopping him; by the time Kirk and McCoy were out of the craft, he had reached the tree, seized a fruit and bitten into it.

"No! I have found my Eden!"

Then he moaned, doubled, and fell.

The group by the shuttlecraft were for a moment paralyzed by shock. Then Chekov turned to Irina. "He too is dead, Irina."

She looked at him in a daze. "And the dream is dead. He sacrificed so much for it. When we landed, and he saw Eden finally, he cried, all of us felt the same. It was so beautiful. And we ran out into it—and . . ."

"Spock to *Enterprise*. Mr. Scott, stand by to beam the injured aboard. Medical team to the Transporter Room."

Everything was normal again on the bridge. Uhura said, "I have Starbase now, Captain."

"Alert them that we have the four and will be beaming them down. And mark the incident closed."

"Yes, sir."

"Bridge to Transporter Room. Scotty, are they there?"

"Three of them, sir."

"Stand by. Mr. Chekov, do you wish to attend?"

Chekov stood hesitantly. "Captain, sir, I wish first to apologize for my conduct during this time. I—did not maintain myself under proper discipline. I endangered the ship and its personnel by my conduct. I respectfully submit myself for disciplinary action.''

"Mr. Chekov," Kirk said with a faint smile. "You did what you had to. As all of us did. Even your friends. You may go."

"Thank you, sir."

He started for the elevator, but as he did so, the doors opened and Irina stepped out. For a moment they looked at each other in silence.

"I was coming to say goodbye," Chekov said.

"And I was coming to say goodbye to you."

They kissed, gently, sadly. Irina said, "Be incorrect, occasionally."

"And you be correct."

"Occasionally."

She turned back to the elevator, but was intercepted by Spock. "Miss Galliulin, it is my sincere wish that you do not give up your search for Eden," he said. "I do not doubt but that you will find it—or make it yourselves."

She bowed her head, entered the elevator and was gone. Chekov and Spock went back to their posts. Chekov still seemed to be caught in the moment; then he became aware of the silence about him, the awareness of the others. He looked around.

Kirk was smiling faintly; he turned to Spock, whose face was expressionless, but who was nodding.

Kirk said, "We reach, Mr. Chekov."

REQUIEM FOR METHUSELAH

Writer: Jerome Bixby
Director: Murray Golden
Guest stars: James Daly, Louise Sorel

≡

Rigellian fever struck aboard the *Enterprise* with startling suddenness, its origin unknown. Permission was asked, and received, of Starfleet Command to abort the current routine mission in order to search for a planet with large deposits of ryetalyn, the only known cure for the disease. By the time they found such a planet, one yeoman had died and four more were seriously ill.

Kirk, McCoy and Spock beamed down at once, leaving Scott at the con. McCoy scanned about him with his tricorder.

"There's a large deposit at bearing two seven three—about a mile away," he reported, his voice grim. "We've got four hours to get it processed, or the epidemic will be irreversible. Everybody on the *Enterprise* . . ."

As he started off with Kirk, Spock's voice stopped them.

"Most strange," he said. "Readings indicate a life form in the vicinity. Yet our ship's sensors indicated that this planet was uninhabited."

"Human?" Kirk said. "But we've got no time for that. Let's get to that ryetalyn deposit."

Again they started off, and again they were halted by a sound—this time a steady whirring behind them. As they turned, they saw floating from behind a rock what could only be a robot: metallic, spherical, about the size of a beachball, studded with protuberances with functions which could only be guessed at. It came toward them at about chest height, flickering menacingly.

The three drew their phasers. A light blinked brightly on the robot's skin, and a bush next to Kirk went up in a burst of flame.

First Kirk and then the other two fired back—or tried to. All three phasers were inoperative. The robot continued to advance.

"Do not kill," a man's voice said. The robot stopped in midair. The owner of the voice came around from behind the same rock: a muscular man of about forty, whose bearing suggested immense dignity, assurance, authority.

"Thanks," said Kirk with relief. "I am Captain James Kirk, of the . . ."

"I know who you are. I have monitored your ship since it entered this system."

"Then you know why we're here, Mr. . . ."

"Flint. You will leave my planet."

"*Your* planet, sir?" Spock said.

"My retreat—from the unpleasantness of life on Earth—and the company of other people."

"Mr. Flint, I've got a sick crew up there," Kirk said. "We can't possibly reach another planet in time. We're sorry to intrude. We'll be happy to leave your little private world as soon as possible, but without that ryetalyn, you'd be condemning four hundred and thirty people to death!"

"You are trespassing, Captain."

"We're in *need*. We'll pay you for the ryetalyn—trade for it—work for it."

"You have nothing I want," Flint said.

"Nevertheless, we've got to have the ryetalyn. If necessary, we'll take it."

"If you do not leave voluntarily, I have the power to force you to leave—or kill you where you stand."

Kirk whipped out his communicator and snapped it open. "Kirk to *Enterprise*. Mr. Scott, lock phasers on landing party coordinates."

"Aye, Captain. All phasers locked on."

"If anything happens to us, there'll be *four* deaths," Kirk told Flint. "And my crew will come down and get the ryetalyn anyhow."

"It would be an interesting test of power," Flint said. "Your enormous forces—against mine. Who would win?"

"If you are not certain," Spock said, "I suggest you refrain from a most useless experiment."

"We need only a few hours," Kirk added.

"Have you ever seen a victim of Rigellian fever?" Mc-Coy said. "It kills in one day. Its effects resemble bubonic plague."

Flint's expression turned remote. "Constantinople, Summer, 1334. It marched through the streets—the sewers. It left the city, by oxcart, by sea—to kill half of Europe. The rats—rustling and squealing in the night, as they, too, died . . ."

"You are a student of history, Mr. Flint?" Spock asked.

"I am." He seemed to rouse himself. "The *Enterprise*—a plague ship. Well, you have two hours. At the end of that time, you will leave."

"With all due gratitude," Kirk said, rather drily. "Mr. Spock, Bones . . ."

"No need," Flint said, indicating the robot. "M-4 will gather the ryetalyn you need. In the meantime, permit me to offer more comfortable surroundings."

"More comfortable" turned out to be a vast understatement. The central room of Flint's underground home was both huge and luxurious. Most impressive were the artworks—framed paintings, dozens of them, hung on the walls, except for one wall which was entirely taken up by books. There were statuary, busts, tapestries, illuminated glass cases containing open books and manuscripts of obvious antiquity, and even a concert grand piano. The place was warm, comfortable, masculine despite all these riches—at once both museum and home.

"Our ship's sensors did not reveal your presence here, Mr. Flint," Spock said.

"My planet is surrounded by screens which create the impression of lifelessness. A protection against the curious—the uninvited."

"Such a home must be difficult to maintain."

"M-4 serves as butler, housekeeper, gardener—and guardian."

McCoy was looking into the illuminated cases with obvious awe. "A Shakespeare First Folio—a Gutenberg Bible—the 'Creation' lithographs by Taranullus of Centaurus VII—some of the rarest books in the Galaxy—spanning centuries!"

"Make yourselves comfortable," Flint said. "Help yourselves to some brandy, gentlemen." He went out, calmly.

"Do we trust him?" McCoy asked.

"It would seem logical to do so—for the moment."

"I'll need two hours," McCoy said worriedly, "to process that ryetalyn into antitoxin."

"If the ryetalyn doesn't show up in one hour, we go prospecting," Kirk said. "Right over Mr. Flint, if necessary."

Spock was now looking at the paintings. "This is the most splendid private art collection I have ever seen," he said. "And unique. The majority are works of three men: Leonardo da Vinci of the sixteenth century, Reginald Pollock of the twentieth century, and even a Sten from Marcus II."

"And this," said McCoy, going over to the bar and picking up a bottle, "is Sirian brandy, a hundred years old. Now where are the glasses? Ah. Jim? I know you won't have any, Spock. Heaven forbid that your mathematically perfect brainwaves be corrupted by this all too human vice."

"Thank you, Doctor. I will have brandy."

"Can the two of us handle a drunk Vulcan?" McCoy asked Kirk. "Once alcohol hits that green blood . . ."

"Nothing happens that I cannot control much more efficiently than you," Spock said, after a sip. "If I appear distracted, it is because of what I have seen. I am close to feeling an unaccustomed emotion."

"Let's drink to *that*," McCoy said. "What emotion?"

"Envy. None of these da Vinci paintings has ever been catalogued or reproduced. They are *unknown* works. All are apparently authentic—to the last brushstroke and use of materials. As undiscovered da Vincis, they would be priceless."

"Would be?" Kirk said. "You think they might be fakes?"

"Most strange. A man of Flint's obvious wealth and

impeccable taste would scarcely hang fakes. Yet my tricorder analysis indicates that the canvas and the pigments used are of contemporary origin.''

"This could be what it seems to be," Kirk said thoughtfully. "Or it could be a cover—a setup—even an illusion.''

"That would explain the paintings," McCoy said. "*Similar* to the real thing . . .''

"One of you, get a full tricorder scan of our host," Kirk said. "See if he's human.''

"The minute he turns his back," McCoy agreed.

Kirk got out his communicator. "Kirk to *Enterprise*. Mr. Scott, run a library check on this Mr. Flint we've encountered here—and on this planet, Holberg 917-G. Stand by with results; I'll contact.''

"Aye, sir.''

"Kirk out. Now let's enjoy his brandy. It *tastes* real.''

But as he lifted the glass to his lips, he once again heard the whirring of the robot, M-4. The men froze warily as the machine entered and moved toward them, stopping to hover over a large, low table. A front panel opened, and out came cubes of a whitish material onto the table. The robot closed the panel and floated back a pace.

McCoy snatched up one of the cubes. "This looks like—it is! Ryetalyn! Refined—ready to be processed into antitoxin!''

"Whatever our host may be, he's come through," Kirk said. "McCoy, beam up to the ship and start processing.''

"That will not be necessary," Flint said, appearing at the top of a ramp. "M-4 can prepare the ryetalyn for inoculation more quickly in my laboratory than you could aboard your ship.''

"I'd like to supervise that, of course," McCoy said.

"And when you are satisfied as to procedures, I hope you will do me the honor of being my guests at dinner.''

"Thank you, Mr. Flint," Kirk said. "I'm afraid we don't have time.''

Flint came a step down the ramp. "I regret my earlier inhospitality. Let me make amends." He half turned, extending a hand.

At the top of the ramp appeared a staggeringly beautiful

girl in loosely flowing robes. She looked down at the three strangers with a mixture of innocence and awe.

The two descended the ramp. The girl was graceful as well as lovely, yet she seemed quite unaware of the charm she radiated.

"I thought you lived alone, Mr. Flint," Kirk said when he could get his voice back.

"No, this is the other member of the family. Gentlemen, may I present Rayna."

The courtesies were exchanged. Then Rayna said, "Mr. Spock, I do hope we can find time to discuss inter-universal field densities, and their relationship to gravity vortex phenomena."

If Spock was as staggered as Kirk was by this speech, he did not show it. "Indeed? I should enjoy such a talk. It is an interest of mine."

"Her parents were killed in an accident, while in my employ," Flint explained. "Before dying, they placed their infant, Rayna Kapec, in my custody. I have raised and educated her."

"With impressive results, sir," McCoy said. "Rayna, what else interests you besides gravity vortex phenomena?"

"Everything. Less than that is betrayal of the intellect."

"The totality of the universe?" McCoy said gently. "All knowledge? Remember, there's more to life than knowing."

"Rayna possesses the equivalent of seventeen university degrees, in the sciences and arts," Flint said. "She is aware that the intellect is not all—but its development must come first, or the individual makes errors, wastes time in unprofitable pursuits."

"At her age, I rather enjoyed my errors," said McCoy. "But, no damage done, obviously, Rayna. You're the farthest thing from a bookworm I've ever seen."

"Flint is my teacher. You are the first other humans I have ever seen."

Kirk stared at her, not sure he liked what he had heard. But it was none of his business.

"The misfortune of men everywhere," McCoy was saying, "is our privilege."

Flint said, "If you would accompany my robot to the laboratory, Doctor, you can be assured that the processing of the ryetalyn is well in hand."

McCoy picked up the ryetalyn cubes and looked uncertainly at M-4. The robot turned silently in midair and glided out, the surgeon in tow.

"Your pleasure, gentlemen?" Flint said. "Chess? Billiards? Conversation?"

Kirk was still staring at Rayna. "Why not all three?" he said absently.

Kirk was no pool shark, and found Rayna far better at it than he was. He lined up a shot, intent. Flint and Spock watched.

Flint said, "I have surrounded Rayna with the beautiful and the good of human culture—its artistic riches and scientific wisdom."

Kirk muffed the shot.

"I have protected her from its venality—its savagery," Flint went on. "You see the result, Captain."

Rayna had lined up a three-cushion shot, which paid off brilliantly. Kirk straightened, feeling resigned.

"Did you teach her *that*?" he asked.

"We play often."

"May I show you, Captain?" Rayna said. She stepped close to him, correcting his grip on the cue.

"You said savagery, Mr. Flint," Kirk said. "How long is it since you visited Earth?"

"You would tell me that it is no longer cruel. But it is, Captain. Look at your Starship—bristling with weapons . . ."

Kirk and Rayna were bending, close together, their arms intertwined on the cue as she set him up for the shot. He found that not much of his mind was on Flint.

". . . its mission to colonize, exploit, destroy if necessary, to advance Federation causes."

Kirk made the shot. This time it was a pretty good one.

"Our missions are peaceful," he said, "our weapons defensive. If we were such barbarians, we would not have *asked* for the ryetalyn. Your greeting, not ours, lacked a certain benevolence."

"The result of pressures that are not your concern."

Spock had wandered over to the piano and sat down, studying the manuscript on the music rack.

"Such pressures are everywhere," Kirk said, "in every man, urging him to what you call savagery. The private hells—the inner needs and mysteries—the beast of instinct. As humans, we'll always be that way." He turned to Rayna, who seemed surprised that anyone would dare to argue with Flint. "To be human is to be complex. You can't escape a little ugliness, inside yourself and from without. It's part of the game."

Spock began casually to pick out the melody of the music manuscript. Flint looked toward him, seemingly struck by a sudden notion, "Why not play the waltz, Mr. Spock?" He turned to Kirk. "To be human is also to seek pleasure. To laugh—to dance; Rayna is a most accomplished dancer."

Sight-reading, Spock began to play. Kirk looked at Rayna. "May I have the pleasure?"

She went into his arms. The first few steps were clumsy, for Kirk was somewhat out of practice, but she was easy to lead. She was wearing a half smile of seeming curiosity. Flint watched them both, outwardly paternal, but also speculatively.

Spock was doing very well, considering that the manuscript looked hastily written; but there was something in his intentness that suggested more than mere concentration on the problems of reading the notation.

As Kirk and Rayna whirled past Flint, she gave Flint a bright, pleased smile, more animated than any expression she had shown before. Flint returned the smile with apparent affection—but there was still that intent speculation underneath.

Then McCoy entered, looking very grim indeed. Spock stopped playing, and the dancing couple broke apart.

"Something wrong?" Kirk asked.

"Nothing to dance about. The ryetalyn is no good! We can't use it. It contains irillium—nearly one part per thousand."

"Irillium would make the antitoxin inert?" Spock said.

"Right. Useless."

"Most unfortunate that it was not detected," Flint said. "I shall go with M-4 to gather more ryetalyn and screen it myself. You are welcome to join me, Doctor." He went out, evidently to summon the robot.

"Time factor, McCoy?" Kirk said. "The epidemic?"

"A little over two hours and a half. I guess we can get in under the wire. I've never seen anything like the robot's speed, Jim. It would take us twice as long to process the stuff."

"Would we have made the error?" Kirk asked grimly.

"*I* made the error, just as much as the robot. I didn't suspect the contaminant until scanning the completed antitoxin showed it up. What if all the ryetalyn on this planet contains irillium?"

"Go with Flint. Keep an eye on procedures."

"Like a hawk," McCoy said, turning away. "That lab's an extraordinary place, Jim. You and Spock should have a look."

He went up the ramp after Flint. Spock got up from the piano bench, picking up the manuscript.

"Something else which is extraordinary," he said. "This waltz I played is by Johannes Brahms. But it is in manuscript, Captain—written in Brahms' own hand, which I recognize. It is an unknown waltz—absolutely the work of Brahms—but unknown."

"Later, Mr. Spock," Kirk said, preoccupied. "I think I will take a look at that laboratory. All our lives depend upon it. If we could get the irillium out of the existing antitoxin . . . Where did Rayna go?"

"I did not see her leave, Captain. I was intent upon . . ."

"All right. Stay here. Let me know when McCoy and Flint return."

Spock nodded and sat down again at the piano. As Kirk went up the ramp, the strains of the waltz began to sound again behind him.

He found the laboratory without difficulty, and it was indeed a wonder, an orderly mass of devices only a few of which looked even vaguely familiar. What use did Flint ordinarily have for such an installation? It implied research work of a high order and constantly pursued. Was there no limit to the man's intellectual resources?

Then Kirk realized that he was not alone. Rayna was

standing on the other side of the lab, before another door. Her hands were clasped before her and her eyes were raised in an attitude of meditation, or of questioning for which she could not find the words. But she seemed also to be trembling slightly.

Kirk went to her, and she turned her head. Yes, she was shivering.

"You left us," Kirk said. "The room became lonely."

"Lonely? I do not know the word."

"It is a condition of wanting someone else. It is like a thirst—like a flower dying in a desert." Kirk halted, surprised at his own outburst of imagery. His eyes looked past her to the door. "What's in there?"

"I do not know. Flint has told me I must never enter. He denies me nothing else."

"Then—why are you here?"

"I—do not know. I come to this place when I am troubled—when I would search myself."

"Are you troubled now?"

"Yes."

"By what?" She looked intently and searchingly into his eyes, but did not answer. "Are you happy here, with Flint?"

"He is the greatest, kindest, wisest man in the Galaxy."

"Then why are you afraid? You *are* afraid; I can see it." He put his arms around her protectively. The trembling did not stop. "Rayna, this place is cold. Think of something far away. A perfect, safe, idyllic world—your presence would make it so. A world that children dream of . . ."

"Did I dream? My childhood—I remember this year—last year . . ."

What had Flint done to this innocent? He felt his expression hardening. She looked bewildered. "Don't be afraid," he said gently. He kissed her. It was meant to be only a brotherly kiss, but when he drew back, he found that he was profoundly shaken. He bent his head to kiss her more thoroughly.

As he did, her gaze flashed over his shoulder, and her eyes widened with horror. "No!" she cried. "No, no!"

Kirk whirled, belatedly aware of the whirring of the

robot. The machine was floating toward him, lights flashing
ominously. He put himself between the robot and the girl. It
advanced inexorably, and he backed a step, trying to lead it
away from Rayna.

"Stop!" Rayna cried. *"Stop!"*

M-4 did not stop. Kirk, backtracking, ducked behind a
large machine and pulled out his phaser; when the robot appeared, he fired point-blank. As he had more than half expected, the weapon failed to work.

"Stop! Command! *Command!*"

Steadily, the robot backed Kirk into a corner. He braced
himself to rush it—futile, without doubt, but there was no
other choice.

Then there was the hissing snap of a phaser, and the
robot vanished.

Spock appeared from around the corner of the massive
machine where Kirk had tried to ambush M-4, stowing his
phaser.

"Whew," Kirk said. "Thank you, Mr. Spock."

"Fortunately the robot was too intent on you to deac-
tivate my phaser," Spock said. "Dr. McCoy and Mr. Flint
have returned with the ryetalyn."

Was Rayna all right? Kirk went to her. She seemed
unharmed. Suddenly she lifted a hand to touch his lips. Then
she turned away, wide-eyed, deep in troubled thoughts.

They were back in the central room—Spock, Rayna,
and a very angry Kirk. Flint was quite calm. Behind his back,
Spock had his tricorder out and aimed at him.

"M-4 was programmed to defend this household, and
its members," Flint said calmly. "No doubt I should have
altered its instructions, to allow for unauthorized but pre-
dictable actions on your part. It thought you were attacking
Rayna. A misinterpretation."

Kirk was far from sure he bought that explanation. He
took a step toward Flint.

"If it was around now, it might interpret quite correctly . . ."

Whirrrr.

The machine was back—or an exact duplicate of it,
floating watchfully near Flint.

"Too useful a device to be without, really," Flint said. "I created another. Go to the laboratory, M-5."

Spock stowed his tricorder over his shoulder. "Matter from energy," he said. "An almost instantaneous manufacture, no doubt, in which your robot was duplicated from an existing matrix."

Flint nodded, but he did not take his eyes from Kirk. "Be thankful that you did not attack me, Captain. I might have accepted battle—and I have twice your physical strength."

"In your own words, that might be an interesting test of power."

"How childish he is, Rayna. Would you call him brave—or a fool?"

"I am glad he did not die," Rayna said in a low voice.

"Of course. Death, when unnecessary, is tragic. Captain, Dr. McCoy is in the laboratory with the new ryetalyn. He is satisfied as to its purity. I suggest that you wait here, patiently—safely. You have seen that my defense systems operate automatically—and not always in accordance with my wishes."

Kirk felt a certain lack of conviction about this last clause.

Flint put his hand on Rayna's arm. "Come, Rayna."

After a last, long look at Kirk, she allowed herself to be led up the ramp. Scowling, Kirk took a stubborn step after them, but Spock held him back.

"I don't like the way he orders her around," Kirk said.

"Since we are dependent upon Mr. Flint for the ryetalyn, I might respectfully suggest, Captain, that you pay less attention to the young lady, should you encounter her again. Our host's interests do not appear to be confined to art and science."

"He loves her?" Kirk said.

"Strongly indicated."

"Jealousy! That could explain the attack. But still—he seemed to *want* us to be together; the billiards game—*he* suggested that we dance . . ."

"It would seem to defy the logic of the human male, as I understand it."

After an uneasy moment, Kirk brought out his communicator. "Kirk to *Enterprise*. Mr. Scott, report on the Rigellian fever."

"Nearly everybody aboard has got it, sir. We're working a skeleton crew, and waiting for the antitoxin."

"A little while longer, Scotty. Report on computer search."

"No record of Mr. Flint. He simply seems to have no past. The planet was purchased thirty years ago by a Mr. Nova, a wealthy financier and recluse."

"Run a check on Rayna Kapec. Status: legal ward, after death of parents."

"Aye, Captain."

As Kirk slowly put the communicator away, Spock said, "There is still a greater mystery. I was able to secure a tricorder scan of Mr. Flint, while you and he were involved in belligerence. He is human. But there are biophysical peculiarities. Certain body-function readings are disproportionate. For one thing, extreme age is indicated—on the order of six thousand years."

"Six thousand! He doesn't look it, not by a couple of decimal places. Can you confirm that, Mr. Spock?"

"I shall program the readings into Dr. McCoy's medical computer when we return to the ship."

"Time factor?"

"We must commence antitoxin injections within two hours and eighteen minutes, or the epidemic will prove fatal to us all."

Kirk frowned. "Why is the processing taking so long this time?"

"The delay would seem to be possibly deliberate."

"Yes," Kirk said grimly. "As if he were keeping us here for some reason."

"Most strange. While Mr. Flint seems to wish us to linger, he is apprehensive. It is logical to assume that he knows our every move—that he has us monitored."

The communicator beeped. "Kirk here."

"Scott, sir. There's no record of a Rayna Kapec in the Federation legal banks."

"No award of custody?"

"No background on her at all, in any computer bank. Like Flint."

"Thanks, Scotty. Kirk out. Like Flint. People without a past. By what authority is she here, then? What hold does he have over her?"

"I would suggest," Spock said, "that our immediate concern is the ryetalyn."

"Let's find McCoy."

As they headed for the door, Rayna entered. She seemed to be agitated. "Captain!" she called.

"Go ahead, Spock, I'll meet you in the laboratory."

When they were alone, Rayna said, "I have come to say goodbye."

"I don't want to say goodbye."

"I am glad that you will live."

Kirk studied her. She seemed innocent, uncertain, yet underneath there was a kind of urgency. She stood motionless, as if in the grip of forces she did not understand.

He went to her. "I know now *why* I have lived." He put his arms around her and kissed her. This second kiss was much longer than the first, and her response suddenly lost its innocence.

"Come with us," Kirk said hoarsely.

"My place . . ."

"Is where you want to be. Where do you want to be?"

"With you."

"Always."

"Here," she said.

"No, come with me. I promise you happiness."

"I have known security here."

"Childhood ends. You love *me*, not Flint."

For a long moment she was absolutely silent, hardly even seemed to breathe. Then she broke free of his arms and ran off. Kirk stared after her, and then started off to the laboratory, his heart still pounding.

The moment Kirk entered, McCoy said, "Flint lied to us. The ryetalyn isn't here."

"But I am picking up readings on the tricorder, Captain," Spock said. "The ryetalin is apparently behind that door."

The door toward which the tricorder was aimed was the same one Rayna had said Flint had forbidden her to enter.

"Why is Flint playing tricks on us?" Kirk demanded,

suddenly furious at the constant multiplication of mysteries.
"Apparently we're supposed to go in and get it—if we can!
Let's not disappoint the chessmaster. Phasers on full!"

But as the weapons came out, the door began to rumble
open of its own accord. A constant, low hum of power was
audible from inside it.

Kirk lead the way. The ryetalyn cubes were conspicu-
ously visible on a table. Kirk went toward them in triumph,
but his attention was caught by a draped body encased on a
slab. The slab carried a sign which read: "RAYNA 16."

The body was the supine form of a woman. The face
was not quite human; it resembled dead white clay, beauti-
fully sculptured and somehow unfinished. Nevertheless, it was
clearly Rayna's.

Hung on the other side of the case was a clipboard with
notes attached. Most of the scribbles seemed to be mathematical.

As if in a dream, Kirk moved on to a similar case. The
figure in it was less finished than the first. Its face seemed to
show marks of sculpture; the features were more crudely defined. Still, it too was Rayna's—Rayna 17.

"Physically human," McCoy said in a low voice, "yet
not human. These are earlier versions. Jim—she's an android!"

"Created here, by my hand," Flint's voice said from
the doorway. "Here, the centuries of loneliness were to end."

"Centuries?" Kirk said.

"Your collection of Leonardo da Vinci masterpieces,
Mr. Flint," Spock said. "Many appear to have been recently
painted—on contemporary canvas, with contemporary materials. And on your piano, a waltz by Johannes Brahms, an
unknown work, in manuscript, written with modern ink—yet
absolutely authentic, as are the paintings . . ."

"I am Brahms," Flint said.

"And da Vinci."

"Yes."

"How many other names shall we call you?" Spock
asked.

"Solomon, Alexander, Lazarus, Methuselah, Merlin,
Abramson—a hundred other names you do not know."

"You were born . . . ?"

"In that region of Earth later called Mesopotamia—in the year 3034 B.C., as the millennia are now reckoned. I was Akharin—a soldier, a bully and a fool. I fell in battle, pierced to the heart—and did not die."

"A mutation," McCoy said, fascinated. "Instant tissue regeneration—and apparently a perfect, unchanging balance between anabolism and katabolism. You learned you were immortal . . . ."

"And to conceal it: to settle and live some portion of a life; to pretend to age—and then move on, before my nature was suspected. One night I would vanish, or fake my demise."

"Your wealth, your intellect, the product of centuries of study and acquisition," Spock said. "You knew the greatest minds of history . . ."

"Galileo," Flint said. "Moses. Socrates. Jesus. And I have married a hundred times. Selected, loved, cherished—caressed a smoothness, inhaled a brief fragrance—then age, death, the taste of dust. Do you understand?"

"You wanted a perfect woman," Spock said. "An ultimate woman, as brilliant, as immortal, as yourself. Your mate for all time."

"Designed by my heart," Flint said. "I could not love her more."

"Spock," Kirk whispered, "you knew."

"Readings were not decisive. However, Mr. Flint's choice of a planet rich in ryetalyn—I had hoped I was wrong."

"Why didn't you tell me?" Kirk asked harshly.

"What would you have said?"

"That you were wrong," Kirk said, "*wrong*. Yes, I see."

"You met perfection," Flint said. "Helplessly, you loved it. But you cannot love an android, Captain. *I* love her; she is my handiwork—my property—she is what I desire."

"And you put the ryetalyn in here to teach me this," Kirk said. "Does she know?"

"She will never know."

Kirk said tiredly, "Let's go, Mr. Spock."

"You will stay," Flint said.

"Why?"

"We have also learned what *he* is, Captain."

"Yes," said Flint. "If you leave, the curious would follow—the foolish, the meddlers, the officials, the seekers. My privacy was my own; its invasion be on your head."

"We can remain silent," Spock suggested.

"The disaster of intervention, Mr. Spock. I've known it—I will not risk it again." Flint's hand went to a small control box on his belt.

Kirk whipped out his communicator. Flint smiled, almost sadly. "They cannot answer, Captain. See."

A column of swirling light began to form slowly in a clear area of the life chamber. As it brightened, the form of the *Enterprise* was revealed, floating a few feet above the floor, tiny familiar lights blinking.

"No!" Kirk cried.

"The test of power," Flint said. "You had no chance."

"My crew . . ."

"It is time for you to join them."

Kirk felt sick. "You'd—wipe out—four hundred lives? Why?"

"I have seen a hundred million fall. I know Death better than any man; I have tossed enemies into his grasp. But I know mercy. Your crew is not dead, but suspended."

"Worse than dead," Kirk said savagely. "Restore them! Restore my ship!"

"In time. A thousand—two thousand years. You will see the future, Captain Kirk." Flint looked at the *Enterprise*. "A fine instrument. Perhaps I may learn something from it."

"You have been such men?" Kirk said. "Known and created such beauty? Watched your race evolve from cruelty and barbarism, throughout your enormous life! Yet now, you would do *this* to us?"

"The flowers of my past. I hold the nettles of the present. I am Flint—with my needs."

"What needs?"

"Tonight I have seen—something wondrous. Something I have waited for—labored for. Nothing must endanger it. At last, Rayna's emotions have stirred to life. Now they will turn to me, in this solitude which I preserve."

"No," said Rayna's voice. They all spun around.

"Rayna!" Flint said in astonishment. "How much have you heard?"

"You must not do this to them!"

"I must." Flint's hand moved implacably back to the belt device.

"Rayna," Spock said. *"What will you feel for him—when we are gone?"*

She did not reply, but the expression of betrayal, tragedy, and bitter hatred which she turned on Flint was answer enough.

"All emotions are engaged, Mr. Flint," Spock said. "Harm us, and she hates you."

"Give me my ship," Kirk said coldly. "Your secret is safe with us."

Flint looked at Kirk levelly. Then there was the slightest suggestion of a shrug; here was a man who had lost battles before. He touched the belt control again.

The column of light with the toy *Enterprise* in it faded and vanished.

"That's why you delayed processing the ryetalyn," Kirk said, in a low, bitter voice. "You realized what was happening. You kept us together—me, Rayna—because I could make her emotions come alive. Now you're going to just take over!"

"I shall take what is mine—when she comes to me," Flint said. "We are mated, Captain. Alike immortal. You must forget your feelings in this matter, which is quite impossible for you."

"Impossible from the beginning," Kirk said in growing fury. "Yet you used me. I can't love her—but I do love her! And *she loves me*!"

Flint sprang. He was quick, but Kirk evaded him. The two combatants began circling like animals. As Kirk passed Spock, the First Officer seized his arm.

"Your primitive impulses cannot alter the situation."

"*You* wouldn't understand! We're fighting over a woman!"

"You are *not*," Spock said, "for *she* is not."

Kirk stepped back, turning his palms out toward his adversary. "Pointless, Mr. Flint."

"I will not be the cause of all this," Rayna said, in a

voice both fiery and shaken. "I will not! I choose! I choose! Where I want to go—what I want to do! I choose!"

"I choose for you," Flint said.

"No longer!"

"Rayna . . ."

"*No*. Don't order me! *No* one can order me!"

Kirk looked at her in awe, and it seemed as though Flint was feeling the same sensation. He extended a hand toward her, and she turned from it. He dropped the hand slowly, staring at her.

"She's human," Kirk said. "Down to the last blood cell, she's human. Down to the last thought, hope, aspiration, emotion. You and I have created human life—and the human spirit is free. You have no power of ownership. She can do as she wishes."

"No man beats me," Flint said coldly.

"I don't want to beat you," Kirk said wearily. "There's no test of power here. Rayna belongs to herself now. She claims her human right of choice—to do as she will, think as she will, *be* as she will."

Finally Flint gave a tired nod. "I have fought for that also. What does she choose?"

"Come with me," Kirk said to her.

"Stay," said Flint.

There were tears in her eyes. "I was not human," she whispered. "Now, I love—I love . . ."

She moved slowly forward toward the two waiting men. She seemed exhausted. She stumbled once, and then, suddenly, fell.

McCoy was at her side in an instant, feeling for her pulse. Flint also knelt. Slowly, McCoy shook his head.

It hit Kirk like a blow in the stomach. "What—happened?" he asked.

"She loved you, Captain," Spock said gently, "and also Flint, as a mentor, even a father. There was not time enough to adjust to the awful powers and contradictions of her newfound emotions. She could not bear to hurt either of you. The joy of love made her human; its agony destroyed her." In his voice there was a note of calm accusation. "The hand of God was duplicated. A life was created. But then—you demanded ideal response—for which God still waits.''

Flint bowed his head, a broken man. "You can't die, we will live forever—together.'' He sobbed. "Rayna—*child* . . .''

Kirk's hand moved, almost blindly, to his shoulder.

Kirk sat at his desk in his own cabin, in half light, exhausted, brooding. The door opened and Spock came in.

"Spock,'' Kirk said, and looked away.

"The epidemic is reduced and no longer a threat. The *Enterprise* is on course 513 mark seven, as you ordered.''

"The very young and lonely man—the very old and lonely man—we put on a pretty poor show, didn't we?'' He bowed his head. "If only I could forget . . .''

His head went down on his arms. He was asleep.

McCoy entered in full cry. "Jim, those tricorder readings of Mr. Flint are finally correlated. Methuselah is dying . . .''

Then he noticed Kirk's position, and added in a low voice, "Thank Heaven—sleeping at last.''

"Your report, Doctor?'' Spock said.

"Flint. In leaving Earth, with its complex of fields in which he was formed and with which he was in perfect balance, he sacrificed immortality. He'll live the remainder of a normal life-span—and die.''

"That day, I shall mourn. Does he know?''

"I told him myself. He intends to devote his last years, and his gigantic abilities, to improving the human condition. Who knows what he might come up with?''

"Indeed,'' Spock said.

"That's all, I guess. I'll tell Jim when he wakes up, or you can.'' He looked at Kirk with deep sympathy. "Considering his opponent's longevity—truly an eternal triangle. You wouldn't understand, would you, Spock? I'm sorrier for you than I am for him. You'll never know the things love can drive a man to—the ecstasies, the miseries, the broken rules, the desperate chances—the glorious failures, and the glorious victories—because the word love isn't written in your book.''

Spock was silent.

"I wish he could forget her." Still silence. "Good night, Spock."

"Good night, Doctor."

Spock regarded Kirk for another silent moment, and then moved deliberately to lock the door behind McCoy. Then he returned to Kirk. His hands floated to Kirk's dropped head, fingertips touching. He said, very gently, *"Forget . . ."*

THE SAVAGE CURTAIN

Writer: Gene Roddenberry and Arthur Heinemann
          (story by Gene Roddenberry)
Director: Herschel Daugherty
Guest stars: Lee Bergere, Barry Atwater

≡

The planet, newly discovered in an uncharted area of space, was clearly not a Class M world. The atmosphere boiled with poisonous reds and greens; the surface was molten lava.

And yet, from one small area Spock picked up persistent readings of carbon cycle life forms—and artificial power being generated in quantities great enough to support a considerable civilization. Hailing on all frequencies at first produced nothing . . . and then, suddenly, the *Enterprise* was being scanned, an incredibly swift and deep probe.

Kirk barely had time to call for alert status when the probing was over. Almost immediately afterward, the image of the planet on the main viewing screen dissolved into a swirling jumble of colors. These slowly gathered together into a face and figure, entirely human, dressed in clothing like those worn in the mid-1880's on Earth. He was sitting on nothing and with nothing visible behind him, as though in limbo. His expression was benign and calm.

"Captain Kirk, I believe?" the figure said. "A pleasure to make your acquaintance, sir."

Kirk, Spock and McCoy stared incredulously at the familiar figure. Finally, Kirk motioned to Uhura.

"Your voice-telegraph device is quite unnecessary, Captain," the figure said. "Do I gather that you recognize me?"

"I . . . recognize what you appear to be."

"And appearances can be quite deceiving." The figure

smiled. "But not in this case, James Kirk. I am Abraham Lincoln."

Kirk considered this incredible claim and apparition, and then turned to his First Officer. "Spock?"

"Fascinating, Captain."

"I've been described in many ways, Mr. Spock," the smiling man said, "but never with that word."

"I was requesting your analysis of this, Mr. Spock."

"They did scan us and our vessel," Spock said, "and doubtless obtained sufficient information to present this illusion."

"Illusion?" the figure said. "Captain, will you permit me to come aboard your vessel? No doubt you have devices which can test my reality."

After a moment's hesitation, Kirk said, "We'd be honored to have you aboard, Mr. President."

The figure reached into its vest pocket, pulled out a large watch on a heavy gold chain and snapped the lid open. "Do you still measure time in minutes?"

"Yes, sir."

"Then you should be over my position in . . . twelve and a half minutes. Until then, Captain . . ." The image on the screen rippled, dissolved and re-formed itself as the planet. Amid the hot reds and poisonous greens of the atmosphere there was now a spot of soft blue. Spock leaned into his hooded viewer.

"An area of approximately a thousand square kilometers, sir," he said. "It's completely Earthlike, including an oxygen-nitrogen atmosphere."

"He called it to the second, sir," Chekov added. "We'll be over it in exactly twelve minutes now."

Kirk touched the intercom button. "Security. Send a detachment to the Transport Room immediately. Phaser side arms—but be prepared also to give presidential honors. Captain out."

"Jim," McCoy said, "you don't really believe he's Abraham Lincoln?"

"It's obvious he believes it, Bones." Kirk stood up. "Mr. Spock, Doctor, full dress uniforms, please. Mr. Sulu, the con is yours."

* * *

In the Transporter Room, Security Chief Dickenson had assembled two security guards, phasers at port. Dickenson himself sported white boots and belt, plus a traditional bos'n's whistle on a gold chain.

Engineering Officer Scott, in full kilt, entered and moved to the Transporter console, fuming. "Full dress! Presidential honors! What's all this nonsense, Mr. Dickenson?"

"I understand President Lincoln is coming aboard, sir."

Scott whirled. "Are you daft, man?"

"All I know, sir, is what the Captain tells me, sir," Dickenson said uncomfortably. "And he said he'd have the hide of the first man who so much as smiles."

McCoy entered, also in full dress, with his tricorder over his shoulder. Scott eyed him dourly; McCoy gave back stare for stare.

"I'd have expected sanity from the ship's surgeon, at least." Scott irritably punched controls on the console. "President Lincoln, indeed! No doubt followed by Louis of France and Robert the Bruce."

Kirk and Spock had come in in time to catch this last remark.

"And if so, Mr. Scott, we'll execute appropriate honors to each," Kirk said. "Gentlemen, I don't believe for a moment that Abraham Lincoln is actually coming aboard. But we are dealing with an unknown and apparently quite advanced life form. Until we know . . . well, when in Rome, we do as the Romans do."

"Bridge to Transporter Room," Chekov's voice said over the intercom. "One minute to overhead position."

"Locking onto something," Scott said. He looked closer, and then gestured at the panel. "Does that appear human to you, Mr. Spock?"

Spock joined him and inspected the console. "Fascinating! . . . For a moment it appeared almost mineral. Like living rock, with heavy fore-claws . . . Settling down into completely human readings now."

"We can beam it aboard any time now, Captain," Scott said.

"Set for traditional ruffles and flourishes. Security, stand ready."

"Phaser team, set for heavy stun," Dickenson said. "Honor guard, ready."

The two security men posted themselves on opposite sides of the Transporter chamber, weapons set, raised and aimed. The four men comprising the honor guard snapped into parade rest. Dickenson raised his whistle to his lips.

"Energize."

The sparkling column appeared, solidified, vanished. The figure left standing there seemed to be inarguably Abraham Lincoln, dressed in the well-remembered 19th century suit, bearded, his face registering the sad wisdom of his presidential years.

Dickenson blew his whistle. Spock pushed a panel button and everyone came to attention. Ruffles and flourishes filled the air.

"Salute!" Kirk said. Everyone did except the two guards, whose phasers remained ready. Lincoln, too, stood gravely at attention through the music. Then Kirk said, "Two!," broke the salute and stepped forward.

"The USS *Enterprise* is honored to have you aboard, Mr. President."

"Strange," Lincoln said, stepping down. "Where are the musicians?"

"Taped music, sir. Starships on detached service do not carry full honor detachments."

"Taped music? Perhaps Mr. Spock will be good enough to explain that to me later." Lincoln extended a hand to Kirk. "A most interesting way to come aboard, Captain. What was the device used?"

"A matter-energy scrambler sir. The molecules of your body were converted to energy, and beamed to this chamber where they were reconverted to their original pattern."

Lincoln hesitated. "Well, since I am obviously here and quite whole, whatever you mean apparently works very well indeed." He looked at the two guards. "If those are weapons, gentlemen, you may lower them. At my age, I'm afraid I'm not very dangerous."

"Readings, fully human, sir," McCoy said.

Kirk signaled the guards to holster their weapons, and then introduced everyone present.

"Please stand at ease, gentlemen," Lincoln said. "I

hope to talk to each of you, but meanwhile, your Captain is consumed with questions and I shall do my utmost to answer them. And I trust your duties will permit time to answer some of mine. At your service, Captain.''

"Mr. Spock." Kirk led his First Officer and his guest off toward the Briefing Room.

"A marvel," Lincoln said. "A total marvel. I can hardly credit my eyes. We thought our *Monitor* the most formidable vessel imaginable—an iron ship that floated on water! You can imagine my amazement at an iron ship that floats on air.''

"Mr. President—"

"Yes, Captain. Forgive my excitement at the novelty of all this.''

"Sir . . . I find some of your comments hard to equate with other statements. For example, you are not at all surprised at the existence of this vessel. But you then exhibit only a 19th century knowledge about it—for example, stating that this vessel 'floats on air.' ''

"I don't understand. What *does* your vessel float on, Captain?''

Kirk exchanged a look with Spock and said patiently, "Sir, the atmosphere surrounding any planet is a relatively thin envelope.''

Lincoln appeared genuinely puzzled. Spock went on: "Given our present altitude, sir, and a present speed converting to 19,271 Earth miles per Earth hour, our velocity counterbalances the pull of this planet's gravity, creating equal but opposite forces which maintain us in orbit.''

This was quite a distance away from the real physical situation, but Spock had evidently decided to choose terms which might be familiar to a 19th century educated man, rather than having to explain what was meant by free fall through a matter-distorted space-time matrix. But even the simplification did not work.

"When the choice is between honesty and disguising ignorance," Lincoln said, "a wise man chooses the former. I haven't the faintest idea what you said.''

"With all respect, sir, that still does not answer my

question," Kirk said. "For example, you knew my name. How is it you know some things about us but not others?"

"Bless me! Yes, I do see the contradiction," Lincoln said, frowning. "Please believe I have neither desire nor intention to deceive you, gentlemen. I must have been told these things, but I . . . I cannot recall when or where."

"Can you guess who it might have been, sir?" Spock said. "What others exist on the planet's surface with you?"

"Others? What others do you mean?"

"That's clearly not Earth down there, Mr. President," Kirk said. "Or do you believe that it is?"

"Strange," Lincoln said thoughtfully, "I never considered that before. No, I do not claim it to be Earth."

"Less than thirty minutes ago, the temperature and atmosphere at any point down there would have made your existence in this form impossible."

"You don't say! I can only assure you that I am what I appear to be, gentlemen: an all too common variety of *Homo sapiens*. Either way, I am too ordinary, James. I am surprised you've always thought so highly of me. The errors, the unforgivable errors I made. McClellan at first appeared to me a veritable Napoleon; Grant seemed a whisky-befuddled barbarian . . ." He shook his head. "There were so many things I could have done to end the war earlier, to save so many lives, so much suffering . . ."

"I'm sure you did all you could—"

"Why do you stop, James? Afraid of showing compassion? It is the noblest of qualities . . . I am certain there is an answer to these contradictions you point up so well." His frown suddenly dissolved. "Yes, that's it, of course. You are both invited to disembark with me. You will receive the answers down there. There is no need to hurry your decision, Captain. I am most anxious to inspect a vessel which at least *appears* to float on air."

"We shall be honored," Kirk said. "Mr. Spock, inform the others. We'll consider this in the Briefing Room in one hour."

Lincoln looked around again. "Fascinating!" he said to Spock, smiling. "If I may borrow your favorite word."

"I'm flattered, sir."

"The smile lends attraction to your features, Mr. Spock."

Kirk turned, but Spock's face was as stony as always. "I'm afraid you're mistaken, sir," Kirk said. "Mr. Spock never smiles."

"Indeed?" Lincoln offered no further comment. Had he seen something behind Spock's expression? It would be in character.

They went up to the bridge, where the main viewing screen still showed a segment of the planet below them. Lincoln stared at it in awe, while Sulu and Chekov stared at him.

"Good Lord!"

"As I recall," Kirk said, "your Union Army observation balloons were tethered six hundred or so feet high, sir. We're six hundred forty-three miles above this planet."

"You can measure great distances that closely?"

"We do, sir," Spock said, moving to his station and checking his instruments. "Six hundred forty-three miles, two thousand twenty-one feet, two point zero four inches at this moment, in your old-style measurement."

"Bless me."

Uhura came onto the bridge. "Excuse me, Captain—"

"What a charming Negress," Lincoln said, then added quickly, "Oh, forgive me, my dear. I know that in my day some used that term as a description of property."

"Why should I object to the term, sir?" Uhura said, smiling. "In our century, we've learned not to fear words."

Kirk said, "May I present our communications officer, Lt. Uhura."

Lincoln shook hands with her, returning the smile. "The foolishness of my own century had me apologizing where no offense was given."

"Actually," she said, "I feel my color much lovelier and superior to yours and the Captain's."

"Superior? Then some of the old problems still exist?"

"No, sir," Kirk said. "It's just that we've learned to each be delighted in what we are. The Vulcans learned that centuries before we did."

"It's basic to the Vulcan philosophy, sir," Spock said. "How an infinite variety of things combine to make existence worthwhile."

"Yes, of course," Lincoln said. "The philosophy of 'nome'—meaning 'all.' " He paused, his frown returning. "Now, how did I know that? Just as I seem to know that on the planet's surface you will meet one of the greatest Vulcans in all the long history of your planet. My mind does not hold the name. But I know that he will be there."

"Excuse me, Captain," Uhura said, "but Mr. Scott is waiting for you in the Briefing Room."

"Oh, yes. Mr. President, with your permission I should like to make Lt. Uhura your guide at this point; I have a meeting."

"I would be delighted."

"Then we'll rejoin you shortly, sir. Mr. Sulu, the con is yours until Mr. Scott returns to the bridge."

In the Briefing Room, as Kirk and Spock entered, McCoy was saying to Spock: "Where the devil are they?"

"Perhaps cooking up a plate of haggis in the galley? They've been everywhere else."

"Sorry, Gentlemen," Kirk said, crossing to the table. "We were delayed."

"Jim, I'd be the last to advise you on your command image—"

"I doubt that, Bones, but continue."

"Do I have to lay it out for you? Practically the entire crew has seen you treating this imposter like the real thing— when he can't possibly be the real article, Captain!"

"Lincoln died three centuries ago and more, on a planet hundreds of light years away." Scott jerked a thumb over his shoulder.

"More in that direction, Engineer," Spock said, pointing down and to the left.

"The exact direction doesn't matter, you pointed-eared hobgoblin! You're the Science Officer," added McCoy, "why aren't you—well, doing whatever Science Officers do at a time like this?"

"I am, Doctor. I am observing the alien."

"At last. At least someone agrees with us he's an alien."

"Yes, he's an alien, of course," Kirk said after a moment's hesitation.

"And potentially dangerous," McCoy pressed on.

"Mad!" said Scott. "Loony as an Arcturian dog-bird."

"Spock and I have been invited to beam down to the planet's surface with him. Comments on that?"

"A big one," McCoy said. "Suddenly, miraculously, we see a small spot of Earth-type environment appear down there. Is it really there or do we just think we see it there?"

"You could beam down into a sea of molten lava," Scott said. "At the moment it's a raftlike mineral crust several hundred meters thick, over a molten iron core. It looks stable, but it was notably unstable in its formative phase."

"And there are transient images of life forms," McCoy said. "Minerallike themselves. Jim, that patch of Earth was created after our ship was scanned. Whoever they are, they examined us, determined our needs and supplied them down there. It smells, Captain. It's a trap."

"But why would they want to destroy only two of us?" Kirk said.

"It would be illogical of them, with such abilities," Spock said. "They could as easily trick us into destroying the entire vessel."

"Spock, are you implying that it's probably safe to beam down?"

"I am not, Doctor. There's no doubt that they want us down there for some hidden purpose. Otherwise they would have revealed some logical reason for all of this."

"Why Lincoln, Spock?" Kirk said. "Any speculation on that?"

"I need not speculate when the reason is obvious, Captain. President Lincoln has always been a very personal hero to you. What better way to titillate your curiosity than to make him come alive for you?"

"Not only to me, Spock."

"Agreed. I felt his charm, too. He is a magnificent work of duplication."

"But he has a *special* emotional involvement for you," McCoy said. "Interesting, since you're the one who will make the decision whether or not to beam down."

"Don't do it, Captain," Scott said.

Kirk thought about it. Finally he said, "The very reason for the existence of our starships is contact with other life. Although the method is beyond our comprehension, we *have* been offered contact. I'm beaming down. As for you, however, Mr. Spock—''

Spock stood. "Since I was included in their invitation to make contact, I must beam down with you, Captain."

McCoy exploded. "You're both out of your heads!"

"And you're on the edge of insubordination, Doctor," Kirk said.

"Would I be insubordinate to remind the Captain that this has the smell of things happening to him which I may not be able to patch back together this time?"

"Aye," Scott growled.

"Your concern noted and appreciated, gentlemen," Kirk said. "Mr. Spock, standard uniform, phasers and tricorder. Mr. Scott, have President Lincoln guided to the Transporter Room; we'll beam down immediately."

The three materialized in what seemed to be a wild canyon. The slopes were steep and boulder-strewn; on the floors there were shrubbery and trees. Kirk looked around.

"Captain!" Spock said. "Our weapons and tricorders did not beam down."

Kirk reached under his shirt and found his communicator still there, although his phaser and tricorder had indeed vanished. "Captain to *Enterprise*, come in . . . *Enterprise*, come in . . ."

Spock was also trying, but quickly gave over in favor of a careful examination of his communicator. "Undamaged," he reported. "Yet something prevents them from functioning."

Kirk swung angrily to Lincoln. "Your explanation, sir."

"I have none, Captain. To me this seems quite as it should be."

"Why have our weapons been taken? Why can't we communicate with our ship?"

"Please believe me. I know nothing other than what I have already told you—"

"The game's over! We've treated you with courtesy, we've gone along with who and what you think you are—"

"Despite the seeming contradictions, all is as it appears to be. I *am* Abraham Lincoln—"

"Just," another voice entered, "as I am who I appear to be."

Another man was approaching them: a tall, distinguished Vulcan. It was obvious that he was old, but as erect and strong as was usual with Vulcans even in age. The dignity and wisdom apparent in his features and bearing matched those of Lincoln's.

"Surak!" Spock said, in outright open astonishment.

"Who?" Kirk said.

"The greatest who ever lived on our planet, Captain. The father of all we became."

Surak stopped and made the Vulcan hand sign. "Live long and prosper, Spock. May you also, Captain Kirk."

"It is not logical that you are Surak," Spock said. "There is no fact, extrapolation from fact, or theory which would make it possible—"

"Whatever I am, Spock, would it harm you to give response?"

Spock slowly lifted his hand and returned the sign. "Live long and prosper, image of Surak, father of all we now hold true."

The newcomer almost smiled. "The image of Surak read in your face what was in your mind, Spock."

"As I tuned and beheld you, I displayed emotion. I beg forgiveness."

Surak nodded gravely. "The cause was more than sufficient. We need speak no further of it. Captain, in my time, we knew not of Earthmen. And I am pleased to see we have differences. May we together become greater than the sum of both of us."

"Spock," Kirk said in an iron voice, "we will not go along with these charades any longer!"

He was answered by still another new voice, seemingly out of the air—an oddly reverberating voice. "You will have the answer soon, Captain."

A strange, shrilling sound, a little like the chiming of bells, followed the voice, and then, directly before the four, there was a rainbow flashing which congealed slowly into a bizarre shape. It was a creature made seemingly of rock, about the size and shape of a man but with clawlike appendages and a mouth which, like a cave, seemed to be permanently open. It was seated in a rock chair carved to fit its body.

"I am Yarnek," the voice reverberated from the open maw. "Our world is called Excalbia. Countless who live on that planet are watching. Before this drama unfolds, we give welcome to the ones named Kirk and Spock."

"We know nothing of your world or customs," Kirk said. "What do you mean by a drama about to unfold?"

"You are intelligent life forms. I am surprised you do not perceive the honor we do you." A claw gestured. "Have we not created in this place on our planet a stage identical to your own world?"

"We perceive only that we were invited down here and came in friendship. You have deprived us of our instruments for examining your world, of our means of defending ourselves and of communicating with our vessel."

"Your objection is well taken. We shall communicate with your vessel so that your fellow life forms may also enjoy and profit from the play. Behold . . . we begin."

At these words, four figures came into view at the edge of the glade, and approached cautiously. One was a squat human in a Mongol costume of about the 13th century; another, also human, in the uniform of a 21st century Colonel; one was a Klingon, and the last a female Tiburon. Except for the Colonel, who was dapper and not unhandsome, they were an ugly-looking lot.

"Some of these you may know through history," Yarnek said. "Genghis Khan, for one. And Colonel Green, who led a genocidal war in the 21st century on Earth. Kahless the Unforgettable, the Klingon who set the pattern for his planet's tyrannies. Zora, who experimented with the body chemistry of subject tribes on Tiburon.

"We welcome the vessel *Enterprise* to our solar system and our spectacle. We ask you to observe with us the confrontation of the two opposing philosophies you term 'good' and 'evil.' Since this is our first experiment with Earthlings, our theme is a simple one: survival. Life and death. Your philosophies are alien to us, and we wish to understand them and discover which is the stronger. We learn by observing such spectacles."

"What do you mean, survival?" Kirk said.

"The word is explicit. If you and Spock survive, you may return to your vessel. If you do not, your existence is ended. Your choice of action is unlimited, as is your choice of weapons, should you wish to use any—you may fabricate anything you desire out of what you find around you. Let the spectacle begin."

"Mr. Spock and I refuse to participate."

"You will decide otherwise," Yarnek said, and then dissolved into the same mist of rainbows from which he had emerged.

"Analysis, Spock. Why do they want us to fight?"

"It may be exactly as explained, Captain. Our concept of good and evil would be strange to them. They wish to see which is strongest."

"And they'll have the answer if it kills us. Do you recall the exact location where we beamed down?"

"We have strayed from it somewhat, Captain. It was in that area, beyond those boulders."

"Ship's coordinates may still be locked in there." He started toward the spot, ignoring the others, Spock following. Lincoln and Surak were soon lost from view; but after a moment, rounding a large boulder, Kirk found himself face to face with them again. After staring at them, Kirk tried again, taking another path—with the same result.

"Mr. Spock?"

"I have no explanation, sir. Unless the creature is compelling us to circle. Quite obviously it is preventing us from reaching that area."

"I'm afraid, Captain," Lincoln said, "that none of us may leave until we do what it demands of us."

From the group of potential antagonists, Colonel Green stepped forward, his hand extended in a gesture of peace. His manner seemed friendly, even intended to charm. "Captain Kirk. May I? I'm Colonel Green. I quite agree with your attitude toward this charade. It's ridiculous to expect us to take part in it."

Kirk looked at him with open suspicion, and Green stopped while he was still a few steps away. "What do you want?"

"Exactly what you do. To get out of here. I have no quarrel with you, any more than you have with me."

"You're somewhat different from the way history paints you, Colonel."

"History tends to exaggerate," Green said with a small laugh. "I suggest we call a halt to this at once, and see if we can't find a way out of our difficulties. My associates are in full agreement with me."

Kirk looked beyond him at the "associates." Zora bowed gravely. Khan was hunkered down on the ground; apparently he was bored. Well, he had never been much of a man for talk. Kahless looked around curiously at the slopes.

"You were tricked into coming here, weren't you?" Green said. "So were we all."

"Where did you come from?"

"I don't remember . . . Isn't that strange? My memory used to be quite remarkable." He came closer, took Kirk's elbow confidentially, drawing him to one side. "But wherever it was, I want to get back. So it seems to me, Captain, that we have common cause, and that our enemy is that creature."

"What do you propose?"

"That we combine forces and reason out some way to overcome it. Are we in agreement?"

Kirk hesitated, studying him. "As I recall, Colonel, you were notorious for striking out at your enemies in the midst of negotiating with them."

"But that was centuries ago, Captain!" Green said, with a louder laugh. "And not altogether true! There is much that I'd change now if I could. Don't let prejudice and rumor sway you."

"Captain!" Spock shouted.

Suddenly everything seemed to be happening at once. Swinging, Kirk saw in a flash that Khan had somehow gotten to higher ground and was holding a boulder over his head in both hands. Then Green's arm was locked around Kirk's neck and he was thrown halfway to the ground. Kirk lashed out, staggering Green, and as he sprang to his feet saw Lincoln wrestling with Khan, who seemed to have missed whomever he had been aiming the boulder at.

Then the brawl was over as suddenly as it had begun, the four antagonists vanished among the boulders and trees of the canyon. Total silence swept over them. Breathing hard,

Kirk joined the other three. All had been battered, Spock severely.

"Is anyone hurt?" Kirk said.

"I fear my clothing is somewhat damaged," Lincoln said. "But how delightful to discover at my age that I can still wrestle."

"Mr. Spock?"

"Quite all right, Captain. However, I suggest that we prepare ourselves for another attack."

"No," Kirk said. "Green was right. That rocklike thing, Yarnek, is the enemy. Not those illusions."

"For an illusion, my opponent had a remarkable grip," Lincoln said, "But I forgot. You consider me an illusion, too."

"The Captain speaks wisely," Surak said. "These four are not our enemy. We should arrive together at a peaceful settlement."

The bell-like trilling began once more, and with it the rainbow swirling. Yarnek was back.

"I am disappointed," the creature said. "You display no interest in the honor we do you. We offer you an opportunity to become our teachers. By demonstrating whether good or evil is more powerful—"

Kirk lunged at the creature. It did not move—but when Kirk seized it, it was as though he had tried to grab a red-hot stove. With a yell he snatched his hands back.

"You find my body heat distressing?" Yarnek said. "You forget the nature of this planet . . . I must conclude that your species requires a cause to fight for. You may now communicate with your ship."

Kirk fumbled for his communicator, and despite the pain of his seared hands, managed to flip it open. "Kirk to *Enterprise*. Come in. Kirk to *Enterprise*. Do you read me?"

"Be patient, Captain," Yarnek said. "They read you."

Suddenly the communicator came alive in a bedlam of shouting voices, backed up by the sound of the ship's alarm. The bridge was obviously in turmoil.

"Mr. Scott!" Uhura called. "The Captain is trying to reach us."

"Engineering!" Scott was shouting. "Give me that again, man, I canna hear you."

"Deterioration has just started, sir."

"What is it, Lieutenant?" Kirk demanded.

"Where?" Scott shouted.

"Red Alert, Captain," Uhura said. "Mr. Scott is standing by."

"In the shielding between matter and antimatter. I don't know what started it."

"What caused the alert?"

"I don't know, sir. Mr. Scott, I have the Captain."

"Check for radiation. Get a repair crew on it at once."

"I have already, sir. We can't seem to stop it."

"Is there danger of detonation?"

"Estimate four hours, sir."

"Mr. Scott, sir, I have the Captain!"

"What? Oh—Captain, Scott here."

"Beam us aboard fast, Scotty."

"I canna, sir. There's a complete power failure. We're on emergency battery power only."

"What's happening?"

"I can't explain it, sir. Matter and antimatter are in Red Zone proximity. No knowing how it started and no stopping it either. The shielding is breaking down. Estimate four hours before it goes completely. That'll blow us up for fair!"

"The estimate is quite correct," Yarnek's hollow voice said. "Your ship will blow itself to atoms within four hours, Captain—unless you defeat the others before then. Is that cause enough to fight for?"

"What if they defeat us?"

"To save your ship and your crew, you have to win."

"Scotty, alert Starfleet Command. Disengage nacelles and jettison if possible. Scotty, do you read me?"

"Your communicators once more no longer function," Yarnek said. "You may proceed with the spectacle." With a chime and a shimmer, the creature was gone.

"The war is forced upon us, Captain," Lincoln said. "History repeats itself."

"Well," Kirk said, "I see nothing immoral in fighting illusions. It's play their game, fight, or lose the ship and every crewman aboard."

Spock looked toward Surak. "And if they're real, Captain?"

Kirk chose to let that go by. "We'll use the top of the defile as a base. It's defensible. They can't approach without our seeing them."

"Are we fighting a defensive war, James?" Lincoln said.

"We don't have the time. But if it goes against us I want a place to retreat to. Right now I want to scout them out, find their weaknesses and attack."

Lincoln smiled. "Do you drink whisky?"

"Occasionally," Kirk said, startled. "Why?"

"Because you have qualities very much like those of another man I admired greatly. One I mentioned before—General Grant."

The reminder of the possible illusory nature of all this was jarring, distracting. "Thank you. We'll need weapons. Spock, I believe the primitive Vulcans made something like a boomerang."

"Yes, Captain. However—"

"Spears, too. Slings. Mr. President, you used slings as a boy—"

"Indeed I did." Lincoln stripped off his coat, pulled out his shirttail and ripped from it a long strip. Again that conflict of realism and illusion.

"Captain," Spock said, "logic dictates that we consider another course." He looked deferentially toward Surak, who thus far had remained a profoundly troubled nonparticipant in the discussion.

"In my time on Vulcan we too faced these alternatives," Surak said. "We had suffered devastating wars that nearly destroyed our planet and another was about to begin. We were torn. And out of our suffering some of us found the discipline to act. We sent emissaries to our opponents to propose peace. The first were killed. Others followed. Ultimately, we achieved peace, which has lasted since then."

"The circumstances were different, Surak."

"The face of war never changes. Look at us, Captain. We have been hurt. So have they. Surely it is more logical to heal than kill."

"I'm afraid that kind of logic doesn't apply here," Kirk said.

"That is precisely why we should not fight—"

"My ship is at stake!"

Surak said, "I will not harm others, Captain."

"Sir," Spock said, "his convictions are most profound on this matter—"

"So are mine, Spock! If I believed there was a peaceful way out of this—"

"The risk would be mine alone, Captain," Surak said. "And if I fail, you would lose nothing. I am no warrior."

There was a moment of silence, while Kirk looked from one Vulcan to the other.

"The Captain knows that I have fought at his side before," Spock said. "And I will now if need be. But I too am Vulcan, bred to peace. Let us attempt it."

"You saw how treacherously they acted," Kirk said.

"Yes, Captain," Surak said. "But perhaps it is our belief in peace which is actually being tested."

"Wellll . . . I have no authority over you. Do as you think best."

"Thank you. May you live long and prosper." Surak gave the Vulcan sign and went off. Kirk watched him depart, doubtful, but also with some awe. Then he shook the mood off.

"The weapons, gentlemen—in case he fails."

Time went past. The three fashioned crude spears, bolos, slings, boomerangs, and gathered rocks for throwing. Spock was visibly on edge; he kept looking after the vanished Surak.

"A brave man," Kirk said.

"Men of peace usually are, sir. On Vulcan he is revered as the Father of Civilization. The father-image has much meaning for us."

"You show emotion, Mr. Spock," Kirk said, and then was instantly sorry he had said it; this was surely no time for needling. But Spock replied only:

"I deeply respect what he accomplished."

"Let's hope he accomplishes something here."

As if on cue, the air was rent by a harrowing scream of agony.

"Surak!" Spock cried.

"Yes," Kirk said grimly. "I would guess that they're torturing him."

"Mr. Spock!" Colonel Green's voice called, from no very great distance off. "Your friend wants you. He seems to be hurt."

"Help me, Spock!" Surak's voice called, raw with pain.

"You can't let him suffer," Green said.

"Sir," Spock said, his face like stone. "They are trying to goad us into attacking rashly."

"I know that."

"And he was aware that this might happen when he went—" Spock was interrupted by another scream.

"I should not have let him go," Kirk said.

"You had no choice, Captain—" Another scream. It cut Kirk like a knife, but Spock went on through it. "You could not have stopped him."

"How can you ignore it?"

"I suspect it, sir. A Vulcan would not cry out so."

"So his suffering doesn't matter?"

"I am not insensitive to it, sir, nor am I ignoring it."

"I don't care whether he is Vulcan or not. He is in agony."

"The fact that he might not be Vulcan does not blind me to the fact."

The cry came again. "But you can listen to that and chop logic about it?" Kirk said. "Well, I can't!"

Kirk strode off toward the antagonists' camp. Spock was after him in one bound, grasping his arm.

"Captain, that is what they want of us. They are waiting for us to attempt a rescue."

"Perhaps we can rescue him, Mr. Spock," Lincoln said. "I suggest that we do exactly what they want."

"Do what they want?"

"Not the way they want it, however. We must first convince them that they have provoked us to recklessness. James? You seem taken aback. I do not mean to presume upon your authority—"

"It isn't that."

"What I propose to do is that I circle around to their rear while you two provide a frontal distraction. It should be sufficiently violent to cover what I do."

"Which is—?"

"Slip into their camp and free him."

"No," Kirk said.

"I was something of a backwoodsman, James. I doubt that you could do what I was bred to."

"I won't have you risk it."

"I am no longer President," Lincoln said, with a slight smile. "Mr. Spock, any comment?"

"No, sir."

"Then," Lincoln said, "one matter further, gentlemen. We fight on their level. With trickery, brutality, finality. We match their evil . . . You forget, James. I know I am reputed a gentle man. Kindly, I believe the word is. But I was Commander in Chief during the four bloodiest years of my country's history. I gave orders that sent a hundred thousand men to death by the hands of their brothers. There is no honorable way to kill, no gentle way to destroy. There is nothing good in war—except its ending. And you are fighting for the lives of your crew."

"Mr. President," Kirk said, "your campaign."

The scream came again. It was markedly weaker.

Khan and Green were on watch as Kirk and Spock worked their way among the boulders to the enemy camp. Kirk made no particular effort at concealment, "accidentally" showing himself several times. By the time they were in range, Zora and Kahless had appeared, weapons at the ready.

Kirk and Spock rose as one, threw spears, and ducked again. One of the spears narrowly missed Khan, who with a wild yell retaliated with a boulder that came equally close.

When Kirk looked again, Green was gone, and a moment later, so were Kahless and Zora. Then Green came back. What did that maneuver mean? But Kirk was left no time to see more; Green threw a spear at him with murderous accuracy, and he was forced to duck again.

Lincoln, creeping up at the rear, almost tripped a mantrap made of a tied-down sapling. Backing off, he deliberately tripped it, and then resumed crawling.

Ahead he could see Surak, bound to a tree, head slumped. No one else seemed to be around.

"Surak!" he called in a low voice. "I will have you

free in a minute." Racing forward, he began to cut the thongs binding the Vulcan. "The others have drawn them away. We will circle around. It was a worthy effort, Surak. No need to blame yourself for its failure."

The thongs parted. As Lincoln put out a hand to help Surak, the Vulcan collapsed at his feet. He was dead.

"Help me, Lincoln!"

Lincoln spun. The voice had been Surak's, but it was coming from Kahless. He and Green were standing in the direction from which Lincoln had just come, grinning, spears ready.

It was only afterward that Kirk was able to sort the battle out. Their four antagonists had charged them, leaping with spears raised. Hit by a rock, Kirk stumbled and fell, and Zora was upon him at once; but whatever expertise she may have had in body chemistry, she was no fighter. Kirk rolled and threw her aside, hard. She was hurt and lay watching him in terror.

Nearby, Spock and Khan were fighting hand to hand. They seemed to be evenly matched, but Kirk had no chance to help—Kahless was upon him. The struggle was a violent, kaleidoscopic, head-banging eternity. When it stopped, very suddenly, it took Kirk several seconds to realize that he had killed the Klingon. Snatching up a spear, he ran at Khan, who broke free of Spock and fled, looking wildly behind him. Green was running now, too. Kirk snatched up a spear and threw it. He did not miss.

Then it was all over. Inside the enemy camp, they found the bodies of Lincoln and of Surak. They looked down with rage and grief. Neither could find anything to say.

Then, once more, the bell-like chiming sounded, and the seated, stony figure of Yarnek emerged from its cocoon of rainbows.

"You are the survivors," the echoing voice said. "The others have run off. It would appear that evil retreats when forcibly confronted. However, you have failed to demonstrate to me any other difference between your philosophies. Your good and your evil use the same methods, achieve the same results. Do you have an explanation?"

"You established the methods and the goals," Kirk said.

"For you to use as you chose."

"What did you offer them if they won?"

"What they wanted most—power."

"You offered me the lives of my crew."

"I perceive," Yarnak said. "You have won their lives."

Kirk boiled over. "How many others have you done this to? What gives you the right to hand out life and death?"

"The same right that brought you here: the need to know new things."

"We came in peace—"

"And you may go in peace." Yarnak faded from view.

Kirk took out his communicator. "Kirk to *Enterprise* . . . Mr. Sulu, beam us aboard."

On the bridge everything seemed to be functioning normally, as though nothing had ever gone wrong.

"Mr. Spock," Kirk said. "Explanation?"

"Conjecture, sir, rather than explanation."

"Well?"

"It would seem that we were held in the power of creatures able to control matter, to rearrange molecules in whatever fashion they desired. So Yarnak was able to create the images of Surak and Lincoln and the others, after scanning our minds, by making use of its fellow creatures as source matter."

"They seemed so real, Spock. To me, especially, Mr. Lincoln. I feel I actually met Lincoln."

Spock nodded. "And Surak. In a sense, perhaps they were, Captain. Created out of our own thoughts, how could they be anything but what we expected them to be?"

"It was so hard to see him die once again. I begin to understand what Earth endured to achieve final peace." Kirk paused. "Mr. Spock . . . is there a memorial to Surak on Vulcan?"

"Yes, sir. A monument of great beauty. However, it is held generally that the true memorial to him is the peace and the friendship that have endured among Vulcans since his time with them."

"The same with Lincoln. I think of all our heroes on Earth, he is the most loved today. We see his dreams around us. We have the brotherhood and equality of men that he hoped for, and we're still learning what he knew instinctively.''

"Men of such stature live beyond their years.''

"They were alive today, Spock. Those were more than rearranged molecules we saw.''

"We projected into them our own concepts of them, sir.''

"Did we?'' After a moment, Kirk shook his head. "There is still much of their work to be done in the galaxy, Spock . . . Mr. Sulu, break orbit for our next assignment.''

ALL OUR YESTERDAYS

Writer: Jean Lisette Aroeste
Director: Marvin Chomsky
Guest stars: Mariette Hartley, Ian Wolfe

The star Beta Niobe, the computer reported, was going to go nova in approximately three and a half hours from now. Its only satellite, Sarpeidon, was a Class M world which at last report had been inhabited by a humanoid species, civilized, but incapable of space flight. Nevertheless, the sensors of the *Enterprise* showed that no intelligent life remained on the planet.

But they did show that a large power generator was still functioning down there. That meant, possibly, that there were still some few survivors after all, in which case they had to be located and taken off before the planet was destroyed.

Homing the Transporter on the power signal, Kirk, Spock and McCoy materialized in the center of a fairly large room, subdivided by shelving and storage cabinets into several areas. One alcove contained a consultation desk, with shelves of books behind it. Another held several elaborate machines which were obviously in operation, humming and spinning and blinking. Kirk stared at these with bafflement, and then turned to Spock, who scanned them with his tricorder and raised his hands in a slight gesture.

"The power pulse source, obviously," the First Officer said. "But what it all *does* is another question."

Along one side was a less puzzling installation: an audiovisual facility containing several carrels (individual study desks) with headsets, projectors and small screens. The nearby wall was pierced by a door and a window. A tape storage area at the end of the room had been caged in, but its door stood ajar.

"May I help you?"

The three officers spun around. Facing them was a dignified, almost imposing man of early middle age. "I am the librarian," he added cordially.

Spock said, "Perhaps you can, Mr . . . ?"

"Mr. Atoz. I confess that I am a little surprised to see you; I had thought that everyone had long since gone. But the surprise is a pleasant one. After all, a library serves no purpose unless someone is using it."

"You say that everyone has gone," Kirk said. "Where?"

"It depended upon the individual, of course. If you wish to trace a specific person, I'm sorry, but that information is confidential."

"No, no particular person," McCoy said. "Just—in general—where did they go?"

"Ah, you find it difficult to choose, is that it? Yes, a wide range of alternatives is a mixed blessing, but perhaps I can help. Would you come this way, please?" With a little bow, Atoz invited them to precede him to the audiovisual area. Apparently, Kirk thought, Atoz thought the three officers were natives, and that they wanted to go where the others had gone. Well, what better way to find out?

It was impossible not to be surprised, however, when Atoz, whom he would have sworn had been behind them, emerged smiling from the tape storage cage.

"How the devil did he get over there?" McCoy said in a penetrating stage whisper.

"Each viewing station in this facility is independently operated," Atoz said, as if that explained everything. "You may select from more than twenty thousand Verisim tapes, several hundred of which have only recently been added to the collection. I'm sure that you will find something here that pleases you." He turned toward Kirk. "You, sir, what is your particular field of interest?"

"How about recent history?" Kirk suggested.

"Really? That is too bad. We have so little on recent history; there was no demand for it."

"It doesn't have to be extensive," Kirk said. "Just the answers to a few questions."

"Ah, of course. In that case, Reference Service is available in the second alcove to your right."

It was not quite so surprising, this time, to find the incredible Mr. Atoz already waiting for them at the reference desk. But there was something else: Kirk had the instant impression that Atoz had somehow never seen them before; a guess which was promptly confirmed by the man's first words.

"You're very late," he said angrily. "Where have you been?"

"We came as soon as we knew what was happening."

"It is my fault, sir," Spock said. "I must have miscalculated. Remember, the ship's sensors indicated there was no one here at all."

"In a very few hours, you would have been absolutely correct," Atoz said. "You three would have perished—vaporized. You arrived just in time."

"Then you know what's going to happen?" McCoy queried.

"You idiot! Of course I know. Everyone was warned of the coming nova long ago. They followed instructions and are now safe. And you had better do the same."

"Did you say they were *safe*?" asked Kirk.

"Absolutely," Atoz said with pride. "Every single one."

"Safe where? Where did they go?"

"Wherever they wanted to go, of course. It is strictly up to the individual's choice."

"And did you alone send all the people of this planet to safety?"

"Yes," Atoz said. "I am proud to say I did. Of course, I had to delegate the simple tasks to my replicas; but the responsibility was mine alone."

"I believe we've met two of them," Kirk said, a little grimly. "You're the real thing, I take it."

"Of course."

McCoy was already scanning Atoz with his tricorder. "As a matter of fact, he is quite real, Jim. And that may explain the report of the ship's sensors; just one remaining man is a difficult object for detection. Sir, you are aware that you will die if you remain here?''

"Of course, but I plan to join my wife and family when the time comes. Do not be concerned about me. Think of yourselves."

Kirk sighed. The man was single-minded almost to the point of mania. But then, that was just the kind of man who'd be given a job like this. Or the kind of man such a job would soon make him. "All right," he said resignedly. "How? What shall we do?"

"The history of the planet is available in every detail," Atoz said, rising and leading them toward the tape carrels. "Just choose what interests you the most—the century, the date, the moment. But, remember, you are very late."

Kirk and McCoy donned headsets, and Atoz selected tapes from the shelves, inserting one in each viewer.

"Thank you, sir," Kirk said. "We will be as quick as we can." He offered a headset to Spock, but the First Officer shook his head and walked off toward the big machine that had mystified him earlier, and which Atoz now appeared to be activating. At the same time, Kirk's screen lighted and he found himself looking at an empty street—it was little more than an alley—which on Earth he would have guessed to be seventeenth-century English. A quick glance to his left revealed that McCoy's screen showed something even less interesting: an Arctic waste. Atoz certainly had peculiar ideas of . . .

A woman screamed, piercingly.

Kirk jumped to his feet, tearing off the headset. The scream came again—not from the headset, obviously, but from the entrance to the observatory-library.

"Help! They're murdering me!"

"Spock! Bones!" Kirk shouted, charging for the door. "Over here, quick!"

Behind him, Atoz' voice cried out: "Stop! I have not prepared you! Wait, you must be . . ."

As Kirk shot out the door, the voice was cut off as if someone had thrown a switch . . .

. . . and he skidded to a halt in the alley he had seen on the screen!

There was no time for puzzlement. The alley was chill

and misty, but real enough and the screams came from around the next corner, followed this time by a man's voice.

"Be sweet, love, and I might have a mind to be generous."

Kirk rounded the corner cautiously. A young man wearing velvet, lace and a sword was struggling with a woman dressed like a gypsy. She seemed to be giving him little trouble; though she was kicking and scratching, his handling was as much amorous as it was brutal. A second, even more foppish young man was lounging against the nearby wall, watching with amusement. Then the woman managed to bite the first one on the hand.

"Ow! Vixen!" He aimed a savage cuff at her cheek. The blow never fell; Kirk's hand closed around his upraised arm.

"Let her go," Kirk said.

The woman wiggled free, and the fop's face hardened. "Come when you are bidden, slave," he said, and aimed a roundhouse blow at Kirk's head. Kirk checked the swing and followed through, and a moment later his opponent was sprawling in the dirt.

The second fop shoved the woman aside and moved threateningly toward Kirk, his hand hovering over his rapier hilt. "You need a lesson in how to use your betters," he said. "Who's your master, fellow?"

"I am a freeman."

This seemed to put the fop almost into good humor again. He smiled nastily and drew his rapier.

"Freedom dresses you in poor livery, like a mountebank—and you want better manners, too, freeman." The rapier point slashed Kirk's sleeve.

"The other's behind you, friend!" the woman's voice called, but too late; Kirk was seized from behind. He elbowed his captor in the midriff and, when he broke away, he had the man's sword in his left hand. These creatures really seemed to know nothing at all about unarmed combat, but it would be as well to put an end to this right now. He drew his phaser and fired point-blank.

It didn't go off.

Dropping it, Kirk shifted sword hands, and closed on the second fop. He was only fair as a swordsman, too; his

lunges were clumsy enough to allow Kirk plenty of freedom
to keep the weaponless first fop on the ropes with left-handed
karate chops. The swordsman's eyes bulged when his companion went down for the third time and began to back away.

"Sladykins! He's a devil! I'll have no more of this."

He disengaged and ran, his friend not far behind. Kirk
picked up and holstered the ineffective phaser and turned to
the woman, who was patting her hair and checking her clothes
for damage. The clothes were none too clean, and neither
was she, although she was pretty enough.

"Thankee, man," she said. "I thought to be limbered
sure when the gull caught me drawing his boung."

"I don't follow you. Are you all right?"

The woman looked him over calculatingly. "Ah, I took
you for an angler, but you're none of us. Well, you're a bully
fine cope for all that. What a handsome dish you served them,
the coxcombs!"

She seemed to be becoming more incomprehensible by
the minute. "I'm afraid you may be hurt," Kirk said. "You'd
better come back into the library with me. You'll be safe
there, and Dr. McCoy can see to those bruises."

"I'm game, luv. Lead and I'll follow. Where's library?"

"Just back there . . ."

But when they got to the alley wall, it was blank. The
door through which Kirk had come had vanished.

He prowled back and forth, then turned to the woman,
who said, puzzled, "What's wi' you, man? Let's make off
before coxcombs come wi' shoulder-clappers."

"Do you happen to remember when you first saw me?
Do you remember whether I came through some kind of
door?"

"I think that rum gull knocked you in the head. Come,
luv. I know a leech who'll ask no questions."

"Wait. It must be here somewhere. Bones! Spock!"

"Here, Captain," the First Officer's voice said at once,
to the woman's obvious alarm. "We hear you, but we cannot
see you. Are you all right?"

"We followed you," McCoy's voice added, "but you'd
disappeared."

"We must have missed each other in the fog."

"Fog, Captain?" Spock's voice said. "We have encountered no fog."

"Mercy on us," said the woman. "It's a spirit!"

"No, don't be frightened," Kirk said hastily. "These are friends of mine. They're—on the other side of the wall. Spock! Are you still in the library?"

"Indeed not," Spock's voice said. "We are in a wilderment of arctic characteristics . . ."

"He means that it's cold," McCoy's voice broke in drily.

"Approximately minus twenty-five centigrade. There is no library that we can see. We are at the foot of an ice cliff, and apparently we came *through* the cliff, since there is no visible aperture."

"There's no sign of a door here either," Kirk said. "Only the wall. It's foggy here, and I can smell the ocean."

"Yes. That is the period you were looking at in the viewer. Dr. McCoy, on the other hand, was watching a tape of Sarpeidon's last ice age—and here he is, and I with him because we left the library at the same instant."

"Which explains the disappearance of the inhabitants," Kirk concluded. "We certainly underestimated Mr. Atoz."

The woman, clearly terrified by the disembodied voices, was edging away from him. Well, that wasn't important now.

"Yes," Spock was saying. "Apparently they have all escaped from the destruction of their world by retreating into the past."

"Well, we know how we got here. Can we get back? The portal's invisible, but we can still hear each other. There must be a portion of this wall that only *looks* solid . . ."

He was interrupted by still another scream from the woman, with whom he was beginning to feel definitely annoyed. He turned to find that her attempt to run out of the alley had been blocked by the two fops, who had returned with a pair of obvious constables.

"My friends are back—a couple of, uh, coxcombs I had a run-in with a little earlier. And they've brought reinforcements."

"Keep looking, Jim," McCoy's voice urged. "You *must* be close to the portal. We're looking too."

"There's the mort's accomplice," one of the fops said, pointing at Kirk. "Arrest him."

"We are the law," one of the constables told Kirk, "and do require that you yield to us."

"On what charge?"

"Thievery and purse-cutting."

"Nonsense. I'm no thief."

"Jim," McCoy's voice said. "What's happening?"

"Lord help us, what's that?" exclaimed the other constable.

"It's spirits!" the woman cried.

The second constable crossed his sword and dagger and held them before him gingerly. He looked frightened, but he resumed advancing. "Depart, spirits, and let honest men approach."

Kirk seized his advantage. "Keep talking, Bones," he said, edging away.

"They speak at *his* bidding," one of the fops said excitedly. "Stop his mouth and they'll quiet!"

"You must be close to the portal now," Spock's voice said.

"Just keep talk . . ."

But the other constable had crept around to the other side. A heavy blow exploded against Kirk's head, and that was the end of that.

The landscape was barren, consisting entirely of ice and rocks, over which the wind howled mercilessly. The ruined buildings surrounding the library had vanished, and so had the library itself. There was nothing but the ice cliff and, on the other side, the rocky glacial plain stretching endlessly into the distance.

Spock continued to feel carefully along the cliff, trying not to maintain contact for more than a few seconds each time. Beside him, McCoy shivered and blew on his hands, then chafed his ears and face.

"Jim's gone!" the surgeon said. "Why can't we hear him?"

"I am afraid that Mr. Atoz may have closed the portal; I doubt that I shall find it now, in any event. We had best move along."

"Jim sounded as if he might be in trouble."

"He doubtless was in trouble, but so are we. We must find shelter, or we will very quickly perish in this cold."

McCoy stumbled. Spock caught him and helped him to a seat on a large bolder, noting that his chin, nose and ears had become whitened and bloodless. The First Officer knew well enough what that meant. He also knew, geologically, where they were; in a terminal moraine, the rock-tumble pushed ahead of itself by an advancing glacier. The chances of finding shelter here were nil. It seemed a curious sort of refuge for a time-traveling people to pick, with so many milder environments available at will.

"Spock," McCoy said. "Leave me here."

"We go together or not at all."

"Don't be a fool. My face and hands are getting frostbitten. I can hardly feel my feet. Alone, you'll have a chance—at least to try to get back to Jim!"

"We stay together," Spock said.

"Stubborn, thickheaded . . ."

His voice faded. Spock looked about grimly. To his astonishment, he saw that they were being watched.

In the near distance was a cryptic figure clad in fur coveralls and a parka, its face concealed by a snow mask out of which two eyes stared intently. After a moment the figure beckoned, unmistakably.

Spock turned to McCoy, to find that he had fallen. He shook the medical officer, but there was no response. Spock put his ear to McCoy's chest; yes, heart still beating, but feebly.

A shadow fell across them both. The figure was standing over them; and again it gestured, *Follow me*.

"My companion is ill."

Follow me.

Logic dictated no better course. Slinging McCoy over his shoulder, Spock stood. The weight was not intolerable, though it threw him out of balance. The figure moved off among the rocks. Spock followed.

The way eventually took them underground, as Spock had already deduced that it would; where else, after all, could there be shelter in this wilderness? There were two rooms—caves, really—and one was a sleeping room, fairly small,

windowless of necessity, furnished most simply. Near the
door was a rude bed on which Spock placed McCoy.

"Blankets," Spock said.

The figure pointed, then helped him cover the sick man.
Spock looked through McCoy's medical pouch, found his
tricorder, and began checking. The figure sat at the foot of
the bed, watching Spock, still silent, utterly enigmatic.

"He cannot stand your weather. Unfortunately, he is
the physician, not I. I'll not risk giving him medication at
this point. If he is kept quiet and warm, he may recover
naturally." He scrutinized the mysterious watcher. "It is quite
agreeably warm in here. Have you a reason for continuing to
wear that mask? Is there a taboo that prohibits my seeing
your face?"

From behind the mask there came a musical feminine
laugh, and then a feminine voice. "I had forgotten I still had
these things on."

She took off the mask and parka, but her laughter died
as she inspected Spock more closely. "Who are you?"

"I am called Spock."

"Even your name is strange. Forgive me—you are so
unlike anyone I have ever seen."

"That is not surprising. Please do not be alarmed."

"Why are you here?" the woman asked hesitantly.
"Are you prisoners too?"

"Prisoners?"

"This is one of the places—or rather, times—Zor Khan
sends people when he wishes them to disappear. Didn't you
come back through the time-portal?"

"Yes, but not as prisoners. We were sent here by mistake; or such is my hypothesis."

She considered this. "The Atavachron is far away,"
she said at last, "but I think you come from somewhere farther than that."

"That is true," Spock said. He looked at her more
closely. This face out of the past, eager yet reposeful, without
trace of artifice, was—could it be what Earthmen called
touching? "Yes—I am not from the world you know at all.
My home is a planet many light-years away."

"How wonderful! I've always loved the books about
such possibilities." Her expression, though, darkened sud-

denly. "But they're only stories. This isn't real. I'm imagining all this. I'm going mad. I always thought I would."

As she shrank from him, Spock reached out and took her hand. "I am firmly convinced that I do in fact exist. I am substantial. You are not imagining this."

"I've been alone here for so long, longer than I want to remember," she said, with a weak smile. She was beginning to relax again. "When I saw you out there, I couldn't believe it."

Spock was beginning to feel something very like compassion for her, which was so unusual that it confused him—which was more unusual still. He turned back to McCoy and checked the unconscious man with the tricorder; this added alarm to the complex.

"I was wrong not to give him the coradrenaline," he said, taking the hypo out of the medical pouch and using it.

"What's happening? Is he dying? I have a few medicines . . ."

"Contra-indicated. Your physiology may be radically different. But I may have given him too much. Well, it's done now."

The woman watched him. "You seem so very calm," she said, "but I sense that he is someone close to you."

"We have gotten used to each other over the years. Aha . . ."

McCoy groaned, stirred and his breathing harshened, as though he were fighting for air. Spock leaned over him.

"Dr. Leonard McCoy, wake up," he said formally but urgently. Then, *"Bones!"*

McCoy's breathing quieted gradually and Spock stepped back. The surgeon's eyes opened, and slowly came to focus on the woman.

"Who are you?" he asked fuzzily.

"My name is Zarabeth."

Somehow, Spock had never thought to ask that.

"Where's Spock?"

"I'm here, Doctor."

"Are we back in the library?"

"We are still in the ice age," Spock said. "But safe, for the moment."

McCoy tried to sit up, though it was obvious that he was still groggy. "Jim! Where's Jim? We've got to find Jim!"

"You are in no condition to get up. Rest now, and I will attempt to find the Captain."

McCoy allowed Spock to settle him back in bed. "Find him, Spock. Don't worry about me. Find him!"

He closed his eyes, and after a moment, Spock nodded silently toward the door. Zarabeth led the way back into the underground living room, then asked, "Who is this Jim?"

"Our Commanding Officer. Our friend."

"I saw only two of you. I did not know that there was another."

"There—is not. He did not come with us. The time-portal sent him to another historical period, much later than this one. If I am to find him, there is only one avenue. Will you show me where the time-portal is?"

"But your friend—in the other room," Zarabeth said. "He is ill."

"It is true that if I leave him, there is the danger that he may never regain the ship." Spock thought it over. It proved to be peculiarly difficult. "He would then be marooned in this time-period. But he is no longer in danger of death, so my primary duty to him has been discharged . . . If I remain here, no one of our party can aid Captain Kirk . . ."

"You make it sound like an equation."

"It should be an equation," Spock said, frowning. "I should be able to resolve the problem logically. My impulse is to try to find the Captain, and yet—" he found that he was pacing, although it didn't seem to help much. "I have already made one error of judgment that nearly cost McCoy's life. I must not make another now. Perhaps it has to do with the Atavachron. If I knew more about how it works . . . Zarabeth, you say that you are a prisoner here. May I ask . . ."

". . . why? My crime was in choosing my kinsmen unwisely. Two of them were involved in a conspiracy to kill Zor Khan. It wasn't enough to execute my kinsmen. Zor Khan determined to destroy our entire family. He used the Atavachron to send us to places where no one could ever find us."

"Ah. Then the solution is simple. Zor Khan exists no

more. You and I can carry McCoy back to the library. I'll
send you and McCoy to the ship, and have Mr. Atoz send
me to wherever Jim . . .''

"No!" Zarabeth cried, in obvious terror. "I can't go
back through the portal now! I will be dead!"

"You cannot go back?"

"None of us can go back," she said, a little more
calmly. "When we come through the portal, we are changed
by the Atavachron. That is its function. Our basic metabolic
structure is adjusted to the time we enter. You can't go back;
if you pass through the portal again, you will be dead when
you reach the other side."

And there it was. He and McCoy were trapped here,
for the rest of their lives. And so was Jim, wherever *he* was.

When Kirk came to, he found himself all too obviously
in jail, and a pretty primitive jail at that, lying on a rough
pallet which squeaked of straw. Fingering his head and winc-
ing, he got up and went to the barred door. There was nothing to be seen but a gloomy corridor and the cell opposite
his. The gypsy was in it.

She seemed to be about to speak to him, but at that
moment there were voices in the near distance and, instead,
she shrank into a far corner of her cell. In another moment
the constable hove into view, leading a man whose demeanor
was all too obviously that of a public prosecutor.

"That's the man," the constable said, pointing to Kirk.
"That's the mort's henchman."

He let the prosecutor into the cell. The man regarded
Kirk curiously. "You are the thief who talks to spirits?"

"Your honor. I am a stranger here."

"Where are you from?"

Kirk hesitated. "An island."

"What is this island?"

"We call it Earth."

"I know of no island Earth. No matter. Continue."

"I'd never seen the lady across the way before tonight
when I heard her scream. As far as I could tell, she was being
attacked."

"Then you deny that you're the wench's accomplice?"

"Yes. I was reading in the library when I heard her

scream." The prosecutor started visibly at the word "library," and Kirk pursued the advantage, whatever it might be. "Perhaps you remember where the library is?"

"Well, well, perhaps your part in this is innocent," the prosecutor said, with some agitation. "I believe you to be an honest man."

"He's a witch!" screamed the woman from her cell.

"Now, wait a minute . . ."

"Take care, woman," the prosecutor said heavily. "I am convinced you're guilty. Do not compound it with false accusation."

"He speaks to unclean spirits! He's a witch. Constable, you heard the voices!"

"It's truth, my lord," the constable said. "I heard the spirit call him. He answered and did call it 'Bones.' "

"He's a witch," the woman insisted. "He cast a spell and made me steal against my wish."

Aghast, Kirk looked into each face in turn. There was no doubt about it; they believed in witches, all of them. The prosecutor, looking even graver than before, asked the constable, with some reluctance, "You heard these—spirits?"

"Aye, my lord. I'll witness to it."

"The 'voices' they heard were only friends of mine," Kirk said desperately. "They were still on the other side of the wall, in the library, my lord."

"I know nothing of this," the prosecutor said agitatedly. "*I* cannot judge so grave a matter. Let someone learned in witchcraft examine him. I will have no more to do with this."

"Look, sir. Couldn't you at least arrange for me to see Mr. Atoz? You do remember Mr. Atoz, don't you?"

"I know of no Atoz. I know nothing of this, nothing of these matters. Take him. I will not hear him."

The constable let the prosecutor out, and together they hurried down the corridor.

Kirk called after them, "Only let me speak to you, my lord!"

They vanished without looking back. Kirk shook the bars, frustrated, angry, hopelessly aware that he was alone and friendless here. Across the corridor, the woman's face was contorted with fear and hatred.

"Witch! Witch!" she shrilled. "They'll burn you!"

They took her away later the next day. Kirk scarcely noticed. He was trying to work out a course of action. He had never seen a jail that looked easier to break, but all attempts to think beyond that point were impeded by a growing headache; and when he got up from the pallet to make sure his hands would fit freely through the bars, he had a sudden spell of faintness. Had he caught some kind of bug?

Down the corridor there was a jingling of keys. The jailer was coming with food. It was now or never.

He was sitting on the pallet again when the jailer arrived; but when the jailer straightened from setting down the bowl of food, Kirk's arm was around his throat, his other hand lifting the ring of keys from his belt. Opening the door from the outside, Kirk pulled the terrified man into the cell and shut the door again.

Releasing his grip, Kirk allowed the jailer a single cry, then knocked him out with a quick chop and rolled him under the pallet. End of Standard Escape Maneuver One. With any luck, that cry should bring the constable, and safe-conduct. Curious how dizzy he felt. On an impulse, he lay down and closed his eyes.

He heard hurrying feet, then the creak of the hinges as the newcomer tried the door. The subsequent muffled exclamation told him that he had been luckier than he knew; the man outside was the prosecutor. Kirk emitted a muffled groan.

Shuffling noises, and then the sound of breathing told him that the prosecutor was bending over him. A quick glance through half-closed lids told them where the nearest wrist was. He grabbed it.

"If you yell, I'll kill you," he whispered with fierce intensity.

The prosecutor neither yelled nor struggled. He merely said, "It will go harder with you if you persist."

"I am being falsely accused. You know it."

"You are to come with me to the Inquisitional Tribunal. There the matter of your witchcraft will be decided."

"There are no such things as witches."

"I shan't say you said so," the prosecutor said. "That is heresy. If they hear you, they will burn you for such beliefs."

"You are the only one who can hear me. Before the Inquisitor, it will be different. I'll denounce you as a man who came from the future, just as I did. Therefore, you too are a witch."

"They would surely burn me as well," the prosecutor agreed. "But what good would that do you?"

"Use your head, man," Kirk said. "I need your help."

"How can I help you? I will do my utmost to plead your innocence. I may be able to get you off—providing you say nothing of the comrades you left behind."

"Not good enough. I want you to help me to return to the library."

"You cannot go back."

"I tell you, I must. My comrades are lost in another time-period. I have to find them. Why don't you go back too?"

"We can never go back," the prosecutor said. "We must live out our lives here in the past. The Atavachron has prepared our cell structure and brain pattern to make life here natural. To return to the future would mean instant death."

"Prepared?" Kirk said. "I am here by accident. Your Mr. Atoz did not prepare me in any way." As he spoke, his temples began to throb again.

"Then you must get back at once. If you were not transformed, you cannot survive more than a few days here."

"Then you'll show me where the portal is?"

"Yes—approximately. But you must find the exact spot yourself. You understand I dare not wait with you. . . ."

"Of course. Let's go."

Five minutes later, Kirk was back in the library. It looked as empty as it had when he had first seen it. He checked the contemporary time with the *Enterprise*, shunting aside a barrage of frantic questions. It was seventeen minutes to nova. Evidently, no matter how much time he spent in the past, the gate at its present setting would always return him to this day. It had to; for the gate, there would be no tomorrow.

He drew his phaser. It had not worked in the past, but he was quite certain it would work here. And this time, Mr. Atoz, he thought grimly, you are going to be *helpful*.

* * *

McCoy was still abed, but he was feeling distinctly better, as his appetite proved. Zarabeth, who had adopted a flowing gown which made her look positively beautiful, was out in her work area, making something she had promised would be a delicacy.

"I hope the *Enterprise* got away in time," McCoy said.

"I hope it will get away. The event is a hundred thousand years in the future."

"Yes, I know. I wonder where Jim is?"

"Who knows?" Spock said. "We can only hope he is well, wherever he is."

"What do you mean, we can only hope? Haven't you done anything about it?"

"What was there to do?"

"Locate the portal," McCoy said impatiently. "We certainly didn't come very far from it."

"We've been through all that already, Doctor. What's the point of rehashing the subject? We can't get back. Wasn't that clear to you?"

"Perfectly. I just don't believe it. I refuse to give up trying."

"It would be suicide if you succeeded."

McCoy sighed. "I never thought I'd see it. But I understand. You want to stay here. I might say, you are highly motivated to remain in this forsaken waste."

And not ten minutes ago, Spock thought, it had been McCoy who had been praising Zarabeth's cooking, and offering other small gallantries. "The prospect seemed quite attractive to you a few moments ago."

"Listen to me," McCoy said, "you point-eared Vulcan . . ."

Before Spock fully realized what he was doing, he found himself leaning forward and lifting McCoy off the bed.

"I don't like that," he said. "I don't believe I ever did. Now I'm sure."

McCoy did not look in the least alarmed. He simply seemed to be studying Spock intently. "What is it, Spock?" he asked. "What's happening?"

Spock let him drop. "Nothing that shouldn't have happened long ago."

"Long ago," McCoy said softly. The intent scrutiny did not waver. "Yes, I guess so . . . Long ago."

The stare disturbed the First Officer, for reasons he did not understand. Wheeling, he went into the underground living room, where Zarabeth was setting a table. She looked up and smiled.

"Ready soon. Would you like a sample?"

"Thank you, but I am not hungry."

She came over and sat down near him. "I can imagine how you must feel. I know what it's like to be sent here against your will."

"My feelings, as you call them, are of no concern," Spock said. "I have accepted the situation."

"I cannot pretend that I am sorry you are here, though I realize that it is a misfortune for you. I am here against my will, too, just as you are."

"I'm sorry I know of no way to return you to your own time."

"I don't mean that I wish to return," Zarabeth said. "This is my time now. I've had to face that. But it has been lonely here. Do you know what it is like to be alone, really alone?"

"Yes, I know what it is like."

"I believe you do. Won't you eat something? Please?"

"If it pleases you." He walked to the table and surveyed it. He felt a faint shock, but it seemed far away. "This is animal flesh."

"There isn't much else to eat here, I'm afraid."

"Naturally, because of the climate. What is the source of heat in this shelter?"

"There is an underground hot spring that furnishes natural steam heat and power."

"And there is sunlight available outside. Excellent. It should be possible to build a greenhouse of sorts. Until then, this will have to do as a source of nourishment." He picked up the most innocuous-looking morsel, surveyed it with distaste, and bit into it. It was quite good; he took another.

"There aren't many luxuries here," Zarabeth said, watching him with evident approval. "Zor Khan left me only what was necessary to survive."

"But he evidently intended you to continue living," Spock said, sampling another dish.

"Yes. He gave me weapons, a shelter, food—everything I needed to live—except companionship. He did not want it said that he had had me killed. But to send me here alone— if that is not death, what is? A very inventive mind, that man."

"But insensitive, to send such a beautiful woman into exile." Instantly, he was badly startled. "Forgive me! I am not usually given to personal remarks."

"How could I possibly take offense?" Zarabeth said.

Spock scarcely heard her. "The cold must have affected me more than I realized. Please—pay no attention. I am not myself."

And that, he thought, was an understatement. He was behaving disgracefully. He had eaten animal flesh—and had enjoyed it! What was wrong with him? He put his hands to his temples.

"I say you are beautiful," he said, feeling a dawning wonder. "But you *are* beautiful. Is it so wrong to tell you so?"

Zarabeth came to him. "I have longed to hear you say it," she said softly.

Then she was in his arms. When the kiss ended, he felt as though a man who had always been locked up inside him had been set free.

"You are beautiful," he said, "beautiful beyond any dream of beauty I have ever had. I shall never stop telling you of it."

"Stay," she whispered. "I shall make you happy."

"My life is here."

"*You lie*," said a voice from the doorway. Spock spun, furious with McCoy and enjoying it.

"I speak the present truth," he said. "We are here, for good. I have given you the facts."

"The facts as *you* know them. But you are also being dishonest with yourself, and that's also something new for you. You accepted Zarabeth's word because it was what you wanted to believe. But Zarabeth is a woman condemned to a terrible life of loneliness. She will do anything to anybody to change that, won't you, Zarabeth?"

"I told you what I know," Zarabeth said.

"Not quite, I believe. You said *we* can't get back. The truth is that *you* can't get back. Isn't it?"

"She would not jeopardize other lives . . . ."

"To save herself from this life alone," McCoy said, "she would lie—and even murder me, the Captain, the whole crew of the *Enterprise*, to keep you here with her." His hand lashed out and caught her by the wrist. "Tell Spock the truth—you would kill to keep him here!"

Zarabeth cried out in terror, and in the next instant Spock found his hands closing around the physician's throat. McCoy did not resist.

"Spock!" he said intensely. "Think! Are you trying to kill me? Is that what you want? What are you feeling? Rage? Jealousy? Have you ever felt them before?"

Spock's hands dropped. His head was whirling. "Impossible," he said. "This is impossible. I am a Vulcan."

"The Vulcan you knew will not exist for another hundred thousand years! Think, Spock—what is it like on your planet now, at this moment?"

"My ancestors are barbarians. Irrational, warlike barbarians . . . ."

"Who nearly killed themselves off with their passions! And now you are regressing to what they were!"

"I have lost myself," Spock said dully. "I do not know who I am. Zarabeth—can we go back?"

"I do not know. I do not know. It is impossible for me to go back. I thought it was true for you."

"I am going to try, Spock," McCoy said. "My life is there, and I want the life that belongs to me. I must go *now*. There isn't much time—I too am changing. Zarabeth, will you help me find my way to the portal?"

"I—Yes. If I must."

"Let's get dressed, then."

The cold seemed more intense than ever, and McCoy, wrapped in a blanket, still had little resistance to it. He leaned against the ice cliff, partially supported by Zarabeth, who once more was almost anonymous in her furs. Spock tapped the cliff, without success.

"There is no portal here," he said. "It's hopeless, Mc-Coy."

"I suppose you're right."

"You're too ill to stay out here in the cold any longer. Give it up."

And then, faintly, they heard Kirk's voice. "Spock! Can you hear me?"

"It's Jim!" McCoy shouted. "Here we are!"

"Stop, we've found them," Kirk's voice said. "Hold it steady, Atoz. Can you hear me any better?"

"Yes," Spock said. "We hear you perfectly now."

"Follow my voice."

McCoy reached out. His hand disappeared into the cliff. "Here it is! Come on, Spock!"

"Start ahead." He turned to Zarabeth. "I do not wish to part from you."

"I can't come with you. You know that."

"What are you waiting for?" Kirk's voice said. "Hurry! Scott says we've got to get back on board right now!"

"They will have to come through together," the voice of Atoz added, "as they went out together. Singly, the portal will reject them."

Spock and Zarabeth looked at each other with despair. He touched her face with his fingertips.

"I did lie," she said. "I knew the truth. I will pay. Good-bye."

Then they were in the library, Kirk pulling them through. Atoz was spinning the dials of the Atavachron frantically, and then, dashing past them, dived into the portal and vanished.

"Atoz!" McCoy called.

"He had his escape planned," Kirk said. "I'm glad he made it." He raised his communicator. "Are you there, Scotty?"

"Aye. It's now or never."

Spock turned toward the portal and raised his fist as if to strike it, but he did not complete the gesture.

"Beam us up. Maximum warp as soon as we are on board."

The library shimmered out of existence, and they were

standing in the Transporter Room of the *Enterprise*. McCoy, still wrapped in his blanket, was once more regarding Spock with his intent clinical stare.

"There is no further need for you to observe me, Doctor," Spock said. "As you see, I have returned to the present. In every sense."

"Are you sure? It did happen, Spock."

"Yes, it happened," the First Officer said. "But that was a hundred thousand years ago. They are all dead. Dead and buried long ago."

The ship fled outward. Behind it, the nova began to erupt, in all its terrifying, inhuman glory.

≡

TURNABOUT INTRUDER

Writer: Arthur H. Singer
 (Story by Gene Roddenberry)
Director: Herb Wallerstein
Guest stars: Sandra Smith, Harry Landers

The *Enterprise* had been proceeding to a carefully timed rendezvous when she received a distress call from a group of archaeologists who had been exploring the ruins on Camus Two. Their situation was apparently desperate, and Kirk interrupted the mission to beam down to their assistance, together with Spock and McCoy.

In the group's headquarters they found two of the survivors, one of whom Kirk knew: Dr. Janice Lester, the leader of the expedition. She was lying on a cot, semi-conscious. Her companion, Dr. Howard Coleman, looked healthy enough but rather insecure.

"What's wrong with her?" Kirk asked.

"Radiation sickness," said Coleman.

"I'd like to put the ship's complete medical facilities to work to save her. Can we get her aboard the *Enterprise*?"

"Exposing her to the shock of Transportation would be very dangerous. The radiation affects the nervous system."

McCoy looked up from his examination of the woman. "I can find no detectable signs of conventional radiation injury, Dr. Coleman," he said.

"Dr. Lester was farthest from the source. Fortunately for me, I was here at headquarters."

"Then the symptoms may not have completely developed."

"What happened to those who were closest to the point of exposure?" Kirk asked.

"They became delirious from the multiplying internal lesions and ran off mad with pain. They are probably dead."

"What form of radiation was it?" McCoy asked.

"Nothing I have ever encountered."

Janice Lester stirred and moaned, and her eyes fluttered open. Kirk came to her side and took her hand, smiling.

"You are to be absolutely quiet. Those are the doctor's orders, Janice, not mine."

Spock had been scanning with his tricorder. "Captain, I am picking up very faint life readings seven hundred meters from here. Help will have to be immediate."

Kirk turned to McCoy, who said, "There is nothing more to be done for her, Captain. Your presence should help quiet her."

As McCoy and Spock went out, Janice released Kirk's hand, and she said with great effort, "I hoped I would never see you again."

"I don't blame you."

Her eyes closed. "Why don't you kill me? It would be easy for you now. No one would know."

"I never wanted to hurt you," Kirk said, startled.

"You did."

"Only so I could survive as myself."

"I died. When you left me, I died."

"You still exaggerate," Kirk said, trying for the light touch. "I have heard reports of your work."

"Digging in the ruins of dead civilizations."

"You lead in your field."

She opened her eyes and stared directly into his. "The year we were together at Starfleet is the only time in my life I was alive."

"I didn't stop you from going on with space work."

"I had to! Where would it lead? Your world of Starship captains doesn't admit women."

"You've always blamed me for that," Kirk said.

"You accepted it."

"I couldn't have changed it," he pointed out.

"You believed they were right. I know you did."

"And you hated me for it. How you hated. Every minute we were together became an agony."

"It isn't fair . . ."

"No, it isn't. And I was the one you punished and tortured because of it."

"I loved you," she said. "We could have roamed among the stars."

"We would have killed each other."

"It might have been better."

"Why do you say that?" he demanded. "You're still young."

"A woman should not be alone."

"Don't you see now, we shouldn't be together? We never should have—I'm sorry. Forgive me. You must be quiet now."

"Yes." Her eyes closed and her head sank back on the cot.

"Janice—please let me help you this time."

In a deadly quiet voice, she said, "You are helping me, James."

He looked at her sadly for a moment and then turned away. The rest of the room, he noticed for the first time, was a litter of objects the group had collected from the ruins. The largest piece seemed to be an inscribed slab of metal, big enough to have been part of a wall. Kirk crossed to it. On its sides, he now saw, were what seemed to be control elements; some kind of machine, then. He wondered what sort of people had used it, and for what.

"A very remarkable object," Janice's voice said behind him.

"Really? What is it for, do you know?"

"Mentally superior people who were dying would exchange bodies with the physically strong. Immortality could be had by those who deserved it."

"And who chose the deserving?"

"In this case," she said, "I do."

The wall flared brilliantly in Kirk's face, and he felt a fearful internal wrench, as though something were trying to turn him inside out. When he could see again . . .

. . . he was looking at himself, through the eyes of Janice Lester.

* * *

Kirk/J left the wall, and coming over to the cot, found a scarf, which he began to fold. Then he bent and pressed it over the woman's mouth and nose.

"You had your chance, Captain Kirk. You could have smothered the life in me and they would have said Dr. Janice Lester died of radiation sickness acquired in the line of duty. Why didn't you? You've always wanted to!"

Janice/K's head moved feebly in denial. The scarf pressed down harder.

"You had the strength to carry it out. But you were afraid, always afraid. Now Janice Lester will take Captain Kirk's place. I already possess your physical strength. But *this* Captain Kirk is not afraid to kill." Kirk/J was almost crooning now, a song of self-hatred. "Now you know the indignity of being a woman. But you will not suffer long. For you the agony will soon pass—as it did for me."

The woman's hand tried to pull his away.

"Quiet. Believe me, it is better to be dead than to live alone in the body of a woman."

The struggling ceased, but Kirk/J did not release his hand until he heard footsteps outside. Then he replaced the scarf and went back to examining the wall. The search party entered only a moment later, looking grim.

"Your report, Dr. McCoy."

"We were too late. There was no way to help them."

"Was it radiation as reported?"

McCoy nodded. "I believe it was celebium. Dr. Coleman does not agree. It's essential to be specific."

"Why? Radioactivity is radioactivity, whatever the source."

"Yes, but in this case there was chemical poisoning involved as well. All the heavy elements are chemically virulent."

"Evidently," Spock added, "the field team broke through a newly exposed crust to a hidden cache of the radioactive element, whatever it was. The damage was instantaneous. They could not get away."

"That," Kirk/J said angrily, "will reflect on Dr. Lester's reputation for thorough preparedness."

"I don't think Dr. Lester can be blamed," McCoy said. "It was a most unfortunate accident, Captain."

"It was careless field work. Dr. Lester will be held responsible—unfair as it may be."

Dr. Coleman looked somewhat fearfully at Kirk/J and went quickly to Janice, bending to examine her. "Dr. Mc-Coy!"

McCoy was there in an instant, tricorder out. "Jim, did you notice any unusual symptoms while we were gone?"

"Nothing at all. She has remained unconscious all the time."

"Dr. Lester is near death," Coleman said.

"Perhaps the shock of knowing what happened to her staff is part of the problem."

"I'm sure it is."

"Beaming her up to the *Enterprise*," McCoy said, "would be less harmful than waiting."

Kirk/J looked questioningly at Coleman, who now seemed frightened. "I don't know," the man said.

"Then we'll go."

At Kirk/J's orders, two medical aides were ready with a stretcher when the party materialized in the Transporter Room. Coleman accompanied the patient to sickbay.

"Mr. Spock, take the ship out of orbit and resume designated course. Dr. McCoy, a word with you, please. You and Dr. Coleman disagree in your diagnosis. Please try to come to an agreement as fast as possible. The matter is especially disturbing—for personal reasons."

"I didn't realize you knew her so well," McCoy said.

"It has been a long time since I saw her. I walked out when it became serious."

"You must have been very young at the time."

"Youth doesn't excuse everything. It's a very unhappy memory."

"Everything possible will be done, Jim."

"Good. Thank you—Bones."

Kirk/J went to the bridge. Uhura, Chekov and Scott were all at their posts, as was Sulu. Spock was intent over his console. Kirk/J looked searchingly at the new faces, and Uhura and Sulu smiled back.

He came slowly to the Captain's position and touched the chair lightly, testing its maneuverability, almost as if with

awe. Then he sat down in it and looked up at the viewing
screen.

"Course, Mr. Chekov?"

"One twenty-seven, Mark eight."

"Mr. Sulu, set speed at Warp Factor Two."

"Warp Factor Two, sir."

"Mr. Spock, would you come here a moment, please?
Thank you. We have a problem with our patient. The two
doctors disagree on their diagnosis."

"That is hardly unusual in the medical fraternity, sir."

"Too bad it doesn't help cure their patients," Kirk/J
said with an edgy smile.

"I think you can rely on Dr. McCoy's advice."

The edginess grew. "Do you have any specific evidence that confirms his opinion?"

"Not precisely, Captain. It is not my function."

"Then don't add to the confusion, Mr. Spock." Kirk/J
arose and strode angrily to the elevator.

In sickbay, he found that Janice/K was regaining consciousness. Moments of quiet were interspersed with sudden
flailing movements, which were restrained by straps, and
moaning. A very frightened Dr. Coleman was pacing beside
her.

"How long has this been going on?" Kirk/J asked.

"It just began."

"You must put a stop to it. If you let Dr. Lester become
fully conscious, she will know what has happened."

"Probably no one will believe it," Coleman said.

"Probably?"

"That's all we can hope for. How could death be explained now?"

Kirk/J went to the head of the cot, Coleman following
on the other side. "I tell you, it can't continue!"

"You killed every one of the staff. You sent them where
you knew the celebium shielding was weak. Why didn't you
kill *him*? You had the perfect opportunity."

"You didn't give me enough time."

"You had every minute you asked for."

"He hung onto life too hard. I couldn't . . ."

"You couldn't because you love him," Coleman said,

his voice beginning to rise. "You want *me* to be his murderer."

"Love *him*?" Kirk/J said, his voice also rising. "I loved the life he led—the power of the Starship Commander. It's my life now."

"I won't become a murderer." Coleman turned and walked quickly toward the door. Kirk/J leaped to block his way.

"You *are* a murderer. You knew it was celebium. You could have treated them for that. You are a murderer many times."

The moaning grew louder. The doors to the medical lab opened and McCoy and Nurse Chapel came to the cot.

"I thought I could quiet Dr. Lester by my presence," Kirk/J said smoothly. "It seems to have had the opposite effect."

"It has nothing to do with you," Coleman said, with ill-concealed agitation. "It's a symptom of the developing radiation sickness."

"Tests with the ship's equipment," McCoy said, "show no sign of internal radiation damage."

"Dr. Coleman," Kirk/J said, "didn't Dr. Lester's staff become delirious before they went off to die?"

"Yes, Captain."

"But, Jim," said McCoy, "Dr. Lester could as easily be suffering from a phaser stun from all the symptoms I detect."

"Dr. Lester and her staff have been under my supervision for two years now," Coleman said stiffly. "If you do not accept my recommendations, responsibility for her health—or her death—will be yours."

Kirk/J looked toward the bed. Janice/K's movements were growing stronger. Then they stopped as her eyes opened; she looked about as if struggling to see and recognize the faces.

"Dr. McCoy," Kirk/J said, "I'm sorry, but I shall have to remove you from the case and turn it over to Dr. Coleman."

"You can't do that! On this ship, my medical authority is final."

"Dr. Coleman wishes to assume full responsibility. Let him do so."

"I will not allow it."

"It has been done." Kirk/J turned to Coleman. "Dr. Lester is your patient. I believe you were about to administer a sedative when I came in."

"No!" the woman cried. "No sedative!" But the job was done.

Starting with the considerable advantage of her year in Starfleet with Kirk, Janice Lester had spent more years studying every single detail of a starship's operation—a knowledge which was now to be put to the test. With a little experience, she could probably become invulnerable to suspicion. But the presence aboard of the personality of James Kirk, even under sedation, was a constant threat to her position. It would be better to leave Janice/K among strangers, who would probably consider her insane.

"Plot a course for the Benecia Colony, Mr. Chekov. How long would it take to reach the colony at present speed?"

"Forty-eight hours, Captain."

"Captain," Spock said, "it will delay our work at Beta Aurigae. It means reversing course."

"It can't be helped. We must take Dr. Lester where she can be treated."

"May I point out, Captain, that Starbase Two is on the direct route to our destination?"

"How long to Starbase Two, Mr. Chekov?" Kirk/J asked.

"Seventy-two hours, sir."

"That's twenty-four hours too long. Dr. Lester's condition is increasingly serious. Continue present course."

"Captain, if the diagnosis of Dr. Lester's illness is the critical problem, the Benecia Colony is definitely not the place for her," Spock said. "Its medical facilities are the most primitive."

"They will have to serve the purpose."

"Starbase Two is fully equipped and staffed with the necessary specialists to determine exactly what is wrong with the Doctor. Isn't that crucial to your decision, Captain?"

"Thank you, Mr. Spock. But the facilities will be of

no use if Dr. Lester is dead. Time is of the essence. Continue on course, Mr. Sulu.''

"Captain," Uhura said, "shall I advise Starfleet Command of the change of plans?"

"No *change* of plan has been ordered, Lieutenant. Our arrival at Beta Aurigae will be *delayed*. Our gravitational studies of that binary system will not suffer, and we may save a life. That is not unusual procedure for the *Enterprise*." Kirk/J arose and went toward the elevator.

"I believe," Spock said, "Starfleet will have to know that our rendezvous with the Starship *Potemkin* will not be kept as scheduled."

"Mr. Spock—if you would concentrate on the areas for which you are responsible, Starfleet would have been informed already."

"Sir, the Captain deals directly with Starfleet on these matters. I assumed that action on my part would be deemed interference."

"Advise Starfleet of the delay, Lieutenant Uhura. Mr. Sulu, maintain course. Increase speed to Warp Six."

Kirk/J escaped from the bridge to the Captain's quarters, but there was no respite there; McCoy was waiting for him.

"Dr. McCoy, are we about to have another fruitless argument about diagnosis?"

McCoy's fist slammed on the top of Kirk's desk. "No, dammit—sir. I'll let my record speak for me."

"Why are you so defensive? There was no implied criticism of you in my order to remove you from the case."

"That's not why I'm here. I'm here because Dr. Coleman's record says he is incompetent."

"That's the opinion of an individual."

"No, sir. It's the considered opinion of Starfleet Command. I checked with them. Dr. Coleman was removed from his post as Chief Medical Officer of his ship for administrative incompetence . . ."

"Administrative duties are not required of him here."

"As well as for flagrant medical blunders."

"Promotions and demotions are sometimes politically motivated," Kirk/J said. "You know that, Doc."

"Not in Starfleet headquarters, *Captain*. At least, not in the Surgeon General's office."

Kirk/J paced for a moment. "I'm afraid the order will have to stand. Dr. Coleman's experience with what happened on the planet had to be the deciding factor. I'm sure you appreciate that."

"I appreciate that you had to make a decision. I, too, have that responsibility, Jim. So I'm asking you to report for a complete checkup."

"Why? What do you base it on?"

"Developing emotional instability and erratic behaviour since returning from the planet."

"You'll never make that charge stick!" Kirk/J said furiously. "Any fool can see why you're doing this!"

"Starfleet Command will be the judge of my motive."

"I won't submit to this petty search for revenge."

"You will submit to Starfleet regulations," McCoy said. "They state that the ship's surgeon will require a full examination of any member of the crew about whom he has doubts—including the Captain. I am ordering you to report for that examination . . ."

He was interrupted by the intercom buzzer.

"Captain Kirk here."

"Lieutenant Uhura, sir. Starfleet Command is requesting additional details of the delay. Shall I handle it?"

"I'll be right there."

The examination could not be postponed indefinitely, however. Knowledge of the Captain's aberrant behaviour was spreading throughout the ship; the crew was becoming increasingly tense. To McCoy's apparent surprise, however, Kirk/J satisfied every test completely.

This stroke of luck was followed by another. Struggling out from under sedation in Dr. Coleman's absence, Janice/K had avoided another injection by persuading Nurse Chapel of her docility—and then had sawed through her restraining straps with a broken medicine glass. Running wildly through the ship holding the glass like a weapon, calling for help and denouncing the Captain as a strutting pretender, she presented the perfect picture of a dangerous madwoman—giving Kirk/J all the pretext he needed to have her put in isolation in a detention cell, with around-the-clock security.

In this, however, he underestimated Spock, of whose sharp observation and penetrating logic the bogus Captain had had only the briefest of experience. The Science Officer knew the limitations of his discipline; he knew, in particular, that the essence of a man's being, his selfhood, was inherently impossible of access to any objective medical test— McCoy himself had often made just this point. Janice/K's denunciation planted a seed in his own mind.

Something had happened to the Captain while he was on the planet. Whatever it was could have taken place only in the short time while he was alone with Dr. Lester. A talk with her might be the only way to shed light on it.

There were two strapping guards outside her detention cell. Spock said to the first, ''How is Dr. Lester?''

''Conscious and quiet, Mr. Spock.''

''Good. I have a few questions to ask her.''

''Did the Captain order it, sir?''

''Why should he?'' Spock said. ''They are my questions. Therefore I am ordering it, Ensign.''

''But the Captain said no one was to speak to Dr. Lester.''

''Has such an order ever included his senior officers?''

''Well, no, sir.'' The ensign activated the door and Spock started in. ''But, Mr. Spock, I believe the Captain meant a guard was to be present.''

''By all means.''

Janice/K's first words on seeing them were ''Thank God! Spock, you've got to listen to me.''

''That is why I came,'' Spock said. ''Apparently something happened while you and the Captain were alone. What was it?''

''She changed bodies with me, with the aid of an ancient machine she'd unearthed. Spock, *I am Captain Kirk*. I know how unbelievable it sounds. But that's how it happened.''

''It is a possibility I had not considered.''

''Unless I can convince you, I have no hope at all of ever getting out of this body.''

''Complete life-entity transfer with the aid of a mechanical device?''

"Yes. Dr. Lester's description of its function is the last moment I remember as myself."

"To my knowledge," Spock said, "such total transfer has never been accomplished with complete success anywhere in the Galaxy."

"It was accomplished and forgotten long ago on Camus II. I am a living example."

"That is your claim. As yet, it is unsubstantiated."

"I know, Spock. Nevertheless I'm speaking the truth. Listen—when I was caught in the interspace of the Tholian sector, you risked your life and even the *Enterprise* to get me back. Help me get back now. And, when the Vians of Minara demanded that we let McCoy die, we didn't permit it. How would I know those things if I were not James Kirk?"

"Such incidents may have been recorded. They could have become known to you."

"You are closer to the Captain than anyone in the universe. You know his thoughts. What does your telepathic sense tell you?"

Spock touched her face and closed his eyes, his own face a study in concentration as he established a mind meld. Then he withdrew his hand and looked at her with new determination.

"I believe you," he said. "My belief is not acceptable evidence. But I will make every effort to make it so. Only Dr. McCoy can help us. Come with me."

"I'm sorry, sir," the guard said. "But Dr. Lester can *not* leave here. You're asking me to violate the Captain's order."

"He is not the Captain."

"Sir, you must be as mad as she is. You're to leave here at once. I follow orders."

"Certainly, Ensign," Spock said. "We must all do our duty."

While he was still talking, he lashed out. The scuffle was brief, but the guard outside the cell was alert—he could be heard calling, "Security to Captain Kirk! The detention cell has been broken into!"

When they emerged, the guard was standing with his back to the opposite wall, phaser leveled. Kirk/J and two more guards were already coming down the corridor, followed by McCoy.

Spock stopped. "Violence is not called for, sir," he said. "No *physical* resistance will be offered."

Kirk/J hit the intercom button. "Security detail to Detention at once. Attention all personnel. First Officer Spock is being placed under arrest on a charge of mutiny. He has conspired with Dr. Lester to take over the ship from your Captain. A hearing will be immediately convened to consider the charges and specifications for a general court-martial." He turned to McCoy. "The board will consist of Scott, you and myself."

"I will not be made party to a court-martial of Spock," McCoy said. "There are better ways to handle it."

"You are not forced to condemn anyone. You are asked—no, you are ordered—to vote your honest convictions. Two out of three carries the final verdict. Convene the board. Guard, return Dr. Lester to isolation. She will be held for sanity tests."

The hearing was held in the briefing room. Kirk/J sat at the head of the table, gavel in hand; McCoy sat quietly to one side. Uhura was making a tape of the proceedings, and Chekov, Sulu and Nurse Chapel were listening intently as Scott began cross-examining Spock.

"Mr. Spock, you are a scientist—a leading scientist of the Galaxy."

"That's very pleasant to hear, Mr. Scott. But it is an exaggeration. I have long since sacrificed basic theoretical investigation for the more immediate excitement of life on the *Enterprise*."

"I meant, your approach to every problem is completely scientific."

"I hope so," Spock said.

"Therefore your statement that you believe this fantastic tale about transference of life entities between the Captain and Dr. Lester is intended to be taken seriously by this court."

"Completely seriously."

"Yet you have no evidence on which to base it."

"I have stated my evidence: telepathic communication with the mind of Captain James T. Kirk."

"You are a reasonable man, Spock," Scott said, exasperated. "But that is not a reasonable statement. Far from it. Far from it. Surely you must have had more than that to go on."

"It was sufficient for me."

"Well, it's not sufficient for a court. Your evidence is completely subjective. You know that, laddie. What has happened to you? We must have evidence we can examine out in the open."

Spock threw a challenging look toward Kirk/J. "You have heard a great deal of testimony—except that of the chief witness. The one who should be the real subject of this inquiry is kept locked away in isolation. Why, *Captain*?"

"She is dangerous insane," Kirk/J said. "We have seen evidence of that."

"She is dangerous only to your authority, *sir*."

"Mr. Spock, my authority was granted to me by Starfleet Command. Only that high authority can take it away."

"Then why be afraid of the testimony of a poor insane woman?"

"This clumsy effort does not threaten my position, Mr. Spock. It does endanger your whole future."

"The witness, sir! Bring on the witness! Let your officers put the questions!"

Kirk/J hesitated a moment. Then he banged his gavel and nodded to a guard, who went out.

"Dr. McCoy."

"Yes, Captain."

"You were at one time disturbed by my orders and reactions, is that not true?"

"Yes, sir."

"But instead of trying to destroy me, you were searching for a way to help me. For the record, tell the court your findings."

"Physically the Captain is in the best of condition. His emotional and mental states are comparable to the time he assumed command of the *Enterprise*."

"Mr. Spock, did you know the results of Dr. McCoy's examination?"

"I know them now," Spock said.

"And what have you to say now?"

"I am disappointed and deeply concerned that there is no objective evidence to support my position—so far."

"Since there is no evidence, will you give up your belief in the insane story of a woman driven mad by a tragic experience?"

Before Spock could reply, the door opened and the woman in question herself was brought in by two guards. Kirk/J pointed to a chair, and she sat down.

"Dr. Lester," he said, "I appreciate your being here. Everyone is deeply aware that you have already been subjected to inordinate emotional stress. Unfortunately, I have had to add to it in the interest of the safety of this crew. I had hoped that any further stress could be avoided. Mr. Spock disagrees. He is of the opinion that your testimony is important in determining the merits of his case. Since we are solely interested in arriving at a just decision, we must ask you a few questions. We shall all try not to upset you." At this, she nodded. "Now. You claim you are James T. Kirk."

"No, I am not Captain Kirk," Janice/K said composedly. "That is very apparent. I doubt that Mr. Spock would have put it that way. I claim that whatever it is that makes James Kirk a living being special to himself is held here in this body."

"I stand corrected. However—as I understand it—I am Dr. Janice Lester."

There was a snicker from the guards.

"That's very clever," she responded. "But I didn't say it. I said the body of James Kirk is being used by Dr. Janice Lester."

"A subtle difference that happens to escape me," Kirk/J said with a smile. "However, I assume that this—this switch was brought about by mutual agreement."

"No. It was brought about by a violent attack by Dr. Lester, with the use of equipment she discovered on Camus II."

"Violence by the lady perpetrated on Captain Kirk? Tsk, tsk. I ask the assembled personnel to look at Dr. Lester and visualize that historic moment."

This time the laughter was general. Kirk/J waited until

it had ridden itself out, then continued, "And do you know any reason why Dr. Janice Lester would want this ludicrous exchange?"

"Yes! To achieve a power her peers would not accord her. To attain a position she does not merit by training or temperament. And most of all she wanted to murder the man who might have loved her—had her intense hatred of her own womanhood not made life with her impossible."

Spock rose angrily. "Sir, this line of questioning is self-serving. There is only one issue: Is the story of life-entity transfer believable? This crew has been to many places in the Galaxy. *You have not.* They are familiar with many strange events. They are trained to recognize that what seems completely unbelievable on the surface is scientifically possible if you understand the basic theory of the event."

"Mr. Spock, do you know of any other case like the one Dr. Lester describes?"

"Not precisely. No."

"Assuming you are correct in your belief, do you expect Starfleet Command to place that person"—his finger stabbed at Janice/K—"in command of this ship?"

"I expect only to reveal the truth."

"Of course you do. And with the truth revealed that I am not really the Captain—and knowing that she will not be appointed Captain—then of course *you* will become the Captain." Kirk/J looked at Spock with apparent compassion. "Give it up, Spock. Return to the *Enterprise* family. All charges will be dropped. The madness that temporarily overcame us all on Camus II will pass and be forgotten."

"And what will happen to Dr. Lester?"

"Dr. Lester will be properly cared for. Always. That is a debt and a responsibility I owe her from the past."

"No, sir!" Spock said emphatically. "I will not withdraw a single charge I have made. You are not Captain Kirk. You have ruthlessly appropriated his body. But the life entity within you is not that of Captain Kirk. You do not belong in command of the *Enterprise*. I will do everything in my power against you."

"Lieutenant Uhura," Kirk/J said with dangerous quietness, "play back the last two sentences of Mr. Spock's tirade."

Spock's voice rang out from the speaker of the recorder: "You do not belong in command of the *Enterprise*. I will do everything in my power against you."

"Mr. Spock, you have heard the statement you put into the record. Do you understand the nature of it?"

"I do. And I stand by it."

"And that is mutiny!" Kirk/J shouted, his face livid. "Deliberate—vindictive—insane at its base—but it is mutiny as charged and incitement to mutiny. Dr. McCoy, Mr. Scott, you have heard it. On the basis of these statements, I call for an immediate summary court-martial by powers granted to me as Captain of the *Enterprise*."

"Just a moment, Captain," Scott said. "I'm not ready to vote Mr. Spock into oblivion so fast. Mr. Spock is a serious man. What he says is to be taken seriously, no matter how wild."

"Come to the point."

"I'm right at the nub of it, Captain. You don't put a man like Mr. Spock out of the service because of a condition akin to temporary insanity. Dr. McCoy, you said the woman may have become mentally deranged due to the radiation she was exposed to."

"Yes, Scotty."

"Couldn't the same thing have happened to Mr. Spock? He was a sight closer to the source of the radiation."

"It's possible."

"Then the mutiny is qualified by the temporary insanity due to the . . . ."

"Thank you, my friend," Spock interrupted. "A noble try. But I was not exposed to the celebium. I took every precaution. And I have been given precautionary treatment since then by Dr. McCoy. I am completely sound in body and mind."

"Mutiny," said Kirk/J, pounding with the gavel. "A summary court-martial on the evidence and the charges is immediately invoked. A recess will be followed by a vote."

"Yes," Spock said. "An immediate vote. This matter must be cleared up at once, before . . . ."

The gavel pounded a loud tatoo. "Silence!"

"Before our chief witness," Spock shouted above the

din, "is left to die on an obscure little colony with the truth locked away inside her!"

Kirk/J rose, his face red with hysteria, almost to the point of apoplexy. "Silence, silence! A recess is declared. The summary court will then be in session. There will be no cross-discussion. No conferences. No collusion. I order the judges to be absolutely silent as they arrive at a decision on the charge of mutiny. When I return we will vote. The evidence presented here can be the only basis for your decision."

He stormed out of the room, leaving everyone stunned. McCoy began to pace. The silence stretched out. At last Scott said, "Who ever heard of a jury being forbidden to deliberate?"

He went out into the corridor, followed by the others, leaving behind Janice/K, Spock and the guards, as well as Uhura.

"What's there to say?" McCoy said.

"Doctor, I've seen the Captain feverish, sick, drunk, delirious, terrified, overjoyed, boiling mad. Until now I've never seen him beet-red with hysteria. I know how I'm going to vote."

"I've been through this with Spock. He is not being scientific. And neither are you."

"It may not be scientific," Scott said, "but if Spock thinks it happened, it must be logical."

"Don't you think I know that? My tests show nothing wrong with the Captain. That's the only fact that will interest Starfleet."

"Headquarters has its problems—and we've got ours. Right now the Captain of the *Enterprise* is our problem."

McCoy frowned. He started to pace again, but was halted by Nurse Chapel.

"Doctor," she said, whispering, "I didn't notice it at the time. But in her first lucid moment, Dr. Lester asked why we were going to miss our rendezvous with the *Potemkin*. How could she know that?"

"Hmm. Especially since the Captain *didn't*. Scotty, the vote is going to be called in a few minutes."

"Let me put one last question. Suppose you voted with

me in favor of Spock. That's two to one and Spock is free.
What do you think the Captain will do?''

"I don't know."

"You know, all right. The vote will stick in his craw.
He'll never accept it.''

McCoy angrily walked away a few steps and then turned
back and looked hard at Scott. "We don't know that."

"I tell you, he won't. Then, Doctor, that's the time to
move against him. We'll have to take over the ship.''

"We're talking mutiny, Scotty.''

"Yes. Are you ready for the vote?''

"I'm ready for the vote.''

Kirk/J was already back in the briefing room when they
reentered. When they were all seated, he stood up. "Lieutenant Uhura, play back the tapes of the conversation in the
corridor.''

Uhura, looking both grief-stricken and guilt-ridden,
moved a switch. Recorded voices said:

"Then, Doctor, that's the time to move against him.
We'll have to take over the ship.''

"We're talking mutiny, Scotty.''

"Yes. Are you ready for the vote?''

"That's enough," McCoy said angrily. "We know what
was said.''

"Enough to convict you for conspiracy with mutineers," Kirk/J said, drawing his phaser. The guards followed
suit. "You are so charged. The penalty is death.''

Chekov and Sulu both jumped forward, talking almost
at once.

"Starfleet expressly forbids the death penalty . . .''

"There is only one exception . . .''

"General Order Four has not been violated by any officer of the *Enterprise* . . .''

"All my senior officers have turned against me," Kirk/J
said. "I am responsible. Execution will be immediate. Go to
your posts. Guards, take them to the brig.''

Only Uhura, Sulu and Chekov were at their posts on
the bridge, a sadly depleted corporal's guard. They were
working, but their expressions were listless, abstracted. Sulu

said at last, "The Captain really must be cracking up if he thinks he can get away with an execution."

"Captain Kirk wouldn't order an execution even if he did crack up," Chekov said. "Spock's right, that can't be the Captain."

"What difference does it make who he is?" said Uhura. "Are we going to allow an execution to take place?"

Chekov clenched his fists. "If Security backs him up, how will we fight them?"

Sulu said, "I'll fight them every way and any way I can . . ."

The conversation was choked off as Kirk/J came onto the bridge, highly elated. When he spoke, the sentences seemed almost to tumble over one another in their haste to get out. "Lieutenant Uhura, inform all sections of the decision. Have each section send a representative to the place of execution on the hangar deck. Mr. Chekov, how far to the Benecia Colony?"

"Coming within scanning range."

"Plot coordinates for orbit. Mr. Sulu, lock into coordinates as soon as orbit is accomplished. Interment will take place on Benecia."

There were no "Ayes," and nobody moved. Kirk/J stared at his officers. "You have received your orders."

Still no response.

"You have received your orders. You will obey at once or be charged with mutiny." His voice began to rise in pitch, losing its male timbre. "Obey my orders or—or . . ."

Then, suddenly, he reeled, staggered, and fell into his chair, seemingly almost in a faint. His body contorted for a moment and then became rigid, his eyes staring wider, but sightlessly.

The others rose in alarm, but the seizure lasted only a moment. Then Kirk/J was out of the chair and leaped for the elevator.

Dr. Coleman was alone in the medical lab when Kirk/J burst in. "Coleman—the transference is weakening."

"What happened?"

"For a moment I was with the prisoners. I won't go back to being Janice Lester. Help me prevent it."

"The only way to prevent it is by the death of Janice Lester. You'll have to carry out the execution."

"I can't," Kirk/J said. "The crew is in mutiny. You must kill him for me."

"I have done everything else for you. But I tell you I will not commit murder for you."

"You can do it for yourself," Kirk/J said urgently. "If I am the Captain of the *Enterprise*, you will regain your position as a Ship's Surgeon. I will see to that."

"I would have been content with you, as you were. I did not need a starship."

"Unless Kirk dies, we will both be exposed as murderers. Does that leave you any choice?"

Reluctantly, Coleman picked up an air hypo, selected a cartridge and snapped it into place.

"The dose must be doubly lethal."

"It is," Coleman said impassively.

Kirk/J led the way to the brig. Judging by the woman's tense expression and the way the others were grouped around her, she too had felt that moment of transitory retransference, and was ready to fight to prolong it should it occur again.

"I have demanded the sentence of execution," Kirk/J said. "However, to prevent any further conspiracy, you will be placed in separate cells. If there is any resistance, a sedative will be administered until you learn cooperation. Dr. Lester is first. Follow Dr. Coleman."

Coleman went back out through the force field. Janice/K held back suspiciously, but then also stepped out into the corridor, Kirk/J behind her. After only a few steps he said loudly, "This woman obviously doesn't know what it means to obey an order."

The hypo flashed in Coleman's hand, but not quickly enough. Janice/K saw it and grabbed that arm with both hands, struggling with all her poor strength to deflect it.

Again the look of dizziness and complete terror overwhelmed Kirk/J; once more his body contorted and grew taut.

The same paralysis gripped Janice/K, its rigidity immobilizing Coleman's arm as her conscious efforts could never have done. Then she screamed.

"Don't! Don't! I have lost to the Captain! I have lost

to James Kirk!'' And then, in a cry of pure madness, ''Kill him! Kill *him*!''

Kirk, whose first move had been to shut off the brig's force field, met Coleman's rush easily; a quick chop and it was over. He turned to Janice, whose face was contorted with hatred and agony. ''Kill him! I want James Kirk dead! Kill him!'' Then, sobbing painfully like a child, ''I will never be the Captain—never—never—kill him . . .''

Coleman, who had been only momentarily stunned, tossed aside the hypo, clambered to his feet and came over to her. She began to collapse, and Coleman took her in his arms.

''You are,'' he said, ''as I have loved you.''

''Kill him,'' Janice said quietly, her eyes vacant. ''Please.''

Spock, McCoy and Scott were all out in the corridor. Kirk seized each of them in turn by the hand. ''Bones, is there anything you can do for her?''

''I would like to take care of her,'' Coleman said pleadingly.

''Of course,'' said McCoy. ''Come with me.'' He led them away toward sickbay.

Kirk looked after them. ''I didn't want to destroy her,'' he said.

''You had to,'' Spock said. ''How else could you have survived, Captain? To say nothing of the rest of us.''

''Her life could have been as rich as any woman's, if only—'' He paused and sighed. ''If only . . .''

''If only,'' Spock said, ''she had ever been able to take any pride in *being* a woman.''

STAR TREK: CLASSIC EPISODES
Adapted by James Blish

SPACE: THE FINAL FRONTIER
THESE ARE THE VOYAGES OF THE *STARSHIP ENTERPRISE*

Explore the final frontier with science fiction's most well-known and beloved captain, crew, and starship, with tales of high adventure. Here are James Blish's classic adaptations of *Star Trek*'s dazzling scripts, available in three volumes – and out now in Bantam paperback.

Star Trek: Classic Episodes Vol. 1 – 0553 29138 6
Star Trek: Classic Episodes Vol. 2 – 0553 29139 4
Star Trek: Classic Episodes Vol. 3 – 0553 29140 8

Enter the magical worlds of *New York Times*
bestselling authors

MARGARET WEIS and TRACY HICKMAN

THE DARKSWORD TRILOGY
Forging the Darksword
Doom of the Darksword
Triumph of the Darksword

ROSE OF THE PROPHET
The Will of the Wanderer
The Paladin of the Night
The Prophet of Akhran

THE DEATH GATE CYCLE
Dragon Wing
Elven Star
Fire Sea

and by Margaret Weis

STAR OF THE GUARDIANS
The Lost King
King's Test
King's Sacrifice

All available in Bantam Paperback

ÆSTIVAL TIDE
by Elizabeth Hand

Four centuries after the Third Shining, the Orsinas rule
absolute in the domed city-state of Araboth. A fortress built at
the ocean's edge, Araboth protects its citizens from the
presumed horrors of Outside. But now, the predictions of
Araboth's collapse seem near fulfilment. As the Prince of
Storms gathers Outside, amidst a giddy atmosphere of decadent
ritual inside, four inhabitants of Araboth will come together in
one last hope for survival. Prisoner and privileged alike, this
small group will face the opening gates to welcome the raging
Æstival Tide.

In a stunning feat of the imagination, Elizabeth Hand Takes us
once again into a world shaken by forces of devastating evil,
sustained by a fragile ray of hope. Breathtaking in its invention,
mesmerizing in the telling, *Æstival Tide* is the intoxicating
sequel to the highly praised *Winterlong*.

'Hand paints some of the most sensuous prose images in a long
time . . . there are those who would kill to have such an
abundance of talent' *Locus*

A Bantam Paperback
0553 40317 6

WINTERLONG
by Elizabeth Hand

In the dark years after the rain of roses, two innocents seek
each other amid the ruins of a once-great city: an autistic girl
given speech by a mad experiment, and a beautiful youth drawn
by the seductive vision of a green-eyed boy whose name is
Death. Now they must take a harrowing journey across a
poisoned garden filled with children who kill, beasts that speak,
and dark gods that walk abroad. For they are destined to take
part in a nightmare ritual of blood, a macabre masque that will
unleash ancient powers and signal the end of human history.

'How rare! A book at once elegant, serene, sensuous and
exciting' *Samuel Delaney*

A Bantam Paperback
0553 40317 6

A SELECTION OF SCIENCE FICTION AND FANTASY TITLES FROM BANTAM BOOKS

THE PRICES SHOWN BELOW WERE CORRECT AT THE TIME OF GOING TO PRESS. HOWEVER TRANSWORLD PUBLISHERS RESERVE THE RIGHT TO SHOW NEW RETAIL PRICES ON COVERS WHICH MAY DIFFER FROM THOSE PREVIOUSLY ADVERTISED IN THE TEXT OR ELSEWHERE.

☐	40068 1	AZAZEL	*Isaac Asimov*	£3.99
☐	40069 X	NEMESIS	*Isaac Asimov*	£4.99
☐	40201 3	PUZZLE OF THE BLACK WIDOWERS	*Isaac Asimov*	£3.99
☐	29138 6	STAR TREK 1	*James Blish*	£3.99
☐	29139 4	STAR TREK 2	*James Blish*	£3.99
☐	29140 8	STAR TREK 3	*James Blish*	£3.99
☐	17452 5	UPLIFT WAR	*David Brin*	£3.99
☐	17162 3	SUNDIVER	*David Brin*	£3.99
☐	17452 5	STARTIDE RISING	*David Brin*	£4.99
☐	17184 4	THE PRACTICE EFFECT	*David Brin*	£3.99
☐	40317 6	WINTERLONG	*Elizabeth Hand*	£4.99
☐	17351 0	STAINLESS STEEL RAT GETS DRAFTED	*Harry Harrison*	£2.99
☐	17396 0	STAINLESS STEEL RAT SAVES THE WORLD	*Harry Harrison*	£2.50
☐	40371 0	KING OF MORNING, QUEEN OF DAY	*Harry Harrison*	£4.99
☐	40274 9	STAR OF THE GUARDIANS Book 1: The Lost King	*Margaret Weis*	£3.99
☐	40275 7	STAR OF THE GUARDIANS Book 2: The King's Test	*Margaret Weis*	£4.99
☐	40276 5	STAR OF THE GUARDIANS Book 3: King's Sacrifice	*Margaret Weis*	£4.99
☐	17586 6	FORGING THE DARKSWORD	*Margaret Weis & Tracy Hickman*	£3.99
☐	17535 1	DOOM OF THE DARKSWORD	*Margaret Weis & Tracy Hickman*	£3.50
☐	17536 X	TRIUMPH OF THE DARKSWORD	*Margaret Weis & Tracy Hickman*	£4.99
☐	40265 X	DEATH GATE CYCLE 1: Dragon Wing	*Margaret Weis & Tracy Hickman*	£4.99
☐	40266 8	DEATH GATE CYCLE 2: Elven Star	*Margaret Weis & Tracy Hickman*	£4.99
☐	17684 6	ROSE OF THE PROPHET 1: The Will of the Wanderer	*Margaret Weis & Tracy Hickman*	£3.99
☐	40045 2	ROSE OF THE PROPHET 2: Paladin of the Night	*Margaret Weis & Tracy Hickman*	£3.99
☐	40177 7	ROSE OF THE PROPHET 3: The Prophet of Akhran	*Margaret Weis & Tracy Hickman*	£4.50
☐	40471 7	STAR WARS 1: Heir to the Empire	*Timothy Zahn*	£3.99

All Corgi/Bantam Books are available at your bookshop or newsagent, or can be ordered from the following address:
Corgi/Bantam Books,
Cash Sales Department,
P.O. Box 11, Falmouth, Cornwall TR10 9EN

UK and B.F.P.O. customers please send a cheque or postal order (no currency) and allow £1.00 for postage and packing for the first book plus 50p for the second book and 30p for each additional book to a maximum charge of £3.00 (7 books plus).

Overseas customers, including Eire, please allow £2.00 for postage and packing for the first book plus £1.00 for the second book and 50p for each subsequent title ordered.

NAME (Block Letters) ....

ADDRESS ....

....